E. Billings, G

Palæozoic Fossils

Volume 1

SALZWASSER
VERLAG

E. Billings, Geological Survey of Canada

Palæozoic Fossils

Volume 1

Reprint of the original, first published in 1865.

1st Edition 2022 | ISBN: 978-3-75258-926-9

Verlag (Publisher): Salzwasser Verlag GmbH, Zeilweg 44, 60439 Frankfurt, Deutschland
Vertretungsberechtigt (Authorized to represent): E. Roepke, Zeilweg 44, 60439 Frankfurt, Deutschland
Druck (Print): Books on Demand GmbH, In de Tarpen 42, 22848 Norderstedt, Deutschland

GEOLOGICAL SURVEY OF CANADA.

SIR W. E. LOGAN, F.R.S., DIRECTOR.

PALÆOZOIC FOSSILS.

VOLUME I.

CONTAINING DESCRIPTIONS AND FIGURES OF NEW OR LITTLE KNOWN SPECIES OF ORGANIC REMAINS

FROM THE

SILURIAN ROCKS.

1861-1865.

BY

E. BILLINGS, F.G.S.

LONDON, NEW YORK, AND PARIS: BAILLIÈRE.

1865.

PREFACE.

The following work consists of descriptions of new species of organic remains from the Lower and Middle Silurian rocks, with re-descriptions, and, in some instances, additional details and illustrations of a few that were previously published either in the annual reports of the Survey or in the scientific journals of the Province. It has been prepared from time to time, according as the new forms were discovered, or as more perfect specimens of those already known were procured. The only systematic arrangement, therefore, that could be followed, was to group the descriptions together in a series of articles. The first portion, consisting of twenty-four pages, was issued in November, 1861,—the second, pages 25 to 56, in January, 1862,—the third, pages 57 to 168, in June, 1862,—the fourth, pages 169 to 344, in February, 1865, while the remainder, completing the volume, will bear date herewith. The first twenty-four pages, and also 57 to 72, have been reprinted with some alterations, the substance of which is specified by Mr. BILLINGS in the appendix on page 419. The figures were all drawn from nature by Mr. H. S. SMITH, the artist of the Survey, and engraved on wood by Mr. J. H. WALKER of this city.

W. E. LOGAN.

GEOLOGICAL SURVEY OFFICE,
Montreal, October, 1865.

GEOLOGICAL SURVEY OF CANADA.

PALÆOZOIC FOSSILS.

NOV. 1861.*

I. *On some new or little-known species of Lower Silurian Fossils from the Potsdam Group (Primordial Zone).* By E. BILLINGS, F.G.S.

The fossiliferous rocks on the north shore of the Straits of Belle Isle, from which a portion of the species hereinafter described were procured, consist of the following in descending order :—

1. LIMESTONES.—Reddish and greenish-coloured limestone, varying in some places to grey, with some red and green shale. The fossils are *Palæophycus incipiens*, *Archeocyathus Atlanticus*, *A. profundus*, *Obolus Labradoricus*, *Obolella chromatica*, *O.? cingulata*, *Olenellus Vermontana*, *O. Thompsoni*, *Conocephalites miser*, *Bathyurus parvulus*, *B. senectus*, *Salterella rugosa*, *S. pulchella*, and *S. obtusa*. There are, besides these, two species of *Orthis* and one of *Orthisina*, and numerous fragments of trilobites, apparently of several undescribed forms. The thickness of these limestones is 141 feet.

2. SANDSTONES.—Grey, red and reddish-grey sandstones, the lower beds holding pebbles of white quartz from the size of a pea to one or two pounds in weight. The only fossil observed is *Scolithus linearis*. Thickness 231 feet.

These rocks rest upon the Laurentian, and their fossils show them to be of the age of the Potsdam group. They were examined by Mr. J. Richardson during the past summer.

Another exposure of rocks of the same age occurs about three miles east of Phillipsburgh in the County of Missisquoi, and extends south into the State of Vermont, where it is largely developed, and constitutes the Red sandrock of the geologists of that state. During several visits made to this exposure last summer, I could find no fossils on the Canadian side of the boundary-line, but several important localities occur in the immediate neighbourhood in Vermont. At one of these, $1\frac{1}{2}$ mile east of Swanton, a number of species have been found by the Rev. J. B. Perry and Dr. G. M. Hall of that town. These gentlemen are engaged in making a careful geological examination of the rocks and fossils of

---

* The following twenty-four pages were reprinted in 1864. See Preface.

their neighbourhood, and have requested me to describe the new species collected by them. At this locality *Palæophycus incipiens*, *Obolella cingulata*, *Olenellus Vermontana* and *O. Thompsoni* occur in the black slates conformably interstratified with the sandstones and magnesian limestones which constitute the principal mass of the formation. It will be observed that several other species are also found here; but the prevailing forms are the four above mentioned, and, as they are most abundant in the limestones of the Straits of Belle Isle, there can be little doubt that the two deposits, although 860 miles distant from each other, are of the same age. The occurrence of *Scolithus linearis* and the general aspect of the fossils, also show that these rocks must be very nearly, if not exactly, in the same geological horizon with the Upper Primal sandstones and slates of Pennsylvania.

PLANTÆ.

Scolithus linearis. (Hall.)

Scolithus linearis.—(Hall.) Pal., N. Y. Vol. I, Pl. I. Figs. 1, *a*, *b*, *c*.

This species occurs at Anse au Loup in the sandstone, but I have not detected it in the limestone of that locality. The form differs from the one which is so common in the Potsdam sandstone of Canada in being larger and straighter. It is perfectly identical with that of the Upper Primal sandstone of Pennsylvania, and also with that of the Potsdam sandstone of Tennessee. (Formation III of Prof. Safford.)

Palæophycus incipiens. (N. sp.)

Description.—This species consists of elongated straight or slightly curved stems from half an inch to three-fourths of an inch in width. The transverse section is irregularly oval, with two acute edges, but it is probable that this flattened form is due to compression. Although numerous specimens lying in the rock were examined, no indication of branching was observed. The specimens are usually from four to six inches in length, but some are more than one foot. They occur abundantly on the surface of certain strata, and the specimens from Anse au Loup are perfectly identical with those which abound in the slates near Swanton in Vermont, holding *Conocephalites*, *Olenellus Thompsoni*, *O. Vermontana*, &c.

Locality and Formation.—Anse au Loup, on the north shore of the Straits of Belle Isle; sandstone of the Potsdam group. Also 1½ mile east of Swanton, in the State of Vermont, in rocks of the same age.

Collectors.—J. Richardson, Rev. J. B. Perry, and Dr. G. M. Hall.

PALÆOPHYCUS CONGREGATUS. (N. sp.)

Description.—Stems cylindrical, from one to four lines in diameter, often crowded together in such abundance as to completely cover the surface of the rock. They lie across each other in every direction, and appear to be so interlaced that where very thick the same stem can seldom be traced for more than one inch in length. They are either straight or crooked, and sometimes present sudden slight enlargements of the diameter, giving them a somewhat nodulose aspect.

Locality and Formation.—One mile south of the boundary line, on the road leading from Moor's Corners in St. Armand to Saxe's Mills in Highgate, Vermont. In the thin beds of the Potsdam group. Red sandrock formation of Vermont.

Collector.—E. Billings.

PROTOZOA.

In the limestone at Anse au Loup there are numerous fossils which from their radiated structure have the aspect of true corals, and yet in polished sections seem to possess the poriferous organization of sponges. I shall therefore leave it an open question as to which of the two divisions they should be referred. There appear to be two closely allied genera, but for the present I shall place all the species in one.

[Since the above was written I have, in 1864, ascertained by treating a silicified specimen of *A. Minganensis* with acid that it contains numerous silicious spicula, and these fossils must, therefore, be classified among the extinct tribes of sponges.]

Genus ARCHEOCYATHUS. (N. gen.)

Generic characters.—Turbinate simple or aggregate ; cup deep. The internal structure, so far as can be made out, consists of an inner wall constituting the inner surface of the cup, and an external wall or epitheca enveloping the whole. Between the two walls there are numerous radiating septa, the interseptal spaces being filled with poriferous or cellular tissue. It is highly probable that the inner wall is permeated by pores communicating with the interseptal tissue.

[The radiating septa are, in *A. profundus*, perforated with small pores. The spicula found in *A. Minganensis* are slender, fusiform, slightly curved, acute at both extremities.]

In *A. Atlanticus* the radiated structure is not so well defined as it is in the others, but still it can be observed in the polished sections. In

A. profundus the septa are well developed, and give to the fossil the aspect of a *Petraia* or *Zaphrentis.* It may be that these two species should be placed in different genera; but as there are numerous fragments of what appear to be intermediate forms, it would seem to be the better course to group them together in the first instance.

ARCHEOCYATHUS PROFUNDUS. (N. sp.)

A. Minganensis, pars, as published in 1861.

Fig. 1.

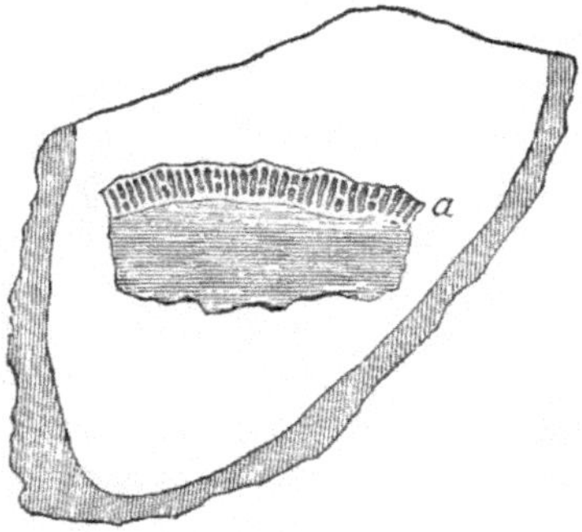

Fig. 2.

Fig. 3.

Fig. 1.—The slender base of attachment. Fig. 2.—A longitudinal section through the base of the cup of a worn specimen; *a*, a transverse section of a fragment where the diameter of the cup is 3½ inches, showing the radiating septa between the outer and inner walls. Fig. 3.—A transverse section across the base below the bottom of the cup.

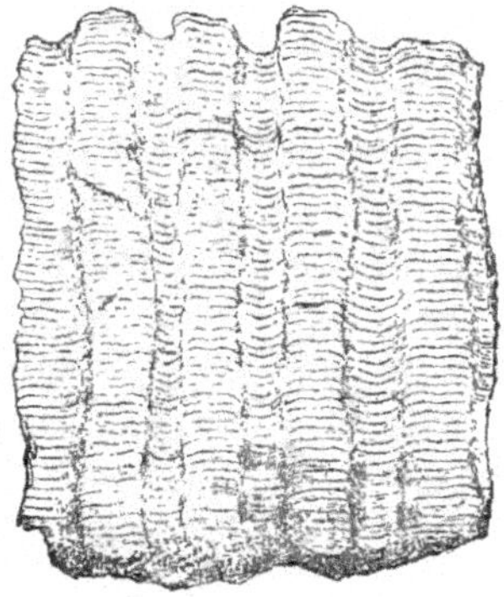

Fig. 4.

Fig. 4.—Fragment of an individual which is 3½ inches in diameter, showing the annulations and the septal striæ.

Description.—Elongate, turbinate, more or less curved, the basal one or two inches slender, then rapidly expanding to a diameter of from one to four inches, then becoming cylindrical. The form is that of a large *Cyathophyllum* or *Zaphrentis.* The cavity of the cup extends in depth nearly to the base. The radiating septa are thin and closely crowded together, there being eight or ten in the width of three lines. The surface is annulated by strong rough ridges from three to six lines distant from each other, the intervening furrows being two or three lines deep. The inner wall of the cup is exceedingly thin, apparently less than half a line.

In none of the specimens is the outer wall preserved except in spots, and there only partially. The large individuals appear to have attained a length of more than one foot with a diameter of from two to four inches.

In 1861 I referred this species to *A. Minganensis*, but further examination induces me to regard it as distinct. The latter is more deeply and distantly annulated, and, besides, it occurs in a higher geological position than does the former, having been found only in the Calciferous formation.

Locality and Formation.—Anse au Loup, on the north shore of the Straits of Belle Isle ; limestone of the Potsdam group.

Collector.—J. Richardson.

ARCHEOCYATHUS ATLANTICUS. (N. sp.)

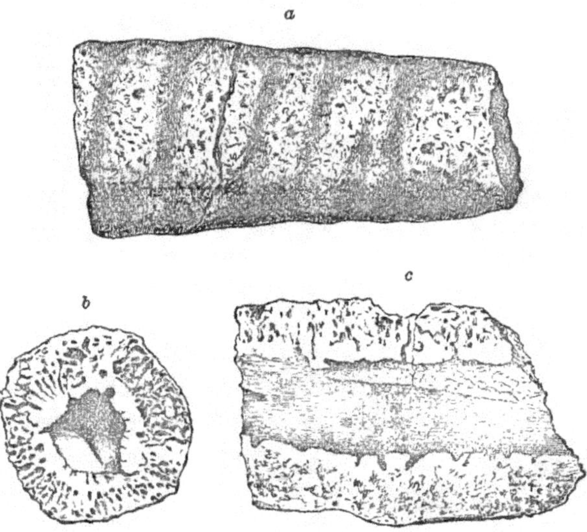

Fig. 5.

Fig. 5.—*a*, a fragment of this species ; *b*, a transverse section ; *c*, a longitudinal section of the same.

Description.—The only specimen of this species in the collection is a fragment four inches and a-half in length, fourteen lines in diameter at the larger and nine lines at the smaller extremity. Where the diameter is eleven lines the cavity of the cup is four and a-half lines across, and the space between the walls three lines. Of the radiating poriferous septa there are about sixty ; they are so irregular that it is only in certain places in finely polished sections that the radiated structure can be detected. On one side where the specimen is weathered the structure presents the appearance of a rather compact cellular tissue. The form appears to be elongate conical, gradually tapering, the surface marked by wide shallow encircling oblique annulations, from three to six lines distant from each other. The outer wall does not seem to be poriferous, but this appearance may be due to the crystalline condition of the rock into which it is converted.

Locality and Formation.—Anse au Loup, on the north shore of the Straits of Belle Isle ; limestone of the Potsdam group.

Collector.—J. Richardson.

BRACHIOPODA.

Obolus Labradoricus. (N. sp.)

Fig. 6.

Fig. 6.—Dorsal valve of *O. Labradoricus.*

Description.—Dorsal valve sub-circular, the hinge-line straight and equal to about three-fourths the width of the shell ; rather strongly and uniformly convex, most prominent at one-fourth the length from the beak, the latter small, neatly pointed, scarcely distinct from the cardinal edge. Surface with fine concentric striæ, which converge slightly on approaching the cardinal edge 15 to 20 in one line, and also with a few coarser concentric undulations of growth, the whole crossed by minute radiating striæ just visible to the naked eye. The shell is black and friable like that of a *Lingula.* Length, 5½ lines ; width, about 6 lines.

Ventral valve unknown.

Locality and Formation.—Anse au Loup, on the north shore of the Straits of Belle Isle. Limestone of the Potsdam group.

Collector.—J. Richardson.

Genus OBOLELLA. (N. gen.)

Generic characters.—Shell ovate circular or sub-quadrate, convex or plano-convex. Ventral valve with a false area which is sometimes minute and usually grooved for the passage of the peduncle. Dorsal valve either with or without an area. Muscular impressions in the ventral valve four; one pair in front of the beak near the middle or in the upper half of the shell, and the others situated one on each side near the cardinal edge. Shell calcareous. Surface concentrically striated, sometimes with thin extended lamellose ridges.

In general form these shells somewhat resemble *Obolus*, but the arrangement of the muscular impressions is different. In *Obolus* the two central scars have their smaller extremities directed downwards, and converging towards each other; but in this genus the arrangement is exactly the reverse.

The three species in which I have seen the muscular impressions are the following:—

1.—*O. chromatica*,—hereinafter described. In this species the central muscular impressions are divergent below.

2.—A species which occurs in the well-known deposit of limestone near Troy in the State of New York. This is probably *Avicula? desquamata.* (Hall) (Pal. N. Y., vol. I, p. 292, plate lxxx, fig. 3.) In two specimens of this species which I have before me the scars are in the upper part of the valve and diverge below. The small scar on each side close to the margin is visible.

3.—A small species from the Potsdam sandstone of the St. Croix River in the Western States, where it occurs associated with the Primordial trilobites described by the late eminent geologist, Dale Owen. In this the central scars are close together, one on each side of the median line and parallel.

The genus appears to be closely allied to *Obolus*, but sufficiently different, on account of the disposition of the muscular impressions, to be classified as distinct therefrom.

OBOLELLA CHROMATICA. (N. sp.)

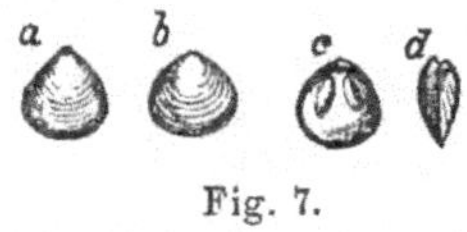

Fig. 7.

Fig. 7. *Obolella chromatica.*—*a.* Ventral valve; *b.* dorsal; *d.* interior of one of the valves, supposed to be the ventral, showing the muscular impressions; *c.* outline restored from detached valves.

Description.—Broad-oval, the rostral extremity obtusely pointed, front broadly rounded, greatest width a little below the middle ; both valves rather strongly and uniformly convex, most tumid at about one third the length from the beak. Ventral valve more acute above than the dorsal, beak depressed below the greatest elevation of the shell, slightly elevated above the margin, with a small area beneath it which is inclined backward at an angle which varies from 45° to 60°. Dorsal valve with an obtusely rounded umbo, the beak scarcely distinct from the cardinal edge and not elevated above the margin. Surface with fine concentric striæ or small minutely rugose ridges of growth of variable size, from 4 to 8 in one line, often smooth from exfoliation, or wearing. Colour of the shell in the reddish limestone a honey yellow, in grey limestone greyish ; when exposed to the weather becomes white and minutely fibrous.

Length and breadth about three lines.

In some specimens the ventral valve is depressed convex, the beak being on a level with the greatest elevation of the shell. The shell is thick and strong, and when well preserved, breaks with a granular fracture. When weathered, a tendency to fibrous exfoliation is manifested.

This species is closely allied to the form that is found so abundantly in the Troy limestone, but the muscular impressions in that one are rather closer together and nearer the beak. (At least they are so in the specimens in my possession.)

Many of the specimens are a little more obtuse in the upper half than those figured. The individuals are exceedingly numerous and differ little in size.

Locality and Formation.—Anse au Loup, on the north shore of the Straits of Belle Isle. In limestone of the Potsdam group.

Collector.—J. Richardson.

OBOLELLA (KUTORGINA) CINGULATA. (N. sp.)

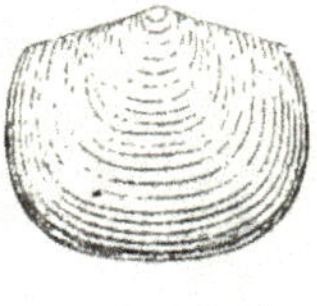

Fig. 8.

Fig. 9.

Fig. 10.

Fig. 8.—Ventral (?) valve of *O. cingulata.* Fig. 9.—Cast of interior of ventral valve. Fig. 10.—Dorsal (?) valve.

Description.—Hinge-line straight, a little less than the greatest width of the shell; sides straight or slightly convex for about one half the length; anterior angles obtusely rounded; front margin either uniformly convex or with a small portion in the middle somewhat straight. Greatest width a little in front of the middle. Ventral valve strongly and uniformly convex, most tumid about the middle; beak depressed below the greatest convexity of the shell; cardinal edges straight or gently concave, diverging from the beak at an obtuse angle. Area unknown. Dorsal valve somewhat flat, most elevated at the beak, in front of which, along the middle of the shell, there is a wide shallow concavity extending to the front margin; on each side of the beak, descending with a somewhat flat slope to the cardinal angles; area unknown, apparently half the height of the ventral area and nearly at right angles to the plane of the margin. Beak erect, obtusely pointed, forming the most elevated part of the shell. Surface with strong concentric sub-lamellose ridges which do not converge to the beak but terminate on the cardinal edges, their course conforming to the margin of the shell. Four or five ridges in the width of one line.

Length of largest dorsal valve seen 6½ lines, greatest width 8 lines. Length of largest ventral valve in a straight line from back to front 7 lines, width 10 lines. The proportional length and width appear to vary. The apical angle of the ventral valve also varies, being in some specimens much more pointed at the beak than in the one above figured. Specimens of all sizes occur from 3 lines in width upwards.*

Locality and Formation.—Anse au Loup, on the north shore of the Straits of Belle Isle. In limestone of the Potsdam group.

Also abundantly in the condition of casts 1½ mile east of Swanton in Vermont.

Collectors.—J. Richardson, Dr. G. M. Hall, and Rev. J. B. Perry.

---

* Since the above was written, I have examined many casts of the interior of this species, and am inclined to the opinion that it is generically distinct from *Obolella chromatica.* From the very considerable elevation of the beak the dorsal valve must have an area and probably a foramen. In one specimen there are two large oval impressions faintly impressed, but still distinctly visible. There is no trace of the lateral scars; and the form, notwithstanding the characters of the surface, conveys the idea of an *Orthisina.* Should, upon further examination, my suspicions turn out to be well founded, I shall call the genus KUTORGINA, after the celebrated European naturalist, KUTORGA. It is not quite certain which is the ventral or which the dorsal valve.

Orthisina festinata. (N. sp.)

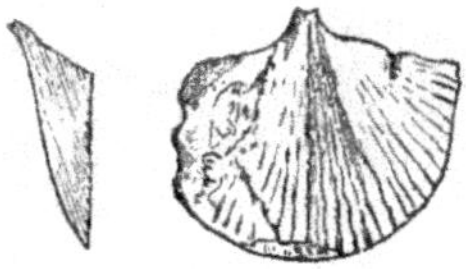

Fig. 11.

Fig. 12.

Fig. 13.

Fig. 11.—Ventral valve and side view of *O. festinata.* Fig. 12.—Area of ventral valve. Fig. 13.—*Camerella antiquata.*

Description.—Subquadrate or semioval, hinge-line equal to the greatest width of the shell. Ventral valve sub-pyramidal, beak elevated, surface with a straight or slightly convex slope in all directions to the margin, area triangular, a little inclined backwards, foramen about as wide as high, closed by a convex deltidium which is perforated at the beak. Dorsal valve nearly flat. Surface with angular bifurcating ribs, five or six in the width of two lines at the margin, crossed by fine concentric striæ, of which there are from seven to ten in one line.

Width on hinge-linge from 10 to 15 lines; length about a third less than the width. Height of beak of ventral valve from two to three lines.

Both valves show longitudinal undulations radiating from the beak to the margin.

This species closely resembles some of the ordinary forms of the genus, but differs internally from any known to me in the Second Fauna in the absence of the dental plates, no traces of which can be perceived in the casts.

Locality and Formation.—1½ mile east of Swanton in Vermont. Potsdam group.

Collectors.—Dr. G. M. Hall, and Rev. J. B. Perry.

Camerella antiquata. (N. sp.)

Fig. 13.

Description.—Ovate or subcircular, beaks obtusely pointed (as seen in the cast), both valves moderately or rather strongly convex. Surface with from 8 to 10 small rounded ribs which do not reach quite to the beaks.

Some of the specimens are proportionally more elongated than others. The front margin appears to be always broadly rounded, and the greatest width at about one-fourth the length from the front margin.

Length from 4 to 6 lines; width either equal to or a little less than the length.

This species resembles *C. varians* of the Chazy, but is more numerously ribbed.

Locality and Formation.—1½ mile east of Swanton, Vermont, in the Potsdam group.

Collectors.—Rev. J. B. Perry, and Dr. G. M. Hall.

Other species of Brachiopoda.

In addition to the above there are in the sandstone of Vermont, 1 mile south of the Province line, two other species, one of which appears to be an *Orthisina*, about the same size and shape as *O. festinata*, but more finely ribbed, and an *Orthis*, somewhat like *O. perveta* of the Chazy.

At Anse au Loup there are also two species of *Orthis*, and apparently one *Orthisina*, all different from the Vermont species.

CRUSTACEA.

Olenellus Thompsoni. (Hall.)

Olenus Thompsoni, (Hall) *12th Reg. Rep. N. Y.*, p. 59. 1859.
Barrandia Thompsoni, (Hall) *13th Reg. Rep. N. Y.*, p. 116. 1861.
Paradoxides Thompsoni, (Emmons) *Man. of Geol.* p. 280. 1860.
Paradoxides Thompsoni, (Barrande) Bul. Geo. *Soc. France.* 2d series, vol. 18, p. 276. 1861.

A well preserved head of this species was collected in the limestone at Anse au Loup.

Olenellus Vermontana. (Hall.)

(The references for this species are the same as P. Thompsoni.)

Several very good specimens of the glabella and head were collected in the limestone of Anse au Loup. It seems to be more abundant there than *P. Thompsoni.*

Conocephalites miser.

Fig. 14.

Description.—Glabella elongate, conical, very convex, most elevated at about the mid-length, slightly narrowed at the neck segment, widest in the middle, narrowly rounded in front, well defined all round by the dorsal furrows. Neck segment strongly convex and bearing a short broad-based spine directed upwards and backwards. Neck furrow extending all across; the posterior glabella furrow well defined across, forming an obtuse angle backward in the median line; median glabellar furrow also running across, but not so strongly defined as the posterior; anterior furrows extending one-third across.

Length of glabella, 2 lines; width in the middle, about half the length.

There is no described species to which this one bears any close relation on account of the peculiar character of the posterior and median furrows running quite across the glabella.

Locality and Formation.—Anse au Loup, on the north shore of the Straits of Belle Isle, in limestone of the Potsdam group.

Collector.—J. Richardson.

Conocephalites Adamsii. (N. sp.)

Fig. 14. Fig. 15. Fig. 16. Fig. 17. Fig. 18.

Fig. 14.—*Conocephalites miser.* Fig. 15.—*C. Adamsii.* Fig. 16.—*C. Teucer.* Fig. 17. —*C. Vulcanus.* Fig. 18.—*C. arenosus.*

Conocephalites.—Adams. *Silliman's Am. Jour. of Science, 2nd series,* vol. 5, p. 109. May, 1848.

Conocephalites.—Billings. *In same Journal, 2nd series,* vol. 32, p. 232, Sept. 1861. *Also in Can. Nat. and Geol.*, vol. 6, p. 324, Aug., 1861.

Description.—Head broad, semicircular, moderately convex; glabella oblong-conical, nearly two-thirds the whole length of the head, the front obtusely rounded or somewhat straight, the anterior angles narrowly rounded, the sides nearly straight from the anterior angle to the neck furrow, just in advance of which is the widest part. The neck furrow well defined all across; the glabellar furrows indistinct, the dorsal furrow is well defined all round the glabella. The cheeks are moderately tumid: a line drawn across the glabella about the mid-length would pass through the eyes. The distance of the eye from the dorsal furrow is equal to the greatest width of the glabella; the eye appears to be very small. The margin in front of the glabella is equal in width to about one-third the whole length of the head; it is bordered by an obtuse narrow elevated rim, just within which is a groove, which is more deeply impressed on each side than directly in front of the glabella, there being at this place a gently convex elevation resembling that which occurs in Barrande's species, *C. Sulzeri* and *C. coronatus*. The ocular ridge is well defined where the surface is preserved, but is rarely visible in the sandstone casts. Most of the specimens are distinctly carinate along the median line of the glabella.

It is possible that there may be a median tubercle on the neck segment, but none of our specimens have this part sufficiently well preserved to shew it.

The following are the dimensions of a specimen of the average size:— Length of head 5 lines; length of glabella 3¼ lines; greatest width of glabella 2 lines; width of glabella at front 1¼ line; distance of eye from side of glabella 2 lines.

Dedicated to Prof. C. B. ADAMS, late State Geologist of Vermont.

Locality and Formation.—Highgate, Vermont, in the Potsdam group, about a mile east of the Highgate Springs.

Collectors.—Rev. J. B. Perry, Dr. G. M. Hall, and E. Billings.

CONOCEPHALITES TEUCER, (N. sp.) ?

Fig. 16.

Compare *C. Billingsi.*—(Shumard.) *Silliman's Am. Jour. of Science.* 2d Series, vol. 32, p. 220. Sept. 1861.

Description.—Head semi-oval; glabella conical, convex, well defined all round by the dorsal furrows, about two-thirds the whole length of the head, widest just in advance of the neck furrow, sides gently convex, front neatly rounded, neck furrow well defined all across; posterior furrows commencing at about one-half the length of the glabella, and running inwards and backwards nearly to the neck furrow and one-third across; median furrows curved backwards, and extending one-fourth across; anterior furrows short; ocular ridges well defined; front margin one-third the whole length of head, with a well defined groove running across, in front of which there is an elevated marginal rim, which rises with a flat slope upwards and forwards; the groove across the margin is situated at about one-fourth the distance from the front of the glabella to the elevated edge of the rostrum; the cheeks are moderately tumid; the neck segment is well developed, with a small median tubercle scarcely the fourth of a line in height, and in some specimens seems to be absent altogether.

Thorax of 13 or 14 segments; axis strongly defined, cylindrical; side lobes about one-third wider than the axis.

The pygidium is very small, being scarcely one-sixth the length of the thorax. The only specimen in which it has been observed attached to the thorax is not sufficiently well preserved to enable me to describe it in detail.

The following are the measurements of two of the specimens:—Length of head $4\frac{1}{3}$ lines; length of glabella 3 lines, width, just in advance of neck furrow, $2\frac{1}{3}$ lines, and at one-third the length from front margin 2 lines.

In a specimen consisting of the thorax and pygidium the whole length is six lines, of which the pygidium occupies apparently a little less than one line. Width at first segment $5\frac{1}{2}$ lines; width of axis at same place $1\frac{1}{2}$ line; width at anterior margin of pygidium about 3 lines.

The position of the eye is not shewn in any specimen that I have seen, but from the width of the portions of the fixed cheeks which remain, it must be distant from the dorsal furrows nearly the width of the glabella.

This species appears to be closely allied to the one above cited from Shumard's paper, so far as the characters of the glabella are concerned. As however the proportions are a little different, I shall dispose of it as above until I can have an opportunity of submitting a specimen to Dr. Shumard.

Locality and Formation.—$1\frac{1}{2}$ mile east of Swanton in Vermont, in the slates of the Potsdam group.

Collectors.—Rev. J. B. Perry, Dr. G. M. Hall, and Sir W. E. Logan.

CONOCEPHALITES VULCANUS. (N. sp.)

Fig. 17.

Description.—Head broad, moderately convex; glabella obtusely conical, with the neck segment triangular and extended backwards in the middle; neck furrow not extending across, being interrupted by a strong carina which runs along the median line; dorsal furrow all round, but not sharply defined. Front margin about one-third the length of whole head with a projecting rim, and a transverse groove situated two-thirds the distance from the front of glabella. Cheeks moderately convex; ocular ridge well defined; a line drawn across the head a little in advance of the mid-length of the glabella, would pass through the eyes; the latter distant from the glabella at least half the whole length of the head. No indications of glabellar furrows visible.

Length of head, $4\frac{1}{3}$ lines; of glabella, including the backward projecting angle of the neck segment, 3 lines; width of glabella just in advance of neck furrow, $2\frac{1}{3}$ lines; distance of eye from glabella, $2\frac{1}{4}$ lines.

This species differs from *C. Adamsi*, in the character of the neck furrows, and in the greater proportional width of the glabella.

It was found along with *C. Adamsi* in the same beds.

Conocephalites arenosus. (N. sp.)

Fig. 18.

Description.—Glabella conical, about three fourths the length of the head, convex, well defined by the dorsal furrows all round, neck furrow all across, posterior glabella furrows represented by obscure indentations which appear to be directed obliquely backwards from near the mid-length to near the neck furrow; there appear to be no median and anterior furrows. Front margin with an elevated rostrum and a transverse groove, the latter passing at about one third from the front of the glabella. Ocular ridge well defined.

Length of head $3\frac{1}{3}$ lines; of glabella $2\frac{1}{2}$ lines; width of glabella at base $1\frac{2}{3}$ line; at one third the length from front $1\frac{1}{3}$ line.

Another head is $4\frac{1}{2}$ lines in length.

The characters of the impressions taken to be the posterior glabella furrows are not well ascertained.

Locality and Formation—In thin bedded, flaggy sandstone by the side of the road leading from Moore's Corners in St. Armand to Saxe's Mills in Highgate, Vermont, about one mile south of the Province line. Potsdam group.

Collector.—E. Billings.

Bathyurus senectus. (N. sp.)

Fig. 19.

Fig. 20.

Fig. 21.

Fig. 19.—Head of *B. senectus.* Fig. 20.—Supposed pydigium of the same. Fig. 21.—*B. parvulus.*

Description.—Glabella sub-cylindrical, clavate, strongly convex, one fourth wider at the front margin than at the neck segment, sides nearly straight, front obtusely rounded and presenting a strong convex elevation, neck furrow extending all across, three pairs of glabella furrows represented by small but distinct and obtuse indentations in the sides. Fixed cheeks rather strongly convex. Eyes of moderate size, semicircular; a line drawn across the head at about one third the length of the glabella from behind would pass through them, and they are distant from the side of the glabella about the width of the neck segment. The front of the head is surrounded by a narrow border which appears to be flat; there appears to be some evidence of a spine on the neck segment.

The pygidium found in the same fragment of stone with one of the specimens of the glabella of this species is in all general characters that of a *Bathyurus*. It is semicircular, convex, axis cylindrical, strongly convex, terminating behind with an abruptly rounded descent, six annulations, the first three or four most strongly defined. The lateral lobes have four segments each, separated by strong rounded furrows; there is a narrow entire margin all round with a distinct groove inside, which appears however to be interrupted at the end of the axis.

The dimensions of the most perfect specimens are as follows:—

Glabella,—length $3\frac{1}{2}$ lines; width at neck segment $1\frac{1}{2}$ line, at the front 2 lines; distance of the eye from the side of the glabella $1\frac{1}{2}$ line. The eye appears to be about $\frac{3}{4}$ of a line in length.

Pygidium,—length 3 lines; width at anterior margin $5\frac{1}{2}$ lines; width of axis 1 line.

Locality and Formation.—Anse au Loup, on the north shore of the Straits of Belle Isle. Limestone of the Potsdam group.

Collector.—J. Richardson.

Bathyurus parvulus. (N. sp.)

Fig. 21.

Description.—Glabella cylindrical, strongly convex, much elevated above the fixed cheeks, uniformly arched from the front margin for half the length backwards, very slightly narrower at neck segment than at front margin, sides straight, nearly parallel, and distinctly defined by the dorsal furrows. Neck furrow extending all across, posterior glabellar furrows indicated by a barely perceptible indentation on each side, no anterior furrows. Front of head surrounded by a narrow flat margin. Eyes distant from the sides of the glabella about the width of the neck segment.

On a side view the head has a convexity equal to about one quarter of a sphere. Length of head $2\frac{3}{4}$ lines; width of glabella $1\frac{1}{2}$ line; width of the flat border surrounding the front of the head about $\frac{1}{3}$ of a line.

A line drawn across the head at about one third of the length from the posterior margin of the glabella would pass through the centres of the eyes. The eyes appear to be about $\frac{1}{3}$ of a line in length.

This species differ from *B. senectus* in the almost total absence of glabellar furrows; and in the nearly equal width of the glabella throughout its whole length.

Locality and Formation.—Anse au Loup, on the north shore of the Straits of Belle Isle. In limestone of the Potsdam group.

Collector.—J. Richardson.

Genus SALTERELLA. (N. gen.)

Generic Characters.—Small, slender, elongate-conical tubes, consisting of several hollow cones placed one within another, the last one forming the chamber of habitation of the animal. The cross section of these tubes is circular or subtriangular, and they are either straight or gently curved; the surface is concentrically or longitudinally striated.

I think these fossils, although no doubt allied to *Serpulites*, sufficiently different therefrom to constitute a distinct genus. Their structure is so compact that they are seldom found compressed, while all species of *Serpulites* are almost invariably in that condition, shewing that they consist in general of something more like a membraneous sack than a hard shelled tube.

This genus is dedicated to J. W. SALTER, Esq., Palæontologist of the Geological Survey of Great Britain.

SALTERELLA RUGOSA. (N. sp.)

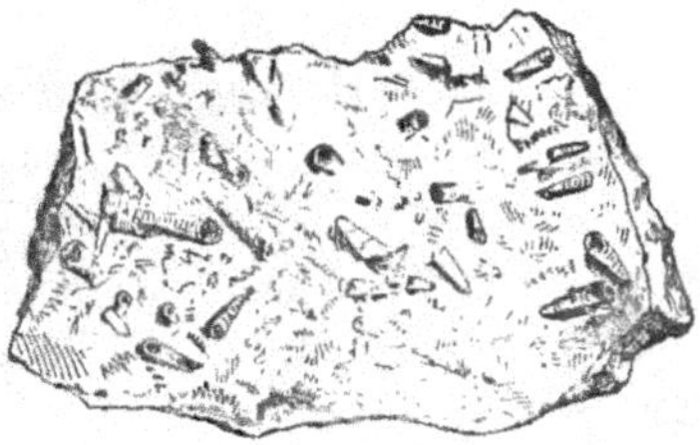

Fig. 22.

Fig.—22. A piece of Limestone with *S. rugosa.*

Description.—This little species is straight, conical, tapering uniformly to an acute point. Length from two to four lines, the greater number of the specimens being under three lines; diameter at large extremity one line in a specimen four lines in length; the smaller ones are often a little more obtuse. Aperture circular, equal to about three-fourths the whole diameter. It is not certain that in any of the specimens observed the surface is preserved; they all appear to be divested of the outer covering, and exhibit four to six imbricating sharp annulations in the length of one line, the edges towards the larger end. These are doubtless the exposed edges of the several sheaths of which the tube is composed. They are usually straight, but some are slightly curved.

This species must be closely allied to *Serpulites Macullochi* (Salter), but upon an average they are smaller than those figured by Salter in the Jour. Geol. Soc. Vol. XV, Pl. 13, fig. 31.

Locality and Formation—Anse au Loup on the north shore of the Straits of Belle Isle, in limestone of the Potsdam group.

Collector.—J. Richardson.

SALTERELLA PULCHELLA. (N. sp.)

Description.—Elongate, conical, gently curved, six to eight lines in length and from one line to one and a-half in width at the aperture. Surface ornamented with small encircling striæ just visible to the naked eye.

This species is larger than *S. rugosa*, always a little curved, not so abundant, and when weathered does not present the sharp imbricating annulations of that species.

Locality and Formation.—Same as *S. rugosa*, but apparently not in the same bed, as the two species are not found together in the same fragments of rock.

SALTERELLA OBTUSA. (N. sp.)

Description.—Six to eight lines in length; diameter at aperture about three lines. The transverse section is always sub-triangular, and in some of the specimens one side appears to be flat like a *Theca*, and I would refer it to that genus only that the tube is composed of successive layers. None of the specimens are perfect, but the form is sufficiently different from that of the other two to indicate a distinct species.

Locality and Formation.—Same as the preceding, but not associated with *S. rugosa*, although it occurs in the same fragments of rock with *S. pulchella*.

2.—*On some new species of Fossils from the Calciferous Chazy, Black River, and Trenton Formations.*

Genus EOSPONGIA. (N. gen.)

ASTYLOSPONGIA (pars).—(Roemer). *Die Silurische Fauna des Westlichen Tennessee*, p. 7, 1860.

Generic characters.—Sub-globular, pyriform or sub-hemispherical sponges, not free, with an internal arrangement of pores (sometimes reticulated), radiating irregularly from the central axis; cup of variable depth.

Dr. Ferdinand Roemer, in his beautiful work on the Silurian Fauna of Western Tennessee, has described three genera of Silurian sponges,—*Astylospongia*, *Palæomanon*, and *Astræospongia*. The first of these, he says, consists of free sponges; hence the generic name. We have several species in the Lower Silurian rocks of Canada, which were evidently attached and not free. Most of the specimens have a well developed pedicle. Some of the others, which exhibit no pedicle, evidently attached themselves while young to some cylindrical body and grew around it. We have several with the stalk of a crinoid passing quite through either in the centre or a little on one side. Others are perforated through the centre as if they had grown around some upright slender body, which has disappeared during the natural process of fossilization. Those with the stalks of crinoids passing through them could not have been free, and the others with the central perforation appear to be of the same species. The structure and general form does not differ from those which exhibit perfect evidence of a pedicle. I propose therefore to separate the species here mentioned from *Astylospongia*, and arrange them under the name of *Eospongia*.

I shall place a new species from the Trenton limestone, corresponding in form to Roemer's *A. inciso-lobata* in *Astylospongia*.

Eospongia Roemeri. (N. sp.)

Description.—Elongate, pyriform or club-shaped; the internal structure in polished sections shows numerous circular tubes, those in the central part of the mass the largest.

The best preserved specimen that I have observed is 5½ inches in length and 3 inches in diameter at two inches from the top. The larger extremity is rounded, with a small depression 1 inch wide and half an inch in depth in the centre. It tapers gradually from 3 inches to a diameter of 1½ inch at the small end where it is broken off. The pores, as shewn in a polished transverse section, are from ½ a line to 2 lines in diameter.

Dedicated to Dr. Ferdinand Roemer.

Locality and Formation—Mingan Islands, Chazy limestone.

Collectors.—J. Richardson, Sir W. E. Logan.

Eospongia varians. (N. sp.)

Description.—This species is depressed turbinate, expanding from the obtusely pointed pedicle to a width of from two to three inches, at a height of from one to two and a-half inches. The upper margin is obtusely rounded. The width of the cup is about one-third of the whole diameter, and about a-half or three-fourths of an inch deep, rounded at the bottom, and with a thick rounded margin. The greatest width of the species is in general near the top, but in those which have grown around the stalk of a crinoid there is a depression below as well as above, so that it is often difficult to say which is the cup or which the base. The transverse polished section shows numerous radiating tortuous channels, often branching, from half to one line in diameter, and usually distant once or twice their width. The vertical section shows other channels ascending and sloping outwards. The weathered surfaces are irregularly striated with obscure rounded often interrupted radiating ridges of from ½ to 1 line wide.

Some of the specimens are nearly flat, but in general they are obscurely turbinate or very depressed pyriform.

Locality and Formation.—Mingan Islands, Chazy limestone.

Collectors.—Sir W. E. Logan, J. Richardson.

Astylospongia parvula. (N. sp.)

Description.—Small, sub-globular, the sides grooved by from five to seven deep furrows, which divide it into as many lobes. The furrows are about half the width of the lobes. There is no trace of either a cup or a pedicle at either extremity. The individuals are from ¼ to ¾ of an inch in diameter.

This species is of the same form as Roemer's *A. inciso-lobota*, with the exception of the absence of the central depression or cup. It is also less than half the diameter of that species.

Locality and Formation.—City of Ottawa. Trenton limestone.

Collector.—E. Billings.

Lingula Perryi. (N. sp.)

Fig. 23.

Fig. 23.—*Lingula Perryi.* Dorsal valve.

Description.—Dorsal valve triangularly oval, the front margin gently convex or nearly straight, the anterior angles broadly rounded, the apex obtusely pointed; the sides from the apex for one half the length, or a little more, gently convex or somewhat straight and diverging at an angle of about 60°. The beak is rounded, prominent and situated about ¼ of a line from the margin of the apex. The most convex part of the shell is at about one fifth the length from the beak; from this point the surface descends with a uniform gentle and very slightly convex slope in all directions to the front margin and anterior angles and half of the sides; in the posterior or upper half with an abrupt slope, becoming concave on each side of the beak. Surface ornamented with fine lamellose ridges distant from each other two or three in one line.

Length of specimen 9 lines; greatest width, at one fourth the length from front margin, about 8 lines.

The shell appears to be smooth between the lamellose concentric striæ, but in more perfect specimens finer striæ may exist. The striæ become more crowded in the upper part, where they curve round to the beak.

This beautiful *Lingula* has somewhat the appearance of *Lingula Belli* of the Chazy Limestone. That species however usually exhibits three flat slopes, one to the anterior margin and one to each side.

Dedicated to the discoverer, Rev. J. B. Perry, of Swanton, Vermont.

Locality and Formation.—Limestone at Highgate Springs, Vermont, apparently of the age of the Black River.

Collector—Rev. J. B. Perry.

Lituites Farnsworthi. (N. sp.)

Fig. 24.

Description.—Tube very slender, forming about three complete whorls; section circular or very nearly so; siphuncle small close to the shell in the median line on the outer or ventral side; septa gently arched and numerous; chamber of habitation deep.

In the best-preserved specimens the first two whorls are in contact, and make a coil one inch across. The whorls then commence to separate, and become more and more distant until at the completion of the third the distance is from 1½ to 2¼ inches. Where the whole spire is 4½ inches across, the diameter of the aperture is one inch; at 3½ inches it is 9 lines. There are usually from 8 to 12 septa in half an inch, but the distance is variable in the same specimen. In the one figured there are 5 or 6 in half an inch in the latter part of the second and commencement of the third whorl, but farther on towards the outer chamber there are 12 or 15 in the same distance. The siphuncle is about ¾ of a line in diameter, and about the same distance from the shell. The chamber of habitation appears to be three or four inches deep. No part of the free portion is straight, the curve continuing, although becoming gradually less, quite to the aperture. Surface of shell unknown.

This species differs from all known American species in being more slender, and in having more numerous septa.

Dedicated to the discoverer, Dr. P. J. Farnsworth, M.D., Phillipsburgh, Canada East.

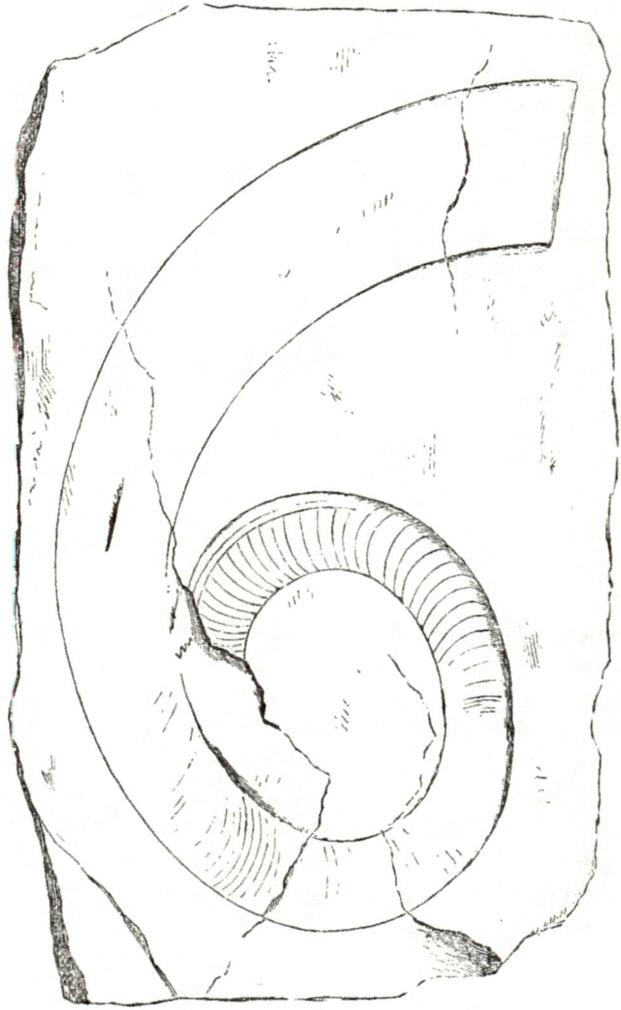

Fig. 24.

Fig. 24.—*Lituites Farnsworthi.* Since the above was engraved, better specimens have been received. The figure does not show the many close septa near the outer chamber, which can be made out, although indistinctly, in the specimen.

Locality and Formation.—Phillipsburgh in the County of Missisquoi, Canada East. In the upper part of the Calciferous sandrock.

Collectors—Dr. P. J. Farnsworth, E. Billings.

Lituites imperator. (N. sp.)

Description.—Very large, the coiled portion alone being $10\frac{1}{2}$ inches across. The first two whorls are $2\frac{1}{8}$ inches and the first three $4\frac{1}{2}$ inches across. The first three are coiled in contact; after which the whorls begin to separate, and at the completion of the fourth are distant about $\frac{1}{4}$ of an inch. The last whorl is then produced nearly in a straight line for about 2 inches, after which (in the only specimen collected) it is not preserved. The dorso-ventral diameter of the tube where broken off is almost $4\frac{1}{2}$ inches. The distances of the septa vary greatly. In the commencement of the third whorl there are three in one inch, but they gradually become more distant until at the end of this whorl there are only two in one inch. The distance then diminishes, and at the middle of the fourth whorl there are four in one inch. (These measurements relate to the outer side.) Beyond this they are not seen, but the siphuncle is preserved to the end of the fourth whorl, and shows the traces of nine septa in the last inch. The siphuncle is exposed in the specimen in two places, both in the fourth whorl. In the first quarter of the length of this whorl it is concealed. In the second quarter it is laid bare for a length of $5\frac{1}{2}$ inches. It is here 4 lines in diameter, and its position is, as nearly as can be, central. In the last quarter of the whorl there is another exposure of about 4 inches, its diameter being five lines, and its position, where last seen, $2\frac{1}{2}$ inches from the ventral or outer margin, and $1\frac{1}{4}$ inch from the dorsal or inner margin. The position therefore of the siphuncle in this species varies in different parts of the same individual. This agrees with Barrande's observations on *Orthoceras mundum*, in which the siphuncle passes from one side to the other in such a maner that ten or twelve species might be made out of different fragments of the same individual. specimen, provided the position of the siphon were alone to be taken into account and the species described by different observers without a knowledge of their connection.*

The only specimen collected is firmly imbedded in the limestone matrix, and is worn away so as to exhibit a complete section along the plane of the coil, showing all the whorls and the siphuncle as above mentioned. The character of the surface cannot thus be observed. But judging from the appearance of the shell as seen in the section the last whorl is crossed by wide shallow undulations, but no traces of these can be seen on the inner whorls, where the shell is also visible.

Locality and Formation.—Phillipsburg in the County of Missisquoi, Canada East. In the upper part of the Calciferous Sandrock.

Collector.—Dr. P. J. Farnsworth.

---

* Barrande. In *Bronn's Neues Jahrbuch*, 1859, p. 608.

Ampyx Halli. (N. sp.)

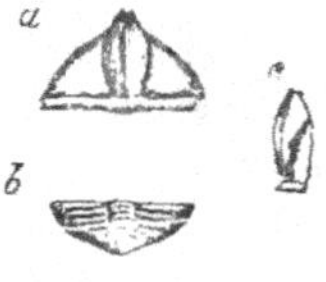

Fig. 25.

Fig. 25.—*Ampyx Halli.* *a*, head; *b*, pygidium; *c*, side view of the head.

Description.—Head somewhat triangular or semioval. Glabella enlongate oval, terminating in front with an acute elevated rostrum, the length of which is not known, and truncated behind by the neck furrow, narrowly convex and rather sharply carinated along the median line. Glabellar furrows represented by two obscure indentations on each side, the posterior at a little less than one line from the neck segment, and the anterior about two lines; the latter are deep pits situated in the dorsal furrow or just in the angle formed by the junction of the base of the glabella with the fixed cheeks. The neck segment is a flat plate inclining upwards and backwards at an angle of about 45°. The neck furrow is well defined all across the whole width of the head, being least distinct in passing over the posterior part of the glabella.

Pygidium semioval with a flat border all round abruptly bent down at nearly a right angle. Axis conical, moderately convex, extending the whole length and causing a slight projection in the posterior margin. Side lobes nearly flat, with five or six flat ribs each with a fine pleural groove extending the whole length. On the axis there appear to be ten or twelve closely crowded annulations occupying five sixths the length, the apex being apparently smooth. On approaching the margin the side ribs seem to curve a little forwards. Length of head, excluding the rostrum, 3½ lines, measured along the base of the glabella. Width of glabella at neck segment 1½ line, and just in front of the anterior pits 2 lines; elevation at neck segment less than one line, and at front of head, so far as seen, about 2 lines. These measurements refer to the largest head seen.

No perfect head has been collected, and I cannot therefore give the length of the rostrum or moveable cheeks.

Dedicated to Dr. G. M. Hall, M.D., of Swanton, Vermont.

Locality and Formation.—St. Dominique, in the County of Yamaska, Canada East, and at Highgate Springs in Vermont. In the Chazy Limestone.

Collectors.—Dr. G. M. Hall, Rev. J. B. Perry, and J. Richardson.

LITUITES APOLLO. (N. sp.)

Description.—Coil 5 or 6 inches across ; the first 2½ whorls in contact, after which they gradually separate so that at the completion of the third whorl they are 1 inch distant from each other. The diameter of the coil is then about 6 inches and the tube about 1½ inches in the lateral diameter of the transverse section, in the dorso-ventral a little less. In the third whorl there are about five septa to the inch. The surface is marked by numerous shallow concave undulations which curve backwards from the umbilicus and make a deep retral sinus on the ventral aspect. The ridges of the undulations are narrowly rounded and not so wide as the concave grooves between them ; the latter are 2 or 3 lines in width. Siphuncle unknown.

This species somewhat resembles *L. undatus* Pal. N. Y. Vol. 1. p. 52. Pl. 13, figs. 1. 1a, but the tube does not taper quite so rapidly and is not flattened on the ventral side as it is in that species, the transverse section being nearly circular and rounded on the ventral as on the lateral aspect.

Locality and Formation.—Mingan Islands, Calciferous formation and also apparently in the Chazy.

Collectors.—Sir W. E. Logan, J. Richardson.

LITUITES PALINURUS. (N. sp.)

Description.—The coil in the largest specimen seen is 4½ inches across and consists of about five whorls very compactly inrolled, each deeply indented by the ventral side of the one next preceding. The transverse section of the tube (with the exception of the indentation on the dorsal side made by the preceding whorl) is nearly circular. The diameter at about the end of the fifth whorl varies from 11 to 15 lines. The septa in the only specimen in which they have been observed are (in the third whorl) five or six to the inch. Surface and siphuncle unknown.

Of this species I have seen only one specimen that shews any part of the free portion of the tube. The separation commences about the middle of the fifth whorl. The length of the produced free portion is not known. No other species known in our rocks is so compactly coiled as this, there being about ¼ of the diameter of each whorl overlapped and concealed by the one next succeeding.

Locality and Formation.—Mingan Islands, Calciferous formation.

Collectors—Sir W. E. Logan, J. Richardson.

Nautilus Pomponius. (N. sp.)

Description—The specimen on which this species is founded consists of the first three whorls, the remainder to the aperture not preserved. These are very compactly inrolled, and form a coil 3 inches across. The tube rapidly expands in the transverse diameter, being at least 2 inches wide at the completion of the third whorl while in the dorso-ventral diameter at the same place it is only 1½ inches. There are four septa to the inch on the outside of the third whorl but the second whorl shows six or seven in the same length. The siphuncle is 2 lines in thickness and with its centre about three lines from the shell on the ventral or outer side of the whorls.

In this species the tube differs from that of any other known to me in the lower limestones in its rate of expansion laterally; the transverse section being oval and the lateral diameter being at least one fourth greater than the dorso-ventral.

Locality and Formation.—Phillipsburgh in the County of Missisquoi, Canada East. In the upper part of the Calciferous formation.

Collectors.—Dr. P. J. Farnsworth, E. Billings.

Orthoceras Menelaus. (N. sp.)

Description.—Shell of medium size, tapering at the rate of 1¼ lines to the inch; section transversely broad-oval or nearly circular; septa from 10 to 12 to the inch where the diameter is from 10 to 15 lines; siphuncle cylindrical, excentric, between 2 and 3 lines in diameter where the shell is from 10 to 15 lines, its centre distant from the margin about once and a half its own thickness. Surface unknown.

The transverse section appears to be broad-oval in all the specimens that I have seen but I am not certain but that this feature is due to pressure. The siphuncle is a cylindrical tube a little dilated where the septa are attached to it and in most of the chambers (in the specimens observed) slightly constricted between the septa.

This species is allied to *O. Murrayi* but differs therefrom in being more nearly circular in the transverse section; in having more numerous septa and the siphuncle more distant from the margin. It seems to be rare.

Locality and Formation.—Wolfe Island near Kingston; Pointe Claire on the Island of Montreal, and the fifth and sixth lots in the ninth concession of the township of Tyendenaga. Black River limestone.

Collectors.—Mr. A. T. Drummond of Kingston, A. Murray and E Billings.

Orthoceras perparvum. (N. sp.)

Description.—Length 3 or 4 inches; diameter at the last septum about 3 lines; section circular; siphuncle very small and very nearly central; septa gently concave, about one line distant, the last three or four much closer together. The chamber of habitation is 1 inch in length and tapers slightly from the last septum towards the aperture which is ½ a line narrower than the diameter at last septum. Surface unknown but the cast of the interior of the chamber of habitation shews a number of very obscure annulations. Fragments of this species resemble *Cyrtoceras exiguum* but the chamber of habitation is twice the depth and the shell does not taper so rapidly. No perfect specimen has been seen but from the fragments that have been collected I think this species must be 3 or 4 inches in length, and is probably curved towards the smaller extremity.

Locality and Formation.—Pallideau Islands. Northern part of Lake Huron. Black River limestone.

Collector.—A. Murray.

Holopea Pyrene. (N. sp.)

Fig. 26.

Description.—Obliquely turbinate; spire depressed conical; whorls about three, ventricose, with a deeply impressed suture, crossed by deep concave undulations which give to the shell a strongly varicose appearance.

The only specimen seen is imperfect consisting of only the apex and 2½ whorls the base of the shell being imbedded in the rock. Width of the part seen 9 lines; width of the undulations about two lines. The form is much like that of *H. obliqua* (Hall) but the deeply furrowed surface shews that it is a very distinct species.

The aspect of this species is very like that of the undulated forms of *Platyceras* and in fact no difference between the genera *Platyceras* and *Holopea* has ever been pointed out.

Locality and Formation.—Paquette Rapids, on the River Ottawa. Black River limestone.

Collector.—Sir W. E. Logan.

Holopea Nereis. (N. sp.)

Description.—Shell turbinate; spire conical; apical angle from 75° to 80°; whorls about four, uniformly ventricose (in the cast of the interior) except in the upper part where there is an angular inflection towards the suture giving an obscurely turreted form. When the shell is preserved this angulation is not so apparent and the suture is indistinct or enamelled. Aperture oval, somewhat effuse below, the upper half of the inner side formed by the penultimate whorl, the lower half by the columella.

Length of largest specimen seen 16 lines, width of last whorl about 12 lines. One small perfect specimen is in length 7 lines; width at the aperture 5 lines; length of the aperture 3 lines.

The casts of this species can always be distinguished from those of *H. obliqua* by the obtuse shoulder-like angulation on the upper side of the whorl. This in a large specimen is about two lines wide at the aperture. When the shell is preserved the suture is seldom visible the surface being continuous from one whorl to another.

Locality and Formation.—Trenton limestone, Ottawa; near L'Orignal and on the Island of Montreal. Black River limestone at Paquette Rapids (Ottawa River).

Collectors.—Sir W. E. Logan, R. Bell, J. Richardson, E. Billings.

Holopea Lavinia.

Description.—Ovate, whorls four or five, depressed convex, the body whorl large equal to about ¾ the whole length. In the cast of the interior the suture is distinct but not very deep. The apical angle is about 80° and in consequence of the moderate convexity of the upper whorls the spire has a somewhat smooth conical appearance only slightly notched in the outline by the depressions of the sutures.

Length about 1½ inches; width at body whorl 1 inch.

This species is closely related to *H. ovalis* of the Calciferous formation. The deep suture of that species gives to the cast a turreted form while in this the spire is more evenly conical.

Locality and Formation.—Twenty-fifth lot in the 5th concession of the township of Admaston. Trenton limestone.

Collector.—J. Richardson.

Holopea Proserpina. (N. sp.)

Description.—Shell very large, about four inches wide at the base and apparently the same in height. Whorls about four, moderately ventricose, the last one a little more than one half the whole length of the shell. Surface with fine lines of growth of variable size, six to eight in one line.

The specimens are all imperfect. The body whorl is very large and appears to be most ventricose at the base; above, sloping to the suture.

The form is very like that of *Cyclonema Hageri* but much larger. *H turgida* has the suture more deeply impressed.

Locality and Formation.—Phillipsburgh in the County of Missisquoi, Canada East. In the upper part of the Calciferous formation.

Collectors.—Dr. P. J. Farnsworth and E. Billings.

CYCLONEMA HAGERI. (N. sp.)

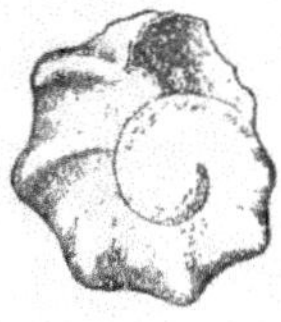

Fig 26.

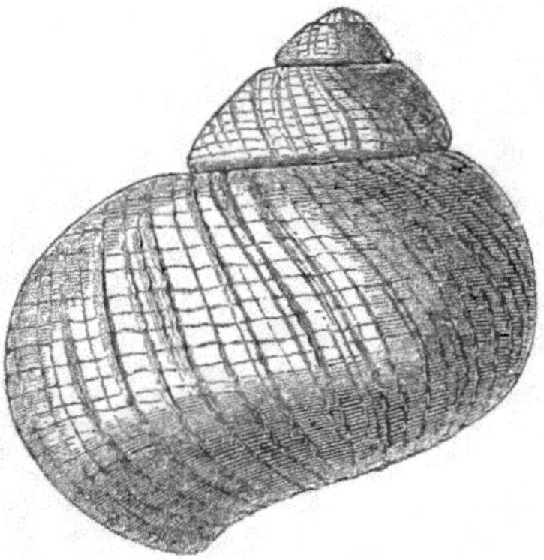

Fig. 27.

Fig. 28.

Fig. 26.—*Holopea Pyrene.* Fig. 27.—*Cyclonema Hageri.* Fig. 28.—*C. Montrealensis.*

Description.—Shell large, obliquely conical; whorls four, ventricose towards the base, somewhat depressed in the middle; suture moderately deep. The apical angle appears to be between 80° and 90°. Surface with strong angular ribs or undulations of growth from half a line to two lines apart becoming more prominent with age. These are crossed by fine spiral ridges from half a line to one line distant.

Height of specimen $2\frac{1}{8}$ inches; width at base 2 inches. The body whorl is at least $\frac{3}{4}$ the whole length.

This species much resembles in form *C. Montrealensis* but is twice the length and breadth.

It is dedicated to A. D. HAGER, Esq., of the Geological Survey of Vermont, who discovered the only specimen I have seen.

Locality and Formation.—Smith's Quarries, Montreal. Trenton limestone.

Collector.—A. D. Hager, Esq.

Cyclonema Montrealensis. (N. sp.)

Fig. 28.

Description.—About one inch in length and breadth; whorls about three, moderately ventricose, most prominent in the lower half; suture rather deep. Aperture ovate, somewhat effuse below, the upper half of the inner side formed by the penultimate whorl. Surface with fine sharp crowded lines of growth just visible to the naked eye. These are crossed by stronger spiral lines four or five in the width of one line with one or two smaller between each of the larger.

Length of the most perfect specimen seen 12 lines; width 11 lines; height of aperture 8 lines; width of aperture 6 lines.

This species is about the size of *C. Halliana*, (Salter) but the whorls are less ventricose and the surface is more closely striated.

Locality and Formation.—Island of Montreal. Trenton limestone.

Collectors.—Sir W. E. Logan, J. Richardson.

Pleurotomaria Eugenia. (N. sp.)

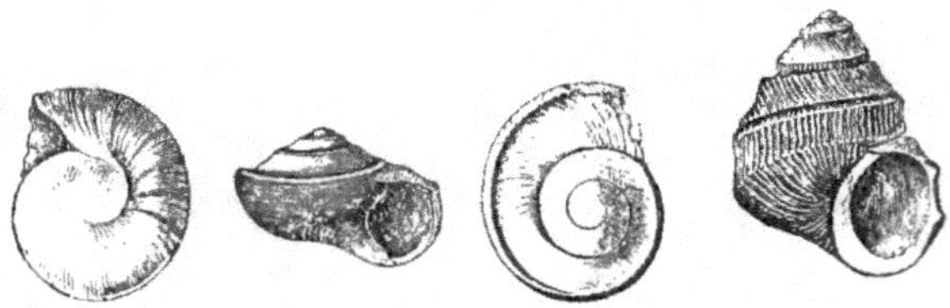

Fig. 29. Fig. 30. Fig. 31. Fig. 32.

Fig. 29.—*Pleurotomaria Eugenia.* Fig. 30 view of the underside. Fig. 31 shewing the aperture. Fig. 32.—*P. Arachne* shewing the spire and band.

Description.—Obtusely sub-lenticular; spire depressed conical; apical angle varying from 115° to 125°; whorls about four, gently convex above near the suture, and concave in the outer one third, the margin surrounded by a flat spiral band placed obliquely on the edge of the outer margin and sloping upwards and inwards. Under-side of whorls strongly and uniformly ventricose; umbilicus closed. Aperture subquadrate; upper side somewhat straight; outside forming an angle of about 100° with the upper at the margin but below the margin uniformly curved down to the middle of the lower side which is somewhat straight and sloping obliquely upwards in the inner half; inner lip obsolete or excessively thin and attached to the surface of the penultimate whorl. Width 9 or 10 lines; height about $\frac{2}{3}$ of the width; band $\frac{3}{4}$ of a line wide at the aperture but gradually diminishing towards the apex.

This species is closely allied to *P. Helena* of the Hudson River formation but differs in being much smaller and in having the upper side of each whorl gently convex on the inner side and concave on the outer side whereas in *P. Helena* the whole of the upper side of the whorl is gently concave.

It differs from *P. calcifera* and *P. rotuloides* in having the umbilicus closed.

Locality and Formation.—Campement d'Ours, near the Island of St. Joseph, Lake Huron. Black River limestone.

Collectors.—A. Murray, R. Bell.

Pleurotomaria Arachne. (N. sp.)

Fig. 32.

Description.—Shell small, turbinate; whorls three or four, ventricose spirally carinated; apical angle about 75°. There is a broad spiral band situated with its upper edge about the middle of the whorl; above this and only separated from it by a sharply elevated thread-like carina there is a second very narrow but well defined concave band, above which the whorl is gently concave for about two thirds the distance to the suture; and in the remaining third to the suture there is a spiral row of small elevated imperfect varices which give to this part of the shell a peculiar nodulose appearance. The suture is deeply canaliculate. Under side of body whorl moderately ventricose. There is a small umbilicus. Aperture oval somewhat effuse below.

Surface with elevated sharp-edged lines of growth, distinctly visible to the naked eye, from eight to ten in the width of one line. On approaching the suture every two or three of these unite into one in order to form the short varices which are situated near the suture. They also unite in the same manner on the lower part of the last whorl as they approach the umbilicus.

Length from 5 to 10 lines. The most perfect specimen examined is 5 lines in length and 4 lines in width at last whorl including the width of the aperture. The latter is $2\frac{1}{2}$ lines in height and 2 lines wide. The larger spiral band is 1 line wide at the aperture and the smaller about $\frac{1}{3}$ of a line. There are three narrow sharply elevated carinæ, one bordering the lower side of the larger band; another separating the two bands and a third bordering the small band on the upper side.

Locality and Formation.—Pointe Claire; Paquette Rapids; and Murray Bay. Black River limestone.

Collectors.—Sir W. E. Logan, Dr. J. W. Dawson, E. Billings.

Pleurotomaria Amphitrite. (N. sp.)

Description.—Shell very large, trochoid, conical, with a flat base. The specimen consists of the body whorl and a portion of the one next above it. Although imperfect there is sufficent to shew that this is a smoothly conical flat-based species belonging to that group of which *P. Ramsayi* of the Calciferous formation is an example. The basal margin is narrowly rounded, the lower side of the body whorl flat and at a right angle (or very nearly so, to the vertical axis of the shell. The upper side of the whorl is gently convex, or nearly flat for a short distance from the aperture and then gradually becomes gently concave. Judging from this form, the spire is most probably an uniformly tapering cone. As the lower side of the body whorl forms an angle of about 60° with the upper side the apical angle would also be about 60°. There is evidence of a wide umbilicus.

Surface with fine crowded sublamellose striæ curving backwards so as to form an acute angle in passing over the margin. Width of the base 4 inches.

This fine shell is allied to *P. Ramsayi*, but is nearly four times as wide at the base.

Locality and Formation. — South point of Large Island, Mingan Islands. Chazy or Black River.

Collector.—J. Richardson.

Murchisonia Vesta. (N. sp.)

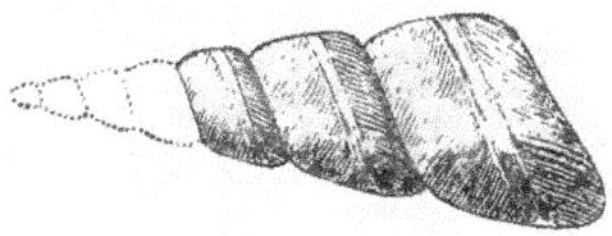

Fig. 33.

Fig. 33.—*Murchisonia Vesta.*

Description.—Elongate, acutely conical, apical angle apparently from 20° to 30° whorls from six to nine, moderately ventricose with an inconspicuous flat spiral band a little below the middle. Surface with fine striæ in the upper part of the whorl curving backwards to the spiral band and in the lower part curving forwards.

The largest specimen seen is a fragment consisting of three whorls 1¼ inches in length, apparently belonging to an individual which if complete would be about 2¼ inches in length; width of spiral band about 1 line; fragments of smaller individuals are common.

This species resembles *M. gracilis* but is not so slender and has the band not in the middle but a little below the middle of the whorl.

Locality and Formation.—Phillipsburgh in the County of Missisquoi, Canada East. In the upper part of the Calciferous formation.

Collectors.—Sir W. E. Logan, Dr. P. J. Farnsworth, E. Billings.

Murchisonia Hyale. (N. sp.)

Description.—Short, turbinate; spire conical; apical angle about 80°; whorls four or five, ventricose with a concave spiral band about the middle. The body whorl is large and uniformly ventricose, most prominent about the middle. The upper whorls are small and uniformly ventricose in the cast. Surface with fine striæ and a few obscure undulations. These curve backwards at an angle of about 45° to the axis of the shell until they reach the spiral band, below which they at first curve forward and then become more vertical.

Length of a specimen of four whorls about 1½ inches; width at base nearly the same; width of spiral band on the last whorl nearly 2 lines.

The only specimen seen is about the size and somewhat of the shape of *Eunema Erigone*. In that species, however, the small whorls are slightly concave above the spiral band but in this they are convex. The band in this species is not so broad, the last whorl is also not so prominent at the base. The manner in which the striæ curve backwards shews that this species has the outer lip notched and it is therefore most probably a *Murchisonia*.

Locality and Formation.—Phillipsburgh in the County of Missisquoi, Canada East. Upper part of the limestone. In beds holding fossils approaching in aspect to these of the Chazy or perhaps the Black River limestone.

Collector.—Dr. P. J. Farnsworth.

Murchisonia Hermione. (N. sp.)

Description.—Spire conical, apical angle about 75°; whorls about four, ventricose, with a strong convex spiral band in the middle, above which is a wide shallow concave band and a similar one below. Between the upper concave band and the suture the whorl is gently convex or nearly flat; below the lower concave band the body whorl is evenly ventricose. The convex band running all the way to the apex gives a strongly angulated appearance to the whorls. The above is the form as seen in a cast of the interior. A small portion of the shell remaining on the body whorl shews a number of small rounded spiral ridges from ½ a line to 1 line apart crossed by very fine but distinct lines of growth. It seems probable that much of the shell is ornamented in this way.

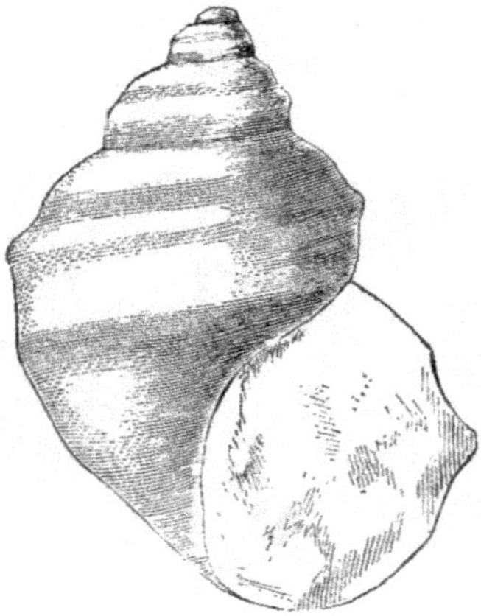

Fig. 34.

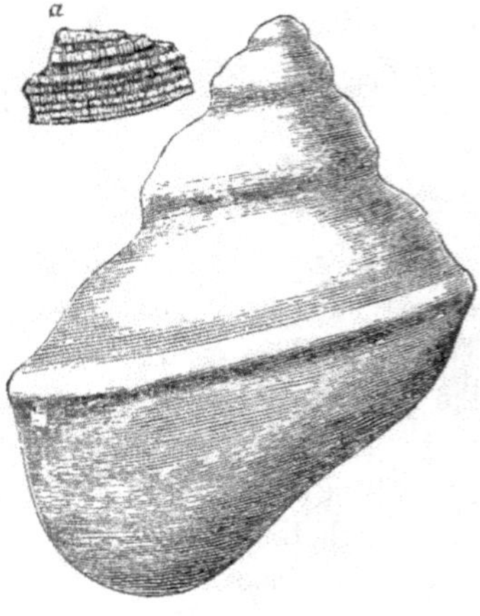

Fig. 35.

Fig. 34.—*Murchisonia Hermione*, front view of a cast of the interior. Fig. 35. posterior view of the same specimen *a*. a portion of the surface a little enlarged.

Length of specimen 2½ inches; width of body whorl and aperture 2 inches; height of aperture 1¼ inches; width of the same about 1 inch.

Locality and Formation.—South point of Large Island, Mingan Islands. Chazy or Black River.

Collector.—J. Richardson.

Murchisonia Procris. (N. sp.)

Description.—Short, conical, very like a small *M. bellicincta* but more obtuse. Whorls five or six, uniformly and rather strongly ventricose; apical angle about 50°. Aperture oval somewhat effuse below. Surface with fine but very distinct lines of growth which have a rugose aspect, from six to eight in the width of one line. About the middle of the whorl there is what appears to be a wide flat spiral band bounded on the lower side by a very distinct thread-like ridge. The upper side of the supposed band is not distinguishable in the specimen owing to the imperfection of the shell.

Length of specimen 1 inch; width of last whorl including aperture 7 lines; width of aperture 4½ lines; height of the same 5½ lines.

Locality and Formation.—Paquette Rapids on the River Ottawa. Black River limestone. Rare.

Collector.—E. Billings.

EUNEMA CERITHIOIDES. (Salter.)

EUNEMA CERITHIOIDES.—(Salter.) *Figures and descriptions of Canadian organic remains.* Decade 1 p. 30.

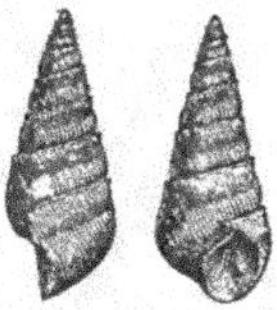

Fig. 36.

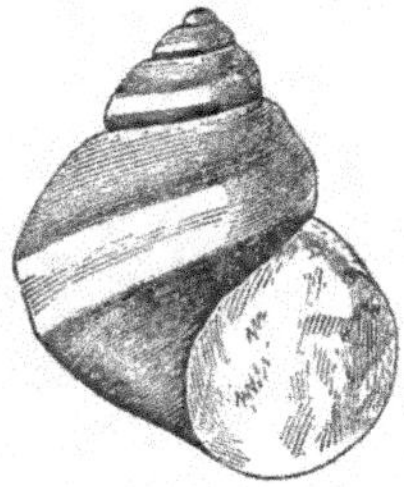

Fig. 37.

Fig. 36.—*Eunema cerithioides*, two views of the same specimen. This figure does not shew the spiral band with sufficient distinctness.
Fig. 37.—*E. Erigone.*

Description.—Spire acutely conical, apical angle about 30°; whorls about seven, slightly convex in the lower half and concave in the upper half; body whorl ventricose below; aperture oval, a little effuse below; outer lip thin; inner lip absent. Surface with fine but distinct lines of growth which in the upper half of the whorl are curved gently backwards and in the lower half slightly forward. A little below the middle of the whorls there is a very obscure flat spiral band.

Length of the only specimen collected 9 lines; width at body whorl 3½ lines; length of the aperture 2½ lines; width of the same 2 lines.

Locality and Formation.—Paquette Rapids on the River Ottawa. Black River limestone.

Collector.—Sir W. E. Logan.

EUNEMA ERIGONE. (N. sp.)

Fig. 37.

Description.—Turbinate, obtusely conical; apical angle about 80°; whorls four or five, ventricose, with a flat spiral band about the middle; suture in the cast deep. The body whorl is most ventricose near the base and moderately convex above to the suture. In the upper whorls there is a shallow concavity just above the flat spiral band. The aperture appears to be obtusely oval. Length of specimen 1¼ inches; width at the aperture about 1 inch; the body whorl occupies about half the whole length; width of spiral band on last whorl 2 lines. Surface unknown.

Of this species I have seen only one specimen and that is a cast of the interior. At first sight it might be taken for a species of *Holopea* but owing to the spiral band it more probably does not belong to that genus.

Locality and Formation.—Near L'Orignal. Black River limestone.

Collector.—R. Bell.

SUBULITES PARVULUS. (N. sp.)

Description.—Shell small, fusiform, much curved below the middle. Spire of four or five whorls, the last one rather more than half the whole length; whorls depressed convex, almost flat; suture not deep. Length about 1 inch; width at about the mid-length 5 lines. Surface unknown.

The greatest width is about the middle or a little below. From this point the shell tapers in both directions, with a rounded slope to the apex and with a broad rounded curve in the base of the last whorl. The side opposite the aperture forms in outline a regular arch from the apex to the lower extremity of the aperture. The height of this arch measured in the middle is a little greater than the width of the shell. The suture is so slightly impressed that when the shell is preserved the spire must be a nearly smooth cone.

There is a species very like this in the limestones of the south side of the Straits of Belle Isle.

Locality and Formation.—Paquette Rapids on the Ottawa River; and near L'Orignal. Black River limestone.

Collectors.—E. Billings, R. Bell.

Genus METOPTOMA, (Phillips.)

METOPTOMA (Phillips).—*Geology of Yorkshire* Part, 2. p. 223, 1836.

Generic characters.—Shell univalve, patelliform, more or less conical; apex anterior, either erect or incurved forwards. External surface either smooth or horizontally or vertically striated or ribbed. Internal surface either smooth or with a crescentiform row of small circular or oval muscular impressions open towards the anterior extremity.

Prof. Phillips confines this genus to such as have "the face under the apex" truncate. There is, however, as is well shewn by our specimens a gradation between those with the aperture oval or circular and those which have it straight in front and curved at the sides and posterior margin. These shells are referred by some to *Capulus* and by others to *Patella* both of which names have been used by me also. But we have now two species from the Quebec group which shew that the muscular impressions do not form one continuous scar as in these two genera but consist of a number of small isolated cavities.

It may be that when the internal characters of Phillips' species become well known, these Lower Silurian forms will be referred to a different genus, but until we have some evidence of a generic difference it would not be safe to give them a separate designation. In all external characters they are identical with the Carboniferous forms.

Metoptoma Niobe. (N. sp.)

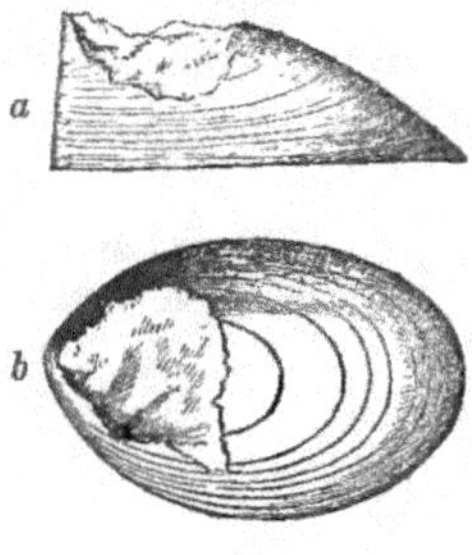

Fig. 38.

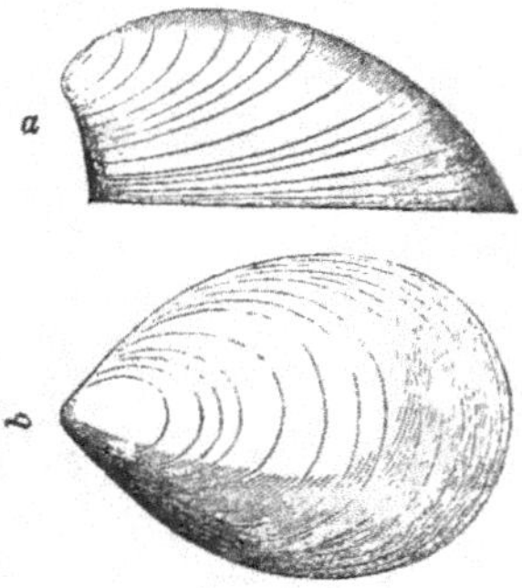

Fig. 39.

Fig. 38.—*Metoptoma Niobe.* *a*, side view; *b*, view of upper side.
39.—*M. Nycteis.* *a*, side view; *b*, view of upper side.

Description.—Oval, subconical, apex much elevated, almost directly above (but a little behind) the anterior margin; posterior margin somewhat narrowly rounded; sides gently convex; anterior extremity more narrowly rounded than the posterior.

On a side view the outline of this shell is subtriangular; the base and anterior extremity straight and forming an angle with each other only a little less than 90°; the dorsal outline very gently curved from the posterior margin for half the length, beyond which it is not known.

The apex is not preserved in the only specimen collected but judging from the straightness of the portion of the anterior extremity that remains it is probably not incurved and forms the most elevated point of the shell. Surface apparently with fine concentric striæ. Length 14 lines; width 9 lines; height so far as is known 5 lines, but judging from the shape it is probably 6 or 7 lines in a perfect shell.

Locality and Formation.—Phillipsburgh, in the County of Missisquoi, Canada East. In the upper part of the Calciferous formation.

Collector.—E. Billings.

Metoptoma Nycteis. (N. sp.)

Fig. 39.

Description.—Ovate, uniformly rounded posteriorly, sides gently convex, anterior extremity more narrowly rounded than the posterior. On a side view the greatest elevation is at about one-third or one-fourth the whole length from the apex; the latter small, acutely rounded, a little overhanging the base and depressed below the greatest elevation about three-sevenths the whole height of the shell. From the most prominent point the outline is gently and uniformly curved to the front margin, from the same point descending with a shorter curve to the apex.

Length at the base, from 12 to 16 lines; greatest width a little behind the middle, from 9 to 12 lines; greatest elevation, from 5 to 7 lines; height of apex above base, 3 or 4 lines. Surface unknown.

Locality and Formation.—Mingan Islands. In the upper part of the Calciferous formation.

Collectors.—Sir W. E. Logan, J. Richardson.

Metoptoma Eubule. (N. sp.)

Description.—Ovate, posterior margin broadly rounded, greatest width at about one third or one fourth the length from the posterior margin, from which point the sides are somewhat straight and converging so as to form an obtuse angle of about 110° at the apex. The shell is rather strongly convex, most elevated in the middle or a little behind the middle and the apex incurved nearly down to the plane of the lateral margin. Surface only imperfectly known, apparently marked with somewhat rugose concentric lines of growth. Length 13 lines; width 14 lines; height 7 lines.

This species resembles *M. Nycteis*, but is comparatively much broader behind, and has the apex not so much elevated.

Locality and Formation.—Phillipsburgh, in the County of Missisquoi, Canada East. Upper part of the limestone. In beds holding fossils approaching in aspect to those of the Chazy or Black River limestone.

Collector.—P. J. Farnsworth.

Metoptoma Orithyia. (N. sp.)

Fig. 40.

Description.—Acutely conical, apex much elevated, base ovate, the margin broadly rounded anteriorly, sides in the anterior half gently rounded, in the posterior half slightly concave and the posterior margin narrowly rounded. The outline in a side view is subtriangular, the apex a little in front in the middle, the anterior slope gently concave or nearly straight and the posterior gently convex. The posterior part of the shell is a little compressed and there is a wide shallow concave depression running from the apex to the base near the posterior edge. Surface unknown. Height about 1 inch, length of base 11 lines, greatest width 7 lines.

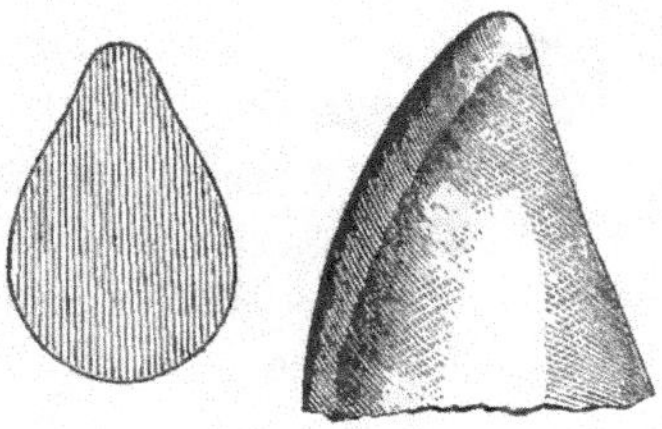

Fig. 40.

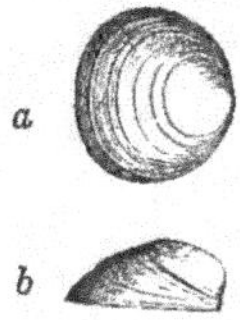

Fig. 41.

Fig. 40.—*Metoptoma Orithyia.* *a*, form of the base; *b*, side view.
41.—*M. Trentonensis.* *a*, view of the upper side; *b*, side view.

Locality and Formation.—Phillipsburgh, in the County of Missisquoi, Canada East. In the upper part of the Calciferous formation.

Collector.—E. Billings.

Metoptoma Erato. (N. sp.)

Description.—Elongate, oval, posterior margin uniformly rounded; sides very gently convex: anterior extremity narrowly rounded or pointed, forming an angle of about 90°. The shell for the greater part is uniformly convex; on approaching the apex compressed at the sides, forming a narrowly rounded or subcarinate umbo. The greatest elevation is in the anterior half of the shell; the apex is obtusely pointed and depressed so that its position is at about half the whole height of the shell. The outline in a side view gently concave at the anterior extremity beneath the apex, while above it is uniformly curved from the apex to the posterior margin. Surface nearly smooth but shewing indications of concentric striæ.

Length 11 lines; width 7 lines; height 3 lines.

Of this species I have seen only three specimens. Two of these seem to be slightly unsymmetrical or have the apex not quite in the median line. It is closely allied to *M. Nycteis*, but is smaller and more depressed.

Locality and Formation.—Paquette Rapids, on the Ottawa River. Black River limestone.

Collector.—E. Billings.

METOPTOMA TRENTONENSIS. (N. sp.)

Fig. 41.

Description.—Shell small, nearly circular, anterior margin obtusely rounded or subtruncate; convex most elevated a little in advance of the middle. The apex varies somewhat in its position. In some specimens it is directly over the anterior margin, and in such it is depressed below the greatest elevation of the shell. In others it is a little behind the anterior margin or nearly central, in which cases it sometimes forms the most elevated point. The shell is thick and the surface marked with fine striæ and often with irregular tumid ridges of growth. The form in some is perfectly circular but in others the anterior margin is nearly straight beneath the apex, or very gently rounded showing an approach to the regularly truncated species. The individuals vary little in size being in general 5 or 6 lines in length and breadth and 2 or 3 lines in height.

This species is more abundant in individuals than any other known in our rocks but apparently confined to particular localities.

Locality and Formation.—Chevrotière and Island of Montreal. Trenton limestone.

Collectors.—Sir W. E. Logan, J. Richardson.

AVICULA HERMIONE. (N. sp.)

Fig. 42.

Fig. 42.—*Avicula Hermione.*

Description.—Ovate, front margin broadly rounded, convex, most prominent in the upper half. Beaks small, closely incurved, umbo narrowly convex but not so much elevated as the middle of the shell. Hinge line and wings unknown. Surface ornamented with strong concentric striæ of variable size usually 6 or 8 in 1 line, but in some places only 3 or 4. These are crossed by small threadlike radiating ridges of which there are 5 or 6 in the width of 2 lines about the middle of the shell.

Length 2 inches; width about the middle 1½ inches.

This species is allied to *A. elliptica* (Hall) but differs in being more convex and pointed above and also in having the surface reticulated by both radiating and concentric striæ.

It seems to be very rare, only one imperfect specimen having been found.

Locality and Formation.—Montreal. Trenton limestone.

Collector.—E. Billings.

Conocardium immaturum. (N. sp.)

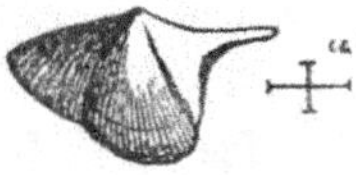

Fig. 43.

Fig. 43.—*Conocardium immaturum*, enlarged.

Description.—This little species is from 2½ to 4 lines in width on the hinge-line and 1½ to 2½ in length measured from the umbones to the ventral margin. The body of the shell is subtriangular, ventricose, the ventral margin rounded, the posterior angle about one fifth more remote from the umbones than the anterior, the umbonial angle acute, apparently 20° or 30°. The anterior wing is triangular compressed, its dorsal margin convex, forming with the anterior margin an angle of about 45°. At the junction of the lower margin of the wing with the ventral margin of the body of the shell there is an obtuse notch, in consequence of the curvature of the two margins mentioned. The posterior wing is small slender and cylindrical at its extremity but towards the body of the shell it rapidly expands into a broad base occupying about ½ the length of the posterior side of the body of the shell. The umbones are small but distinctly elevated above the hinge line. The beaks are closely incurved.

Surface covered with fine radiating ribs, just visible to the naked eye. Of these, 10 can be counted on the anterior wing and about double the same number on the body.

The following are the dimensions of the most perfect specimen observed. Width on hinge line including both wings 2½ lines; from the umbones to extremity of anterior wing 1½ lines; from the umbones to extremity of posterior wing 1 line; from umbones to ventral margin 1½ lines; width of ventral margin 1¼ lines; the anterior ventral angle is about ¼ of a line more remote from the umbones than the posterior angle.

None of the specimens examined are quite perfect, and it seems probable that in some the posterior wing may be proportionally a little larger. In the one figured, a piece appears to have been broken off.

D. D. Owen has figured a small species, under the name of *Pleurorhynchus antiqua*, in his Report on the Geology of Wisconsin and Iowa, Pl. 2 B. Fig. 19. His figure shows the body of the shell and the anterior wing, but not the posterior siphonal wing. Judging from so much as is exhibited, the ventral margin of the body of the shell does not project so far below the lower margin of the anterior wing as it does in this species. Owen found his specimen in the Lower Silurian rocks at Lower Fort Garry, on the Red River, in the Hudson Bay Company's territory.

It may be that this species belongs to an undescribed genus, but until the interior can be seen, we are compelled to place it in *Conocardium* on account of its external characters.

Locality and Formation.—Paquette Rapids, on the Ottawa River. Black River limestone.

Collectors.—Sir W. E. Logan, E. Billings.

MODIOLOPSIS MEYERI. (N. sp.)

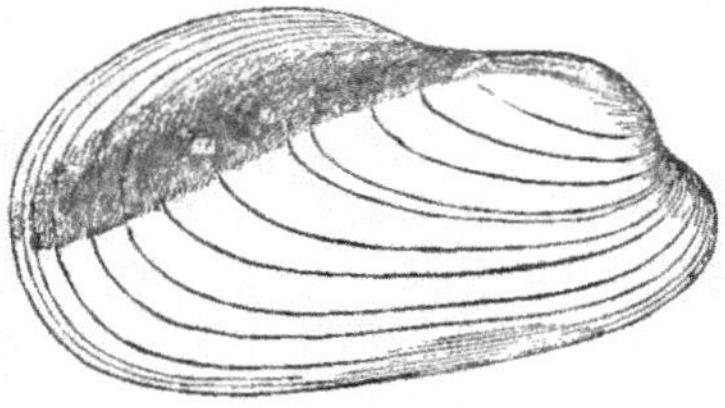

Fig. 44.

Fig. 44.—*Modiolopsis Meyeri.*

Description.—Transversely sub-ovate, alated posteriorly, rather strongly ventricose. The umbones are a little flattened and the beaks strongly incurved. From the umbones a strong oblique gibbosity extends diagonally downwards and backwards, becoming obsolete near the lower posterior angle. The hinge line is straight and about half the whole transverse length of the shell. The posterior half of the dorsal margin is elevated into a rather prominent rounded alation, thence descending with an uniform gentle curve to the posterior extremity, which is narrowly rounded and confined to the lower half of the shell. Ventral margin gently convex; anterior extremity small, about one-seventh the whole transverse length.

The length from posterior to anterior extremity is about 2 inches; from greatest elevation of dorsal margin in the posterior half to ventral margin, 1 inch; from umbones to ventral margin, ¾ of an inch.

Differs from *M. Modiolaris* in its greater gibbosity, and from *M. Gesneri* in the convex ventral margin, and absence of a byssal sinus.

Locality and Formation.—City of Ottawa. Trenton limestone.

Collector.—E. Billings.

MODIOLOPSIS GESNERI. (N. sp.)

a

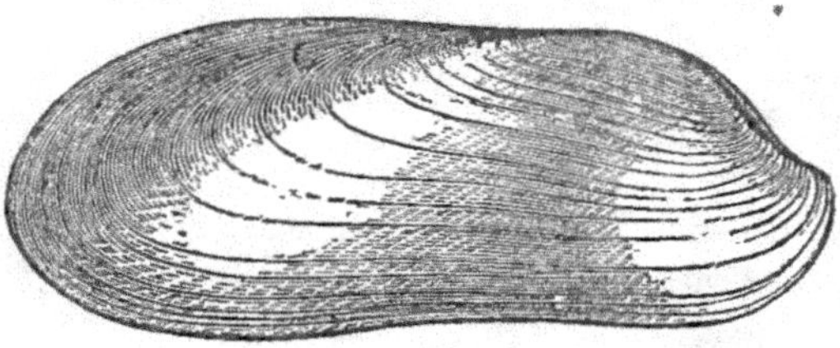

b

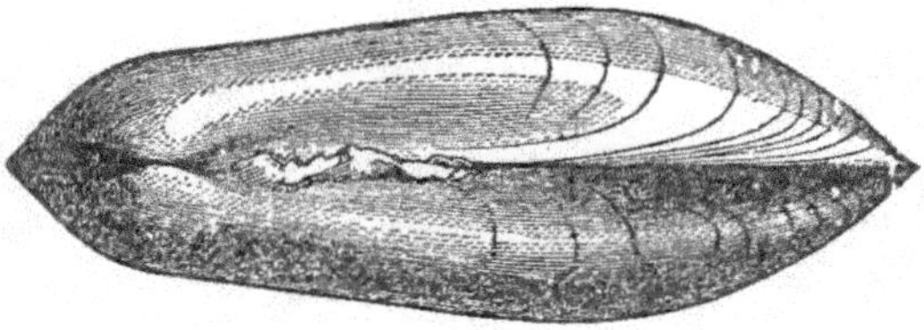

Fig. 45.

Fig. 45—*a*, View of right valve and *b*, hinge line of *M. Gesneri.*

Description.—Transversely elongate, arcuate, ventricose in the posterior half; a wide, shallow byssal sinus extending from the umbones to the ventral margin where it occupies the posterior two-thirds of the anterior half of the shell. Umbones somewhat flattened by the byssal sinus; beaks closely incurved; dorsal margin from the umbones to within about one-fourth of the whole length from the posterior extremity gently arched, or nearly straight, and nearly parallel with the ventral margin; then descending with a gentle curved slope to the posterior extremity, which is narrowly rounded; ventral margin, with the exception of the concave curve caused by the byssal sinus, nearly parallel with the dorsal. Anterior extremity small, about one-sixth of the whole transverse length of the shell. Surface with concentric ridges of growth of variable size, four or five in one line, with stronger ones sometimes two or three lines apart.

Transverse length, 2¾ inches; from the umbones to ventral margin, 10 or 12 lines.

Differs from *M. Modiolaris* in being more ventricose in the posterior half, and in having a more deeply impressed byssal sinus, and in having the dorsal and ventral margins more nearly parallel.

Locality and Formation.—City of Ottawa, Trenton limestone ; also at the Petite Chaudière Rapids, two miles from Ottawa, in the Black River limestone.

Collectors.—J. Richardson, E. Billings.

Modiolopsis Maia. (N. sp.)

Fig. 46.

Description.—Small, transverse, ventricose ; posterior extremity obliquely truncated ; umbones somewhat flattened ; beaks small, closely incurved, almost in contact with each other. Dorsal margin behind the umbones straight, gradually ascending until about one third of the whole transverse length from the posterior extremity, forming an obtuse angle of about 120° with the posterior margin which descends with a gently curved slope to the posterior angle, the latter obtusely rounded and situated in the ventral third of the shell. Ventral margin nearly straight in the posterior two thirds narrowly curved upwards at the posterior angle, more broadly curved up to the anterior angle which is narrowly rounded and situated a little below the middle of the shell and projecting about $\frac{1}{6}$ the whole transverse length in front of the umbones. A wide, very shallow byssal sinus extends from the beak obliquely backwards to the ventral margin, the middle $\frac{1}{3}$ of the length of which it occupies. A strong umbonial gibbossity runs diagonally backwards and downwards, becoming obsolete just before reaching the posterior ventral angle. Between this and the posterior extremity of the hinge line there is a concave slope. The greatest gibbosity is about the mid-length of the shell and nearer the dorsal than the ventral margin.

Surface not well exhibited in the specimen observed but shewing a few concentric lines of growth.

Transverse length 6 lines ; umbones to ventral margin 3 lines ; posterior extremity of hinge line to ventral margin $3\frac{1}{3}$ lines.

Locality and Formation.—East of Blue Point, Lake St. John, on the Saguenay. Trenton limestone.

Collector.—J. Richardson.

Modiolopsis Nais. (N. sp.)

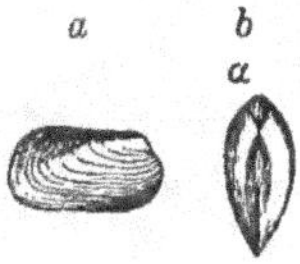

Fig. 46.

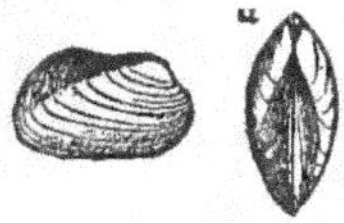

Fig. 47.

Fig. 46.—*Modiolopsis Maia.* *a*, right valve ; *b*, hinge line.
47.—*M. Nais.* *a*, right valve ; *b*, hinge line.

Description.—Shell, small, oblong, dorsal and ventral margins straight and nearly parallel, posterior extremity slightly wider than the anterior, obliquely and rather abruptly truncated with a moderate curvature. Anterior margin sloping from the umbones at an angle of about 130° ; anterior extremity about $\frac{1}{5}$ the whole transverse length, narrowly rounded and situated just below the middle. Umbones small, slightly flattened by the nearly obsolete byssal sinus ; beaks small, closely incurved but not in contact. The valves are moderately ventricose and the umbonial ridge scarcely prominent, the slope from it to the dorsal margin even, gently convex with a barely perceptible concavity just at the posterior dorsal angle.

Surface with rather strong sublamellose concentric ridges of growth, with finer ones between.

Transverse length 5 lines ; umbones to ventral margin $2\frac{1}{4}$ lines ; slightly more extended posteriorly ; depth of both valves 2 lines.

Locality and Formation.—Paquette Rapids, on the Ottawa River. Black River limestone.

Collector.—Sir W. E. Logan.

Modiolopsis Adrastia. (N. sp.)

Description.—Sub-triangular, 2 or 3 inches in transverse length, gradually tapering from the umbones to the posterior extremity, which is pointed or narrowly rounded. Ventral margin straight, gradually curved upwards at both extremities ; anterior margin somewhat straight, descending with an oblique slope below the middle to the narrowly rounded anterior extremity, forming an angle of between 60° and 70° with the ventral margin. Umbones inconspicuous, somewhat flattened ; beaks small, closely incurved ; valves only moderately ventricose, usually rather compressed. Surface with numerous rounded concentric undulations, two or three in one line.

Transverse length of best specimen 2½ inches; umbones to ventral margin 15 lines.

This species differs from most others of this genus in tapering to a narrowly rounded posterior extremity, and in its undulated surface.

Locality and Formation.—St. Joseph's Island, Lake Huron. Black River limestone.

Collector.—A. Murray.

CTENODONTA ABRUPTA. (N. sp.)

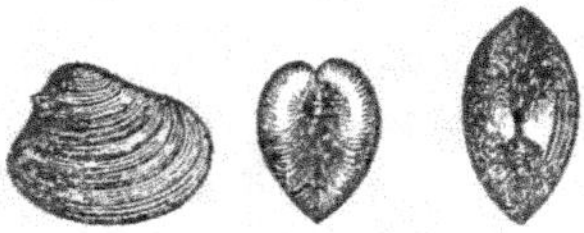

Fig. 48.

Fig. 49.

Fig. 48.—*Ctenodonta abrupta.* *a*, left valve; *b*, posterior extremity; *c*, hinge line.
49.—*Cyrtodonta Leucothea.*

Description.—Sub-triangular, ventricose, umbones large, beaks closely incurved, the posterior extremity abruptly truncated. In the outline, the anterior and posterior dorsal margins form a right angle (very nearly) with each other. The anterior extremity is broadly rounded and is placed altogether in the lower half of the shell. The ventral margin is usually rounded, but is sometimes nearly straight in the posterior half. The posterior ventral angle is small, narrowly rounded, and near the ventral margin; ligament short and very prominent. Surface with concentric lines of growth of variable size, some of them rather fine.

Width, 6 or 7 lines; length from umbones to ventral margin, 5 or 6 lines; depth of both valves, 4 lines.

In the above description I have called the side on which the ligament is placed, the posterior extremity, although it is very abruptly truncated and the beaks seem to curve towards it.

Locality and Formation.—Paquette Rapids, Ottawa River. Black River limestone. Also in the Trenton, at the City of Ottawa.

Collectors.—Sir W. E. Logan, E. Billings.

CYRTODONTA LEUCOTHEA. (N. sp.)

Fig. 49.

Description.—Shell small, rhomboidal, greatly alated and abruptly truncated posteriorly. Umbones depressed, convex; beaks closely incurved but scarcely in contact. Dorsal margin behind the umbones straight, in front of the umbones also nearly straight or gently concave, the umbonial angle about 135° ; posterior extremity broader than the anterior, gently rounded, nearly at right angles with the dorsal ; ventral margin nearly straight for three-fourths the whole length, narrowly curved upwards at each extremity. Anterior margin consisting of the portion of the dorsal margin in front of the umbones above mentioned. From the umbones a prominent broad gibbosity extends obliquely downwards to the lower posterior angle, between this gibbosity and the posterior dorsal angle a gentle slope becoming perceptibly concave on approaching the angle. Surface nearly smooth.

Width of dorsal margin, from umbones to posterior dorsal angle, 2 lines; from umbones to anterior ventral angle, $1\frac{1}{4}$ lines ; length of ventral margin, 3 lines ; of posterior margin, $2\frac{3}{4}$ lines ; depth of both valves, 2 lines.

Locality and Formation.—Paquette Rapids, on the River Ottawa. Black River limestone.

Collector.—Sir W. E. Logan.

LINGULA PROGNE. (N. sp.)

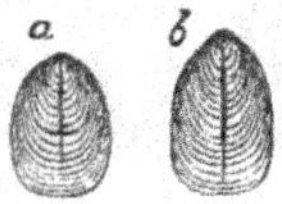

Fig. 50.

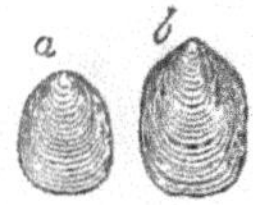

Fig. 51.

Fig. 50.—*Lingula Progne.* *a*, dorsal valve ; *b*, ventral valve.
51.—*L. Kingstonensis.* *a*, dorsal valve ; *b*, ventral valve.

Description.—Shell oblong-oval ; both valves gently and uniformly convex ; front margin broadly rounded or somewhat straight ; anterior angles rounded ; sides and the anterior two thirds of the length with the exception of the anterior angles straight or gently convex, parallel ; in the posterior third converging with a slightly convex slope to beaks. The ventral valve is somewhat pointed at the beak with an apical angle of about 70° ; the apex of the dorsal valve is obtusely rounded. Surface with concentric undulations, more numerous in some specimens than in others. In addition to these there are fine concentric striæ and longitudinal radiating lines, the latter not visible at all on some of the specimens until the surface is partially exfoliated. Colour black, shining.

Length 5 or 6 lines ; width about $\frac{3}{5}$ of the length. A specimen found at Montreal $9\frac{1}{2}$ lines in length and 5 lines in width appears to belong to this species.

All of the specimens that have come under my observation are more or less flattened by pressure, but the true form of the shell appears to be gently and uniformly convex.

Locality and Formation.—Montreal, in the Trenton limestone. Collingwood, in the Utica Slate.

Collectors.—Sir W. E. Logan, A. Murray, J. Richardson.

LINGULA KINGSTONENSIS. (N. sp.)

Fig. 51.

Description.—Ovate or sub-pentagonal; anterior angles rounded; front margin somewhat straight or gently convex; sides nearly straight and parallel from the anterior angles until within one third the length from the apex, then converging with a gently convex slope to the beaks; apex acutely rounded; apical angle about 90°. Surface with a smooth glistening aspect, and marked by minute concentric undulations of the shell. Colour dark brownish-black. Length from $2\frac{1}{2}$ lines to 6 lines; width a little variable, from $\frac{2}{3}$ to $\frac{4}{5}$ the length,

Somewhat resembles *L. Huronensis* but is smaller and more compressed and does not exhibit the three flat planes of that species. It is more closely allied to *L. Progne* from which it differs in being proportionally shorter and broder. The specimens examined are nearly all flattened by pressure but some of them which preserve the natural form very nearly appear to be uniformly depressed convex.

Locality and Formation.—Long Island near Kingston. Black River limestone.

Collectors.—J. Richardson and Mr. A. T. Drummond of Kingston.

LINGULA BRISEIS. (N. sp.)

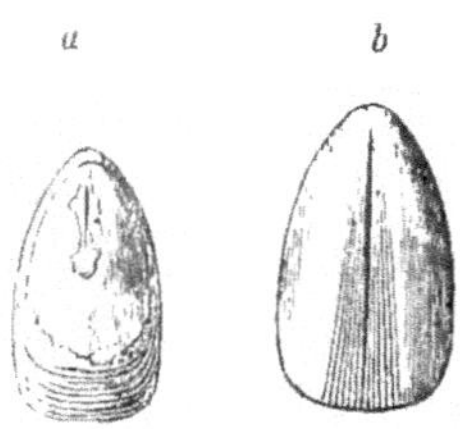

Fig 52.

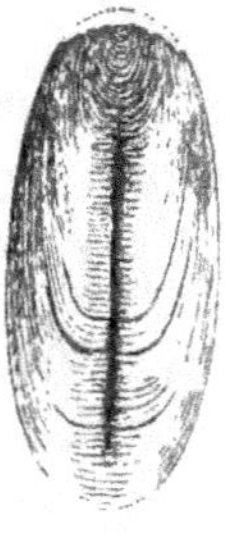

Fig. 53.

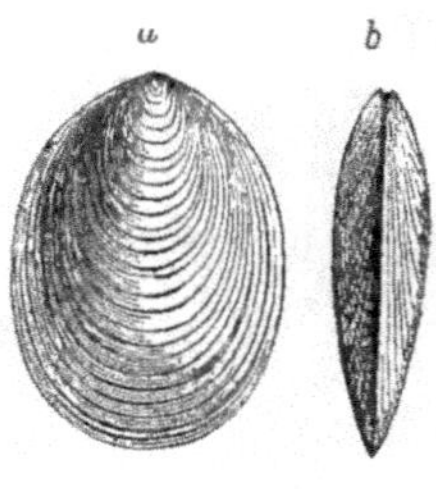

Fig. 54.

Fig. 52.—*Lingula Briseis.* *a* and *b*, views of two specimens.
53.—*L. Philomela.*
54.—*L. Cobourgensis.* *a*, view of ventral valve. *b*, longtiudinal section.

Description.—Elongate, conical; anterior angles rounded; front margin nearly straight or gently convex; sides somewhat straight and parallel in the lower half, then converging with a very moderate curve to the beaks; apex acutely rounded. Both valves appear to be very slightly convex and with a slight barely perceptible concavity near the sides. Surface when perfect to the naked eye nearly smooth and with a glistening lustre; under the lens shewing very fine longitudinal striæ; these become more apparent when the shell is partially exfoliated. There are also numerous obscure undulations of growth. One of the valves shews in the cast of the interior a strong groove along the median line sometimes extending nearly the whole length of the shell. Colour of shell light brown.

Length of largest specimen seen 9 lines; width at one fourth the length from the base 5 lines at one fourth the length from the apex 3⅜ lines.

Specimens from 5 lines up to 9 lines in length occur associated together in the same locality.

This species resembles *L. Progne* but is of a more nearly conical shape, the side commencing to converge towards the apex from a point about the middle or a little below.

Locality and Formation.—Near Olivier's Mills on the River Bayonne. Lower part of Trenton limestone.

Collector.—J. Richardson.

Lingula Philomela. (N. sp.)

Fig. 53.

Description.—Very elongate, oval; width a little less than half the length; front margin rather narrowly rounded with a small space in the middle straight or sinuate; sides for about two thirds the length straight or very gently convex; the apical extremity appears to be obtusely angular but this still remains doubtful as no specimens with this part perfect have been collected. The shell is rather strongly convex, most prominent at or about the mid-length. There is shallow concave sinus extending all along the median line from near the apex to the front margin. Surface with fine crowded imbricating striæ of variable size, the smaller just visible to the naked eye and the larger partaking of the nature of squamose interruptions of growth. Colour in the black limestone black. A specimen in grey limestone shewing the interior in a state of exfoliation is light greyish-brown, but this may be owing to some circumstance in the fossilization of the shell.

Length 16 lines; width 7 lines.

Locality and Formation.—Montmorenci Falls, and Island of Montreal. Trenton limestone.

Collectors.—Sir W. E. Logan, J. Richardson.

LINGULA COBOURGENSIS. (N. sp.)

Fig. 54.

Description.—Almost regularly oval; greatest width about the middle; length one-fourth greater than the width; anterior extremity uniformly rounded; apex obtusely angular; both extremities sub-equal; sides gently convex. Both valves are moderately convex, and one of them has sometimes an irregular furrow extending from near the beak along the median line for one-half or three-fourths the length. Colour, dark brown, with some shades of light brown or yellow; general aspect smooth and shining, with fine concentric undulations of growth, which become fine, elevated, sharp, closely crowded striæ, on each side of the beak; longitudinal striæ are visible on some specimens.

Length, about 1 inch; width, about $\frac{3}{4}$ of an inch; depth of both valves, 3 or 4 lines. Smaller specimens occur associated with the larger.

Although the specimens appear to be abundant, I have never seen one with the beaks entire. *L. obtusa* (Hall)is a smaller shell, wider in front and of a black colour.

Locality and Formation.—Cobourg, Trenton limestone. Also at Collingwood, in the same formation.

Collectors.—T. Devine, Esq., Crown Lands Dept., Mr. J. F. Smith, Toronto, R. Bell.

LINGULA DAPHNE. (N. sp.)

LINGULA ATTENUATA, (Hall,) *Pal. N. Y.*, Vol. 1, p. 94, Pl. 30, figs 1*a* 1*b*, *Not L. attenuata*, (Sowerby.)

Description.—Shell ovate, broadest in the anterior half, moderately pointed in the rostral half; front margin uniformly rounded; sides in the lower half gently convex, and in the upper somewhat straight or slightly curved and converging to an angle of between 50° and 70° at the apex. The valves are uniformly convex, the greatest tumidity being in the upper half. Surface with fine concentric striæ and occasionally minute undulations of the shell resembling striæ to the naked eye.

Length, from 4 to 8 lines; width varying from $\frac{3}{5}$ to $\frac{3}{4}$ the length.

This species has been referred to *L. attenuata*, Sowerby, but it differs therefrom in having the front uniformly rounded. In the English species the front margin is nearly straight in the middle, and the sides in the lower half also nearly straight and parallel.

Locality and Formation.—Montreal. Trenton limestone.

Collectors.—Sir W. E. Logan, J. Richardson.

Discina Circe. (N. sp.)

Fig. 55.

Fig. 56.

Fig. 55.—*Discina Circe.* Fig. 56.—*D. Pelopea.*

Description.—Circular; lower valve with the apex central or very nearly so; peduncular groove acutely oval, extending from the apex about two-thirds the distance to the margin. The foramen is probably situated at the outer extremity of the groove, but it cannot be seen in the specimen examined. The upper valve (supposed to be that of this species,) has the apex situated about one-third the semi-diameter from the margin. In both valves the apex is smooth.

Surface with rather strong, sub-lamellose concentric striæ, which become more distant and coarser from the apex outwards. At the margin there are four or five ridges in 1 line, but next to the apex double that number in the same space. The ridges are somewhat irregular, being in some places slightly undulated, and occasionally branched, two or more running into one. The grooves are rather wider than the ridges, and the lamellose aspect of the latter appears to be due to their being more abruptly elevated on the inner side, or the side towards the apex than on the outside.

Width of the specimen of the lower valve examined, 9 lines; length of peduncular sulcus, 3¼ lines; width of same, ½ a line. Another specimen (an upper valve) is 7 lines wide.

The lower valve is depressed, conical, and appears to have been about 2 lines in height, but as it is somewhat distorted by pressure, the true elevation cannot be determined. The upper valve seems to be less convex than the lower.

The species described by Prof. Hall, under the name of *Orbicula lamellosa*, (Pal. N. Y., Vol. 1, p. 99, pl. 30, figs. 10 *a b*,) appears to be a smaller and more finely striated species. It may be that the figures represent a young individual of this species; but, at all events, the name proposed by Prof. Hall cannot be retained, as it was pre-occupied by another and very distinct species, *D. lamellosa.* (Brod. Zool. Proc. 1833, p. 124.)

This species also resembles *D. Forbesii* (Davidson,) a Wenlock limestone species, but differs in having the apex of the lower valve central, instead of eccentric.

Locality and Formation.—Belleville, Trenton limestone. Also Flat Point, Lake St. John, in the same formation.

Collectors.—E. Billings, (Belleville), J. Richardson, (Lake St. John.)

DISCINA PELOPEA. (N. sp.)

Fig. 56.

Description.—Upper valve circular, depressed conical. Apex about half the semi-diameter from the posterior margin. Surface with fine concentric striæ when perfect, but when partially exfoliated, smooth and places polished shining. Colour, black; width, 6 lines. Lower valve unknown.

This species is about the size and shape of *D. lamellosa*, (Hall) but has the apex rather nearer the margin. It differs from *D. circe* in the same character, and also in being smaller and not so strongly striated.

Locality and Formation.—Montreal. Trenton limestone.

Collector.—Sir W. E. Logan.

TREMATIS MONTREALENSIS. (N. sp.)

Fig. 57.

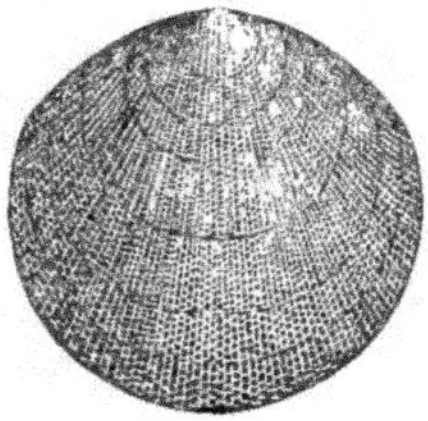

Fig. 58.

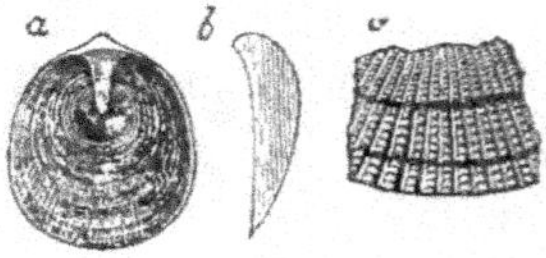

Fig. 59.

Fig. 57.—*Trematis Montrealensis.* Lower valve, shewing the small penduncular notch.

58.—*T. Ottawaensis.* Upper valve.

59.—*T. Huronensis.* *a*, lower valve; *b*, longitudinal section, shewing the curvature of both valves; *c*, a portion of the surface enlarged.

Description.—Lower valve transversely broad, oval, depressed, convex, nearly flat; foramen consisting of a very small notch in the posterior margin; surface with a few concentric striæ and undulations; shell, jet black and where not striated, presenting a polished, shining appearance.

Width of specimen, 7 lines; length, 5 lines; height, about 1 line.

The greatest convexity is at about one-third the diameter from the posterior margin.

Of this species we have only a single valve. The anterior margin, for about half a line in width is abruptly bent down, and it is not certain that this is the result of accident.

T. Terminalis has the lower valve more elevated and a deeper notch for a foramen; *T. Huronensis* has the lower valve concave.

Locality and Formation.—Montreal. Trenton limestone.

Collector.—Sir W. E. Logan.

TREMATIS OTTAWAENSIS.

Fig. 58.

Description.—Nearly circular; length a little greater than the width; upper valve moderately and uniformly convex, most elevated about the middle; apex small, obtusely pointed, slightly elevated, marginal. Surface with fine, radiating striæ, which increase by interstitial addition, sometimes closely crowded together, in which case there are ten or twelve in the width of one line; occasionally more distant, or from four to eight in one line. The intermediate grooves are divided into square compartments by cross ridges, which connect the radiating ridges, but are not continuous, those in one groove not corresponding in position with those in the adjacent grooves, so as to form uninterrupted concentric lines. In specimens with the striæ closely crowded together, only the radiating lines are distinctly visible, but the others can always be detected in good specimens, on close examination.

Length, from 12 to 15 lines; width a little less than the length. Lower valve unknown.

The species figured by Prof. Hall, under the name of *Orbicula filosa* resembles this, but has the surface much more finely striated and not reticulated. This is also a larger species.

A large number of specimens of this species were found in one spot 4 or 5 yards in extent, in a thin stratum of argillaceous shale between beds of Trenton limestone at Ottawa. None of them were perfect, and they appeared to be all of the same value.

Locality and Formation.—City of Ottawa. Trenton limestone.

Collector.—E. Billings.

TREMATIS HURONENSIS. (N. sp.)

Fig. 59.

Description.—Obtusely oval. Lower valve gently concave; foramen a deep triangular notch in the posterior margin, extending inwards a little more than half the distance to the centre. Upper valve, moderately convex, most elevated in the posterior half, with a small rounded beak, incurved down to the plane of the posterior margin. Surface with fine very obscure radiating striæ, ten or twelve in the width of one line, crossed by fine concentric striæ about the same distance apart. This arrangement of the striæ gives to the surface a finely punctuated aspect.

Length, 6 or 7 lines; width, 5 or 6 lines.

The shell is thin and of a light brown or dun colour. When a little worn, it has a smooth, glistening appearance, and the punctures and striæ are then scarcely visible.

Trematis cancellata (G. B. Sowerby,) must be closely allied to this species. It is thus described: "Shell orbicular, very flat, being more gibbous near the posterior extremity; surface covered with close-set, elevated lines radiating from the apex, which are crossed by the elevated lines of growth, so that the entire surface has a finely reticulated appearance; the fissure in the ventral valve is small and close to the hinge; shell very thin; length and breadth, ¾ of an inch." (Sharpe, Jour. Geo. Soc., Vol. 4, p. 69.) I have not seen Sowerby's original description and figure, bnt from the above it would appear that *T. cancellata* has a small foramen, while *T. Huronensis* has a large one, and also the radiating and concentric striæ not elevated.

Locality and Formation.—Pallideau Islands, Lake Huron. Black River limestone.

Collector.—A. Murray.

Genus ARTHROCLEMA. (N. gen.)

Generic characters.—The only species of this genus at present known consists of a cylindrical jointed stem with several long slender branches which are also usually jointed. The surface exhibits numerous small oval pores resembling those of *Ptilodictya*.

These fossils have somewhat the appearance of species of *Ptilodictya*, but differ in having the stems cylindrical instead of compressed.

Generic name from "*arthron*" a joint and "*klema*" a twig.

ARTHROCLEMA PULCHELLA. (N. sp.)

Fig. 60.

Description.—The central or principal stem of this species is from 3 to 6 inches in length and from ½ a line to 2 lines in thickness. The joints are distant from 2 to 4 lines from each other. There are two branches to each joint situated exactly opposite to each other on the opposite sides of the main stem. These also send off smaller branches from their opposite sides, the whole being arranged in one plane like the mid-rib and veins of a leaf. The young branches are not jointed but the full grown ones are.

The pores are oblong-oval about six in the length of one line. In general there is, on each side of the joint, an enlargement of the stem, the segments in such cases having somewhat the form of an hourglass.

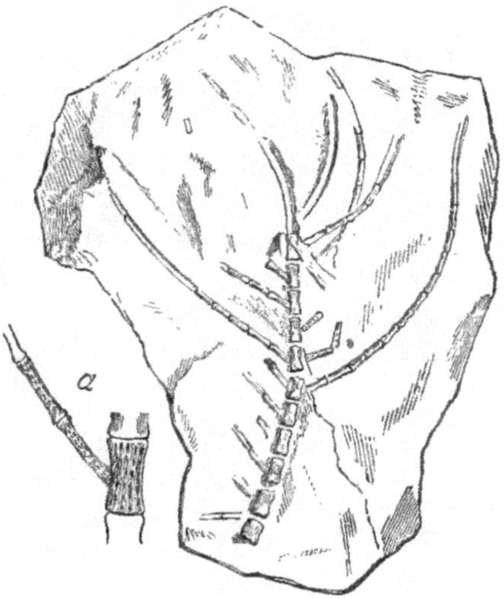

Fig. 60.

Fig. 60.—*Arthroclema pulchella.* A specimen of the usual size partly imbedded in stone ; *a*, enlargement of one of the joints of the main stem and of a portion of one of the branches.

Locality and Formation.—Trenton limestone, City of Ottawa. Also near Peterborough, Canada West.

Collectors.—E. Billings and W. Rogers.

STROMATOPORA COMPACTA. (N. sp.)

Description.—This species forms small sub-globular masses, from 1 to 2 inches in diameter. The concentric lamellæ are thin and closely packed together, there being in some specimens from 6 to 12 layers in the thickness of 2 lines.

This species differs from *S. rugosa* in being much smaller and more compact. It occurs in localities where *S. rugosa* is not found, but at Paquette Rapids it is associated with that species in the same beds.

Locality and Formation.—Island of Montreal, and Paquette Rapids, on the Ottawa river. Black River limestone.

Collectors.—Sir W. E. Logan, J. Richardson.

SERPULITES DISSOLUTUS. (N. sp.)

Description.—This species is usually from 2 to 3 inches in length, and from 1½ to 3 lines in width at the larger extremity. The form is elongate, slender, tapering to an acute point, generally pressed quite flat, often showing on each side an elevated wire-like margin, running the whole length, as if two of the opposite sides of the tube were thicker and stronger than the other two. In such specimens there is an irregular depression along the middle, between the two thickened margins. Colour, jet black, shining ; surface apparently smooth.

The best preserved specimen that I have seen is 2½ inches in length, and 1¾ lines in width at the larger extremity. Another specimen with a portion of the smaller extremity broken off is 2⅝ inches in length ; 3¼ lines wide at the larger and 1 line wide at the smaller (broken) extremity. This specimen, when perfect, must have been a little more than three inches in length.

This species is often found in slender, hair-like, jet-black, shining fragments, consisting of the separated thickened sides of the tube. No perfectly entire specimens have been collected.

Locality and Formation.—Montreal, Ottawa, Lachine, Naquareau. Trenton limestone.

Collectors.—Sir W. E. Logan, J. Richardson, E. Billings.

BATHYURUS SMITHII. (N. sp.)

Description.—The specimen upon which this species is founded consists of the glabella and the greater part of the fixed cheeks of a minute trilobite, discovered by Mr. J. F. Smith, of Toronto, two or three years ago, in the neighborhood of Peterborough, C.W. The glabella is obtusely conical, strongly convex, most elevated in the middle, separated from the cheeks by a deep dorsal furrow, which runs all round ; front margin obtusely rounded ; sides gently convex ; neck furrow extending all across. Cheeks moderately tumid. Eyes at about the mid-length of the head, and distant about half the width of the glabella from the dorsal furrow.

Length of glabella, 1 line ; width of the same, a little more than half a line ; length of eye, apparently about ¼ of a line.

On account of the rather great convexity of the glabella, this species resembles a *Menocephalus*. I refer it to *Bathyurus*, provisionally.

Locality and Formation.—Peterborough. Black River limestone.

Collector.—Mr. J. F. Smith.

3.—*On some New Species of Fossils from the Quebec group.*

1.—SYNCHRONISM OF THE POINT LÉVIS LIMESTONES.

As there has been a good deal of discussion, with much diversity of opinion, on the subject of the geological age of the rocks at Point Lévis, it may not be out of place, here, to review the evidence upon which the position assigned to them in the recent publications of the Survey, is founded. The question is intimately connected with the characters of the Fauna of the Potsdam group, and I shall therefore, in the first place, give a list of the papers relating thereto, with the species described in each.

1847.—PROF. J. HALL described *Scolithus linearis*, *Lingula prima*, and *L. antiqua*. The first of these was stated to occur in the Potsdam sandstone of the valley of Lake Champlain, " in the partially altered sandstone of the same age, at the base of the Green Mountains, in Adams, Mass.," in New Jersey, Pennsylvania, Maryland, Virginia, and Tennessee. The two species of *Lingula* were found in New York. (Pal. N.Y., vol. i.)

1851.—DR. H. A. PROUT described *Graptolithus Hallianus*, from the Potsdam sandstone of Wisconsin. (Am. Jour. Sci. (2) xi, p. 187.) This species has been since referred, by Prof. J. Hall, to the genus *Dendrograptus*.

1851.—SIR W. E. LOGAN read a paper before the Geological Society of London " On the Occurrence of a Track and Foot-prints of an Animal in the Potsdam sandstone of Lower Canada." He stated that his " attention was first drawn to the track by Mr. Abraham, then editor of the Montreal Gazette, who duly appreciated its possible geological importance, and inserted a notice of it in his daily journal." (Jour. Geo. Soc., vol. vii, p. 247.)

1852.—PROF. R. OWEN described and figured the tracks above mentioned under the names of *Protichnites septem-notatus*, *P. octo-notatus*, *P. latus*, *P. multinotatus*, *P. lineatus* and *P. alternans*. As to the affinities of the creature which made the tracks, he says the *Limulus* " comes nearest to his idea of the kind of animal which has left the impressions on the Potsdam sandstone." (Jour. Geo. Soc., vol. viii, p. 214.)

1852.—DR. D. D. OWEN described *Orbicula prima*, *Lingula ampla*, *L. pinnaformis*, *Dikelocephalus Minnesotensis*, *D. Pepinensis*, *D. Miniscaensis*, *D. Iowensis*, *D. granulosus*, *Lonchocephalus Chippewaensis*, *L. hamulus*, *Crepicephalus Wisconsensis*, *C. Minniscaensis*, and *Menocephalus Minnesotensis*, from the Potsdam sandstone of Wisconsin. He also cites with doubt *Obolus Apollinis*, *L. antiqua* and *L. prima* with *Orthis* and Crinoidal stems from the same beds. (Geol. Rep. on Wisconsin, Iowa and Minnesota.)

1859.—J. W. SALTER described *Conocephalites antiquatus* from "a cast in a brown sandstone, said to be a bouldered fragment from Georgia." (Jour. Geo. Soc., vol. xv, p. 554.)

1860.—DR. B. F. SHUMARD announced the discovery of the Potsdam sandstone and Calciferous sandrock or their equivalents in Burnet county, in the State of Texas, and described one species, (*Orthis Coloradoensis*,) from the former. (Trans. Acad. Nat. Sci., St. Louis, vol. i, pp. 627, 672.)

1860.—SIR W. E. LOGAN described and figured a track in the Potsdam sandstone under the name of *Climactichnites Wilsoni*. This track was discovered by Dr. James Wilson of Perth. (Can. Nat. Geol., vol. v, p. 279.) Dr. J. W. Dawson has described and figured the various tracks of *Limulus* on the sand of the existing sea-beaches, showing very clearly that both *Protichnites* and *Climactichnites* may be the tracks of crustaceans. (Can. Nat. Geol. vol. vii, p. 273.)

1860.—F. H. BRADLEY described *Conocephalites minutus* from the Potsdam sandstone at Keeseville, N. Y. He also reported the occurrence of the cast of a *Pleurotomaria* and a crinoidal joint in the same beds. (Am. Jour. Sci. (2) xxx, p. 241.)

1861.—DR. B. F. SHUMARD described from the Potsdam of the locality in Burnet county in Texas, above mentioned, *Discina microscopica*, *Camerella* (sp. ?), *Capulus* (sp. ?) *Agnostus Coloradoensis*, *Arionellus* (*Bathyurus*) *Texanus*, *A.* (*Bathyurus*) *planus*, *Conocephalites depressus*, *C. Billingsii* and *Dikelocephalus*, *Roemeri*. (Am. Jour. Sci. (2) xxxii, p. 213.) In this paper Dr. Shumard mentions the previous discovery, by Dr. Ferd. Roemer, of trilobites in Texas which had been referred by Barrande to the fauna of the Primordial zone. I have not access to Roemer's work at present, or I would notice his species here.

1862.—DR. F. V. HAYDEN and F. B. MEEK gave an account of their discovery of the Potsdam sandstone around the Black Hills and other localities along the eastern side of the Rocky Mountain range. They described *Obolella nana*, *Theca* (*Pugiunculus*) *gregarea* and *Arionellus Oweni* from the Black Hills and Big Horn Mountains. They also cite species either identical with or closely allied to *Lingula prima* and *L. acuminata*, from the same localities. (Am. Jour. Sci. (2) xxxiii, p. 73, Jan. 1862; also Proc. Acad. Nat. Sci. Phila., Dec. 1861, p. 435).

1862.—DR. B. F. SHUMARD revised several of D. D. Owen's species, and also described *Dikelocephalus latifrons*, *Arionellus bifurcatus*, and *Conocephalites minor* from the Potsdam of Wisconsin. He also made the first announcement of the occurrence of the genus *Agnostus* in this formation. The species noticed by him "appears to be identical with or at least very nearly allied to" *A. Orion* which occurs at Point Lévis. (Trans. Acad. Sci., St. Louis, vol. ii, May, 1862).

1863.—PROF. J. HALL revised a number of the above named species from the Potsdam sandstone of Wisconsin, and described the following new ones: *Lingula Winona*, *L. Moisa*, *L. Aurora*, *Discina inutilis*, *Obolella? polita*, *Orthis Pepina*, *Platyceras primordialis*, *Euomphalus vaticinus*, *Theca primordialis*, *Serpulites Murchisoni*, *Dikelocephalus limbatus*, *D. spiniger*, *D. Misa*, *D. Osceola*, *Conocephalites Eos*, *C. Perseus*; *C. Shumardi*, *C. nasutus*, *C. Oweni*, *C. Eryon*, *C. anatinus*, *C. Pattersoni*, *C. binodosus*, *C. Winona*, *C. diadematus*, *C. optatus*, *C. nactus*, *Chariocephalus Whitfieldi*, *Illænurus quadratus*, *Triarthrella Auroralis*, *Agnostus Josepha*, *A. parilis*, *A. disparilis*, *Aglaspis Barrandei*, *Pemphigaspis bullata*, and *Amphion matutina*. The new genera of trilobites described in this paper are *Pemphigaspis Aglaspis*, *Triarthrella*, *Illænurus*, *Chariocephalus* and *Ptychaspis*. In the last of these is placed Owen's two species, *Dikelocephalus Minnesotensis* and *D. granulosus*. All the species are illustrated by excellent figures. (16th Reg. Rep.)

1864.—PROF. A. WINCHELL, of Michigan, described *Orthis Barabuensis*, *Straparollus (Ophileta) primordialis*, *Pleurotomaria Advena*, *Ptychaspis Barabuensis*, *Palæophycus articulatus*, and *P. informis*, from the Potsdam sandstone of Sauk County, Wisconsin. He also reports from the same locality, *Scolithus linearis*, *D. Minnesotensis* and *D. Pepinensis*.

In addition to the above, Prof. Hall has described from the Potsdam group in Vermont *Olenellus Vermontana*, *O. Thompsoni* and *Bathynotus Holopyga*. There will also be found in this work the following twenty-two species,—*Scolithus Canadensis*, *Palæophycus incipiens*, *P. congregatus*, *Archeocyathus Atlanticus*, *A profundus*, *Obolus Labradoricus*, *Obolella chromatica*, *O. (Kutorgina) cingulata*, *Orthisina festinata*, *Camerella antiquata*, *Conocephalites miser*, *C. Adamsi*, *C. Vulcanus*, *C. Teucer*, *C. arenosus*, *Bathyurus senectus*, *B. parvulus*, *B. vetulus*, *B. perplexus*, *Salterella rugosa*, *S. pulchella*, and *S. obtusa*.

There are also in Canada certain beds, at present considered to form the upper layers of the Potsdam, which hold *Lingula acuminata*, *Ophileta compacta*, *Pleurotomaria Canadensis*, and a small orthoceratite. It may be that these beds should be placed in the base of the Calciferous, and, therefore, in the following comparisons the fossils they hold will not be taken into account.

Assuming that the above are all the described species of this series of rocks, the fauna of the Potsdam as at present known would appear to consist of—

Plantae,	6	species.
Protozoa,	2	"
Graptolitidæ,	1	"
Brachiopoda,	21	"
Gasteropoda,	5	"
Annelida,	5	"
Crustacea,	67	"
	107	

The six species of Plantæ are supposed to be fossil sea-weeds, and there can be no doubt that at least four of them are ; but as to the two species of *Scolithus* there is much difference of opinion. By some they are thought to be casts of annelide-burrows, and by others fucoids. Much further of observation is required to determine the affinities of these obscure but very remarkable fossils. The two species of *Archeocyathus* may possibly belong to an extinct order of corals, but for the present they are placed among the *Protozoa.* The Graptolitidæ, Brachiopoda, Gasteropoda, and Annelida are mostly of genera or sub-genera, which have a great vertical range, and can scarcely be made available to determine, by their generic relations, the age of any geological horizon, although certain species of each genus may be confined to, and characteristic of, particular groups of strata. In the following comparisons, therefore, they will not be taken into account further than to notice that none of the species are as yet known to ascend into the Calciferous formation. The trilobites belong to the following genera :

Aglaspis,	1	species.
Arionellus	4	"
Bathyurus	4	"
Bathynotus	1	"
Chariocephalus	1	"
Conocephalites.	23	"
Crepicephalus	2	"
Dikelocephalus	10	"
Menocephalus	1	"
Lonchocephalus	2	"
Olenellus	2	"
Ptychaspis	1	"
Triarthrella	1	"

The above constitute the dominant family of the trilobitic fauna of the Potsdam.

Agnostus	4	"
Amphion	1	"
Illænurus	1	"
Pemphigaspis	1	"
Protichnites	6	"
Climactichnites	1	"
	67	

In the above list, I have left all the species in the genera to which they were originally referred by their authors respectively. Some alterations have been proposed by Prof. Hall and Dr. Shumard, which will no doubt be adopted either wholly or in part. Without objecting to any of these changes, it seems the better course, for the present, to admit D. D. Owen's four genera, until more perfect specimens can be procured.

On a comparative examination of all the genera in the above list it will be seen, that *Agnostus*, *Illænurus* and *Pemphigaspis* are peculiar types, and, in their organization, stand apart, as it were, from all the others. *Amphion* is a well defined genus, now, for the first time, found in rocks so ancient as the Potsdam, although it occurs in the Calciferous, and is known in Bohemia, by a single species (*A. Lindauri*, *Barr.*) in the lowest beds characterized by the second fauna. These four genera are represented, so far as at present known, in the Potsdam by only seven species, and constitute but a small portion of the whole fauna of the period. We may also set aside *Protichnites* and *Climactichnites*, because they consist only of tracks, and we know too little about them to form any idea of the affinities of the family to which they belong.

After making the deductions, above mentioned, there remain thirteen genera, and these all belong to one great family, which appears to have attained its greatest development in the Potsdam period, and to have gradually declined afterwards, until the era of the Trenton limestone, when it became extinct. The different generic groups, of which this family is composed, are most closely allied, and run into each other in such a manner as to render subdivision almost impossible, showing that they all had one common origin. There appear to be, furthermore, innumerable varietal passages between the species, while, in certain localities, the individuals occur in such vast multitudes, although always in fragments, as to constitute of themselves the principal mass of the rock. The aspect of the family is that of a portion of the first fauna of Barrande, and it seems probable that it existed in a period somewhat later than that of the large species of *Paradoxides*, which form so striking a feature in the Primordial zone of Europe. In Bohemia, Sweden, Wales and Spain, some of the genera do indeed occur in the rocks of that ancient horizon, but they do not constitute the principal and dominant section of the fauna. In the Potsdam, on the other hand, thirteen out of seventeen genera (excluding the genera founded on tracks), and fifty-three out of sixty species, belong to this family, while the individuals are so exceedingly numerous that they perhaps furnish ninety per cent. of the whole.

Without noticing the Calciferous formation, for the present, we may proceed next to the examination of the fauna of the Quebec group. In the table shewing the succession of Canadian rocks, on page 20 of the

Geology of Canada, this group is divided into the Sillery and Lévis formations. The Sillery, consisting of a vast deposit of sandstones and slates, has, as yet, furnished only two species of fossils,—a small *Lingula*, too imperfectly preserved to be determined, and *Obolella pretiosa*. The Lévis formation holds a large, interesting and well marked fauna, which persistently maintains the same combination of types, and consequently exhibits the same aspect along a chain of exposures extending from Newfoundland to Vermont, a distance of nearly 1000 miles. The same rocks have been traced through Vermont into New York, and will, perhaps, yet be found to continue on to the Gulf of Mexico. The formation, however, in its extension into the United States has, as yet, furnished only a few fragmentary fossils. The localities in Canada, where organic remains abound, are of limited extent, and widely separated from each other, although they all occur in the same line of outcrops. The perfect identity of the species which are common to exposures so far apart as are Cow Head in Newfoundland, and Point Lévis and Phillipsburgh in Canada, is truly wonderful; while the rock specimens, whether of slate or limestone, are often absolutely indistinguishable from each other by any lithological characters. From this formation we have 219 described species, distributed as follows:

Zoophyta	1	species.
Graptolitidæ	53	"
Brachiopoda	28	"
Lamellibranchiata	2	"
Gasteropoda	42	"
Cephalopoda	20	"
Crustacea	73	"
	219	

In the above, I have not included any of the Newfoundland fossils except those which occur in the slates and limestones at Cow Head. The rocks of this locality are precisely of the same age as those of Point Lévis: but the other fossiliferous exposures, such as those at Portland Creek, Table Head, Point Rich, and Pistolet Bay, hold a somewhat different, although closely related, fauna. They may well be placed in the Quebec group, but not in the Lévis formation. The Quebec group, in fact, consists of several formations differing from each other lithologically and palæontologically, and yet forming a connected series. In the Lévis formation, the following genera of trilobites occur:

Arionellus	2	species.
Bathyurus	12	"
Bathyurellus	6	"
Conocephalites	1	"
Dikelocephalus	14	"
Menocephalus	3	"
Loganellus	1	"

The above belong to the dominant family of the trilobitic fauna of the Potsdam.

Agnostus	3	"
Amphion	5	"
Ampyx	1	"
Asaphus	4	"
Cheirurus	8	"
Endymionia	1	"
Holometopus	1	"
Harpes	1	"
Harpides	1	"
Illænus	5	"
Nileus	1	"
Lichas	1	"
Remopleurides	1	"
Shumardia	1	"
	73	

In this list I have placed all the species in the genera to which they were originally referred, except the species of *Loganellus*, which was described as an *Olenus*. The two species of *Arionellus* may possibly belong to Prof. Hall's newly proposed genus *Ptychaspis*. In the genus *Bathyurus* there are two species, (*B. conicus* and *B. Cordai*,) which evidently have the characters of Owen's genus *Crepicephalus*. In *Dikelocephalus Sesostris*, we have also a form which I consider to be perfectly congeneric with *D. Miniscaensis*, one of the types of *Ptychaspis*. *Menocephalus* is not recognized by Hall and Shumard among the fossils of the Potsdam sandstone of Wisconsin, where the specimen on which Owen proposed the genus was procured. *Crepicephalus* is also placed by them in *Conocephalites*, where, indeed, it is perfectly admissible, provided the great extension given to this latter genus be sustained. I think, however, the number of species is becoming so great that, sooner or later, *Conocephalites* will be broken up into a number of genera. Be this as it may, we have, in the Lévis formation, the leading generic types of the dominant family of the Potsdam trilobites, although (in accordance with the views of different authors) not all under the same names. All the species (39 in number) that I have referred to *Arionellus*, *Bathyurus*, *Bathyurellus*, *Conocephalites*, *Dikelocephalus*, *Menocephalus* and *Loganellus*, belong to that family. Comparing the trilobitic fauna of the Potsdam with that of the Lévis formation, we thus find that in the former, thirteen out of seventeen genera, and fifty-three out of sixty species; and in the latter, seven out of twenty-one genera with thirty-nine out of seventy-three species belong to the same zoological group. This shows that, while this peculiar type of trilobites strongly connects the two faunæ, during the period of the Lévis formation it was on the decline.

Passing now to the upper part of the Lower Silurian we may, for our present purpose, regard the Chazy formation as being characterized by a distinct fauna; but the Black River, Birdseye, Trenton, Utica Slate, and Hudson River, should all be grouped together. The fauna of this latter series may be called the Trenton fauna, as it attains its greatest development in that formation.

In the Chazy fauna the dominant family of the Potsdam trilobites is reduced to a single genus and species—*Bathyurus Angelini.* The genus *Amphion* also passes from the Potsdam to the Chazy, but is not known above that formation in this country.

In the Trenton fauna the dominant family of the Potsdam is represented by only two genera (*Bathyurus* and *Triarthrus*). The latter has not been found below the Trenton; but it, nevertheless, is a genus of the primordial type. Barrande has placed it in his third family, which includes *Paradoxides*, *Arionellus*, *Conocephalites*, *Olenus*, &c. (Système Silurien, p. 340.) In Canada we have four species of this genus, all in the Utica slate, *T. Beckii*, *T. spinosus*, *T. glaber* and *T. Canadensis*. The first of these is found, in New York, in the Trenton as well as in the Utica slate. Of the three species of *Bathyurus*, two (*B. Smithi and B. extans*) occur in the Black River limestone; while the third (*B. spiniger*) is common to the Black River and Trenton.

In order to save space the generic relations of the several trilobitic faunæ above noticed may be abbreviated as in the following lists.

Trenton Fauna.

Asaphus, 10; Acidaspis, 2; **Bathyurus, 3;** Bronteus, 1; Calymene, 3; Cheirurus, 3; Dalmanites, 3; Encrinurus, 1; Harpes, 3; Illænus, 7; Lichas, 1; Proetus, 1; *Triarthrus*, 4; Trinucleus, 1. Total, 43.

Chazy Fauna.

Asaphus, 2; **Amphion, 1;** Ampyx, 1; **Bathyurus, 1;** Cheirurus, 3; Harpes, 1; Illænus, 6; Lichas, 1; Remopleurides, 1; Sphærexochus, 1. Total, 18.

Lévis Fauna.

Agnostus, 3; Amphion, 5; Ampyx, 1; **Arionellus, 2;** Asaphus, 4; **Bathyurus, 12;** *Bathyurellus*, 6; Cheirurus, 8; **Conocephalites, 1; Dikelocephalus, 14;** Endymionia, 1; Holometopus, 1; Harpes, 1; Harpides, 1; Illænus, 5; **Menocephalus, 3;** Nileus, 1; Lichas, 1; Remopleurides, 1; Shumardia, 1; *Loganellus*, 1; **Crepicephalus; Ptychaspis; Bathynotus.** Total, 73.

Calciferous Fauna.

Asaphus, 1; **Amphion, 2; Bathyurus, 6**; *Bathyurellus*, 2; *Dolichometopus*, 3. Total, 14.

Potsdam Fauna.

Agnostus, 4; Aglaspis, 1; Amphion, 1; Arionellus, 4; Bathyurus, 4; Bathynotus, 1; Chariocephalus, 1; Climactichnites, 1; Conocephalites, 23; Crepicephalus, 2; Dikelocephalus, 10; Illænurus, 1; Menocephalus, 1; Lonchocephalus, 2; Olenellus, 2; Pemphigaspis, 1; Protichnites, 6; Ptychaspis, 1; Triarthrella, 1. Total, 67.

In the above lists the genera printed in black-letter are those that occur in the Potsdam; those in italics belong to the primordial type, but have not yet been found in the Potsdam. All the others are members of the second fauna of Barrande, except, indeed, *Endymionia* and *Shumardia*, which are new genera, whose geological range is as yet undetermined. *Crepicephalus*, *Ptychaspis* and *Bathynotus* are placed in the Lévis faunæ, but with their number not indicated, because the species are included in *Dikelocephalus* and *Bathyurus*. The lists show, so far as the proposition can be demonstrated by *genera alone*, that the true place of the Lévis formation is between the Potsdam and the Trenton groups, not below the Potsdam, as is still maintained by some observers.

If we examine how far these several faunæ are connected together by species, we find :—

1. Not a single species of the large fauna of the Potsdam is known to pass upwards.

2. Of the Calciferous fauna, four species (*Asaphus canalis*, *Amphion Salteri*, *Bathyurus Cordai* and *B. conicus*) pass upwards into the Lévis formation. And one of these (*A. canalis*) ascends into the Chazy.

3. Of the Lévis fauna, two species (*A. canalis* and *Cheirurus prolificus*) pass upwards into the Chazy.

4. One trilobite only (*Asaphus platycephalus*), and that doubtfully identified, is common to the Chazy and Trenton. It is also worthy of notice that the peculiar group of the genus *Cheirurus*, with a spine on the head, has only been found, in America, in the Lévis formation, and in the Chazy, (see *C. perforator*, p. 275; *C. Glaucus* and *C. Satyrus*, p. 323.) And further that the genus *Remopleurides* has, as yet, been found in America only, in the same two formations.

Proceeding, next, to the other orders and classes, such as the Brachiopoda, Gasteropoda, Cephalopoda, &c., it is quite clear that the Lévis fauna is, upon the whole, distinct from all the others, although a few species are common to it and the Calciferous, or to it and the Chazy.

The Calciferous species, which are certainly found in the Lévis formation, are *Lingula Mantelli*, *Camerella calcifera*, and *Pleurotomaria calcifera*. There are, besides these, a few which I do not consider to be positively identified with Calciferous species, but which, nevertheless, in such specimens as have been collected, agree so well with the figures in the Pal. N. Y., that it would be unsafe to give them new names. They have been referred by me heretofore to *Ophileta uniangulata*, *Maclurea matutina*, *M. sordida* and *Holpea dilucula*.

Of Chazy species we find, at Phillipsburgh, the plates of a Cystidean, which I cannot distinguish from those of *Palæocystites tenuiradiatus*, a peculiar and remarkable fossil, and highly characteristic of the Chazy limestone. It is, probably a distinct species, but in detached plates it is impossible to point out any difference. *Camerella varians* is also common to the Chazy and Lévis faunæ. The remarkable genus *Calathium* is represented in the Lévis formation by *C. pannosum*, and in the Chazy by *C. Canadensis*. This genus commences in the Calciferous, and runs up to the Chazy. *Stenopora fibrosa* can scarcely be mentioned as a characteristic fossil, but it is found in beds below the Lévis, and passes upwards to the upper Silurian. There are no species common to the Lévis and Trenton faunæ, except the one last mentioned.

It will be seen by referring to Art. 6, p. 207 and its continuation, p. 361, that in Newfoundland the Lévis formation does not there immediately overlie the true Calciferous, but is separated therefrom by two other series of strata of considerable importance. The first of these, consisting of Divisions I, K, L, M, is 1084 feet in thickness, and holds a fauna which is, upon the whole, distinct from that of the Lévis formation. The trilobites are :

Bathyurus	2	species.
Bathyurellus	1	"
Asaphus	1	"
Illænus	2	"
Amphion	1	"
	7	

Of these, *Asaphus canalis* and *Amphion Barrandei* occur in the Lévis formation. *Orthis Electra* is also found in these beds: but all the other fossils are either new species, or species that occur in the Chazy and Calciferous. Overlying this series of strata is another 277 feet in thickness, with a different fauna, the details of which will be found at the place cited. Then follows 700 feet of sandstone, overlying which is the Lévis formation, at Cow Head. It would thus appear that the rocks at Point Lévis not only overlie, but, also, when the series is complete, are at least 2000 feet above the true Calciferous. That so many trilobites belonging to the dominant type of the Potsdam should occur in such a horizon appears to me to be a most extraordinary fact. Judging from the fossils alone, I should say that the Lévis formation immediately snccceds the Calciferous, but the physical evidence seems to show that such is not the case.

2.—Descriptions of New Species of Fossils.

In a paper published in the Canadian Naturalist and Geologist, vol. v, p. 201, August, 1860, I made a provisional division of the specimens in which the fossils were first found at Point Lévis, and designated them simply as limestones Nos. 1, 2, 3 and 4. I think it advisable to retain these divisions here, but it is quite clear that they all belong to the same series of beds. No. 1 is a peculiar greyish-white limestone and holds a number of species that have not been discovered in any locality except at Point Lévis. Sir W. E. Logan has shown that there are nine bands of the limestone and that my Nos. 1 and 3, belong to his band No. 3, and also that his No. 4 includes my No. 2. There are several species common to these two bands, but a great deal more must be done in the way of collecting fossils at Point Lévis before all the questions that have arisen with regard to the fauna of that locality can be satisfactorily disposed of.

The following is Meek and Hayden's description of *Obolella nana.*

"Obolella nana." (Meek and Hayden.)

"Shell very small, subcircular, or transversely suboval, moderately convex, rather thick; front broadly rounded; sides more narrowly rounded. Beak of dorsal valve short and obtuse. Ventral valve proportionally a little longer than the other, about as long as wide, and having a slightly more prominent beak; without a distinct mesial ridge within; scars of adductor muscles ? located behind the middle and diverging towards the front. Surface marked by a few concentric furrows; exfoliated specimens showing small obscure regularly disposed radiating striæ on the inner laminæ.

"Length of dorsal valve, 0·15 inch; breadth of do., 0·17 inch; convexity, 0·15 inch. Length and breadth of ventral valve of a smaller specimen, each 0·14 inch.

"In first sending on to the Academy a description of this little shell, we had referred it with doubt to the genus *Obolus*, stating, at the same time, that its muscular scars, so far as they could be made out from the only specimen we had seen showing the interior, seemed to present differences from the type of Eichwald's genus. Since seeing Mr. Billings's figures of his genus *Obolella*, recently published, we are fully satisfied that he is right in separating these shells from the genus *Obolus*.

" Our species is so closely allied to *Obolella chromatica* of Billings, the type of the genus, (see " New species of Lower Silurian Fossils, page 7,) that we were inclined to regard it as specifically identical until we had an opportunity to compare it with specimens of Mr. Billings's species, kindly sent us by him. On comparing it with these, we find it is more convex, and proportionally broader, while its concentric markings are stronger. The substance of its shell is also thicker, and differs in showing radiating striæ on the inner laminæ of exfoliated specimens.

" *Locality and Position.*—Central portions of the Black Hills, from the Primordial or Potsdam sandstone."

OBOLELLA PRETIOSA. (N. sp.)

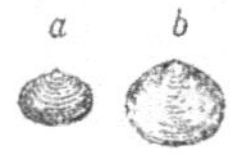

Fig. 61.

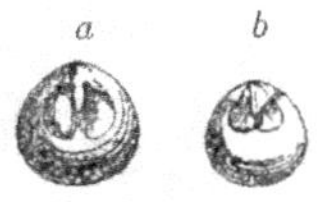

Fig. 62.

Fig. 63.

Fig. 61.—*Obolella pretiosa.*—*a.* Ventral valve of a small specimen; *b.* dorsal valve of a specimen of the average size.

62.—*O.*——— *desiderata.*—*a.* Cast of the interior of what is supposed to be the ventral valve; *b.* cast of interior of dorsal valve.

63.—*O*——— *Ida.*—*a.* Dorsal, and *b.* ventral valve.

Description.—Transversely broad oval; width greater than the length; front margin broadly rounded; lateral margins more narrowly rounded than the front; greatest width about the middle, or a little below; beak of ventral? valve minute, pointed, apparently not depressed below the greatest elevation of the shell; apical angle very obtuse, about 150 ; cardinal slope straight, or sometimes gently concave on each side of the beak, for a length equal to one-fourth or one-third the whole width of the shell, and then imperceptibly becoming curved round to the lateral margins. The other valve only differs in outline by having the apex more obtuse. Both valves are moderately and uniformly convex; the greatest elevation being about the middle, or a little above it. Surface with very fine squamose concentric striæ. In some of the specimens a few radiating striæ are visible. These, however, may be in some instances due to distortion, as the shell is very thin.

Some of the specimens are inequilateral, or have the umbo and beak a little on one side of the median line, and thus present the aspect of a small lamellibranchiate shell.

Length from 2 to 3 lines; width usually about one-fourth or one-fifth greater than the length. The specimens are often much distorted, and sometimes nearly circular; but all the well-preserved individuals that have come under my observation are transversely sub-elliptical, the width being greater than the length.

This species differs from *O. chromatica*, *O. Ida*, and *O. desiderata*, in its proportions, and from the first of these particularly in having a thin instead of a thick shell. In this latter character also it differs from *O. nana* (Meek and Hayden). On comparison of specimens, I cannot see any difference between this species and one figured by Dr. Emmons in his American Geology, Pl. I, fig. 10, the size, proportions, and surface characters being precisely the same, so far as I can judge. The Virginian species, as may be seen by Emmons' figure and also by specimens in my possession, is (like ours) sometimes inequilateral. It occurs in Augusta County, Virginia, in soft-whitish grey slates associated with graptolites.

Locality and Formation.—Our species occurs in the greenish and olive-colored slates near the bridge of the Grand Trunk across the Chaudière, and also in similar slates, but of a darker color, at Cape Rouge, above Quebec. These slates are interstratified with the Sillery sandstones, which are at present classified as the upper part of the Quebec group, but the question as to whether such is their true position or not, is considered an open one. The only fossils found in the Sillery, up to the present time, are this species and a small *Lingula* which will be described as soon as good specimens can be procured.

Collector.—J. Richardson.

Obolella desiderata. (N. sp.)

Fig. 62, *a*, *b*.

Description.—Shell small, moderately convex. Ventral valve ovate; greatest width a little in front of the middle; front angles and margin uniformly rounded, the front margin sometimes with a portion in the middle straightish; the upper half slightly narrowed towards the beak. Dorsal valve nearly circular.

Length and breadth from 3 to 4 lines.

The specimens that have been collected are all, with the exception of three or four, pressed quite flat. Those not distorted by pressure show a moderate amount of convexity, the greatest elevation being at about one-third the length from the beak. The beaks appear to be depressed down to a level with the hinge line, but upon this point there yet remains some uncertainty.

From some nearly perfect casts of the interior, the following characters can be made out. In one of the valves (supposed to be the ventral), a strong rounded groove commences just beneath the beak, and runs along the median line to about the centre of the shell. On each side of the principal groove is a large ovate muscular impression, extending from near the mid-length of the shell a little more than half way to the beak. These impressions are bounded and distinctly defined at their lower extremities by the two small diverging grooves above mentioned. Their outer and upper margins are distinctly defined. In the rostral part of the shell there are two small grooves which take their origin close to the beak, one on each side, and run towards the front, diverging to the outside of the upper part of the two large muscular impressions. The characters of the interior of the dorsal valve are somewhat similar to those of the ventral valve, but the median groove is shorter, and there is a thickening of the shell just below the beak, which presents the appearance of a false area inside of the cavity of the umbo. It is probable that the two small grooves above mentioned are connected with the small muscular impressions, which, in *O. chromatica*, are distinctly seen outside of the two larger. The condition of our specimens, however, is such, that this point must remain open for further investigation.

This species differs from *O. chromatica* in the form of the muscular impressions, which are larger and nearer the median line. *O. pretiosa* is of a different form, the width being greater than the length. *O. Ida* is much smaller, more convex, and not so nearly circular. *O. nana* (Meek and Hayden), Proc. Acad. Nat. Sci., Philadelphia, vol. 13, p. 435, Dec. 1861, is also wider than it is long.

The two large muscular impressions in this species appear to converge towards the front in some of the specimens, as in the genus *Obolus*, while in *O. chromatica* they diverge. But, notwithstanding this difference, the large size of these scars, and the general aspect of the shell, appear to be sufficient to authorise us to place it in *Obolella*.

Locality and Formation.—Point Lévis; in the graptolitic slates, Quebec group.

Collectors.—Sir W. E. Logan, J. Richardson.

Obolella Ida. (N. sp.)

Fig. 63, *a*, *b*.

Description.—Shell small, obtusely ovate, greatest width at or a little in front of the middle, abruptly narrowed to the beaks, sides and front margin uniformly rounded, the front slightly less convex than the sides. Both valves equally and rather strongly convex, most elevated at about one-third the length from the apex, thence sloping with a gentle curve to the sides and front margin, abruptly descending on each side of the beak and umbones. Ventral valve slightly more pointed above than the dorsal; umbo narrowly convex; beak apparently depressed to the level of the lateral margin. Dorsal valve obtusely angular or narrowly rounded at the beak, the latter not visibly distinct from the cardinal edge; umbo obtusely convex. Surface with a somewhat shining aspect, with a very fine concentric striæ; a few radiating striæ are visible on two of the specimens. Shell apparently very thin.

Length of a perfect ventral valve, 2 lines; width, 1⅞ lines. The length and width of the dorsal valve are about equal.

This species somewhat resembles a *Lingula*, but in general its aspect is so much like that of an *Obolella*, that although the internal characters have not been observed, I think it best to refer it to the latter genus. It is one-third smaller and not so thick-shelled as *O. chromatica*, and differs from that spécies in having the beaks depressed down to the level of the lateral margin instead of a little elevated.

It differs from *O. pretiosa* in having the umbones more tumid, the beaks not so sharply pointed, in its greater convexity, smaller size, and less proportional width. *O. desiderata* is larger, and more obtuse in the rostral half. *O. nana* (Meek and Hayden) is proportionally broader.

Locality and Formation.—Point Lévis. In limestones Nos. 1 and 3, Quebec group.

Collector.—Sir W. E. Logan, J. Richardson, and R. Bell.

Lingula Irene. (N. sp.)

Fig. 64. *a*, *b*.

Description.—Nearly circular or very broadly ovate; beak small and apparently acute; apical angle about 90°. Sides for about one-fourth the length next the beak straight or very nearly so, sometimes slightly concave and occasionally with a barely perceptible convex curve. In the anterior two-thirds, the sides and front margin are uniformly curved so as to give to the front part of the shell a circular contour. Surface with fine but distinct subsquamose concentric striæ, of which there are from six to ten in the width of one line. Length of largest specimen seen, 7 lines; width, 6½ lines. Another specimen is 5½ lines in length, and 5¼ in width.

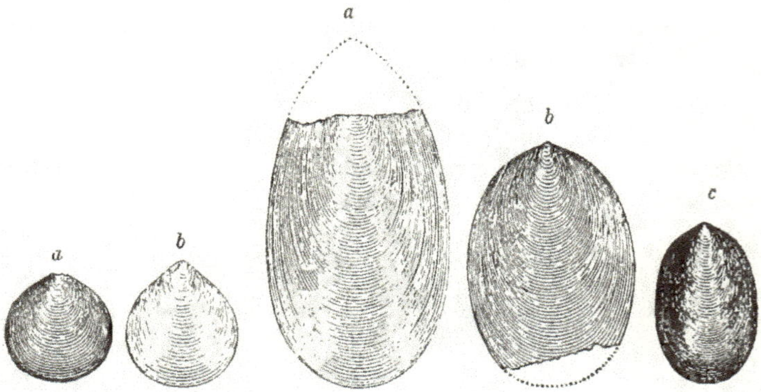

Fig. 64. Fig. 65.

Fig. 64.—*Lingula Irene.*—*a.* Specimen found in a boulder of magnesian limestone near Montreal, supposed to be from the calciferous sandrock; *b.* Specimen from the graptolitic slates, Point Lévis.

Fig. 65.—*L——— Quebecensis.*—Three specimens of different sizes.

The specimens in the slate at Point Lévis are usually pressed quite flat, but some of them show a considerable amount of convexity in the upper half. A single valve from the Calciferous sandrock at the eastern end of the Island of Montreal is rather strongly convex, especially on the umbo. It is 7 lines in length, and 6½ in width, its proportions, contour, and surface characters being precisely like those of the largest specimen from Point Lévis.

This resembles *L. curta* of the Trenton limestone and Utica slate, but is proportionally broader.

Locality and Formation.—Point Lévis; in the graptolitic slates of the Quebec group. A specimen not distinguishable specifically from those of Point Lévis was found by Mr. Ramsay in a boulder of the Calciferous sandrock near the city of Montreal.

Collectors.—Mr. Ramsay, J. Richardson, J. Weston.

Lingula Quebecensis. (N. sp.)

Fig. 65. *a, b, c.*

Description.—Shell large, elongate-oval; extremities nearly equal; front margin narrowly and uniformly rounded; sides very gently convex;

apex obtuse, slightly angular in the ventral and broadly rounded in the dorsal valve. In perfect specimens both valves are moderately convex, most elevated in the upper half, especially along the middle, for a short distance from the beak, about one-fourth of the width next the margin on each side of the umbones compressed. Surface with fine concentric striæ, from eight to ten in the width of one line.

Length from 15 to 18 lines ; width from 10 to 12 lines.

The above description relates to the specimens collected in the black graptolitic slates at the water's edge, a short distance below the ferry at Point Lévis ; but in the thin-bedded limestones interstratified in the slates on the road-side near the ferry-landing, others were collected of a smaller size, but with precisely the same form and proportions. The largest found at this locality is 12 lines in length and 8 lines in width. Numerous smaller ones, from 3 to 10 lines in length, occur along with the larger, in the same beds. At present I believe all of these belong to the same species ; but should a separation hereafter be deemed advisable, it is proposed to retain the name *L. Quebecensis* for the larger form, which is associated with the graptolites.

This species resembles *L. quadrata,* but is more nearly oval, and proportionally not so broad.

Locality and Formation.— Point Lévis. In the graptolitic slates and thin-bedded limestones of the Quebec group.

Collector.—J. Richardson.

LEPTÆNA SORDIDA. (N. sp.)

Fig. 66.

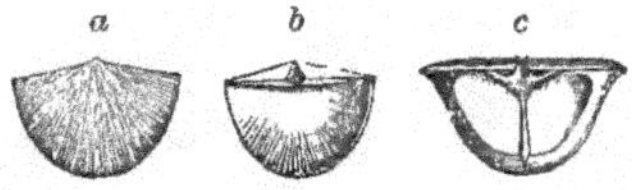

Fig. 67.

Fig. 66.—*Leptæna sordida.*—*a,* Ventral and *b,* dorsal aspects.

67.—*L*——— *decipiens.*—*a,* Ventral and *b,* dorsal aspects ; *c,* interior of dorsal valve.

Description.— Shell small, obtusely semi-oval ; length equal to about five-sixths of the width ; cardinal angles either rounded or slightly projecting ; sides either straight or slightly convex, and either parallel or only very slightly converging in the upper half of the shell ; front half broadly and uniformly rounded.

Ventral valve strongly and uniformly convex, or depressed hemispherical ; a small portion at the cardinal angles compressed. Area very large, forming an obtuse angle with the plane of the lateral margin.

Dorsal valve gently concave; area slightly inclining forwards, forming with the area of the other valve an angle of about 100°.

Foramen of ventral valve about as wide as it is high, the apical third closed by a thin deltidium. Area of the dorsal valve crossed by a groove as in *L. decipiens.*

The surface of this species appears to be smooth, but as all the specimens are silicified it is possible that this may be the result of some circumstance in the process of fossillization.

Width about 3 lines, length 2½ lines. Many of the specimens are a little larger.

Locality and Formation.—Point Lévis. In the upper part of the limestone No. 2, Quebec group.

Collectors.—Sir W. E. Logan, J. Richardson, R. Bell.

Leptæna decipiens. (N. sp.)

Fig. 67. *a, b, c.*

Description.—Shell rather small, about the size of *L. sericea*, semi-oval, widest on the hinge-line, usually narrowed from the cardinal angles forward; front margin rounded; length from two-thirds to three-fourths of the width. Ventral valve convex, somewhat flattened in the upper half; umbo narrow and slightly elevated, the convexity extending therefrom gradually widening towards the front; the cardinal angles compressed and sometimes slightly reflected; front half curved towards the dorsal valve with a rounded slope. The area is rather large, somewhat concave, forming an obtuse angle with the plane of the lateral margin. Foramen triangular, usually open, but sometimes with a rudimentary deltidium over a small part at the beak.

Dorsal valve concave, with a distinct mesial sinus commencing at the beak and gradually widening forward, becoming obsolete before reaching the front margin. Area well developed, flat, rather more than one-third the width of that of the ventral valve, forming a right angle with the plane of the lateral margin.

Interior of ventral valve with a well-defined ridge running all round, parallel with and at about one-third the length of the shell from the margin. The dental plates are rudimentary, and seem to converge towards each other, thus exhibiting a tendency to form a small chamber in front of the beak.

Interior of dorsal valve with a semicircular ridge similar to that of the ventral valve, but apparently a little nearer the margin. In some specimens a mesial ridge extends from near the foramen towards the front, terminating at the semicircular ridge with a strongly elevated projection. At the hinge-line there is a sort of foramen passing between the dental sockets and forming a concave groove across the area nearly to the beak. On each side of this foramen there is a small projection similar to those that are seen in the dorsal valve of *Orthis*. It is barely possible that these these may represent the divaricator processes, but at present I am inclined to the opinion that they do not. I think the muscles were attached to the surface at the bottom of the groove which passes between them.

Surface with fine striæ alternating in size exactly as in *Strophomena alternata*.

Width from 4 to 6 lines. Length from 3 to 4 lines. Area of ventral valve from ½ to ⅝ of a line in height at the foramen.

Locality and formation.—Point Lévis. In the upper part of lime stone No. 2, Quebec group.

Collectors.—Sir W. E. Logan, J. Richardson.

ORTHIS GEMMICULA. (N. sp.)

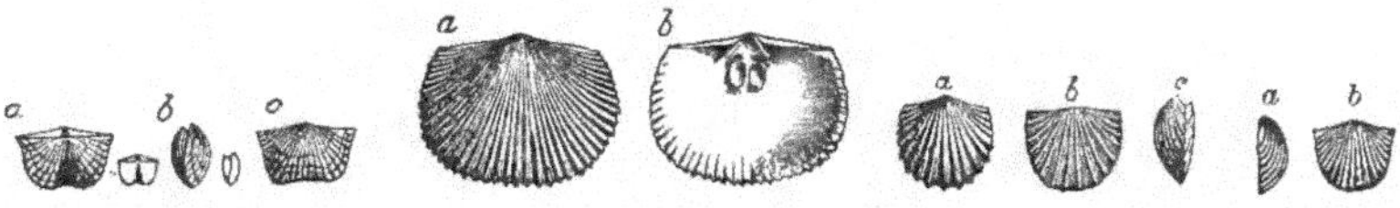

Fig. 68. Fig. 69. Fig. 70. Fig. 71.

Fig. 68.—*Orthis gemmicula; a, b, c,* three views of a specimen enlarged. The small figures show the natural size.

69.—*O.*— *Tritonia; a,* dorsal valve; *b,* interior of the same.

70.—*O.*— *orthambonites; a, b, c,* ventral, dorsal and side views.

71.—*O.*— *Euryone; a, b,* ventral valve.

Description.—Shell very small, transversely oblong or semioval; hinge line equal to or a little greater than the width of the shell; cardinal angles either rectangular or slightly produced, forming small acute ears; sides either straight or gently convex, and subparallel or converging towards the front; front margin either rounded, straight or sinuate, and often with a deep notch in the middle. Ventral valve very convex, most elevated in the upper half and along the middle, where it is often obtusely carinated, descending with a gently concave or somewhat flat slope to the sides; cardinal angles compressed; beak small, pointed, depressed to about half the height of the valve; area about half the height of the valve, forming with the plane of the lateral margin an angle of about 110°; foramen scarcely so wide as high; dorsal valve convex with a deep angular sinus which divides the valve into two tumid lobes. Surface when very perfect with fine concentric striæ crossed by stronger radiating striæ which give to the shell a beautifully cancellated appearance; when not perfect, either smooth or with only the radiating striæ.

Width from 1 to 1½ lines; length from ¼ to ⅓ less than the width.

This is the smallest species of *Orthis* known in the Lower Silurian rocks of Canada. Numerous perfect single valves and a few with both valves connected were procured by treating fragments of limestone holding the silicified fossils with acid. The form varies somewhat after the manner of *O. Lynx*, being sometimes transversely oblong with the sides subparallel and often narrowed towards the front, and with or without short ears at the cardinal angles. The front is often rounded, but in general it is either somewhat straight or with a wide angular notch in the middle crossed by the deep mesial sinus of the dorsal valve. In the foramen there is seen in several of the specimens a projection which seems to be a large divaricator process, but in others this is not seen.

Locality and Formation.—Point Lévis. In the upper part of the limestone No. 2, Quebec group.

Collectors.—Sir W. E. Logan, J. Richardson.

ORTHIS TRITONIA. (N. sp.)

Fig. 69. *a*, *b*.

Description.—Dorsal valve transversely sub-elliptical, hinge-line nearly equal to the greatest width of the shell, cardinal extremities rounded but somewhat angular, sides gently convex, anterior angles broadly rounded, front margin very gently convex. The shell is moderately convex, most elevated at about one third the length from the beak, compressed near the cardinal angles; beak small, incurved down nearly to the plane of the margin; umbo broadly rounded, projecting a little over the hinge-line. Surface with angular bifurcating ribs, several times divided between the umbo and the front margin, becoming very fine on approaching the cardinal angles, from four to six in the width of two lines at the front margin. There is a very obscure mesial depression, which scarcely affects the contour of the surface but is still perceptible, running all the way to the beak, on approaching which it becomes attenuated to a single impressed line. The area is small, consisting simply of the thickness of the shell; the foramen wide but very low.

In the interior of the valve the anterior pair of occlusor muscular impressions consist of two small but deep pits of an oval shape, one line in length and half a line in width, situated close to the median line and about their own length from the beak. Above each of those are two very small pits which may represent the posterior pair. There is no divaricator process, the umbo being simply hollowed out into a triangular cavity, to the bottom of which the muscles for opening the valve were attached.

Length 5 lines; width 7 lines.

Ventral valve unknown.

Of this species we have only a single but very perfect dorsal valve. It resembles the dorsal valve of *O. plicatella*, but is not so convex. It differs from *O. pectenella* and *O. subquadrata* in external aspect, while in the interior it exhibits no divaricator process. I know of no species in the Lower Silurian rocks which has the muscular impressions situated so near the hinge-line.

Locality and Formation.—Point Lévis. In the upper part of the limestone No. 2, Quebec group.

Collectors.—Sir W. E. Logan, J. Richardson.

Orthis orthambonites. (Pander.)

Orthis calligramma, *var.* Orthambonites. Murchison and De Verneuil. *Geol. Rus.* Vol. II. p. 207, Pl. XIII. fig. 8.

Fig. 70. *a, b, c.*

Description.—Shell rather small, coarsely ribbed, semioval or suborbicular; ventral valve convex, and dorsal valve nearly flat; hinge-line straight and nearly equal to the greatest width of the shell; front angles and margin broadly and nearly uniformly rounded; sides in the upper half of the shell somewhat straight or gently convex. Ventral valve strongly convex, most elevated in the upper half; beak incurved down nearly to the level of the plane of the lateral margin; umbo prominent neatly rounded, overhanging the hinge-line; cardinal angles somewhat compressed; area small, concave, not extending the whole width of the shell; foramen small, about as wide as it is high. Dorsal valve nearly flat, gently convex in the upper half, sloping to the cardinal angles and front margin, with a wide barely perceptible mesial sinus; area small, nearly at a right angle to the plane of the margin; foramen small, extending to the beak; the latter scarcely distinct from the hinge-line. In the interior of this valve the margin all round the front and lower half of the sides is deeply crenulated by the coarse ribs. In the upper half there is a low obtuse mesial ridge which on approaching the foramen divides, a branch going to each of the crural processes. In the foramen there is a thin plate-like divaricator process. The occlusor muscular impressions are small and situated close to the mesial ridge in the upper half of the valve.

Surface of each valve with from fourteen to eighteen strong undivided ribs separated by deep furrows equal to them (the ribs) in width.

Width of dorsal valve about 3½ lines; length of the same about 3 lines. Owing to the projection of the umbo, the ventral valve has the length and width more nearly equal.

The specimens agree so nearly with the figures of *O. calligramma*, var. *Orthambonites*, in the work above cited, that I have no hesitation in referring them to that species. In Russia it occurs in the orthoceratite limestone abundantly in the neighbourhood of St. Petersburgh.

Locality and Formation.—Point Lévis. In the upper part of limestone No. 2, Quebec group.

Collectors.—Sir W. E. Logan, J. Richardson, R. Bell.

Orthis Euryone. (N. sp.)

Fig. 71. *a*, *b*.

Description.—Shell small, semi-oval; hinge line equal to the greatest breadth of the shell; cardinal extremities rectangular or nearly so; sides straight, gently convex or gently concave, and either parallel for about one fourth the length or slightly converging; front angles and front margin forming a uniform broadly rounded curve; a small portion in the middle of the front margin sometimes straight. Ventral valve strongly and uniformly convex, not carinated along the middle; a small portion at the cardinal angles compressed; umbo large, broadly convex, overhanging the hinge line; beak very small; area small, lying nearly in the plane of the lateral margin, in most specimens rather strongly concave; foramen narrow, its width less than the height. Surface with from twenty-five to thirty-five small but very distinct ribs. Dorsal valve nearly flat, with a wide shallow mesial sinus extending from the front margin two-thirds the length of the shell.

Width, 3 lines; length, 2½ lines.

This species differs from *O. orthambonites* in having the ventral valve more broadly convex, and in having nearly double the number of ribs. It is more abundant than that species, and the individuals differ very little from each other either in size or form.

Locality and Formation.—Point Lévis; in the upper part of limestone No. 2, Quebec group.

Collectors.—Sir W. E. Logan, J. Richardson, R. Bell.

ORTHIS ELECTRA. (N. sp.)

O—— PARVA?—Billings, Can. Nat. Geol., vol. 6, pp. 312, 315, 346.

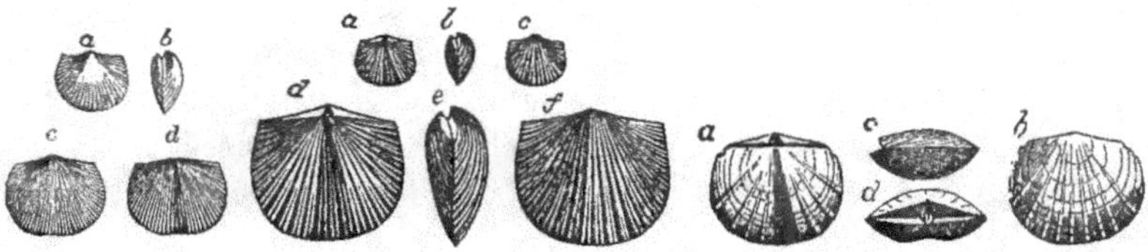

Fig. 72. Fig. 73. Fig. 74.

Fig. 72.—*Orthis Electra*,—*a*, *b*, Ventral and side views of a specimen with the valves in place; *c*, view of a detached ventral valve; *d*, view of a dorsal valve.

73.—*O*—— *Hippolyte*,—*a*, *b*, *c*, Different views of a small specimen; *d*, *e*, *f*, a large specimen restored from detached valves.

74.—*O*—— *Evadne*,—*a*, *b*, *c*, *d*, Different views of a specimen.

Description.—About the size and nearly of the shape of *O. perveta* (Conrad), to which species it is closely allied. Shell semi-oval or suborbicular; greatest width about the mid-length; cardinal angles a little more than 90°, rarely rectangular, sometimes appearing to be slightly rounded; hinge-line usually a little less than the greatest width of the shell; sides gently convex, sometimes straight for a short distance below the cardinal angles; anterior angles rounded; front margin usually convex, but sometimes with a portion in the middle straight. Ventral valves strongly and narrowly convex along the middle in the upper half, descending with a somewhat flat or gently convex slope to the sides and cardinal angles, the latter not much compressed. The front half of the valve becomes more broadly convex, but in general the carination, which commences at the beak, can still be perceived, although nearly obsolete. Beak small, only a little projecting over the hinge-line, depressed to about one third the height of the shell; area small, at its base forming an angle of a little over 100° with the plane of the lateral margin, strongly concave in the upper part; foramen small, about as wide as it is high.

Dorsal valve very gently convex, with an indistinct wide shallow mesial sinus, which in some specimens is scarcely perceptible. Area small, forming an obtuse angle with the plane of the lateral margin; foramen small but well defined to the very point of the beak; the latter scarcely distinct from the cardinal edge.

In the interior of the ventral valve the muscular impressions are not distinguishable in any specimen that I have seen, but just in front of the umbonial cavity there is a strong oval or subcircular callosity about 1 line in width in shells which are 3 or 4 lines in length. Above this the umbonial cavity is deeply excavated and the dental plates scarcely at all developed. In the interior of the dorsal valve a lower obtuse ridge runs along the median line from the foramen for half the length of the shell forward, when it becomes obsolete. No divaricator process can be seen in the foramen of any specimen observed, although this part appears to be perfectly preserved in many of the detached valves examined.

Surface covered with fine bifurcating striæ from six to eight in the width of one line.

Width from 3 to 6 lines; length about $\frac{1}{5}$ or $\frac{1}{6}$ less than the width.

As before mentioned, this species is very closely allied to *O. perveta*, the geological position of which appears to be about the Chazy, Black River, and the base of the Trenton limestones. The only differences that can be made out from a comparison with specimens from Tennessee and the figures given by Hall in the Palæontology of New York, are, that in *O. perveta* the dorsal valve is more convex than it is in *O. electra*, and the beak of the ventral valve not so depressed, while at the same time it is more extended. At present I have no means of comparing the interiors of the two species. When such a comparison can be made, should no greater differences be disclosed than are afforded by the external characters, I would be disposed to unite the two under one name. The specimens of *O. perveta* from Tennessee vary greatly in form and convexity, and yet, in all, the dorsal valve is more convex that it is in *O. Electra*. The European species *O. parva* is also most closely allied to *O. Electra*, only differing therefrom, so far as can be determined by comparison with figures, in having the beaks more strongly incurved. Its geological position must be very nearly the same.

These species belong to a group of finely striated *Orthides*, which made its appearance in the beginning of the Silurian period, and flourished in all the after geological ages up to the Carboniferous.

Locality and Formation.—Point Lévis. The specimens from which the description was drawn up are silicified shells, procured in the upper part of limestone No. 2. But in the white, grey, and yellowish masses which hold the greater number of the species of trilobites, a species resembling this occurs rarely, but not sufficiently well preserved to enable us to say whether or not it is the same.

Collectors.—Sir W. E. Logan, J. Richardson, R. Bell.

Orthis Hippolyte. (N. sp.)

Fig. 73. *a, b, c, d, e, f.*

Description.—Sub-quadrate, hinge-line equal to the greatest width of the shell; cardinal angles rectangular, or a little obtuse, sometimes slightly rounded; sides in the upper one-third, straight, or gently convex; front angles and margin broadly rounded. Ventral valve strongly convex in the small, and moderately so in large specimens; more or less carinated along the middle, with a flat slope towards the sides; greatest elevation about the middle or a little above; beak depressed to about half the height of the shell; area of moderate size, forming an angle of about 125° with the plane of the lateral margin; foramen rather small. Dorsal valve gently convex in the upper half, with a broad, shallow mesial sinus extending from the front margin to the umbo, a flat slope to the cardinal angles; area almost linear; beak scarcely distinct from the cardinal edge.

Surface with moderately strong, angular, radiating, bifurcating ribs, three or four in the width of one line at the front margin, becoming finer towards the cardinal angles; usually, one, two, or three small ones in the spaces between the larger, which do not reach the beak.

Width, from 3 to 6 lines; length from one-fifth to one-third less than the width.

This species is allied to *O. orthambonites*, but it has the ribs always sub-divided, and it varies greatly in size. It is also more distinctly carinated along the middle.

Locality and Formation.—Limestone No. 2, at Point Lévis. Also in the upper part of the limestone at Phillipsburgh.

Collectors.—Sir W. E. Logan, J. Richardson.

Orthis Evadne. (N. sp.)

Fig. 74. *a, b, c, d.*

Description.—Subquadrate; hinge-line straight, equal to the greatest width of the shell; sides in the upper two thirds nearly straight, or gently convex; front angles rounded; front margin rounded, or with a portion in the middle equal to half the whole width nearly straight. Ventral valve moderately convex, greatest elevation a little in front of the middle, the upper half somewhat flat and sloping to the hinge-line, the front half the most convex, the surface descending from the middle to the front margin and sides with an abruptly rounded slope; umbo very slightly elevated above the general surface; area of moderate size, flat, extending to the cardinal angles, forming with the plane of the lateral margin an obtuse angle of about 135°; foramen open to the beak, about as wide as high. Dorsal valve gently convex, with a wide shallow mesial depression extending to the beak; area half the size of that of the ventral valve; interrupted in the middle by a double divaricator process similar to that of *Leptæna sericea;* forming with the ventral area an angle of about 90°.

Surface of the specimen not well preserved, but it appears to have a number of fine distinct ribs with smaller ones between as in *S. alternata*, the whole crossed by numerous rugose concentric squamæ of growth.

Length of the specimen 4½ lines; width 5½ lines; height of the ventral area of the foramen ¾ of a line.

Of this singular species only a single specimen with the valves attached has been collected. The ventral valve is remarkably like that of a *Leptæna* or *Strophomena*, but the dorsal valve is that of an *Orthis* externally, while the place of the foramen is occupied by a divaricator process which has so far as it can be seen the structure of the same organ in *L. sericea.* It seems to belong to a group connecting *Orthis* with *Strophomena.*

Locality and Formation.—Point Lévis. In the upper part of limestone No. 2, Quebec group.

Collectors.—Sir W. E. Logan, J. Richardson, R. Bell.

Orthis Mycale. (N. sp.)

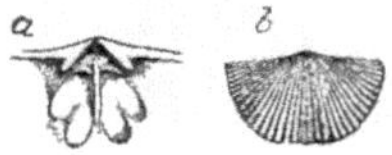

Fig. 75.

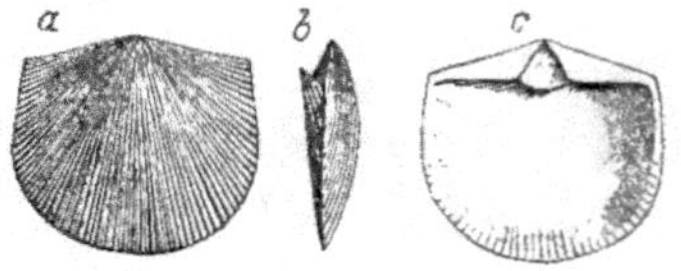

Fig. 76.

Fig. 75.—*Orthis Mycale.*—*b*, Dorsal valve; *a*, muscular impression enlarged.
76.—*O*—— *Eudocia.*—*a*, Ventral view; *b*, side view; *c*, interior of ventral valve.

Description.—Shell transversely semi-oval, proportionally very wide; hinge-line equal to the greatest width of the shell; cardinal angles somewhat acute, about 75°; sides straight, gently convex or gently concave for about half the length, then gradually curved round to the front margin, which is gently rounded or straight in the middle. Ventral valve moderately convex, with the cardinal angles largely compressed; beak depressed below the greatest height of the shell; area small, forming with the plane of the lateral margin an angle of about 130°; foramen about as wide as high. Dorsal valve moderately convex, largely compressed at the cardinal angles, a wide, shallow mesial sinus extending to the beak; umbo inconspicuous; foramen wide, triangular, and without a divaricator process; area almost linear, lying nearly in the plane of the lateral margin. Surface with fine bifurcating ribs, 4 or 5 in the width of one line, with usually a much finer one between each two of the larger.

Width 5 lines; length 3 lines.

This species is much broader than *O. Electra*, and has the dorsal valve more convex.

Locality and Formation.—Point Lévis; in the upper part of limestone No. 2, Quebec group.

Collectors.—Sir W. E. Logan, J. Richardson.

ORTHIS EUDOCIA. (N. sp.)

Fig. 76. *a*, *b*, *c*.

Description.—Semi-oval; hinge-line equal to the greatest width of the shell; cardinal angles apparently rectangular; sides somewhat straight, and sub-parallel for two-thirds the length; front angles and margin uniformly rounded. Ventral valve gently convex; greatest height in the upper half, sloping with a slightly convex descent to the sides and front margin; beak nearly of the same height as the shell, very slightly depressed; area moderate, flat, extending to the cardinal angles, forming with the plane of the lateral margins an obtuse angle of about 120°; foramen large, extending to the beak. Dorsal valve flat, with a slight concavity in front of the beak, along the middle. Surface with fine striæ of unequal size, about 8 in the width of one line, at the front margin; of these, usually about three are much stronger than the others.

Width 8 lines; length of ventral valve 7 lines; height of area at the beak 1½ lines. The dorsal valve is a little shorter than the ventral.

Closely allied to *O. tricenaria*, from which it differs only in having the ventral valve less elevated, and the surface finely striated, instead of coarsely ribbed.

Locality and Formation.—Point Lévis; in the upper part of limestone No. 2, Quebec group.

Collectors.—Sir W. E. Logan, J. Richardson.

Genus STRICKLANDIA. (Billings.)

STRICKLANDIA, (Billings) *Canadian Naturalist and Geologist*, Vol. 4, p. 434, April, 1859.
RENNSELÆRIA, (Hall) pars. *Twelfth Annual Report of the Regents of the State of New York*, p. 39, October, 1859.

This genus was proposed by me, in the work above cited, to include such shells as those known in England under the names of *Pentamerus lens*, *P. liratus*, and *P. lævis.* They differ from *Pentamerus* in having the valves usually sub-equal, and no longitudinal septa or triangular chamber in the interior of the dorsal valve. Both valves have an area, but in the dorsal it is usually linear, or only slightly exceeding the thickness of the substance of the shell in height. The ventral valve has usually a concave mesial sinus more or less developed, and the dorsal valve a mesial fold corresponding thereto. The hinge line in some of the species, such as in *S. lævis* and *S. microcamerus*, have the hinge line straight and much extended.

Among the brachiopoda found in the limestone nodules of Point Lévis there are two species which have all the internal characters of this genus. The form is also the same, except that in one of them, *S. Arachne*, the area of the ventral valve is so much developed as to give the whole shell the external appearance of an *Orthis.* It has, however, the mesial fold and sinus, and the shell exhibits a tendency to vary, by the extension of the middle of the front margin, which is also a peculiarity of the typical species. De Verneuil has described in the Geology of Russia, vol. 2, p. 129, Pl. 2, fig. 1 *a–g*, a species under the name of *Spirifer Tcheffkini*, which appears to me to be a *Stricklandia*, and to stand between *S. Arachne* and *S. brevis.* The surfaee is reticulated in nearly the same way, and the form (in a general sense,) is similar, with the exception that the ventral area is very slightly developed, or almost linear. Judging from the external characters alone, for the interior is not described, I should say that *S. Tcheffkini* belongs to *Stricklandia.* Should this surmise turn out to be well-founded, then these three: *S. Arachne*, *S. Tcheffkini*, and *S. brevis* will form a very complete series, leading to *S. lens*, *S. Gaspensis* and others, which constitute the bulk of the genus. I strongly suspect that *Camerella Calcifera* should be referred to *Stricklandia.*

Stricklandia? Arachne. (N. sp.)

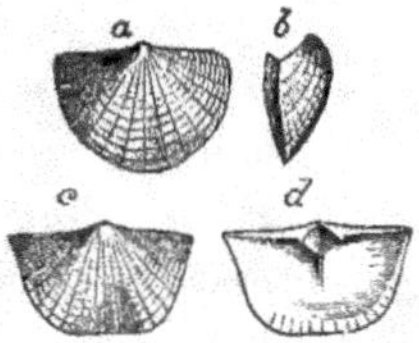

Fig. 77.

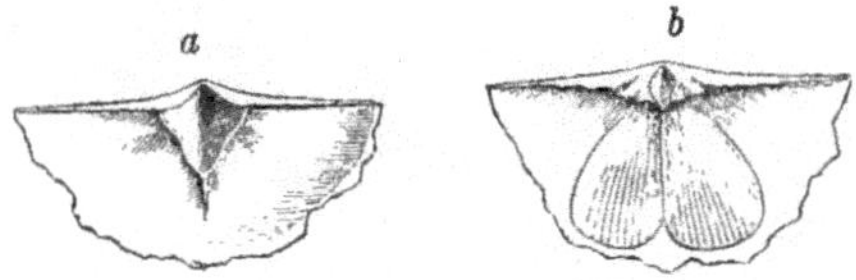

Fig. 78.

Fig. 77.—*Stricklandia Arachne; a*, ventral view; *b*, side view; *c*, ventral valve of another specimen of a somewhat different form; *d*, interior of *c*. All these figures enlarged two diameters.

Fig. 78.—*S? Arethusa; a*, interior of a portion of the ventral valve; *b*, interior of part of the dorsal valve.

Description.—Semi-elliptical or sub-rhomboidal, hinge line equal to or greater than the width of the shell; sides converging towards the front, and either straight or gently convex; front margin rounded, or with a portion in the middle straight. Ventral valve strongly convex, sub-pyramidal, greatest elevation a little in front of the beak; a faint mesial sinus along the middle, not reaching the beak; area rather large, slightly concave, forming an angle of about 100° with the plane of the lateral margin; foramen triangular, its width at the base equal to the height. Dorsal valve depressed, convex, with an obscure mesial elevation; area about one-fourth the size of that of the ventral valve; foramen open to the beak.

Surface with obscurely rounded ribs, five or six in the width of one line, these are separated by fine, sharp furrows, and crossed by distinct concentric striæ, from six to eight in the width of one line, giving to the surface a reticulated appearance.

The largest specimen seen is 3 lines wide and 2 lines in length.

In the interior of the ventral valve there is a small triangular chamber beneath the beak, supported by a short mesial septum. In the interior of the dorsal valve there is no mesial septum.

Locality and Formation.—Point Lévis; in the upper part of limestone No. 2, Quebec group.

Collectors.—Sir W. E. Logan, J. Richardson.

Stricklandia Arethusa. (N. sp.)

Fig. 78. *a*, *b*.

Description.—Of this species we have only discovered some fragments, but these are quite sufficient to show that it is distinct from any that has been heretofore described. The form appears to be semi-elliptical, both valves moderately convex; the hinge line straight and sometimes two inches wide; surface smooth. The area of the ventral valve is about one line in height at the beak; The foramen triangular, and about as wide as it is high. In the interior there is a small triangular chamber just in front of the foramen, with an obtuse tooth on each side. The area of the dorsal valve is somewhat smaller than that of the ventral, and the foramen is nearly of the same size. In front of the foramen there are two indistinct ovate muscular impressions, one on each side of the median line, with a slightly developed mesial septum between them. These scars are longitudinally striated, and there are some faint indications of subdivision of each. They, no doubt, represent the two pairs of occlusor scars of the generality of the brachiopoda.

The speeimens are silicified, and were procured by dissolving nodules of limestone in hydrochloric acid. Several of the fragments obtained in this way show that all the front half of both valves is very thin and fragile, and that in one, most probably the ventral valve, there is a shallow rounded mesial sinus, with a corresponding elevation in the dorsal. This species appears to be allied to *Stricklandia* (Pentamerus) *microcamerus* (M'Coy), and appears to be preserved in the same way, *i. e.*, only the parts around the beak and hinge line remaining. I have specimens of what appear to be portions of the two valves of M'Coy's species, and although the two seem to be closely allied, yet ours has the muscular impressions in the dorsal valve much larger.

Locality and Formation.—Point Lévis; in the upper part of limestone No. 2, Quebec group.

Collectors.—Sir W. E. Logan, J. Richardson.

GASTEROPODA.

Genus Metoptoma. (Phillips.)

In my paper on the fossils of Point Lévis, in the Canadian Naturalist and Geologist, vol. 5, these shells were referred to *Patella*, and afterwards to *Capulus*: I think it more probable that they belong to *Metoptoma*. A number of other undescribed species are known to me in the Lower Silurian rocks of Canada.

Metoptoma Melissa. (N. sp.)

Description.—Shell obliquely conical, the base uniformly broad oval, a little narrower at the front than at the posterior margin, tapering from the base upwards to the apex, which in the cast is acute, erect and situated at about one-third the length from the anterior margin. Surface unknown.

Length of the specimen at the base, 9 lines; width, 8 lines; height, 8½ lines.

Locality and Formation.—Point Lévis. In limestone No. 2, Quebec group.

Collectors.—J. Richardson, R. Bell.

Metoptoma Hyrie. (N. sp.)

Cyrtodonta.—(Billings.) *Canadian Naturalist and Geologist*, vol. 5, p. 201.

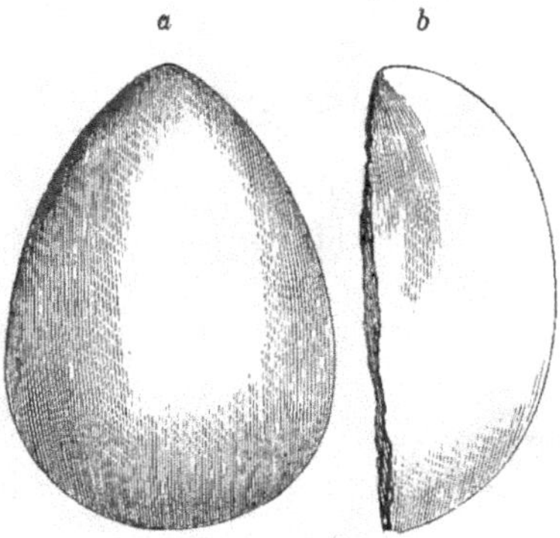

Fig. 79.

Fig. 79.—*Metoptoma Hyrie.*—*a*, View of the upper side; *b*, side view.

Description.—This species is almost identical with *M. Nycteis*, described and figured at page 37, 38, of this series of papers. The only difference is that the beak is incurved down nearly to the plane of the lateral margin, whereas in *M. Nycteis* it is elevated about two-thirds the whole height. The form is an uniform oval, narrowed to an acutely rounded point at the beak; sides gently convex; posterior margin broadly rounded; greatest width about the middle, or a little nearer the beak. On a side view the outline is nearly regularly arched from the beak to the front, the greatest height being a little nearer the beak than the mid-length. Surface unknown.

Length of large specimen, 21 lines; width, 14 lines; height, 9 lines. The specimens vary somewhat in their proportions.

Locality and Formation.—Point Lévis; in limestone No. 2, Quebec group.

Collectors.—Sir W. E. Logan, J. Richardson, R. Bell, T. Weston.

METOPTOMA ORPHYNE. (N. sp.)

Description.—This species, like *M. Melissa*, is almost completely conical, but more obtuse. The base is oval, slightly more narrowed in front than behind. Apex erect, acute, and a little in advance of the centre. The surface of the cast exhibits eight or nine shallow concave undulations running round the shell, parallel with the plane of the base, each about one line wide.

Length, 12 lines; width, about 9 lines; height, 8 lines.

Locality and Formation.—Point Lévis; in limestone No. 2, Quebec group.

Collector.—R. Bell.

METOPTOMA AUGUSTA. (N. sp.)

Description.—Shell irregularly conical, the anterior side flattened, and the posterior rounded. Apex a little in advance of the middle, and apparently a little curved backwards. The flattened anterior side gives to this species the aspect of a large *Calceola*. The front margin is not preserved, but appears to have been nearly straight, the sides gently convex, and posterior margin broadly rounded. Surface unknown.

Length, 1½ inches; width, 1¼ inches; height, 13 lines.

I am not quite sure that this is a symmetrical species. Only about half of the specimen is preserved, and the flat anterior side does not appear to be at a right angle to the longitudinal axis of the shell.

Locality and Formation.—Point Lévis; in limestone No. 2, Quebec group.

Collector.—T. Weston.

METOPTOMA VENILLIA. (N. sp.)

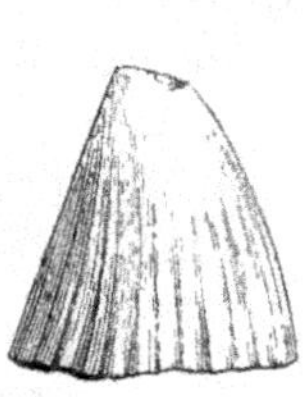

Fig. 80.

a b

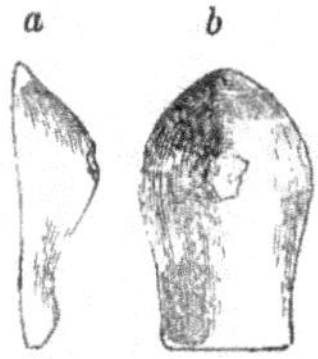

Fig. 81.

Fig. 80.—*Metoptoma Venillia.*—Side view.

81.—*M———— anomala.*—*a*, Side view; *b*, view of the upper side.

Description.—Conical; base ovate; uniformly rounded at the sides and posterior margin slightly narrowed from the middle to the front. Apex nearly central, situated a little in advance of the middle. Surface of the cast vertically marked with obscure concave furrows about one line wide.

Length of base, 9 lines; width, 8 lines; height, 11 lines.

This species has nearly the form of *M. Melissa*, but it can be easily recognised even in fragments by its sulcated surface. The furrows run from near the apex straight to the base.

Locality and Formation.—Point Lévis; in limestone Nos. 1 and 2, Quebec group.

Collectors.—R. Bell, J. Richardson.

METOPTOMA ANOMALA. (N. sp.)

Fig. 81. *a, b.*

Description.—The base of this species is oblong and pentagonal, one extremity, supposed to be the anterior, straight, and at a right angle to the sides, the latter nearly straight or gently concave, and parallel or nearly so for two-thirds the length; when, forming an obtusely rounded angle, they converge to meet in a rounded point in the middle of the posterior extremity. The apex is situated at about one-third the length from the posterior margin, and from this point the anterior portion of the shell is roof-shaped, obtusely carinated, and descending with a flat slope to the sides. On a side view, the outline ascends to the apex with a straight slope, at an angle of about 45° with the plane of the lateral margin; from the apex forwards it descends with a concave slope for half the whole height, and, just before reaching the anterior margin, becomes parallel with the base. Surface unknown.

Length 8 lines; width 5 lines; height at the apex 3 lines; height at front margin 1½ lines.

Locality and Formation.—Point Lévis; in limestone No. 2, Quebec group.

Collectors.—J. Richardson, R. Bell.

PLEUROTOMARIA VAGRANS. (N. sp.)

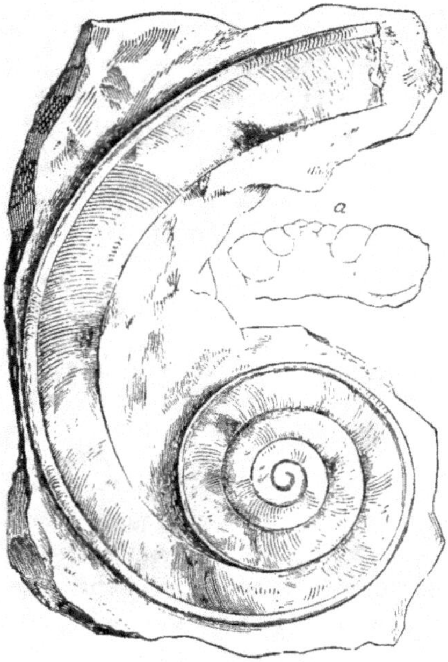

Fig. 82.

Fig. 82.—*Pleurotomaria vagrans.*—View of the upper side; *a*, transverse section of the spire. In the principal figure, the band is too wide.

Description.—Discoidal; spire nearly flat; whorls four or five, slender, gradually increasing in size, on the upper side gently and nearly uniformly convex, a narrow spiral band on the outer edge which is obtusely angular; outside of whorls gently convex; lower side narrowly rounded along the middle, umbilicus wide, extending to the apex. The last whorl is separated from the others, and produced singly to a length of four or five inches, gradually losing its curvature as it increases in length. Surface with fine striæ, and a few obscure undulations curving backwards from the suture outwards. Width of the uncoiled portion of the spire when consisting of four whorls, 15 lines; width of outer whorl 3¼ lines; width of last whorl at four inches from the spire, 5 lines; depth about 4 lines.

Locality and Formation.—Point Lévis; in limestone No. 2, Quebec group.

Collectors.—Sir W. E. Logan, J. Richardson, R. Bell.

Pleurotomaria Postumia. (N. sp.)

Description.—Discoidal; spire varying from gently convex to flat, or even a little concave; whorls five or six, very slender, very slightly convex on the upper side; outer edge very acute and a little turned upwards; outer and lower side gently convex and forming an angle of from 60° to 80° with the upper side; lower side rounded, and sometimes obtusely carinated along the middle; umbilicus very wide, extending to the apex. Surface unknown.

Width of a specimen of six whorls 18 lines; width of last whorl 3 lines; depth about the same.

Locality and Formation.—Point Lévis; in limestone No. 2. Also, at Phillipsburgh in limestone of the same age. Quebec group.

Collectors.—Sir W. E. Logan, R. Bell, Dr. J. B. Farnsworth.

CEPHALOPODA.

Orthoceras Autolycus. (N. sp.)

Description.—Section circular, tapering at the rate of about 1¼ lines to the inch. Septa moderately concave, from eight to ten in one inch. Siphuncle about one line in diameter, marginal, in contact with the shell.

This species is common, but always found in fragments. It appears to be about 1 foot in length, and 1½ inches in diameter at the larger extremity. It is slightly curved, as are most of the Orthoceratites in the Chazy and Calciferous formations. The siphuncle is small and lateral, in contact with the shell on the side of the convex curvature. The chamber of habitation seems to be deep, for in a small specimen only 7 lines in diameter it is 1 inch in length, and, besides this, a portion seems to be broken away. The larger extremity exhibits a number of broad, shallow annulations, which cross the shell obliquely, and in some specimens seem to be interrupted on the side of the convex curve. Surface markings of shell unknown.

Locality and Formation.—Point Lévis; in limestone No. 2. Quebec group.

Collectors.—Sir W. E. Logan, J. Richardson, R. Bell.

CRUSTACEA.

Genus SHUMARDIA. (N. gen.)

Generic Characters.—Head semicircular, with a convex, sub-cylindrical glabella; no eyes visible in the only species known. Pygidium about as large as the head, with a prominent cylindro-conical axis; side lobes and axis more or less distinctly ribbed. Thorax unknown.

The only species of this genus known to me is a minute trilobite, evidently allied to the genus *Agnostus*, from which it differs in having the pygidium regularly ribbed like an *Asaphus* or *Calymene*.

This genus is dedicated to the eminent American palæontologist and geologist, Dr. B. F. Shumard.

SHUMARDIA GRANULOSA. (N. sp.)

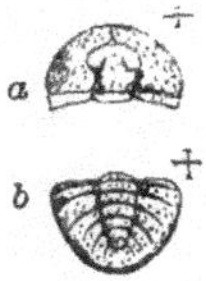

Fig. 83.

Fig. 83.—*Shumardia granulosa*, enlarged four diameters. *a*, the head; *b*, the pygidium.

Description. — Minute, ovate. Head nearly semicircular, length a little more than half the width, strongly convex. Glabella irregularly sub-cylindrical, broadly rounded in front, three-fourths the whole length of the head, with a large tubercle on each side at the anterior extremity, and a very minute one on each side next to the neck furrow, the latter extending all across. Dorsal furrows on each side of the glabella very deep, and angular at the bottom as far as the large anterior tubercles; around these and the front of the glabella, not so deep, yet still distinctly defined. From the middle of the front of the glabella, a well defined angular furrow runs straight forward to the middle of the anterior margin of the head. In the bottom of this furrow there appears to be a small triangular tubercle, which gives to the glabella, in some specimens, but not in all, the appearance of having a projecting angular point in the middle of its front margin. The two large tubercles mentioned seem to be simply a lateral expansion of the anterior one-fourth of the glabella, making its width at this place one-third greater than it is at the mid-length.

The neck segment is well defined and prominent. Cheeks exceedingly convex, most elevated along the middle or along a line half way between the glabella and the margin. The neck furrow extends all across the cheeks at the posterior margin.

Pygidium semi-oval, narrowly rounded behind, very convex, about as wide as the head, but one-third longer; axis acutely conical, strongly convex about three-fourths the whole length and a little less than one-third of the whole width, well defined all round by the dorsal furrows. The axis is divided into six segments, the anterior of which is subdivided by a small furrow which runs across it and extends into the anterior segment of the side-lobes. In the side-lobes there are five segments, the last one sometimes obscurely defined: these do not extend quite to the margin.

Surface of both head and pygidium covered with small granular tubercles, more distinctly developed in some individuals than in others. Some specimens of the pygidium have a space all round the margin smooth.

Length of head about 1 line; width about $1\frac{3}{4}$ lines. Length of pygidium $1\frac{1}{3}$ lines. These measurements refer to the largest specimens seen. In many the proportional length and width differ a little from the above.

The pygidium and head have never been seen in connection, but several of each occur together in the same small specimen of stone, and it seems therefore almost certain that they belong to each other.

Locality and Formation.—Point Lévis. In the thin-bedded limestone interstratified in the graptolitic slates, Quebec group.

Collector.—J. Richardson.

Genus ENDYMION. (N. gen.)

Generic Characters.—In the only species of this genus at present known, the head is semi-oval and convex; glabella ovate, convex, with a large elongate, oval tubercle on each side. The facial suture appears to terminate at the posterior angle or just outside of it, and running forward to cut the anterior margin on a line passing through the middle of the cheek, parallel with the longitudinal axis of the body. On this point, however, there is yet some doubt, as the moveable cheek has not been seen, and what appears to be the facial suture may be a fracture. Thorax distinctly trilobed; axis convex; side-lobes flat; six or seven segments; the pleuræ with a well-defined groove crossing them diagonally outwards and downwards. Pygidium semi-oval, distinctly trilobed, with the axis and side-lobes divided into segments by well defined furrows.

This genus is allied to both *Trinucleas* and *Ampyx*. From the former it differs in the absence of the punctured border of the head; from the latter, in the form of the glabella, which has a large tubercle on each side, and is destitute of a rostrum.

ENDYMION MEEKI. (N. sp.)

Fig. 84.

Fig. 84.—*Endymion Meeki*, enlarged two diameters.

Description.—Broad oval; length to width about as 5 is to 4. Head transversely semi-oval; glabella convex, depressed semi-cylindrical in the posterior half of the length, then expanding to twice the width of the neck-segment, front obtusely rounded; glabellar furrows represented by two obscure indentations on each side, of which one is situated at about the mid-length, and the other half-way between this and the neck-segment. Neck furrow extending all across. Neck segment convex, and well defined. On each side of the glabella there is an elongated fusiform lateral lobe or large tubercle, separated from the main body of the glabella by the dorsal furrows, which are moderately deep. These lateral lobes are also separated from the cheeks by a furrow distinctly defined, but broader than the dorsal furrows. The anterior extremities of the lobes are acute, and situated on a line drawn across the glabella at about one-fourth of the length from the front margin thereof. The posterior extremities are a little truncated by the neck furrow. The glabella is about four-fifths the whole length of the head. The cheeks are moderately tumid, and crossed at the base by the neck furrow, which runs nearly out to the posterior angle, and then seems to turn forward as if it were continued all round the head.

Thorax distinctly trilobed, with six segments visible in the specimen, it remaining doubtful whether or not there is a seventh situated where a fracture crosses the body, just behind the first segment next the head. Axis of thorax semi-cylindrical, very convex, a little wider in the middle than at the extremities; less than one-third the whole width of the body. Side lobes, as far as seen, flat. Pleural groove crossing the pleuræ outwards and downwards in the outer third of the length, gradually becoming parallel with the posterior side, and then curving slightly forwards.

Pygidium semi-oval, apparently about one-third the length of the head; the axis convex, acutely conical, and of five segments. Side-lobes flat, with three obscure furrows, which do not reach the margin. The pygidium seems to have a smooth border abruptly turned down all round, but this remains doubtful. Surface smooth. About the middle of the glabella there is a small rounded tubercle.

Length of specimen, 5 lines. Width at posterior margin of head, about 4 lines. Length of head, $2\frac{1}{4}$ lines. Length of thorax, $1\frac{3}{4}$ lines. Length of pygidium, about 1 line.

In the specimen, the glabella and the whole of the left cheek are very perfect. A fracture crosses the thorax, just behind the first segment, and it is barely possible that in this place there was a segment which is not preserved. My own impression is, that there are only six segments. The axis is perfect, except at the fracture. The left side lobe is also perfect, with the exception of the ends of the pleuræ, where some obscurity exists. The right cheek, the greater part of the right side of the thorax and pygidium, are not preserved.

This species is dedicated to the excellent American palæontologist, Mr. F. B. Meek.

Locality and Formation.—Point Lévis; in the upper part of limestone No. 2, Quebec group.

Collectors.—Sir W. E. Logan, J. Richardson.

Holometopus Angelini. (N. sp.)

a b

Fig. 85.

Fig. 85.—*Holometopus Angelini.*—*a*, Side view of head; *b*, a nearly perfect head.

Description.—Head semicircular, moderately convex, length about equal to half the width. Glabella five-sixths of the length of the head, narrow, and depressed cylindrical, with the sides parallel to the posterior half, then gradually enlarging to twice the width at the front, which is broadly rounded; anterior angles of glabella rather obscure, but apparently acutely rounded. The sides of the glabella are separated from the cheeks by the deep dorsal furrows, which are obscurely angular at the bottom and wide above; they extend as far as the anterior angles, but do not run round the front. Cheeks tumid; eyes small, apparently crescentiform, situated about their own diameter from the posterior margin, and about the same distance from the side of the glabella. Neck furrow extending all across the base of the glabella. The facial suture in its course in front of the eye at first curves a little outwards and then forwards, cutting the anterior margin of the head on a line drawn parallel with the longitudinal axis of the body, a little outside of the eye. Surface smooth.

Length of head of largest specimen seen, about 2¾ lines. Length of glabella, 2⅖ lines. Width of head, 5½ lines. Diameter of the eye, ¾ of a line.

The posterior angles and margin of the head are not preserved.

This species closely resembles *H. limbatus* (Angelin), but that species has the anterior angles of the glabella broadly, instead of acutely rounded.

Locality and Formation.—Point Lévis; in the upper part of limestone No. 2, Quebec group.

Collector.—J. Richardson.

4.—*New Species of Fossils from different parts of the Lower, Middle and Upper Silurian Rocks of Canada.*

Scolithus Canadensis. (N. sp.)

Description.—This species consists of numerous cylindrical or irregularly prismatic stems, (or rather the cavities in the rock once occupied by such stems,) from one to two lines in diameter, and from one to six inches in length, and either straight, or more or less curved. In some specimens several of the stems are in contact with each other, and when this is the case and the stems have an angular shape they very much resemble the coral *Tetradium.* The larger stems are more often straight than the smaller. The true *Scolithas linearis* is generally larger, and the stems straight and parallel with each other. I have seen no specimens of that species in our Canadian rocks, although it does occur in the lowest red sandstone in Labrador, on the north shore of the straits of Belle Isle; to which place our survey has extended. In the Canadian species the individuals are usually irregularly scattered through the rock, lying in all directions.

Locality and Formation.—Townships of Landsdowne and Bastard, Ste. Geneviève Island, near Ste. Anne, Beauharnois, and at various other localities in the upper part of the Potsdam formation. I have also collected this species on the east side of Snake Mountain, in Vermont.

Collectors.—Sir W. E. Logan, A. Murray, J. Richardson, R. Bell, E. Billings.

Palæophycus Beverleyensis (N. sp.)

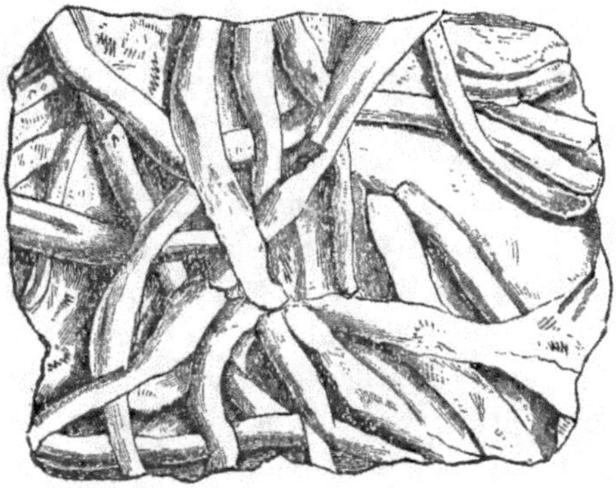

Fig. 86.

Fig. 86. *Palæophycus Beverleyensis.*

Description.—In this species the stems are in general from two to 2½ lines in thickness, cylindrical or sub-angular, and either straight or more or less curved, crowded together in great profusion on the surface of the strata, and crossing each other in all directions. The stems appear to be simple, or not branched, throughout their whole length, but upon this point there is some doubt, as occasionally two or more may be seen joining in such a manner that they suggest the idea of branching, although it cannot be distinctly ascertained. It is at all events certain that where a stem is well preserved and stands out in full relief, no appearance of division can be seen. It is only where they are closely crowded together that they seem to be subdivided. Some of the stems can be traced a length of 6 or 8 inches, and they retain the same thickness throughout. They appear to have been long, slender, soft marine plants, which by some cause were thrown down upon the surface of the strata in tangled masses, and there petrified.

On comparing this species with *P. congregatus* (see p. 3) the difference can be seen at the first glance. In that species the stems vary greatly in thickness, and are generally crooked, instead of gracefully curved.

Locality and Formation.—Near Beverley in the township of Bastard. In the upper part of the Potsdam sandstone, associated with *Lingula acuminata, Ophileta compacta, Pleurotomaria Laurentina,* and fragments of small Orthoceratites.

Collectors.—H. Murray, R. Bell.

Palæophycus Funiculus. (N. sp.)

Description.—This species consists of long, slender, cylindrical wire-like stems, about 1½ lines in thickness, gently curved and sparsely scattered about the surface of the strata. Sometimes they are found in considerable numbers lying across each other, but never in such dense reticulating layers as those formed by *P. Beverleyensis* and *P. Beauharnoisensis.* Single stems one foot or more are often seen without any others near them, and being, when not distorted by pressure, very nearly cylindrical, they somewhat resemble a round, smooth crinoidal column.

Locality and Formation.—Edwardstown, near Norton's Creek Mill, in the County of Napierville. Calciferous formation. It also occurs near L'Orignal, in the County of Prescott, in loose slabs.

Collectors.—J. Richardson, E. Billings.

Palæophycus obscurus. (N. sp.)

Description.—This species consists of cylindrical, rod-like stems, usually from ½ to ¾ of an inch in thickness. They are usually straight, and found in broken pieces from 3 to 12 inches in length, being most common in the thin beds of shale between the strata of limestone. They are sometimes more or less crooked, but never, so far as I have observed, gracefully curved. They very much resemble in size and form *P. tubularis* (Hall), Pal. N.Y., vol. i., pl. 2, fig. 1, and may possibly be the same species. At present I think them different, and propose to name them as above, provisionally.

Locality and Formation.—City of Ottawa. In the Trenton limestone.

Collectors.—J. Richardson, E. Billings.

Palæophycus Beauharnoisensis. (N. sp.)

Description.—This species is evidently allied to *P. Beverleyensis*, differing therefrom principally in the greater size and more rigid aspect of the stems. These vary in thickness from 1 to 4 lines, but the most common size is from 2 to 3 lines. They are either straight or slightly curved, nearly cylindrical, somewhat angular, often with one or more deep longitudinal grooves. They cover large surfaces of the rock, crossing each other at all angles. Some of the stems can be traced to a length of two feet. They often appear to be somewhat flattened, and show some indications of branching at an acute angle.

Locality and Formation.—Beauharnois. Calciferous sandrock.

Collectors.—Sir W. E. Logan, J. Richardson.

Genus LICROPHYCUS. (N. gen.)

Generic Characters.—Composed of numerous elongated sub-cylindrical stems springing from a common root, the stems either remaining single or sending off branches at an acute angle.

The genus *Buthotrephis* (Hall) should, I think, be confined to those fucoids which consist of a central principal stem, more or less branched above, as in *B. antiquata*, *B. subnodosa*, &c. The species which form tufts consisting of a number of stems rising from a single root, appear to be sufficiently different to constitute a distinct genus.

LICROPHYCUS OTTAWAENSIS. (N. sp.)

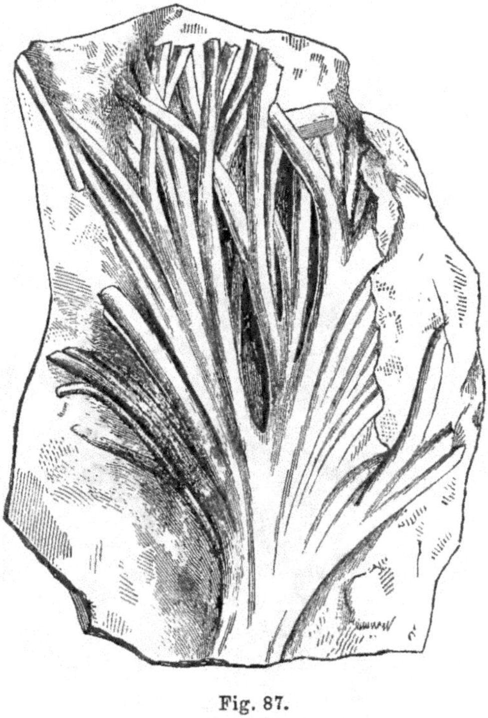

Fig. 87.

Fig. 87.—*Licrophycus Ottawaensis.*

Description.—This species consists of elongated slender flexible stems, springing from a common root, and dividing into numerous branches, which are given off at a very acute angle. The stems are from $1\frac{1}{2}$ to 2 lines in thickness, and gently curved from the centre outwards, forming a tuft from 4 to 8 inches in height and about the same in the greatest width. In the best preserved specimen observed, the original stem is cylindrical, and about 4 lines in thickness at the base, where it is broken off. At 1½ inches in height, it is 9 lines in diameter, and here consists of a bundle of from 20 to 30 stems closely aggregated into one solid cylindrical mass. The stems then separate and curve gracefully outwards, forming a tuft 7 inches wide at the height of 4 inches. The length of the whole is about 7 inches. The stems have a smooth sub-cylindric aspect, and appear to have been of a succulent or soft structure, so that, when thrown down and buried in the sediment, they were pressed and partly blended into each other.

This is a very striking, easily recognized, and persistent species. Specimens from Ottawa, where it is most abundant, may be identified at the first glance with those from Peterboro.

Locality and Formation.—City of Ottawa, Peterboro, and Belleville. Trenton limestone.

Collectors.—E. Billings, M. Rogers.

Licrophycus minor. (N. sp.)

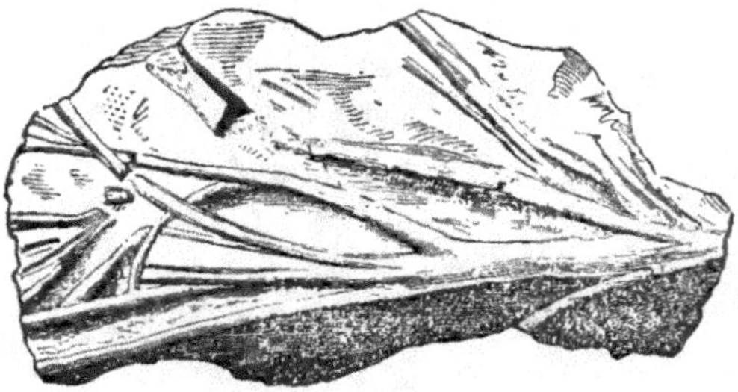

Fig. 88.

Fig. 88.—*Licrophycus minor.*

Description.—In this species the stems are about one line in thickness, branching at an acute angle, straight or curved. Length, 3 or 4 inches; width, across the whole tuft, from 1½ to 2 inches. It is closely allied to *L. Ottawaensis*, but is much smaller, and in general the branches are straighter, and appear to have been of a more firm consistence, as they are not so much compressed.

Locality and Formation.—City of Ottawa; in the Trenton limestone.

Collector.—E. Billings.

Lycrophycus Hudsonicus. (N. sp.)

Description.—This species forms large fan-shaped tufts one foot wide, consisting of long, branched, cylindrical, usually much curved stems from 2 to 3 lines in thickness. It resembles *L. Ottwaensis*, but differs in the greater flexibility of the stems, the effect of which is to produce wide straggling expansions instead of compact tufts.

Locality and Formation.—Manitouwaning Bay, Lake Huron; in the upper part of the Hudson River group.

Collector.—R. Bell.

Licrophycus Hiltonensis. (N. sp.)

Description.—This species consists of numerous sub-cylindrical straight or curved stems, which spring from a common root, and are many times branched above. The original stem divides close to the root into several branches, each of which as it increases in length gives off new branches at an acute angle, the new ones suddenly becoming of the thickness of the old; the latter usually more or less curved. The stems are in general about half an inch in thickness. At five inches from the base fourteen stems can be counted in one specimen on the surface of the rock, occupying a width of seven inches. The length of this group is nine inches.

This species closely resembles *B. succulens* (Hall), Pal. N. Y. vol. 1, Pl. 22, fig. 2a, but the stems are twice the size. The species figured on Pl. 21 of the same work as an undetermined Palæophycus appears to be a fragment of this species.

Locality and Formation.—Near Hilton Village, Island of St. Joseph, Lake Huron. Black River and base of the Trenton.

Collectors.—A. Murray, R. Bell.

Rusophycus Grenvillensis. (N. sp.)

Description.—This species is found in the form of irregular oblong-ovate or depressed hemispherical masses, one end usually divided into two parts by a furrow of more or less depth. The whole mass is generally crossed by numerous undulating wrinkles, which have a direction transverse to that of the furrow. The more common dimensions are from 3 to 4 inches in length, and from 2½ to 3½ in width, but occasionally specimens occur much larger and also smaller. One of these is 9½ inches by 5½, and in addition to the principal groove exhibits two or three other obscure furrows on each side. This may constitute a distinct species.

This curious fossil is evidently generically identical with that figured by Prof. Hall in the 2nd vol. Pal. N. Y., Pl. 9, under the name of *Rusophycus bilobatus*, but differs therefrom specifically in being proportionally shorter, while the furrow does not run the whole length, as it does in the Clinton species.

Locality and Formation.—Head of the Grenville Canal; in the Chazy sandstone.

Collector.—Sir W. E. Logan.

ZOOPHYTA.

PETRAIA APERTA. (N. sp.)

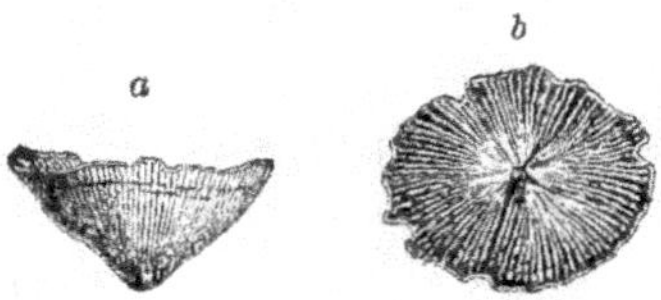

Fig. 89.

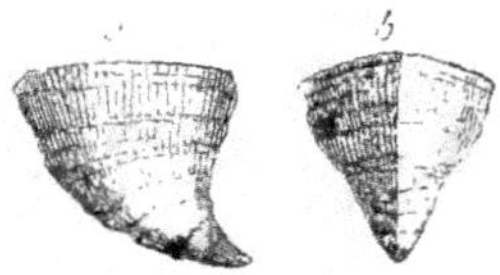

Fig. 90.

Fig. 89.—*Petraia aperta.*—*a*, Side view; *b*, interior of cup.
90.—*P* —— *angulata.*—*a* and *b*, Two views of this species.

Description.—Corallum simple, turbinate, short, widely expanding; cup deep, broadly concave in the bottom, with a distinct septal fossette on one side. Radiating septa from 100 to 150. Surface with a few annulations of growth, and finely marked with the longitudinal septal striæ, of which there are from 5 to 7 in the width of one line. The specimens are from 4 to 6 lines in height, and from 8 to 12 lines in width at the margin. Depth of the cup about half the height. The point of attachment is very nearly central.

In the 1st vol. of the Palæontology of New York, Pl. 12, Prof. Hall has figured two species under the name of *Streptelasma profunda.* It is possible that the specimen represented by his fig. 4, on the plate quoted, may be an individual of this species, but the figure does not exhibit any indications of a cup, or any external characters to prove that it belongs to this genus, or indeed that it is a coral at all. The other five figures are sections of a species of *Petraia.* He describes *P. profunda* as having the cup extending nearly to the base of the coral, and having from 36 to 60 radiating septa. In the Black River limestone in Canada, there is a species which agrees very well with Prof. Hall's description, but it is decidedly distinct from the one for which I now propose the name *P. aperta.* This latter has over 100 radiating septa.

Locality and Formation.—Paquette Rapids, on the river Ottawa; Black River limestone.

Collector.—E. Billings.

PETRAIA ANGULATA. (N. sp.)

Fig. 90, *a*, *b*.

Description.—Of this species we have only three small specimens. They are irregularly conical, moderately curved, expanding from an acute point to a width of seven lines at a height of about eight lines, acutely angulated on the side opposite the concave curve. Surface with a few obscure annulations of growth, and besides engirdled with numerous smaller obscure lines, from four to six in one line. The cup appears to be about four lines deep in a specimen eight lines in length. There appear to be three or four septal striæ on the outside in the width of one line. The specimens being imbedded in stone, the number of the septa cannot be ascertained.

The distinctive character of this species consists in its acutely angular shape.

Locality and Formation.—West end of Anticosti; Hudson River group.

Collector.—J. Richardson.

PETRAIA PYGMEA. (N. sp.)

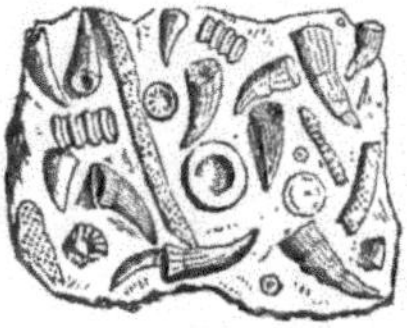

Fig. 91.

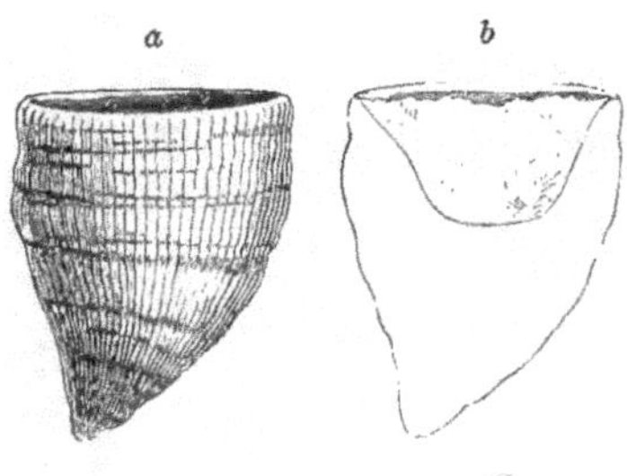

Fig. 92.

Fig. 91.—*Petraia pygmea.*—A small slab of limestone with several specimens of this species, with some other fossils, imbedded in its surface.

92.—*P* —— *latuscula.*—*a*, Side view; *b*, longitudinal section.

Description.—Very small, elongate, conical, slender, slightly curved, often in more than one direction; radiating septa alternating in size, about fourteen of the larger with an equal number of the smaller, at the margin of individuals of the average size. Surface with a few obscure undulations of growth. Cup moderately deep.

Length, from 3 to 4 lines; width of the cup at the margin, about 1 line; depth of the cup, from ½ to ⅜ of a line.

This little species occurs in immense numbers in the Middle Silurian on the Island of Anticosti.

Locality and Formation.—Challoupe River, Anticosti; division 4, Middle Silurian.

Collector.—J. Richardson.

PETRAIA LATUSCULA. (N. sp.)

Fig. 92, *a*, *b*.

Description.—Corallum of medium size, short, turbinate, nearly straight slightly curved towards the base, expanding to a width of from 8 to 10 lines in a length of from 5 to 8 lines, then becoming cylindrical or nearly so. Cup rather deep. Radiating septa, as indicated by the external markings, about 50. Surface with a few obscure undulations of growth; the longitudinal striæ representing the septa are usually obscure, but in some specimens distinctly marked.

The most abundant specimens are from 5 to 10 lines in length, and from 8 to 10 lines in width at the margin. In one specimen 13 lines in length, the width of the cup is 10 lines and the depth 5 lines.

Locality and Formation.—The Jumpers, Anticosti; division 4. Middle Silurian.

Collector.—J. Richardson.

ZAPHRENTIS CANADENSIS. (N. sp.)

PETRAIA CANADENSIS.—Report on the Geology of Canada, now in the press, p. 208, fig. 205.

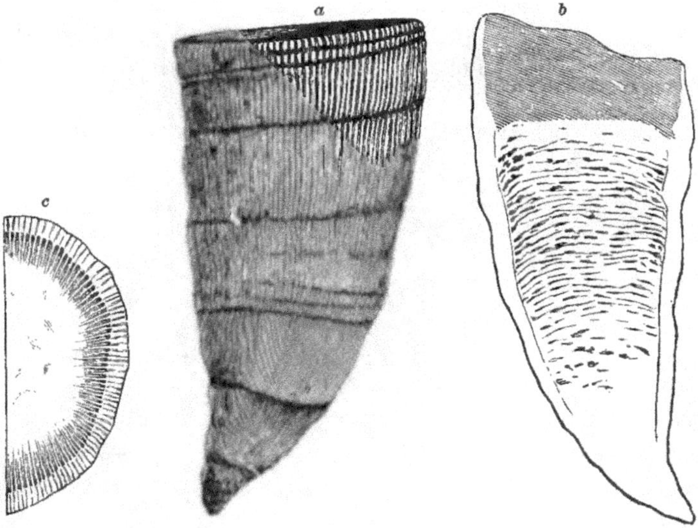

Fig. 93.

Fig. 93.—*Zaphrentis Canadensis.*—*a*, side view ; *b*, longitudinal section, shewing the form of the cup and internal structure ; *c*, transverse section of one half of a specimen just above the bottom of the cup.

Description.—Corallum turbinate, more or less curved, often nearly straight, expanding to a width of from 1 inch to 1½ inches in a height of 3 or 4 inches. Cup from ¾ to 1 inch in depth, the bottom flat or irregularly convex, and its width (at the bottom) equal to three-quarters of the whole diameter. Radiating septa at the margin of the cup in a specimen 3½ inches in length and ½ inch in diameter, about 150, alternating in size. In the same specimen, the radiating septa close to the bottom of the cup extend inwards 2 lines from the outer wall, the latter being 1 line in thickness. In a longitudinal polished section, all the central portion is seen to be filled by transverse diaphragms, three or four in two lines. Surface with a few obscure undulations of growth, and, when worn, with distinct septal striæ.

The specimens are numerous, and vary in their length, diameter, and amount of curvature; some are strongly curved in the lower, and straight in the upper half. The septal fossette has not been observed, and it is therefore doubtful whether or not it belongs to the genus. Young specimens $\frac{3}{4}$ of an inch in length, and also the smaller extremities of the adult, are destitute of transverse diaphragms.

This species in its external characters very much resembles *Petraia rustica* (Billings), Report for 1857, and is found associated with it in the same beds. The internal structure at once shows it to be distinct. I referred it to the genus *Petraia*, and it is figured under that name in the work cited at the head of this description, judging it to be distinct from *P. rustica* on account of the form of the cup; but since that part of the work was printed I have had specimens split by a lapidary, and find that it more probably belongs to *Zaphrentis*.

Locality and Formation.—Drummond Island, Lake Huron. Hudson River group.

Collector.—A. Murray.

AMPLEXUS CINGULATUS. (N. sp.)

Description.—Corallites very elongate, cylindrical, varying from 3 to 8 lines in diameter, annulated at various distances by prominent usually sharp-edged rings of growth, with concave spaces between. Radiating septa from 50 to 80, according to the size of the corallite, extending inwards about one-sixth of the diameter. The inner area occupies full five-sixths of the whole diameter; the transverse septa or tabulæ thin, slightly undulating, from $\frac{1}{4}$ to $\frac{3}{4}$ of a line apart. Surface with about two longitudinal septal striæ in one line, the ridges between which are often divided by a smaller stria.

The annulations are distant from each other from 2 to 14 lines, the most common distance being about half an inch. They are usually sharp-edged, but often in the younger corallites they are either obtusely rounded or represented by mere enlargements of the diameter of various forms and distances.

This species appears to be gregarious, as great numbers are found on the same slabs of limestone, lying across each other in all directions and broken into fragments from 1 to 4 inches in length.

Locality and Formation.—Ance à la Barbe, Bay of Chaleurs. Middle Silurian.

Collector.—Sir W. E. Logan.

Ptychophyllum Canadense. (N. sp.)

Description.—Corallum large, obtusely pedicillated, the base turbinated for a height of one or two inches, then abruptly expanding so as to form a wide circular horizontal disc, from four to eight inches in diameter. Radiating septa from eighty to one hundred. These are closely crowded together at the centre of the fossil, but become more widely separated as they recede towards the margin. At 2½ inches from the centre in one specimen they are 2½ lines apart; at four inches in another larger individual they are 3½ lines distant from each other. Judging from the cast of a cup of this species, the septa must be elevated a little above the surface of the disc; the intervening spaces being slightly concave. In several specimens the base, instead of showing an acute point of attachment, is excavated into a cup-like cavity, ¾ of an inch in depth. The central portion of the upper side seems to be only slightly elevated above the general surface of the widely expanded disc. The under side of a large specimen which is somewhat worn is covered with numerous concentric flexuous raised lines, three or four in the width of one line. In another it is smooth as if protected by a dense epitheca.

Locality and Formation.—South-west point, Anticosti; in division 4, Middle Silurian. Associated with *Pentamerus oblongus*.

Collector.—J. Richardson.

Cyathophyllum Pennanti. (N. sp.)

Description.—Forming large colonies from 2 inches to 2 feet in diameter, consisting of long, slender, often straight corallites, 4 or 5 lines in diameter. The young appear to bud from the side of the adult, and also in some instances from the cup. The surface of the corallites is in general somewhat smooth, but in colonies which have had a disturbed growth it is more irregular, being annulated with obscure accretion ridges, and presenting occasional swellings or enlargements of the diameter. In some there are a few lateral projections which connect the contiguous corallites, as in the genus *Eridophyllum*. In the transverse section there are seen about 60 radiating septa, one half of which seem to reach very nearly to the centre. In the longitudinal section, the transverse diaphragms in the central half form, with the radiating septa, a tissue of square or oblong cells. In some places where the transverse diaphragms alone are visible, the cells are greatly elongated horizontally. The outer vesicular area is filled with oval or irregularly reniform cells, with curved sides, and some acute angles, from 4 to 8 cells in the width of one line.

This species must be closely allied to the well known *C. articulatam* of the Upper Silurian rocks of Europe, but differs therefrom in not being so strongly annulated, and in exhibiting a tendency to form connections between the corallites by the development of small radiciform projections, as in the genus *Eridophyllum.*

The colonies are large, and when split open, the long, slender, cylindrical, and parallel corallites (which are always in contact with each other or very nearly so,) present an aspect very like that of some species of Devonian corals from Canada West, such as *Diphyphyllum arundinaceum.*

Locality and Formation.—L'Anse a Gascon, Bay of Chaleurs: Middle Silurian.

Collector.—Sir W. E. Logan.

CYATHOPHYLLUM WAHLENBERGII. (N. sp.)

Description.—Corallum aggregate, growing in colonies one foot or more in diameter; composed of numerous long cylindrical corallites, three or four lines in diameter, and either closely crowded together or separated from one to four lines. The young branch from the sides of the adult, and are at first very slender, but reach the full size at a length of one or two inches. The corallites are annulated with numerous irregular constrictions, often with sharp-edged elevations between. There appear to be about 60 radiating septa, which do not quite reach the centre. In weathered specimens the interseptal spaces are seen to be divided into oblong or square cells by very thin transverse septa.

Resembles *C. articulatum* (Wahlenberg), but is a smaller species. It is larger, and more strongly annulated than *C. flexuosum* (Lonsdale).

Locality and Formation.—East Point, Anticosti; in division 3, Anticosti group, Middle Silurian.

Collector.—J. Richardson.

CYATHOPHYLLUM PELAGICUM. (N. sp.)

Description.—Corallum aggregate; forming large colonies, from 6 to 15 inches in diameter, consisting of long slender cylindrical corallites, 3 or 4 lines in thickness, closely crowded together. Radiating septa about 60, of an alternating size, the small reaching $\frac{1}{3}$ and the larger $\frac{2}{3}$ the distance from the outer wall to the centre. Central area about one-third the whole diameter; crossed by thin, often flexuous, transverse diaphragms, of which there are 2 or 3 in one line. The inner wall is thin, and the radiating septa seem to be abruptly terminated by it. The young corallites bud from the side of the adult, and gradually attain their full size. Surface with fine transverse striæ of different sizes, usually five or six in one line, crossed by obscure septal striæ.

The inner wall is excessively thin, and in some individuals appears to be absent altogether; but in many it is distinctly visible. The size of the inner area varies, as it does in all species of this genus, but in general it is one-third the width of the corallite.

Locality and Formation.—Becsie River Bay, Anticosti; in Division 2, Anticosti group, Middle Silurian.

Collector.—J. Richardson.

Cyathophyllum interruptum. (N. sp.)

Description.—Corallum apparently simple, turbinate, curved, gradually expanding to a width of 1½ inches in a length of 5 inches; irregularly annulated by sudden constrictions and expansions of growth, from ¾ to 1¼ inches apart. The transverse section, where the diameter is 1½ inches, shows about 120 radiating septa, which seem to reach half-way to the centre. On the outside, where the surface is a little worn, the septal striæ are well indicated, and the interseptal spaces divided into square compartments by the transverse diaphragms. There are about 3 septal striæ in 1 line. The cup appears to be about ¾ of an inch deep, and at the bottom about ⅓ the whole diameter of the fossil. The internal structure in the longitudinal section cannot be made out in the specimens observed, being obscured by crystallization.

This species somewhat resembles *C. truncatum* (Linnæus), but is more deeply annulated. The rings on the upper side project at about a right angle from the side, sometimes ½ an inch, and gradually slope on the lower side to the narrowest part of the next constriction below, so that the individual is constructed as if several corallites had been set into each other.

Locality and Formation.—L'anse à le Barbe, Bay of Chaleurs, Middle Silurian.

Collector.—Sir W. E. Logan.

Cyathophyllum Anticostiense. (N. sp.)

Description.—Corallum rather large, cylindro-turbinate, slightly curved at the base. Cup irregularly conical, its depth about half the diameter of the corallite; the walls thick; the margin effuse or obtusely rounded, the inner surface of the cup descending with a convex slope from the outer edge inwards. In the longitudinal section the inner area is about one-third the whole diameter; the tabulæ thin, much undulated, three or four in the width of one line; the outer area filled with small cells, which curve upwards and outwards, the rows leaving the inner area at an angle of 45° or somewhat less, and cutting the outer surface at an angle of from 60° to 90°, or thereabout. There are from 120 to 150 radiating septa, most of which reach the inner area. In worn specimens the surface is stongly sulcated longitudinally by the septal striæ, and the transverse walls of the cells which fill the intermediate spaces are seen closely crowded together, there being four or five in one line. They present the peculiar zigzag arrangement seen in most species of *Heliophyllum*.

In size this species resembles *C. angustum* (Lonsdale), but in that species the vesicular tissue forms on the surface, where seen in the interseptal spaces, "regular square cells," whereas, in this, they form zigzag transverse lines.

Length, from 4 to 8 inches. Diameter of cup, from 2 to 2½ inches.

Locality and Formation.—South-west Point, Anticosti; in Division 4, Anticosti group, Middle Silurian.

Collector.—J. Richardson.

Cyathophyllum Euryone. (N. sp.)

Description.—Turbinate, curved at the base, expanding to a diameter of one inch at the height of from one to one and a half inches, then becoming cylindrical; radiating septa about one hundred; cup with a flat or gently convex bottom, which is in width about half the whole diameter; inner area full half the whole width, with flat or convex tabulæ; outer area with the cells ascending in lines which meet the exterior at an angle of about 45°; the vesicles acutely oval, from one to one and a half lines in length, with a thickness of one-third or one half a line. Surface, in a worn specimen, strongly sulcated by the septal striæ, of which there are four or five in one line.

Of this species I have seen only one specimen, of which the length is 3 inches, and the diameter 1 inch.

It occurs in the same formation with *C. Anticostiense*, but differs therefrom in the form of the cup, which has a flat bottom instead of being conical; and also in the greater diameter of the inner area.

Locality and Formation.—The Jumpers, Anticosti; in Division 4, Anticosti group, Middle Silurian.

Collector.—J. Richardson.

Cyathophyllum Eriphyle. (N. sp.)

Description.—Corallum simple, elongate, cylindro-turbinate, large. Cup rather deep, conical. Inner area about one-third the whole diameter, with the transverse septa well defined but undulating, in some places nearly in contact, and in others separated from half a line to one line or a little more. Outer area with large acutely-lentiform cells sloping upwards and outwards, from three to six lines in length. Surface with a thin epitheca, the edges of the septa shewing, as it were, through it, about one line distant from each other, and often with what appear to be one or two smaller septa between each two of the larger. There are also numerous annulations of growth, of various sizes, the larger distant from four to nine lines from each other, and each being slightly more prominent on its upper than on its lower edge. Fine transverse annulating striæ, from six to eight in one line, are also visible where the surface is well preserved. The radiating septa are not distinctly visible in the specimens, but they appear to be about a line apart at the margin.

Length from 4 to 10 inches. Diameter from 2 to 2½ inches.

This species differs from both *C. angustum* and *C. Anticostiense* in the greater size of the vesicles composing the internal structure.

Locality and Formation.—Anse à la Vieille, Bay of Chaleurs. Middle Silurian.

Collector.—Sir W. E. Logan.

Cyathophyllum nymphale. (N. sp.)

Description.—Corallum turbinate, curved at the base, expanding to a width of three inches in a length of two and a half. Cup shallow, concave, with a small projection in the middle, indicating the inner area. Radiating septa, as indicated by the sulci on the exterior, about one hundred. Inner area well defined in the longitudinal polished section, about one-sixth the whole diameter; the tabulæ very thin and numerous, apparently five or six in one line. The outer area consists of an exceedingly compact vesicular structure, the largest cells being scarcely half a line in length. Outer surface with strong convex longitudinal ribs about one line in width, the sulci separating them, sharply rounded or angular at the bottom.

The only specimen of this species that I have seen is of a remarkable shape. On one side of the cup the margin curves downwards, and on the other, upwards. It is barely possible that the concave extremity which I have called the cup may be the base, the small projection in the middle being the point of attachment. In that case, this species would be a *Ptychophyllum*. The supposed base is worn away in the specimen, so that this point cannot be determined at present. The extraordinary compactness of the internal structure separates this from any described species from the Silurian rocks of America.

Locality and Formation.—Anse à la Vieille, Bay of Chaleurs. Middle Silurian.

Collector.—Sir W. E. Logan.

Cyathophyllum Pasithea. (N. sp.)

Description.—The specimen upon which this species is founded is cylindrical, 21 lines in length and 10 lines in diameter. In the longitudinal section, the inner area is 3½ lines in diameter, filled with large cells, the tabulæ being very thin and not extending across but irregularly coalescing, thus forming acutely lenticular vesicles, from 1 to 3 lines in length, arranged in curving lines, the convex side towards the base of the corallite. In the outer area the vesicular tissue is very fine, but distinct, and indicated in the polished section by two sets of lines, one curving upwards and the other downwards, crossing each other nearly at a right angle. There are six or seven lines in the width of one line, and the cells are on an average about one-sixth of a line across. In the transverse section there are seen about 70 radiating septa, which extend about two-thirds of the way to the centre. The surface is longitudinally marked with distinct ridges, about three in one line, separated by fine deep sulci. It is also transversely annulated by strongly projecting rings of growth, most prominent and angular on their upper sides. Of these there are six in the length of 21 lines.

This species differs so widely from all the others described in this paper, that a comparison is scarcely necessary. Owing to the peculiar construction of the cells in the outer area, that is to say, curving downwards as well as upwards, I suspect that it will turn out to be a *Heliophyllum*.

Locality and Formation.—Anse à la Vieille, Bay of Chaleurs. Middle Silurian.

Collector.—Sir W. E. Logan.

Cystiphyllum maritima. (N. sp.)

Description.—The only specimen of this species I have seen is turbinate, gently curved, 2½ inches in length, and about the same in width at the upper extremity. Surface annulated with several deep undulations of growth, and longitudinally striated with very distinct septal sulci, about four in the width of one line in the upper half, and five or six towards the smaller extremity. The cup is about ¾ of an inch in depth, obtusely conical, and distinctly sulcated on the inside by the septal striæ. In a longitudinal polished section, the structure appears to be very compact, or composed of very small cells, two or three in the width of one line, but owing to the peculiar state of preservation of the specimen these cannot be well observed.

I have some doubts whether this species should not be referred to the genus *Cyathophyllum*, since the strongly striated surface of the cavity of the cup would indicate that the radiating septa are more fully developed than they are in *Cystiphyllum*. The species to which it bears the nearest resemblance is *C. Greyi* (Edwards and Haime) from the Wenlock limestone at Dudley. It appears to be a larger and more strongly striated species than that, and therefore I shall give it a distinct name for the present, provisionally.

Locality and Formation.—Anse à la Vieille, Bay of Chaleurs. Middle Silurian.

Collector.—Sir W. E. Logan.

Strombodes gracilis. (N. sp.)

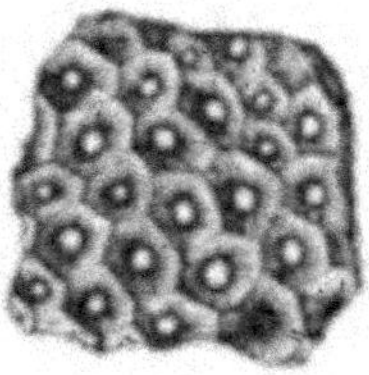

Fig. 94.

Fig. 94.—*Strombodes gracilis.*

Description.—Corallum in large masses, consisting of cells from 2 to 3 lines in diameter, most of them pentagonal. Cup about 1 line in depth, with an irregularly rounded central style ½ line in height, and one-third or one-half the whole width of the corallite. There appear to be 30 or 40 septal striæ on the inner side of the cup.

Resembles *S. diffluens* (Lonsdale) but is much smaller.

Locality and Formation.—Manitouwaning, Lake Huron. Middle Silurian.

Collector.—A. Murray.

BRACHIOPODA.

Lingula Canadensis. (N. sp.)

a

b

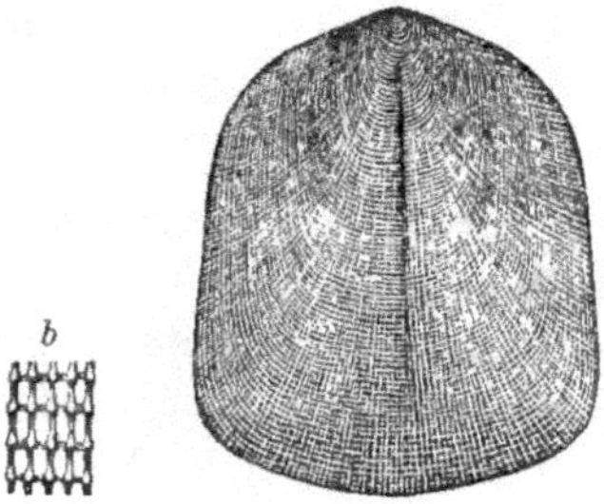

Fig. 95.

Fig. 96.

Fig. 95.—*Lingula Canadensis.*—*a*, Dorsal (?) valve ; *b*, portion of surface enlarged
96.—*L*——— *Forbesi.*

Description.—Shell large, oblong, sub-pentagonal; front margin gently convex or nearly straight; anterior angles narrowly rounded; sides straight, and nearly parallel for about two-thirds the whole length, then converging to the beaks; apical angle about 130°; cardinal edges on each side of the beak nearly straight. The valves are moderately convex, most tumid in the upper half, descending to the sides and front margin with three flat slopes. Surface with fine, thread-like, elevated, longitudinal ridges, five or six in the width of one line at the front margin; these are crossed by much finer concentric ridges, ten or twelve in one line, which are continued over the longitudinal ridges, and give to the surface a minutely nodulose appearance.

Length about 1½ inches; greatest width, at the anterior angles about 1 inch, and at the posterior angles about 1 line less.

This species resembles in form, surface characters, and geological position, the large *L. tenuigranulata* (McCoy). That species is, however, proportionally a little longer, and is, besides, much more finely striated, there being twenty-six longitudinal striæ in the width of one line.

Locality and Formation. — Anticosti, Black Point. Hudson River group.

Collector.—J. Richardson.

Lingula Forbesi. (N. sp.)

Fig. 96.

Description.—Elongate, oval; front narrowly and regularly rounded; sides gently convex; apex somewhat acutely rounded. Both valves are rather strongly and uniformly convex. Surface with fine concentric striæ.

Length of specimen of average size, 9 lines; width about 5 lines.

Locality and Formation.—English Head, Anticosti; Hudson River group. And also at Junction Cliff, Anticosti; in Division 1, base of the Middle Silurian.

Collector.—J. Richardson.

Genus Strophomena.

The following descriptions are copied from a paper published in the *Canadian Naturalist and Geologist*, Vol. V., February 1860 :—

In the Silurian rocks of Canada and the neighboring countries, there are many species or varieties of that group of the genus *Strophomena* of which *S. alternata* may be regarded as the typical form. These are all closely related, and yet exhibit such differences that only those naturalists who entertain wide views upon the subject of the value and significance of specific distinctions, would feel inclined to unite them under one common name. The forms of this group most common in the Lower and Middle Silurian rocks are, *S. alternata*, *S. incrassata*, *S. deltoidea*, *S. camerata*, *S. tenuistriata* and some others to be described hereafter in this paper. The first of these ranges from the Chazy limestone upwards perhaps to the Niagara rocks, but is most abundant in the Trenton limestone and Hudson River group. It is also very widely distributed, as it occurs in all parts of the Continent, where the last two formations have been recognized, and is also found in the Lower Silurian in England and Ireland. *S. incrassata* has exactly the same form as some of the varieties of *S. alternata* but is never, as far as I have been able to ascertain, more than half the average size of this latter species. It seems to be confined to the Chazy and the Black River limestone or the lower part of the Trenton, and has therefore, a geological distribution different from that of *S. alternata*, a fact which would appear to constitute an additional ground for classifying it as a distinct species. *S deltoidea* is a Trenton limestone form abundant in certain localities, but not generally distributed. Thus in the

State of New York, according to Professor Hall, "it abounds at Trenton Falls and at Sugar River in Lewis County," but "is scarcely known as occurring in the Champlain valley."* In Canada it is found at Lachine and at several other places, but there are hundreds of good exposures of the rock in the Province that have been carefully examined, where not a single specimen has been seen, although in all the localities *S. alternata* is more or less common. *S. camerata* occurs at one spot in the vicinity of Ottawa, but I have never met with it elsewhere. *S. tenuistriata* may be collected in the hard black limestone around the base of the mountain of Montreal, particularly in the neighborhood of the McTavish monument, and also at Ottawa and two or three other places, but does not occur at all in the majority of the localities of the Trenton limestone. These three species, therefore must have been capable of existing in certain places only, on the bottom of the ocean during the period of the accumulation of this rock, while *S. alternata* flourished everywhere. Whether or not, therefore, they are to be regarded as distinct species, this much at least seems probable, that they were by some peculiarity in their habits or in their organization, unfitted for so wide a range through the seas as that enjoyed by *S. alternata*.

The question, whether or not these supposed species are really distinct, cannot be answered until naturalists shall have discovered some general law of life by an appeal to which they may in all cases determine what is a species as distinguished from a mere variety. It is scarcely necessary to state that such a law if it do exist at all may remain unknown to man for ages, and in the meantime nearly all determinations of species from varieties where the forms are very closely related may be regarded as not positively established. The physical geologist is more interested in the results of investigations which show that certain forms are confined to particular geological horizons than in those, whose sole object is to determine the exact zoological relations of such forms. If it be true, for instance, that that particular form of the genus called *Strophomena incrassata* is confined to the limestones lying next under the Trenton in the fossiliferous series, it makes no difference to the geologist, whether it be in reality a distinct species of itself or only a variety of some other species. Its value to him as a guide, while tracing out the geographical distribution of these Rocks, is not at all affected by the zoological question. In demonstrating the physical structure of the country, he can reason upon varieties with as much safety as upon true species, provided that such varieties are confined to and consequently characteristic of particular portions of the geological edifice. It is therefore, of great importance, not only to ascertain to what

---

* Palæontology of New York, vol. 1, p. 107.

particular level each variety is confined, but also to determine whether or not such species as range through several formations exhibit any and what change in form on passing from one group of rocks to another. Should it be hereafter proved that the supposed species above quoted, constitute on purely zoological grounds, but one extensive and variable species, still it would be convenient for geological purposes to have a separate name for each variety that can be shewn to be characteristic of a particular geological horizon.

Before entering upon the description of the new species, I shall give a general account of such characters as are common to all the forms of the group typified by *S. alternata*.

Strophomena alternata. (Conrad.)

In all the forms of this important type, the convexity of the ventral valve has a peculiar contour which may be seen not only in the Lower Silurian but also in the Upper Silurian and even in such Devonian species as *S. Pattersoni*, *S. inequiradiata*, *S. demissa*, *S. concava*. That part of the valve which is usually called the visceral disc occupies all the central region of the shell and terminates in a point at the beak. Just in front of the beak it forms a more or less well defined low rounded umbo on each side of which there is a flattened or sub-concave depression extending obliquely outwards to the margin just in front of the cardinal angles. These latter are usually reflected or a little curved upwards from the plane of the lateral margins. The visceral disc is somewhat flattened, gently convex or only slightly elevated throughout the greater part of its extent. In the upper half of the shell it is bounded by the depressions that have been mentioned as existing between the umbo and cardinal angles, but in front and at the sides it terminates where the shell begins to be bent down to form the deflected margin which runs all round the edge and becomes obsolete on approaching the cardinal angles. This margin varies in width from one-twelfth to two-thirds the whole length of the shell and therefore the disc in some of the varieties occupies nearly the whole superficies of the valve, but in others, less than half. In the very young shells in most of the specimens that I have seen, there is no deflected margin and occasionally adult individuals may be found, which on a side view give the outline of an uniform flattened arch from beak to front. In by far the greater number of specimens however the deflected margin is well defined. The contour of the front of the visceral disc varies according to the form of the deflected margin and is thus either broadly rounded or more or less pointed. In *S. rhomboidalis*, which also belongs to this group, the front of the disc, and its sides also, are often nearly straight.

The dorsal valve is flat or only gently concave beneath the visceral disc of the ventral valve, but all round, its curvature conforms to that of the deflected margin.

In the true *S. alternata* the areas of the ventral and dorsal valves are inclined towards each other at an angle varying from 75° to 80°, but this angle never amounts to 90°. It will be observed that in some of the new species hereinafter described it is greater than 90°.

The surface in most of the species exhibits two sets of radiating striæ, the larger of which are about one-twelfth of a line wide in large specimens, and the smaller half that size, from one to ten of the smaller between each two of the larger, the more common numbers being from three to five. Sometimes also the shell is marked with a series of concentric wrinkles.

Of the above characters, those which are confined to the upper half of the shell such as the form of the beak, the umbo, the concave depressions or hollows on each side of the umbo, and the reflected cardinal extremities, are common to all the species, and in order to avoid repetition will not be particularly dwelt upon in the following descriptions. The radiating striæ are also very constant in the aspect they present. The only parts which appear to afford permanent variations of much value are the front of the visceral disc, the deflected margin and the hinge line, The proportional length and breadth of the shell seems also to be of much importance especially if accompanied by a variation in two or three of the other characters.

STROPHOMENA NITENS. (Billings.)

STROPHOMENA NITENS.—*Canadian Naturalist and Geologist*, vol. 5, p. 53, Feb. 1860.

Fig. 97.

Fig. 77.—*Strophomena nitens.* *a*, is a section showing the curvature and obtuse angles formed by the inclination of the areas.

Description.—Transversley semi-oval, sides somewhat straight for one third or a little more of the length from the cardinal angles, and slightly converging towards each other ; front angles broadly rounded ; front margin gently convex or nearly straight for about one third the width in the middle portion. Width on hinge-line from nine to twelve lines. Length from six to eight lines.

The beak, umbo depressions on each side of the umbo and cardinal angles of the ventral valve the same as in *S. alternata.* The deflected margin forms an angle of between 100° and 110° with the general plane of the visceral disc, and occupies on the median line (in all the specimens I have seen) from one third to nearly one half the whole length of the shell.

The dorsal valve is quite flat, or even a little concave, just in front of the beak, but elsewhere curved to correspond with the ventral valve.

The area of the ventral valve lies nearly in the plane of the lateral margins, and the area of the dorsal valve forms with it an angle of about 95°. The height of the area of the ventral valve at the foramen is three fourths of a line in a specimen nine lines wide, and of the dorsal valve about one third of a line. Foramen of ventral valve partly closed by a V-shaped deltidium, the lower open part of which is closed by the strongly projecting deltidium of the dorsal valve.

The width of the foramen, is about equal to its height.

The surface is the same as in *S. alternata*, and, when a little worn presents a smooth shining silken lustre.

When compared with *S. incrassata*, *S. alternata*, *S. deltoidea*, S. *camerata*, or *S. tenuistriata*, it will be seen that this species is shorter in proportion to the width than any of them, and also that the inclination of the areas towards each other differs in forming an obtuse instead of an acute angle.

Locality and Formation.—This species occurs at Charleton Point, Anticosti, in the upper part of the Hudson River group.

Collector.—J. Richardson.

Strophomena Ceres. (Billings.)

Strophomena Ceres.—*Canadian Naturalist and Geologist*, vol. 5, p. 54, Feb. 1860.

Description.—Semi-oval, sides rather straight and a little converging for one third their length; front angles and margins broadly rounded. Width on hinge line twelve to fifteen lines; length ten to twelve lines.

The ventral valve varies greatly in the amount of its convexity. In some specimens it is depressed convex, and these have almost precisely the aspect of the more flattened forms of *S. alternata.* Others are slightly convex, nearly hemispherical, uniformly arched from beak to front, no devected margin distinct from the visceral disc, the latter occupying the whole of the shell, except a small triangular space at the hinge-angles. Between these two extremes there are individuals which present all the intermediate degrees of convexity, and some in which the deflected margin can be detected with a width equal to half the whole length of the shell.

The surface is the same as that of *S. alternata*.

The area of the ventral valve is one line high in a specimen fourteen lines wide, and lies very nearly in the plane of the lateral margin. The foramen is as wide as high, and closed by a strongly convex deltidium, the lower margin of which is concave to admit the equally convex deltidium of the dorsal valve, whose area is almost half a line wide and forms an obtuse angle of between 90° and 100° with that of the ventral valve. The beak of the ventral valve exhibits in some specimens a small round perforation.

This species differs from *S. nitens* in being in general a little longer proportionally, larger, and more uniformly convex, with scarcely a distinct deflected margin. In *S. nitens* the length is in general only two thirds of the width, but in this species it is always over five sixths.

The angle formed by the inclination of the areas being obtuse instead of acute furnishes the only character as far as I can ascertain by which it can be separated from *S. alternata*.

Locality and Formation.—Charleton Point, Hudson River group, and also at East Point in the Middle Silurian, Anticosti.

Collector.—J. Richardson.

STROPHOMENA LEDA. (Billings.)

STROPHOMENA LEDA.—*Canadian Naturalist and Geologist*, vol. 5, p. 55, Feb. 1860.

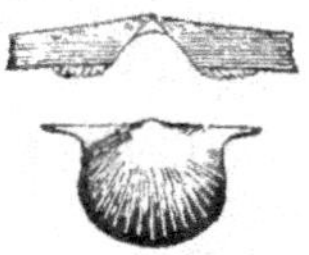

Fig. 98.

Fig. 99.

Fig. 98.—*Strophomena Leda* with a portion of the hinge area of the ventral valve enlarged to shew the striated teeth.

99.—A specimen without ears supposed to be of the same species.

Description.—Shell rather small and thin, semi-oval, the front and front angles regularly rounded, sometimes a little narrower at the base of the ears than at one third the length from the hinge line, the latter usually exceeding the greatest width of the shell, and forming projecting spiniform ears. Width excluding the ears, five to nine lines; length five-sixths of the width; ears one line and a half in length each, in a well preserved specimen five lines wide.

The ventral valve is in the small specimens, depressed convex and nearly uniformly arched from beak to front; the umbo well defined, but the concave depressions on each side rather obscure; no deflected margin. The large specimens (nine lines wide) are sometimes strongly convex. Dorsal valve concave, its curvature corresponding to that of the ventral valve. Surface as in *S. alternata*.

Area of ventral valve half a line in height in a specimen seven lines wide, lying nearly in the plane of the margin, apparently a little sloping outwards, forming an angle of about 100° with that of the dorsal valve, which latter is scarcely one-fourth of a line wide. Foramen not distinctly observed but apparently wider than high.

The detached and empty ventral valves exhibit two rather large triangular hinge teeth, one on each side of the foramen, covered with striæ on the outside in a manner similar to that of the area of those species to which Professor Hall has given the generic name of *Strophodonta*.

The spiniform ears are often either broken or worn away.

Varieties.—Several specimens nine lines wide without ears, and others of the same size strongly convex, and with an indistinct deflected margin, occupying from one-third to one-half the length of the shell, appear to belong to this species.

The species when the ears are broken away has exactly the appearance of *S. alternata*, only that it is never more than half the size. The characters of the hinge areas and teeth taken together with the small size and hinge ears, are abundantly sufficient to show that it is distinct from *S. alternata*. It is a longer shell than *S. nitens*, and is in general destitute of a deflected margin. It is smaller, thinner and less convex than *S. Ceres*.

Locality and Formation.—Anticosti, in strata situated from 800 to 1000 feet above the base of the Middle Silurian, and 250 feet below the rocks containing *Pentamerus oblongus*.

Collector.—J. Richardson.

Stophomena Philomela. (Billings.)

Strophomena Philomela.—*Canadian Naturalist and Geologist*, Vol. V., p. 56, Feb. 1860.

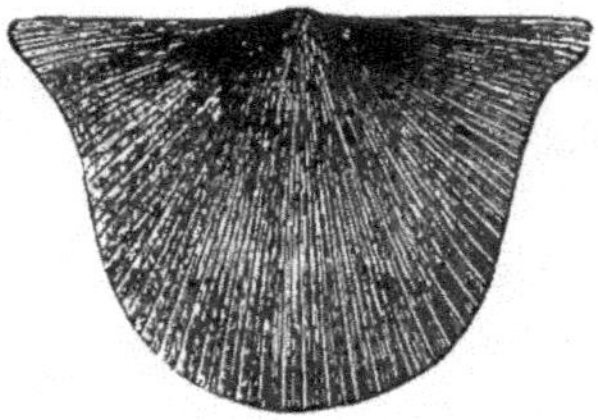

Fig. 100.

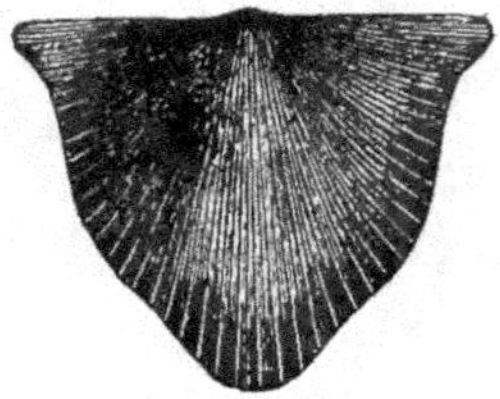

Fig. 101.

Fig. 100.—*Strophomena Philomela.*
101.—The same with a mesial fold.

Description.—Shell rather large; hinge line exceeding the greatest width, forming short rounded ears; sides gently concave, converging towards each other; front margin and angles regularly rounded, sometimes with a projecting lobe in the middle. Width on hinge line from eighteen to twenty four lines. Length from two-thirds to four-fifths the width.

In the ventral valve the umbo and depressions on each side are well defined and exactly like those of the convex form of *St. alternata.* The visceral disc is moderately and broadly convex; the deflected margin from one-fourth to one-third the whole length of the shell, passing into the disc with a short rounded curve. Dorsal valve with the curvature corresponding to that of the ventral valve.

The area of the ventral valve is a little more than half a line in height at the foramen in a specimen two inches wide, and it inclines a little outwards apparently forming an angle of from 160° to 170°, with the plane of the lateral margins. The foramen appears to be almost completely closed, but this character has not been ascertained with certainty owing to the imperfection of the specimens examined. The hinge teeth are striated as in *S. Leda.* The area of the dorsal valve is almost linear, or at the most not half the width of that of the ventral valve.

The surface does not differ from that of *S. alternata*, so far as I have been able to ascertain.

Varieties.—One specimen has been found associated with the others of this species in which the length and breadth are almost equal. It has no ears, although it is longer in proportion to the width, and yet it does not appear to differ sufficiently to constitute a distinct species. Another specimen has a rounded fold in the front margin which becomes [obsolete at one third the length of the shell.

This species by its projecting ears, narrow areas, and striated hinge teeth is most closely related to *S. Leda*, from which it differs in being four times the size. It has so much of the aspect of *S. alternata*, that at present we have no means of distinguishing it from that species without an examination of the hinge area and teeth.

Locality and Formation.—Middle Silurian, Anticosti, associated with *Pentamerus oblongus.*

Collector.—J. Richardson.

The above four species, *S. nitens*, *S. Ceres*, *S. Leda*, and *S. Philomela* are closely allied to *S. alternata.* The three following have the ventral valve concave, and belong to a very different group, of which *S. filitexta* (Hall) may be regarded as a typical form.

STROPHOMENA FLUCTUOSA. N. S.

STROPHOMENA FLUCTUOSA.—*Can. Nat. and Geol.*, Vol. V., p. 57, Feb. 1860.

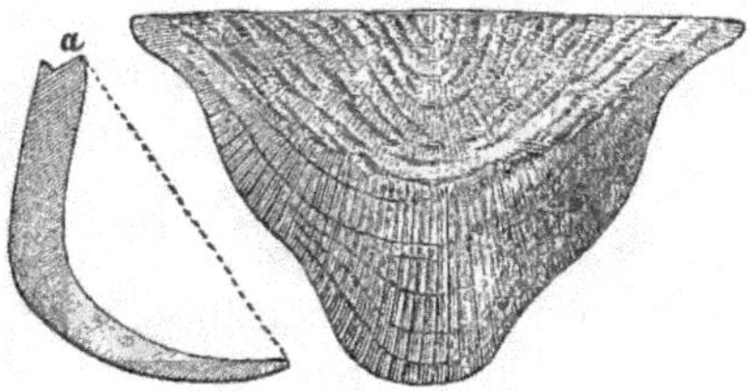

Fig. 102.

Fig. 102.—*Strophomena fluctuosa.* *a*, section, the dotted line represents the plane of the lateral margin, and it is drawn to shew that the area of the concave or ventral valve is at a right angle to it.

Description.—Triangular, or semi-oval, usually widest at the hinge-line, and more or less narrowly rounded, pointed, trilobed, or nasute in front.

Dorsal valve convex, the visceral disc being in general equal to one third the superficies of the whole valve, nearly flat, the remainder abruptly curved down all round so that the lower half of the length of the shell is sometimes at right angles with the upper half. The cardinal angles more or less compressed and often a little reflected, usually forming angular or narrowly rounded ears. Ventral valve concave, the curvature corresponding to that of the dorsal valve.

Area of dorsal valve lying in the plane of the lateral margin, about one third of a line high. Area of ventral valve forming a right angle with the marginal plane, in large specimens one line or a little more in height at the beak, and gradually decreasing towards the extremities of the hinge-line.

Foramen of ventral valve triangular; the width at the base somewhat exceeding the height, completely closed by a convex deltidium, the basal margin of which is rendered a little concave by the convex margin of the similar deltidium which closes the foramen of the dorsal valve.

Surface with a set of fine rounded elevated radiating striæ distant from each other usually about half a line, sometimes a little less and occasionally one line. Between each two of these there are from two to ten much finer striæ; the whole crossed by fine crowded concentric lines. In most of the specimens the whole of the upper half of the shell is covered with short undulating wrinkles, which sometimes have a concentric arrangement and often form concentric rows converging from the hinge-line towards the centre of the shell, crossing each other. The specimens from the Trenton limestone are usually without these undulations, but in those from the Hudson River group this character is prominently exhibited.

This shell is somewhat variable in its characters. The visceral disc of the dorsal valve is sometimes confined to a small area around and in front of the beak and along the hinge-line, and in such cases the deflection takes place at one fifth or one fourth the length from the beak. Occasionally a broad rounded elevated mesial fold extended into a linguiform projection of the middle of the front margin gives to the dorsal valve a trilobate character. The area of the ventral valve is in general at right angles to the plane of the lateral margins, but sometimes it slopes a little forward. In some the hinge-line is greatly extended, the cardinal extremities forming projecting triangular ears.

Width on hinge-line from one inch to one inch and a half Length variable, from two thirds of the width to four fifths or a little more.

Strophomena deltoidea (Conrad) has the ventral valve convex and may be always distinguished from this even when the hinge-line cannot be seen by the small rounded umbo close to the beak. *S. camerata* and *S. tenuistriata* (Conrad) have also the ventral valve convex. (See Plate 31 A, Vol. I. Pal. N. Y.)

Locality and Formation.—Trenton limestone, City of Ottawa, rare; more common in the Hudson River group, Anticosti.

Collectors.—E. Billings, J. Richardson.

STROPHOMENA THALIA. N. s.

SSROPHOMENA THALIA.—*Can. Nat. and Geol.*, Vol. V., p. 57, Feb. 1860.

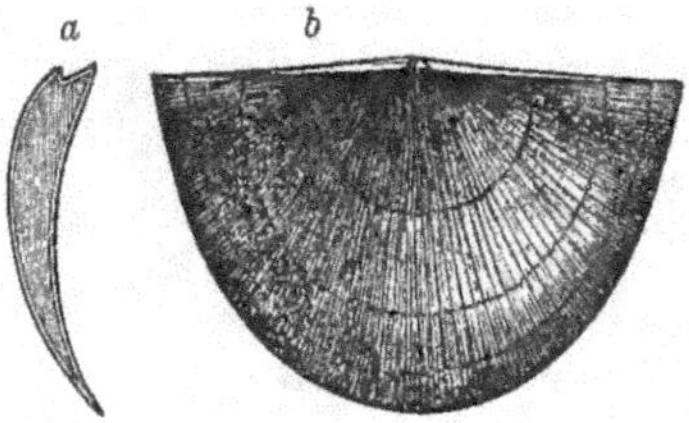

Fig. 103.

Fig. 103.—*Strophomena Thalia.* *a*. longitudinal section ; *b*, ventral aspect.

Description.—Semi-oval or subtriangular, often narrowly rounded or somewhat pointed in front, hinge-line usually greatly exceeding the width of the shell, and forming with the sides an angle of from 70° to 80°. Width at hinge-line from one to two inches, length about five eighths the width.

Dorsal valve moderately convex, depressed towards the cardinal angles, which are a little recurved ; umbo flat. On a side view the outline forms a gentle and nearly uniform curve from the front for about four fifths the length, when it descends with a flat slope to the beak, which it reaches at an angle of from 45° to 60°.

Ventral valve concave, the greatest depth about the middle or a little nearer the beak.

Area of ventral valve moderate, forming an angle of about 100° with the plane of the margin, its height in a specimen two inches wide, one line ; foramen triangular, closed by a convex deltidium, its width at the base about one fifth greater than the height. The beak is not perforated in any specimen that I have seen. Area of dorsal valve nearly in the plane of the margin, its width about one third of that of the ventral valve.

Surface with moderately coarse radiating striæ, which increase both by bifurcation and interstitial addition, usually unequal but sometimes uniform in size, from ten to fifteen in the width of two lines, crossed by excessively fine crowded concentric lines.

This species is allied to *S. fluctuosa*, but differs in having the areas of the ventral and dorsal valves inclined at an angle which is rather less than a right angle. In its outline it forms nearly an uniform arch instead of being abruptly bent like *S. fluctuosa*.

The dorsal valve of *S. recta* (Conrad) is said to have a slight mesial depression, while the ventral valve is flat. *S. plano-convexa* (Hall) has also a slight mesial depression in the dorsal valve, and is flat or even a little convex in front of the beak of the ventral valve, where this species is concave. It has also a perforated beak, and an area more approximated to the plane of the lateral margins than it is in *S. Thalia*. The three species are, however, notwithstandnig these differences, closely related.

Locality and Formation.—City of Ottawa, Trenton limestone.

Collector.—E. Billings.

Strophomena Hecuba. N. s.

Strophomena Hecuba, *Can. Nat. and Geol.*, Vol. V. p. 60, Feb. 1860.

Fig. 104.

Fig. 104.—*Strophomena Hecuba*, dorsal valve.

Description.—Subtriangular with usually a linguiform projection in front. Width on hinge-line about two inches ; length varying from a little less to a little more than the width.

Dorsal valve very convex, nearly regularly arched from beak to front, only a small space at the hinge extremities compressed, the whole of the remainder of the shell exceedingly ventricose, usually a rounded fold in front which becomes obsolete at one fourth the length, area sublinear, scarcely half a line in width in the largest specimens.

Ventral valve depressed convex near the beak, and concave all round near the margin, area about one line wide and forming an angle of about 115° with the plane of the lateral margins. Foramen not observed.

Surface marked with fine radiating striæ ten or twelve in the width of one line, every third, fourth or fifth one of which is twice the size of the intermediate fine ones. The whole surface is besides (in most specimens) ornamented with indistinct concentric wrinkles from one fourth of a line to two lines in width. There are probably fine concentratic striæ, although I have not, (owing to the partially exfoliated state of the specimens examined) been able to detect them.

This species varies considerably in the amount of the convexity of the dorsal valve and in the size of the mesial fold in front. Some have a wide flat space in the umbonial region, and in such, on a side-view, the outline of the shell rises from the beak at an angle of about 45° only, while in others, which are more ventricose, this angle is full 60° with the plane of the margin.

Sometimes the sides are strongly compressed, so that the shell becomes subcylindrical and greatly produced in front, the length exceeding the width. In some specimens the striæ are nearly all of the same size, but in general they alternate as in the finest marked specimens of *S. alternata*

Resembles *S. Thalia*, but that species has the ventral valve concave nearly to the beak. It is more uniformly gibbous than *C. fluctuosa.*

Locality and Formation.—Anticosti, Hudson River group.

Collector.—J. Richardson.

The following species are considered to be either new or closely allied to some that are not very well known among American collections :—

STROPHOMENA JULIA. (N. sp.)

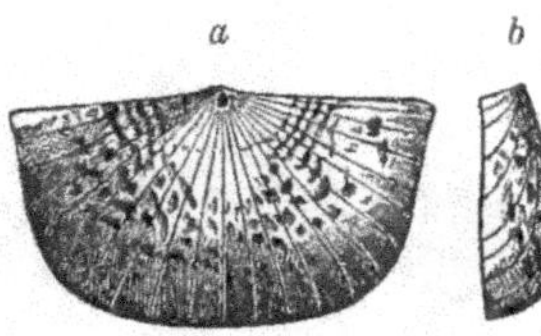

Fig. 105.

Fig. 105.—*Strophomena Julia.*—*a*, Ventral view ; *b*, side view, enlarged two diameters.

Description.—Shell small, transversely oblong, greatest width at the hinge-line ; sides somewhat straight ; front angles obtusely rounded ; front margin straight or gently convex. Ventral valve convex ; the front margin and the anterior half of the sides abruptly curved down to form a deflected border, the length of which is equal to one-third of the whole length of the shell. The visceral disc, or all that part of the shell which is not included in the deflected border, is gently convex, most elevated in the middle, somewhat flattened at the cardinal angles. Beak scarcely distinct from the cardinal edges, a little depressed below the greatest height of the shell, perforated by a well-defined circular aperture. Area proportionally rather large, flat, nearly at right angles to the plane of the lateral margins, slightly overhanging the hinge-line. Foramen apparently as wide as it is high, closed by a convex deltidium. Dorsal valve flat, all except the margin, which is curved to correspond with the ventral valve. Surface with about 30 fine, but distinct, radiating striæ, about one-half of which reach the umbo; the intervening flat spaces with much finer striæ, just visible to the naked eye. A small space on the umbo is smooth, and much of the remainder of the shell covered with small irregular undulations.

Width of a ventral valve, on the hinge-line, 7 lines; length about 4 lines. Width of a dorsal valve of another specimen, 6 lines; length 3½ lines.

Of this species only two detached valves have been collected. It is evidently closely allied to *Leptæna Loveni* (De Verneuil, *Bul. Geol. Soc. France*, 2d series, vol. v., p. 339, pl. 4, fig. 5), but is proportionally broader, and differs greatly in the curvature of the valves, as may be seen by the figures above given. *L. Loveni* has also a deep sinus in the middle of the front half of the ventral valve, and a corresponding fold in the dorsal.

Locality and Formation.—The Jumpers, Anticosti. In Division 4, Anticosti group, Middle Silurian.

Collector.—J. Richardson.

STROPHOMENA IMBREX. (Pander.)

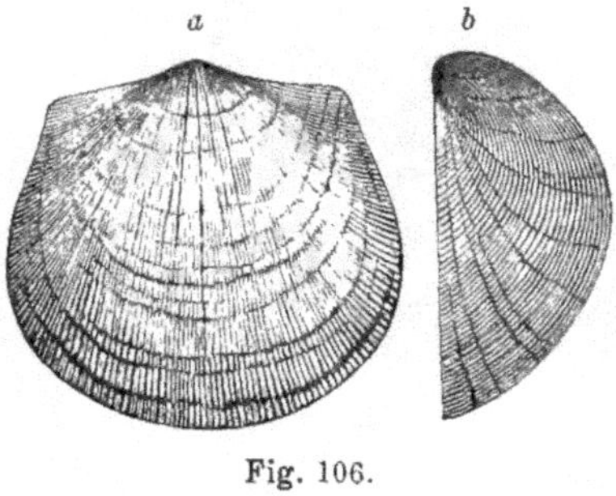

Fig. 106.

Fig. 106.—*Strophomena imbrex ?—a*, Ventral valve; *b*, side view of one of the forms of this species.

Remarks.—This species only differs from *Strophomena alternata* in the curvature of the valves and in the surface characters. The visceral disc is gently convex and shaped like that of *S. alternata*, but the shell is usually suddenly bent, and the deflected margin greatly, produced often at a right angle to the upper part. The length of the margin and the angle of curvature vary extremely. The surface is covered with fine rounded or sub-angular striæ, which are always more or less flexuous. In some, they are of a uniform size all over; in others, they alternate in size, and have from two to six smaller between each two larger. These are crossed by fine concentric striæ, and often the visceral disc exhibits a number of obscure concentric undulations, as in *S. deltoidea*. The shell has a silken lustre, in certain conditions of preservation. Our specimens agree so nearly with the descriptions of *S. imbrex*, that for the present it would not be advisable to give it a new name. *S. camerata* (Conrad) appears to be the same species, only smaller and found at a lower horizon, *i.e.*, in the Trenton.

Locality and Formation.—This species occurs in great abundance at Cape Robert, Anticosti; in the Hudson River group. It is there associated with *S. Hecuba*.

Collector.—J. Richardson.

STROPHOMENA ANTIQUATA. (Sowerby.)

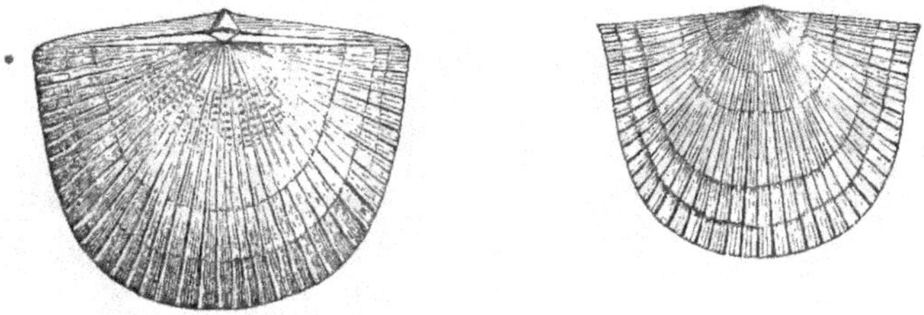

Fig. 107.

Fig. 107.—*S. antiquata.* *a*, dorsal, and *b*, ventral views.

Remarks.—This species belongs to the resupinate group along with *S. filitexta* and *S. planoconvexa.* The ventral valve is gently concave, and the dorsal as gently convex. The surface exhibits several concentric squamose ridges of growth, and is covered with strong rounded and rugged, often flexuous radiating ridges, which increase both by subdivision and intercalation. Between these larger ridges there are from two to six smaller radiating striæ, the whole crossed by very fine concentric lines and irregular undulations of the shell.

It is with much doubt that I refer our specimens to this species. I have not access to any detailed description except that given by McCoy in the British Pal. Foss., and he makes no mention of either the concentric striæ or the fine radiating lines between the large ridges.

Locality and Formation.—Prinsta Bay, Anticosti. In Division 3, Anticosti group; also at the Forks of the Chatte River in Gaspé.

Collectors.—J. Richardson, A. Murray.

STROPHOMENA RECTA. (Conrad.)

STROPHOMENA RECTA (Conrad). *Proc. Acad. Nat. Sci. Philadelphia*, Vol. I, p. 332, 1843.
LEPTÆNA RECTA (Hall). *Pal. N. Y.*, Vol. I, p. 113, Pl. 31, B, Figs. 6, *a*, *b*.

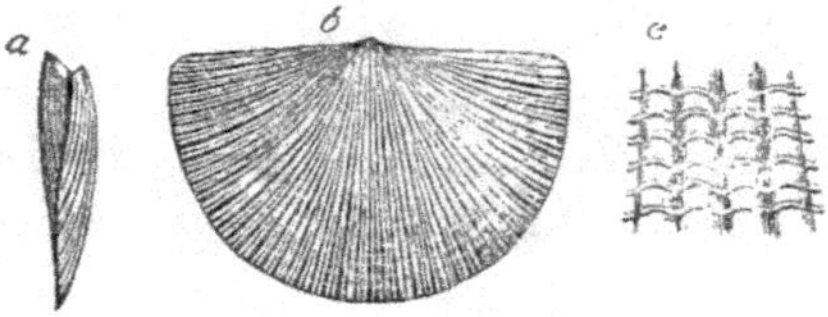

Fig. 108.

Fig. 109.

Fig. 108.—*Strophomena recta.* *a*, side view, *b*, ventral view; *c*, portion of face enlarged.

109.—*S.* ——— *subtenta.* Dorsal valve supposed to be of this species.

Description.—Semielliptical, both valves nearly flat, hinge-line equal to, a little greater, or a little less than the width; sides somewhat straight for about half the length, and either parallel or slightly converging forwards; all the front half of the shell uniformly rounded, sometimes only gently convex or somewhat straight in the middle of the front margin. Ventral valve slightly convex in the umbonial region, and elsewhere flat or gently concave; beak scarcely distinct from the cardinal area, slightly depressed below the umbo; area of medium size, flat, extending the whole length of the shell, forming an obtuse angle of from 110° to 135° with the plane of the lateral margin; foramen triangular, width at the base greater than the height, closed by a convex deltidium which does not quite reach the hinge-line, but has its lower margin concave. Dorsal valve uniformly very depressed convex or nearly flat, slightly concave at the cardinal angles and with a barely perceptible mesial depression along the middle, which commences very near the beak and extends one third or one half the length of the shell; beak very small and minutely elevated above the cardinal edge; area varying in size, from less than one half to nearly equal that of the ventral valve.

Surface with fine rounded slightly crenulated radiating striæ of different sizes, the smaller coming in by implantation at varions distances from the beak. In some specimens the striæ are more nearly of one uniform size than in others; at the front margin there are usually four of the larger and four or five of the smaller striæ in the width of one line. When the surface is perfectly preserved, it is seen to be beautifully cancellated by fine apparently squamose striæ, which are undulated slightly upward in passing over the ridges. There appear to be from ten to twelve concentric striæ in the width of one line.

Width of largest specimen collected 1 inch; length 9 lines; height of ventral area 1 line.

Both Conrad and Hall describe the two areas as being nearly equal. In only one of our specimens is the dorsal area preserved, and in that it is about one fourth the width of the ventral area. The specimen figured in the 1st vol. of the Palæontology of New York has a width on the hinge-line about equal to twice the length of the shell. In none of ours is the length more than two thirds the width. Notwithstanding these differences, I venture to refer ours to Conrad's species, as in all other respects they agree with the figures and descriptions.

This shell is closely allied to *S. pecten*, and may yet be found to be connected therewith by intermediate forms. On examining a large number of good specimens of *S. pecten*, I find that that species varies a good deal. In some of the individuals the radiating striæ are straight in all parts of the shell. In others, those in the middle are straight, but those near the cardinal angles more or less convex. The concentric striæ also vary in fineness from ten to twenty in the width of one line. The curvature of the ventral valve also varies, it being in some individuals gently convex all over except near the cardinal angles, and in others convex at the umbo and concave all round. The proportions vary, the hinge-line being often much extended and the shell narrowest towards the front, or it is equal to or even a little less than the greatest width. The area of the dorsal valve is sometimes nearly equal to that of the ventral, but often less than half the size. The ventral valve is always depressed convex or nearly flat, but never concave except near the cardinal angles. It almost always exhibits a mesial depression exactly like that of *S. recta*.

Not only does *S. pecten* agree with *S. recta* in the form of the valves and characters of the surface, but it varies in the same way, and the two species must be regarded as not only congeneric, but even as most closely allied, if not absolutely identical. The only difference exhibited by our specimens is that in *S. rectus* the deltidium of the ventral valve extends down nearly to the hinge-line, and thus almost entirely closes the foramen, while in *S. pecten* it only closes a small portion at the apex.

Some of the specimens of *S. pecten* have a minute perforation in the beak of the ventral valve, and there are indications of a similar aperture in *S. recta*.

The Russian species *O. asmusi* (De Verneuil), figured and described in the Geology of Russia, seems to be closely allied to *S. recta*.

Locality and Formation.—This species has only been found at one locality in Canada, as far as I am aware,—the top of the Barrack Hill in the city of Ottawa, in the upper beds of the Trenton limestone.

Collector.—E. Billings.

Strophomena subtenta. (Conrad.)

Strophomena subtenta. (Conrad.)
Leptæna subtenta. (Hall.) Pal. N. Y., vol. 1, p. 115, pl. 31 b, fig. 9 *a b*.

Fig. 109.

Remarks.—This species occurs at Anticosti, in the Hudson River group, rarely, only three detached valves having been collected. It is a resupinate form, with a gently convex dorsal valve, and the surface marked by fine rounded radiating striæ increasing in number by implantation several times between the beak and the front margin, and crenulated by fine concentric striæ. The hinge-line and cardinal angles are strongly corrugated by six or seven short oblique wrinkles. The form and surface markings correspond very nearly with the figures and description given in the work cited. Conrad's specimens were from Cincinnati, most probably from the Hudson River group, and ours is found in the same formation, associated with an abundance of *Rhynchonella capex*, so numerous in rocks of this age in the Western States.

Locality and Formation.— English Head, Anticosti. Hudson River group.

Collector.—J. Richardson.

Strophomena Arethusa. (N. sp.)

Description. — Of this shell only three separated valves have been collected, and, although somewhat distorted, and pressed nearly flat, the remarkable characters of the surface show them to be distinct from any described species of the Silurian rocks of America. The form is semi-elliptical; hinge-line equal to the greatest width of the shell; cardinal angles rectangular or nearly so; sides straight or gently convex, and parallel in the upper half; all the front half of the shell broadly rounded. Width 10 lines; length 8 lines.

The shell is very thin and fragile. The surface is covered with minute closely-crowded radiating striæ, barely visible to the naked eye. Under the glass there appear to be about 20 of these in the width of one line. They are slightly undulated; the new ones come in by implantation, and the whole are crossed by extremely minute concentric striæ. The striæ are of a uniform size, and so small that to the eye the shell appears at first sight to be smooth. On account of the distorted condition of the specimens, I cannot determine which valve is the convex one, but it appears to be the ventral.

Locality and Formation—Observation Cape, Anticosti. Hudson River group.

Collector.—J. Richardson.

ORTHIS IPHIGENIA. (N. sp.)

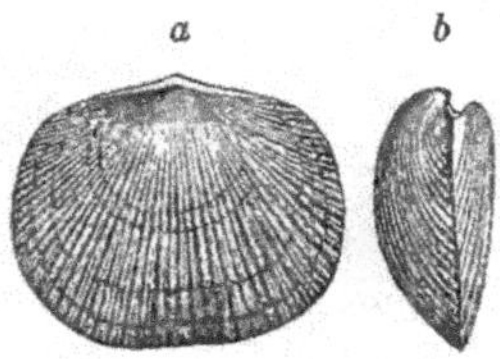

Fig. 110.

Fig. 110.—*Orthis Iphigenia.*—*a*, Ventral view; *b*, side view.

Description.—Transversely sub-elliptical; hinge-line one-third shorter than the greatest width of the shell; cardinal angles rounded; sides irregularly or uniformly rounded; greatest width about the middle or a little in front thereof; front margin broadly rounded or very gently convex. Ventral valve depressed convex, greatest elevation on the umbo just in front of the beak, descending with a flat or gently concave slope to the cardinal angles; the central region either gently convex, flat, or gently concave; a wide concave shallow mesial sinus, which usually terminates abruptly at from 1½ to 3 lines from the front margin; area small, about half the width of the shell, slightly concave, and a little overhanging the hinge-line; umbo with its most elevated point distant from the beak a little less than the height of the area; beak small, depressed about one-third below the most elevated point of the shell, scarcely distinct from the cardinal edge; foramen triangular, its width at the base about equal to the height. Dorsal valve moderately and uniformly convex; a small portion at the cardinal angles compressed and often slightly reflected; area a little less than that of the ventral valve, overhanging the hinge-line; umbo small, obtusely rounded; beak forming a small elevation upon, but scarcely distinct from the cardinal edge.

Surface with sub-angular radiating striæ, 5 or 6 in the width of 2 lines in the middle of the shell, and about 4 at the front margin. These striæ are subdivided at about one-third the length from the beak, and again at about two-thirds.

Width of a large specimen 1 inch; length ¾ of an inch; width of the area 6 lines; height of the same 1 line.

It will be seen from the details given in the above description, that this species is most closely allied to *O. subquadrata*, and perhaps should be regarded in the light of a variety thereof. There are, however, certain differences which are very persistent, although not great. In *O. subquadrata* the dorsal valve has always a mesial sinus, and the ventral, a mesial fold; the area is always more than one half the width of the shell; the most elevated point of the ventral valve is distant from the beak a little more than the height of the area, and the shell is somewhat larger. In this species there is a sinus in the ventral valve, instead of a fold, and the dorsal valve is uniformly convex or exhibits no sinus; the area is about one-third the whole width, and the greatest elevation of the ventral valve is nearer the beak than it is in *O. subquadrata*. This latter species ranges from the Trenton to the Hudson River group, but *O. Iphigenia* occurs only in the Trenton.

Locality and Formation.—City of Ottawa; Trenton limestone.

Collectors.—E. Billings; A. T. Drummond, Esq., of Kingston.

Orthis porcata. (McCoy.)

Orthis porcata (McCoy). *Silurian Fossils of Ireland*, p. 32, Pl. 3, Fig. 14, 1846. Also in the *British Palæozoic Fossils*, p. 223, Pl. 1, H, Figs. 41, 42, 1851–55.

Orthis inflata (Salter). *Memoirs of the Geol. Surv. of Great Britain*, Vol. 2, p. 372, Pl. 27, Fig. 3, 1858.

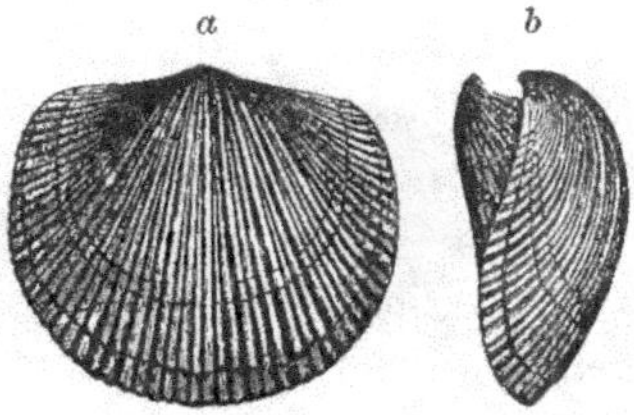

Fig. 111.

Fig. 111.—*Orthis Porcata.* *a*, ventral, and *b*, side view.

Description.—Shell varying from a medium to a large size; semi-elliptical or subquadrate; hinge-line equal to or a little less than the greatest width; cardinal angles rounded or rectangular; sides gently convex or straight and subparallel; all the front half of the shell uniformly rounded, sometimes a portion in the middle of the front margin nearly straight. Ventral valve somewhat flat; the beak strongly elevated, usually a wide shallow concavity extending from the umbo to the front margin, where it is often nearly as wide as the whole shell; a flat, gently convex or gently concave slope from the umbo to the cardinal angles. In some specimens, the middle portion of the shell, instead of being gently concave, is either flat or gently convex. The most elevated point is usually from half a line to one line from the beak; the latter small, scarcely distinct from the cardinal edge and depressed a little below the umbo. The area is large, and very nearly equal to the width of the shell in those specimens which have the cardinal angles rectangular, and somewhat shorter when they are rounded; it is also either flat or gently concave, and the upper part slightly overhangs the hinge-line. The foramen is triangular, open to the beak, its width at the base about equal to the height. Dorsal valve uniformly convex, varying greatly in the amount of its gibbosity, the cardinal angles flattened and usually a little reflected; greatest elevation a little above the middle; umbo obtusely rounded; beak small, scarcely distinct from the cardinal edge; area one half the size of that of the ventral valve, with a wide triangular foramen open to the beak, and having in the middle a strong divaricator process: it is either flat or gently concave, and slightly overhangs the hinge-line.

The surface in most of the specimens is covered with strong radiating striæ, which are twice and sometimes thrice divided before reaching the margin. In the middle of the shell there are about six striæ in the width of two lines, and at the margin about four. Those at the cardinal angles are sometimes a little smaller, and often a little larger than the others.

The usual width is from 12 to 18 lines; length about one fourth less than the width. Height of the ventral area from 1½ to 2 lines.

The principal difference between this species and *O. subquadrata* consists in the more uniform and greater convexity of the dorsal valve, and in the absence of a mesial fold and sinus.

Some of the specimens are much more coarsely ribbed than others, having only three ribs to two lines at the front margin, and four or five in the middle of the shell. In very perfect specimens fine concentric lines of growth are obscurely visible crossing the radiating ridges.

Locality and Formation.—Trenton limestone at Ottawa and near L'Orignal; also at Anticosti in the base of the Anticosti group, Middle Silurian. This species also occurs in the Bala group in numerous localities in Wales and Ireland.

Collectors.—E. Billings, R. Bell, J. Richardson.

ORTHIS RETRORSA. (Salter.)

ORTHIS RETRORSA (Salter). *Memoirs of the Geol. Surv. of Great Britain*, Vol. 2, p. 373 Pl. 27, Fig. 3, 1858.

ORTHIS CARLEYI (Hall). 13th Rep. Reg. N. Y., p. 120, January 1861, dated April 10th 1860.

a b

Fig. 112.

a b

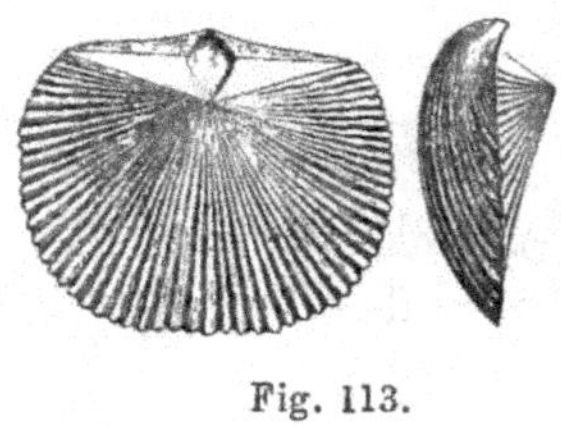

Fig. 113.

Fig. 112.—*Orthis retrorsa* (Salter). *a*, dorsal, and *b*, side view.

Fig. 113.—The same species from Cincinnati (*O. Carleyi*, Hall). It is undoubtedly identical with the English species, and also with the Ottawa species, only a little larger.

Description.—This species only differs from *O. porcata* in having the area of the ventral valve inclining forward, instead of overhanging the hinge-line. The specimens collected at Ottawa are much smaller than those figured in the works above cited, but are in every other respect specifically identical. The area varies much in its size and in the amount of its inclination.

Locality and Formation.—City of Ottawa; Belleville; and near L'Orignal. It also occurs at Cincinnati in Ohio, in the Hudson River group, and at numerous localities in Wales, in the Bala group.

Collectors.—Sir W. E. Logan, R. Bell, E. Billings.

ORTHIS MARIA. (N. sp.)

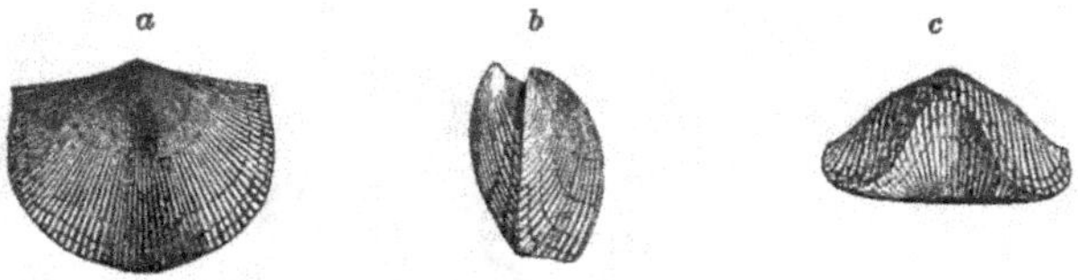

Fig. 114.

Fig. 114.—*Orthis Maria.* *a*, ventral view; *b*, side view; *c*, view of the front margin.

Description.—Transversely oblong; hinge-line equal to or a little less than the greatest width; cardinal angles either rectangular or moderately rounded; sides gently convex and subparallel; anterior angles rounded; front margin with a portion of the middle usually straight. Ventral valve irregularly depressed pyramidal, with a deep rounded mesial sinus which becomes obsolete before reaching the beak; the latter small, pointed, not incurved, scarcely distinct from the cardinal edge, and forming the most elevated point of the valve. From the beak to the cardinal angles the shell descends with a flat or sometimes gently concave slope. Area rather large, its height at the beak equal to one eighth of its length, slightly concave, nearly at a right angle to the plane of the margin, but slightly overhanging the hinge-line. Dorsal valve rather strongly convex, with its front much elevated in the middle by a large rounded mesial fold which becomes obsolete at the umbo; cardinal angles compressed and slightly reflected; umbo large, obtusely rounded, overhanging the hinge-line; beak very small but distinct, situated on the cardinal edge and not elevated; area about one third the size of that of the ventral valve, lying nearly in the plane of the margin, slightly concave and sometimes a little overhanging the hinge-line. Foramen of ventral valve triangular, its width at base about two thirds the height, apparently open to the beak, but this point not clearly ascertained. Surface with rather fine radiating striæ, 3 or 4 in the width of a line at the middle of the front margin; gradually becoming finer towards the cardinal angles, one half running all the way to the beak, and the other half dying out at from a half to two thirds the distance. Width of average-sized specimen 9 lines; length 6 lines; height of area of ventral valve 1⅓ lines.

The front margin is usually straight in the middle, but sometimes it is rounded as in the specimen above figured.

Locality and Formation.—Gramache Bay, Anticosti. In Division 1, Anticosti group; Middle Silurian.

Collector.—J. Richardson.

ORTHIS LAURENTINA. (Billings.)

ORTHIS LAURENTINA (Billings). *Report G. S. C.* for 1857, p. 297.

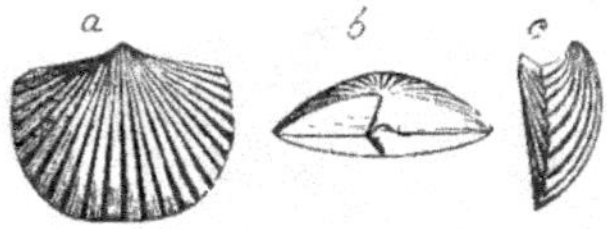

Fig. 115.

Fig. 115.—*O. Laurentina.* *a*, ventral valve; *b*, area; c, side view.

Description.—Semielliptical, broader than long in the proportion of about seven to five; hinge-line straight, slightly exceeding the width of the shell; the dorsal valve flat, very slightly convex, the most elevated point being at the beak, a perceptible depression along the middle; cardinal area low, triangular, inclining backwards at an angle of 100°, or a little more, to the plane of the lateral margin; foramen partly closed. Ventral valve convex, most elevated at one third the length from the beak, which is small, pointed and depressed about one third below the greatest height of the valve; cardinal area rather large, triangular, somewhat concave, extending to the beak, but closed by a convex deltidium all but a small triangular space at the base. Surface with from twenty to twenty-five prominent, subangular radiating ridges, which gradually enlarge from the beak to the base, separated by the same number of sulci equal to the ridges in breadth and depth, two ridges in one line at the front margin. Some of the specimens are obscurely subquadrate. Width of large specimen seven lines; length five lines; height of ventral area at the beak 1⅓ lines; width of foramen at the base ⅔ of a line.

This species is closely allied to both *O. tricenaria* and *O. disparalis.* Indeed these three would be by some good naturalists all united. The only differences that I can perceive are that this species is smaller than

O. tricenaria and has the foramen partly closed. *O. disparalis* has a more erect beak. I think them all one species; but as others would not, and as this name has got into use, I shall retain it for the present.

Locality and Formation.—Junction Cliff, Anticosti. In Division 1, Anticosti group; Middle Silurian.

Collector.—J. Richardson.

ORTHIS MEROPE. (N. sp.)

Fig. 116.

Fig. 116.—*Orthis Merope.* *a*, ventral view; *b*, area; *c*, side view.

Description.—Shell small; width at the hinge-line twice the length; cardinal angles acute, from 60° to 70°; sides and front margin forming a regular semielliptical curve. Ventral valve pyramidal, most elevated at the beak, thence sloping nearly uniformly in all directions to the sides and margin; area large, at right angles to the plane of the margin, sometimes inclining slightly forward or backward; foramen large, extending to the beak. Dorsal valve nearly flat, with an obscure mesial sinus. Surface with from 25 to 30 strong, angular undivided ribs.

Width 3 lines; length 1½ lines.

Locality and Formation.—City of Ottawa. In the lowest beds of the Trenton limestone.

Collector.—E. Billings.

Genus PORAMBONITES. (Pander.)

The following species is placed in the genus *Porambonites* provisionally. Its internal characters are very similar to those of *Rhynchonella*, but externally it differs in having an open foramen in each valve and the beaks nearly equal. In these two latter characters it agrees with *Porambonites*, from which again it differs in having the shell ribbed and the surface not pitted.

A small generic group might be made to include *P. Ottawaensis* and the two species figured in the Geology of Russia under the names of *Spirifer rectus* and *S. Panderi.*

PORAMBONITES OTTAWAENSIS. (N. sp.)

Fig. 117.

Fig. 117.—*Porambonites Ottawaensis.* *a*, *b*, *c*, *d*, Different views of a specimen; *e*, interior of ventral valve; *f*, interior of dorsal valve; *g*, side view of a specimen, which, being empty, shows the form of the oral arms.

Description. — Ovate or sub-triangular; valves of nearly an equal length; apical angle about 90°; sides straight for a little more than one-half the length from the beaks, in the front half rounded; front margin gently convex, or with a portion in the middle either straight or concave, according as it is affected by the mesial fold and sinus. Ventral valve convex, most elevated at one-fourth the length from the beak; a concave mesial sinus commences at the front margin and extends in some specimens nearly to the umbo, in others dying out at two-thirds the length of the shell; area small, scarcely one-third the width of the shell, strongly concave, overhanging the hinge-line; beak small, incurved down to one-third the greatest elevation of the valve; foramen triangular, its width about equal to its height. The form of the dorsal valve is similar to that of the ventral, but it is a little larger, and has a mesial fold which in general is only slightly elevated; area not quite so high as that of the ventral valve, and lying nearly in the plane of the margin, but a little curved over the plane; foramen triangular, open to the beak. On each side of the umbo both valves are abruptly deflected, so that they descend to the margin at a right angle. Surface on the umbo and flat space on each side, smooth; three obscurely angular ribs on the mesial fold and two on the sinus; from three to five ribs on each side; none of the ribs reach the beaks. A few squamose zigzag concentric striæ are visible.

In the interior of the ventral valve, the dental plates form two thin vertical septa, extending about one-fourth or one-third the length of the shell. The teeth are well developed. The umbo between the dental plates is hollow quite to the beak, as in *Rhynchonella.* There is no trace of a deltidium.

In the interior of the dorsal valve, the bases of the oral arms consist of two short plates, concave on their upper, and convex on their lower sides.

They are separated from each other by a narrow fissure which extends quite to the beak. Beneath, they are supported by two very slightly developed vertical and parallel plates. From their anterior extremities two slender calcified oral processes extend about one-fifth the length of the shell, curving upwards nearly to the inner surface of the ventral valve. In the cavity of the umbo there is no divaricator process, as there is in *Orthis*.

This species is closely allied to *P. rectus* (Pander) = *Spirifer rectus* (De Verneuil) in the geology of Russia, but is not so numerously ribbed.

The specimens are about 6 lines in length, and the same in width.

Locality and Formation.—Pauquette Rapids, on the River Ottawa. Black River limestone.

Collector.—E. Billings.

Rhynchonella fringilla. (N. sp.)

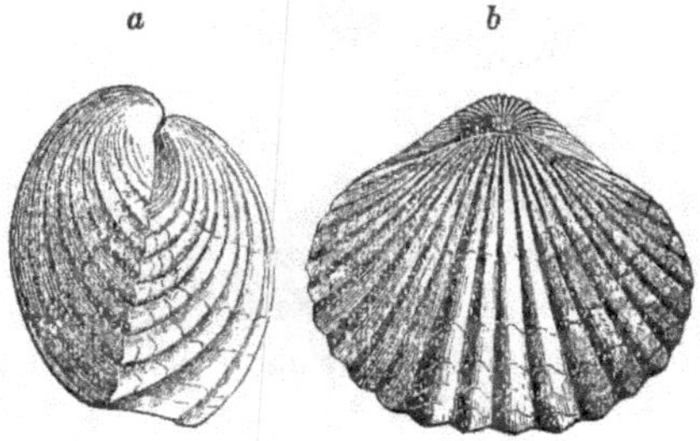

Fig. 118.

Fig. 118.—*Rhynchonella fringilla.*—*a*, Side view; *b*, dorsal view.

Description. — Shell large, strongly convex, transversely elliptical, greatest width about the middle, length about one-eighth less than the width. Ventral valve convex, with a wide concave mesial sinus, which extends to the umbo, bordered on each side by two or three ribs more prominent than the others, 4 or 5 strong depressed convex ribs in the sinus, and from 8 to 10 on each side; beak closely incurved down to the umbo of the dorsal valve, a smooth space on each side next to the hinge-line. Dorsal valve a little larger than the ventral, with an obtusely rounded umbo, and the beak deeply buried beneath that of the ventral valve; a large depressed convex mesial ridge extending from the umbo to the front, where it elevates the margin; 4 or 5 ribs on the mesial elevation, those on the outside sometimes subdivided at about half their length into 2 or 3; on each side of the mesial ridge there are from 8 to 10 ribs.

Length 15 lines, width 17 lines, depth of both valves 13 lines.

Very numerous small specimens from 6 lines in length and upwards, occur with the larger.

This species is closely allied to *R. capax* (Conrad), Hudson River group, being of nearly the same form and size. That species, however, has only 5 or 6 ribs on each side, ornamented by concentric striæ, while this has 8 or 10 smooth ones.

Locality and Formation.—Gull Cape, Anticosti. In Division 4, Anticosti group, Middle Silurian.

Collector.—J. Richardson.

Rhynchonella Anticostiensis. (Billings.)

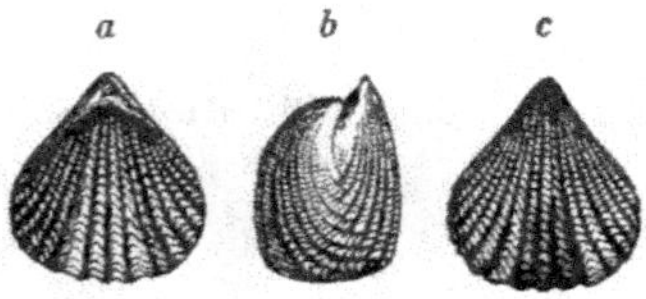

Fig. 119.

Fig. 119.—*Rhynchonella Anticostiensis.*—*a, b, c,* Different views of a specimen.

Description.—Sub-pentagonal; apical angle about 80°; sides nearly straight or slightly convex for rather more than half the length from the beak, then curving to the edge of the mesial sinus; front nearly straight for the breadth of the sinus; side view, oblong; front, dorsal and ventral sides nearly straight; umbo of dorsal valve abruptly curved in to the base of the beak of the ventral valve, which is conical, erect, and scarcely incurved. Ventral valve with a deep mesial sinus becoming obsolete at two-thirds the length from the base; dorsal valve with a strong mesial elevation which, on approaching the umbo, disappears, and is succeeded by a scarcely perceptible sinus, which continues to the summit. Surface with 18 or 20 radiating angular ridges, crossed by close zigzag imbricating striæ; 3 ribs in the ventral sinus, and 4 on the dorsal mesial elevation.

Length 7 lines, width near the front 6 lines.

This species resembles *Atrypa subtrigonalis* (Hall; Palæontology of New York, vol. 1, pl. 33, fig. 12), but has a larger and more erect beak, while the side view exhibits a broadly truncated base, with the dorsal and ventral outlines more nearly straight.

Formation and Locality.—Hudson River group. English Head, Anticosti.

Collector.—J. Richardson.

Rhynchonella glacialis. (N. sp.)

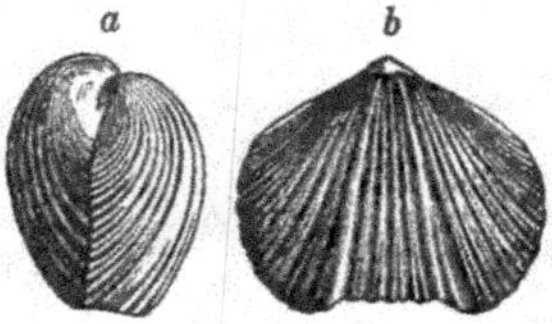

Fig. 120.

Fig. 120.—*Rhynchonella glacialis.*—*a*, Side view; *b*, dorsal view.

Description.—Shell rather large, transversely elliptical, greatest width about the middle, length about one-eighth or one-ninth less than the width. Ventral valve varying from moderately to strongly convex, most prominent in the upper half; umbo narrow, sub-carinated; beak small, closely incurved down to the umbo of the dorsal valve; mesial sinus wide, concave, extending to the umbo. Dorsal valve about equal to the ventral in the amount of its convexity; beak hidden beneath that of the ventral valve; umbo divided by a narrow sinus, which commences under the beak of the ventral valve, and, extending about one line therefrom, gradually divides, the branches being obscurely indicated all the way to the front, on either side of the mesial ridge; the latter convex and moderately elevated at the front margin, becoming obsolete near the umbo, on which its place is occupied by the sinus above mentioned. Surface of both valves with somewhat obscure bifurcating ribs. On the dorsal valve there are two or three ribs in the sinus at the umbo which are extended on to the mesial ridge, and subdivide into from 6 to 8 before reaching the front. The ribs on each side and also on the ventral valve divide in the same way, becoming less conspicuous towards the front. In perfect specimens the surface also exhibits some concentric striæ near the front, but in general the ribs have a smooth aspect.

This species is allied to *R. fringilla*, and occurs along with it in the same beds, but differs from it in its somewhat smaller size and divided ribs. The young of the two species differ in the same respects.

Locality and Formation.—Gull Cape, Anticosti. In Division 1, Anticosti group; Middle Silurian.

Collector.—J. Richardson.

Genus Athyris. (McCoy.)

This genus, as originally described by McCoy and D'Orbigny, consists of a large and important assemblage of species ranging from the Middle Silurian up to the Permian inclusive. It appears to be capable of subdivision, and accordingly several generic names have been proposed for the various sub-groups. The arrangement that I follow is that published by Davidson in his Introduction to the classification of the Brachiopoda. According to this, Athyris stands for that group of imperforate species which has *A. tumida* for the type, and is precisely equal to Meristella (Hall), proposed in 1861. Spirigera includes the perforated group with *S. concentrica* for the typical form.

If Professor Hall's suggestions be followed, then Spirigera must be suppressed altogether and Athyris take its place, and thus stand as the generic name of a group of shells for which it is decidedly inappropriate. I cannot see the least reason whatever for this change, except that it would make a vacancy for Prof. Hall's genus Meristella. If we follow Davidson, there can be no misnomer, for both Athyris and Spirigera will stand for groups for which they are in no way inappropriate, and no injustice will be done to either McCoy or D'Orbigny.

Athyris umbonata. (N. sp.)

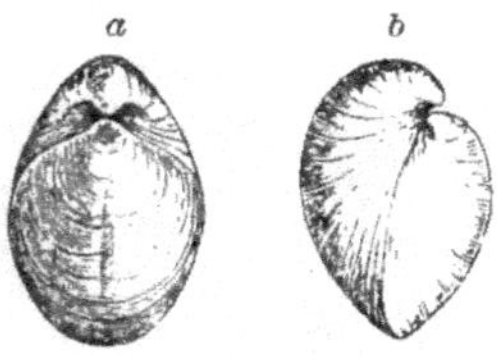

Fig. 121.

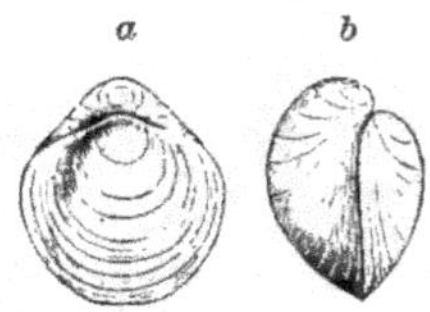

Fig. 122.

Fig. 121.—*Athyris umbonata.* *a*, dorsal, and *b*, side view.
122.—*A.*—— *Prinstana.* *a*, dorsal, and *b*, side view.

Description.—Elongate ovate; sides usually forming a continuous gentle curve from the umbo of the ventral valve to the front margin, sometimes a little angulated at the hinge extremities; front margin either rounded or with a small portion in the middle straight. Ventral valve strongly convex, forming a continuous curve from beak to base, spiral in the upper half, gently curved in the lower. Umbo large, rounded, very prominent. Beak abruptly incurved down to the umbo of the dorsal valve. There is usually a faint indication of a mesial sinus in this valve, which however only amounts to a flattening of the shell along the middle of the lower two thirds. Dorsal valve moderately convex, most elevated at one third the length from the beak; umbo obtusely rounded, beak concealed; hinge-line curved but distinct for two thirds the whole width. Surface smooth or with many obscure accretion ridges; in a few individuals these latter are strongly developed, but in general the aspect is that of a smooth shell. Length from 6 to 9 lines, width varying from two thirds to eight ninths of the length.

This species is more elongated than *A. Prinstana*, and has the umbo of the ventral valve more strongly developed. The two species appear to be connected by intermediate links; but in a large number of specimens two groups can be selected having upon the whole a distinct specific aspect.

Both are allied to the several species of this group found in the Clinton and Niagara rocks of New York, and especially to *A. naviformis* (Hall), which differs in being radiately striated and in having a deep mesial sinus.

Locality and Formation.—Junction Cliff, Anticosti. In Division 1, Anticosti group; Middle Silurian.

Collector.—J. Richardson.

ATHYRIS PRINSTANA. (N. sp.)

Fig. 122. *a, b.*

Description.—Shell subcircular, moderately convex, smooth; apical angle about 105°; cardinal slopes straight or nearly so for one fourth the length of the shell, greatest width about the middle or a little in front thereof; sides gently convex; front rather more narrowly rounded than the sides. Ventral valve evenly convex, most elevated in the upper half; the outline thence to the beak forming a smooth spiral curve; a somewhat straight or gently convex slope to the front margin; umbo large rounded; beak small, closely incurved, very nearly if not absolutely in contact with the umbo of the dorsal valve. Dorsal valve uniformly depressed convex, most elevated at about one third the length from the beak; umbo small, rounded; hinge-line nearly straight and equal to about two thirds the whole width of the shell. Surface smooth. Length 7 lines; width about the same; depth of both valves 5 lines.

Locality and Formation.—Prinsta Bay, Anticosti. In Division 1, Anticosti group; Middle Silurian.

Collector.—J. Richardson.

Athyris Julia. (N. sp.)

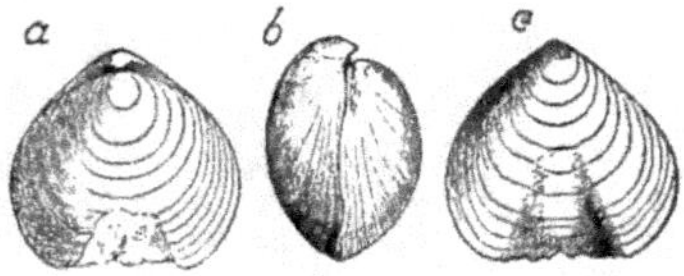

Fig. 124.

Fig. 124.—*Athyris Julia.* *a*, dorsal, *b*, side, and *c*, ventral view.

Description.—Shell of medium size, moderately convex, subovate' greatest width a little in front of the middle; sides rounded; front margin truncated; apical angle about 90°; cardinal slopes straight for nearly one third the length of the shell. Ventral valve moderately convex, most elevated about the middle, thence uniformly arched to the beak, more abruptly curved to the front margin. Umbo small, prominent; beak pointed, incurved over the hinge-line, but not in contact with the umbo of the dorsal valve; a wide, flat, shallow mesial sinus which indents the anterior one fourth. Dorsal valve uniformly convex all over except a short flat mesial elevation in front. Surface with a smooth polished aspect, but when closely examined exhibiting numerous obscure concentric striæ.

Length of specimen 7 lines; width the same; depth of both valves 5 lines.

Locality and Formation.—The Jumpers, Anticosti. In Division 4, Anticosti group; Middle Silurian.

Collector.—J. Richardson.

The following species with its varieties are referred to the genus *Athyris* provisionally. The shell structure resembles that of *Atrypa reticularis*, but the muscular impressions are more like those of *Athyris* than those of *Atrypa.* In some polished sections I have detected traces of internal spiral appendages, but have not ascertained their position. Should it be found that they are situated as in *Atrypa*, it may become necessary to refer this species to that genus. The fossil called (by Prof. Hall) *Orthis erratica* belongs to the same group, and so do, most probably, *Rhynchonella modesta* and *R. recurvirostra*.

Athyris Headi. (N. sp.)

a b

Fig. 125.

a b

Fig. 126.

a b

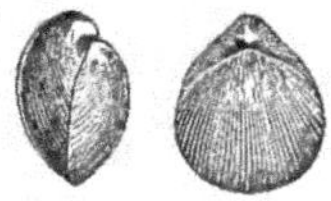

Fig. 127.

Fig. 125.—*Athyris Headi.* *a*, dorsal view ; *b*, side view of a specimen of the typical form. Fig. 126.—*a*, dorsal view ; *b*, side view of a specimen from Lake St. John (var. *A. borealis*). Fig. 127.—*a*, dorsal view ; *b*, side view of a specimen from Anticosti var. *A. Anticostiensis*).

Description.—Broad oval or sub-pentagonal ; both valves convex ; sides and front margin occasionally somewhat straight. Ventral valve rather strongly convex, most elevated about the middle or a little above ; beak closely incurved, in contact with the umbo of the dorsal valve ; umbo somewhat carinated ; an obscure mesial sinus which is usually so slightly impressed as to constitute only a flattening of the shell extends from the front margin to within one third of the length from the beak, where it becomes obsolete ; on each side of the sinus the shell descends with a somewhat flat slope to the sides. Dorsal valve not so convex as the ventral ; often with an obscure mesial sinus.

Surface with fine rounded radiating ridges, closely crowded together, of a nearly uniform size, from eight to ten in the width of two lines.

Length about 10 lines ; width a little less than the length.

This species is dedicated to the late John Head, Esq., by whose unfortunate death science has sustained a grievous loss.

Locality and Formation.—On the south shore of the St. Lawrence opposite Three Rivers. Hudson River formation.

Collectors.—J. Head, Esq., J. Richardson.

Varieties of Athyris Headi.

Var. A. Borealis, Fig. 126. This form is found on Lake St. John, on the River Saguenay. It differs from the typical form in being more elongate-oval and in having a more tumid umbo. Hudson River formation. Collected by J. Richardson and R. Bell.

Var. A. Anticostiensis. Smaller than the typical form, more nearly circular and with a more tumid umbo. Occurs in the Hudson River formation near English Head, Anticosti. Collected by J. Richardson.

Camerella Ops. (N. sp.)

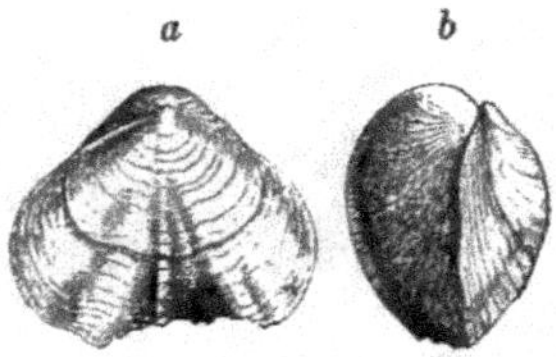

Fig. 128.

Fig. 128.—*Camerella Ops.*—*a*, Dorsal, *b*, side view.

Description.—Sub-globular, transversely sub-elliptical, greatest width a little in front of the middle, sides rounded, front margin undulated by the coarse ribs and mesial sinus. Ventral valve very convex, strongly tumid in the upper half; umbo large, rounded; beak incurved down beneath that of the opposite valve; mesial fold obscure, extending to the umbo with a shallow, wide, obscure sulcus on each side. Dorsal valve smaller than the ventral, most convex in the upper half; beak small, not incurved, but depressed below the greatest elevation of the shell; a small area beneath it, inclining outwards at an obtuse angle with the plane of the margin; mesial sinus deep, rounded in the bottom, becoming obsolete at about two-thirds the length of the shell, an obscure rounded fold on each side. Surface with a smooth aspect, but, when closely examined, exhibiting numerous fine undulating concentric striæ. There are a few obscure undulations, indicating ribs at the front margin.

Locality and Formation.—The Jumpers, Anticosti. In Division 4, Anticosti group; Middle Silurian.

Collector.—J. Richardson.

LAMELLIBRANCHIATA.

Cyrtodonta Harrietta. (N. sp.)

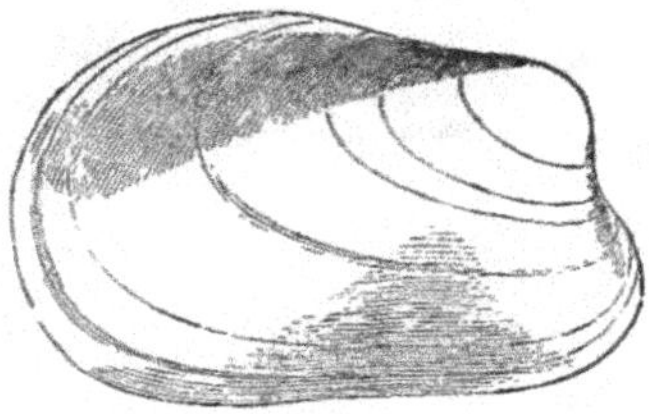

Fig. 129.

Fig. 129.—*Cyrtodonta Harrietta.*—Right valve.

Description.—Transversely oblong; dorsal and ventral margins subparallel; posterior extremity broadly and nearly uniformly rounded; anterior extremity short, narrowly rounded, occupying only the ventral half of the height of the shell, its most projecting point extending only about one-twelfth the whole transverse length of the shell beyond the umbones. Ventral margin slightly concave; dorsal margin most elevated at a little more than one-third the length of the shell from the posterior extremity; most projecting point of the posterior extremity a little below the half height of the shell. Beaks small, spirally incurved forwards down to the hinge-line nearly; shell strongly convex in the umbonial region, most prominent at about one-fourth the length from the umbones; the most convex region extends from the umbones obliquely backwards and downwards; a wide shallow byssal sinus in the anterior two-thirds of the length, slightly sinuates the ventral margin, and becomes obsolete at one-half the height of the shell. Surface unknown.

Transverse length 21 lines; height at the umbones 11 lines; at the most elevated point of dorsal margin 12 lines; depth of single valve 7 lines.

Locality and Formation.—English Head, Anticosti. Hudson River group.

Collector.—J. Richardson.

Cyrtodonta Emma. (N. sp.)

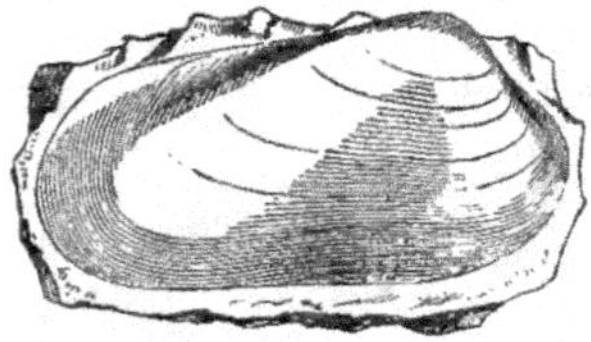

Fig. 130.

Fig. 130.—*Cyrtodonta Emma.*—Right valve.

Description.—Transversely elongate, ovate, slightly narrowed from the umbones backwards. Anterior extremity occupying the lower two-thirds of the height, rounded, and projecting a little more than one-sixth of the whole transverse length in advance of the umbones; posterior extremity rounded, with indications of an oblique truncation in the upper half. Dorsal and ventral margins sub-parallel, but slightly converging backwards. Beaks, as is apparent by the cast of the interior, closely incurved, umbones rather strongly convex, slightly flattened by a shallow byssal sinus, which extends to the ventral margin and renders the same gently concave. The greatest convexity of the shell is at one-third the length, or a little more, from the anterior extremity. The dorsal margin is slightly compressed in its posterior half.

Surface of shell unknown, but probably concentrically striated. The casts of the interior shew some strong concave or sub-angular concentric wrinkles on the umbones, and curving round in front of them.

Transverse length 18 lines; height at the umbones 9 lines; at the posterior extremity of the hinge-line, 7 lines; depth of a single valve 5 lines.

Locality and Formation.—English Head, Anticosti. Hudson River group.

Collector.—J. Richardson.

Cyrtodonta ponderosa. (N. sp.)

Description.—Oblong, oval, somewhat sub-rhomboidal, dorsal and ventral margins sub-parallel; the hinge-line straight with a well-defined area, sometimes two lines in width; the posterior half of the margin forms a rounded obtuse angle (130° to 145°) with the hinge-line, then straight but declining a little downwards for a length a little greater than that of the hinge-line when it forms another rounded angle of about 150° (the measure varying a little) with the posterior edge, which is somewhat straight or gently curved to the most projecting point of this extremity. Ventral margin gently convex or straight for half the length in the middle portion, curving upwards to the posterior extremity, and anteriorly ascending with a broad, rounded curve; anterior margin descending abruptly to meet the curve of the ventral margin. Sometimes a small anterior ear, but in general the outline from the umbones downward shows no interruption. Umbones not very large, rounded; beaks incurved, sometimes in contact, and sometimes 1 or 2 lines apart. From the umbones a broadly rounded gibbosity runs obliquely to the lower posterior angle.

Surface concentrically marked with strong sub-lamellose lines of growth, often rugose towards the posterior extremity. Shell always very thick and ponderous.

An average-sized specimen is 2 inches in length and 4 in width. The proportions vary somewhat, some being shorter and more nearly oval than others.

Locality and Formation.—Cape Smyth, Lake Huron. Hudson River group.

Collector.—R. Bell.

CYRTODONTA HINDI. (N. sp.)

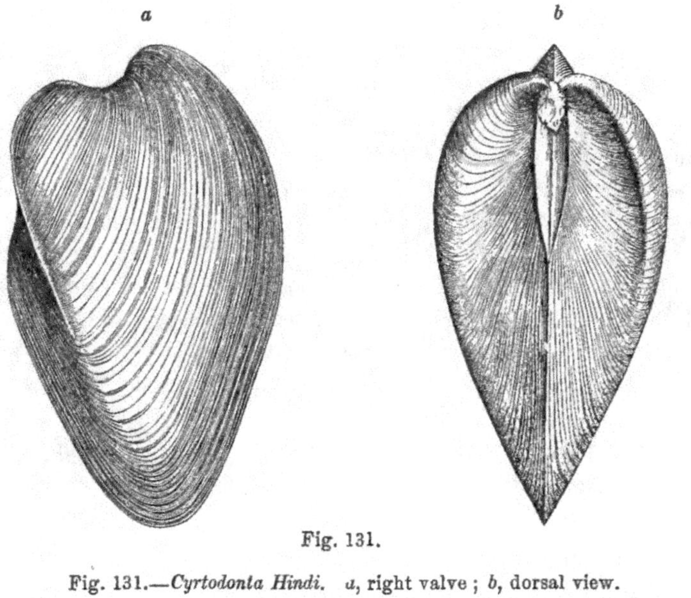

Fig. 131.

Fig. 131.—*Cyrtodonta Hindi.* a, right valve; b, dorsal view.

Description.—Obliquely ovate, or sub-rhomboidal, tapering from the middle to a narrow rounded point at the posterior extremity, strongly ventricose in the anterior half; beaks closely incurved; a sharp umbonial ridge running from the beak nearly to the posterior extremity; from this ridge the surface descends with a concave slope to the hinge-line and dorsal margin; hinge-line straight, with a well-developed concave area. The anterior extremity is small and rounded; the ventral margin strongly convex in the anterior half and somewhat straight behind.

Of this fine new species I have seen only the one figured.

Dedicated to the discoverer, Prof. H. Y. Hind, of Trinity College, Toronto.

Locality and Formation.—Near Toronto; Hudson River group.

Collector.—Prof. H. Y. Hind.

CTENODONTA IPHIGENIA. (N. sp.)

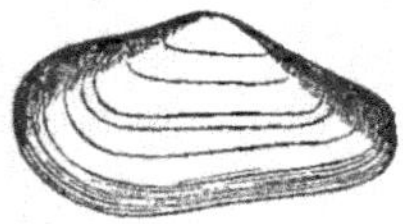

Fig. 132.

Fig. 132.—*Ctenodonta Iphigenia.* Right valve.

Description.—Transversely sub-ovate; umbones a little behind the mid-length; anterior extremity large and broadly rounded; from the umbones the shell tapers to a narrow, rounded posterior extremity which occupies the lower one third next the ventral margin. The greatest convexity is a little in front of the middle. A portion of the ventral margin in the posterior two thirds of the length is gently concave. The umbones are somewhat flattened by a wide shallow byssal sinus which descends to the ventral margin. There is a somewhat sharply angular umbonial ridge running from the beaks to the posterior extremity. Between this ridge and the hinge-line there is an elongated imperfect lunette. The beaks appear to be closely incurved. Surface unknown.

Transverse length about 1 inch; distance from the umbones to the ventral margin half an inch.

Of this species we have only a single specimen,—a right valve. It resembles *C. nasuta*, but differs from that species by having a strong posterior umbonial ridge.

Locality and Formation.—Cape Smith, Lake Huron; Hudson River formation.

Collector.—R. Bell.

GASTEROPODA.

METOPTOMA ALCESTE. (N. sp.)

Fig. 133, *a*, *b*.

Description.—Shell conical or sub-pyramidal; base sub-ovate or sub-circular, broadly rounded in front, sides gently convex, anterior margin with a small space in the middle nearly straight. Apex at about one fifth the length from the anterior margin, much elevated, the anterior side gently convex or nearly flat with a strong rib running from the apex to the middle of the front margin. This is the appearance of the fossil as seen in the cast of the interior, no specimens with the shell preserved having been collected.

Length of base of large specimen 13 lines; width about the same; height 14 lines. In some specimens the greatest width is about one third the length from the anterior margin, but in others it is a little in advance of this position.

The rib in this species resembles that so frequent in species of Bellerophon, and it may be that the side which is called anterior in these descriptions is the posterior side.

Locality and Formation.—English Head, Anticosti; in the Hudson River group.

Collector.—J. Richardson.

METOPTOMA ESTELLA. (N. sp.)

a *b*

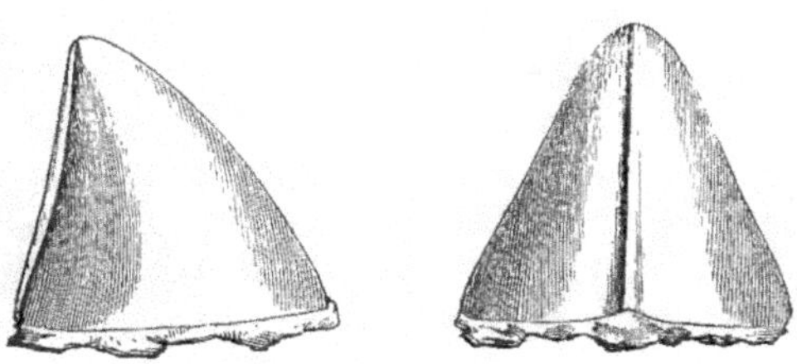

Fig. 133.

a *b*

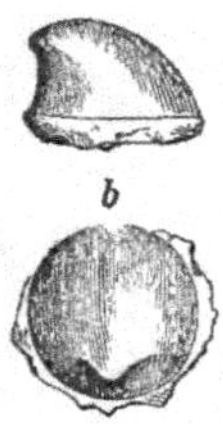

Fig. 134.

Fig. 133.—*Metoptoma Alceste.* *a*, side view; *b*, anterior view.
134.—*M.* ——— *Estella.* *a*, side, and *b*, vertical view.

Description.—Base very nearly circular, length slightly exceeding the width; apex pointed, depressed or slightly incurved so that the point of it is almost vertically above the middle of the front margin. On a side view the outline from the middle of the posterior margin to the apex forms almost a complete quarter of a circle with a tendency to become spiral on approaching the apex. Beneath the apex the outline is concave to the middle of the front margin. The form of the shell is a cone with the apex incurved.

Length 6 lines; width about $5\frac{1}{4}$ lines; height 3 lines.

Locality and Formation.—English Head, Anticosti; Hudson River group.

Collector.—J. Richardson.

Pleurotomaria Elora. (N. sp.)

Fig. 135.

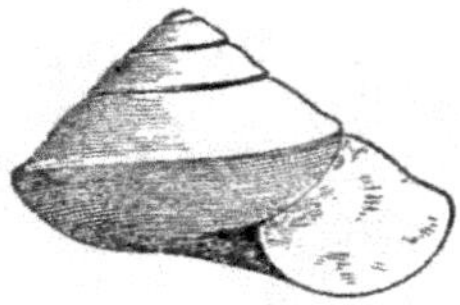

Fig. 136.

Fig. 135.—*Pleurotomaria Elora.*
136.—*P.* ———— *Galtensis.*

Description.—Spire conical, rather strongly elevated; whorls in the cast depressed convex on the upper side, with a sharp-edged margin all round, just within which there is a slight concavity, most distinct on the last whorl. Base nearly flat; umbilicus about one third the whole width, deep, extending to the apex.

Width of a specimen of the average size 18 lines; height 10 lines. There are from four to six whorls.

Locality and Formation.—Elora; Guelph formation.

Collector.—R. Bell.

Pleurotomaria Galtensis. (N. sp.)

Fig. 136.

Description.—Shell in the cast depressed conical, sub-lenticular; apical angle about 100°. Whorls from four to six, nearly flat on the upper side, gently convex on the inner and very slightly concave near the outer side. Margin all round angular. Under side strongly convex. Umbilicus small, about one fifth the whole width in the cast. Aperture rounded on the lower side, concave on the inner side, and nearly straight above.

Width 14 lines; height about 10 lines.

Locality and Formation.—Galt; Guelph formation.

Collector.—R. Bell.

PLEUROTOMARIA DEIOPEIA. (N. sp.)

Description.—Shell obtusely conical; apical angle about 90°; whorls about four, with a narrowly rounded outer margin, above which they are gently convex or somewhat flat all the way to the suture. On the under side the body whorl is gently convex. The suture is deep, and the upper whorls project a little over those below them. Surface beautifully ornamented with fine angular revolving ridges, of which there are five or six in the width of one line. These are crossed by finer lines, which curve backwards to the outer edge, crossing obliquely and producing a rhomboidal cancellation. There appears to be a rounded band on the outer edge of the whorls, with a gentle concavity just above it.

Height 15 lines; width about 20 lines; height of body whorl 8 lines.

Locality and Formation.—Elora; in the Guelph formation.

Collector.—R. Bell.

MURCHISONIA XANTHIPPE. (N. sp.)

Fig. 137.

Fig. 138.

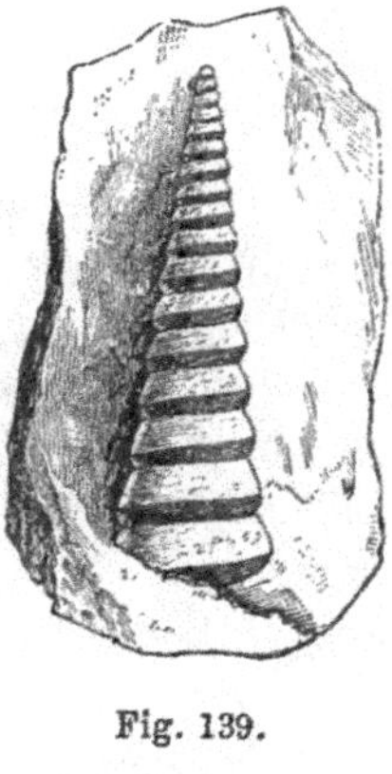

Fig. 139.

Fig. 137.—*Murchisonia Xanthippe*, drawn from a gutta-percha cast.
138.—*M.*——— *Vitellia*, do. do.
139.—*M.*——— *Estella*, do. do.

Description.—Spire acutely conical; apical angle from 40° to 50°; whorls six or seven, acutely angular along the middle (screw-shaped), the last one large, and, including the aperture, nearly one half the whole length of the shell. The most projecting part of each whorl is just about the middle; above this mesial angulation the surface of the shell descends with a gently concave or nearly flat slope directly to the suture; below the angulation the slope is similar to that above, but appears to be more nearly flat. On the body whorl the angular edge is bevelled on its upper surface by a narrow flat spiral band about one third of a line in width, so situated that it slopes upwards and inwards. This whorl is more concave on the upper side than the others. Below the margin there is a wide shallow concave band about two lines in width, but so slightly depressed as to be scarcely distinguishable. The body of the whorl below the margin is large and obtusely conical, and the aperture appears to have been caniculated or effuse at the lower angle. Surface unknown, but probably finely striated. The aperture is not preserved in the specimen, but it is evidently large, straight or gently concave on the upper side, and with the outer lip moderately convex.

Length about 18 lines; width of body whorl about 10 lines.

This group belongs to the Lower Silurian group of *Murchisonia*, of which *M. perangulata* of the Black River limestone is the type.

Locality and Formation.—Galt. Guelph formation; Middle Silurian.

Collector.—E. Billings.

MURCHISONIA VITELLIA. (N. sp.)

Fig. 138.

Description.—Spire conical, apical angle about 60°; whorls 5 or 6, strongly ventricose, obtusely angular, and with a flat spiral band along the middle; above the band descending with a flat or very slightly concave slope for three-fourths the distance to the suture; in the remaining one-fourth very gently convex; suture deep; below the band moderately and uniformly convex. The upper whorls appear to become regularly convex, both above and below the band. The band is gently concave or nearly flat, and its plane is nearly parallel with the longitudinal axis of the shell. Surface with fine striæ curving backwards above, and forwards below the band. Aperture unknown.

Length of the only specimen collected about 18 lines. Width of the last whorl 16 lines.

Locality and Formation.—Galt. In the Guelph formation; Middle Silurian.

Collector.—E. Billings.

Murchisonia Estella. (N. sp.)

Fig. 139.

Description.—Spire very acutely conical, elongated, slender, screw-shaped; whorls numerous, angulated a little below the middle; above the angular edge descending with a flat or slightly concave slope about two thirds the distance to the suture, just before reaching which there is a barely perceptible convexity; suture deep. Below the angulation the slope is flat all the way to the suture. The angular edge is apparently sharp, and if there be a band it must be a very narrow one.

A fragment consisting of 15 whorls is 18 lines in length; 5½ lines wide at the larger and 1 line at the smaller extremity. Another specimen consisting also of 15 whorls is 17 lines in length, 5½ lines at the larger and 1 line at the smaller extremity. The dimensions of these two (the only ones collected) are therefore the same. The angulation is situated a little above the lower third of the length of the whorls.

This species is allied to *M. longispira* (Hall), Pal. N. Y., Vol. 2, p. 345, Pl. 83, Fig. 2, *a*, but is more acutely angular in the whorls.

Locality and Formation.—Galt. In the Guelph formation; Middle Silurian.

Collectors.—E. Billings, R. Bell.

Murchisonia Mylitta. (N. sp.)

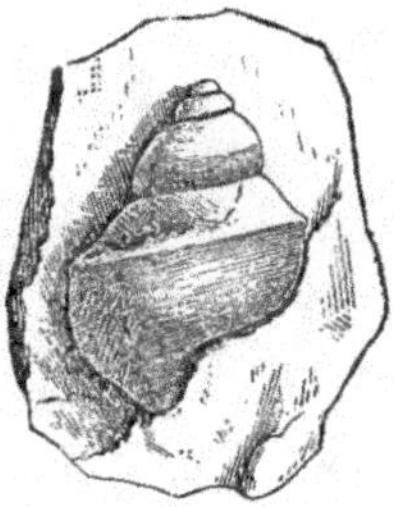

Fig. 140.

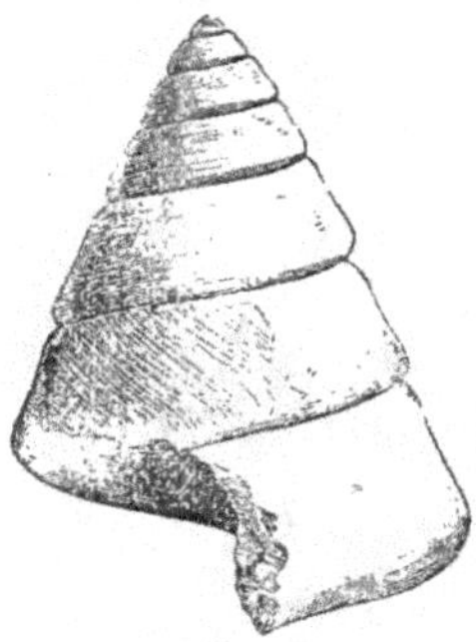

Fig. 141.

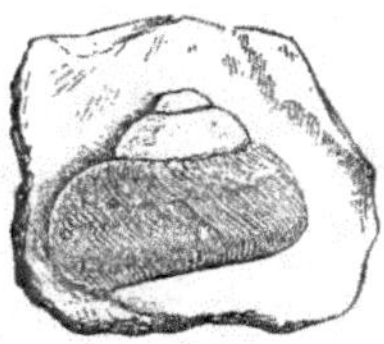

Fig. 142.

Fig. 140.—*Murchisonia Mylitta.*
141.—*M.* ——— *Hercyna.*
142.—*Holopea Harmonia.*

Description.—Shell short; whorls 4 or 5, ventricose, with a narrow spiral band a little above the middle on the last. Above the band the surface descends with a flat slope to the suture; below the band the whorls are uniformly ventricose. The last whorl appears to be about two-thirds of the whole length of the shell. The band has a distinct but narrow carination on its upper side. Surface nearly smooth, but, on a small portion of the shell which remains, very fine striæ are visible. The band, as indicated in the cast, is narrow and slightly concave.

Length about 1 inch; width about 8 lines; width of the band on the last whorl about ⅔ of a line.

The surface resembles a short *M. bellicincta*, from which it differs in the form of the whorls, by being flat above the band. The shell is thin, and the band not visible on any of the whorls except the last, in the only specimen collected.

Locality and Formation.—Elora. In the Guelph formation; Middle Silurian.

Collector.—R. Bell.

Murchisonia Hercyna. (N. sp.)

Fig. 141.

Description.—Conical; apical angle about 65°; whorls 5 or 6, somewhat flat. Base nearly flat; outer edge of body whorl narrowly rounded; upper side of whorls flat or very slightly concave along the middle; the spire is slightly turretted, the lower edge of each whorl projecting a little over the upper edge of the one next below it. Umbilicus very small in the cast, and when the shell is preserved it must be nearly if not entirely closed. Surface, judging from a small portion of the shell remaining, with fine striæ, which curve gently backwards from the suture to the lower edge of the whorl. The upper whorls appear in the cast of some of the specimens, to be gently convex, instead of flat.

Locality and Formation.—Galt. In the Guelph formation.

Collector.—E. Billings.

Holopea Harmonia. (N. sp.)

Fig. 142.

Description.—Shell turbinate; apical angle about 80°; whorls 3 or 4, the last one with a wide flat band along the middle, equal to a little more than one-third the whole height of the whorl; above the band the shell ascends with a gently convex or nearly flat slope to the suture. On the under side the last whorl is gently convex, and the base of the shell is thus somewhat flat. The upper whorls are apparently gently convex or flattened, but they are not well preserved in the only specimen collected.

Surface with fine obtusely-angular striæ, six or seven in the width of one line, making a sigmoid curve backwards until the bottom of the last whorl is attained, when they turn a little forward and run into the umbilicus. The latter is not seen in the specimen, but it must be small.

Length 8 lines; width 9 lines.

Locality and Formation.—Galt. In the Guelph formation; Middle Silurian.

Collector.—J. Richardson.

HOLOPEA GUELPHENSIS. (N. sp.)

Fig. 143.

Fig. 143.—*Holopea Guelphensis.*

Description.—Shell turbinate; apical angle about 80°; whorls 3, uniformly ventricose, the last one large; aperture elliptical, its height about one-fifth greater than its width; umbilicus small, its width in the cast being about one-fifth the width of the aperture. Surface unknown.

Length about 1 inch; width of last whorl, including the aperture, 9 lines. The two apical whorls occupy about one-sixth of the whole length.

Locality and Formation.—Galt. In the Guelph formation; Middle Silurian.

Collector.—A. Murray.

HOLOPEA GRACIA. (N. sp.)

Description.—Shell turbinate; apical angle about 90°; whorls four, moderately and nearly uniformly ventricose, most prominent at about the lower third; suture not very deep. Length 13 lines; width 12 lines. The body whorl occupies about one half the whole length of the shell. Umbilicus and surface unknown.

This species very closely resembles *H. Guelphensis*, but differs therefrom in having the body whorl proportionally not so large, while the most convex part of all the whorls is in the lower one-third, instead of in the middle.

Locality and Formation.—Galt. In the Guelph formation; Middle Silurian.

Collector.—E. Billings.

Straparollus Hippolyta. (N. sp.)

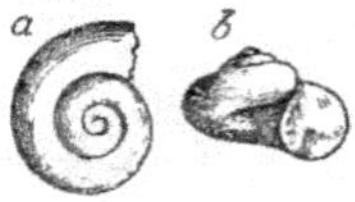

Fig. 144.

Fig. 145.

Fig. 144.—*Straparollus Hippolyta.* *a*, view of the spire; *b*, front view.
145.—*S.* ——— *Daphne.*

Description.—Shell small, sub-discoid; whorls about three, the apical two being very small; suture deep. Height from 3 to 4 lines; width from 6 to 8 lines. The whorls are uniformly rounded above, below, and on the outside. In some specimens they appear to be a little flattened vertically. The second whorl is elevated about half its own height above the body whorl. The two apical whorls are just visible above the second on a side view. As the whorls are nearly cylindrical but a little flattened vertically, the aperture must be transversely oval. In a specimen 7 lines wide, the width of the aperture, as shown in a cast of the interior, is 3 lines, and its height about 2½ lines.

Locality and Formation.—Galt. In the Guelph formation; Middle Silurian.

Collectors.—R. Bell, E. Billings, J. Richardson.

Straparollus Daphne. (N. sp.)

Fig. 145.

Description.—Obtusely conical; apical angle about 100°; whorls six or seven, very slender, and, as shown in the cast of the interior, very nearly cylindrical. Umbilicus very wide, showing all the whorls quite to the apex. Height of largest specimen seen about 6 lines; width about 9 lines; thickness of last whorl in a specimen 8½ lines wide and showing 5 whorls in the umbilicus, 2½ lines.

This species has only been found in the condition of casts of the interior, and it is not quite certain what is the form of the whorls on the outside of the spire. As seen in the umbilicus, they are uniformly rounded on the inner and lower sides, and a little depressed vertically so that the form of the aperture must be transversely ovate.

Locality and Formation.—Galt. In the Guelph formation; Middle Silurian.

Collectors.—A. Murray, R. Bell.

CEPHALOPODA.

ORTHOCERAS DARWINI. (N. sp.)

Description.—The only specimen of this species collected is 3½ inches in length; section apparently transversely oval; lateral diameter at the larger extremity about 2 inches, at the mid-length 1½ inches, and at the smaller extremity 1 inch. The dorso-ventral diameter at the smaller extremity is 9 lines, but at the larger, in consequence of the imperfection of the specimen, it cannot be ascertained. In 2½ inches of the length there are 19 septa. These appear to be nearly flat or only gently concave. The siphuncle appears to be moniliform, 2 lines in thickness, and with its centre 6 lines from the dorsal and 3 lines from the ventral margin. The surface of the cast is longitudinally sulcated by obscure furrows about 1 line apart, showing that the shell itself must be marked in a similar manner. The specimen is slightly curved.

It is not certain to what extent the transversely ovate form of the section of this species may be due to compression. From the fact that the septa do not appear to be distorted, I think the measurements above given indicate the natural proportions.

Locality and Formation.—New Hope. In the Guelph formation; Middle Silurian.

Collector.—E. Billings.

ORTHOCERAS SELWINI. (N. sp.)

Description.—This specimen is 3 inches in length; lateral diameter at the larger extremity 14 lines; at the smaller 9 lines; the dorso-ventral diameter seems to be a little less, but one side of the specimen is imperfect. In a length of 3 inches there are 24 septa. The siphuncle appears to be moniliform; the inflations between the septa discoid, and 4 lines in diameter; the centre of the siphuncle 3 lines from the ventral margin.

Locality and Formation.—Galt. In the Guelph formation; Middle Silurian.

Collector.—R. Bell.

CYRTOCERAS LYSANDER. (N. sp.)

Description.—Shell elongate, slightly curved, and very gradually tapering. Section transversely ovate; septa varying from moderately to rather strongly concave, from 15 to 20 in one inch; siphuncle about a line in diameter, and almost in contact with the shell on the ventral side; chamber of habitation apparently more than 1 inch in depth; surface

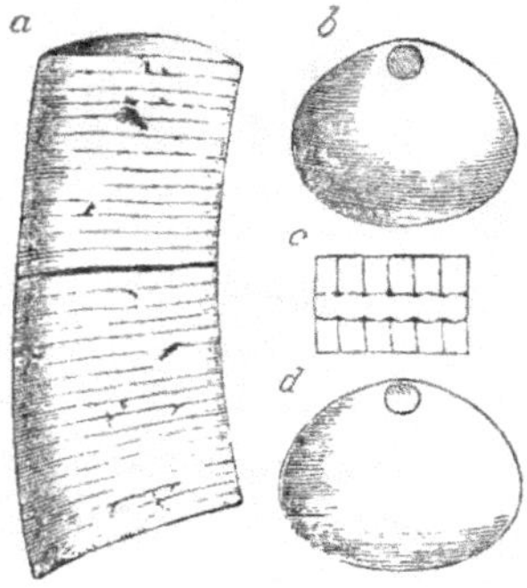

Fig. 146.

Fig. 146.—*Cyrtoceras Lysander.*—*a*, Side view of a fragment; *b*, *d*, transverse sections, showing some difference in form; *c*, a portion of the ventral side ground down to the siphuncle.

with fine engirdling undulations, 3 or 4 in one line, so obscurely developed that, on a superficial glance, the shell seems to be somewhat smooth.

A fragment of this shell 18 lines in length tapers about $\frac{3}{4}$ of a line. The relative proportion of the dorso-ventral and lateral diameters of the section is somewhat variable. The following are the measurements of the sections of several fragments apparently belonging to different individuals: $9\frac{1}{4}$, $7\frac{1}{4}$; 9, 7; 8, $6\frac{1}{2}$; $8\frac{1}{2}$, $6\frac{1}{2}$. In these figures the larger number is the lateral diameter, and the smaller the dorso-ventral. In some fragments the ventral side is narrowly rounded along the middle, but in others it is like the dorsal side gently convex.

Locality and Formation.—Cape Smyth, Lake Huron. Hudson River group.

Collector.—R. Bell.

Cyrtoceras Orodes. (N. sp.)

Description.—Section nearly circular, the dorso-ventral diameter slightly greater than the lateral. Aperture 15 lines in diameter; shell at 9 lines from the aperture, 11 lines in diameter; depth of chamber of habitation 9 lines. The septate portion of the specimen is 21 lines in length measured on the ventral side, and in that distance there are 12 septa. The specimen is so gently curved that in a length of 30 lines the arch formed by the ventral outline is only 5 lines in height in the middle.

This shell differs from *C. Orestes* in being more gently curved, and in having the aperture expanded.

Locality and Formation.—New Hope. In the Guelph formation; Middle Silurian.

Collector.—E. Billings.

PHRAGMOCERAS HECTOR. (N. sp.)

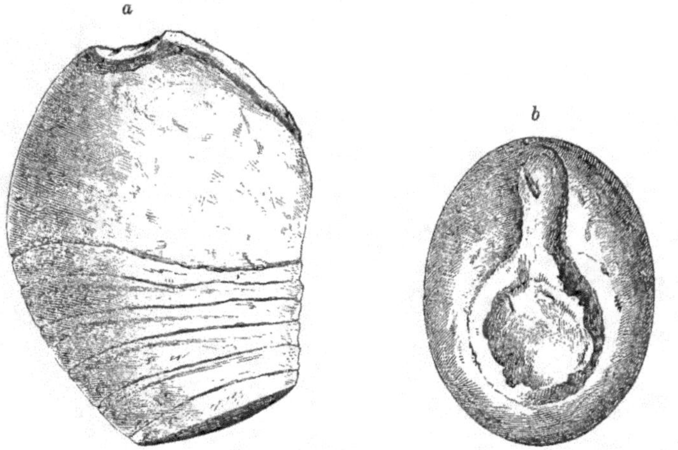

Fig. 147.

Fig. 147.—*Phragmoceras Hector.* *a*, side view of the specimen; *b*, view of the cast of the interior.

Description.—Chamber of habitation large, sub-hemispherical but laterally compressed so that at the last septum the dorso-ventral diameter is 20 lines to a lateral diameter of 15 lines. The first 2½ inches of the ventral contour is curved to a radius of about 18 lines. The chamber of habitation is 14 lines in depth. The septa are about 3 lines distant on the ventral, and 1½ lines on the dorsal aspect. In the cast of the interior the ventral lobe of the aperture leaves a large ovate protuberance about 6 lines across. The dorsal lobe is about 7 lines in length and 2½ lines in width, and extends quite to the dorsal margin.

Locality and Formation.—New Hope. In the Guelph formation; Middle Silurian.

Collector.—E. Billings.

ASCOCERAS NEWBERRYI. (N. sp.)

Description.—Shell small, ovate, apex narrowly rounded; contracted towards the aperture; greatest diameter a little above the middle of the septate portion, at which point the lateral diameter is greater than the dorso-ventral in the proportion of 10 to 8. There are, apparently, three septa. The first of these crosses the back of the shell about two lines above the apex; then traverses the side, proceeding obliquely upwards at an angle of about 45° to the longitudinal axis, and crosses the ventral

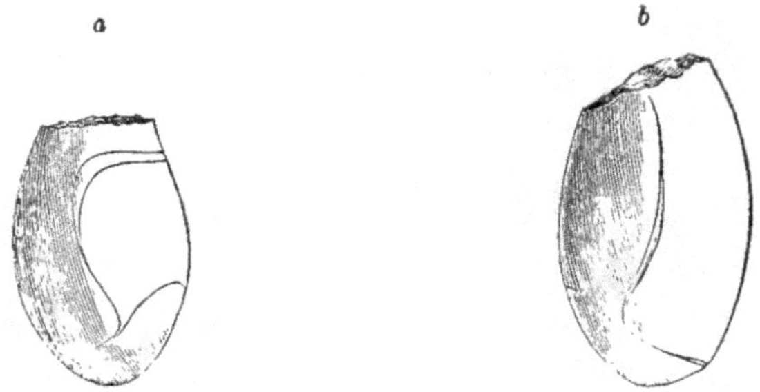

Fig. 148.

Fig. 148.—*Ascoceras Newberryi.* *a*, *b*, side views of two different specimens.

at four lines above the apex. The other two are first seen on the side, where they seem to be combined and originate from the first in a single suture; thus united, they ascend the side about four lines, curving slightly backwards: they then separate gradually, and at eleven lines above the apex turn abruptly forwards and cross the ventral side, the greatest distance between them being just at the turn, where they are separated one line. The aperture is not preserved in any of the specimens collected.

This description is founded on the most perfect specimen seen, of which the above Fig. 148, *a*, is a view of the right side, a little restored. The other three specimens are more or less worn and distorted. From these it seems that all three of the septa are united, or in some way so concealed, in the suture described as the first septum, that they cannot be seen in perfect specimens. The siphuncle is seen in the base or apex of two of the specimens, not quite half way between the centre and the dorsal margin. It is about 1 line in diameter.

Length of the best preserved specimen 12 lines; dorso-ventral diameter at the point where the septum crosses the ventral side 7 lines, and at the most ventricose part below 8 lines. Greatest lateral diameter 10 lines. This specimen is from English Head, Anticosti.

Another specimen from Gemache Bay (fig. 000, *b*) is a little longer, and as it is a little worn both on the dorsal and ventral sides, the proportions appear to be somewhat different; but when perfect they must be very nearly the same. It will be seen by the figure (*b*) that the upright sutures at first separate, and then seem to unite again. This might constitute a specific difference; but on account of the worn condition of the specimen, the markings are very obscure, and this appearance may be deceptive.

In form, this little species resembles *A. Canadense*, from which it differs greatly in the course taken by the first septum across the ventral side.

This species is dedicated to the eminent American geologist and palæontologist, Dr. J. S. Newberry.

Locality and Formation.—English Head, Anticosti; on the south side of the St. Lawrence, opposite Three Rivers; and also at Point Rich, Lake Huron. In the Hudson River group. The specimen represented by fig. 148, *b*, above, is from Junction Cliff, Anticosti, in Division 1, base of the Anticosti group, Middle Silurian. It is not quite certain that this latter is of the same species.

Collectors.—J. Richardson, R. Bell.

Additional species from various localities.

CYRTIA MYRTEA. (N. sp.)

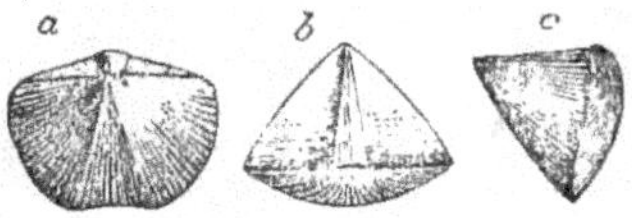

Fig. 149.

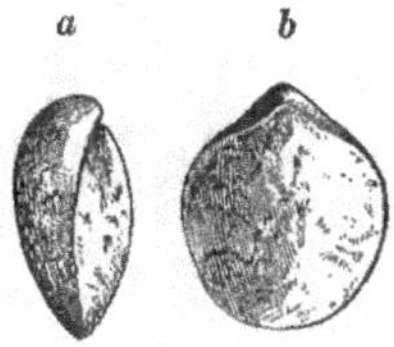

Fig. 150.

Fig. 149.—*Cyrtia Myrtea.*—*a*, Ventral view; *b*, view of the area; *c*, side view.
150.—*Charionella Hyale.* *a*, side, and *b*, dorsal view.

Description.—Ventral valve pyramidal, much elevated; area large, flat, at right angles to the plane of the margin; beak acutely pointed, not incurved; foramen narrow, closed all the way to the beak by a strongly convex deltidium; a shallow mesial sinus, which is gently concave, commences at the front margin, with a width equal to a little more than one-third the length of the hinge-line, and runs all the way to the beak, where it diminishes to a point. The dorsal valve is sub-elliptical; cardinal angles slightly rounded; sides gently convex and converging towards the front margin; the latter with a gentle concavity in the middle, formed by the mesial sinus; area small, lying in the plane of the margin. This valve is gently convex, with an obscure depressed convex mesial fold.

Surface with fine radiating striæ, about 8 in the width of one line.

Width on the hinge-line 7 lines; length of dorsal valve 5 lines; height of ventral area 4 lines.

Locality and Formation.—South-west Point, Anticosti. In Division 4, Anticosti group, Middle Silurian.

Collector.—J. Richardson.

CHARIONELLA ? HYALE. (N. sp.)

Fig. 150, *a*, *b*.

Description.—Ovate, both valves about equally convex; length one-eighth greater than the width; apical angle about 100°; cardinal edge on each side of the beak gently concave or nearly straight; sides gently convex; greatest width about the middle or a little above it; front margin rounded. Ventral valve moderately convex, most elevated in the upper half; umbo narrow, obtusely sub-carinate; beak small, only slightly incurved, with apparently a perforated apex, and a deltidium below it. Dorsal valve uniformly depressed convex, with indications of an obtuse carination along the middle. Surface unknown.

Length of largest specimen collected 8 lines; width 7 lines; depth of both valves 4 lines.

The specimens are all in the condition of casts, and as there are no indications of a hinge-plate, I have referred the species to *Charionella*, provisionally.

Locality and Formation.—Galt. In the Guelph formation; Middle Silurian.

Collectors.—J. Richardson, R. Bell.

Genus TRIMERELLA. (N. gen.)

Generic Characters.—Shell large, ovate or circular; valves moderately or strongly convex; beaks solid and transversely striated, as in the genus *Obolus*. Interior of each valve with three longitudinal septa of variable length which support a horizontal flat or concave plate. In the surface of this plate the muscular apparatus was either wholly or in part attached. On each side there appears to be a small ovate muscular impression, as in *Obolus*. Surface of the shell with concentric accretion ridges or striæ. Shell thick.

This genus is allied to *Obolus*, from which it differs in the possession of the longitudinal septa.

TRIMERELLA GRANDIS. (N. sp.)

Description.—Shell large, ovate, greatest width a little in advance of the mid-length; sides gently convex, front margin broadly or uniformly rounded; apical extremity apparently obtusely pointed. Both valves moderately and uniformly convex; greatest tumidity a little above the middle; umbo of dorsal valve broadly rounded. Judging from some of

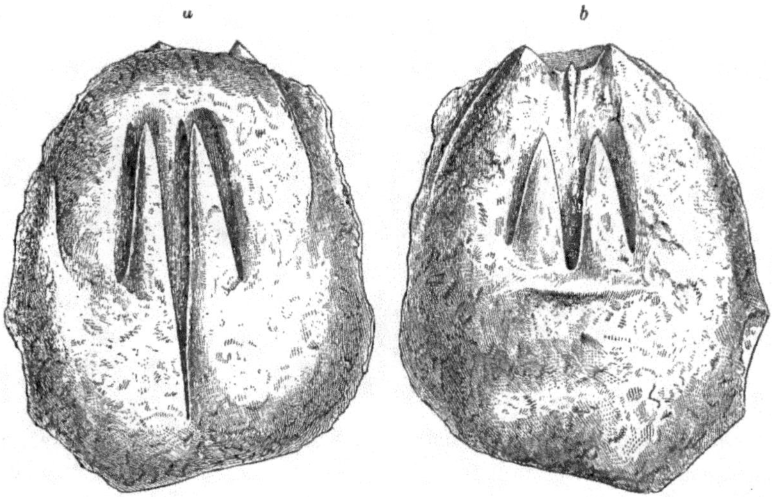

Fig. 151.

Fig. 151.—*Trimerella grandis*. *a*, cast of interior of the supposed dorsal valve; *b*, other side of the same cast, showing the characters of the interior of the ventral? valve.

the impressions, the ventral valve has a flat, solid, transversely-striated area forming an obtuse angle with the plane of the lateral margin. Surface of shell with obscure concentric accretion ridges.

Length of large individual about 3 inches; width about 2½ inches.

The casts of the interior of this species vary greatly in the length of the conical projections between the septa. Although not common, they have been found of all sizes from the length of 8 to 36 lines. The specimen above figured is one of the various forms. It yet remains to be ascertained how many species there may be.

Locality and Formation.—Galt; New Hope and Elora. In the Guelph formation; Middle Silurian.

Collector.—J. Richardson, J. Dalgleish, R. Bell, E. Billings.

TRIMERELLA ACUMINATA. (N. sp.)

Fig. 152.—*Trimerella acuminata.*

Remarks.—The fragment figured below appears to belong to a distinct species, differing from *T. grandis* in having the apical extremity much more pointed, and the longitudinal septa running all the way to the beak. The specimen is too imperfect for description, and it is figured under the above name only provisionally. It occurs with *T. grandis.*

Obolus Galtensis. (N. sp.)

Fig. 151.

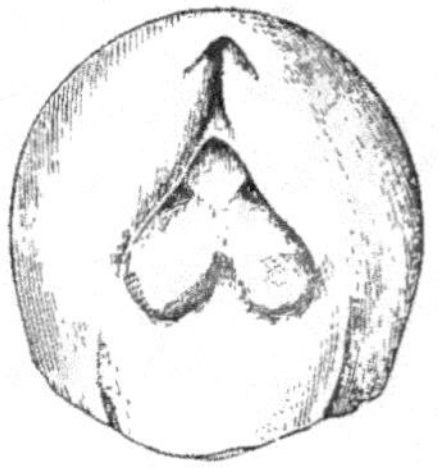

Fig. 152.

Fig. 152.—*Obolus Galtensis.*

Description.—Ovate, both valves moderately convex; sides gently, and front margin broadly rounded; apical extremity of ventral valve 70°; greatest width a little below the middle. The area of the ventral valve is flat, with a concave groove along the middle; and while in one specimen it lies nearly in the plane of the margin, in another it slopes a little outwards.

The largest specimen seen is 25 lines in length and 18 in width.

Locality and Formation.—Galt. In the Guelph formation; Middle Silurian.

Collectors.—E. Billings, R. Bell.

Orthoceras Piso. (N. sp.)

Description.—Section circular, tapering eight lines in a length of five inches; septa moderately concave, about twelve to the inch; siphuncle moniliform, dilated, between the septa, to a diameter of about 1½ lines, its centre distant about three lines from the margin, where the diameter of the fossil is 10 lines. The shell is preserved on the specimen, and appears to be quite smooth, but this may have been caused by cleaning it from the adhesive shale in which it was found imbedded. It is most probably marked with fine engirdling striæ.

The specimen is 5 inches in length; width at the larger extremity 14 lines, and at the smaller 6 lines.

Locality and Formation.—Cape Smyth, Lake Huron. In the Hudson River group.

Collector.—R. Bell.

Pleurotomaria ? Viola. (N. sp.)

Description.—A cast of the interior consisting of five whorls is twenty three lines wide at the base and eighteen lines in height; umbilicus nine lines wide, and on inside exhibiting all the whorls quite to the apex. The whorls are sub-cylindrical, gradually increasing in size; transverse section showing the form of the aperture elliptical, the width about one fourth greater than the height. Width of the aperture about eight lines; height six lines.

It is difficult to say whether this fossil should be called a *Pleurotomaria* or a *Murchisonia.* The cast resembles a short *Murchisonia* with slender cylindrical whorls and a very wide umbilicus. On the outer side there is some appearance of an angulation, as if there were a band on the margin of the shell.

Locality and Formation.—Galt; in the Guelph formation.

Collector.—E. Billings.

Pleurotomaria Valeria. (N. sp.)

Description.—Large, conical; whorls five or six, very gradually increasing in size, with a sharp-edged margin all round. On the upper side, as nearly as can be ascertained from the cast, the whorls have an obtusely rounded angulation at about one third their width from the outer edge; above this angulation they are flat or gently concave to the suture; below it, also flat, and descending with an abrupt slope to the outer edge. The latter presents a sharp angle of about 90°. Just below it a gently concave band about one and a-half lines wide. The remainder of the under side of the whorls is gently convex, uniformly rounded into the umbilicus. The aperture, as shown in the cast, is transversely ovate, depressed convex above and below, narrowly rounded on the inside and angular on the outside. Umbilicus about one half the whole width.

Width 28 lines; height 15 lines; width of umbilicus 14 lines; width of aperture 9 lines; height of the same 6 lines.

This shell somewhat resembles *P. Elora,* but differs in being angulated on the upper side of the whorls.

Locality and Formation.—Galt; in the Guelph formation.

Collector.—E. Billings.

Pleurotomaria Agave. (N. sp.)

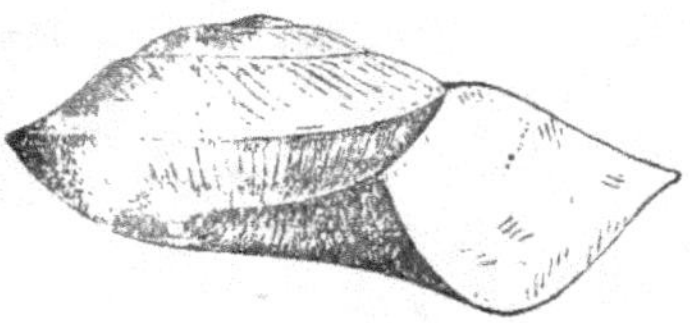

Fig. 153.

a b

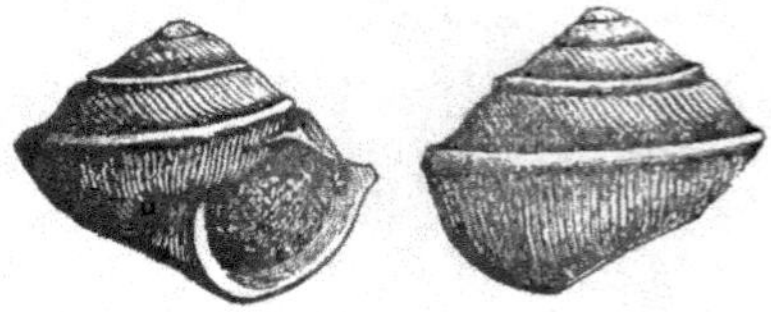

Fig. 154.

Fig. 153.—*Pleurotomaria Agave.*
154.—*P Dryope.* *a* and *b*, different views of the same specimen.

Description.—Lenticular, with an acute margin; apical angle from 125° to 145°; whorls three, forming a nearly smooth slope from the apex to the margin. On the upper side the last whorl is gently concave in the outer half, or two-thirds of the width, and slightly convex or flat above; in some specimens the concavity occupies the whole width; upper whorls gently convex or flat; apex generally rounded. The margin in the last whorl is thin, sharp, and a little turned upwards. On the underside the whorls are convex, most prominent a little within the mid-width where they are obtusely rounded angular. Umbilicus a little more than one-third the whole width, exposing the rounded inner edges of all the whorls to the apex. Aperture rhomboidal. Surface with fine striæ curving backwards to the margin.

Width of an average specimen 22 lines; height 10 lines; width of last whorl, on the upper side at the aperture, 7 lines. The width appears to be from 15 to 24 lines; the most common 20 lines.

P. lapicida (Salter) is smaller and has the aperture more nearly elliptical, and a much narrower umbilicus.

P. Americana (Billings) has the outer margin rounded.

P. aperta (Salter) has the whorls more slender, and the umbilicus wider.

Locality and Formation.—Naquareau River, above Red River; Trenton limestone.

Collector.—J. Richardson.

Pleurotomaria Dryope. (N. sp.)

Fig. 154. *a, b.*

Description.—Shell turbinate; spire depressed conical; apical angle about 100°; whorls three. On the upper side the whorls are concave for three-fourths their width; the inner one-fourth next the suture convex.

The margin is truncated by a flat band, about half a line in width and nearly vertical, sloping a little inwards and upwards. On the under side the whorls are strongly convex, obscurely angulated at the edge of the umbilicus ; there are indications of a faint concave band just below the margin. Umbilicus small ; when measured across from the angulated line of the last whorl, it is one-third the whole width, but it contracts to one-tenth the whole width in passing through this whorl, and seems to diminish only slightly thence to the apex. The whorls in the umbilicus are rounded. The aperture is sub-circular ; rounded on the inner and lower side, and angular at the edge, its height about equal to its width. The second whorl is slightly turretted above the last. Surface with fine and coarse striæ, the latter being minute undulations of growth, about four in one line, all curving backwards to the margin both above and below.

Width, from 10 to 12 lines ; height, from 7 to 9 lines.

Locality and Formation.—Pauquette's Rapids, on the Ottawa River ; Black River limestone.

Collector.—E. Billings.

Pleurotomaria Vitruvia. (N. sp.)

Description.—Shell sub-lenticular ; spire depressed conical, smooth ; apical angle from 120° to 130° ; whorls three. On the upper side the whorls make a nearly smooth flat slope from the apex to the margin, which is narrowly rounded, and shows some indications of a band. Below the margin convex, gradually increasing in prominence to the edge of the umbilicus which is rather sharply angulated. In the umbilicus the whorls are nearly flat, and sometimes forming an indistinct staircase to the apex. The umbilicus is about one-third the whole width, abruptly ascending from the angulated edge to the apex. Surface nearly smooth.

The whole of the aperture has not been observed, but several silicified fragments show that the inner lip is nearly straight and approaching the vertical, slightly convex in its upper, and concave in the lower half, giving an obscure sigmoid curve. It is much extended downwards, making the depth of the body whorl at the angle of the umbilicus at the aperture more than one-third the whole height of the shell.

Width from 12 to 18 lines ; height from 9 to 12 lines.

This species is allied to both *P. Americana* and *P. Progne*, but differs from the former in having the whorls flat in the umbilicus instead of rounded, while the latter has the umbilicus closed.

Locality and Formation.—Pauquette's Rapids, on the Ottawa River ; Black River limestone.

Collector.—E. Billings.

MURCHISONIA ALEXANDRA. (N. sp.)

MURCHISONIA VENTRICOSA (Salter). Dec. 1, p. 23, pl. 5, fig. 2.

Description.—Shell rather large, turbinate, acutely conical; apical angle from 45° to 50°; whorls about six, strongly ventricose, with a flat band in the upper third. The aperture appears to be large and ovate; the inner lip is thin and folded over so as to conceal the minute umbilicus. Surface finely striated. Length about 30 lines; width of body whorl 15 lines.

This species is about the size and somewhat of the shape of *M. bellicincta.* The principal difference is in the form of the upper part of the whorl. The lower two-thirds or three-fourths of the whorl is nearly uniformly convex, but the upper third descends abruptly to the deep suture. The band is quite flat, and being situated on the upper sloping part, gives to the whorl a truncated appearance. The lower edge of the band is defined by a small acute carina, seldom visible in specimens which are worn.

In *M. ventricosa* (Hall) the whorls are strongly angulated in the middle, as in *M. perangulata.*

Locality and Formation.—Pauquette's Rapids, on the Ottawa River; Black River limestone.

Collector.—Sir W. E. Logan.

METOPTOMA SUPERBA. (N. sp.)

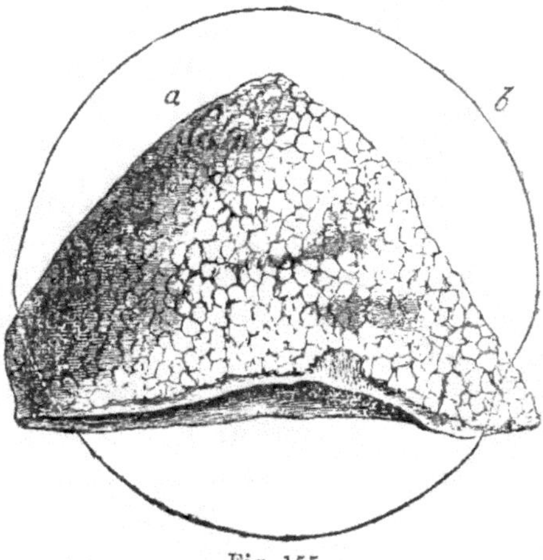

Fig. 155.

Fig. 155.—*Metoptoma superba.* Side view of a specimen which [illegible] with small concretions of silex, the interior being perfectly empty. The line, *b*, shows the form of the aperture.

Description.—Shell large, depressed conical; aperture circular; apex central, or very nearly so. An obscure carination runs from the apex to the margin on one side, but elsewhere the shape is evenly conical. The inside of the shell is quite smooth, but the outside appears to be concentrically striated, at least it is so near the margin, where it is exposed for about a line in height. The concentric striæ are crossed by coarser striæ, radiating from the apex to the margin, two or three in one line.

Diameter of the aperture 27 lines; height of the shell 18 lines.

Locality and Formation.—Pauquette's Rapids, on the Ottawa River; Black River limestone.

Collector.—E. Billings.

ORTHOCERAS DRUMMONDI. (N. sp.)

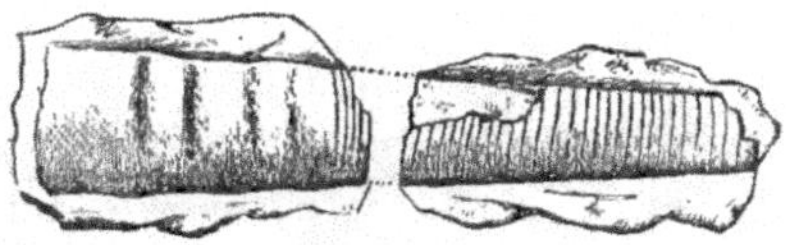

Fig. 156.

Fig. 156.—*Orthoceras Drummondi.*

Description.—Shell small, apparently slightly curved; section elliptical, nearly circular, the lateral diameter being a little greater than the dorso-ventral; tapering at the rate of a little more than a line to the inch; from twenty to thirty septa in a length of one inch, those near the chamber of habitation more closely crowded than those towards the apex; siphuncle small, slightly dilated between the septa, situated close to the margin, but not in contact with the shell; chamber of habitation proportionally deep, with several obscure shallow undulations or constrictions of the shell. Surface unknown.

This species appears to be only two or three inches in length. Only two specimens have been found however. The chamber of habitation is 10 lines in depth where the diameter of the aperture is 5 lines.

Locality and Formation.—Near Kingston; Black River limestone.

Collector.—A. T. Drummond, Esq., of Kingston, to whom the species is dedicated.

ORTHOCERAS VELOX. (N. sp.)

Description.—Shell rather large, slightly curved, tapering at the rate of from twelve to fifteen lines in one foot of the length; section circular; septa moderately concave, from six to nine in one inch; siphuncle large, cylindrical, marginal, in contact with the shell, its thickness about equal to one-third the whole diameter of the shell. The surface of the shell is marked with coarse, unequal, engirdling striæ, distinctly impressed, from twelve to twenty in an inch. These striæ cross the shell obliquely, curving towards the apex on the ventral side. Chamber of habitation unknown.

Judging from the fragments that have been collected, this orthoceratite must attain a length of four or five feet. The following are the dimensions of several specimens:

1. Length 13 inches; diameter of shell at the longer extremity 32 lines, and of the siphuncle 10 lines; diameter of shell at smaller extremity 15 lines, and of the siphuncle 5 lines.

2. Length 10 inches; diameter of shell at the larger extremity 26 lines, siphuncle 8 lines; diameter of shell at smaller extremity 16 lines, siphuncle 5½ lines.

3. Length 6 inches; diameter of shell 22 and 15 lines; siphuncle 7½ and 5 lines.

The siphuncle is sometimes found separate, and is always strongly marked by oblique encircling lines, indicating the positions of the junction of the septa with it. The smaller extremity is also filled with the organic deposit so characteristic of species of this type.

This species must be closely allied to *O. rapax*, but has a more slender siphuncle.

Locality and Formation.—Mingan Islands, Islands of Montreal and Bizard, in loose blocks near Cornwall; Chazy limestone.

Collectors.—Sir W. E. Logan, J. Richardson, E. Billings.

ORTHOCERAS DIFFIDENS. (N. sp.)

Description.—Apparently about one foot in length; section circular; tapering at the rate of from one and a half to two lines to the inch; septa from four to five to the inch, rather strongly concave. The siphuncle is moniliform, the segments between the septa subglobular or ovate, the diameter of each being equal to about one-fifth the whole diameter of the shell. The position of the siphuncle, as shown in three different individuals, is, with its centre, about half way between the centre of the shell and the margin; it is a little more distant from the margin than it is from the centre of the fossil.

This species, both internally and externally, closely resembles *O. Allumettense*, so common in the Black River limestone. The siphuncle of that species, however, is in general larger, being usually one-third the whole width, rarely one-fourth.

Length, from 8 to 12 inches; diameter at aperture, 1 to 1½ inches.

Locality and Formation.—Mingan Islands; Chazy.

Collector.—J. Richardson.

Cyrtoceras Isodorus. (N. sp.)

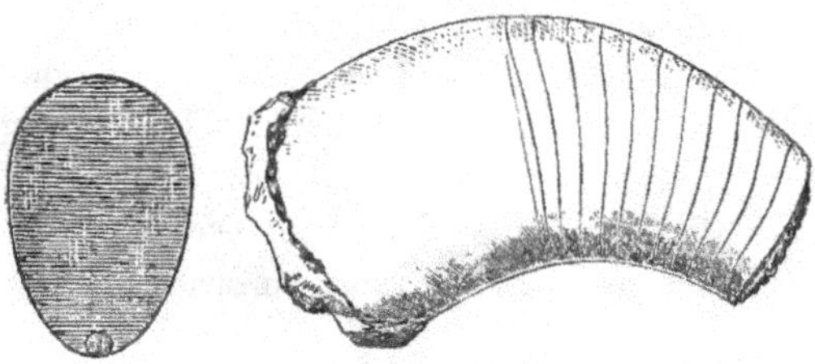

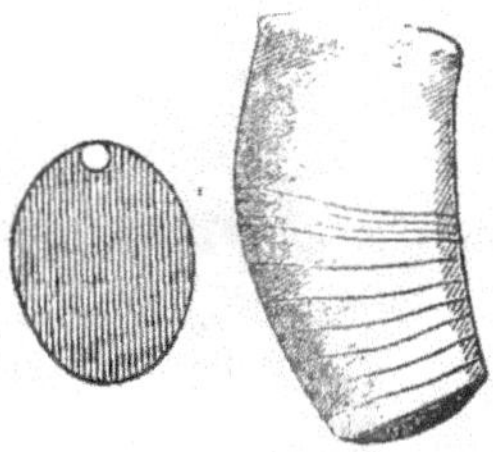

Fig. 157. Fig. 158.

Fig. 157.—*Cyrtoceras Isodorus.* *a*, Section at the last septum; *b*, side view.
158.—*C. Huronense.* *a* and *b*, Section at the last septum and side view.

Description.—Shell rather strongly curved, laterally compressed. Section ovate, the dorso-ventral diameter, at the last chamber, being to the lateral in the proportion of ten to seven; the greatest lateral diameter nearer the dorsal than the ventral side; the aperture slightly more strongly compressed laterally than the septate portion; the dorsal side more obtusely rounded than the ventral. Septa one line distant on the side. Siphuncle, small, in contact with the shell on the ventral side. Chamber of habitation of moderate depth.

The specimen is 2 inches in length measured along the curve of the ventral side. Dorso-ventral diameter at the aperture 10 lines, lateral 6 (?) lines; dorso-ventral diameter at last chamber 10 lines, lateral 7 lines; dorso-ventral diameter at the eleventh septum 6 lines, lateral 5 lines. Depth of chamber of habitation 10 lines. The ventral contour is curved to a radius of 15 lines; the radius of the dorsal curve is about 12 lines. The siphuncle is a little less than a line in diameter, and appears to be slightly inflated between the septa.

This species somewhat resembles *C. simplex*, and indeed, fragments of the two, if collected together, could hardly be separated. The former is slightly more curved, more narrowly rounded on the ventral side, and tapers more gradually than the latter. It is more curved on the dorsal side, and larger than *C. Huronense.*

The aperture is not clearly shown in the specimen, but it is evidently compressed laterally, and even seems to be (although obscurely) of the key-hole shape of *Phragmoceras præmaturum.*

Locality and Formation.—St. Joseph Island; Black River or Trenton limestone.

Collectors.—A. Murray, R. Bell.

Cyrtoceras Huronense. (N. sp.)

Fig. 158. *a*, *b*.

Description.—Shell rather small, constricted at the aperture; the ventral outline more curved than the dorsal; section elliptical, the dorso-ventral diameter being about one-fifth greater than the lateral, at the last chamber, and at the aperture apparently one-third greater. In one specimen the last three septa next the chamber of habitation occupy a space of only one line, but the next seven occupy six lines, measured on the side. In another specimen there are nine septa in six lines, and in a third, ten septa in seven lines. Siphuncle small, close to the shell on the ventral side. Chamber of habitation of moderate depth.

One of the specimens, which consists of the cast of the interior of the chamber of habitation, with the last nine septa next thereto, is 16 lines in length, measured along the ventral curve. Dorso-ventral diameter at the smaller extremity $5\frac{1}{2}$ lines, lateral $4\frac{1}{2}$ lines; dorso-ventral diameter at the last septum $7\frac{1}{2}$ lines, lateral 6 lines; dorso-ventral diameter of the aperture 6 lines, lateral 4 lines. Depth of the chamber of habitation measured on the side 6 lines, diameter of siphuncle about $\frac{1}{2}$ a line.

The ventral outline, for 16 lines next to the aperture, is curved to a radius of about 14 lines. The dorsal contour is only slightly concave.

Locality and Formation.—St. Joseph Island; Black River or Trenton limestone.

Collectors.—R. Bell, A. Murray.

Cyrtoceras Ligarius. (N. sp.)

Description.—Shell large, gently curved; section ovate, most obtusely rounded on the dorsal side; septa eleven in two inches; chamber of habitation moderately deep and apparently with a constriction near the aperture. Siphuncle unknown.

The specimen is 3 inches in length, curved on the ventral side to a radius of about 4 inches; but on the dorsal side the septate portion is nearly straight, while the chamber of habitation is slightly curved. Dorso-ventral diameter at the last septum, and also at the aperture, about 20 lines. The lateral diameter cannot be clearly ascertained, but it appears to be at the last septum, about 18 lines. Depth of the chamber of habitation, about 15 lines. The dorso-ventral diameter at the eleventh septum appears to be about 14 lines.

This species is very like *C. macrostomum* (Hall), Pal. N. Y., vol. i, pl. 42, fig. 1b, but is a larger form, and does not taper so rapidly. The diameter at the aperture in the two species is the same very nearly, but at three inches therefrom it is 14 lines in one specimen, and a little less than 12 in Prof. Hall's figures.

Locality and Formation.—Drummond Island; Hudson River formation.

Collector.—A. Murray.

CYRTOCERAS JUVENALIS. (N. sp.)

Description.—Short, ventricose, rather strongly curved. Section nearly circular, near the aperture the dorso-ventral diameter a little longer than the lateral; at the last septum circular, or very nearly so; the ventral side is slightly more narrowly rounded than the dorsal. Septa about four in three lines where the diameter is seven lines.

Surface obscurely reticulated. The transverse striæ are minute, not sharp, accompanied by a few obscure undulations of growth, and make a backward bend on the median line of the ventral aspect. The longitudinal lines are straight, three or four in the width of one line, not strongly developed, but still distinctly visible.

The specimen is 21 lines in length along the ventral curve, which has a radius of 10 lines. Dorso-ventral diameter at the larger extremity (supposed to be very near the aperture) 7¾ lines, lateral 7½ lines; at 6 lines nearer the apex (supposed place of last septum) the dorso-ventral diameter is 8¾ lines, lateral nearly 9 lines; from this point the shell tapers to a diameter of 5½ lines in the length of about 1 inch, the section still remaining circular, or nearly so.

Locality and Formation.—Montreal; Trenton limestone.

Collector.—McLachlin.

CYRTOCERAS ORESTES. (N. sp.)

Description.—Shell strongly curved; in the first four and a-half inches of its length (measured on the outside) forming nearly a half circle with a radius of twenty-one lines; the larger extremity with a more gentle curve than the smaller. Dorso-ventral diameter at the last septum fourteen lines; lateral diameter at the same place twelve lines; depth of chamber of habitation fourteen lines. Where the dorso-ventral diameter is nine lines, the septa are nearly two lines distant on the ventral margin. Siphuncle about one line in diameter, and with its centre distant about one line from the ventral margin.

Locality and Formation.—Tenth lot of the first concession of the Township of West Flamborough. Niagara limestone; Middle Silurian.

Collector.—R. Bell.

Cyrtoceras Postumius. (N. sp.)

Description.—Shell of medium size; section elliptical, the transverse diameter being greater than the dorso-ventral in the proportion of about ten to six and a half; nearly uniformly curved, the first two and a half inches on the outside forming a segment of a circle, of which the radius is 2 inches, thence to the apex more rapidly curved. Septa gently concave, three in two and a half lines at about the mid-length. Siphuncle close to the ventral or outer curve, apparently in contact with the shell, moniliform or expanded into obliquely-depressed globular chambers, each one line in diameter.

The specimen is 3⅝ inches in length, measured along the outer or ventral side. Transverse diameter at the aperture 10 lines; dorso-ventral diameter 6½ lines; dorso-ventral diameter at the apex 3 lines. The chamber of habitation is not perfect, but, judging from what remains, it must be at least ¾ of an inch in depth.

Locality and Formation.—Cape Smyth, Lake Huron; Hudson River formation.

Collector.—R. Bell.

Cyrtocerina. (N. gen.)

Generic Character.—*Fossil Nautilidæ* having the general characters of *Cyrtoceras*, but with a large siphuncle on the dorsal side (or on the side of the concave curve).

The above sub-generic name is proposed for the reception of two remarkable species of *Cyrtoceras*, which appear to be separated from the main body of the genus by their short thick form and the position of the siphuncle. One of the species occurs in the Black River limestone, and the other in the upper part of the Quebec group.

Cyrtocerina typica. (N. sp.)

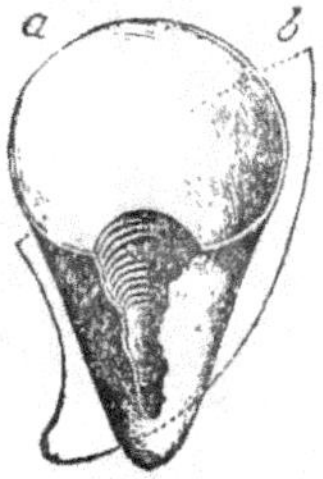

Fig. 159.

Fig. 159.—*Cytocerina typica.* *a*, dorsal view of a specimen consisting of the septate portion (in part), and showing the cavity of the siphuncle. Owing to the position in which the specimen was drawn, the section, instead of oval, appears to be circular being fore-shortened. The outline figure *b*, is the side view.

Description.—This species is founded on a simple specimen, consisting of a portion of the septate part of the shell. Section oval, narrowly rounded on the ventral side; dorso-ventral diameter (as measured on the plane of the last septum preserved in the specimen) twelve lines, lateral diameter nine lines; diameter of siphuncle three lines, tapering to a point at the apex; length following the ventral curve eighteen lines. Septa moderately concave and crossing the shell obliquely, so that the dorsal margin is much nearer the apex than the ventral, the distances in the specimen, for the septum observed being seven and eighteen inches respectively. The distance of the septa from each other has not been positively ascertained, none of them, except the last, being preserved. The inside of the siphuncle is transversely grooved, and it is possible that these grooves may represent the edges of the septa. If they do, then the septa must be very thin, and closely crowded together, as there are on an average about five grooves in a length of one line.

The species, so far as its characters can be made out, is a short thick strongly curved form, with a large siphuncle in contact with the shell on the dorsal side.

Locality and Formation.—Paquette's Rapids; Black River limestone.

Collector.—E. Billings.

ILLÆNUS VINDEX. (N. sp.)

Fig. 160.

Fig. 160.—*Illænus vindex.* *a*, Upper side of the head. *b*, Front view of the same.

Description.—Head sub-triangular, the front narrowly rounded, thence nearly straight on each side to the posterior angles, which terminate in short, stout, sharp spines; glabella depressed, semi-cylindrical, with concave sides for a little more than half the length, then enlarged to nearly twice the width, in front nearly vertical. The eyes are conical, close to the posterior margin, sloping outwards and upwards at an angle of 45°, their bases distant from the dorsal furrow about three-fourths the width of the glabella at its narrowest place.

Thorax with ten segments; axis rather strongly convex, not quite one-third the whole width; side lobes flat for half their width next the axis, then bent down at an angle of about 45°.

Pygidium transversely oblong; posterior margin gently convex; sides truncated for two-thirds of the whole length, and forming with the anterior margin, an angle of about 100° ; axis short, about half the whole length, moderately convex, not very strongly defined at the apex, but still distinct. Surface punctate.

Length of the best preserved head in a straight line, not following the curvature, 6 lines ; width at the posterior margin to the extremities of the spines 16 lines ; width between the apices of the eyes 14 lines ; width of the posterior half of the glabella 3 lines ; and of the anterior half 6 lines ; height of the head 6 lines ; height of the ocular cones about 2½ lines ; diameter of the same at about half their height 1 line.

Another specimen, consisting of the thorax and pygidium in connection, but without the head, gives the following measurements :

Length of the thorax 5 lines ; entire width 10 lines ; width of the axis 3½ lines.

Length of the pygidium in a straight line from the anterior to the posterior margin 5 lines ; width between the posterior angles 8 lines ; between the anterior angles 6 lines. The pygidium is rather strongly convex.

I. conifrons has the posterior portion of the glabella proportionately more narrow and prominent, and the front conical instead of rounded. These two species, however, are most closely allied.

Locality and Formation.—Mingan Islands ; Chazy.

Collectors.—Sir W. E. Logan ; J. Richardson.

Sphaerexochus parvus. (N. sp.)

S. parvus.—Billings. *Geology of Canada*, p. 133, fig. 66.

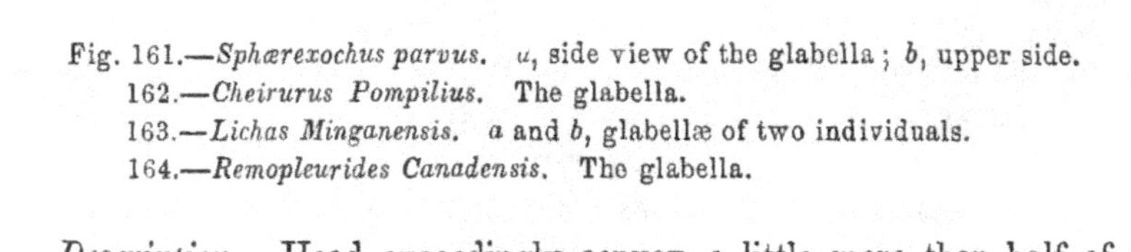

Fig. 161. Fig. 162. Fig. 163. Fig. 164.

Fig. 161.—*Sphærexochus parvus.* *a*, side view of the glabella ; *b*, upper side.
162.—*Cheirurus Pompilius.* The glabella.
163.—*Lichas Minganensis.* *a* and *b*, glabellæ of two individuals.
164.—*Remopleurides Canadensis.* The glabella.

Description.—Head exceedingly convex, a little more than half of a sphere, length and width about equal ; posterior glabellar lobes ovate, perfectly isolated, about one-third the width of the glabella ; middle and anterior glabellar furrows visible only on close examination, each extending about one-third across; neck segment narrow; neck furrow extending all across.

Length and width of largest specimen seen, 4 lines.

This species is only known by detached glabellæ, and these so closely resemble *S. mirus* (Beyrich) that I have some doubts as to whether they should receive a new name. Forms very similar occur in the Quebec group.

Locality and Formation.—Island of Montreal; Chazy limestone: also, south side of Large Island, Mingan Islands; Chazy, or Black River.

Collectors.—J. Richardson, E. Billings.

Cheirurus Pompilius. (N. sp.)

Fig. 162.

Description.—Of this species only the glabella, with portions of the fixed cheeks attached, and the neck segment broken off, has been found. The glabella is rectangular; sides straight and parallel; front gently convex, with a very narrow marginal rim. There are three pairs of glabellar furrows, all extending about one-third across and inclining a little backwards. The posterior lobes are isolated. The anterior lobes occupy nearly two-fifths the length of the glabella, and the others about one-fifth each. The cheeks are punctured. The glabella is only moderately convex, not abruptly elevated in front.

Length of the glabella, without the neck segment, about 7 lines; width 6 lines.

Locality and Formation.—South side of Large Island, Mingan Islands; Chazy, or Black River.

Collector.—J. Richardson.

Lichas Minganensis. (N. sp.)

Fig. 163. *a, b.*

Description.—Head very convex, abruptly tumid in front; width of the middle lobe, at the neck furrow, about two-fifths the whole length of the head, exclusive of the neck segment; the furrows on each side of said lobe nearly parallel for about half the length, then curving outwards so as to make the width of the lobe in front equal to the length. The side lobes are of a reniform shape, truncated behind by the neck furrow, about two-thirds the length of the head, and in their greatest width about equal to the width of the median lobe in its posterior half. Length of the largest specimen, exclusive of the neck segment, eight lines. Surface with numerous rounded tubercles, the largest of which are about half a line in diameter.

This species very closely resembles *L. Jukesii* from the Quebec group, but in that species the middle lobe is expanded at the neck-furrow and contracted in the mid-length.

Locality and Formation.—In the white limestone on the south side of Large Island, Mingan Islands; Chazy, or Black River.

Collectors.—Sir W. E. Logan, and J. Richardson.

Remopleurides Canadensis. (N. sp.)

Fig. 164.

Description.—Head gently convex, somewhat abruptly elevated in front; width of space between the eyes equal to the length of the head, neck segment well defined by the neck furrow, and with a tubercle in the middle. The eyes are two-thirds the length of the head; their posterior and anterior corners at about an equal distance from each other (two-thirds the length of the head); the median projection of the glabella in front of the eyes is about one-fifth the length of the head. Surface under the lens finely tubercular. There are two pairs of very obscure glabellar furrows, and two smooth lines behind them representing the third or posterior pair.

Length 4 lines; length of the eyes $2\frac{2}{3}$ lines. Only one specimen of this species has been collected.

Locality and Formation.—Front concession of the Township of Clarence; Chazy.

Collector.—J. Richardson.

Harpes Ottawaensis. (N. sp.)

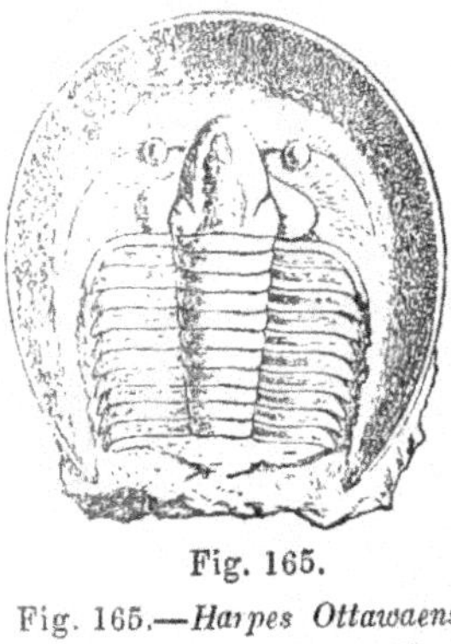

Fig. 165.

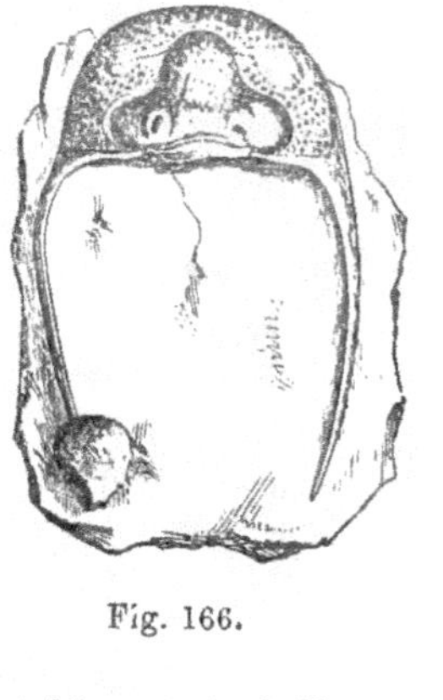

Fig. 166.

Fig. 165.—*Harpes Ottawaensis.*
166.—*H. Dentoni.* The glabella distorted in posterior half.

Description.—Head strongly convex with a wide punctured border, which extends backwards to about the thirteenth segment of the thorax.

If a line be drawn across touching the posterior edge of the neck-segment, the contour in front of that line is nearly a perfect semi-circle. Glabella regularly conical, its length about five-ninths that of the head; posterior furrows distinct, entering at about one-half the distance from the ocular ridge to the posterior margin of the neck segment, thence running obliquely inward and backwards at an angle of about 45°, apparently not quite one-third the width; two anterior furrows on each side, represented by obscure pits; neck furrow narrow; neck segment convex, strongly elevated on the fixed cheeks. The eyes are small, and situated on a line drawn across the glabella at the anterior fourth; ocular ridge well defined, smooth, prolonged, with a backward curve outside of the eye. Thorax a little more than half the width of the head; the axis strongly convex and gradually apering backwards; side lobes flat; pleuræ with a wide groove along the middle, a small portion of their outer extremities turned backward. Surface of thorax, glabella, and a sub-reniform space on each side of the base of the glabella, smooth; the border with circular punctures about one-tenth of a line in width, and separated by smooth rounded interspaces half their own width; the punctures larger and more distant at the inner edge of the border; on the elevated part of the cheeks they have a sub-reticulated arrangement.

Length of the head, including the border, 8½ lines; width at neck-segment, 16 lines; length of glabella 5 lines; width of the same at the base 4 lines; length of the posterior prolongations of the border behind a line drawn across at the neck-segment 9 lines; distance of the eye from the side of the glabella 1 line.

The crust on all the middle part of the glabella is broken away, but the part of it which remains on the side is smooth even when viewed through a pocket lens.

Harpes Dentoni has the surface differently marked, the eye more distant from the glabella, and the lateral spines proportionally longer.

Locality and Formation.—City of Ottawa; Trenton limestone.

Collector.—Dr. J. M. Grant, Ottawa.

HARPES DENTONI. (Billings.)

Fig. 166.

(*Canadian Nat. and Geo.*; vol. 8, p. 36: 1863.)

Description.—The head of this species, exclusive of the posterior prolongation of the border, is nearly semi-circular. The border itself is not wholly preserved in the specimen, so that its width cannot be ascertained. The length of the head without the border is six lines, and its width on a line running across the neck segment one inch. The margin is prolonged backwards thirteen lines from the neck furrow. The head is rather strongly convex, its elevation at about mid-length of the glabella being about four lines in the specimen, although a little depressed by distortion. The glabella is strongly convex, being elevated nearly one line above the level of the cheeks; it is obtusely rounded in front, and appears to be nearly as broad where a line drawn through the eyes crosses it as it is at the neck furrow, but on this point there is some doubt as the posterior portion is crushed. The neck furrow is well defined across the glabella, and curves a little forward on the median line. The neck segment is well developed. On each side of the base of the glabella, there is an irregularly semi-oval space, the outer margin of which, is abruptly sunk about half a line below the general surface of the cheeks. This space is bordered on its posterior margin by the neck furrow;—on the outer and anterior side, by a nearly vertical elevation of the crust of the cheek, the outline of the space making an obtusely rounded curve on the outside and then turning inward and forwards to the glabella, which it reaches at an acute angle on a line crossing the eyes. There appears to be a slightly impressed glabellar furrow on each side, which commences at about one line from the neck furrow, at about one-third the width of the glabella from the side of the same, and runs obliquely forwards and outwards, reaching the side at about one line behind the eye. In front of this, there appear to be two small depressions in the side of the glabella, close to the surface of the cheek and opposite the eye. A line drawn across the head through the eyes would cross the glabella at about one third its length from the front. The eyes are small tubercles, scarcely half a line in diameter, and situated about two lines from the side of the glabella. A small thread-like ocular ridge runs from the eye forward, nearly to the front of the glabella, but does not appear to cross the small dorsal furrow which runs round the sides and front. The neck-segment forms a vertical elevation along the posterior margin of the head, half a line in height, and curving backwards gradually passes into the posterior prolongations of the head. These, as far as they can be seen, are nearly vertical, but sloping a little inwards and upwards.

The surface of the whole head is covered with small irregularly polygonal pits, separated from each other by sharp-edged walls. On the cheeks these pits are, on an average, about one-fourth of a line across, but they vary in size, some of them being much smaller than the others. They seem to be in general a little smaller on the glabella than on the cheeks. Where a portion of the crust is broken away from the front of the head, a cast of the inner surface can be observed. It is covered with small round tubercles, about three in one line.

This species differs from *Harpes antiquatus*, the only species hitherto described from the Lower Silurian Rocks of Canada, in having the glabella more obtusely rounded in front, and in the remarkable characters of the surface, which is reticulated, all over the head, by the sharp lines separating the angular punctures; while in *H. antiquatus* the glabella is smooth or only minutely punctured.

Dedicated to Mr. Wm. Denton, of Painesville, Ohio, who discovered it.

Locality and Formation.—Ottawa; Trenton limestone.

Stenopora Huronensis. (N. sp.)

Description.—Corallines forming large rounded masses, sometimes one foot in diameter and nine inches in height, covered with small conical elevations from two to four lines in diameter, the most prominent about two lines in height, and being distant from each other from one to six lines, (measuring from the centre of each). The tubes are small, there being about four or five in the width of one line, larger on the summits of the elevations, where, also, they exhibit a tendency to an arrangement in lines radiating from the apex of the elevations. In some of the weathered sections an obscure lamellar concentric structure is exhibited, similar to that of *Stromatopora concentrica.*

Locality and Formation.—Cape Smyth, Lake Huron; Hudson River formation.

Collector.—R. Bell.

5.—*New Species of Fossils from the limestones of the Quebec Group from Point Lévis and other localities in Canada East.*

Orthis Battis. (N. sp.)

Description.—Shell of medium size, semi-elliptical; hinge line about one-fourth more than the length; cardinal angles varying from about 80° to 90°; sides straight and either parallel or a little converging for one-half or three-fourths the whole length; anterior angles and margin rounded; ventral valve with the umbonial region narrowly convex; much compressed towards the cardinal angles; a deep rounded mesial sinus one-third the whole width and dying out at about half the length from the front margin; sometimes an incipient fold in the middle of the sinus; area low; beak minute, a little depressed below the umbo. Dorsal valve moderately convex, with a short mesial fold corresponding to the sinus in the other valve. Surface with fine striæ apparently four or five in one line with indications of concentric striæ.

Width on the hinge line 6 or 7 lines. The area of the ventral valve seems to be less than a line in height. All the specimens are imbedded in stone so that the area and foramen cannot be seen.

This species resembles *O. Maria*, (ante, p. 137, fig. 114,) but is not so convex.

Locality and Formation.—Point Lévis ; limestone No. 2, Quebec.

Collectors.—Sir W. E. Logan, and T. Devine, Esq.

CLISOSPIRA. (N. gen.)

Generic Characters.—Aperture widely expanded all round in a plane which is at a right angle (or nearly so) to the longitudinal axis of the spire, the latter conical. The cavity occupied by the animal appears to be, at least in the lower part, not spirally coiled, as in the ordinary gasteropods, but straight and central, with the lip spread out all round, trumpet-like. There is some evidence that towards the apex of the spire, it is spirally coiled, but neither of the two specimens collected has this part preserved. The suture is distinct in the spire, but seems to become obsolete on approaching the lip.

The specimens are so imperfect, that the affinities of this curious fossil are not very apparent. Even the shell has a different aspect from that of any gasteropod I have seen in the Lower Silurian rocks, being nearly black with a horny texture.

CLISOSPIRA CURIOSA. (N. sp.)

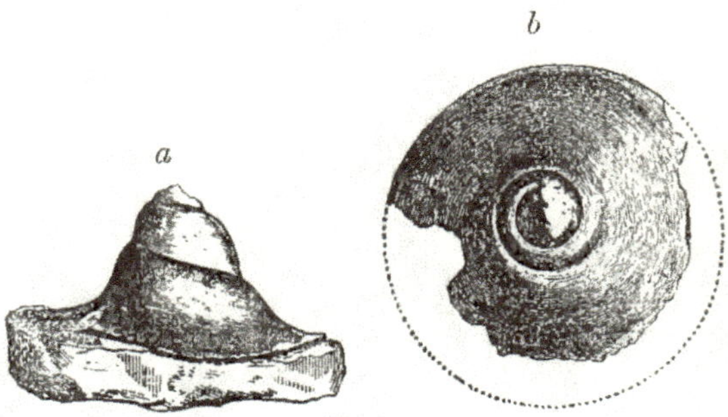

Fig. 167.

Fig. 167.—*Clisospira curiosa.* *a*, side view ; *b*, view of the specimen, looking down upon it from above.

Description.—Aperture trumpet-like, expanded to a width of about one inch ; spire central, or nearly so, sinistrally coiled, about five lines in diameter at the height of six lines, about seven lines at the base, or where it passes into the wide lip. The whorls are depressed convex, and the suture, where the shell is preserved, only slightly impressed. The spire is nearly vertical on one side and sloping on the side opposite. The shell is nearly black, and of a lamellar structure.

The least of the two specimens collected has only two whorls, and part of the third preserved, so that the characters of the apical portion are unknown. The shell is somewhat exfoliated, and does not shew the surface markings. When placed with the aperture downwards, and viewed from above, the lip is seen as a nearly circular disc-like expansion, the spire forming a central elevation.

Locality and Formation.—Near St. Antoine, above Quebec, in a boulder with *Subulites Psyche;* Quebec group.

Collector.—J. Richardson.

Holopea leiosoma. (N. sp.)

Fig. 168.

Fig. 169.

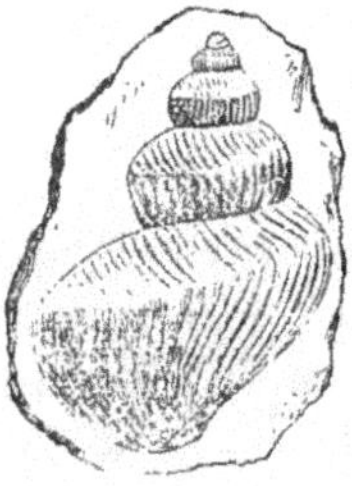

Fig. 170.

Fig. 171.

Fig. 168.—*Holopea leiosoma.* View of the upper side.
169.—*Subulites Psyche.*
170.—*Murchisonia Jessica.*
171.—*M. Cassandra.*

Description.—Shell small, sub-globular, consisting of two whorls; the last one constituting nearly the whole bulk; the apical whorl very small, scarcely elevated above the general surface. The aperture is not exposed in the specimen examined, but it must be nearly circular, as the whorls appear to be uniformly ventricose and smooth.

Width about 6 lines; height about 4 lines. As the base of the shell of the specimen is imbedded, the precise proportions cannot be ascertained. This species closely resembles *H. gibberula*, but has the whorls more uniformly ventricose.

Locality and Formation.—Point Lévis; in limestone No. 3, Quebec group.

Collector.—J. Richardson.

Cyclonema Phædra. (N. sp.)

Description.—Shell of about three ventricose whorls; apical angle about 65°; surface with numerous spiral striæ, or minute carinæ, three or four in the width of one line, with concave spaces between, those on the margin the strongest. These are crossed by very fine striæ parallel with the aperture.

The specimen is imperfect and partly imbedded. Its height appears to have been about 8 lines. The surface characters are similar to those of *C. bilix*, but the whorls are more convex, and the suture more deeply impressed.

Locality and Formation.—Near St. Antoine, above Quebec, in a boulder with *Subulites Psyche;* Quebec group.

Collector.—J. Richardson.

Subulites Psyche. (N. sp.)

Fig. 169.

Description.—This species is only known by several fragments. Whorls five or six, depressed convex, with the suture slightly impressed, resembling, in these respects, all the other species of the genus. The largest specimen examined, consists of the last three whorls, the apical two or three broken off. Its length is 21 lines, and diameter of last two whorls, 12 lines. When perfect it must have been about 2½ inches in length.

It is larger than *S. puella*, but not so slender in its proportions, and it is much smaller than *S. subfusiformis* of the Trenton limestone.

Locality and Formation.—Near St. Antoine, above Quebec, in a boulder, with trilobites of the Quebec group.

Collector.—J. Richardson.

Ophileta profunda. (N. sp.)

Description.—The specimen is twelve lines in diameter, and consists of three whorls, including a minute one in the centre. Upper side of whorls uniformly convex; suture distinct; outer side gently convex, most tumid a little above the mid-height; umbilicus about three-fourths the whole width with an acutely rounded edge; inner side of whorls in the umbilicus gently convex. Surface unknown.

The spire is depressed below the outer whorl, so that the specimen is doubly concave. The width of the specimen is 12 lines, and as the last whorl is broken off, it was, when perfect, probably several lines wider; width of last whorl, where broken off, 4½ lines; height 6½ lines.

Locality and Formation.—Point Lévis; in limestone No. 2, Quebec group.

Collectors.—J. Richardson and R. Bell.

OPHILETA ABDITA. (N. sp.)

Description.—From one to three inches across, consisting of from three to five slender whorls, uniformly rounded on the upper side. Spire flat, or concave, umbilicus probably wide and concave, but not observed.

The specimens are all partially imbedded, shewing only the upper side. The best preserved 2½ inches across; the last whorl, where broken off, 7 lines wide. It appears to have five whorls. This may be a variety of the *M. profunda*, but the whorls are more slender, and it has a different aspect. It occurs along with *M. profunda* at Point Lévis, and also at Philipsburgh.

MURCHISONIA JESSICA. (N. sp.)

Fig. 170.

Description.—Shell of medium size; apical angle between 50° and 60°; whorls about four, strongly convex, with a rounded angle a little above the middle, thence to the suture depressed convex, below the angle more uniformly ventricose. The body whorl is large, forming more than half the length of the shell. The suture is deep and the whorls strongly projecting. Surface unknown, the specimen being a cast of the interior, on which, however, are impressed numerous obscure grooves which cross the whorl from the suture backwards to the angle, and then gently forwards.

This shell is closely allied to *M. ventricosa* (Hall), but differs in not being so oblique, and in having the shell undulated.

Locality and Formation.—Point Lévis; in limestone No. 2, Quebec group.

Collector.—J. Richardson.

MURCHISONIA CASSANDRA. (N. sp.)

Fig. 171.

Description.—Shell rather small, apical angle between 50° and ; whorls about five, strongly and uniformly ventricose, with a narrow indistinct band about the middle. Surface unknown.

Length of the specimen 9 lines ; width at the body whorl 7 lines. Has the shape of *M. bellicincta*, but is smaller and not so acute.

Locality and Formation.—Point Lévis ; in limestone No. 2, Quebec group.

Collector.—J. Richardson.

MURCHISONIA SYLVIA. (N. sp.)

Description.—Apical angle about 80° ; whorls four, strongly ventricose, with a median band which forms on the cast of the interior an obscure rounded angulation. Surface of the cast with narrow, faint grooves crossing from the suture backwards to the band, and then forwards.

Length of largest specimen 10 lines ; width at the body whorl about the same.

Differs from *M. Cassandra* in being proportionally shorter and more oblique.

Locality and Formation.—Point Lévis ; in limestone No. 2, Quebec group.

Collectors.—J. Richardson, R. Bell, T. C. Weston.

PLEUROTOMARIA QUEBECENSIS. (N. sp.)

Fig. 172.

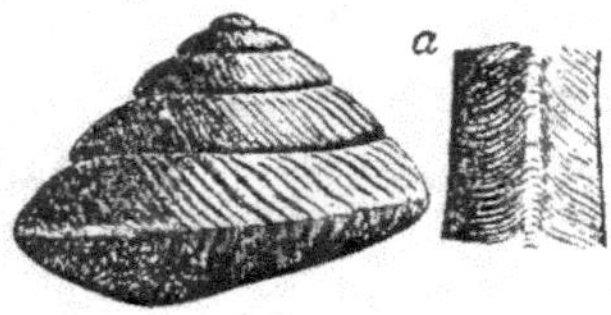

Fig. 173.

Fig. 174.

Figs. 172–174.—*Pleurotomaria Quebecensis.* Fig. 174. A polished section through a specimen, showing the wide umbilicus. *a*, magnified view of the margin of the body-whorl.

Description.—Shell pyramidal, varying in height, consisting of five or six slender whorls. The whorls are usually nearly flat on the upper side, the surface forming a straight slope from the acute apex to the angular margin of the body-whorl ; sometimes gently convex with a tendency to become slightly concave in the lower half. On the under side the most convex part of the whorl is close to the umbilicus, the edge of which is obtusely rounded angular. From the margin to the umbilicus the whorls are depressed convex. The margin of the body-whorl is somewhat acutely angular, narrowly rounded. The umbilicus is wide, being at least half the whole width. Surface with fine striæ, which curve backwards from the suture to the margin, and then forwards to the umbilicus. The specimens usually show numerous shallow undulations following the course of the fine striæ.

Width of a large specimen 18 lines.

Besides the form above described there are several others, which are either varieties, or closely allied species. I propose to classify them, as follows, provisionally :—

1. *P. rotundispira.*—Spire not so much elevated as that of *P. Quebecensis*, and rounded at the apex.

2. *P. Missisquoi.*—About 2 inches wide ; whorls more convex, both above and below. This form occurs at Phillipsburgh in the upper part of the limestone.

3.—A form with wide whorls, resembling *P. Canadensis*, and not distinguishable therefrom in imperfect specimens. Occurs at Phillipsburgh.

All these are closely related to *P. Americana*, *P. Progne*, *P. calcifera*, *P. Canadensis*, *P. aperta*, and many others ; different localities, apparently, having one or more varieties.

Locality and Formation.—*P. Quebecensis* and *P. rotundispira* occur at Point Lévis in limestone No. 2, Quebec Group.

Collectors.—Sir W. E. Logan ; T. Devine ; J. Richardson.

CYRTOCERAS METELLUS. (N. sp.)

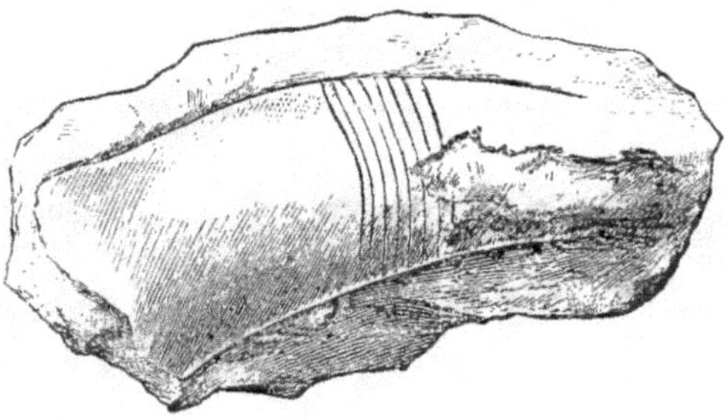

Fig. 175.

Fig. 176.

Fig. 175.—*Cyrtoceras Metellus.* Side view.
176.—*C. Dictys.* " "

Description.—Shell gently curved ; section circular, or nearly so ; septa about eighteen to the inch ; chamber of habitation proportionally very deep. Siphuucle unknown.

The specimen is $2\frac{1}{2}$ inches in length, curved on the ventral side to a radius of $2\frac{1}{4}$ inches; diameter at the aperture 11 lines, and at $1\frac{3}{4}$ inches from the aperture 8 lines; depth of chamber of habitation 14 lines.

This species resembles *C. Syphax* very closely; but as the chamber of habitation is nearly twice the depth, the form of the animal must have been different. I venture, therefore, to classify it as a distinct species, but should this separation turn out to be erroneous, I beg that both forms may be referred to *C. Metellus*.

Locality and Formation.—Point Lévis; limestone of the Quebec group.

Collectors.—R. Bell, T. C. Weston.

Cyrtoceras Dictys. (N. sp.)

Fig. 176.

Description.—Shell moderately curved; section elliptical, the dorso-ventral being, as nearly as can be ascertained, one-fourth greater than the lateral; septa between forty and fifty to the inch, with several slight undulations; shell apparently smooth.

The best specimen collected is a portion of the larger extremity. It is 11 lines in length; the dorso-ventral diameter is 7 lines at the larger extremity and 5 at the smaller; the ventral contour is arched to a radius of about 16 lines, but it is most probable that towards the apex it becomes more sharply curved.

Although a number of fragments of this species have been observed, I have not been able to ascertain the position of the siphuncle. The dimensions of the chamber of habitation are also undetermined.

This species is distinguished by its numerous thin and closely crowded septa.

Locality and Formation.—Point Lévis; limestone of the Quebec group.

Collectors.—J. Richardson, R. Bell.

Cyrtoceras Alethes. (N. sp.)

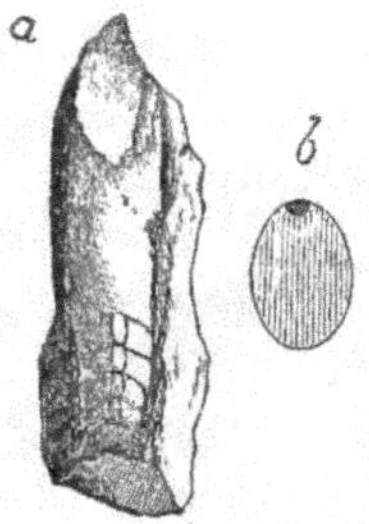

Fig. 177.

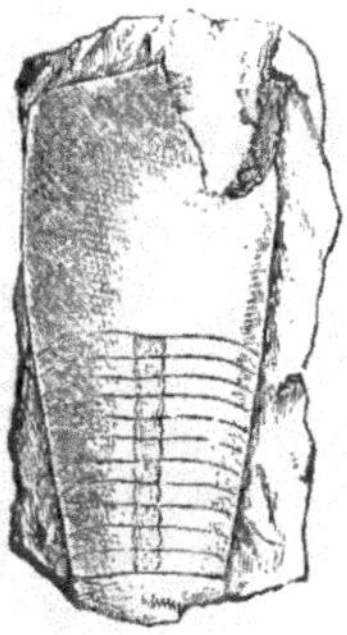

Fig. 178.

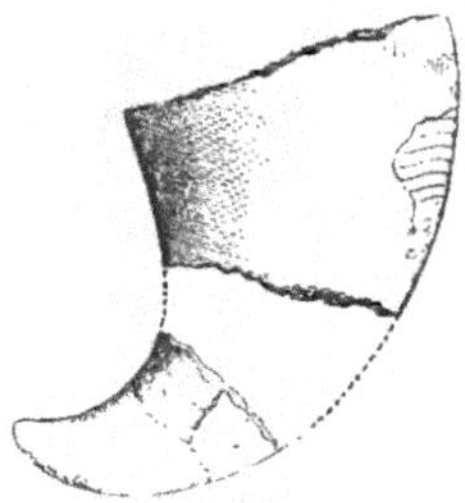

Fig. 179.

Fig. 177.—*Cyrtoceras Alethes.* *a*, ventral view ; *b*, section ; *c*, side.
178.—*C. Syphax.* Ventral view.
179.—*Cyrtocerina Mercurius.* Side view.

Description.—Shell small, slender, gradually tapering, gently curved ; section elliptical, the dorso-ventral diameter being about one-fourth, or one-third greater than the lateral ; septa about fourteen or fifteen to the inch ; siphuncle small, in contact with the shell on the ventral side. Chamber of habitation proportionately very deep. Surface unknown.

The only specimen collected is 13 lines in length ; dorso-ventral diameter at the aperture 5 lines ; lateral diameter 3½ lines ; dorso-ventral diameter at the smaller extremity of the specimen 3 lines ; depth of chamber of habitation 9 lines. It is possible that the specimen may be a little distorted by lateral compression. The diameter of the siphuncle is about half a line, and its section is not quite circular, being flattened on the ventral side, where it is in contact with the shell. The curvature of the ventral side, so far as it can be ascertained, for the portion preserved, is that of a circle with a radius of 15 lines. It is probably more sharply curved near the apex.

This species differs from all the ordinary forms of this genus found in the Lower Silurian rocks of Canada in its slender proportions and comparatively distant septa. A small species, *C. exiguum*, occurs in the Black River limestone somewhat like it, but with a circular section.

Locality and Formation.—Point Lévis ; in limestone No. 2. Quebec group.

Collector.—R. Bell.

Cyrtoceras Syphax. (N. sp.)

Fig. 178.

Description.—Shell only slightly curved; section nearly circular, the dorso-ventral diameter being a little greater than the lateral; chamber of habitation gently contracted from the middle to the aperture; siphuncle small, in contact with the shell on the ventral side; septa, eleven in seven and a half lines.

Several specimens of this species have been collected, the best preserved of which has the following dimensions: Length 16 lines; lateral diameter of the aperture 7½ lines; lateral diameter at the smaller extremity 5 lines; depth of chamber of habitation 8½ lines. The siphuncle is about a line in diameter, and its section is nearly semi-circular, being much flattened on the side next the shell.

Locality and Formation.—Point Lévis; limestone of the Quebec group.

Collectors.—J. Richardson, R. Bell.

Cyrtocerina Mercurius. (N. sp.)

Fig. 179.

Description.—Shell short, abruptly tapering, rather strongly curved; section elliptical, the dorso-ventral diameter being, as nearly as can be ascertained, one-third or one-fourth greater than the lateral. The septa, measured on the surface on the ventral side near the chamber of habitation, are about half a line distant, but on the dorsal side near the apex they must be much closer together.

Associated with the two specimens represented by fig. 179, in the same rock, were found two other fragments. One of these fragments shows a section of the siphuncle, and that its position is in contact with the shell on the dorsal side, while its dorso-ventral diameter is about three-fourths the lateral diameter of the shell. In a polished longitudinal section through this fragment, there are ten septa in the length of two lines. This would be double the number shown by the other in the same space, but in this latter the measurement gives the distance on the surface where they (the septa) come out obliquely, and are consequently not so approximated.

This species must be very closely allied to *C. typica.* The septa, as shown by one of the fragments of the former, are the same in number, in the same length as the grooves on the inside of the siphuncle of the latter.

The siphuncle of this species is larger than that of the other. The transverse sections differ in being more narrowly rounded on the ventral than on the dorsal aspect in *C. typica*, while in *C. Mercurius* both the ventral and dorsal sides have the same form of convexity.

The specimens are, however, very imperfect, and further, discoveries may render some modifications of the descriptions of these two remarkable cephalopods necessary.

The dorso-ventral diameter of one of these specimens next to the chamber of habitation is 9 lines; lateral diameter 6 lines; dorso-ventral diameter of the siphuncle in the same specimen 4 lines; lateral diameter 3 lines.

Locality and Formation.—Point Lévis; limestone of the Quebec group.

Collectors.—R. Bell, T. C. Weston.

DIKELOCEPHALUS DEVINEI. (N. sp.)

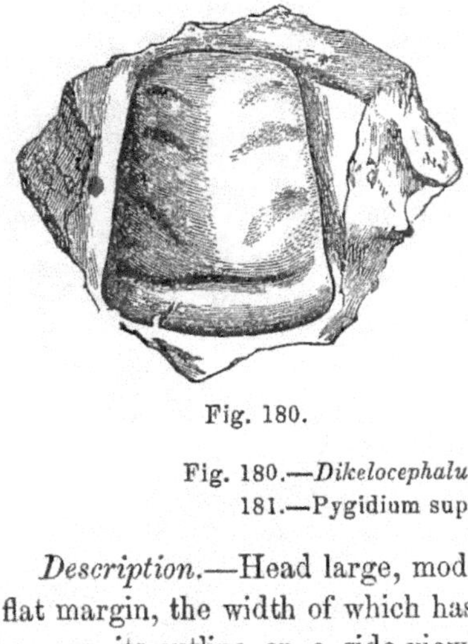

Fig. 180.

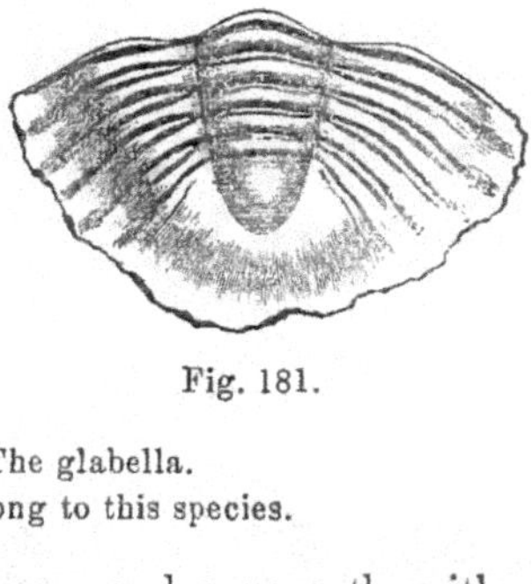

Fig. 181.

Fig. 180.—*Dikelocephalus Devinei.* The glabella.
181.—Pygidium supposed to belong to this species.

Description.—Head large, moderately convex, and apparently with a flat margin, the width of which has not been ascertained. Glabella oblong, convex, its outline on a side view uniformly arched from the front, backwards, to about the mid-length, then nearly straight; sides straight and converging towards the front, which is also nearly straight, or gently convex, and about one-fourth narrower than the base; neck furrow wide, but somewhat obscure, deepest on each side of the middle, a little turned forwards at the ends, which do not quite reach the dorsal furrows; posterior glabellar furrows, with their anterior extremities, just behind the mid-length, directed obliquely backwards and inwards at an angle of 45°; two anterior pairs of furrows, all very obscure; neck segment wide, depressed convex, with a minute tubercle in the middle. The margin of the head appears to be wide and somewhat concave. At each of the anterior angles of the glabella there is a shallow depression. The dorsal furrows are narrow and obscurely impressed. Pygidium strongly convex in the central region, the marginal third becoming gradually flattened; margin not preserved; axis narrow, conical, strongly convex, five strong rounded rings, besides the terminal one, which is about one-third the length of the whole axis and gradually declines backwards; side lobes, with the four anterior ribs well defined, and each divided into two by a deep groove, which commences close to the axis; at their outer extremities the ribs gradually die out; there are indications of a fifth and terminal pair of ribs. It is probable that the pygidium is bordered by a flat smooth margin.

Surface of the head and pygidium smooth.

Length of the largest glabella seen 14 lines; width at the neck segment 11 lines; width at the anterior margin 8 lines.

This trilobite probably attains a length of 4 or 5 inches.

The pygidium and head have not been seen in connection, but several of each were found in the same piece of stone, and so associated, that I have no doubt of their being rightly referred.

This species is closely allied to *D. magnificus*. It is dedicated to T. Devine, Esq., of the Crown Land Department.

Locality and Formation.—Point Lévis, in limestone No. 2; Quebec group.

Collectors.—Sir W. E. Logan, T. Devine, and T. C. Weston.

DIKELOCEPHALUS HISINGERI. (N. sp.)

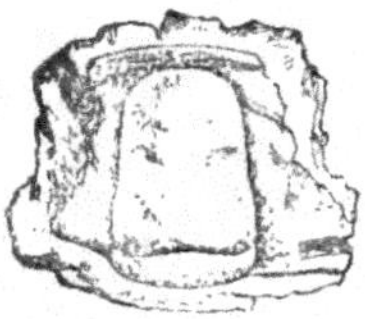

Fig, 182.

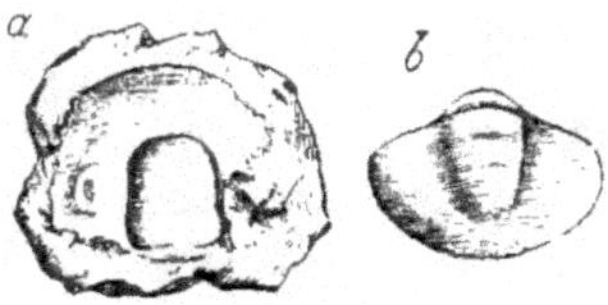

Fig. 183.

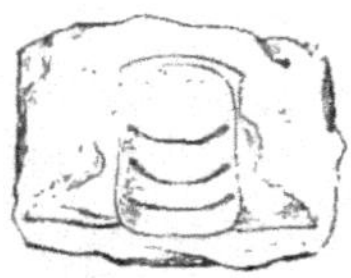

Fig. 184.

Fig. 182.—*Dikelocephalus Hisingeri.*

183.—*D. affinis*, variety of *D. Oweni.*—*a*, glabella; *b*, supposed pygidium.

184.—*D. Sesostris.*

Description.—Glabella oblong, truncato-conical, narrowed towards the front, convex; the outline on a side view rather abruptly elevated in front, then gently arched to the neck furrow; sides straight; anterior angles rounded ; front margin gently convex ; dorsal furrows well defined to the front ; neck-furrow most strongly impressed on each side of the middle ; posterior glabellæ-furrows oblique, situated behind the mid-length ; two pairs of anterior furrows ; all the furrows very obscure. The anterior margin of the head is thin, narrow, destitute of a rim, and turned upwards. The eyes appear to be small, and situated on a line drawn across the glabella, a little behind the anterior third. They are distant from the dorsal furrow about one-fourth the width of the glabella, and have a well defined ocular ridge.

Length of the best preserved glabella 7 lines ; width at neck segment 5½ lines ; width at the front margin 4 lines ; width of the margin of the head in front of the glabella 1 line ; distance of the eye from the side of the glabella 1½ lines.

The form of the glabella in this species is almost exactly the same as that of *D. Devinei*, and yet I think the two are distinct, for the following reasons :—

One of the specimens of *D. Devinei* shows that the margin of the head in front of the glabella has a width equal to one-half the whole length of the glabella, whereas in this species it is only one-seventh.

Locality and Formation.—Point Lévis, in limestone No. 1 ; Quebec group.

Collector.—T. C. Weston.

Dikelocephalus affinis. (N. sp.)

Fig. 183, *a*, *b*.

Description.—Glabella oblong, sub-quadrate, length one-fifth greater than the width; sides straight and nearly parallel ; front angles rounded; front margin gently convex. The front margin of the head is gently convex, and has a width equal to nearly one-third the length of the glabella. It has a row of small punctures, at one-third its width from the glabella, as there is in *D. Oweni*. There do not appear to be any glabellar furrows. The glabella is very gently convex, and there does not seem to be any marginal rim to the front of the head.

The pygidium, found with it, is convex and has a broad obtusely conical axis, one-third the whole width and two-thirds the whole length. Front margin gently convex, and all behind the angles uniformly rounded. Length two-thirds the width. Both axis and side lobes are nearly smooth, but exhibit faint indications of segmentation. It is not at all certain that this pygidium belongs to the species.

This may be only a variety of *D. Oweni*; but owing to the greater proportional width and smoothness of the glabella, and the absence of a marginal rim to the head, it has a different aspect.

Locality and Formation.—Point Lévis; in limestone No. 2, Quebec group.

Collector.—T. Devine, Esq.

DIKELOCEPHALUS SESOSTRIS. (N. sp.)

Fig 184.

Description.—Glabella oblong, sub-cylindrical; most convex along the median line; front abrnptly but not strongly elevated; outline, on a side view, nearly straight for two-thirds the length, then rather suddenly curved down to the front; sides a little concave about the mid-length, nearly straight and parallel; anterior angles rounded; front margin gently convex or straight in the middle. Neck furrow extending all across and turned forwards at the extremities, not quite reaching the dorsal furrows; posterior furrows, with their anterior extremities, a little behind the middle, extending across with a strong backward curve; anterior furrows, with their anterior extremities, just behind a line drawn across at the anterior third, then curving backwards, sometimes absent or only impressed near the sides. In general all the furrows terminate without reaching the sides of the glabella. The dorsal furrow is distinctly impressed, but very narrow. The eyes are small, their centres situated just in front of the mid-length, and almost in contact with the side of the glabella. The anterior margin of the head is narrow, thin, and turned upwards, as it is in *D. Hisingeri.*

Length of glabella 5 lines; width 4 lines; width of the front margin of the head ½ a line.

This species, together with the two that I have placed in the genus *Arionellus*, under the names *A. cylindricus* and *A. subclavatus*,* will certainly fall into the newly proposed genus *Ptychaspis*,† if that generic name be sustained. *Ptychaspis* seems to me to differ scarcely at all from *Bathynotus.* ‡ A species, almost identical with *D. Sesostris*, occurs in the upper part of the Potsdam at Whitehall, New York.

Locality and Formation.—Point Lévis; in limestone, No. 1, Quebec group.

Collectors.—T. Devine Esq., T. C. Weston.

---

* Geology of Canada, p. 237.

† *Ptychaspis* (Hall). 16th *Rep. Reg.* N. Y., p. 170, 1863. A genus proposed to include species of the type of *D. Miniscaensis* (Owen). Potsdam sandstone.

‡ *Bathynotus* (Hall). 13th *Rep. Reg.* N. Y., p. 117, 1861.

DIKELOCEPHALUS SELECTUS. (N. sp.)

Description.—The form of the glabella in this species is the same as that of *D. Sesostris*, with the following differences: The neck furrow and the posterior glabellar furrow are straighter, and terminate in the dorsal furrow. The width of the front margin of the head before the glabella, is one-fourth the length of the glabella, and has a depressed convex rim, one line wide, in a specimen in which the glabella is five and a half lines in length. The eye is somewhat larger than that of *D. Sesostris*, and with its centre situated just behind a line drawn across the head at the mid-length.

These differences give to the glabella a distinct aspect, but further discoveries may show that this, with the one mentioned as occurring at Whitehall, in New York, are all varieties of *D. Sesostris*.

Locality.—In the same bed with *D. Sesostris*.

DIKELOCEPHALUS MISSISQUOI. (N. sp.)

Description.—Pygidium resembling that of *D. magnificus;* anterior margin rounded in the middle half, then curving backwards and gradually merging into the sides, which become nearly straight, and spreading outwards at an angle of about 30° with the longitudinal axis; with this direction they extend backwards a short distance beyond a line drawn across at the apex of the axis or middle lobe. The posterior margin of the pygidium is not preserved in the specimen. Axis short, conical, convex, with apparently three rounded segments, besides a terminal one, which is triangular and gradually merges into the general surface behind. Side lobes gently convex in the central region, gradually becoming flat behind. There are four depressed convex ribs on each side, all spreading a little outwards.

Length 6 lines, and as the posterior margin is not preserved, when perfect it was a little longer; greatest width, on a line drawn across at 4 lines from the front margin 9 lines; length of axis about 3 lines; width of the same at the front margin 2 lines.

As before stated, this pygidium resembles that of *D. magnificus*. It differs in having the ribs at the side nearly flat and considerably divergent, giving a much greater proportional width.

Locality and Formation.—Phillipsburgh; (limestone) B 2, section Geo. of Can., p. 844, Quebec group.

Collector.—Dr. J. M. Hall.

Dikelocephalus pauper. (N. sp.)

Description.—Glabella small, truncato-conical, narrowed towards the front, moderately convex, the outline on a side view nearly straight, or gently convex for two-thirds the length, then abruptly curved down to the front; sides nearly straight, converging forwards; front gently convex, or nearly straight in the middle; anterior angles narrowly rounded; neck furrow extending all across, the extremities turned forwards, but scarcely touching the dorsal furrow; anterior furrows represented by two small oblique pits on each side; neck segment wide, a little turned forwards at the ends. The margin of the head in front of the glabella, is in width about one-sixth of the length of the glabella, and has a thickened rim or border.

Length of largest glabella seen 3½ lines; width at the neck segment 3 lines; width at the front 2¼ lines; width of the margin, in front of the glabella ¾ of a line.

This species is of the same type with *D. Sesostris*, but differs from it in being always smaller, in having the glabella narrowed towards the front, or truncato-conical instead of oblong, and in the form of the glabellar furrows which do not extend across, but are small but distinct pits. It is more common than *D. Sesostris.*

Locality and Formation.—Point Lévis; limestone, No. 1; Quebec group.

Collectors.—Sir W. E. Logan, T. Devine, Esq., J. Richardson, R. Bell.

Genus Loganellus. (Devine.)

Generic Characters.—The trilobites, for which this genus was proposed, are ovate, with a conical or sub-cylindrical glabella, having two or three more or less distinctly marked, usually oblique furrows on each side; facial suture behind the eye curving outwards, and cutting the posterior margin inside of the angle; in front of the eye, also curving more or less outward to the front margin. Thorax broad; side lobes flat; pleuræ about twelve; pleural groove running along the middle, nearly to the extremities. Pygidium with a well-defined axis; side lobes depressed, and with from four to six ribs.

The genus is allied to both *Olenus* and *Dikelocephalus*. It differs from the former in being composed of larger species, and in having the facial suture curving outwards in front of the eye. Angelin has described the Swedish species of *Olenus* under eight sub-genera, and this might form a ninth, differing as much from any of them as they do from each other. Several of those which I have placed in *Dikelocephalus* will probably fall into this genus, if it shall be sustained, but at present I do not wish to change their generic references until more is known about them. The typical species of *Dikelocephalus* have the last glabellar furrow, and sometimes the second one, extending all across. This genus was proposed by Mr. Devine, in April, 1863, but the species was placed provisionally in the genus *Olenus*. I think it best to leave it there until we shall have obtained more information concerning the affinities of the numerous species of this group, now only known to us by fragments. It seems probable that some of the species from the Potsdam sandstone, referred by Dr. Shumard and Prof. Hall, to *Conocephalites*, may belong to *Loganellus*. The following is Mr. Devine's description:*

OLENUS ? LOGANI. (Devine.)

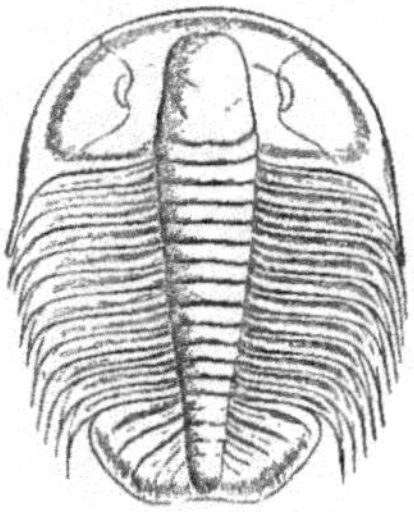

Fig. 185.

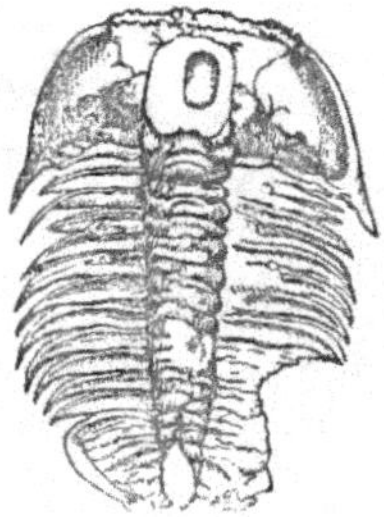

Fig. 186.

Fig. 185.—*O. Logani.* The anterior part of the glabella, in this figure, is slightly too narrow.

Fig. 186.—An imperfect specimen, shewing the hypostoma in place.

"*Description.*—The general form is oval. Head, exclusive of spines semicircular, more than twice as wide as long; truncate in front, and prominently convex in the middle, with a narrow equal border, one half a line in width, extended at the posterior angles with the free cheeks into moderate diverging spines; posterior margin marked by a shallow furrow, reaching from the glabella outward to the free cheeks; eyes not large, smooth, and equi-distant from the front and posterior margins, and about one line from the glabella; the ocular ridge prominent, extending from the eye obliquely forward to the glabella, meeting the latter at about one line from the front thereof; facial suture running obliquely from the eye

* Description of a new Trilobite, from the Quebec group; by T. DEVINE, F.R.G.S., C. L. Dept. Quebec: Can. Nat. and Geol., vol. 8, p. 95, April, 1863.

and cutting the front and posterior margins far outwards. The free cheeks are not quite so smooth as the central lobe of the head, but no radiation or other marking is visible.

"Glabella bell-shaped; width, less than one-third of the entire head; broadly rounded in front, reaching nearly to the front margin; depressed convex at the neck lobe; neck furrow well defined, extending across, and directed obliquely forward at each side—two oblique glabellar furrows at each side in front of the latter, making an angle, anteriorly, of about 45° with the axis; the furrows are well marked interiorly, but very obscure at the sides, and are separated by about one-half the width of the glabella, forming three lateral lobes of nearly equal size, each larger than the neck lobe. In some specimens there are three glabellar furrows on each side, the front one making a greater angle, anteriorly with the axis, than either of the others.

"Pleuræ twelve; moderately convex outward from the axial furrow, each marked by an equal deep groove to the tips, which are of a horny aspect, recurved and extended into long spines; sides parallel as far back as the eighth segment, then gradually converging to the pygidium.

"Axis convex, gradually tapering to the extremity of the tail, about two-thirds of the width of the pleuræ anteriorly—less at the pygidium; twelve body rings, and five or six caudal joints; the body rings notched above, posteriorly, and slightly swelled at the axial furrows.

"Pygidium entire, semi-circular, truncate behind; lateral lobes depressed convex, on a level with the pleuræ; four broad ribs on each side of the middle lobe, recurved towards the extremities; margin smooth and entire, anterior angles moderately rounded.

"*Dimensions of largest specimen:*

Entire length	16 lines.
Length of head	5 "
" of thorax	8 "
" of axis of tail	3 "
Width at base of head	11 "
" at eighth segment	10 "
" at front of pygidium	8 "
" at axis at same place	1½ "
Length of glabella	4 "
Width at neck lobe	3½ "
" at front of glabella	2½ "
" between the eyes	4 "
" of margin in front of glabella	0½ "
" of border	0¼ "

" *Locality.*—Point Lévis; band of limestone A 3, referred to in Sir W. E. Logan's 'Remarks on the Fauna of the Quebec group of rocks and the Primordial Zone of Canada,' addressed to Mr. J. Barrande, dated Montreal, 31st December, 1860, and printed in the Canada Naturalist and Geologist of that year. 'I have in the mean time referred this species to *Olenus*, although at one time inclined to refer it to *Cononcephalites* (*Sub-genus*). Should it be found necessary to institute an intermediate generic form, whatever place naturalists may assign it in the animal kingdom, I propose that it be named *Loganellus Quebecensis*.'

" Dedicated to Sir W. E. LOGAN, F.R.S., &c., &c., Director of the Canadian Geological Survey."

MENOCEPHALUS SALTERI. (Devine.)

MENOCEPHALUS SALTERI. (Devine.) *Can. Nat. and Geo.*, vol. viii, p. 210, June, 1863.

Fig. 187.

Fig 187.—*Menocephalus Salteri.* (Devine.) A specimen perfect with the exception of the moveable checks. Enlarged two diameters.

Description.—" Form oblong-oval. Entire length three lines, and width at posterior margin of the head one and one-fifth line; front of head and posterior margin of tail, broadly rounded; sides parallel.

" Head semi-circular, two-fifths of the entire length, strongly convex, posterior margin marked by a well-defined furrow, which curves round the lateral angles anteriorly.

" Glabella ovate, narrow at the base, and broadly rounded in front, extending anteriorly beyond the fixed cheeks, prominently convex with a very narrow flat rim forming an arch round the front.

" Thoracic segments six or seven, flat, lying close to each other, with a broad deep groove extending outwards to the tips, which are bent down.

" Axis—tapering regularly from the front of the head to the posterior margin of the tail, convex, as wide as the pleuræ in front and less posteriorly; the rings of the axis run into the grooves of the pleuræ, marked by a deep grove.

" Tail semi-circular, the lateral lobes marked by two or three ribs with a deep groove as in the pleuræ, owing to which and the smallness of the specimen, it is difficult to perceive the line of separation between the body and the tail.

"The eyes and free cheeks are absent in all specimens.

"Affinities—in form and number of pleuræ it resembles *Cyphoniscus socialis* (Salter), but differs from it in details of structure; the pleuræ are of a different type, having the groove running along the middle, straight outwards, and not obliquely outwards and downwards, as in Salter's figure. The pygidium is entire, but it is as deep grooved as the pleuræ, the whole form is not so convex, and the pleuræ are not facetted. It appears from the outward edge of the fixed cheeks that the facial suture cuts the margin in front and posterior margin far outward. The head of *Menocephalus Salteri* resembles closely that of *Bathyurus Saffordi*, in the flat arched border in front of the glabella and in the three convex lobes into which the head is divided.

"Dedicated to J. W. Salter, Esq., Palæontologist of the Geological Survey of Great Britain.

"This beautiful little crustacean was found at Point Lévis in the Quebec group of rocks, in the same band of limestone as *Olenus Logani*.'

Bathyurus strenuus. (N. sp.)

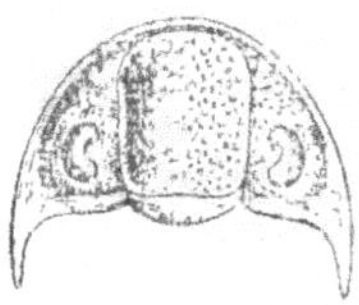

Fig. 188.

Fig. 189.

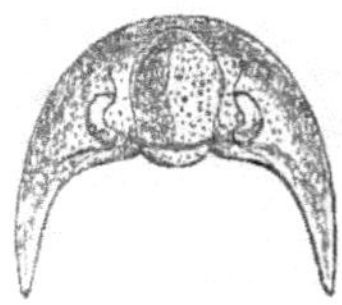

Fig. 190.

Fig. 188.—*Bathyurus strenuus*. The head.
189.—*B. arcuatus*. Side view of the head. Fig. 190.—Upper side of the same.

Description.—Head convex, broadly rounded in front, with short posterior spines; length nearly two-thirds the width. Glabella large, oblong, nearly as long as the head, convex, most elevated just in front of the neck furrow, thence arched down to the front margin; sides parallel; front angles rounded, front margin somewhat straight in the middle; neck furrow narrow, well defined all across and continued on the cheeks beyond the eyes; dorsal furrow slightly impressed but distinct along the sides of the glabella to the front margin; neck segment depressed convex, widest in the middle. Eyes moderate, reniform; their length nearly half the width of the glabella; about one-third or one-half their own length from the sides of the glabella: their anterior angles close to a line drawn across the head at the mid-length. There is a narrow wire-like rim all round the edge of the head. The cheeks and eyes rather strongly elevated. Surface in some specimens smooth and in others tuberculated except near the margin.

Length of the head 6½ lines; width across the neck-furrow 11 lines; length of glabella 6¼ lines; width of the same 4 lines; length of the eye 1¾ line.

Locality and Formation.—Near St. Antoine above Quebec, in a boulder along with *Subulites Psyche:* Quebec group.

Collector.—J. Richardson.

BATHYURUS ARCUATUS. (N. sp.)

Fig. 190.

Description.—Head convex, broadly rounded in front, posterior angles produced backwards forming long flat spines. Glabella convex, sub-angular along the middle, narrowed from the anterior third backwards, rounded in front, nearly the whole length of the head. Neck furrow all across the glabella and continued on the cheeks beyond the eyes. Neck segment moderately convex, projecting backwards in the middle. Eyes prominent, reniform, one third the whole length of the head, close to the neck furrow, about half their own length distant from the side of the glabella. The margin of the head is thin and abruptly turned upwards in front of the glabella, a concave space just within the edge extends all round and is continued into the posterior spines. Surface of glabella and part of the cheeks around the eyes tuberculated; margin and spines apparently smooth.

Length of the largest head collected 4¾ lines; width of the same at the neck furrow 9¾ lines; the cheek spines are about the length of the head.

Locality and Formation.—Near St. Antoine above Quebec, in a boulder with *Subulites Psyche:* Quebec group.

Collector.—J. Richardson.

BATHYURUS PERSPICATOR. (N. sp.

Fig. 191.

191.—*B. perspicator.*

Description.—Head convex, broadly rounded and with a short rounded projection in front of the glabella; eyes large; cheeks with short posterior spines, directed a little outwards. Glabella large, nearly as long as the head, convex, sometimes flattened between the eyes, thence arched down to the front; sides in the posterior two-thirds or three-fourths nearly parallel, slightly converging backwards; front somewhat angularly rounded; neck furrow narrow extending all across and continued on the cheek beyond the eyes; neck segment depressed convex, widest in the middle. Eyes reniform, close to the side of the glabella, a little more than one-third the whole length of the head; their posterior angles about one-fifth their own length from the neck furrow. Surface of the glabella smooth, cheeks sometimes tuberculated.

Length of a specimen 4 lines; width across the neck furrow 6 lines; length of the glabella 3½ lines; width of the same between the anterior angle of the eyes 2½ lines; width at neck furrow 2 lines; length of posterior spines about 2 lines; length of the eye 1½ line.

Locality and Formation.—Near St. Antoine above Quebec, in a boulder with *Subulites Psyche:* Quebec group.

Collector.—J. Richardson.

Cheirurus solitarius. (N. sp.)

Description.—This species is founded on a single small specimen consisting of the head and seven segments of the thorax, the whole being only three lines in length. Head convex, semi-circular, the posterior angles with short spines; glabella strongly convex, abruptly tumid in front, greatest elevation a little behind the mid-length; front rounded; sides straight for two-thirds the length, sub-parallel, slightly converging backwards; anterior angles broadly rounded; neck furrow all across; two glabellar furrows on each side dividing all of the glabella in front of the neck furrow into three nearly equal parts; the anterior furrows nearly at right angles; the posterior entering obliquely backwards and distinct one-third across, and then obscurely marked backwards to the neck furrow; all the furrows extending about one-third across. Eyes reniform, their length equal to half the width of the glabella, their posterior angles about half their own length from the neck furrow and about the same distance from the side of the glabella. The cheeks are rather small; the terminal spines appear to be two-thirds the length of the head; the glabella is full one third the width of the head, and extends the whole length of it, and even seems to overhang the margin. The axis of the thorax seems to be wider than the side lobes, but the latter are obscurely preserved in the specimen.

Length of the head 1½ line; width at the neck furrow 3 lines.

Locality and Formation.—Near St. Antoine, above Quebec in a boulder with *Subulites Psyche:* Quebec group.

Collector.—J. Richardson.

6.—*New species of Fossils from the Quebec Group in the northern part of Newfoundland.*

The north-western coast of Newfoundland, from Cape Norman in the Straits of Belle Isle to Bonne Bay on the Gulf of St. Lawrence, a distance of about 180 miles, is composed altogether of Lower Silurian limestones, slates, quartzites, and sandstones. These rocks form a belt of low country lying along the coast and extending inland to the foot of a range of mountains which, at least in the southern part, are composed of Laurentian gneiss. The width of this belt, of Silurian rock, for about 100 miles north of Bonne Bay appears to be from 5 to 10 miles, but further north it becomes broader, and may spread across to the eastern shore of the island.

The fossils, as well as the stratigraphical position, shew that these rocks belong to the Potsdam and Quebec groups. The Potsdam group has here a thickness of about 2000 feet, and is composed, for the greater part, of sandstones, quartzites and slates, the remainder being dolomites and limestones. The Quebec group is 6600 feet in thickness, the lower 3200 feet, consisting almost altogether of limestones above which there is a deposit of 1400 feet of sandstones, slates and conglomerate limestones, and this in its turn, is overlaid by 2000 feet of greenish sandstones and red shales. The following table of the different members of this series of rocks is abridged from the measured sections published in the *Geology of Canada*, on pages 865–868, 869–871, and 879:

QUEBEC GROUP.

Q.	Greenish sandstones and red shales.... Sillery......................		2000
P.	Grey and white limestone conglomerates with much black shale. The black shale holds the compound graptolites, and the limestone some of the trilobites and other fossils of Point Lévis. Many of the species are identical with those of Division N,............	700	
O.	Grey calcareous sandstones and black shales,......................	700	
			1400
N.	Black bituminous limestones, ...	277	
M.	Light bluish-grey limestones, ...	658	
L.	Light bluish-grey limestones............................	191	
K.	Grey and whitish magnesian limestones,..........................	100	
I.	Light yellowish-gray magnesian limestones, ...	135	
			1361

In the above five divisions (I to N inclusive) the Gasteropoda and Cephalopoda have the aspect partly of Calciferous and partly of Black River and Trenton fossils. One Chazy Brachiopod (*Camerella varians*) occurs in N. One trilobite (*Asaphus canalis*), a calciferous and Chazy species, occurs in I, K, L and in G, H, below. Several of the trilobites in M and N occur at Point Lévis. The bulk of the whole fauna is new.

H. Greyish-blue limestones, ...	265	
G. Dark grey limestones, ...	400	
F. Dark grey geodiferous limestones, ...	500	
E. Dark grey limestones, ...	500	
D. Magnesian limestones, ...	174	
		1839

These five divisions (D to H inclusive) represent the Calciferous formation.

POTSDAM GROUP.

C. Quartzites, limestones, dolomites and blackish-blue soft shales,.......	932	
B. Quartzites, limestones, dolomites and micaceo-arenaceous shales,.....	483	
A. Blackish blue soft shale with quartzites in the upper half............	605	
		2020
		8620

In this table the thickness of the rocks, in all the divisions from A to G inclusive, is given as ascertained at Bonne Bay, and for I, K, L, M and N as measured at Table Head. The volume of the same strata in the region further north is not so great. The Potsdam group at the Straits of Belle Isle, for instance, is only 1147 feet in thickness, whereas at Bonne Bay it is 2020, the difference being made up by a greater development of shale at the latter locality. Divisions O and P were measured at Cow Head, and the greenish sandstones and red shales of Q at the south arm of Bonne Bay. For further details relating to the structure of the whole region, from Bonne Bay to the Straits of Belle Isle, reference must be made to the *Geology of Canada.*

For a catalogue of the fossils and remarks on their distribution, see the end of this article.

PROTOZOA.

Among the fossils collected in the limestones of the Quebec group, in the northern part of Newfoundland, are fragments of several species resembling, in their external characters, many of those of the Mesozoic rocks, which are usually considered to be sponges. The specimens are so imperfect that their internal structure cannot be determined with anything like the precision required to decide upon their true position. They appear to me, however, to differ from all the known genera, and I shall therefore dispose of them provisionally, for the present, as follows :—

Genus CALATHIUM. (N. gen.)

Generic characters.—The species for the reception of which this genus is proposed, have a cylindro-turbinate form, and are perforated by small tubular canals, which are arranged in longitudinal and transverse rows, so as to give to the mass a more or less regularly reticulated appearance. The apertures of the canals are round, oval, or quadrangular. The cup seems to be deep. Structure of the partitions between the canals, unknown.

CALATHIUM FORMOSUM. (N. sp.)

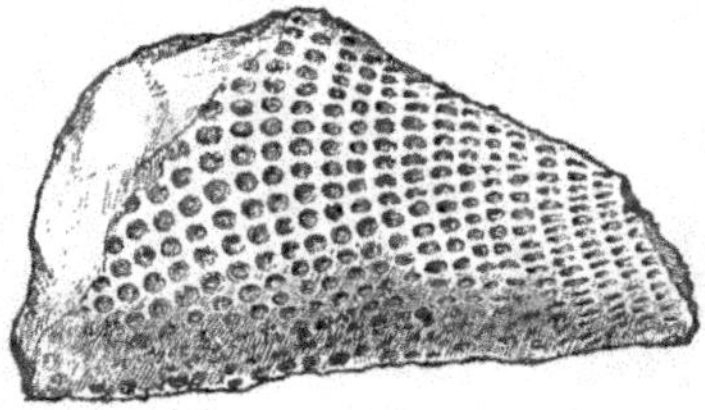

Fig. 192.

Fig. 193.

Fig. 192.—*Calathium formosum.*
Fig. 193.—*C——— affine.*

Description.—The only specimen of this species, that has been collected, is cylindro-turbinate, length 21 lines, diameter at the larger extremity 14 lines, and at the smaller 4 lines. The apertures are nearly 1 line wide in the upper part, and half their own width distant from each other. In the lower part they are somewhat smaller and closer together. The longitudinal rows ascend obliquely, inclining a little to the left. The transverse rows cross the others at right angles.

Locality and Formation.—G, Cape Norman, Newfoundland: Quebec group.

Collector.—J. Richardson.

CALATHIUM AFFINE. (N. sp.)

Fig. 193.

Description.—The specimen is about 9 lines in length, and tapers from 9 lines in diameter at the larger end, to 3 lines at the smaller. There are six transverse rows of tubes in three lines. The longitudinal rows appear to be somewhat more numerous, but owing to the condition of preservation they are not clearly seen. The fossil seems to be composed of a series of rough transverse plates, but this is owing to the circumstance of the partitions between the longitudinal rows having been destroyed.

This species seems to be quite distinct from *C. formosum*, in having the tubes smaller and closer together, and in tapering more abruptly.

Locality and Formation.—G, Cape Norman, Newfoundland: Quebec group.

Collector.—J. Richardson.

CALATHIUM ANSTEDI. (N. sp.)

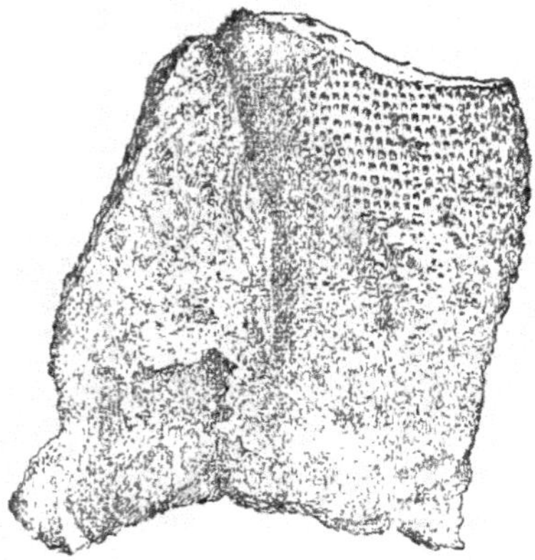

Fig. 194.

Fig. 194.—*Calathium Anstedi.* A fragment consisting of two individuals growing from the same base.

Description.—Turbinate, conical, expanding to the width of sixteen lines in a length of two inches, several individuals sometimes growing from the same base. Cup deep and narrow. Surface (and probably the whole mass) reticulated with nearly square canals, of which there are from four to six in the width of two lines, the apertures separated by thin walls, about one-fourth of a line in thickness. The rows of pores ascend the sides in straight lines, or nearly straight. The transverse rows are at right angles to the vertical rows.

Of this species only three specimens were collected, the best preserved of which is represented by fig. 194. This consists of the lower portions of two individuals which grew together. Length of the largest 2 inches; width at the upper extremity (broken off) 16 lines. The cup at this place seems to be 6 lines in diameter, and the walls 4 lines in thickness.

Another specimen is $2\frac{1}{2}$ inches across the larger extremity, and must have been from 5 to 6 inches in length.

Locality and Formation.—H, Pistolet Bay on Schooner Island, Newfoundland: Quebec group.

Collector.—J. Richardson.

CALATHIUM FITTONI. (N. sp.)

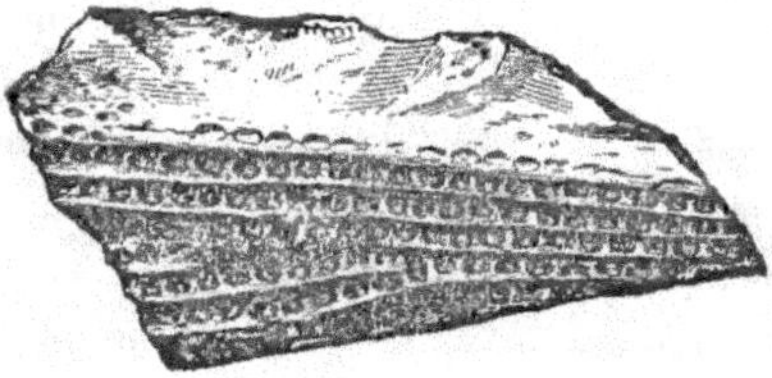

Fig. 195.

Fig. 195.—*Calathium Fittoni.* A fragment of the inside of the cup.

Description.—Elongate, apparently sub-cylindrical, gradually expanding. There are five or six vertical rows of canals in a width of six lines, and about the same number of transverse rows. The apertures are sub-ovate or sub-quadrangular. The walls between the vertical rows are about half a line in thickness, but those between the transverse rows are not so thick.

This species, judging from several fragments, is more than 4 inches in length, and probably 2 inches in greatest width. It may belong to a different genus.

The best specimen is a fragment of the inside of the cup. It is represented in fig. 195.

Locality and Formation.—K, Point Rich, Newfoundland : Quebec group.

Collector.—J. Richardson.

Genus TRACHYUM. (N. gen.)

Generic characters.—The species on which this genus is proposed have a close texture without large canals. One of the species has a deep cup, but the other is a rudely cylindrical mass without any internal cavity. As it is evidently a fragment, it is most probably the basal portion broken off below the cup. In case it should turn out to belong to a different genus, I beg that the name may be retained for species congeneric with the best preserved of our specimens, *T. Cyathiforme.*

TRACHYUM CYATHIFORME. (N. sp.)

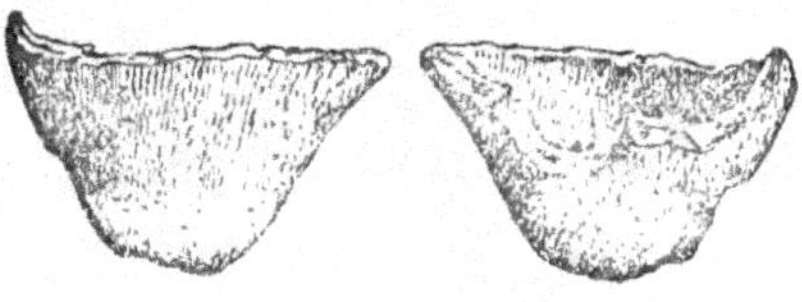

Fig. 196.

Fig. 196.—*Trachyum Cyathiforme.* Two views of the same specimen.

Description.—Obtusely turbinate, expanding to the width of twelve lines at a height of nine lines; base obtusely rounded; cup wide and deep; walls thin. The substance appears to be composed of thin parallel fibres running from the base upwards, about twelve in the width of one line. The thickness of the walls in a specimen nine lines in height and twelve in width is about one line at the margin, and two lines at the bottom. The cup therefore occupies nearly the whole bulk.

Locality and Formation.—G, Cape Norman, Newfoundland: Quebec group.

Collector.—J. Richardson.

TRACHYUM RUGOSUM. (N. sp.)

Description.—The only specimen collected is a rudely cylindrical mass three inches in length and eighteen lines in diameter. It has three or four deep engirdling constrictions, and is composed of the same fibrous structure as *T. Cyathiforme*, with which it was found in the same bed.

The above name is proposed for it provisionally.

ZOOPHYTA.

It is remarkable that throughout so vast a series of fossiliferous limestones as that of the Quebec group, there should be an almost total absence of corals. Four species only have been detected, and these are represented by only eleven fragments, in a collection of fossils which numbers more than a thousand specimens. Of these, the only one that can be certainly determined is *Stenopora fibrosa* (Goldfuss); one good specimen was found in Division H, at Table Head, and another in P, Cow Head: the latter at least 2000 feet above the former. At Cow Head there were collected some fragments of what seems to be a species of *Petraia* allied to *P. corniculum*, but the specimens are very obscurely preserved, and it is quite possible that they may belong to one of the genera of sponges, *Archeocyathus* or *Calathium*.

The other two species appear to belong to the genus *Stromatopora*. They are the following:

STROMATOPORA COMPACTA. (Billings.)

A single specimen, not distinguishable from this species (see *ante*, p. 55,) was found in Division L, at Point Rich.

STROMATOPORA RUGOSA. (Hall.)

Specimens of a species, which appears to be only a variety of *S. rugosa*, were collected in Division G, Cape Norman.

I have placed the genus *Stromatopora* here instead of among the Sponges, as it appears to me, from some recent examinations that I have made, to be a coral allied to *Fistulipora*.

CRINOIDEÆ.

A few fragments of crinoidal columns were collected at different levels, from Division G, upwards. No remains of *Cystideæ* were collected, and only one star-fish,—described below.

ASTERIADÆ.

STENASTER HUXLEYI. (N. sp.)

Fig. 197.

Fig. 197.—*Stenaster Huxleyi.* View of the upper side of the only specimen collected.

Description.—Deeply stellate, four or five inches across ; body small, less than half an inch in diameter ; rays long, flexuous, sub-cylindrical, apparently angulated along the medium line on the upper side, uniformly tapering to an acute point. On the dorsal side the rays are covered by a multitude of small sub-angular plates, each from one-fourth to one-third of a line wide. The central part of the body is not well preserved in the only specimen collected; but it is evident from a view of the plates which remain, that they are here larger and more convex than those of the rays.

Diameter of the body 5 lines. Length of each ray $1\frac{5}{8}$ inches. Width of the rays at their junction with the body 3 lines. Depth of the rays from the dorsal to the ventral side of the body apparently somewhat less than the width. The total breadth of the specimen, if the rays were straightened out, would thus be about $4\frac{1}{4}$ inches.

From the manner in which the rays are curved, it is evident that they possessed a considerable amount of flexibility. The specimen is somewhat distorted by pressure, but a small portion of one of the rays near the body seems to retain its natural shape, and it is here obtusely angulated along the median line. The transverse section of the ray should be, therefore, sub-pentagonal. There is still, however, some doubt on this point. The under side is unknown.

Dedicated to the distinguished Naturalist Prof. T. H. HUXLEY.

Formation and Locality.—Point Rich, Newfoundland: Quebec group.

Collector.—J. Richardson.

BRYOZOA.

No Bryozoa have been collected at Newfoundland.

BRACHIOPODA.

LINGULA NYMPHA. (N. sp.)

(Compare *L. Philomela,* ante, p. 49.)

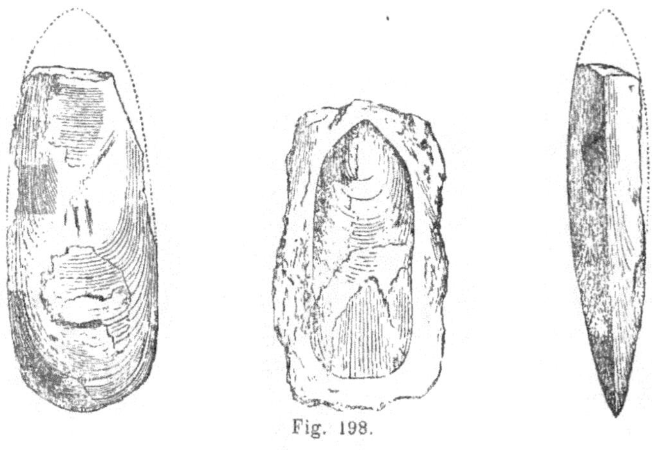

Fig. 198.

Fig. 198.—*Lingula Nympha.* Views of two specimens.

Description.—Very elongate, ovate; width to the length about as 9 to 24; front broadly rounded, with a portion in the middle straight; sides straight and parallel; apex of dorsal valve about 90°; cardinal slopes on each side of the beak nearly straight, or gently convex, forming an obtuse rounded angle with the sides at about one-fourth the length. The shell is strongly convex in the upper half, and wedge-shaped in the lower half. Surface concentrically marked, with fine striæ, and a few obscure radiating lines, as in most species of this genus.

Length of large specimen 2 inches; width 9 lines. This species is closely allied to *L. Philomela* (ante, p. 49), but has the sides straighter, is proportionately more convex in the upper half, and is destitute of the groove along the median line.

It is not so nearly pentagonal as *L. Lyelli.*

Locality and Formation.—N, Table Head, Newfoundland: Quebec group.

Collector.—J. Richardson.

Lingula Iole. (N. sp.)

Fig. 199.

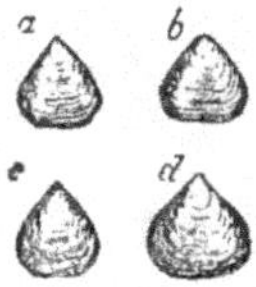

Fig. 200.

Fig. 199.—*Lingula Iole.* *a, b, c, d, e,* views of five different specimens.
200.—*L. Cyane.* *a, b, c, d,* views of four different specimens.

Description.—Shell small, ovate, ventral valve longer and more acute in the rostral half than the dorsal; apical angle from 45° to 60°; greatest width usually at about one-fourth the length from the front, thence tapering to the beaks with gently convex sides; front angles evenly rounded; front margin obtusely rounded. Dorsal valve with the beak obtuse, and a rather convex umbo. Both valves rather strongly and uniformly convex; the ventral valve sometimes obscurely carinated on approaching the beak. Surface obscurely striated, presenting a somewhat smooth shining aspect.

Length of ventral valve $3\frac{1}{2}$ lines; width $2\frac{1}{2}$ lines. Length of dorsal valve $2\frac{3}{4}$ lines; width $2\frac{1}{2}$ lines.

This species is closely allied to *L. Cyane*, and occurs along with it in the same beds, but differs in being more uniformly convex, in not being so wide, and in not presenting the sub-pentagonal aspect of that species.

Locality and Formation.—P, four miles north-east from Portland Creek, Newfoundland: Quebec group.

Collector.—J. Richardson.

Lingula Cyane. (N. sp.)

Fig. 200, *a–d*.

Description.—Shell small, sub-ovate or obscurely pentagonal. Ventral valve longer than the dorsal; beak acute: apical angle about 60°; greatest width below the mid-length; the upper half uniformly tapering, with nearly straight margins to the beak; sides in the lower half gently convex and sub-parallel; anterior angles rounded; a portion in the middle of the front margin nearly straight. The dorsal valve is a little shorter than the ventral, and more obtuse in the upper half. Both valves are rather strongly convex, but slightly flattened along the median line from the mid-length to the front margin. Surface with fine concentric striæ scarcely visible to the naked eye, and with a few larger undulations of growth. One specimen, under the magnifier, shews fine radiating striæ.

Length of ventral valve 3½ lines; width, 3 lines; length of dorsal valve 3 lines; width the same.

Locality and Formation.—P, four miles north-east from Portland Creek, Newfoundland: Quebec group.

Collector.—J. Richardson.

OTHER SPECIES OF LINGULA.

L. Quebecensis, *ante*, p. 72, occurs in Division P, on the south side of Cow Head.

Acrotreta gemma. (N. sp.)

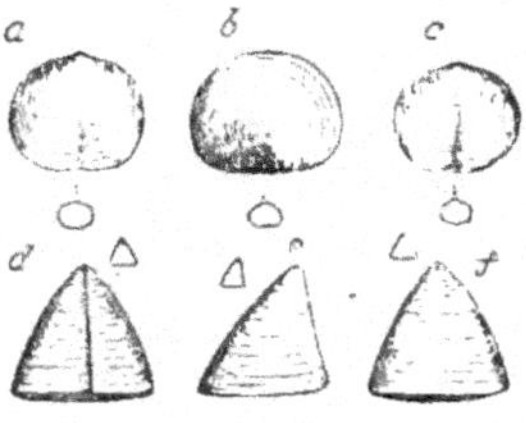

Fig. 201.—*Acrotreta gemma.* The small outline figures indicate the natural size; *a* and *c*, dorsal valves; *b*, ventral valve, as seen from above; *d*, area of a ventral valve which shews a central groove: *f*, area of another specimen which exhibits no groove; *e*, side view.

Fig. 201.

Description.—Shell very small, about 1 line in diameter; one valve nearly flat, and the other, acutely conical. Dorsal valve very gently convex, nearly circular; sides and front margin uniformly rounded; posterior margin very obtusely angulated at the beak, on each side of which, a portion of the cardinal edge equal to one-fourth of the whole width of the shell, is nearly straight; umbo very small; beak apparently depressed to the hinge line and not projecting beyond it; cardinal angles compressed, broadly rounded; a wide shallow mesial sinus extends from the front margin about half way to the beak; elsewhere the valve is gently convex, or nearly flat.

Ventral valve acutely conical, with a flat triangular area which is perpendicular to the plane of the lateral margin, its base half the width of the whole shell. In the apex of this valve there is a minute circular aperture, and in one specimen a dark line extends from it down the middle of the area, which appears to represent the foraminal groove of this genus; but in two other specimens of the ventral valve, with the area well preserved, there is no indication of a groove. Surface with very fine concentric striæ.

Width of dorsal valve, about 1 line; length, about $\frac{8}{9}$ of a line. The height of the ventral valve is about 1 line.

The form of this species is very like that of *A. subconica* (Kutorga), but that species is twice the size of this, and has the area distinctly grooved.

Locality and Formation.—P, four miles north-east from Portland Creek, Newfoundland; Quebec group.

Collector.—J. Richardson.

Orthis delicatula. (N. sp.)

Description.—Shell thin and flat, semi-elliptical, hinge line straight, equal to about twice the length of the shell: sides and front uniformly rounded. Ventral valve with a narrow mesial elevation in the upper half, elsewhere flat; beak and umbo slightly elevated above the hinge line; area narrow or linear. The dorsal valve is almost flat with a shallow mesial groove. Surface with very fine radiating striæ, about ten in the width of one line. Width of an average specimen, 4 lines; length 2 lines.

Locality and Formation.—N, Table Head and Pistolet Bay; P, four miles north-east of Portland Creek, Newfoundland; Quebec group.

Collector.—J. Richardson.

Other species of Orthis.

1. Orthis Electra, *ante*, p. 79, occurs at Table Head, Port aux Choix, and Point Rich in Divisions H and I. At Table Head some of

the specimens are silicified, and I have been able thus to compare both the interior and exterior with the originals, on which the species was founded.

2. O. HIPPOLYTE, *ante*, p. 81, occurs at Cow Head in Division P.

Besides the above there are several small convex finely striated species of the type of *O. perveta* and *O. elegantula*. The specimens are so badly preserved that it would be useless to name them. They occur at Port aux Choix, Table-Head, Point Rich, and Bonne Bay.

STROPHOMENA AURORA. (N. sp.)

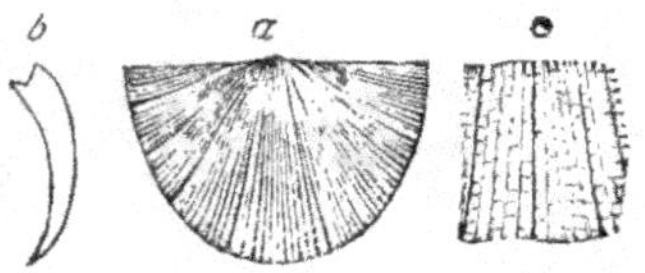

Fig. 202.

Fig. 202.—*Strophomena aurora; a*, ventral valve ; *b*, section ; *c*, portion of the surface enlarged.

Description.—Semi-elliptical, length varying from a little more than one-half the width, to four-fifths of the width, widest at the hinge line; contour usually an uniformly elliptical curve from the cardinal angles all round. Ventral valve convex, narrowly and often acutely carinated on the umbo, depressed and sub-concave towards the cardinal angles. Area moderate, forming an obtuse angle of about 125° with the plane of the lateral margin. Dorsal valve concave, with a mesial sinus commencing at the beak and growing wider and shallower towards the front margin ; area apparently about half the size of that of the ventral valve, and forming a right angle therewith. Surface with rather strong angular striæ of different sizes, the smaller coming in between the larger, both by intercalation and sub-division, the whole crossed by fine concentric striæ, more distinct in specimens which have the radiating striæ well separated than in those which have them close together. The striæ are about the size of those of *S. alternata*, but more angular. The concentric striæ are just visible to the naked eye when the surface is well preserved. On most specimens they cannot be seen at all, as a very small amount of weathering or exfoliation removes them. In some there are several strong angular folds radiating from the beak to the front margin, with usually one of the larger striæ running along the crest of the fold, and a number of the smaller in the intervening concave space.

The convexity of this species, as indeed it is in all others of the genus, is variable. Usually the ventral valve is depressed convex, the outline forming an even, flattened arch, from beak to front, but often it is strongly arched and angulated about the middle. The carination of the umbo sometimes extends quite to the front margin, and in such instances it has a strong angular elevated stria along its crest in the median line of the shell. Width from 7 lines to 1 inch. Length from $\frac{5}{8}$ to $\frac{4}{8}$ the width.

A separated dorsal valve, apparently belonging to this species, has the divaricator process undivided, as in the genus *Orthis*.

Locality and Formation.—K, L, M, N, Point Rich and Table Head, N, Burnt Cape, Pistolet Bay; P, four miles north-east from Portland Creek, Newfoundland; Quebec group.

Collector.—J. Richardson.

OTHER SPECIES OF STROPHOMENA AND LEPTÆNA.

1. *Strophomena imbecilis.*—Subquadrate or semi-elliptical, about half an inch wide, with extremely fine radiating striæ. The specimens are all imperfect, but show that this is a new species. P, four miles north-east from Portland Creek.

2. *Leptæna decipiens?* *Ante*, p. 73, a single valve not distinguishable from this species, was found in P, four miles north-east from Portland Creek.

CAMERELLA PARVA. (N. sp.)

Description.—Shell small, ovate, length about one-third greater than the width; apical angle about 60°; sides gently convex; front broadly rounded. Ventral valve rather strongly convex, uniformly arched from beak to front; mesial groove narrow, concave in the bottom, dying out at two-thirds the length from the front. Dorsal valve broad, ovate, not so long as the ventral, and more uniformly but not so strongly convex; mesial fold narrow, rounded, dying out at about half the length. Surface apparently smooth. Length of ventral valve about 2 lines.

The specimens are imperfect. The beak of the ventral valve is not well exposed, but seems to be strongly incurved.

Locality and Formation.—N, Table Head; P, four miles north-east from Portland Creek, Newfoundland.

Collector.—J. Richardson.

Camerella varians. (Billings.)

(*Canadian Nat. and Geol.* vol. iv, p. 445 : Dec. 1859. *Geol. Can.*, p. 127.)

Remarks.—This species, or one almost identical with it, occurs along with *C. parva* both at Table Head and four miles north-east from Portland Creek; also in the nodules of white limestone on the south side of Cow Head. It was first discovered in the Chazy limestone at the Mingan Islands, and was afterwards collected near the village of Chazy in New York, in the same formation, by J. Richardson.

Camerella calcifera. (Billings.)

(*Canadian Nat. and Geol.*, vol. vi. p. 31 : Aug. 1861. *Geol. Can.*, vi. p. 231.)

Remarks.—This species occurs in the nodules of white limestone on the south side of Cow Head in Division P. It is very characteristic of the limestone at Point Lévis and Phillipsburgh. At all these localities it is associated with *Bathyurus Saffordi*. It occurs also at St. Timothy, near the head of the Beauharnois Canal, and at Norton's Creek, in the upper part of the Calciferous formation.

Rhynchonella Corinthia. (N. sp.)

Description.—Transversely elliptical; width one-fourth, or one-third greater than the length. Ventral valve strongly convex, with a wide rounded mesial sinus which dies out at the umbo. Dorsal valve strongly and uniformly convex, with a wide rounded but not greatly elevated mesial fold. Surface with numerous small angular ribs, which bifurcate two or three times before reaching the margin; from three to five in one line, usually seven in two lines. Width about 8 lines; length 6 lines.

Of this species only a few fragments have been collected, but they are sufficient to show that it is different from any yet described. The form of the valves is that of a *Rhynchonella*, somewhat resembling the globose individuals of *R. plena*. But the bifurcation of the ribs is suggestive of *Orthis*. The beaks are not visible in any of the specimens.

Locality and Formation.—N, Table Head, Newfoundland; Quebec group.

Collector.—J. Richardson.

LAMELLIBRANCHIATA.

Euchasma Blumenbachium. (Billings.)

(Conocardium Blumenbachium.—*Can. Nat. and Geol.*, Vol. IV, p. 350. *Geol. of Can.*, p. 113.)

Remarks.—This species occurs in Divisions G and H, at Port aux Choix, Table Head, and Cape Norman.

Genus Eopteria. (N. gen.)

Generic Characters.—The general form of the species for which this genus is proposed is precisely like that of *Pterinea*, except that both valves are equally convex, and the hinge appears to have an external ligament like that of *Unio*. On this latter point, however, there remains some doubt, as the hinge is only partially seen in one specimen.

Eopteria typica. (N. sp.)

Description.—Hinge line straight; anterior wing small, posterior large; umbones near the anterior extremity. Body of the shell strongly and obliquely convex, sub-cordiform; ventral margin rounded; posterior margin descending from the extremity of the hinge line at an angle of about 100°, nearly straight or slightly concave, until approaching the posterior ventral angle, where it forms a narrowly-rounded curve to the ventral margin. The posterior wing is not much compressed. The greatest gibbosity is about the middle of the shell, and extends obliquely from the umbones backwards and downwards to the posterior ventral angle. Surface with coarse radiating striæ, about four in a width of three lines at the ventral margin.

Length of hinge line about 12 lines; length from the umbones to the posterior ventral angle about 13 lines.

Resembles an ordinary form of *Pterinea*, but is more convex than the generality of the species of that genus.

Locality and Formation.—G, Port aux Choix, Newfoundland; Quebec group.

Collector.—J. Richardson.

Ctenodonta Angela. (N. sp.)

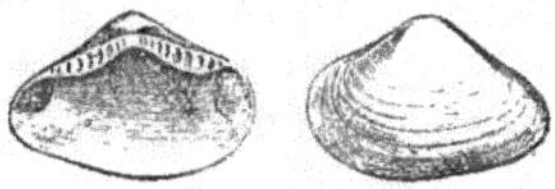

Fig. 203.

Fig. 203.—*Ctenodonta Angela*; left valve, interior and exterior.

Description.—Shell small, sub-ovate or sub-rhomboidal; anterior extremity broadly rounded; posterior narrowly rounded; ventral margin in the posterior two-thirds somewhat straight, in the anterior third obtusely convex; umbones prominent, situated about the middle of the dorsal margin; beak small, closely incurved; a shallow, barely perceptible byssal sinus extending from the umbo obliquely to the posterior half of the ventral margin. If a line be drawn between the most projecting points of the anterior and posterior extremities, it will divide the shell into two nearly equal parts: of these, the upper or dorsal half is triangular, the umbones forming the apex with an angle of about 120°, the posterior slope a little longer than the anterior: the ventral half of the shell is semi-ovate, the anterior end the largest. The shell is very thick, and rather strongly convex. Surface with obscure concentric striæ. Transverse length 8 lines; umbones to ventral margin 5 lines.

Ctenodonta contracta (Salter) has the posterior extremity more pointed, but in no other respect differs from this species.

Locality and Formation.—M, Table Head, Newfoundland; Quebec group.

Collector.—J. Richardson.

GASTEROPODA.

Holopea Ophelia. (N. sp.)

Fig. 204.

Fig. 204.—*Holopea Ophelia.* Different views of the same specimen.

Description.—Shell small, turbinate, apical angle between 80° and 90°; whorls three, including a minute one at the apex, smoothly ventricose, most prominent at about the lower third. Aperture sub-ovate, the outer lip broadly convex, the inner lip, from the umbilicus downwards, slightly curved, and folded over the minute umbilicus; the upper and inner half of the aperture formed by the penultimate whorl.

Length 6 lines; width, from the outer lip through, about the same; height of the aperture, 4 lines. On a posterior view the two apical whorls constitute only one-fifth the whole length. The last whorl forms nearly the whole bulk.

In some of the specimens there seems to be a spiral band about the middle of the whorl, as in *Pleurotomaria.*

Locality and Formation.—L, Point Rich, Newfoundland; Quebec group.

Collector.—J. Richardson.

Genus STRAPAROLLINA. (N. gen.)

Generic characters.—Shell turbinated, with round or obscurely angulated whorls; spire varying from obtusely to acutely conical; aperture nearly circular, sometimes with a notch in the inner lower angle of the lip.

This group appears to stand between *Straparollus* and *Holopea*. The species known are *S. pelagica* and those figured in the *Geology of Canada* on p. 144, under the names of *Straparollus asperostriatus*, *S. Circe*, and *S. Eurydice*.

STRAPAROLLINA PELAGICA. (N. sp.)

Fig. 205.

Fig. 205.—*Straparollina pelagica.*

Description.—Shell turbinate, pyramidal; spire of four or five moderately-ventricose whorls; apical angle between 65° and 70°; base convex. The body whorl is obscurely rounded angular at the margin, just above which there are indications of a faint concave band; thence moderately ventricose to the suture. Below the margin the whorls are depressed convex or somewhat flattened. The umbilicus is about one-fourth the whole width, with an angular elevated carina on the edge; whorls within the umbilicus nearly flat, all of them exposed to the apex. Surface obscurely striated parallel to the edge of the aperture, the latter obscurely rhomboidal.

Length of the largest specimen 10 lines; width 9 lines.

Locality and Formation.—G, H, Pistolet Bay, and Cape Norman, Newfoundland; Quebec group.

Collector.—J. Richardson.

SUBULITES DAPHNE. (N. sp.)

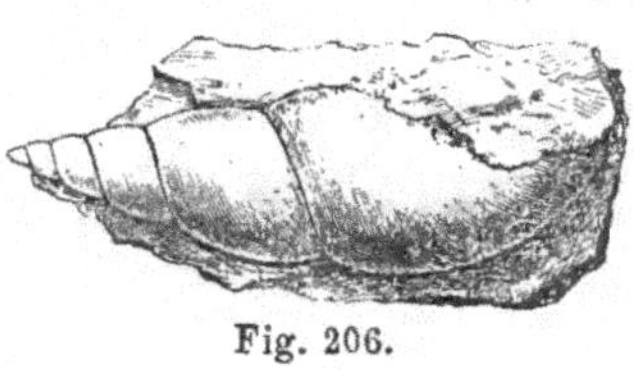

Fig. 206.

Fig. 206.—*Subulites Daphne.*

Description.—Shell rather small, slender, fusiform, of about six gently convex, or nearly flat whorls; apical angle 35°. Surface unknown.

The only specimen collected is a cast of the interior. Length 19 lines; length of the body whorl, measured along the inner side of the aperture from the suture to the lower angle of the aperture, 11 lines; greatest diameter, near the upper edge of the body whorl, 5¼ lines.

Locality and Formation.—L, Point Rich, Newfoundland.

Collector.—J. Richardson.

PLEUROTOMARIA VIRGO. (N. sp.)

Fig. 207.

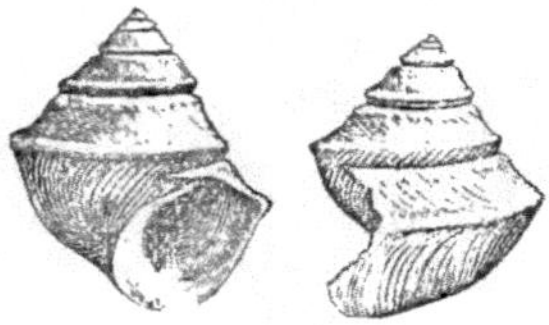

Fig. 208.

Fig. 209.

Fig. 207.—*Pleurotomaria virgo.*
208.—*P. selecta.* Front and side views.
209.—*P. virguncula.*

Description.—Shell small, turbinate; spire evenly pyramidal; apical angle about 80°; whorls about four; the last one strongly ventricose. Along the middle of the last whorl there is a concave spiral band, and, separated from this by a narrow thread-like ridge, a deep groove; above which, flat or very slightly concave to the suture. In the upper whorls the band gradually becomes concealed in the suture, the groove remaining distinct. The base below the band is moderately convex, except on approaching the aperture, where it is strongly so. Aperture rhomboidal, obtusely angular at the band; the upper half of the inner side formed by the penultimate whorl; the lower half by a thickened slightly effuse lip. Umbilicus minute, but visible. Surface with fine backward curving striæ. Length 7 lines; width 6 lines.

Smaller than *P. selecta*, the band concave instead of convex, and with a groove above it.

Locality and Formation.—H, I, K, L, Table Head, Newfoundland; Quebec group.

Collector.—J. Richardson.

PLEUROTOMARIA SELECTA. (N. sp.)

Fig. 208.

Description.—Shell with the spire pyramidal, and the whorls strongly angular; apical angle about 75°. Whorls five, angular in the middle or a little below; a narrowly rounded band on the edge; above which, concave or nearly flat to within one-fifth of the suture, where there is an obscure thread-like carina; then nearly horizontally bevelled into the suture. The whorls are turretted about one-fourth their width above each other. The body whorl just below the margin has a slightly concave band; below which, strongly convex. Aperture rhomboidal; the upper half of the inner side formed by the penultimate whorl; the lower half by a thickened effuse lip. The umbilicus is closed. Surface with rather strong backward curving striæ.

Length 9 lines; width 8 lines.

This species is exactly like *M. Dryope* (see p. 170), but has the spire more elevated.

Varieties.—Associated with *P. selecta* are specimens with the spire not quite so much elevated; apical angle 85°; the band on the margin narrower; the upper edge of each whorl having the plane of the bevel into the suture more oblique, or sloping upwards instead of nearly horizontal. The whorls are also less distinctly turretted.

Locality and Formation.—H, I, K, L, Table Head, Newfoundland; Quebec group.

Collector.—J. Richardson.

Pleurotomaria virguncula. (N. sp.)

Fig. 209.

Description.—Shell small with an evenly pyramidal spire; apical angle between 80° and 95°; whorls four; base convex. The body whorl has a double band along the middle, consisting of two concave grooves and three sharp narrow carinæ, the one separating the two grooves being the most prominent and constituting the margin. Above the double band is another, rather strongly concave, and from one-third to half the width of the upper side of the whorl. The upper side of this latter band is limited by a fourth carina, above which the edge of the whorl is bevelled into the suture. On the upper whorls only three of the carinæ and two of the grooves are visible, and the latter are there also usually of equal width. The apex is acutely terminated. The base is rather strongly convex. Aperture sub-rhomboidal, rounded on the inner side and angular at the band. Inner lip greatly thickened. Umbilicus minute, and in some specimens closed by the callous of the lip. Surface with fine striæ.

Length from 4 to 8 lines; width a little less than the length.

Locality and Formation.—H, I, K, L, Table Head, Newfoundland; Quebec group.

Collector.—J. Richardson.

Pleurotomaria sponsa. (N. sp.)

Description.—Shell small, turbinate, with four ventricose whorls; apical angle from 75° to 85°; the general form like that of a *Holopea*. The whorls are nearly uniformly convex, most tumid a little below the middle, where there is a narrow convex distinctly elevated band, above which the whorl is depressed convex to the suture. In the upper whorls the band is either close to the suture on the lower edge of the whorl, or else concealed. Under side rather strongly convex, with an angular carina at the edge of the umbilicus; the latter small, about one-sixth the whole width of the base. Surface apparently smooth, but probably finely striated.

Length from 4 to 8 lines; width a little less than the length.

None of the specimens have the aperture perfect, but they show, that of the inner side, the upper half is formed by the penultimate whorl, and the lower half by a slightly reflexed lip.

Locality and Formation.—N, Table Head, Newfoundland; Quebec group.

Collector.—J. Richardson.

Pleurotomaria Etna. (N. sp.)

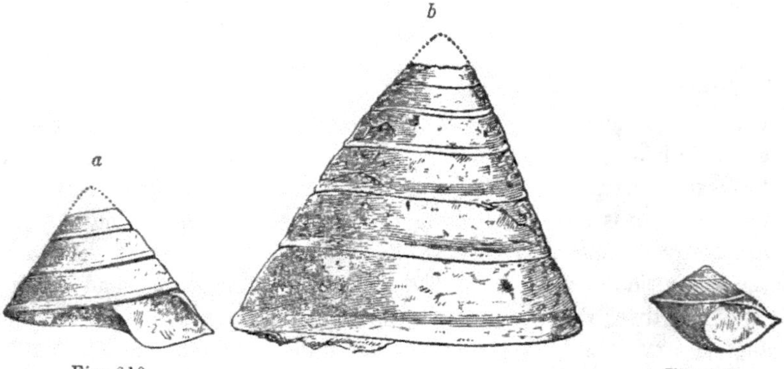

Fig. 210. Fig. 211.

Fig. 210.—*Pleurotomaria Etna.* *a*, *b*, views of a small and a large specimen.
211.—*P. Hortensia.*

Description.—Shell pyramidal; apical angle varying from 65° to 90°. Whorls from four to seven; on the upper side nearly flat, a fain groove just above the lower edge; on the under side flat and nearly horizontal, rounded at the umbilical edge. Umbilicus about one-third the whole width, exposing all the whorls to the apex. Aperture rhomboidal; outer lip conforming to the slope of the spire; lower lip straight and nearly horizontal on the outside, rounded at the inner angle; inner lip gently convex or straight, forming an obtuse angle with the lower. Surface finely striated.

This species belongs to the type of *P. Ramsayi*, from which it is at once distinguished by the wider umbilicus. It is more closely allied to *P. Amphitrite* (see p. 32), differing therefrom in being smaller, and in having a groove near the suture.

Width at the base of largest specimen (a fragment) 2 inches; height a little less than the width.

Locality and Formation.—G, Cape Norman, H, Ta le Head, Newfoundland; Quebec group.

Collector.—J. Richardson.

Pleurotomaria Hortensia. (N. sp.)

Fig. 211.

Descrip ion.—Shell discoidal, with a sharp projecting margin having a concave band just within the edge, both above and below. Spire depressed conical with a rounded apex. Whorls in the upper two-thirds of their width gently convex, becoming more flattened on approaching the concave band; the apical whorl convex its whole width. On the under side the whorls grow gradually more convex from without inwards, most tumid at two-thirds their width, thence rather abruptly rounded into the umbilicus, which is scarcely one-third the whole width.

The specimen consists of two whorls, and is probably the apical portion of a larger individual. Its width is 4½ lines; height 3 lines. The margin is at about half the whole height.

Closely allied to *P. Harpya*, but has a smaller umbilicus.

Locality and Formation.—H, Table Head, Newfoundland; Quebec group.

Collector.—J. Richardson.

Pleurotomaria Harpya. (N. sp.)

Description.—Lenticular, whorls wide, depressed convex both above and below; umbilicus one-half the whole width.

This species is founded on a specimen which is a cast of the interior. Width 28 lines; height about 7 lines. There are three whorls, allowing for a small one 2 lines across in the centre. The other two increase from a width of 1½ lines to 9 lines in making two turns. A vertical polished section shows that the outer margin is thin and sharp, and that the aperture is most probably not rhomboidal but transversely elliptical, the outer angle acute and the inner probably narrowly rounded. The form is thus like that of *P. lapicida* (Salter), differing therefrom in being larger and in having a wider umbilicus; the whorls also are not so flat above, and not so convex below.

Locality and Formation.—G, Cape Norman, Newfoundland; Quebec group.

Collector.—J. Richardson.

PLEUROTOMARIA HYALE. (N. sp.)

Description.—Shell rather small, lenticular; spire depressed convex, the whorls slightly elevated above each other at the suture, flat or with a barely perceptible convexity on the upper side; base a little more strongly convex than the spire. Umbilicus either very narrow or completely closed. Surface unknown.

Width about 9 lines; height 4 to 6 lines.

The character of the margin has not been clearly ascertained, but it appears to be acute, and probably has a very narrow band on the edge. The shape may be described as ventricose-lenticular, both spire and base moderately convex, and the peripheral edge being at about the mid-height, or a little above. It resembles *P. Progne*, *Geol. Can.*, p. 181, f. 176, but is a smaller species, and has the whorls slightly elevated above each other at the sutures.

Locality and Formation.—F, Keppel Island and Port aux Choix, Newfoundland; Quebec group.

Collector.—J. Richardson.

PLEUROTOMARIA NORMANI. (N. sp.)

Fig. 212.

Fig. 212.—*Pleurotomaria Normani.*

Description.—The specimen on which this species is founded is an imperfect cast of the interior. Width at the base twenty-four lines;

height fourteen lines ; apical angle about 105° ; whorls five or six, gently convex, a rather strongly impressed, narrow, concave band, just within the outer margin.

The umbilicus appears to be about half the whole width, but it cannot be well seen in the specimen. Judging from the appearance presented by a small portion of the shell which is preserved, the suture, in perfect specimens, must be represented by a close seam, not deeply impressed, as in the above figure,

This specimen is evidently another form of the *P. Canadensis* group, with a more elevated spire ard a narıower concave band than the others.

Locality and Formation.—G, Cape Norman, Newfoundland ; Quebec group.

Collector.—J. Richardson.

PLEUROTOMARIA NUMERIA. (N. sp.)

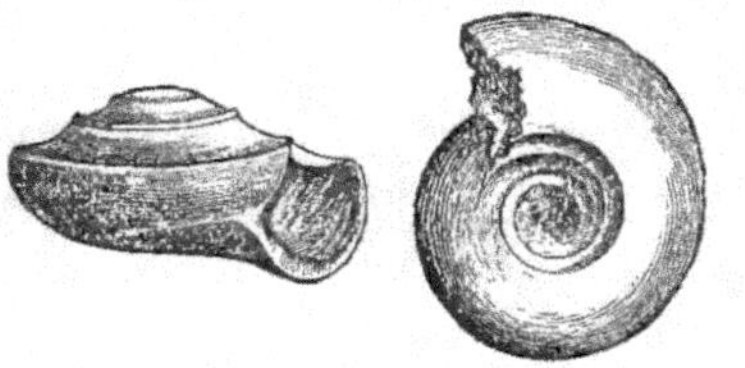

Fig. 213.

Fig. 213.—*Pleurotomaria Numeria.* *a*, front view ; *b*, view of the underside.

Description.—Sub-lenticular ; spire usually much depressed ; whorls on the upper side nearly flat or gently concave, with a slightly elevated marginal edge, sometimes abruptly elevated half a line above each other at the suture. Lower side of whorls strongly convex and angulated at the edge of the umbilicus, descending into the umbilicus with a flat and nearly vertical slope. Umbilicus about one-third the whole width, exhibiting all the whorls within. There are about four whorls. Aperture rhomboid-oval ; outer lip in old specimens vertical, in young specimens inclining a little inwards ; upper lip nearly horizontal ; lower side of aperture rounded, but the lip thickened, and often angulated. Surface unknown.

Width of a large specimen 12 lines : height 6 or 7 lines ; width of aperture 3 or 4 lines.

Locality and Formation.—G, Cape Norman, Newfoundland ; Quebec group.

Collector.—J. Richardson.

Pleurotomaria Agarista. (N. sp.)

(Perhaps a variety of *P. Numeria.*)

Description.—Spire depressed conical; whorls about four, flat or gently convex on the upper side, a narrow elevated band on the outer edge of the last one, just within which is a shallow groove; above, gently convex to the suture. On the underside the whorls are strongly convex; in the umbilicus, flat and vertical (except the last, which is gently convex): the outside, in the last whorl, just below the margin, nearly vertical, but sloping a little inwards. Aperture rhomboidal; upper side angular at the suture, outside of which, sloping downwards to the margin, at an angle of about 30° to the horizontal axis; below the edge nearly vertical, but sloping inward; lower and inner lips rounded. Umbilicus one-third the whole width, exhibiting all the whorls within, in a winding staircase arrangement.

Width 14 lines; height 9 lines.

This species agrees with *P. Numeria* in every respect, except that it has a more elevated spire, and the whorls more convex on the upper side.

Locality and Formation.—H, Table Head, Newfoundland; Quebec group.

Collector.—J. Richardson.

Pleurotomaria ? Calphurnia. (N. sp.)

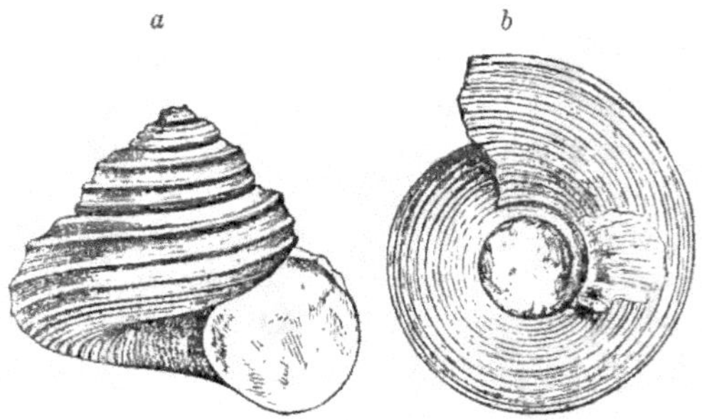

Fig. 214.

Fig. 214.—*Pleurotomaria Calphurnia.* *a*, front view; *b*, view of the base. This is a more than commonly elevated specimen.

Description.—Shell turbinate, with three or four spirally grooved rounded whorls. Spire varying from depressed to elevated conical; apical angle from 80° to 100°. Aperture somewhat circular, slightly indented by the penultimate whorl. In the upper whorls there are four concave spiral grooves or bands, separated by three angular carinæ. The lower sides of the whorls are covered with numerous sharp spiral carinæ, two or three in the width of one line. Umbilicus open, disclosing the whorls to the apex. On one of the specimens there are indications of fine transverse lines of growth.

Width of the largest specimen at the aperture 16 lines; height from the lower side of the aperture to the apex 14 lines; width of the aperture 7 lines.

This species resembles a strongly carinated *Cyclonema*, and may be, perhaps, a species of that genus.

Locality and Formation.—G, Cape Norman, Newfoundland; Quebec group.

Collector.—J. Richardson.

MURCHISONIA CATHARINA. (N. sp.)

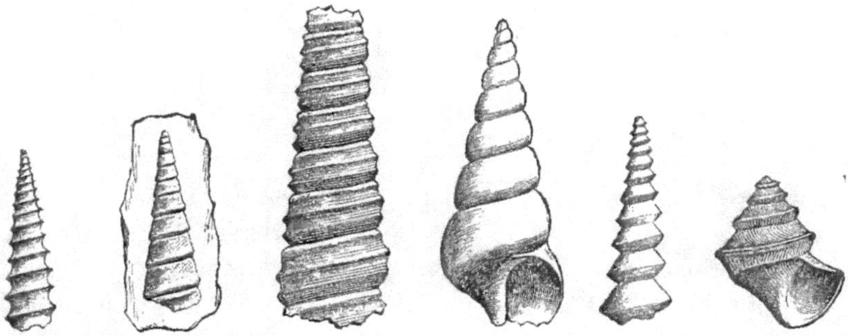

Fig. 215. Fig. 216. Fig. 217. Fig. 218. Fig. 219. Fig. 220.

Fig. 215.—*Murchisonia Catharina.*
216.—*M. acrea.*
217.—*M. Adelina.*
218.—*M. simulatrix.* A variety of *M. gracilis.*
219.—*M. Cicelia.*
220.—*M. sororcula.* A variety of *M. perangulata.*

Description.—Shell small, slender; whorls about fifteen, extremely and sharply angular in the middle, the space between each two of the carinæ being deep and uniformly concave. The form of the spire is that of a deeply threaded screw. The suture appears to be about half way between the carinations in the bottom of the concave space. Apical angle from 10° to 15°. Surface unknown.

Length of a specimen with fourteen whorls, from the apex downwards, 10 lines; width of the last whorl 3 lines.

Locality and Formation.—K, Table Head, Newfoundland; Quebec group.

Collector.—J. Richardson.

MURCHISONIA ACREA. (N. sp.)

Fig. 216.

Description.—Shell rather small and slender, somewhat turretted; whorls from twelve to fifteen, flat or sub-concave, each with the lower edge rounded and sub-angulated, projecting a little over the one below; all above this projection flat or gently concave, and sloping to the suture, close to which there is a slight convexity. Surface characters unknown.

A specimen of eleven whorls is 11 lines in length; diameter at the last whorl 3½ lines. Apical angle from 15° to 20°.

This species belongs to that group, of which *M. Anna*, so characteristic of the Calciferous, is an example. It resembles a small *Turritella.*

Locality and Formation.—G, Port aux Choix, Newfoundland; Quebec group.

Collector.—J. Richardson.

MURCHISONIA ADELINA. (N. sp.)

Fig. 217.

Description.—Shell elongate, tapering at the rate of about one line to the inch. Whorls from fifteen to twenty, nearly flat or gently convex, with three equi-distant slightly elevated carinæ, separated by concave spiral grooves. Suture rather deep. The only surface markings visible are fine revolving lines on the carinæ and in the grooves between. The central carina is usually a little more prominent than the others, and all appear to be acutely edged, when perfect.

Length about 3 inches; diameter at last whorl 6 lines.

Locality and Formation.—G, Cape Norman, Newfoundland; Quebec group.

Collector.—J. Richardson.

MURCHISONIA SIMULATRIX. (N. sp.)

Fig. 218.

Description.—Shell small and rather slender, with from ten to thirteen nearly uniformly ventricose whorls, which are slightly the most ventricose in the lower half. Aperture ovate, formed on the upper and inner side by the penultimate whorl, not free; no umbilicus. The band is narrow and obscure, situated just below the middle of the whorl. The surface is in general smooth, but in perfect specimens obscurely marked by fine striæ, curving backwards to the band.

Length from 18 to 30 lines ; diameter of last whorl from 6 to 8 lines.

This species is closely allied to *M. gracilis* (Hall), but differs in the position of the band, and in the form of the aperture. In the Trenton species, the band is in the middle of the whorl, and the lip is continuous all round the inner side of the aperture.

M. Vesta has the whorls less convex.

Locality and Formation.—H, I, K, L, M, N, Table Head and Point Rich, Newfoundland ; Quebec group.

Collector.—J. Richardson.

MURCHISONIA CICELIA. (N. sp.)

Fig. 219.

Description.—Shell rather small and slender ; spire of from ten to fifteen whorls, which are strongly and sharply angular at about the lower third, with a straight slope to the suture above. Space between each two carinæ angular, not concave as in *M. Catharina.* Surface unknown Apical angle from 15° to 20°.

This species belongs to the same group with *M. perangulata* (Hall) of the Black River and Trenton, from which it is distinguished by its elongated and slender form. It is also allied to *M. Estella* of the Guelph limestone, see p. 155, ante.

Length about 12 lines ; width of last whorl about 3½ lines.

Locality and Formation.—L, Table Head and Point Rich, Newfoundland ; Quebec group.

Collector.—J. Richardson.

MURCHISONIA SORORCULA. (N. sp.)

Fig. 220.

Description.—Shell turbinate, with about five acutely angular whorls ; apical angle from 55° to 65° ; base strongly convex. The whorls are strongly angular along the middle, above gently concave to the suture ; the band situated on the edge of the angulation. The body-whorl below the angle has a single carina, between which and the margin there is a concave band, usually a little more than half the width of the upper side of the whorl. Aperture angular on the outside, rounded on the inner side, partly formed by the penultimate whorl, the lower-inner lip thickened. No umbilicus. Surface with fine sharp backward curving striæ.

This species is a variety of that group to which *M. perangulata* (Hall), *M. serrulata* (Salter), *M. gyrogonia* (McCoy), and others belong. From the first of these it differs in having no umbilicus. The second has two carinæ below the angle on the body-whorl. The third, as figured by McCoy, has the whorls more oblique.

Locality and Formation.—H, I, K, L, M, Table Head and Point Rich, Newfoundland ; Quebec group.

Collector.—J. Richardson.

MURCHISONIA AUGUSTINA. (N. sp.)

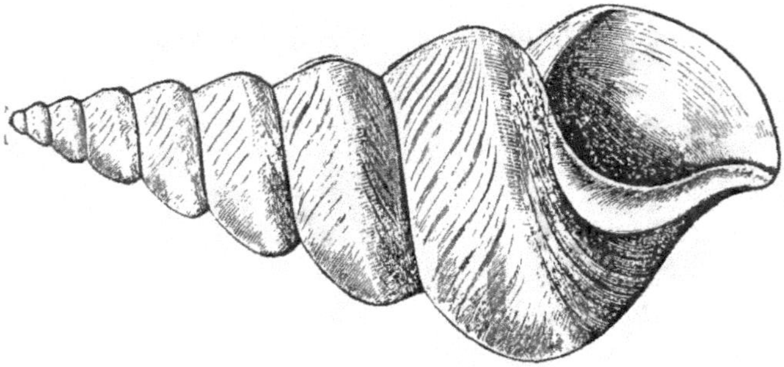

Fig. 221.

Fig. 221.—*Murchisonia Augustina.* A variety of *M. bellicincta.*

Description.—Shell large, with from eight to ten strongly convex whorls, which are obscurely angulated, and with spiral band, just below the middle. Aperture sub-ovate, with indications of a canal at the lower angle. The lip is free all round ; on the upper side in contact with the penultimate whorl, and on the inner side with a fold which forms an angular canal, and leaves open a small umbilicus. Surface with obscure undulations curving backwards to the band, and probably fine striæ, although none can be seen on the specimens (which are silicified). The band is situated on the angular part of the whorl, and appears to be smooth.

Length of a specimen of the average size from the apex to the anterior angle of the aperture 3½ inches ; width across the last whorl and aperture about 20 lines.

The casts of this species closely resemble, both in size and form, those of *M. bellicincta* (Hall), so common in the Trenton, the only difference being that the whorls are slightly angulated below the middle, instead of uniformly ventricose. The surface, when perfect, of *M. bellicincta*, is covered with fine thread-like striæ, distinctly visible on the band (which is on the middle of the whorls), and never (in any of the specimens that I have seen) undulated.

M. arenaria, of the Calciferous, is more closely allied, but appears to me to be a different species, being much shorter.

Locality and Formation.—H, I, K, L, M, N, West side of Pistolet Bay, Burnt Cape, Table Head, and Point Rich, Newfoundland; Quebec group.

Collector.—J. Richardson.

MURCHISONIA AGILIS. (N. sp.)

Description.—The casts of the interior of this species are elongated gradually tapering, with apparently about fifteen short and nearly uniformly depressed ventricose whorls.

A fragment 24 lines in length tapers from a diameter of 3 lines at the larger extremity to 4 at the smaller. It has nine whorls.

Another specimen of twelve whorls tapers from 6 lines to a point in 25 lines.

This species somewhat resembles *M. gracilis*, but differs in having the whorls shorter, not so convex, and the suture not crossing so obliquely; surface unknown.

Locality and Formation.—G and H, Cape Norman and Table Head, Newfoundland; Quebec group.

Collector.—J. Richardson.

MURCHISONIA PLACIDA. (N. sp.)

Description.—Shell small, short, of about four uniformly ventricose whorls; an obscure narrow band at the lower third of the last whorl; apical angle about 47°. Surface unknown. There is a minute umbilicus. Length about 8 lines; width at the aperture about 5½ lines.

Locality and Formation.—G, Cape Norman, Newfoundland; Quebec group.

Collector.—J. Richardson.

Genus MACLUREA. (Lesueur.)

Remarks.—In the Palæontology of New York, vol. i., there are two species of this genus, *M. sordida* and *M. matutina*, described and figured as occurring in the Calciferous formation. The original specimens were evidently very imperfect, and it appears to have been not possible to give the details of the specific characters. The figures barely show enough to indicate the genus. I have heretofore referred to *M. matutina*, with doubt, a species found in the Calciferous at the Mingan Islands, and have also thought that I could recognize it in the limestone of the Quebec group at Phillipsburgh. It has now, however, become apparent, from the collections made in Newfoundland, that there are several distinct species, all having nearly the form and proportions indicated by the figures in the work above cited; but it is, at present, impossible to decide that any one of them is truly *M. sordida* or *M. matutina.* I propose, therefore, to describe them all as new, and to leave it for future discoveries to determine whether or not those which occur at the typical locality, in New York, are represented among them.

In the following descriptions the shell is regarded as being sinistral; the flat side is thus the spire and the umbilicated side the base.

Although I think that the genus *Ophileta* is founded on species of *Maclurea*, with very slender whorls, I retain it for the present provisionally.

MACLUREA CRENULATA. (N. sp.)

a *b* *c*

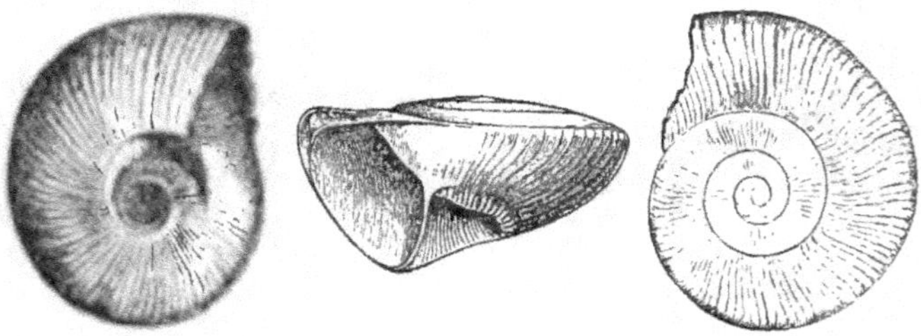

Fig. 222.

Fig. 222.—*Maclurea crenulata.* *a*, base; *b*, front; *c*, spire.

Description.—Shell hemispherical; spire flat, of three or four rather slender whorls, outer edge narrowly rounded angular; umbilicus about one-third the whole width, with a sharp crenulated edge; inner side of the whorls, in the umbilicus flat and nearly vertical; all the whorls exposed in a spiral staircase form to the apex. The base forms an irregular hemisphere, highest at the aperture.

Surface finely striated, and usually with some rugose lines of growth. These latter are sometimes absent, and the shell has then a smooth aspect.

A single specimen of an operculum was found in the same piece of limestone, with several shells of this species. It is a flat thin plate, with a muscular process, as in *M. Logani.*

The edge of the umbilicus is exhibited in more than fifty specimens, and in all it bears a sort of a rounded band, which is beautifully crenulalated transversely, as in most of the species of *Solarium.*

The inner whorls of the spire are sometimes a little elevated above the others. The upper side of the whorls is quite flat, when the shell is preserved, and usually so in the casts of the interior, but sometimes rounded.

Width of a specimen of the average size 15 lines; height 7 lines; width of the umbilicus 4 lines, varying from one-fourth to one-third the whole width of the shell.

Numerous small silicified specimens of this species were collected at Table Head and Point Rich, where it appears to range through a thickness of about 900 feet.

Closely allied to *M. oceana*, but differs in having the edge of the umbilicus acute and crenulated instead of narrowly rounded; in having the inner side of the whorl in the umbilicus flat instead of convex; the umbilicus also is narrower, and the operculum thin, with a well developed muscular process. The lowest strata in which it has been found are about 300 feet higher than the highest holding *M. oceana.*

Locality and Formation.—I, K, L, M, N, Table Head and Point Rich, Newfoundland; Quebec group.

Collector.—J. Richardson.

MACLUREA OCEANA. (N. sp.)

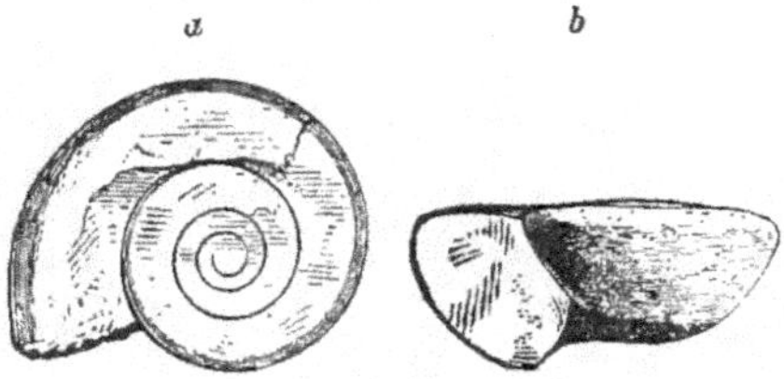

Fig. 223.

Fig. 223.—*Maclurea oceana.* *a*, the spire; *b*, front view.

Description.—Shell from one to four inches across; whorls four or five, rather slender; umbilicus about half the whole width (in small specimens; it has not been seen in those of large size). Spire flat; the outer edge narrowly rounded; the suture compressed and thread-like when the shel is preserved, but, as seen in the cast of the interior, deeply impressed. The outer side of the body-whorl is gently convex, and sloping to the edge of the umbilicus at an angle of from 60° to 70° with the plane of the flat side of the shell. The height of the aperture appears to be a little less than half the whole width of the shell. The edge of the umbilicus is acutely rounded, not acute as in *M. Emmonsi* and *M. affinis.* The inner side of the whorls in the umbilicus is gently convex, and somewhat sloping; the edge exposed in staircase form to the apex. Surface unknown, but most probably finely striated.

In a specimen 13 lines across, consisting of three complete whorls, the outer whorl is 4 lines wide; height of the aperture 6 lines; width of the umbilicus 5½ lines.

In a specimen 33 lines wide, consisting of four whorls, the outer whorl is 9 lines wide; aperture and umbilicus not exposed.

The proportions of this species are very nearly those of *M. crenulata*, and, in the condition of casts, the two cannot be distinguished from each other. When the shell is preserved, the differences become at once apparent.

In *M. crenulata* the umbilicus is narrower; the edge bears a crenulated band; the inner side of the whorl, in the umbilicus flat; and the height of the aperture is a little more than half the whole width of the shell.

The operculum found with it has no muscular process, as in *M. Logani.*

This species occurs also in a somewhat lower geological position than *M. crenulata.*

Locality and Formation.—F, G, H, Port aux Choix, Table Head, Cape Norman, and Pistolet Bay, Newfoundland; Quebec group.

Collector.—J. Richardson.

MACLUREA AFFINIS. (N. sp.)

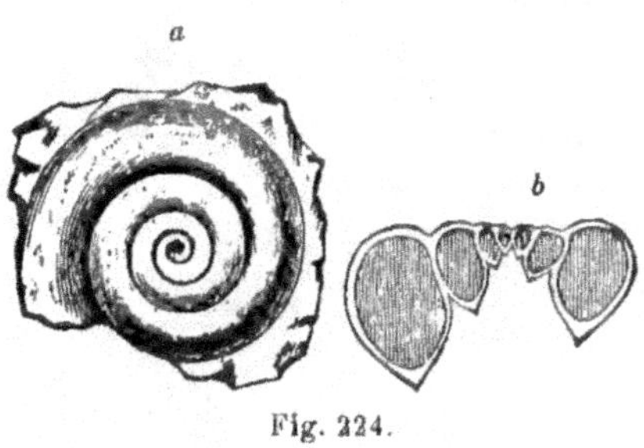

Fig. 224.

Fig. 224.—*Maclurea affinis.* *a*, the spire; *b*, section.

Description.—Shell small; width from $1\frac{1}{2}$ to 2 inches; spire flat, of four or five slender whorls, which, as seen in the casts of the interior, are uniformly convex on the upper side, the suture being deeply impressed. Umbilicus somewhat more than three-fifths the whole width; the edge, as shown in a vertical polished section, acute; the inner sides of the whorls, in the umbilicus, convex; all the whorls seen, in staircase form, to the apex. Surface unknown.

Width 18 to 24 lines; height 6 to 8 lines; width of last whorl 5 to 6 lines.

Differs from *M. Emmonsi* in having more slender whorls. It also resembles *M. ponderosa*, but this latter is vastly larger.

In perfect shells the whorls may be flat above, although in the casts they are rounded.

Locality and Formation.—F, Keppel Island, Newfoundland; Quebec group.

Collector.—J. Richardson.

Maclurea ponderosa. (N. sp.)

Description.—Shell large; from four to six inches across; of four or five whorls. Spire flat, the central whorls often a little elevated above the outer ones; the margin obtusely rounded. Base truncated hemispherical; umbilicus about half the whole width, with an acute edge; sides of the whorls in the umbilicus moderately convex. Surface with strong squamose striæ parallel to the edge of the aperture. Shell remarkably thick, usually exhibiting a tendency to exfoliation.

No very perfect specimens of this species have been collected, although it occurs in vast numbers in several localities. The edge of the umbilicus in ordinary specimens is acutely rounded, but in good vertical polished sections it is very acute. Such sections also show that, in some, the edge of the whorls is exposed, in the umbilicus, in staircase form, to the apex, but in others it is quite certain that it (the edge) is concealed by the preceding whorl.

In most specimens the whorls on the upper side are uniformly depressed convex, with a moderately deep suture, but sometimes they are nearly flat.

A specimen of four whorls is about 5 inches across.

This species, in size and proportions, much resembles *M. Magna*, but differs from it in having the whorls a little more slender in the horizontal direction, and deeper in the vertical, in having the edge of the umbilicus more acute and always a thicker shell. The vertical section is almost exactly like that of *M. affinis*, as represented above in fig. 224, which, on comparison, will be found constantly a little different from similar sections of *M. Magna.*

The only differences I can perceive between *M. affinis* and this species, are in the much greater size and thickness of shell of the latter.

Locality and Formation.—P, Cow Head, Newfoundland; and also near Phillipsburgh, Canada East. It occurs most abundantly at Correy's farm, about five miles north of Phillipsburgh, on the road to Bedford, in band C 1, of the Phillipsburgh series.

Collectors.—J. Richardson, at Cow Head; E. Billings, at Phillipsburgh.

MACLUREA ACUMINATA. (N. sp.)

Fig. 225.

Fig. 225.—*Maclurea acuminata.* A cast of the interior.

Description.—Shell from two to four inches across; spire flat, the middle sometimes a little convex; suture closely compressed, in the cast of the interior deeply excavated; outer edge thin and acute; whorls three or four. The base is depressed hemispherical; umbilicus very small, and in some specimens apparently closed altogether. Surface with fine striæ, those on the base seem to be rather coarse.

This species is easily recognized, even when in the condition of casts, by its margin, which is often much more acute than is represented in the above figure.

The largest specimen collected is 3½ inches across, and consists of about 3½ whorls, the last one being 12 lines wide at the aperture. The height is about one-third the width.

Locality and Formation.—K, L, M, N, Table Head and Point Rich, Newfoundland; Quebec group.

Collector.—J. Richardson.

MACLUREA SPECIOSA. (N. sp.)

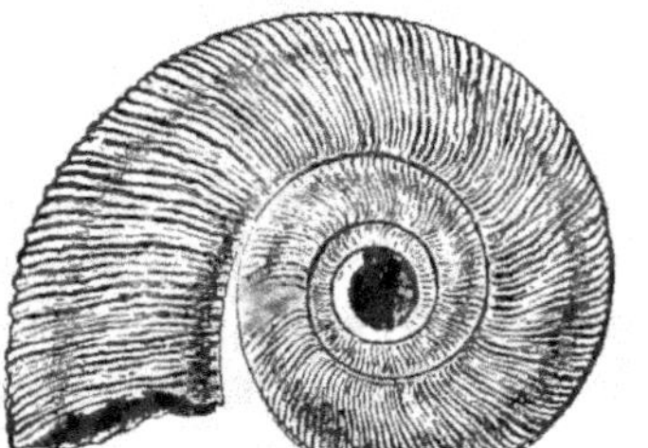

Fig. 226.

Fig. 226.—*Maclurea speciosa.* The spire.

Description.—Shell about two inches across, consisting of four or five slender whorls. Spire flat or very slightly convex in the middle, upper side of the whorls with a concave band, occupying the outer half, the inner half elevated, and either convex or with the most prominent part slightly flattened. The margin is nearly acutely angular. The outer side of the whorl, below the margin, is either flat or gently concave, and sloping inwards at an angle of about 70°, with the plane of the spire in the body-whorl, but from 60° to 70° in the smaller whorls. The umbilicus is about five-sixths of the whole width, the edge rounded angular in the last whorl; acutely angular in the inner whorls. The slope of each whorl into the umbilicus is gradual, and sometimes a little concave near the edge, then convex, and lastly, nearly vertical. All the whorls are exposed to the apex. The aperture is obscurely rectangular in the last whorl, but more nearly oval in the inner whorl; the width a little greater than the height.

Surface with strong rugose transverse striæ, and often with shallow concave grooves, from two to three in two lines.

The casts of the interior somewhat resemble those of *M. transitionis*, but are distinguishable by the form of the upper side of the whorl, the margin of which, instead of being uniformly rounded, as in the species cited, is obliquely truncated by an obscure flat band, which slopes outwards and downwards at an angle of 15° to 30° with the plane of the spire. The acute edges of the margin of the shell and umbilicus are more obtuse or obsolete in the cast.

The last whorl is sometimes a little vagrant.

A specimen 13 lines in width is 4 lines in height.

Locality and Formation.—G, H, I, K, L, M, Point Rich, Table Head, Cape Norman, Schooner Island in Pistolet Bay, entrance to the north arm of Bonne Bay, Newfoundland; Quebec group.

Collector.—J. Richardson.

Maclurea transitionis. (N. sp.)

Description.—Shell small, about two inches across, of about four slender whorls. Spire flat; the suture in casts of the interior deeply impressed; the outer margin rounded; the outer side of the last whorl depressed convex and nearly vertical. The umbilicus is nearly the whole width of the shell, with an acute edge. The inner side of the whorls in the umbilicus has two slopes. The first, commencing at the edge of the umbilicus, extends about one-third the width of the whorl, inclined at an angle of 45° or somewhat less, to the plane of the spire; it is usually gently concave. The second, inside of the first, is gently convex, and inclined at an angle of from 70° to 80°. Surface unknown.

Width of an average specimen 20 lines; width of last whorl 6 lines; height of last whorl about 6 lines.

When the upper side alone of this species is seen, it cannot be distinguished from *M. affinis;* the size of the shell and proportions being about the same. The umbilicus, however, is altogether different. Some of the specimens have thicker whorls, and approach *M. Emmonsi* in form.

Locality and Formation.—K, L, Table Head and Point Rich, Newfoundland; Quebec group.

Collector.—J. Richardson.

MACLUREA EMMONSI. (N. sp.)

Fig. 227.

Fig. 227.—*Maclurea Emmonsi.* *a*, front view of a small specimen; *b*, spire of a large specimen; *c*, spire of *a*.

Description.—Shell from one to three inches across, usually about two inches; spire flat, of three or four whorls, somewhat rapidly increasing in size; outer edge obtusely rounded; umbilicus from one-half to three-fourths the whole width with an acute edge. On the upper side the smaller whorls are, in some specimens, quite flat, and in others convex; the outer margin of the last whorl, in all the specimens seen, is obtusely rounded. The edge of the umbilicus, in the perfect shell, is thin and quite sharp, with a concave band just below it; in the casts it is acutely rounded. With the exception of the concave band, the inner side of the whorls in the umbilicus is gently convex. The whorls are all seen in the umbilicus, but the edge projects only slightly. The height of the shell is nearly two-thirds its width. Surface unknown, but probably finely striated.

Width of an average specimen 24 lines; height 15 lines; width of umbilicus 11 lines; width of last whorl 9 lines.

This species differs from *M. crenulata* in being of a more rotund form, the outer edge of the body whorl obtusely rounded, the umbilicus wider, and the edge not crenulated.

M. transitionis may be only a variety.

Locality and Formation.—I, K, L, M, N, Point Rich and Table Head, Newfoundland; Quebec group.

Collector.—J. Richardson.

OTHER SPECIES OF MACLUREA.

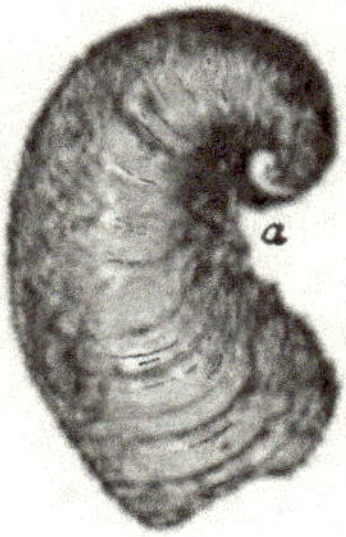

Fig. 228.

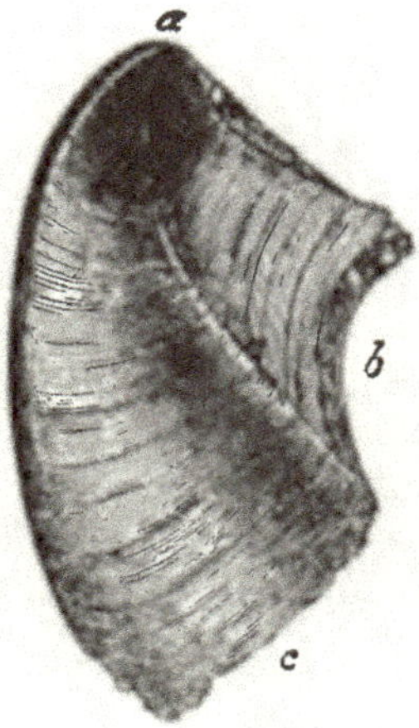

Fig. 229.

Fig. 230.

Figs. 228, 229, 230.—Opercula of different species of *Maclurea.*

At Cape Norman, associated with *M. oceana*, the three forms of operculum above figured were found, evidently belonging to distinct species. The one represented by fig. 229, occurs abundantly and in a fine state of preservation. The outer surface is divided into two sub-triangular areas by a suture running from the nuclear angle *a*, to the lower inner angle. The inner or smaller area is striated parallel to the inner concave edge *b*; the outer area parallel to the lower gently convex edge *c*. It is about two lines in thickness at the lower edge, but becomes gradually thicker to the upper, the most elevated point being at the nuclear angle, *a*, where the thickness is ten lines in the specimen figured. On the inside, the upper and outer edges are bordered by a thick elevated margin. There is no muscular process, as there is in the operculum found with *M. crenulata*.

The operculum represented by fig. 228 is of a sub-cylindrical spiral form, and exhibits no sutures on its outer surface, the striæ being continuous all across. There is no muscular process.

Figure 230 has no suture, and although more nearly related to fig. 228 than it is to the other, is still quite distinct therefrom.

There was also another operculum found at Pistolet Bay, which is nearly straight, and two inches long by six lines in width.

These four opercula, differing so widely from each other, prove that there are also as many distinct species of *Maclurea* to which they belong. Accordingly at Cape Norman we find fragments of what appear to be forms different from those above described. I propose to name them as follows:

MACLUREA SYLPHA. (N. sp.)

Description.— This species is founded on a silicified fragment consisting of the middle three whorls of a specimen which appears to have been somewhat larger and more nearly globular than any of those above noticed. Spire flat; width across the three whorls, 12 lines; last whorl 4 lines wide; height of the aperture as nearly as can be ascertained 10 lines; width of the umbilicus, 7 lines. The umbilicus, which is quite empty in the specimen, is cylindro-conical; the edge scarcely at all projecting, and the sides of the whorls flat. It extends quite to the apex.

MACLUREA PSYCHE. (N. sp.)

Description.—A specimen 18 lines wide, has the aperture $10\frac{1}{2}$ lines in height; umbilicus 6 lines wide. The spire is flat, but the number of whorls cannot be made out. The edge of the umbilicus is narrowly rounded as it is in *M. oceana*; inner side of the whorl gently convex. In general aspect resembles a sub-globular form of *M. oceana*, differing therefrom in having a narrower umbilicus which does not ascend to the apex, and in having the aperture more extended in the vertical direction.

Maclurea rotundata. (N. sp.)

a b

Fig. 231.

Fig. 231.—*Maclurea rotundata.* *a*, front view of a cast of the interior; *b*, view of the base.

Description.—Shell about two inches across, strongly convex; spire flat, the inner whorls sometimes a little elevated above the outer; whorls about three, flat on the upper side; margin narrowly rounded; umbilicus half the whole width, with the edge narrowly or acutely rounded; whorls in the umbilicus gently convex. Surface unknown.

Width of specimen figured 18 lines; height of aperture 12 lines; width of umbilicus 9 lines; width of last whorl at the aperture 7 lines.

This species is closely allied to *M. Emmonsi* from which it differs in having the upper side of the whorls flat, even in casts of the interior, and in its somewhat narrower umbilicus. *M. Psyche* has the umbilicus still narrower and penetrating only half the height of the shell.

Locality and Formation.—Bonne Bay, entrance to the north arm, and also east arm, south-west side, Newfoundland; Quebec group.

Collector.—J. Richardson.

Ophileta Nerine. (N. sp.)

a b

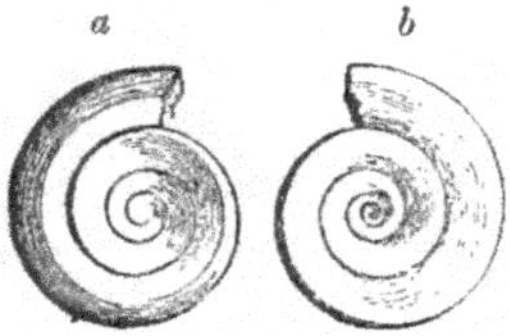

Fig. 232.

Fig. 232.—*Ophileta Nerine.* *a*, base; *b*, the spire.

Description.—Smaller than *O. compacta;* spire gently concave; margin acutely rounded. Lower side deeply concave, with the whorls strongly angular along the middle; the edges of all the whorls seen in the umbilicus. In the smaller specimens the outer side of the whorls slope inward at an angle of about 75°, but in the larger ones it is more nearly vertical. The inner slope of each whorl (from the angular edge which runs along the middle on the lower side), into the umbilicus, is flat; the slope outwards (or the outer side of the whorl) is gently convex.

In a specimen 8½ lines wide, there are four whorls; width of last whorl at the aperture 2 lines; depth about the same. The largest specimen seen is 15 lines wide. Surface finely striated parallel with the aperture.

This species is certainly closely allied to *O. compacta*, and it is not without much hesitation that a new name is proposed for it. The following are the differences:—In *O. compacta* the spire is always flat, and the lower side of each whorl (or that side which slopes into the umbilicus) concave. In this species the spire is always gently concave, and the lower side of the whorl flat. *O. compacta* is, also, a much larger species, being usually from 20 to 30 lines, while of *O. Nerine*, although found in immense numbers, the largest seen is 15 lines wide, and all the others seen, from 3 to 8 lines wide.

Although a new name is proposed, I think it only a variety, and further that *O. compacta* and *O. complanata* are also varieties of the same species.

Locality and Formation.—F, Bay of St. John, Newfoundland; Quebec group.

Collector.—J. Richardson.

OPHILETA UNIANGULATA. (Hall.)

EUOMPHALUS UNIANGULATUS, (Hall.) Pal. N. Y., vol. 1, p. 9, pl. iii, figs. 1, 1*a*.

Remarks.—This species occurs at Cow Head in Division P. It occurs also in the limestones at Point Levis in Band 4, and at Bedford in C 1, Geol. of Can. p. 845.

Helicotoma Proserpina. (N. sp.)

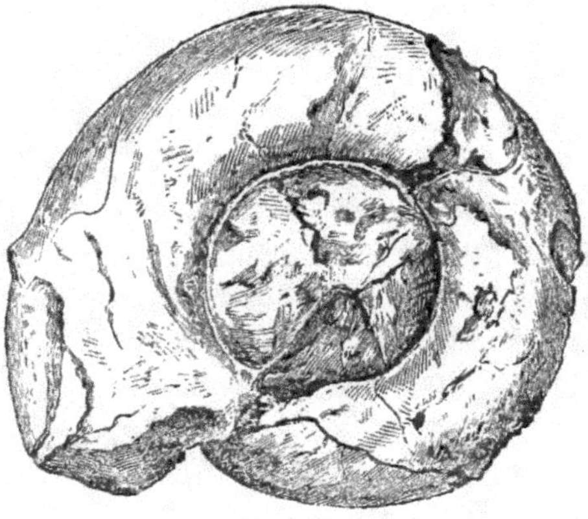

Fig. 233.

Fig. 233.—*Helicotoma Proserpina.* The under side.

Description.—Shell large, consisting of about four sub-cylindrical whorls; spire nearly flat, the inner whorls being only slightly elevated above each other; suture apparently deeply impressed. On the upper side the whorls are slightly flattened along the middle, rounded at the edges. On the under side they are strongly and uniformly convex. The outer side is somewhat flattened and approaching the vertical, but rounded above and below. The umbilicus is about half the whole width.

Width of the specimen 30 lines; height of the last whorl 9 lines; width 8 lines.

This species is founded on a single specimen, which retains a part of the shell, but so covered by adherent matter that the surface characters cannot be ascertained. On the outside of the last whorl there are visible some oblique undulations which cross from the margin downwards and forwards. These, no doubt, indicate the course of the striæ, which, most probably, curve backwards to the margin, both above and below.

Locality and Formation.—G, Cape Norman, Newfoundland; Quebec group.

Collector—J. Richardson.

Helicotoma Tritonia. (N. sp.)

Description.—The specimen is a fragment consisting of four whorls; width 19 lines; height about 6 lines. Spire gently concave; whorls sub-cylindrical, on the upper side, with a narrow elevated ridge at the margin, or a little within it, then gently convex to the suture ; close to the marginal ridge there is a distinct groove following it all the way to the centre of the disc. On the outside the whorls are gently convex and sub-vertical, apparently sloping a little outwards in the last whorl, and inwards in the smaller ones. On the under side the whorls are rather strongly convex, obscurely rounded, descending with a somewhat flat slope into the umbilicus, which is wide and concave. Where the shell is preserved, on the outside of one of the inner whorls, it shews four or five narrow, thread-like ridges, following the whorl longitudinally.

This species must be closely allied to *H. Proserpina*. It differs from it in having a marginal ridge on the upper side, and in the form of the whorls on the lower side not so prominently rounded.

Locality and Formation.—G, Cape Norman, Newfoundland ; Quebec group.

Collector.—J. Richardson.

HELICOTOMA GORGONEA. (N. sp.)

Description.—Shell large, depressed conical. Whorls about four, nearly cylindrical. On the upper side (as ascertained by a vertical polished section), the whorls are turretted, each rising about one-fourth its own diameter above the preceding. On the under side strongly and uniformly convex, or cylindrical ; umbilicus not quite half the width, exposing all the whorls to the apex in stair-case arrangement.

Width 2½ inches ; width of the last whorl at the aperture 9 lines ; height about the same.

The specimen shews the under side, the spire being imbedded in limestone. The whorls below, and in the umbilicus (which is nearly empty), are uniformly cylindrical, apparently a little flattened along the middle of the lower side, but above, as seen in the section, they seem to be obtusely angulated half way between the margin and the suture. The inner upper side of each is also impressed by the one next above it.

This species, so far as its form can be made out, resembles closely some of the large *Euomphali* with cylindrical and slightly angulated whorls, which abound in the Devonian and Carboniferous series.

It may be that this species is only a variety of *H. Proserpina.*

Locality and Formation.—H, Table Head, Newfoundland ; Quebec group.

Collector.—J. Richardson.

Helicotoma Eucharis. (N. sp.)

Fig. 234.

Fig. 234.—*Helicotoma Eucharis.* *a*, upper side; *b*, front view.

Description.—Shell small, of three whorls, including a minute one in the centre. Spire nearly flat, the inner whorls a little elevated above the outer; margin narrowly rounded; upper side of whorls flat and sloping a little downwards to the suture, the outer edge being more elevated than the inner. Outer side of the whorls gently convex. Umbilicus a little more than half the whole width; the edge acutely rounded; the whorls within, gently convex.

Surface with fine striæ, which curve backwards to the marginal edge.

Width, 4½ lines; height of the aperture, 3 lines. Of this species only two specimens have been found. One of them has the edge of the umbilicus quite acute, but in every other respect the two are identical. Both have indications of a shallow concave band just below the margin of the last whorl.

Locality and Formation.—L, M, Table Head, Newfoundland; Quebec group.

Collector.—J. Richardson.

Ecculiomphalus distans. (N. sp.)

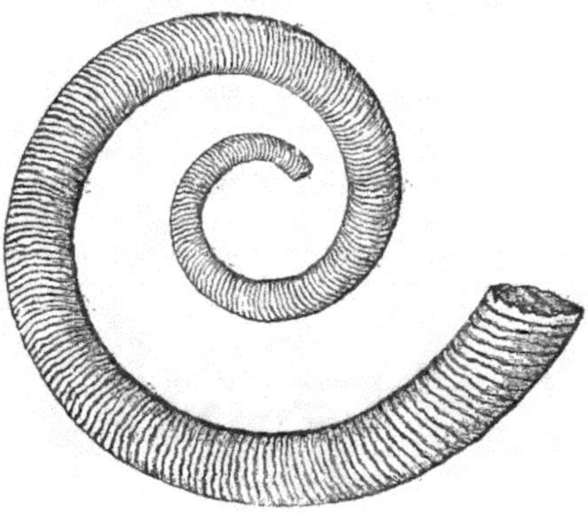

Fig. 235.

Fig. 235.—*Ecculiomphalus distans.* Lower side.

Description.—Shell slender, coiled in a regularly spiral curve, whorls three or four, distant from each other about once and a half their width. Surface coarsely striated transversely.

The specimen is imbedded in a piece of limestone, the lower side being exposed. There are two complete whorls preserved, which appear to be the second and third, the first or inner one absent. Width of the whole coil, 27 lines; width of the inner whorl (supposed to be the second,) 10 lines; thickness of the last whorl at the aperture, (or where broken off,) 4½ lines.

On the lower side the whorls are uniformly convex; on the outer side more depressed, but still it is moderately convex; inner side apparently a little flattened; upper side, judging from the fractured extremity, with a carina at about the outer third, inside of which there seems to be a flat slope. The form of this side, however, still remains doubtful.

Locality and Formation.—P, north-east side of Cow Head, Newfoundland; Quebec group.

Collector.—J. Richardson.

Ecculiompalus Atlanticus. (N. sp.)

Description.—Tube slender, forming two whorls, closely coiled, but not in contact. Under side of the whorls nearly uniformly rounded; upper side angular near the outer edge.

The spire of the best specimen seen, is 11 lines across; width of the aperture, 3 lines; height about the same; distance of the last whorl from the preceding one, at the aperture, about 1 line. In other specimens, the whorls are not so much separated.

This species is smaller than *E. intortus*, and has more slender whorls.

Locality and Formation.—F, Bay of St. John, G, Keppel Island, Newfoundland; Quebec group.

Collector.—J. Richardson.

Ecculiomphalus superbus. (N. sp.)

Description.—Shell large, gently curved, surface with strong angular transverse striæ, about five in two lines. A single imperfect specimen only has been collected. Its length, following the outside, is six inches; width at the aperture, 15 lines; depth about 12 lines. The under side is obscurely angular along the middle, and the upper apparently rounded. About two inches of the larger extremity nearly straight, and the remainder curved to a radius of about fifteen lines. Its form is exceedingly like that of *E. Canadensis*, but it is larger and more strongly striated.

Locality and Formation.—P, two miles north-east from Portland Creek, Newfoundland; Quebec group.

Collector.—J. Richardson.

METOPTOMA INSTABILIS. (N. sp.)

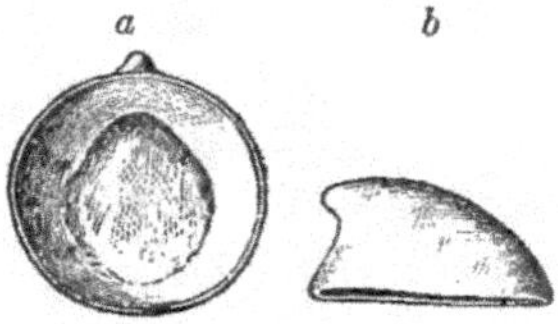

Fig. 236.

Fig. 236.—*Metoptoma instabilis.* *a*, under side; *b*, side view.

Description.—Shell small, depressed conical; apex acute, slightly incurved, situated over the anterior margin; aperture circular; surface finely striated parallel to the base.

Width of an average specimen, 8 lines; height, 4 lines.

The above relates to a symmetrical individual, but there are many specimens with the base more or less oval, and the apex turned either to the right or left, besides being more flattened on one side than the other. I regard these as being all deformed individuals of the same species.

Locality and Formation.—L, Table Head, Newfoundland; Quebec group.

Collector.—J. Richardson.

CEPHALOPODA.

ORTHOCERAS PISCATOR. (N. sp.)

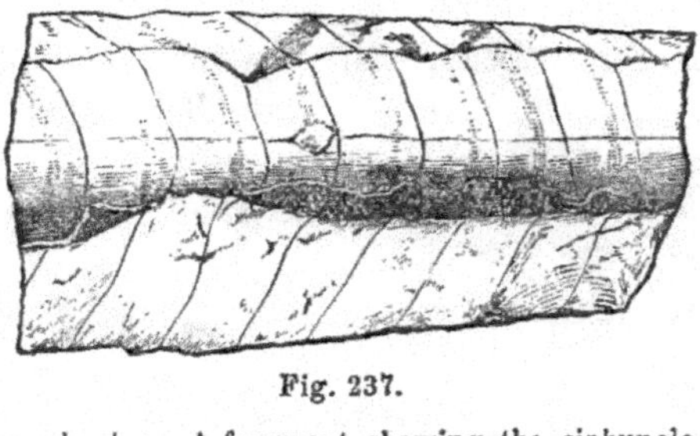

Fig. 237.

Fig. 237.—*Orthoceras piscator.* A fragment shewing the siphuncle and some of the septa.

Description.—This is a large, elongated, gradually tapering species, with a large lateral siphuncle. A specimen, three feet in length, tapers from a diameter of about four inches at the larger extremity, to one inch at the smaller. The siphuncle in the same length tapers from about sixteen lines to nine lines; and it is thus more than one-half the whole diameter near the apex, but less than one-third near the chamber of habitation. The section is circular, or nearly so.

In one specimen, where the diameter is nine lines, there are six septa to one inch in length. In another specimen of a siphuncle, seven inches in length, eleven lines in diameter at the larger and seven at the smaller, there are twenty-three septa. In the large specimen, where the diameter is three inches, there are four septa in fourteen lines. The average appears to be between three and four septa to the inch, from a diameter of two inches and upwards. The detached siphuncles are usually a little flattened on the ventral side along the line of the contact with the shell. Surface unknown.

Locality and Formation.—I, K, L, M, N, Table Head and Point Rich, Newfoundland; Quebec group.

Collector.—J. Richardson.

ORTHOCERAS SERVILE. (N. sp.)

Description.—Section ovate, in the proportions of about fifteen to ten. The rate of tapering for the shorter diameter supposed to be the dorso-ventral, is about one line and a half to the inch. The lateral diameter diminishes at the rate of three lines to the inch. Only two of the septa are visible in the specimen; they are at the larger extremity, and are distant about one line from each other. Surface with fine engirdling striæ. Siphuncle unknown.

Length of the specimen 3 inches; lateral diameter at the larger extremity 15 lines, at the smaller 6 lines; dorso-ventral diameter about 10 and 4½ lines.

This is a short, compressed, rapidly tapering species, belonging to the theca-shaped group to which *O. hastatum* (Black River limestone), and *O. xiphias* (Trenton) belong.

Locality and Formation.—L, Point Rich, Newfoundland; Quebec group.

Collector.—J. Richardson.

ORTHOCERAS EXPLORATOR. (N. sp.)

a b

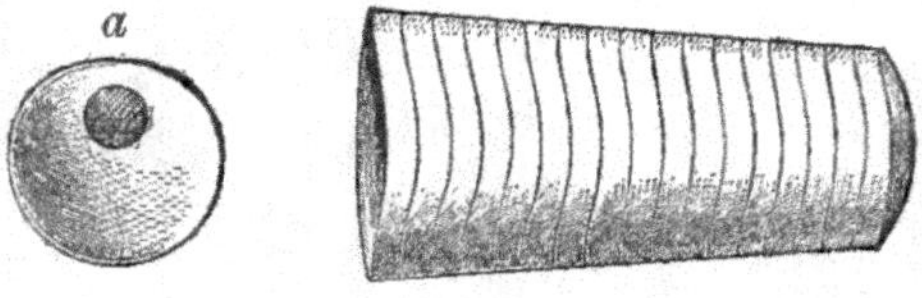

Fig. 238.

Fig. 238.—*Orthoceras explorator.* a section shewing the siphuncle; b side view of the specimen.

Description.—Section nearly circular, slightly flattened on the ventral side; tapering at the rate of about one line and a half to the inch; septa about twelve to one inch, where the diameter is from seven to eight lines, gently undulated towards the apex on the ventral side; siphuncle cylindrical, two lines in diameter where the diameter of the shell is eight lines, situated at about one line or less from the shell on the ventral side. Surface unknown.

Locality and Formation.—H, Pistolet Bay on Schooner Island, Newfoundland; Quebec group.

Collector.—J. Richardson.

ORTHOCERAS PRIAMUS. (N. sp.)

a b

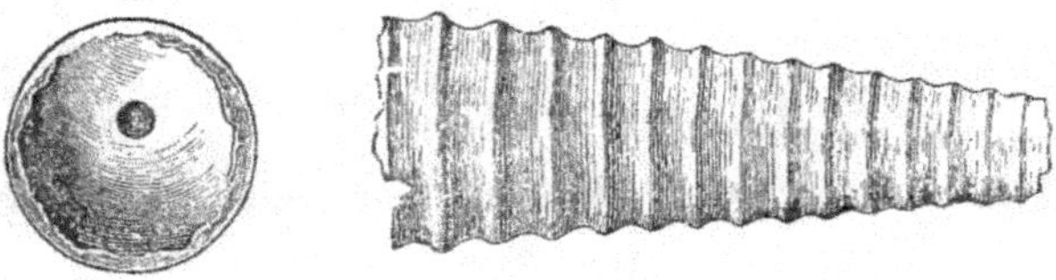

Fig. 239.

Fig. 239.—*Orthoceras Priamus.* a, section; b, side view of a fragment with the shell preserved.

Description.—Shell annulated, of medium size; section circular; siphuncle cylindrical, very slightly, if at all, inflated between the septa, its diameter between one-sixth and one-seventh the whole diameter of the shell, near the centre; septa from about five to eight to the inch; annulations narrowly rounded, with uniformly concave spaces between, fifteen in a length of two inches; surface with fine thread-like, engirdling striæ, from eight to ten in one line, covering the annulations, as well as the interspaces.

Length of the best preserved specimen 2 inches ; diameter at the larger extremity 9 lines, and at the smaller 4 lines ; diameter of the siphuncle $1\frac{1}{3}$ lines. The centre of the siphuncle is about 1 line from the centre of the septum.

Another specimen, 5 inches in length, tapers from 14 lines to 3 ; and has 9 septa in the 2 inches at the larger extremity, and 8 in 1 inch at the smaller.

In external characters this species closely resembles *O. decrescens* (Black River and Trenton), but differs in the form of the siphuncle, which is cylindrical instead of moniliform.

Locality and Formation.—L, Point Rich, M, Table Head, Newfoundland ; Quebec group.

Collector.—J. Richardson.

Orthoceras Allumettense (Billings).

O. Allumettense (Billings.) *Report G. S. C.*, 1857, p. 351.

Remarks.—This species occurs at Table Head, in Divisions M and N ; at Point Rich, in M ; and on the west side of Pistolet Bay, in N. In Canada it occurs in the Chazy and Black River formations ; but has not been found above the Black River limestone. The specimens from Newfoundland are all one-half larger than the largest that have been collected in Canada. In other respects, I cannot make out any difference.

Orthoceras hæsitans. (N. sp.)

Variety of O. Bigsbyi (Stokes) ; *O. tenuifilum* (Hall.)

Description.—Section apparently nearly circular, the transverse diameter a little greater than the dorso-ventral ; siphuncle inflated between the septa, a little less than one-half the whole diameter ; septa distant about one-sixth the whole diameter.

Only two specimens have been collected ; and both of these are curved to a radius of about one foot. The siphuncle in one of these specimens is in contact with the shell at the smaller extremity, where the diameter is about one inch, and distant from it about one line, where the diameter is nearly two inches. In the other it is two lines distant from the shell throughout.

Both specimens are somewhat distorted by pressure, and, therefore, the dimensions cannot be given precisely. They are each about 5 inches in length, 2 inches in diameter at the larger, and 15 lines at the smaller extremity.

The only difference between this species and *O. Bigsbyi* is, that in the latter the siphuncle is in general a little more than half the whole diameter, whereas in this species it is less than one-half.

Locality and Formation.—I, Point Rich, M, Table Head, Newfoundland; Quebec group.

Collector.—J. Richardson.

ORTHOCERAS LAMARCKI. (Billings.)

O LAMARCKI. (Billings.) *Can. Nat. and Geol.*, vol. iv, p. 362, Oct. 1859. *Geol. Can.*, p. 121, fig. 38.

Remarks.—This species, or a very closely allied variety of it, occurs abundantly, in silicified fragments at Cape Norman, in Division G, at Pistolet Bay, on Schooner Island, in Division H, and at the River of Ponds, in G, Newfoundland. It resembles *O. Priamus*, but is more nearly cylindrical, the rate of tapering being on an average about one line to the inch. The siphuncle is stated in the original description, to be full one-third of the whole diameter, but in the majority of the specimens from Newfoundland it is about one-fourth. I would classify these, from this locality, as a distinct species, were it not that among them there is one with the siphuncle full one-third the whole diameter, and several with it between one-fourth and one-third.

ORTHOCERAS FLAVIUS. (N. sp.)

Description.—Shell of medium size; section apparently circular; siphuncle cylindrical, in contact with the shell; septa from nine to thirteen to the inch. Surface and rate of tapering unknown.

The best preserved specimen is 3 inches in length, about 9 lines in diameter at the smaller extremity, and 10½ lines at the mid-length, shewing a rate of tapering of about 1½ lines to the inch. The specimen, however, is distorted by pressure. The siphuncle is 3 lines in diameter in the lateral direction, and 2½ in the dorso-ventral. It is nearly of the same size throughout. There are 10 septa to the inch. Another siphuncle of the same length, is 4 lines in diameter at the larger, and 3 lines at the smaller extremity. It has 13 septal rings to the inch.

O. explorator has the siphuncle not in contact with the shell, and one-third smaller, but in other respects resembles this species.

Locality and Formation.—I, Point Rich, Newfoundland; Quebec group.

Collector.—J. Richardson.

Piloceras Canadense. (Billings.)

P. Canadense. (Billings.) *Can. Nat. and Geol.*, vol. v, p. 171.

Remarks.—Several specimens of the siphuncle of this species were collected at Cape Norman and Port aux Choix, in divisions F and G. In Canada it has been found only in the Calciferous formation.

Piloceras Wortheni. (N. sp.)

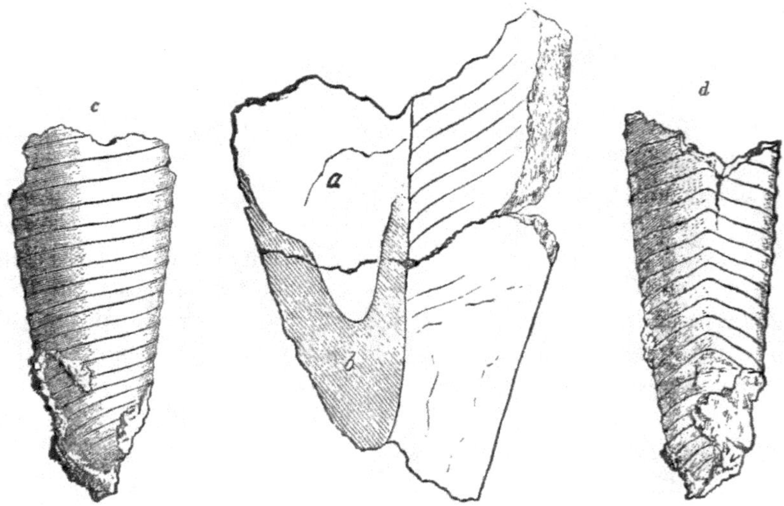

Fig. 240.

Fig. 240.—*Piloceras Wortheni.* The central figure is a longitudinal section, *a*, the cavity, and *b*, the solid part of the siphuncle ; *c*, side, and *d*, ventral view of a detached siphuncle.

Description.—Siphuncle nearly straight, from two to four inches in length ; tapering at the rate of two and two-thirds lines to the inch, for two inches from the larger extremity in a specimen two and a half inches in length, then more rapidly to the apex ; septa from eight to twelve in one inch ; section broadly elliptical, the dorso-ventral diameter about one-fifth greater than the lateral. The septa cross the sides obliquely, sloping towards the aperture, in proceeding from the dorsal to the ventral side. Surface unknown.

One of the specimens shews that on the ventral side, the siphuncle is in contact with the shell. Another specimen, a longitudinal polished section of which is represented by fig. 240, shews that at two inches from the apex, the shell must be at least one inch from the siphuncle on the dorsal side; and, as the specimen is mutilated on that side, the distance may be greater. The septa are excessively thin, and at their junction with the siphuncle are curved towards the apex, forming an attachment similar to that observed in the ordinary species of *Orthoceras* and *Nautilus*.

In a specimen 30 lines in length, the dorso-ventral diameter at the larger extremity is 14 lines; lateral, 11 lines, at 1½ inches nearer the apex, the dorso-ventral diameter is 11 lines, and the lateral, 9 lines. Thence more rapidly tapering to the apex. In the first 18 lines there are 12 septa or 8 to the inch on an average, but in the apical inch there are 12 or 13. In other specimens they are a little closer together.

In *P. Canadense* the siphuncle is in general, more curved, and the septal ridges cross it, sloping from the dorsal side downwards in proceeding to the ventral side. In this species they slope in the opposite direction (assuming always that the most curved side is the ventral).

Dedicated to A. H. WORTHEN, State Geologist of Illinois.

Locality and Formation.—H. Port aux Choix, Newfoundland; Quebec group.

Collector.—J. Richardson.

PILOCERAS TRITON. (N. sp.)

Description.—Larger than *P. Canadense*, with a straighter siphuncle and more distant septa.

The best preserved siphuncle collected, is 5½ inches in length; dorso-ventral diameter, at the larger extremity 2 inches; lateral 21 lines; in the apical 18 lines, there are 10 septa; in a length of 2 inches next the large end, there are only 7.

In *P. Canadense*, where the lateral diameter is 12 lines, there are 7 septal rings on the siphuncle, but in this species at the same diameter there are only 5, and further up they are 3½ lines distant from each other.

Locality and Formation.—H and I, west side of Pistolet Bay, Newfoundland; Quebec group.

Collector.—J. Richardson.

PILOCERAS GRACILE. (N. sp.)

Description.—This name is proposed for a species, of which a portion only of a siphuncle has been found. It differs from all the others in being proportionably more slender and elongated, and in having more distant septa.

Length of the specimen, imperfect at both ends, 5 inches ; dorso-ventral diameter, at the larger extremity 15 lines ; lateral diameter, 13 lines ; dorso-ventral diameter, at 4 inches from the larger extremity, 11 lines ; the rate of tapering being thus about 1 line to the inch ; septa about 4 lines distant from each other.

Locality and Formation.—H, Schooner Island in Pistolet Bay, Newfoundland ; Quebec group.

Collector.—J. Richardson.

Other Species of Cephalopoda.

At all the localities, from Division F, upwards, fragments of undetermined orthoceratites occur, many of which will, no doubt, turn out to be undescribed. It is remarkable that no species of *Cyrtoceras* has been collected in these rocks in Newfoundland, while they abound at Point Levis. Of other genera I propose to name the following species, provisionally :

1. *Nautilus insolens.*—About 6 inches across ; whorls all seen in the umbilicus ; aperture 3 inches wide and 2½ inches in the dorso-ventral diameter ; siphuncle apparently near the centre, 3 lines in diameter consisting of segments, which are constructed or shaped like a dice-box. The septa have not been distinctly observed, but judging from the length of the segments of the siphuncle they appear to be 3 or 4 lines apart. The section is broadly elliptical, flattened along the ventral aspect, rounded at the sides. The specimens are all more or less distorted. It occurs in Division L, at Point Rich.

2. *Nautilus desertus.*—The specimen is a fragment, consisting of the two central whorls of a strongly annulated species. Diameter 16 lines ; dorso-ventral diameter of the last whorl, where broken off, 6 lines ; lateral diameter 9 lines ; distance of the annulations from each other 3 lines. The whorls envelope each other to the depth of one-sixth the dorso-ventral diameter ; they are moderately convex on the ventral aspect and narrowly rounded on the side. It occurs in Division L, Point Rich.

3. *Nautilus calciferus.*—Whorls slender, compactly inrolled, the outer a little impressed by the inner ; septa twelve to the inch on the ventral aspect, where the diameter of the coil is three inches ; siphuncle small, close to the shell in the median line of the ventral aspect.

A specimen 3 inches across, consisting of about 3 whorls, has the last whorl 13 lines in the dorso-ventral diameter, and the siphuncle about 1½ lines in thickness.

This species has more numerous septa than has *L. Palinurus*, (*ante*, p. 25.)

It occurs, both at Port aux Choix and Cape Norman, in F and G.

4. *Nautilus versutus.*—The specimen is 5½ inches across, and consists of about four whorls. Septa, in the last whorl, ten to the inch. The ventral side of the last whorl is broad and nearly flat, the sides narrowly rounded. Siphuncle unknown.

The last whorl has a breadth of 27 lines on the ventral aspect, and a dorso-ventral diameter of 18 lines.

It is evident, that in perfect specimens this species must exhibit a wide shallow umbilicus, exposing all the whorls. Its form must be much like that of *N. Pomponius*, (*ante*, p. 26), but has more numerous septa. It was found on the west side of the east arm of Bonne Bay, apparently in Division H.

5. *Lituites Pluto.*—The specimen is a portion of the free whorl. It is 7 inches in length; apparently about 20 lines in diameter at the larger extremity, and 16 at the smaller. There are about 12 septa to the inch throughout. It is curved to a radius of about 12 inches. It occurs at Point Rich, in Division L.

CRUSTACEA.

Bathyurus Saffordi and B. Cordai. (Billings.)

a b

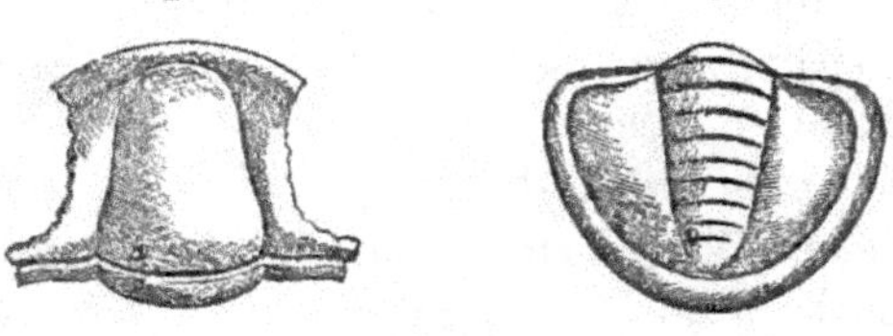

Fig. 241.

Fig. 242.

Fig. 241.—*Bathyurus Saffordi.* *a*, the glabella; *b*, the pygidium.
242.—*B. Cordai.* The glabella.

Remarks.—*B. Saffordi* occurs at Cow Head, in Division P, in white limestone, associated with great abundance of *Maclurea ponderosa.* It is the most common trilobite at Point Lévis and Phillipsburgh, in the limestones of the Quebec group.

B. Cordai also occurs at Cow Head, in P, but in a greyish limestone. Some imperfect specimens of a species which appears to be identical with it were found at Bay St. John, in Division F. It occurs at Point Lévis and Phillipsburgh, along with *B. Saffordi*, but is not so common as that species.

In a blue limestone, evidently belonging to the Calciferous formation at Comstock, in the State of New York, numerous specimens of the glabella of a trilobite, which can scarcely be distinguished from *B. Cordai*, have been collected.

BATHYURUS NERO. (N. sp.)

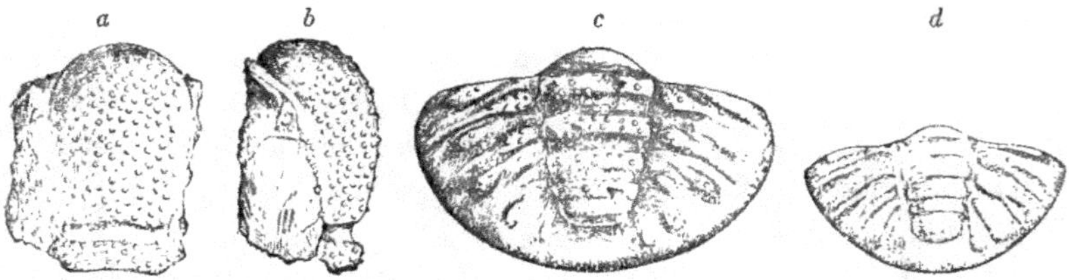

Fig. 243.

Fig. 243.—*Bathyurus Nero.* *a*, upper side of the glabella; *b*, side view of a specimen, with an arched outline; *c* and *d*, pygidia.

Description.—Oblong-ovate, about three inches in length and two in width. Head strongly convex, with the posterior angles produced backwards into long stout spines. Glabella oblong, a little wider in front than at the neck segment; sides nearly straight and sub-parallel; well defined all round by the dorsal furrows; strongly convex or semi-cylindrical; abruptly elevated in front; the outline, on a side view, nearly straight, with the exception of the front, or gently arched as in fig. *b;* neck furrow concave, rather deep, extending all across; neck segment rounded, well defined. Pygidium semi-elliptical, strongly convex, broadly rounded behind; front margin slightly convex; length a little greater than half the width; axis very convex, about four fifths the length and a little less than one third the width of the pygidium; obtusely rounded and abruptly elevated at the apex, with five strong transverse rings; sides with four ribs, besides the half rib at the front margin; these ribs are, in small specimens, divided or simply forked by a groove, for half their length next the margin; in large specimens the groove becomes deeper, and crosses the rib obliquely from behind, forwards and outwards, leaving a large tubercle next the axis in front, and another behind the groove, near the margin.

The whole of the surface, so far as yet observed, is covered with strong tubercles.

No entire specimens have been seen; but the detached cheeks, found in the same hand specimens of rock, show that the posterior angles of the head are spinose, as above mentioned.

Locality and Formation.—F, Keppel Island; G, Port aux Choix and Cape Norman; H, Port aux Choix, Schooner Island, in Pistolet Bay, and Table Head; N, west side of Pistolet Bay, Newfoundland; Quebec group.

Collector.—J. Richardson.

BATHYURUS TIMON. (N. sp.)

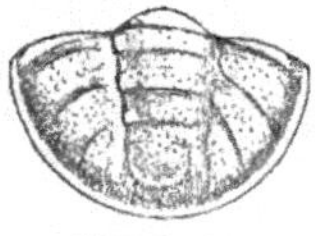

Fig. 244.

Fig. 244.—*Bathyurus Timon;* pygidium.

Description.—Pygidium rather strongly convex, semi-elliptical; length about two thirds of the width; a smooth, narrow, concave margin all round. Axis concave, semi-cylindrical; a little less than one third the whole width; gently tapering, obtusely rounded, and abruptly elevated at the apex, with five strong rounded rings, the last two of which are only partially separated; side lobes with three broad but strongly elevated ribs, the last one sub-triangular.

In small specimens, the grooves between the ribs are narrow and angular, but with age they become wider and concave in the bottom, as in the above figure. Surface, when well preserved, finely tubercled.

Associated with these pygidia is a single specimen of a glabella, as strongly convex as that of *Menocephalus globosus*. From the surface characters, and its occurrence in the same beds, I think it belongs to this species.

Locality and Formation.—G, H, Port aux Choix, Newfoundland; Quebec group.

Collector.—J. Richardson.

BATHYURUS CAUDATUS. (N. sp.)

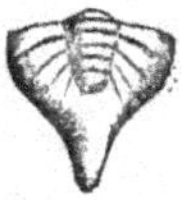

Fig. 245.

Fig. 245.—*Bathyurus caudatus;* pygidium, the anterior margin restored.

Description.—Pygidium strongly convex, with a strong triangular spine behind. Axis conical, a little less than one third the whole width, strongly convex, well defined all round by the dorsal furrow, the apex rounded, four or five rings. Side lobes, with four or five broad and short ribs, which extend about half way to the margin. There is a smooth border all round, which is not concave, but apparently slightly convex; this is extended backwards, and forms the terminal spine.

The specimen is imperfect at the anterior margin, and it is not quite certain whether there are four or five ribs.

Locality and Formation.—G and H, Port aux Choix, Newfoundland; Quebec group.

Collector.—J. Richardson.

BATHYURUS BREVICEPS. (N. sp.)

Fig. 246.

Fig. 246.—*Bathyurus breviceps*, enlarged two diameters.

Description.—Glabella short and wide, strongly convex, rounded and abruptly elevated in front; sides, nearly parallel; neck furrow extending all across. The front margin has a narrow flat rim which is elevated at an angle of about 45°; between the rim and the front of the glabella a narrow deep groove. The dorsal furrows are deep, but narrow, all round the glabella. The fixed cheeks are convex. The eye appears to be small and situated about the mid-length, and distant from the dorsal furrows about half the width of the glabella. There are no glabellar furrows. The surface appears to be smooth.

Length of glabella, 1 line; width, a little less than 1 line. The groove and marginal rim in front of the glabella occupy about ¼ of a line. Total length of the head, 1¼ lines.

Locality and Formation.—N, Table Head, Newfoundland; Quebec group.

Collector.—J. Richardson.

Genus. BATHYURELLUS. (N. gen.)

Generic characters.—Trilobites of a medium size, oblong, ovate; head, thorax, and pygidium, sub-equal; head convex with the posterior angles sometimes produced backwards into spines; glabella conical, usually convex, and without glabellar furrows; eyes, lunate; facial suture in front of the eye curving outwards, then either straight forwards or curving inwards on approaching the margin, behind the eye running outwards sub-parallel to the neck furrow, and cutting the margin before reaching the outer angle. Thorax distinctly tri-lobed, about nine segments; pygidium with the axis usually short and not strongly grooved; side lobes, with short ribs sometimes indistinctly developed; a broad smooth border all round, which is sometimes concave.

This genus should perhaps be regarded as a sub-genus of *Bathyurus*. The typical species of this latter, such as *B. extans*, *B. Nero*, and *B. Cybele*, have a sub-cylindrical glabella rounded in front, strongly convex, and with obscure glabellar furrows. In this genus the glabella is conical or pointed in front, and exhibits no trace of furrows. The pygidium also differs in not being strongly convex, in having a shorter axis, and in general a wider border.

In Newfoundland we first find this genus in Division F, in rocks which appear to be of the age of the lower part of the Calciferous formation, and it ranges upwards to Division P, through a thickness of more than 3000 feet. It occurs in Newfoundland, near Quebec, and at Phillipsburgh. At Swanton, in Vermont, a species has been found in the Trenton, which may belong to this genus.

BATHYURELLUS ABRUPTUS. (N. sp.)

Fig. 247.

Fig. 248.

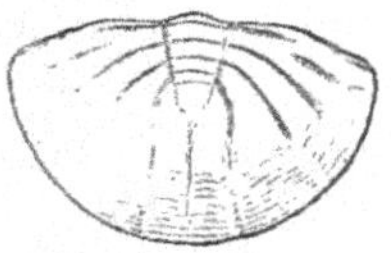
Fig. 249.

Fig. 250.

Fig. 247.—*Bathyurellus abruptus*. The glabella and fixed cheeks.
248.—*B. marginatus*. The glabella and part of the fixed cheeks.
249.—Supposed pygidium of *B. marginatus*.
250.—Pygidium most common, with *B. abruptus*, enlarged two diameters.

Description.—Glabella cylindro-conical, sides parallel, front rather narrowly rounded and scarcely at all elevated or defined from the smooth anterior margin. Neck furrow narrow, extending all across. Neck segment rather broad, and depressed convex. Judging from the form of the palpebral lobe the eye is large and semi-annular, and a little more than one-half the length of the glabella, the posterior angle close to the neck furrow, and the anterior angle almost in contact with the side of the glabella a little in advance of the mid-length. Around the front of the head there is a smooth border which is somewhat concave, and varies in width from one-fifth to one-fourth of the length of the glabella. On a side view the head is rather strongly convex, the outline gently arched along the median line of the posterior two-thirds of the glabella, and then descending with a convex slope to the smooth anterior margin, which is slightly concave between the apex of the glabella and the edge of the head. There is scarcely a marginal rim to the head of this speoies so far as yet observed.

The pygidium, represented by fig. 250, has a strongly convex and rather acutely conical axis, a little less than half the whole length, and a little less than one-third the whole width. The side lobes have three or four short and very obscure furrows near the anterior margin, but elsewhere, are smooth, and descend with a concave slope to the margin. The anterior angles seem to be abruptly bent downwards, and just behind the deflected portion there is a short curved groove, the convex side forwards, deeper than the others. This groove dies out before reaching the axis on the one hand, and, on the other, before reaching the margin. There is, however, an obscure rounded fold, in front of the groove, which reaches the margin.

No perfect specimens of this peculiar pygidium have been discovered, but as nearly as can be ascertained, its form is obscurely sub-quadrate, the posterior margin obtusely rounded, the sides somewhat parallel, but diverging from each other forwards. The central portion next the anterior margin is strongly convex, and the peculiar slope of the wide margin gives it a shape resembling that of a duck's bill.

Length of the largest pygidium collected 6 lines; width about the same. Length of the largest glabella 4 lines.

Locality and Formation.—F, G, and H, Port aux Choix, and Keppel Island, Newfoundland; Quebec group.

Collector.—J. Richardson.

Bathyurellus marginiatus. (N. sp.)

Fig. 248.

Description.—Glabella cylindro-conical, narrowly rounded in front, rather strongly convex, uniformly arched along the median line; width, a little more than half the length; neck segment depressed convex; neck furrow narrow, extending all across. The front of the head has a flat horizontal margin—its width equal to one-sixth the whole length of the head. From this to the glabella, there is a convex ascent—the width of the margin and ascent being one-third the whole length of the head. The glabella is two-thirds the whole length of the head. Eyes and cheeks, unknown.

This species differs from *B. abruptus*, in having the glabella proportionally shorter.

The pygidium, fig. 249, supposed to be that of this species, is nearly flat, and very much resembles that of a *Bronteus*. It is nearly semicircular, width not quite double the length; axis small, convex, conical, not quite half the whole length, with four or five obscure annulations; side lobes nearly flat, with four wide ribs. The anterior rib has a short pleural groove close to the anterior margin next the axis, and another at about the middle of its width, but in the outer half of its length. The other ribs are undivided, and curve backwards, so that the posterior two (consisting of one from each side) are parallel with the median line.

Only one specimen of the head of this species has been observed. The pygidium appears to be somewhat common.

Locality and Formation.—F, G, and H, Keppel Island, Port aux Choix, and Table Head, Newfoundland; Quebec group.

Collector.—J. Richardson.

BATHYURELLUS NITIDUS. (N. sp.)

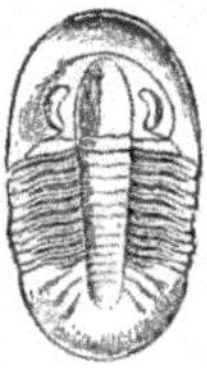

Fig. 249.

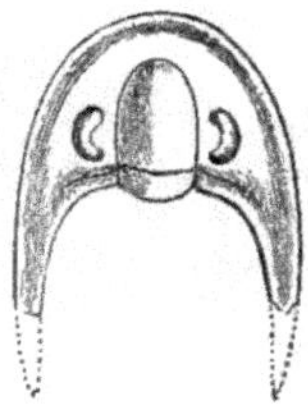

Fig. 250.

Fig. 249.—*Bathyurellus nitidus.* Drawn from a partially rolled-up specimen.
250.—*B. formosus.* The eyes in this figure are a little too large.

Description.—Oblong ovate. Head convex, with a wide concave border; front uniformly rounded; posterior angles apparently without spines. Glabella conical, strongly convex, its outline on a side view forming a gradually rising arch from the front to the mid-length, then nearly horizontal to the neck furrow, the latter narrow and slightly impressed; dorsal furrows distinctly defined, but narrow all round; sides straight and parallel for half the length, then gently curving forwards to form a somewhat pointed apex. Eyes large, lunate, half the length of the glabella, their posterior ends about half their own length from the posterior margin of the head; their anterior ends a little in advance of the mid-length of the glabella. They are distant about their own width from the sides of the glabella, or a little less. Just outside of the eyes is an obscure linear groove, which forms a semicircle round them and the front of the glabella.

Thorax, with nine segments; axis strongly convex, semi-cylindrical, less than one-fourth the whole width, with straight sides, slightly converging backwards. Pleuræ flat, apparently falcate at their extremities; the genal angle at about half the length; the pleural groove running along the middle of the ribs, nearly to the extremity.

Pygidium much less convex than the head, semicircular, with a wide smooth slightly concave border; axis short, conical, half the length of the pygidium, obscurely defined at the apex; two or three obscure ribs near the anterior margin; side lobes, with obscure indications of ribs near the axis.

The whole surface appears to be smooth.

The head of this species is somewhat like that of *B. marginatus*, but differs in the form of the margin. It is closely allied, but still distinct.

Length of the largest specimen observed about 11 lines; length of the head 4½ lines; of the glabella 3 lines; of the eye 1½ lines; width of the head 6 lines; length of the thorax 3 lines; length of the pygidium 3½ lines.

Locality and Formation.—P, Cow Head, Newfoundland; Quebec group.

Collector.—J. Richardson.

Bathyurellus formosus.

Fig. 250.

Description.—This species has a strongly convex head, terminating with strong and long posterior spines, and with a narrow concave border. The form of the head is precisely the same as that of *B. nitidus*, with the exception of the spines and the difference in the width of the margin. The eye is also smaller. From *B. validus*, it is distinguished by the greater convexity and straightness of the sides of the glabella.

In *B. nitidus* all the space in front of the glabella is concave, forming what I have designated the wide concave border. In *B. formosus* only one-third of the same space, next the margin, is concave; the remainder, extending to the glabella, has a convex upward-slope.

In both *B. fraternus* and *B. validus* the border is, also, narrow and concave, but the glabella in the anterior two-thirds is scarcely at all elevated above the general convexity of that part of the head, whereas in *B. formosus* it is strongly convex.

Locality and Formation.—P, Cow Head, Newfoundland; also, in a boulder near Quebec, with *Subulites Psyche* and other fossils; Quebec group.

Collector.—J. Richardson.

BATHYURELLUS FRATERNUS. (N. sp.)

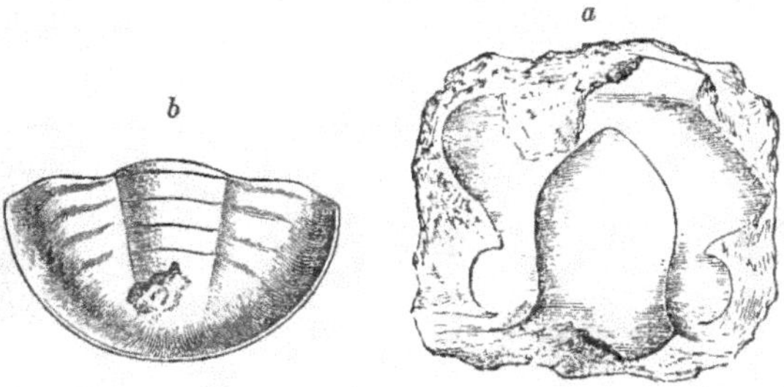

Fig. 251.

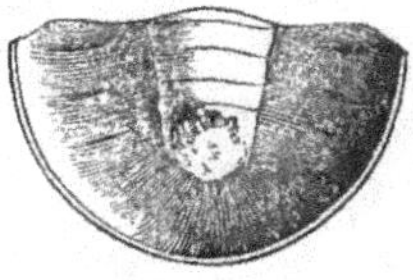

Fig. 252.

Fig. 251.—*Bathyurellus fraternus.* *a*, the glabella; *b*, the pygidium.
252.—*B, validus.* The pygidium.

Description.—Head strongly convex, with a narrow concave border. Glabella conical, only slightly elevated above the general convexity of the head in the anterior two-thirds, rather strongly elevated in the posterior third, slightly narrowed between the eyes, greatest width at about two-thirds the length from the neck segment, thence with gradually converging sides to the apex which is pointed or very angularly rounded. Dorsal furrow linear, but distinctly visible all round the glabella. Eyes semicircular, their anterior angles situated just behind a line drawn across the glabella at the mid-length, their centres distant from the sides of the glabella about their own length. No neck furrow is visible in the specimen, but this part is badly preserved.

The pygidium, found associated with the glabella above figured, is very nearly semicircular, moderately convex, and with a narrow deeply concave margin all round. The axis a little less than one-third the whole width at the front margin, and moderately convex, but becomes gradually less prominent backwards, until it merges into the general surface at about two-thirds or three-fourths the length. It is crossed by four linear grooves, but the segments between the grooves are scarcely at all elevated. The side lobes have also four obscure grooves, all terminating at the deeply concave marginal border.

Length of the head 13 lines; length of the glabella 10½ lines; greatest width of the glabella, at one-third the length from the apex, 6 lines;

length of the eye 3 lines. Length of a pygidium 9 lines; width of the same 15 lines.

This species resembles *B. nitidus*, but differs therefrom in having smaller eyes, a less convex glabella, and a narrower margin around the front of the head. *B. formosus* has the glabella convex and elevated above the general surface of the head. It is more difficult to distinguish this species from *B. validus*.

Locality and Formation.—P, Cow Head, Newfoundland; Quebec group.

Collector.—J. Richardson.

Bathyurellus validus. (N. sp.)

Fig. 252.

Description.—The form of the glabella and fixed cheeks of this species are the same as those of *B. fraternus*. The head is strongly convex, and the posterior angles are prolonged in broad, flat spines, as in *B. formosus*. The pygidium is semicircular, with a moderately convex axis, and a very wide and deeply concave margin, which occupies nearly the whole of the side lobes and space behind the axis.

Length of the head 17 lines; width about 30 lines.

Should it turn out that *B. fraternus* has the posterior angles of the head as in this species, then the only difference would be in the pygidium. They should then, perhaps, be united under one specific name; in which case I beg that *B. validus* be retained.

The beds in which *B. validus* occurs, are about 2000 feet below those holding *B. fraternus*.

Locality and Formation.—L, Point Rich, Newfoundland; Quebec group.

Collector.—J. Richardson.

Genus Dolichometopus. (Angelin.)

The following two species are placed in Angelin's genus, *Dolichometopus*, provisionally. But they, with several others such as *Bathyurus capax* and *B. armatus*, may constitute a new genus.

DOLICHOMETOPUS ? CONVEXUS. (N. sp.)

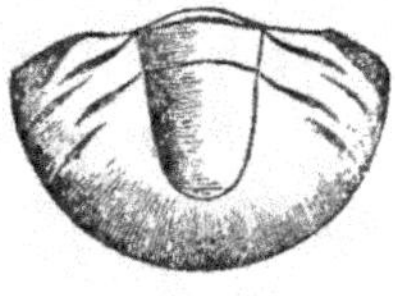

Fig. 253.

Fig. 253.—*Dolichometopus ? convexus. (N. sp.)*

Description.—Pygidium rather strongly and uniformly convex, nearly semicircular, the length a little more than half the width, the anterior angles obliquely truncated for about one-fifth the whole width, sides and posterior margin uniformly rounded; axis a little less than one-third the whole width, nearly two-thirds the whole length, moderately convex in front and scarcely elevated above the general surface at the apex. The specimen is somewhat worn, but still it exhibits traces of two or three ribs in the anterior part. There is no concave border.

Length 9 lines; width 12 lines.

Locality and Formation.—G, Port aux Choix, Newfoundland; Quebec group.

Collector.—J. Richardson.

DOLICHOMETOPUS ? GIBBERULUS. (N. sp.)

Fig. 254.

Fig. 254.—*Dolichometopus ? gibberulus*, enlarged two diameters.

Description.—The specimen, on which this species is founded, is a small pygidium, very like that of *B. convexus*, but with the axis shorter and more prominent. The form is nearly semicircular, strongly convex; sides and posterior margin uniformly rounded; anterior angles obliquely truncated for about one-fourth the whole width; axis conical, strongly convex, distinctly defined at the apex, about half the whole length, with a single linear groove near the anterior margin; side lobes smooth, with the exception of two incomplete grooves just behind the anterior margin.

Length 2 lines; width 3 lines.

Locality and Formation.—G, Port aux Choix, Newfoundland; Quebec group.

Collector.—J. Richardson.

Asaphus canalis? (Conrad.)

Isotelus canalis. (Conrad) ms. (Hall.) *Pal. N. Y.*, vol. 1, p. 25, pl. iv, figs. 17, 18, 19.

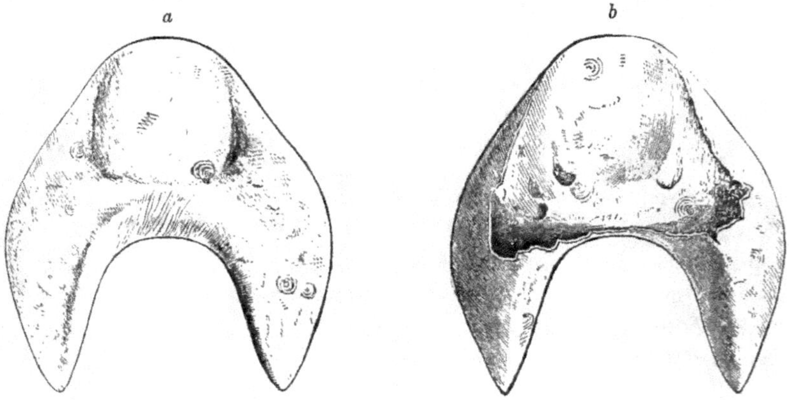

Fig. 255.

Fig. 255.—*Asaphus canalis.* a, the lower side of the hypostoma; b, the upper or inner side.

Remarks.—The specimen above figured is the hypostoma of a large *Asaphus*, of a species that has a great vertical range in the rocks of Newfoundland. No entire specimens have been found, but fragments occur in all the Divisions from *F* to *M* inclusive. The pygidium is characterized by a wide concave margin all round, but in other respects has the form of *A. platycephalus.* A pygidium resembling it occurs in the Chazy limestone, both in Canada, and at the village of Chazy in the State of New York. It is also found in the Calciferous formation at Mingan, and in the Counties of Leeds and Grenville, in Canada West. Several large, and nearly entire, individuals, have been collected in the Chazy sandstone at L'Orignal, Aylmer, and on the Island of Montreal. The specimens from all these localities agree so well with Prof. Hall's description and figure, above cited, of *A. canalis* (Conrad), that I have referred them to that species provisionally.

It will be observed that the above figures do not show the two wings that project, one on each side, from the anterior extremity of the hypostoma of an *Asaphus.* A perfect specimen from Point Rich explains their absence. They are very small, and situated on the upper side, from which they project nearly at right angles to the plane of the hypostoma; consequently, in a view of the lower side (fig. 255, *a*), they cannot be seen. Fig. 255, *b*, shows the upper side, but in this specimen they are broken off. Prof. Hall's fig. 18, above cited, shows a portion of the anterior half of a hypostoma with the same rounded front margin that is seen in our specimens. The two small muscular pits are well preserved in one of our specimens, but they are scarcely visible in the one figured.

It may be here remarked that in the Chazy limestone a perfect hypostoma, quite different from the above, has been found, showing that in that formation there are at least two species of *Asaphus*.

Locality and Formation.—Port aux Choix, Point Rich, Table Head, and Bonne Bay, Newfoundland,—F, to M, inclusive; Quebec group.

Collector.—J. Richardson.

Asaphus Huttoni. (N. sp.)

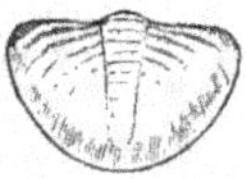

Fig. 256.

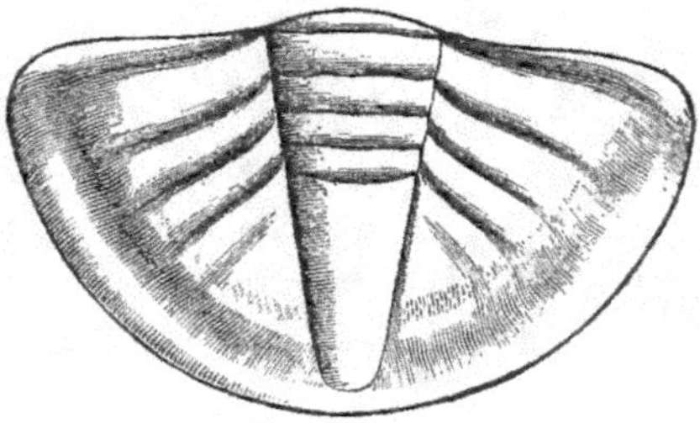

Fig. 257.

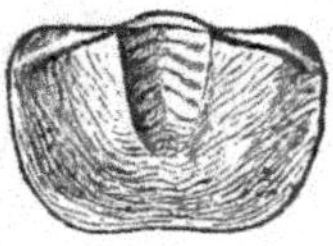

Fig. 258.

Fig. 256.—*Asaphus Huttoni.* Fig. 257.—*A. Morrisii.* Fig. 258.—*A. quadraticaudatus.*

Description.—Pygidium semi-ovate moderately convex, length a little greater than half the width. Axis narrow, convex, well defined, one-fifth the whole width at the anterior margin, tapering to one-half at the apex; the front half with about eight very obscure ribs; the posterior half apparently smooth. Side lobes, with about eight obscure ribs in the anterior two-thirds, which die out at one-third the width of each lobe from the margin; the posterior third on each side of the apex of the axis smooth. There is a smooth border all round which is gently concave on approaching the margin. The border is one-sixth the whole width. The anterior margin is straight for the middle third; the outer third on each side is gently convex and facetted.

Resembles *A. Morrisii,* but is more numerously ribbed. It is more nearly allied to *A. Canadensis* (Chapman), of the Utica slate, but that species is more strongly and distinctly ribbed.

Length of the specimen, 5 lines; width, 7 lines.

Locality and Formation.—N, Table Head, Newfoundland; Quebec group.

Collector.—J. Richardson.

ASAPHUS MORRISII. (N. sp.)

Fig. 257.

Description.—Large, oblong-ovate. Pygidium nearly semicircular, length a little greater than half the width; axis narrow, moderately convex, very distinctly defined by the dorsal furrows, about one-fifth the whole width at the front margin, thence tapering to an obtuse point near the posterior margin, not well defined at the end. There is a smooth concave border all round, the width of which is about one-third of the width of the side lobes at the anterior margin. There are about ten obscure rounded rings on the axis; those in the posterior half of the length being in general scarcely distinguishable. The side lobes have five ribs each besides the half rib at the anterior margin. The length of the axis varies in different individuals from four-fifths to five-sixths the whole length. The anterior angles are strongly facetted.

The hypostoma is oblong, with two short rounded lobes in front, and a shallow notch between. The muscular impressions are deep, transverse, and situated at one-third the length from the front margin. The posterior two-thirds gently convex. Surface of hypostoma crossed by deep undulating striæ.

Width of the largest pygidium seen, 3½ inches; length, 2¼ inches.

Locality and Formation.—N, Table Head, P, four miles N. E. from Portland Creek, Newfoundland; Quebec group.

Collector.—J. Richardson.

ASAPHUS QUADRATICAUDATUS. (N. sp.)

Fig. 258.

Description.—Obscurely sub-quadrate, the middle two-thirds convex, the outer third gradually becoming flattened or gently concave towards the edge; anterior margin apparently nearly straight, facetted on the outer third; angles narrowly rounded; sides in the anterior half sub-parallel, in the posterior half and angles broadly rounded; posterior margin with the middle-third either straight or gently concave. Axis well defined, stoutly conical, rather convex, a little less than one-third the whole width, and about two-thirds the whole length; width of the obtusely rounded apex half the width at the front margin. The surface is marked by rather coarse sub-concentric fissure-like striæ. On the side lobes there is a single pleural groove at the front margin, and another forming a half rib at the anterior end of the axis. In small specimens the axis is without any trace of ribs, but in the largest seen there are indications of eight or nine very obscure grooves on the sides, extending obliquely inwards and forwards; none on the side lobes. The apex of the axis is sometimes indistinctly defined.

The largest specimen seen is 10 lines in length, and 17 in width.

Locality and Formation.—N, Table Head, and P, four miles N.E. from Portland Creek, Newfoundland; Quebec group.

Collector.—J. Richardson.

NILEUS MACROPS. (N. sp.)

Fig. 259.

Description.—Head sub-semicircular, length a little greater than half the width, rather strongly convex, posterior corners sub-angular or very narrowly rounded; eyes semiannular, their length equal to three-fourths the whole length of the head, their posterior angles about one-fifth their length from the margin; they are situated near the side of the head. There is a small rounded tubercle about the centre of the upper side of the head.

Thorax of seven segments; axis obscurely defined, and a little more than half the whole width.

Pygidium transversely sub-oval, length scarcely half the width, uniformly depressed convex, broadly and uniformly rounded behind, and apparently facetted on the anterior margin near the angle.

Several imperfect specimens have been collected. They are about 12 lines in length, and 7 in width. Length of the head 4 lines, and of the eye 3 lines.

This species differs from *N. scrutator* in having the eye much larger, and from *N. armadillo* in having only seven instead of eight segments in the thorax.

Locality and Formation.—N, Table Head, Newfoundland; Quebec group.

Collector:—J. Richardson.

Nileus scrutator. (N. sp.)

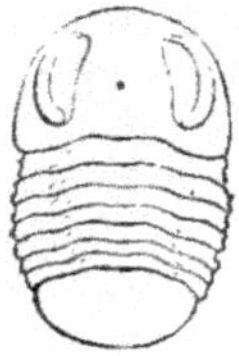

Fig. 259.

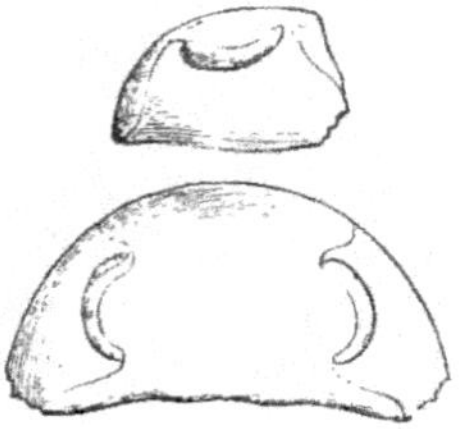

Fig. 260.

a b

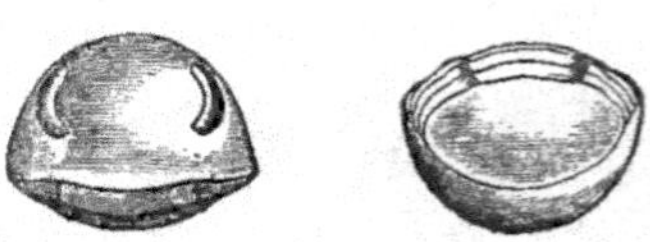

Fig. 261.

Fig. 259.—*Nileus macrops.*
260.—*N. scrutator.* Upper and side views of the head.
261.—*N. affinis.* *a*, head of a coiled up specimen; *b*, under side of the same shewing the pygidium and the thick fold or doublour under the front part of the head.

Description.—Head nearly semicircular, rather strongly convex, a little less than a quarter of a sphere, posterior angles narrowly rounded, length about half the width. Eyes moderately large, crescentiform ; their length about three-eighths the whole length of the head ; their posterior corners situated about half their own length from the posterior margin ; the distance between them, measured from the most projecting point of the outer curve at the base of the visual surface of each, one-eighth greater than the length of the head (the latter measured along the curve) ; the height of the visual surface about one-third the length of the whole eye ; distance from the posterior angle of the cheek to the eye a little greater than half the length of the head. When perfect the visual surface of the eye is closely covered with minute lenses or tubercles not visible to the naked eye, but which can be distinctly seen with an ordinary pocket magnifier. The eye-lid is depressed convex. The anterior corners of the eyes are a little closer to each other than are the posterior. The facial suture departing from the anterior corner of the eye at first curves slightly outwards and then inwards, and runs all round close to the front margin, but does not cut it. Behind the eye it runs outwards, and cuts the posterior margin at a point half way from the eye to the posterior angle of the head.

Pygidium semi-oval, anterior angles rounded, all pressed convex, not tri-lobed, a shallow concave depression all round close to the sides and posterior margin ; length equal to half its width. Surface smooth.

The best preserved head is nine lines in length and about seventeen in width ; length of the eye about three and a half lines ; distance of posterior angle of the eye from the margin two lines.

An obscurely preserved specimen, apparently of this species is three inches in length and one and three-quarters in width. There appears to be seven segments in the thorax.

Another specimen, also badly preserved, is two and a quarter inches in length, and one and five-eighths in width. It has seven segments in the thorax.

This species differs from *N. armadillo* (Dalman) which occurs in Angelin's *Regio* C, in Sweden in having the eyes smaller, and seven instead of eight articulations in the thorax.

Locality and Formation.—N, Table Head, P, Portland Creek, Newfoundland; Quebec group.

Collector.—J. Richardson.

Nileus affinis. (N. sp.)

Fig. 261, *a. b.*

Description.—This species differs from *N. scrutator* in having the eyes proportionally a little larger, the anterior angles nearer the front margin, the cheeks outside of the eye narrower and the head not so wide. The visual surface of the eye is also smooth, not minutely tuberculated as it is in *N. scrutator*.

Locality and Formation.—P, Cow Head, Newfoundland; also on the Island of Orleans; Quebec group.

Collectors.—Sir W. E. Logan (Island of Orleans), and J. Richardson (Cow Head).

Illænus fraternus. (N. sp.)

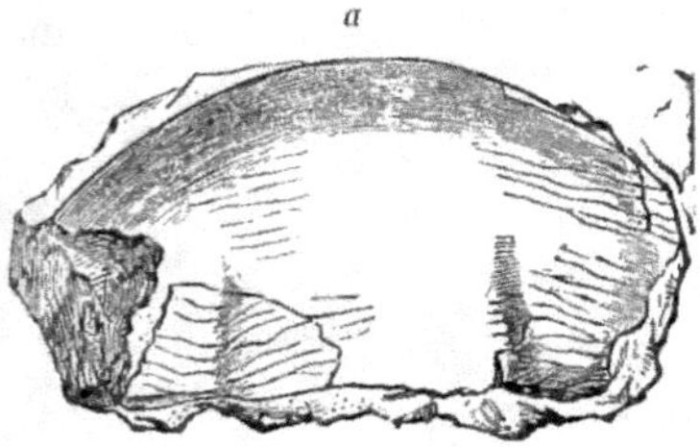

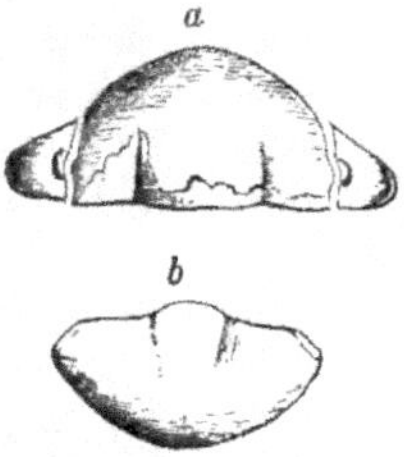

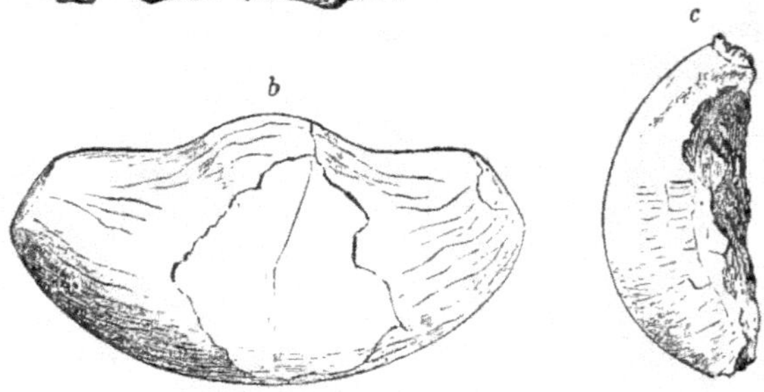

Fig. 262. Fig. 263.

Fig. 262.—*Illænus fraternus.* *a*, part of the head; *b*, pygidium.
263.—*I. consimilis.* *a*, part of the head; *b*, pygidium; *c*, side view of *a*; some of the specimens are more abruptly arched.

Description.—Head very convex, forming about one-fourth of a sphere, the posterior third distinctly tri-lobed by the dorsal furrows which are distant from each other about one-third the whole width. Eyes near the posterior margin, and distant from the dorsal furrows about one-half the width of the central lobe. Pygidium rather strongly convex, nearly semicircular, its length a little more than half the width at the front margin, the posterior three-fourths of the margin uniformly rounded to the curve of a semicircle very nearly, the anterior third obliquely truncated; axis one-third the whole length, not defined at the extremity.

A specimen of the head without the fixed cheeks measures along the curve on the median line, nine and a half lines; width of the middle lobe, four lines; length of dorsal furrows, about three lines; distance of the eye from the dorsal furrow, two lines; distance from the posterior angle of the eye to the posterior margin, a little less than one line; the length of the eye is about one and a half lines. A detached cheek which occurs in the same fragment of stone with several imperfect heads has the outer angle well rounded and distant two and a half lines from the eye. In the pygidium, the fold of the crust below extends about half the length, and in the cast of the inner surface there is a rounded groove extending from near the apex of the axis backwards becoming obsolete before reaching the margin.

Surface of the head and pygidium with numerous flexuous fissure-like striæ, three or four in one line, having a rudely concentric arrangement sub-parallel with the margin.

This species is certainly most closely allied to *I. crassicauda* both in form and surface markings. It seems however to be a smaller species, for though the specimens are numerous, none that I have seen could have been, when perfect more than one and a half inches in length. *I. crassicauda* has the posterior part of the pygidium very tumid, and a sharp elevated rim bordering the anterior margin of the head, characters which are not possessed by *I. fraternus*.

Locality and Formation.—L, Point Rich; and N, Table Head; P, four miles N. E. from Portland Creek, Newfoundland; Quebec group.

Collector.—J. Richardson.

Illænus consimilis. (N. sp.)

Fig. 263. *a, b, c.*

Description.—This is a large species, and closely allied to *I. Americanus* of the Trenton limestone. The length of the head (measured along the surface following the curve) is about two-thirds the whole width; glabella defined by the dorsal furrows for about one-third the whole length, and its width equal to about half the whole length. The anterior two-thirds of the head form a broad, moderately and uniformly convex front, inclined at an angle of from 80° to 90° to the plane of the posterior third. The glabella is very gently convex, and the space between it and the facial suture on each side is nearly flat. The anterior margin is gently convex nearly all round the front, a little concave just outside of the facial suture, and has a small, sharp, elevated rim on the edge, which becomes obsolete just before reaching the posterior angles, the latter narrowly rounded. Eyes apparently depressed, lunate, distant from the dorsal furrows about half the width of the glabella, and half their own length from the posterior margin. They appear to be about 2½ lines in length in individuals of full size.

Thorax with ten segments; axis a little more than one-third the whole width, and tapering a little backwards; side lobes flat on each side for a little more than half their width; pleural angle well defined, about 45°.

Pygidium semi-elliptical, greatest width equal to about twice the length;

angles truncated for one-fourth the length, at an angle of about 80° ; all the rest of the margin broadly rounded ; axis obscurely defined, about one-third of the length ; more distinct in the cast of the interior, where it is conical and narrowly rounded at the apex with an obscure ridge proceeding from it to the posterior margin.

Surface with concentric fissure-like, rudely concentric striæ. The pygidium is sometimes nearly smooth. Width of the largest pygidium seen 2 inches ; length 1 inch.

I have not seen a perfect head of this species, but several deprived of the cheeks. One specimen only, retains the thorax and the pygidium in connection, but without the head. A perfect cheek was found detached, but in the same piece of stone, with several pygidia and portions of the head.

As before stated, this species is most closely allied to *I. Americanus*. The only differences that I can see, are the following: In this species the middle lobe of the head is nearly flat, and the surface marked with coarse concentric striæ. In *I. Americanus* the middle lobe is more convex, and the surface covered with short, wave-like wrinkles, not striæ. This latter species, however, is an exceedingly rare form, and a larger collection might furnish some with intermediate characters.

Locality and Formation.—L, Point Rich, M and N, Table Head, Newfoundland ; Quebec group.

Collector.—J. Richardson.

ILLÆNUS TUMIDIFRONS. (N. sp.)

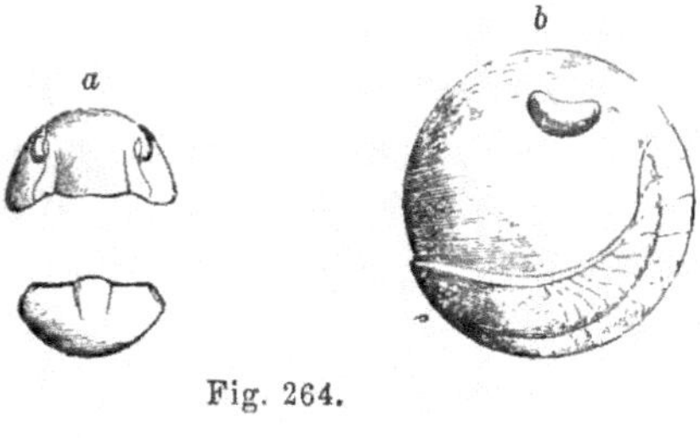

Fig. 264.

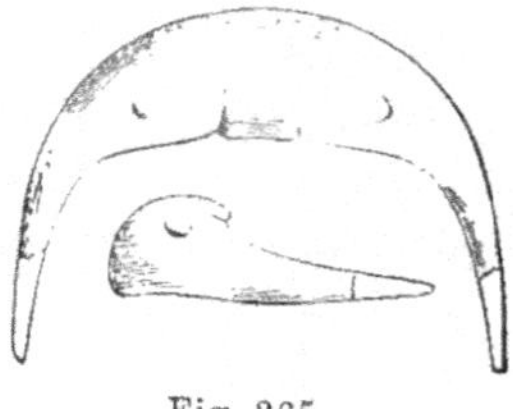

Fig. 265.

Fig. 264.—*Illænus tumidifrons.* *a*, the head and pygidium ; *b*, a rolled up specimen, enlarged four diameters.
Fig. 265.—*I. arcuatus.* Upper and side views of the head.

Description.—Head exceedingly convex, equal to nearly half of a sphere ; the front part very convex and projecting over the margin ; the posterior angles rounded ; middle lobe well defined, convex, extending one-third the whole length ; eyes moderate, lunate, close to the dorsal furrows, and distant from the posterior margin about half the width of the central lobe. They are not conical, but depressed hemispherical, abruptly elevated on the outside, and on the inside even with the surface.

Thorax with ten segments; axis well defined, convex, slightly tapering backwards, with straight sides, about one-third the whole width; side lobes flat to the angle of the pleuræ, which is situated at about half the width of the lobes.

Pygidium sub-semicircular, its length a little greater than half the width; anterior angles obliquely truncated, all the rest of the posterior margin uniformly rounded; axis convex, conical, well defined at the sides, but not at the apex, about one-third the length.

Surface having a smooth aspect, but when closely examined presenting the usual concentric fissure-like markings.

With one exception, all of the specimens of this species that I have are small, being mostly the heads and tails of individuals which, when perfect, were about one inch in length. There are in the collection three small perfect ones, rolled up, about 4 lines wide. One imperfect pygidium is 9 lines in length, and probably belonged to an individual 1½ inches in length.

This species differs from *I. fraternus*, in having the eyes nearer the dorsal furrows, and more distant from the posterior margin, and also in the great convexity of the front part of the head.

It is, like the last, most probably a geographical variety of *I. crassicauda*.

Locality and Formation.—P, Cow Head, Newfoundland; Quebec group.

Collector.—J. Richardson.

ILLÆNUS ARCUATUS. (N. sp.)

Fig. 265.

Description.—Head very short, curved into the shape of a crescent, the angles produced backwards into stout spines, which terminate acutely. Glabella quadrate, extending a little more than half the length of the head, measured along the surface. The posterior half of the head is somewhat flat or gently convex; the anterior half is abruptly curved down, and the margin a little inrolled or brought under the most projecting part of the front. Eyes small, depressed hemispherical, distant from the dorsal furrows the width of the glabella, and half that distance from the posterior margin.

Length of the head, in the best preserved specimen, in a straight line, is 4 lines; length, following the curve of the surface, 7 lines; width at the posterior margin 13 lines; between the points of the spines 15 lines; width of glabella 2½ lines; distance of the eye from the neck furrow 2½ lines; distance of the centre of the eye from the posterior margin 1¼ lines; length of the eye a little more than half a line. The spines extend about 6 lines backwards from a line drawn across the head at the posterior margin.

This extraordinary trilobite is clearly allied to *I. Bayfieldi* and *I. consobrinus*, more particularly to the latter. There are some specimens of the latter with the head shorter and broader than the one figured, and approaching this species in form. Still the extreme arcuation of the head, and the contraction of the cheeks into cylindrical spines, distinguishes this sufficiently to authorise a separate name.

Locality and Formation.—P, Cow Head, Newfoundland; Quebec group.

Collector.—J. Richardson.

Illænus consobrinus. (N. sp.)

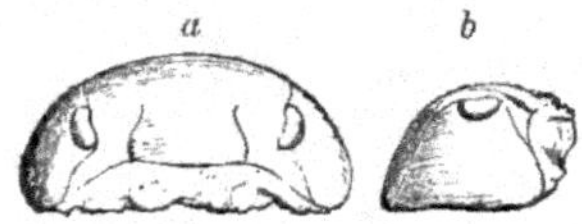

Fig. 266.

Fig. 266.—*Illænus consobrinus.* *a*, the upper side of the head, *b*, side view of the same.

Description.—Head short, proportionally very wide, strongly arched from the posterior to the anterior margin, most elevated point at one-third the length, from behind; anterior margin gently convex in the middle half and more abruptly towards the angles; the latter well rounded. The middle lobe or glabella is about one-third the whole width in a straight line from angle to angle, gently convex, and extends one third the whole length (measured along the curve of the surface); dorsal furrows well defined, the eyes are rather small, lunate, depressed convex on the outside, level with the surface on the inside, distant from the dorsal furrows half the width of the glabella, a little less than their own length from the dorsal margin, and the width of the glabella from the posterior angles to the head. Surface with the usual concentric striæ.

The best preserved specimen measures in a straight line between the posterior angles, 9½ lines. Length of the head measured on the curve 8½ lines; width of glabella 4 lines; distance of the centre of the eye from the dorsal furrow 2 lines; length of the eyes 1¼ lines; distance of its posterior angle from the margin 1 line; distance from the eye to the cheek-angle 4 lines.

These proportions vary somewhat in different individuals.

Thorax and pygidium unknown.

This species is allied to both *I. latus* (McCoy), and *I. Bayfieldi.* From the former it differs in having the eye more remote from the cheek-angle.

From the latter in having the eye one half the size, and more distant from the posterior margin.

Locality and Formation.—P, Cow Head, Newfoundland; Quebec group.

Collector.—J. Richardson.

Genus Endymionia. (Billings.)

Endymion. (Billings), ante p. 93.

Remarks.—Since the publication of this genus, I have learned that the name *Endymion* is in use for a genus of plants. I therefore propose to change it to *Endymionia.*

Endymionia meeki. (Billings.)

Remarks.—This speces occurs abundantly in division N, at Table Head, and the west side of Pistolet Bay; also in P, four miles N. E. from Portland creek.

Holometopus Angelini. (Billings.)

Remarks.—This species occurs with *E. Meeki* at all the localities of that species above mentioned and also at Cow Head.

Harpides Atlanticus. (N. sp.)

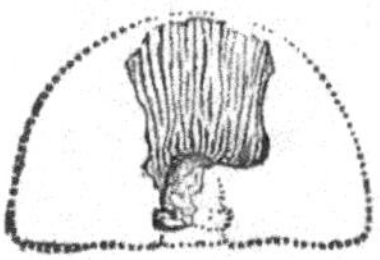

Fig. 267.

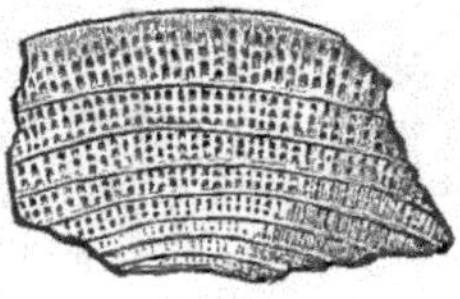

Fig. 268.

Fig. 267.—*Harpides Atlanticus.* Part of the glabella and margin.
Fig. 268.—*H. concentricus.* A fragment of the margin, enlarged two diameters.

Remarks.—Of this species only the fragment, above figured, has been observed. The glabella is conical, and apparently with a single lobe on each side next the neck-furrow. The margin is gently concave, its width equal to one and a-half the length of the glabella, with coarse, rounded, radiating striæ, or small ribs. It must be very closely allied to *H. rugosus* (Angelin), a species which occurs in Norway and Sweden, in Angelin's Regio, B C, at the base of the second fauna.

Locality and Formation.—P, four miles N. E from Portland Creek, Newfoundland ; Quebec group.

Collector.—J. Richardson.

HARPIDES CONCENTRICUS. (N. sp.)

Fig. 268.

Remarks.—This name is proposed for a species, of which a fragment of the margin is above figured. It occurs with *H. Atlanticus.*

LICHAS JUKESII. (N. sp.)

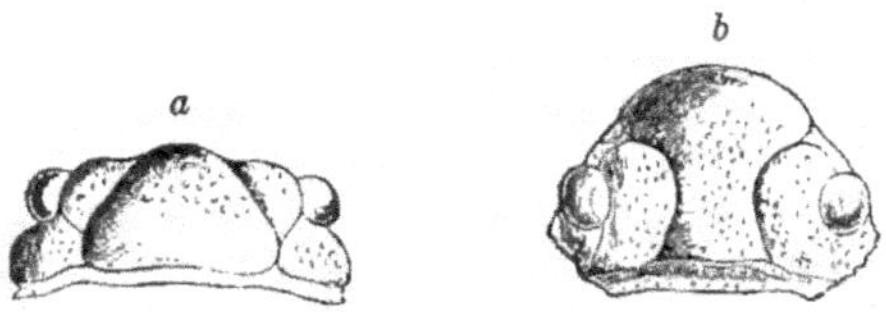

Fig. 269.

Fig. 270.

Fig. 269.—*Lichas Jukesii.* *a*, front view of the head ; *b*, upper side.
Fig. 270.—*Shumardia glacialis.* A nearly perfect head.

Description.—Head semi-elliptical or subtriangular, convex, flattened on the top, abruptly elevated in front ; posterior angles with short spines directed obliquely outwards and backwards at an angle of about 45°, with the median line of the body. That part of the head which is situated between the eyes is longitudinally divided into three lobes. The width of the middle lobe at the neck furrow is about equal to half the length of the head, but it becomes nearly one-third narrower just in advance of a line drawn across the eyes. It then rapidly expands until at the front margin, its width is equal to the length of the head. The other two lobes are each, at the neck furrow, about half the width of the middle lobe ; they become a little wider and more tumid just in front of the eye, and then contracting, end in an obtuse point before reaching the margin. The middle lobe is abruptly elevated in front, somewhat tumid and projecting a little over the margin. The width of the neck segment appears to be nearly equal to the length of the head. Neck furrow well defined. The cheeks are subtriangular, convex, and terminated at the outer angles by the spines above mentioned. The eyes are very prominent, globular, about one-third the length of the head, situated close to the side of the outer of the longitudinal lobes, and scarcely their own length from the posterior margin. There is a narrow rim all round the sides and front of the head.

Length of largest specimen seen 4 lines; width between the eyes 4 lines; height 3 lines.

Surface with small tubercles.

Locality and Formation.—P, Cow Head, Newfoundland; Quebec group.

Collector.—J. Richardson.

SHUMARDIA GLACIALIS. (N. sp.)

Fig. 270.

Description.—Head convex, semicircular, the posterior angles produced backwards into spines, the length of which is unknown. Glabella clavate, strongly convex, sub-carinate along the median line, broadly rounded in front; sides straight and converging backwards; width at neck segment a little more than half the width at the front; length about two-thirds the whole length of the head; neck furrow extending all across and apparently continued on the cheek to the angles; three small indentations on each side representing the glabellar furrows. The dorsal furrows are deep and wide as far as the anterior angles, but are only slightly impressed round the front of the glabella. Cheeks and space in front of the glabella rather strongly convex. From each of the anterior angles of the glabella a short curved line or fold runs outwards half the width of the cheeks. No eyes. Surface covered with fine fissure-like striæ.

Width of largest specimen seen 6 lines; length 3 lines; width of glabella at front 1½ lines, length 2 lines.

Locality and Formation.—P. Portland Creek and Pistolet Bay, Newfoundland; Quebec group.

Collector.—J. Richardson.

CHEIRURUS VULCANUS. (N. sp.)

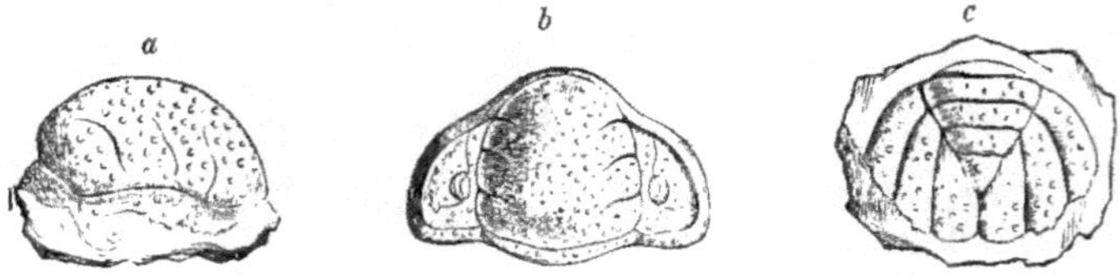

Fig. 271.

Fig. 271.—*Cheirurus Vulcanus.* a, side view of the glabella; b, upper side of the head; c, a pygidium found along with a and b.

Description.—Glabella in large specimens exceedingly convex, sometimes abruptly elevated just in front of the neck furrow. The contour is ovate or obtusely conical, rounded in front and sides gently convex, a little narrower in front than behind. Neck furrow extending all across; posterior pair of glabellar furrows with a sigmoid curve, originating in the dorsal furrows a little behind the mid-length of the head, then sloping gently backwards with a curve which is concave towards the front in the lower half and convex in the upper half, the inner extremities separated by about one-fourth the width of the glabella. The two anterior pairs are one third the width of the glabella, and are both convex towards the front. Cheeks small and drooping, rounded at the angles with a narrow slightly elevated rim, which runs round the front of the glabella. Eyes very small and close to the side of the glabella, opposite the front part of the posterior glabellar lobe.

Length of the largest glabella seen including neck segment 10 lines; width at the neck segment 8 lines; elevation in the middle 5 lines.

Surface with numerous small rounded tubercles; the casts are usually smooth.

The pygidium associated with the fragments of the head of this species is depressed convex, with a triangular axis ending in a point backwards, with four transverse grooves, and three broad depressed convex ribs on each side, the last two parallel with the median line and the others nearly so.

Locality and Formation.—P, Cow Head, Newfoundland; Quebec group.

Collector.—J. Richardson.

CHEIRURUS MERCURIUS. (N. sp.)

Fig. 272.

Description.—Glabella obtusely conical, convex, front half tumid, sides straight or gently convex, sub-parallel, front broadly rounded. Neck furrow extending all across; posterior pair of glabellar furrows nearly straight and sub-parallel with the neck furrow, extending all across, but the middle third not so deeply indented; the two anterior pairs are short and obscurely marked.

The eye appears to be small, close to the side of the glabella, and just opposite the end of the posterior glabellar furrow. The cheeks seem to have the form of *C. Vulcanus.*

Associated with this species are some specimens only differing by having the last pair of glabellar furrows not connected in the middle.

Locality and Formation.—P, Cow Head, Newfoundland: Quebec group.

Collector.—J. Richardson.

CHEIRURUS PROLIFICUS. (N. sp.)

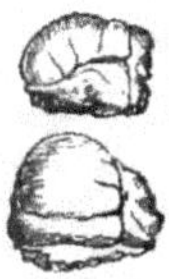

Fig. 272.

Fig. 273.

Fig. 272.—*Cheirurus Mercurius.* Upper and side views of the glabella.
273.—*C. prolificus.* Upper and side views of the head.

Description.—Head short, convex, about quarter of a sphere; cheeks triangular, drooping, rounded at the angles; glabella conical, narrowly rounded in front, sides gently convex, neck furrow extending all across, three pairs of glabellar furrows, the last with the inner extremities separated by a little less than one-third the width, the others a little shorter, all slightly curved, the convex side forwards. The eyes are small and opposite the second lobe from the neck furrow, and a little nearer the side of the glabella than to the centre of the cheek. The posterior and outer cheek margins have a narrow elevated rim. Surface of cheeks and glabella finely tuberculated.

Width of an average sized head 6 lines; length 4 lines.

This species is closely allied to both *C. Vulcanus* and *C. Mercurius*, and occurs in great numbers in the same fragments of limestone with them.

The following are the differences: in *C. Vulcanus* the eye is opposite the front part of the last lobe of the glabella, but in this species it is opposite the second; in *C. Mercurius* the last glabellar furrows are straight, and extend across.

Locality and Formation.—P, Cow Head, Newfoundland; Quebec group.

Collector.—J. Richardson.

CHEIRURUS POLYDORUS. (N. sp.)

Fig. 274.

Fig. 274.—*Cheirurus Polydorus.*

Description.—Glabella oblong, depressed cylindro-convex, sides straight and sub-parallel, front nearly straight in the middle, angles obtusely rounded, neck furrow extending all across, three glabellar furrows on each side about equidistant from each other, the inner extremities of all being a little more than one-fourth from the sides, and all curving a little backwards. The posterior margin has a smooth rounded rim just within which there is a narrow groove; outer margin or sides (at least near the angle) with a similar rim; angles produced backwards with rounded spines the length of which is unknown. Eyes small, opposite the second glabellar lobe from the neck furrow, and about one-fourth the width of the glabella distant from the dorsal furrow. Cheeks closely punctate.

Length of the best preserved glabella 5½ lines; width 4 lines.

Locality and Formation.—N, Table Head, P, Portland Creek; Quebec group.

Collector.—J. Richardson.

Cheirurus perforator. (N. sp.)

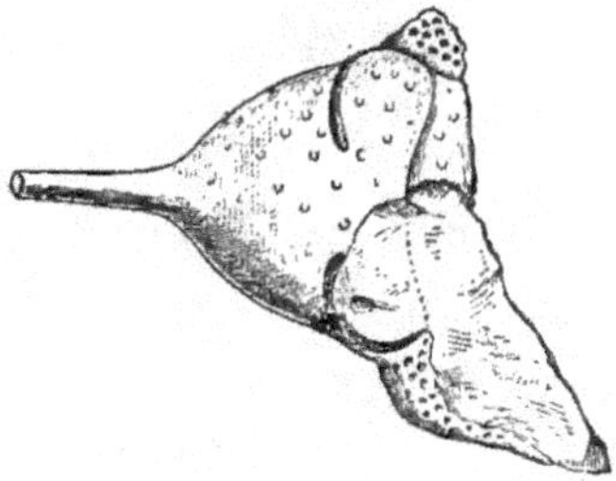

Fig. 275.

Fig. 275.—*Cheirurus perforator.* The front half of the glabella with portions of the fixed cheeks.

Description.—Large, glabella strongly elevated in front, obtusely conical with deep linear furrows, and a long cylindrical rostrum. Cheeks coarsely punctured, and glabella with a few rounded tubercles.

The only specimen of this remarkable trilobite discovered, is the anterior part of the glabella, with a small portion of the cheek on each side. The length, from the base of the rostrum, backwards as far as preserved, is 9½ lines, measured along the median line of the upper side. At 5 lines from the base of the rostrum there is a pair of deep linear glabellar furrows, very gently curved (the convexity forward), their upper extremities distant from each other about 3 lines, the lower extremity about 1 line from the cheek, and 7 lines from the base of the rostrum; length of each furrow 5 lines. About 3 lines behind there is a second furrow not so much curved which extends to the cheek below, and appears to run all across (but this point is not determined owing to the imperfection of the specimen). It seems probable that if this specimen were perfect, the total length of the glabella would be from 12 to 15 lines, and there may be, thus, another pair of furrows besides the neck furrow.

I at first supposed this remarkable fossil to be an *Ampyx*, and had so described, but fortunately, before printing, other species of the same type were discovered, which shew that it is a *Cheirurus* with the unusual appendage of a large spine on the head.

Locality and Formation.—N, Table Head, Newfoundland; Quebec group.

Collector.—J. Richardson.

Cheirurus Sol. (N. sp.)

Fig. 276.

Fig. 276.—*Cheirurus Sol.* The glabella.

Description.—Glabella small, sub-circular; length three-fourths of the width, moderately convex; front and sides rounded; neck furrow extending all across; posterior pair of glabellar furrows situated just behind the mid-length; second pair half-way between the posterior pair and the front; anterior pair cutting the front margin, and having about one-third of the whole width of the glabella between them at the margin, extending obliquely backwards and inwards at an angle of about 45° with the median line. All of the furrows extend inwards a little more than one-third the whole width of the glabella. The space along the median line which is not crossed by the glabellar furrows is more convex than the remainder of the glabella. Surface finely tubercular. Length of glabella 2 lines; width $2\frac{2}{3}$ lines.

Locality and Formation.—N, Table Head, and P, four miles N. E. from Portland Creek, Newfoundland; Quebec group.

Collector.—J. Richardson.

Amphion Barrandei. (N. sp.)

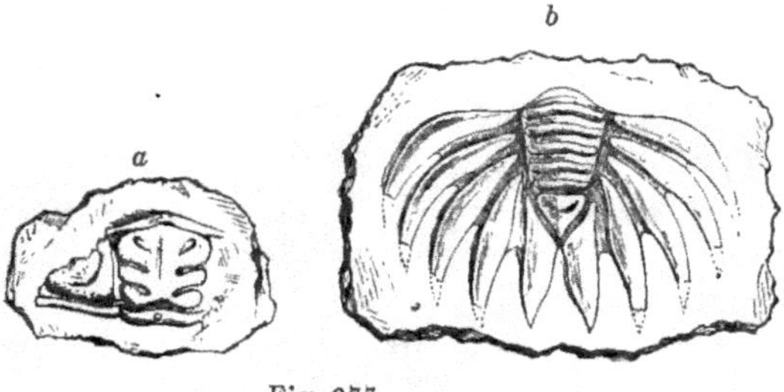

Fig. 277.

Fig. 278.

Fig. 277.—*Amphion Barrandei.* *a*, an imperfect head; *b*, the pygidium.
278.—*A. Canadensis.* Figured here for comparison.

Description.—Head moderately convex; glabella quadrate, a little narrower behind than at the front; sides straight separated from the cheeks by the narrow well-defined dorsal furrows, neck segment with a tubercle in the middle; neck furrow extending all across; two glabellar furrows on each side extending one-third across; anterior lobes equal to half the whole glabella, and subdivided by two short oblique furrows pointing inwards and backwards, situated half way between the median line and the anterior angles, and near but not cutting the front margin; a third small pit in the middle of the front margin is visible in casts of the interior. The eyes appear to be small and situated opposite the posterior half of the second lobe, and a little less than one-third of the length of the head from the side of the glabella.

Pygidium moderately convex, axis conical, convex, well defined, with six segments (the last one triangular terminating in an acute point, and having a rudely semicircular pit just above the middle); side lobes with five ribs on each side, all extending beyond the margin and terminating in flattened pointed spines. The last two ribs are parallel with the axis; the next two diverge a little, but are still nearly parallel; the three anterior pairs diverge more widely, the anterior being at right angles to the axis for about half the length, the outer half curved backwards. In some specimens the anterior ribs are broadly curved, for the inner half. The spinose terminations of the ribs are separated from each other about the width of the rib. The length of the pygidium, measuring to the tips of the spines, is a little more than half the width.

The surface appears to be finely tubercular.

This species is closely allied to *A. Lindaueri* (Barrande),* which occurs in rocks lying at the base of the second Fauna in Bohemia, but differs in the form of the triangular or last segment of the axis, and in having the ribs more divergent. It differs from *A. Canadensis* in having the ribs more divergent, and in being less convex.†

A. Salteri has three glabellar furrows on each side, but none in the front margin.

Locality and Formation.—I, K, L, Point Rich; L, M, N, Table Head and Bonne Bay; P, Portland Creek and Cow Head, Newfoundland; Quebec group.

Collector.—J. Richardson.

---

* (BARRANDE.) *Système Silurien du centre de la Bohême*, page 820, pl. xxx.

† In *A. Canadensis*, the last or triangular segment of the axis is minute in young specimens, but becomes gradually larger and elongated as the individual increases in size.

AMPHION JULIUS. (N. sp.)

Fig. 279.

Fig. 279.—*Amphion Julius.* The pygidium.

Description.—Pygidium rather convex, semicircular; axis elongate-conical, strongly convex, with about ten rings, the last three or four obscurely defined. The side lobes have five strong ribs, each terminating in a short slender spine. The grooves between the ribs are deep, and a little less than the width of the ribs. The last rib on each side originates at the mid-length of the axis, and lies parallel and close thereto. The others become gradually more divergent to the first. The true margin of the pygidium does not extend beyond the apex of the axis, but the ribs project a little further, forming a fringe of ten slender, sharp spines. The last three or four ribs of the axis are so obscurely separated that they seem to form a single triangular segment. Length of the axis of the best preserved specimen 3½ lines; width of the same at the anterior margin 1½ lines; length of the spines about 1 line.

This pygidium has a greater number of rings in the axis than there is in any described species of *Amphion.* It is barely possible that this may be a *Cromus;* but it has fewer ribs in the side lobes than any species of that genus figured by Barrande.

Locality and Formation.—P, Cow Head, Newfoundland; Quebec group.

Collector.—J. Richardson.

AMPHION INSULARIS. (N. sp.)

Description.—Pygidium strongly convex, with five pairs of ribs lying close together and curved backwards, so that for the greater part they are sub-parallel with the axis. The margin, being imperfect all round the characters of the extremities of the ribs, cannot be made out. The axis has five well defined articulations besides the terminal one, which latter is triangular, and extends backwards in a long point between the last pair of ribs.

Length of the specimen 4 lines; width at the anterior margin apparently about 5 lines.

Associated with this pygidium is a glabella, which may possibly belong to it. It is strongly convex; front rounded; neck furrow all across; two pairs of glabellar furrows, inclining a little backwards and extending inwards about one fourth the width or a little more.

Length of the glabella 2½ lines; width 2 lines.

Locality and Formation.—G, Port aux Choix, Newfoundland; Quebec group.

Collector.—J. Richardson.

TRIARTHRUS FISCHERI. (N. sp.)

Fig. 280.

Fig. 280.—*Triarthrus Fischeri.* The glabella and fixed cheeks.

Description.—This species has the form of those common in the Utica slate. From *T. Beckii* it differs in being destitute of the tubercles along the median line of the axis; from *T. spinosus* in the absence of the spines at the head and thorax; from *T. Canadensis* also in being destitute of spines; and from *T. glaber* in having the eyes more distant from the glabella. It seems to be smaller than the species above compared, none of the specimens indicating a length of more than eight lines.

Locality and Formation—N, Table Head and Pistolet Bay; P, Portland Creek, Newfoundland; Quebec group.

Collector.—J. Richardson.

TELEPHUS AMERICANUS. (N. sp.)

Fig. 281.

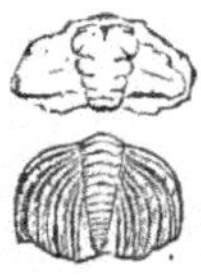

Fig. 282.

Fig. 283.

Fig. 281.—*Telephus Americanus.* The glabella.
282.—*Encrinurus mirus.* Glabella and pygidium.
283.—*Remopleurides Panderi.* The glabella.

Description.—Glabella obtusely conical, length one sixth greater than the width, rather strongly convex; front uniformly rounded; sides parallel; neck segment and furrow forming nearly one third of the whole length; the furrow narrow and extending all across. The fixed cheeks are crescentiform, rounded on the outside, terminating posteriorly at the front edge of the neck furrow and extending around one-third of the width of the front of the glabella; an obscure groove just outside of the middle of the cheek, parallel with the margin in the front half, but running out to the edge before reaching the posterior corner. In front of the glabella there are two small projecting points. The surface is obscurely tubercular, and there is a small tubercle on the middle of the neck segment.

Length from 2 to 3 lines.

The detached glabellæ occur in considerable numbers, but I have seen none of the other parts in connection with any of them. There are no fragments that can be identified as belonging to this trilobite, except the glabella.

Locality and Formation.—N, Table Head, and P, four miles N. E. Portland Creek and Pistolet Bay, Newfoundland; Quebec group.

Collector.—J. Richardson.

Genus ENCRINURUS. (Emmrich.)

The following species, of which we have only some fragments, exhibits characters belonging to several genera, such as *Encrinurus* (Emmrich), *Cromus* and *Dindymene* (Barrande). I shall place it in the first named genus provisionally, for the present.

ENCRINURUS MIRUS. (N. sp.)

Fig. 282.

Description.—Head semi-elliptical, width apparently more than twice the length. Glabella clavate, moderately convex, front margin irregularly rounded with a notch in the middle, width at neck-segment half the width of the front, sides straight, neck furrow extending all across, three glabellar furrows on each side, extending one-third across, the anterior furrow with a branch making a notch in the front lobe, the lobes gradually diminishing in size backwards. Fixed cheeks broad, gently convex. Eyes distant from the dorsal furrows about the width of the glabella at the second lobe, and placed about opposite the last glabellar furrow; they appear to be small, and are connected with the front furrow by an ocular ridge. Movable cheeks unknown.

Pygidium with an elongate-conical, convex axis with from twelve to fourteen distinctly defined rings or segments. Side lobes with four narrow, convex ribs, the last pair commencing at about the mid-length of the axis, and extending backwards parallel and close thereto, the next also nearly parallel, and the anterior two pairs with the posterior half of their length parallel or converging. Between each two of the principal ribs there is a smaller one which is only slightly elevated, and seems to become obsolete before reaching the margin. There is evidence that the four principal ribs terminate in short spines.

Glabella with a few small tubercles; cheeks coarsely punctate; pygidium with three or four tubercles on the principal ribs. The surface in all the specimens is, however, not well preserved.

Length of the best preserved fragment of the head, 3 lines; width of the glabella at the front lobe, 2¼ lines; at the neck-segment, about 1 line; length of the axis of a pygidium, 3½ lines; width of the same at the anterior margin, 1½ lines.

The specimens of the pygidium are all imperfect, but when in their natural position, I think the ribs converge backwards, and that they all terminate in small spines. One specimen clearly shews some of these spines.

Locality and Formation.—N, Table Head and Pistolet Bay, P, Portland Creek, Newfoundland; Quebec group.

Collector.—J. Richardson.

Remopleurides Panderi. (N. sp.)

Fig. 283.

Description.—Head small, the space between the eyes transversely elliptical, and about one-fourth wider than the length of the whole head. The neck segment is distinctly defined by the neck furrow, and apparently half the width of the space between the eyes. The dorsal furrows extend forward a little more than one-third the length of the head from the neck-furrow, and appear to have each a small pit in the bottom. The eyes are semicircular and two-thirds the length of the head, their posterior corners situated at the front edge of the neck furrow and close to the dorsal furrows. The dorsal furrows are distant from each other at their anterior extremities about one-third the distance between the outer curve of the eyes; they are a little more widely separated behind. The front part of the glabella which forms the projection characteristic of this genus, is one-fifth the length of the head, and is about as wide as the space between the neck furrows.

Only two specimens have been collected, each a little less than 2 lines in length.

No glabellar furrows are visible.

Locality and Formation.—N, Table Head, Newfoundland; Quebec group.

Collector.—J. Richardson.

Remopleurides ? Schlotheimi. (N. sp.)

Paradoxides or Olenellus. *Geol. Can., p.* 871, 872.

Fig. 284.

Fig. 284.—*Remopleurides ? Schlotheimi. a, b,* two specimens of the glabella, both distorted.

Description.—Glabella cylindro-conical, rounded and abruptly elevated in front; neck furrow extending all across; three pairs of glabellar furrows all inclining inwards and backwards, the middle pair only, continued across. The eyes are semi-annular, about half the length of the glabella or a little less, their anterior and posterior angles touching the sides of the glabella.

The specimens are all more or less distorted, and hence the true proportions of the parts cannot be determined. In all of them the space between the side of the glabella and the eye (sometimes called the palpebral lobe) is on a level with the median line of the glabella, thus forming a nearly flat horizontal plane across from one eye to the other. A fine thread-like groove runs round the lobe close to the eye. The surface appears to be quite smooth.

The pygidium found in association with the glabella above figured, somewhat resembles that of *Dikelocephalus magnificus.* It is ovate with an acutely conical axis, the side-lobes with five or six well defined ribs each. The axis is about half the whole length, and the ribs of the side-lobes incline backwards like those of a *Remopleurides.* The specimens are too obscurely preserved to be figured.

When compared with the head of *Olenellus Thompsoni*, the resemblance was so perfect, that I once thought this species was congeneric therewith. Hence the reference in the Geology of Canada above cited. I now think that both it and *Dikelocephalus magnificus* should be referred to *Remopleurides*, or perhaps to some closely allied form.

Locality and Formation.—N, Table Head and Pistolet Bay; P, four miles N. E. from Portland Creek, Newfoundland; Quebec group.

Collector.—J. Richardson.

AMPYX LÆVIUSCULUS. (N. sp.)

Fig. 285.

Description.—Pygidium triangular, nearly smooth; axis rather strongly convex, well defined and prominent to the apex, crossed by some obscure grooves, which, however, are so indistinct that to a superficial view the surface seems to be quite smooth. The posterior margin is broadly bevelled, sloping at an angle of 45°, the upper angle of the bevel rounded. Side lobes gently convex, smooth, with the exception of a single linear groove close to the anterior margin.

Width of the largest pygidium collected 5¼ lines; length 2¼ lines; width of the axis at the front margin 1½ lines; thickness of the posterior margin or width of the sloping plane of the bevelled edge ⅔ of a line.

This species differs from *A. normalis*, in having the pygidium proportionally wider, a more prominent axis and a thicker posterior margin.

Locality and Formation.—N, Table Head, Newfoundland; Quebec group.

Collector.—J. Richardson.

AMPYX NORMALIS. (N. sp.)

Fig. 285.

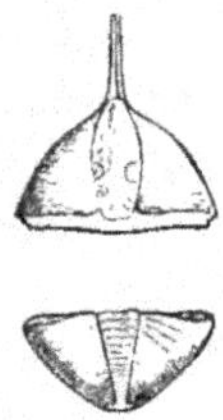

Fig. 286.

Fig. 287.

Fig. 285.—*Ampyx læviusculus.*—A pygidium enlarged one-fourth.
286.—*A. normalis.*—The head (without the movable cheeks), and the pygidium.
287.—*A. semicostatus.*—A pygidium enlarged two diameters.

Description.—Head, without the movable cheek, triangular, the width about one-third greater than the length; fixed cheeks, gently convex, smooth; neck segment consisting of a flat plate, inclining backwards. The glabella elongate-ovate, greatest width about the mid-length, one fourth narrower at the neck segment, the apex extending a little over the front margin of the head; the rostrum, apparently, when perfect, equal to the whole length of the head, not round but fluted; two or three ovate or nearly circular scars, one each side of the glabella in the posterior half.

Pygidium triangular, width twice the length, the two posterior sides gently convex, and the margin abruptly bent down or bevelled nearly vertically, the upper edge of the bevel angular and with indications of a slightly elevated linear rim; axis very depressed convex or nearly flat, its width at the anterior margin about one-fourth of the whole width, extending the whole length or nearly so, crossed by obscure undulating furrows. Side lobes gently convex.

Length of the head without the rostrum, 5 or 6 lines; length of the pygidium about 4 lines.

The pygidium of this species resembles, at first sight, that of *A. læviusculus*. The latter, however, is proportionally wider, the posterior bevelled, margin thicker, and the upper edge of the bevel rounded instead of angular.

It differs from *A. nasutus* (Dalman), principally in having the rostrum fluted instead of round.

Locality and Formation.—N, Table Head and Pistolet Bay; P, four miles N. E. from Portland Creek, Newfoundland; Quebec group.

Collector.—J. Richardson.

Ampyx Rutilius. (N. sp.)

Description.—Pygidium subtriangular, length about one-third of the width, nearly vertically bevelled behind, the upper edge of the bevel with an acute linear rim. Axis cylindro-conical, strongly convex, extending the whole length, with about ten rounded rings. Side lobes nearly flat, slightly concave near the margin, with nine ribs very distinctly defined the whole width.

Width of the specimen 4 lines; length 1⅓ lines. This pygidium resembles that of *A. Halli*, (*ante*, p. 24), but in that species each of the ribs on the side lobes has a pleural groove, whereas in this species they have no such groove.

It differs from *A. semicostatus*, in having more numerous ribs, which also extend the whole width. It occurs along with it in the same beds, and it may be necessary hereafter to unite the two; but, at present, they appear to me to be decidedly distinct.

Locality and Formation.—P, four miles N. E. from Portland Creek, Newfoundland; Quebec group.

Collector.—J. Richardson.

Ampyx semicostatus. (N. sp.)

Fig. 287.

Description.—Pygidium sub-triangular, posterior margin broadly rounded, obtusely angular at the apex; length two-fifths of the width; axis cylindro-conical, strongly convex, extending the whole length, with five or six distinctly defined rounded annulations; dorsal furrows on each side of the axis, deep and well defined. The side lobes are rather tumid in the middle, but concave towards the margin, the latter with a distinctly elevated angular rim and nearly vertically bevelled; there are five or six ribs extending about half-way from the margin to the axis. In very small specimens only two or three are visible.

Locality and Formation.—N, Table Head and Pistolet Bay; P, four miles N. E. from Portland Creek, Newfoundland; Quebec group.

Collector.—J. Richardson.

Agnostus Galba. (N. sp.)

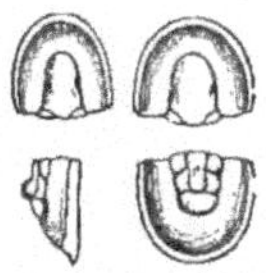

Fig. 288.

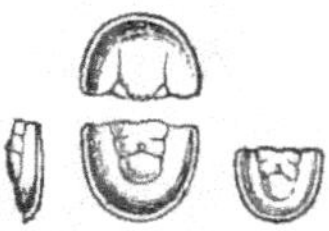

Fig. 289.

Fig. 288.—*Agnostus Galba.* Enlarged about two diameters.
289.—*A. Fabius.* Enlarged two diameters.

Description.—Head strongly convex, with a narrow rim; front margin rounded; glabella convex, well defined all round, strongly elevated above the general surface, smooth, no tubercle nor furrows; in some specimens a slight indentation on each side at about the mid-length; a small triangular lobe on each side at the posterior margin. The proportional length of the glabella varies slightly, but it is, in general, about two-thirds of the whole length of the head.

Pygidium, in contour and convexity, like the head. Axis strongly convex, well defined all round by the dorsal furrows; a furrow runs all across at one-third the length from the apex; a short one on each side at two-thirds the length from the apex. The tubercle forms a longitudinal medium lobe in the anterior two-thirds of the axis. It (the tubercle) is, at the anterior margin, slightly elevated above the general convexity of the axis; it is less elevated just over the anterior of pair furrows; but, behind this point, it rises to twice the height, and terminates abruptly at the posterior furrow. The anterior lobes of the axis are distinctly separated from the tubercle by a narrow groove; the second two are not.

Surface apparently smooth, but in one of the specimens there are indications of small wrinkles which unite with each other so as to give a reticulated aspect, somewhat similar to that of *A. reticulatus* (Angelin).

Length of head and pygidium from 1 to 2 lines each.

This species is allied to *A. Americanus*, but has the axis of the pygidium shorter, and no tubercles on the head.

A. glabratus (Angelin) has two short spines on the posterior angles of the pygidium, but in all other respects resembles this species very closely.

A. tardus (Barrande) is also very closely allied to this species, differing only in the shorter axis of the pygidium, and in having the tubercle of an uniform height its whole length.

Locality and Formation.—M, and N, Table Head and Pistolet Bay; P, four miles N. E. from Portland Creek, Newfoundland; Quebec group.

Collector.—J. Richardson.

Agnostus Fabius. (N. sp.)

Fig. 289.

Description.—Head uniformly and moderately convex, semi-elliptical, front margin broadly rounded; a very narrow, flat rim all round the front and sides; glabella a little more than one-third the whole width, scarcely at all elevated above the general surface, not defined in front, and only obscurely so in the posterior half, by the dorsal furrows, which are parallel and become obsolete about the middle of the head. On each side of the glabella, at the posterior margin, there is, in the dorsal furrow, a small triangular lobe.

The pygidium is proportionally a little more elongated than the head; posterior margin uniformly rounded; a narrow, flat rim all round to the anterior angles. The axis is a little more than one-third the whole width, about one-fourth narrower at the apex than at the front margin; the apex rounded, or with a portion in the middle somewhat straight; sides nearly straight, well defined by the dorsal furrows; two pairs of transverse furrows, the posterior reaching the median line, where there is a small rounded tubercle, situated a little behind the mid-length (of the axis); the anterior furrows half way between the tubercle and the front margin, their position, however, slightly variable; their inner extremities separated by about one-third the width of the axis. Surface apparently smooth.

Length of the largest head seen, about 2 lines; length of the largest pygidium observed, about $1\frac{1}{2}$ lines.

Differs from both *A. Galba* and *A. Americanus* in the form of the tubercle on the axis of the pygidium, and also in not having the glabella defined all round by the dorsal furrows, as it is in the two species compared.

The different individuals differ somewhat in the amount of the convexity.

Locality and Formation.—N, Table Head and Pistolet Bay ; P, four miles N. E. from Portland Creek, Newfoundland ; Quebec group.

Collector.—J. Richardson.

ENTOMOSTRACA.

LEPERDITIA TURGIDA. (N. sp.)

Description.—Small and strongly convex ; dorsal margin straight ; anterior and posterior dorsal angles obliquely truncated at an angle of about 45°, and for nearly half the breadth ; ventral margin most convex in the posterior two-thirds, thence gently convex and sloping upwards. The greatest breadth is a little behind the mid-length. The right valve is strongly convex, most inflated in the posterior two-thirds, and nearer the ventral than the dorsal margin. Left valve smaller and less convex than the right.

Length of the largest and most perfect right valve observed, 2 lines ; breadth of the same, a little behind the mid-length, $1\frac{2}{3}$ lines. Numerous specimens of all sizes, from the length of $\frac{1}{2}$ a line up to 2 lines, occur on the same slabs. The smaller ones are more nearly ovate than the larger.

This species has a general resemblance to *L. Canadensis* (Jones), but is always more tumid, and can be distinguished therefrom, after having been studied, at a glance.

Locality and Formation.—G and H, Port aux Choix and Cape Norman, Newfoundland ; Quebec group.

Collector.—J. Richardson.

LEPERDITIA CONCINNULA. (N. sp.)

Description.—Rather small, ovate, dorsal margin straight ; anterior extremity rounded and slightly narrower than the posterior ; the latter more broadly rounded, obliquely truncated at the dorsal angle, where, also, there is a short spine or projection situated on the angle. The ventral margin is somewhat straight, sub-parallel with the dorsal, but slightly converging towards the anterior extremity. At both extremities the margin of both valves is compressed and sometimes seen to have a shallow concave groove running round parallel to the edge. The valves are moderately convex. The tubercle is situated at about one-third the length from the anterior extremity, and at one-third the breadth below the hinge line. Surface apparently smooth.

Length of a large specimen 3 lines; width 2 lines.

Resembles *L. Canadensis* (Jones), but has a more nearly straight ventral margin, and is not so convex.

Locality and Formation.—L, Point Rich, M. Table Head, Newfoundland; Quebec group.

Collector.—J. Richardson.

Leperditia ventralis. (N. sp.)

Description.—Right valve sub-ovate; dorsal margin straight; angles obliquely truncated; ventral margin convex, most projecting a little behind the mid-length; margin at both extremities compressed; strongly convex in the lower half, most tumid at the ventral margin, which is so abruptly folded under as to appear carinated. Left valve unknown. Surface apparently smooth.

Length 4½ lines; greatest width 3 lines. A single well-preserved right valve was collected, and it was associated with imperfect specimens of what is probably the left valve. These latter are more nearly ovate, and less convex than the right valve.

This species is distinguished by the strongly convex and sub-carinated ventral margin.

Locality and Formation.—N, Bonne Bay, north-west arm, and also at the entrance to the east arm, Newfoundland; Quebec group.

Collector.—J. Richardson.

Beyrichia Atlantica. (N. sp.)

Description.—Small sub-ovate or reniform, greatest convexity along the median line; a single shallow depression, extending from the dorsal margin about half the breadth, situated about the mid-length. The best preserved specimen is elongate-ovate, strongly convex, rounded at both ends, and slightly truncated obliquely at the dorsal angles.

Length 1 line; width ½ a line.

Allied to *B. Logani* (Jones), but is proportionally more elongated.

Locality and Formation.—L, Point Rich, M, Table Head, Newfoundland; Quebec group.

Collector.—J. Richardson.

(There yet remain to be noticed, a number of species of Graptolites and several other fossils from Newfoundland, not yet determined. These will be published in a continuation of this article further on.)

7.—*New species of Fossils from the Quebec Group, in Eastern Canada, with some others previously described, and some from other formations.*

The species described in this article were, most of them, discovered after the article concluded on page 206 was printed. The limestone in Stanbridge, range 6, lot 20, from which many of the new species were collected, belongs to the base of division D, section Geol. of Can., pp. 844, 852, 853.

BRACHIOPODA.

LINGULA IRIS. (N. sp.)

Fig. 290.

a *b*

Fig. 291.

Fig. 292.

Fig. 290.—*Lingula Iris.*
291.—*Orthis? apicalis.* *a*, ventral valve; *b*, side view of the same.
292.—*Orthis Corinna.* Ventral valve.

Description.—Shell small, sub-ovate; sides parallel, or nearly so, in the lower two-thirds gently convex or somewhat straight; in the upper one-third converging to the beak with a convex slope; beak narrowly rounded; anterior angles rounded; anterior margin, with a portion in the middle, somewhat straight. The only specimen collected is gently convex, a somewhat flat space along the middle, and a flat, or gently convex slope on each side to the margin in the upper two-thirds.

Surface with obscure, radiating and concentric striæ.

Length 4½ lines; width 3¼ lines.

Locality and Formation.—Point Lévis, limestone No. 2; Quebec group.

Collector.—T. C. Weston.

ORTHIS? APICALIS. (N. sp.)

Fig. 291. *a*, *b*.

Description.—Shell small, shaped like an *Acrotreta.* Ventral valve pyramidal, the height at the beak in some individuals equal to the whole width of the shell; hinge line straight, equal to the greatest width; sides and front uniformly rounded; area large, its height sometimes equal to its width, striated parallel to the hinge line, usually a little concave, sometimes at a right angle to the plane of the margin, but often sloping a little backwards; foramen large, apparently open, and about one-third the whole width. Dorsal valve moderately convex. Surface with fine, sharp rugose striæ, and a few concentric sub-squamose lines.

The form of the dorsal valve is usually semicircular, the front margin shewing some traces of a wide, shallow sinus. The proportional length and width, however, varies to a small extent.

Width on the hinge line about 2 lines; length about 1 line.

Locality and Formation.—Point Lévis, limestone No. 1; Quebec group.

Collector.—T. C. Weston.

Orthis Corinna. (N. sp.)

Fig. 292.

Description.—Small, transversely oblong or ovate; hinge line equal to, or a little less than, the greatest width; cardinal angles either rounded or rectangular. Ventral valve rather convex, most elevated near the beak, usually flat or concave from the beak to the cardinal angles, a wide, shallow sinus from the front margin upwards, which dies out before reaching the umbo. The beak appears to be a little depressed below the umbo, but it is not preserved in the specimens observed. Area wide, flat, sloping a little backwards. Dorsal valve moderately convex, with an obscure fold in the front half. Surface with very fine radiating striæ, six to nine in the width of one line.

Width from 5 to 6 lines; length varying from two-thirds to three-fourths the width.

The sides in the upper half are sometimes straight and parallel, and sometimes rounded. Anterior angles rounded. The front margin is usually straight, or a little concave, in the middle.

Locality and Formation.—Stanbridge, range 6, lot 20; Quebec group.

Collector.—T. C. Weston.

Orthis ? Armanda. (N. sp.)

a. b. c.

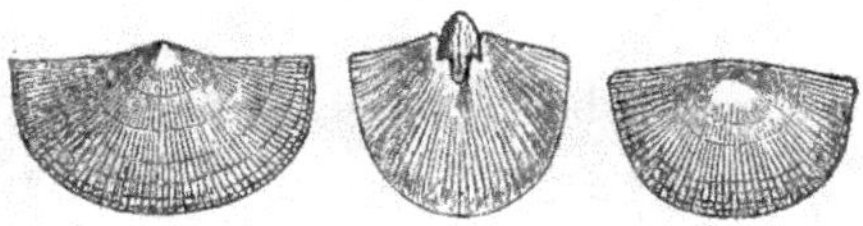

Fig. 293.

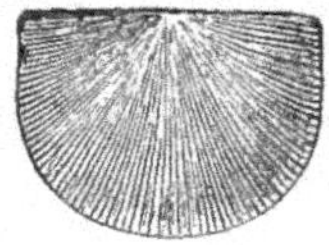

Fig. 294.

Fig. 293.—*Orthis Armanda.* *a*, ventral valve of a wide variety; *b*, ventral valve of a narrower form, showing a cast of the interior of the beak and umbo; *c*, dorsal valve.
294.—*Orthis Minna.*

Description.—Shell of medium size, varying in width; hinge line straight; cardinal angles 90°, or often a little less; sides straight, and either parallel or a little converging from the hinge line forward for one-fourth or one-half the length; anterior angles and front margin rounded. Ventral valve pyramidal, varying in height, the beak usually the most elevated point, thence with a convex or straight slope to the anterior angles and margin, the slope to the cardinal angles either flat or gently concave. Dorsal valve depressed convex, concave towards the cardinal angles; beak scarcely elevated above the hinge line.

The area of the ventral valve is rather large, sometimes three lines in height, often less, very variable in this respect, either at right angles to the plane of the margin, or inclined thereto sometimes as low as 45°. Foramen moderate, apparently open. In the interior the dental plates seem to form an imperfect triangular chamber, thus differing somewhat from the usual forms of the genus.

Surface with fine sharp distinct striæ several times sub-divided, from six to ten in the width of one line at the margin. These striæ are usually crenulated by concentric lines, especially towards the front margin.

Width on the hinge line from 6 to 10 lines; length varying from one-half to three-fourths of the length.

Locality and Formation.—Phillipsburg (limestone), B. 2, section Geol. of Can., p. 844; Quebec group.

Collectors.—E. Billings, Dr. P. J. Farnsworth.

Orthis minna.

Fig. 294.

Description.—Shell rather large, sub-quadrate; hinge line straight, equal to the greatest width; cardinal angles rectangular; sides in the upper half straight and parallel; front angles and margin broadly rounded.

Ventral valve flat or gently concave ; area narrow. Dorsal valve depressed convex with a wide, shallow mesial sinus nearly the whole length ; cardinal angles compressed , beak apparently incurved down to the hinge line ; area linear. Surface with fine bifurcating striæ four to six in the width of one line.

Width from 10 to 12 lines ; length 6 to 8 lines. The width appears to be in general one-fourth greater than the length.

This species appears to be allied to *O. platys* of the Chazy limestone, but has the ventral valve gently concave or flat, instead of depressed convex.

Locality and Formation.—Stanbridge, range 6, lot 20 ; Quebec group.

Collector.—T. C. Weston.

CAMERELLA BREVIPLICATA. (N. sp.)

Fig. 295.

Fig. 296.

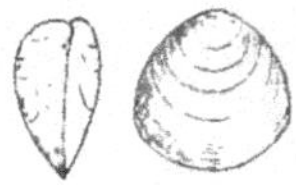

Fig. 297.

Fig. 295.—*Camerella breviplicata.* Dorsal and side views.
296.—*C.? costata.* Dorsal ? valve.
297.—*C. polita.* Ventral and side views.

Description.—Shell with both valves convex, ovate, greatest width at about one-third of the length from the front, thence narrowed with straight or gently convex sides to the beak ; anterior angles rounded ; front margin usually broadly rounded, but sometimes with a portion in the middle straight. Dorsal valve slightly more convex than the ventral, most tumid in the upper third ; beak closely incurved ; umbo broadly rounded. The ventral valve is like the dorsal, except that it seems to have a small beak a little elevated above the hinge line, and is less convex.

Surface smooth, from eight to ten short plications at the front margin, usually one-fourth the length of the shell, sometimes less.

Length of the largest specimen collected 4 lines, width about the same, sometimes a little less.

Locality and Formation.—Stanbridge, range 6, lot 20 ; Quebec group.

Collector.—T. C. Weston.

Camerella ? costata. (N. sp.)

Fig. 296.

Description.—Broad ovate, greatest width about the mid-length, uniformly convex, with from ten to twelve strong, angular undivided ribs, which extend to the beaks.

The best preserved specimen of this species that has been collected, is partly imbedded in the matrix. It is transversely ovate or sub-circular, the width one-fourth greater than the length, the sides and front uniformly rounded, rather strongly convex, the greatest elevation at one-fourth the length from the beak ; umbo broadly rounded. It appears to be a dorsal valve.

Length 6½ lines ; width 8 lines.

It is quite uncertain that this species is a true *Camerella*. It may be congeneric with *Porambonites Ottawaensis* (*ante*, p. 240).

Locality and Formation.—Stanbridge, range 6, lot 20 ; Quebec group.

Collectors.—J. Richardson, T. C. Weston.

Camerella polita. (N. sp.)

Fig. 297.

Description.—Shell ovate, smooth and moderately convex, greatest width at about one-fourth the length from the front margin, thence tapering with gently convex sides to the beaks ; front angles and margin rounded. Dorsal valve most convex just in front of the umbo ; beak incurved down to the hinge. Ventral valve less convex than the dorsal ; beak small, pointed, a little elevated above the hinge.

Surface smooth.

Length of largest specimen collected 3 lines ; width about the same.

This species has nearly the same form as *C. breviplicata*, but differs therefrom in being smooth, in being less convex, in having the front margin thinner and usually more rounded. The form varies from ovate to sub-circular. The young individuals of *C. breviplicata* have two or three incipient folds in the front margin by which they may be readily distinguished from this species.

Locality and Formation.—Stanbridge, range 6, lot 20, and on the upper end of the island of Orleans ; Quebec group.

Collectors. T. C. Weston, E. Billings.

LAMELLIBRANCHIATA.

EOPTERIA RICHARDSONI. (N. sp.)

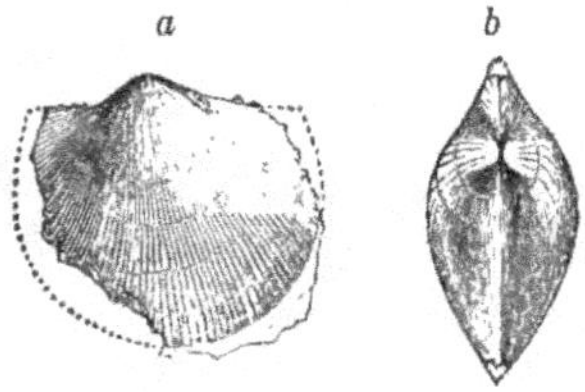

Fig. 298.

Fig. 298.—*Eopteria Richardsoni.* *a*, left valve; *b*, cardinal view.

Description.—Shell obliquely sub-circular, length and width about equal, uniformly convex; anterior cardinal angle compressed; beaks small, closely incurved, situated a little behind the mid-length of the hinge line; surface with fine radiating striæ.

The only specimen collected is imperfect, but, it appears, that the whole of the ventral and posterior margin is broadly rounded. Both valves are equally convex, most tumid a little above the middle. The anterior cardinal angle is compressed and apparently rectangular or perhaps a little rounded. The posterior angle is not distinctly seen, but it seems to be scarcely at all compressed. The hinge line behind the beaks is exhibited as a rounded ridge with no evidence of a suture, (at least none can be seen in this specimen). There are about six striæ in the width of one line near the margin.

Eopteria typica (*ante*, p. 221,) has coarse ribs and is narrowly rounded at the lower posterior angle.

Length and width about 9 lines.

Dedicated to the discoverer.

Locality and Formation.—Near St. Antoine above Quebec, in a boulder with *Subulites Psyche;* Quebec group.

Collector.—J. Richardson.

EOPTERIA? ORNATA. (N. sp.)

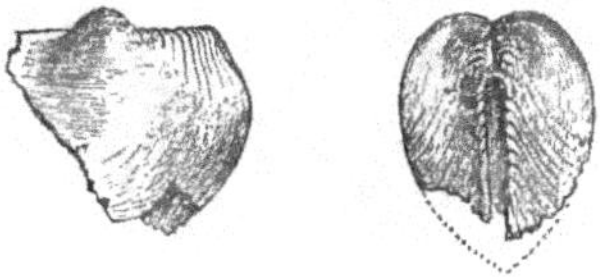

Fig. 299.

Fig. 299.—*Eopteria? ornata.* *a*, side view of the anterior extremity; *b*, anterior extremity shewing the gape: enlarged two diameters.

Description—The specimen is the anterior extremity of a silicified individual, which was procured by dissolving a small piece of limestone on hydrochloric acid. Hinge line, so far as preserved straight, projecting before the umbones; anterior angle about 90°, not rounded but angular; most projecting point of anterior extremity narrowly rounded, and situated about one-third the height below the angle; below this broadly rounded with an oblique and gentle curve until a point nearly beneath the umbones on the ventral margin is attained: all behind this not preserved. Both valves are rather strongly convex. The anterior angle in front of the beaks is compressed and the dorsal edges of the hinge are transversely corrugated. On an anterior view the shell is seen to be gaping, the edges within the fissure crenulated as shewn in fig. *b*, above. Surface with strong, sharp, concentric ridges, from eight to ten in one line.

The specimen when perfect was probably about 8 lines in length.

This species is placed in the genus *Eopteria* provisionally until more shall become known about its affinities.

Locality and Formation.—Point Lévis. In the upper part of limestone No. 2, Quebec group.

Collector.—Sir W. E. Logan.

GASTEROPODA.

MURCHISONIA MISSISQUOI. (N. sp.)

Description.—Shell large, elongate, acutely conical, tapering at the rate of about one inch in a length of three inches. Whorls narrow, strongly convex, with three or four carinæ on each, the spaces between concave. Surface unknown.

Length about 4 inches. The largest whorl seen appears to be about 1½ inches across.

This species is closely allied to *M. Adelina*, (*ante*, p. 231, fig. 217,) but is not so nearly cylindrical, and is a larger species.

It is only known by three fragments, and an entire individual obscurely seen in section.

Locality and Formation.—Stanbridge, range 6, lot 20 ; Quebec group.

Collector.—T. C. Weston.

METOPTOMA QUEBECENSIS. (N. sp.)

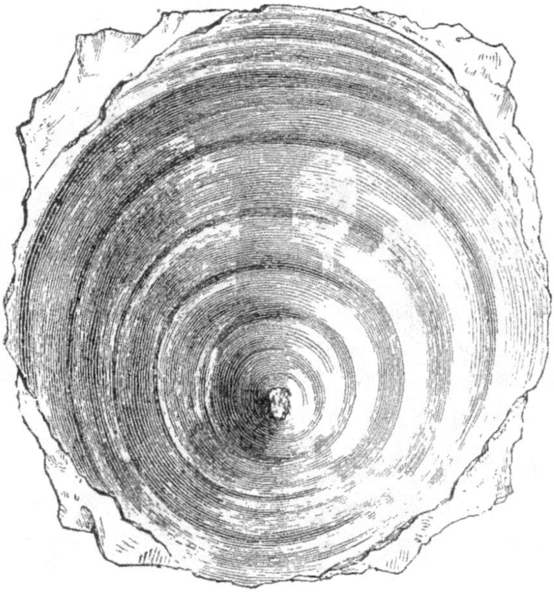

Fig. 300.

Fig. 300.—*Metoptoma Quebecensis.* View of the upper side of an imperfect specimen.

Description.—Shell with the base elliptical, length from one-eighth to one-sixth greater than the width ; conical, or, rather, campanulate, the margins showing a tendency to spread out horizontally ; apex eccentric, situated about one-sixth the whole length from the centre. The height appears to be from one-third to one-half the length. Surface with a few wide shallow concave undulations of growth. It also appears to be finely striated, but no specimens with it perfectly preserved have been collected.

M. melissa (*ante*, p. 86,) has the cone more acute, and proportionately more elevated, besides being more narrowly rounded on the anterior, than on the posterior aspect. It is also a smaller species.

Length of a large specimen 3½ inches; width 3 inches.

Locality and Formation.—Point Levis; limestone of the Quebec group.

Collectors.—T. Devine, Esq., T. C. Weston.

HELICOTOMA MISER. (N. sp.)

H. perstriata. *Geol. Can.* pp. 233, 862.

Description.—Shell small, with four slender, but strongly carinated whorls. Spire flat, the whorls on the upper side, with two strong, acutely angular carinæ of equal height, separated by a deep, concave groove, which is visible quite to the apex. The inner carina is situated a little more than one-third of the width of the whorl from the suture. The outer carina rises vertically from the periphery. From the inner carina, there is a flat slope, extending down to the bottom of the deeply excavated suture at an angle of 45°. From the edge of the outer carina there is a vertical descent, one-fourth the depth of the whorl, forming a flat band at a right angle to the plane of the spire. This band is bounded on its lower side, by an angular carina, the upper side of which forms an abrupt projection at a right angle to the band. Below this carina, the whorl appears to be vertical, or nearly so for one-fourth its depth, and then rounded into the umbilicus, this lower rounded part being ornamented by fine sharp striæ following the whorls. No striæ across the whorls are visible on this specimen, but, no doubt, they exist.

Diameter 6 lines; width of the last whorl at the aperture 1¾ lines; depth about the same. The umbilicus is not visible in the specimen, but it is probably about one third the whole diameter.

Only one specimen has been seen, and this is perfect above, but has its base imbedded in the matrix.

I have heretofore referred this species to *H. perstriata* of the Calciferous formation, but now think it may be separated as a closely allied species. In that species the inner whorls of the spire are a little elevated above the outer; and the concave groove between the two carinæ on the upper side of the whorls, as well as the slope into the suture, are longitudinally striated. The band below the outer carina is not quite vertical, one third the depth of the whorl, longtitudinally striated and obscurely divided into two bands by an elevated line along the middle. None of these characters are possessed by *H. miser.*

Locality and Formation.—Point Levis; in limestone No. 2, Quebec group.

Ophileta? bella. (N. sp.)

O. uniangulata. *Geol. Can., p.* 860; *ante*, p. 246.

a b c

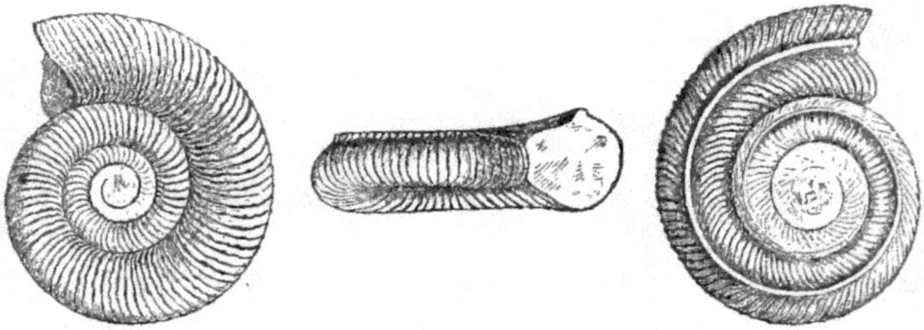

Fig. 301.

Fig. 301.—*Ophileta bella.* Different views of a nearly perfect specimen.

Description.—From one to two inches across; lower side flat or gently concave; upper side concave, with a strongly elevated narrow spiral band; whorls, four or five. On the lower side, the whorls are usually moderately convex, but sometimes they are flattened on the inner half. The outer side of the whorls are convex. On the upper side, the spiral band sometimes runs along the middle of the whorl, as in fig. 301, *c*, but its position varies between the middle and the outer edge. The aperture has an angular notch above with the apex at the termination of the band: on the lower side, a flexure backwards. Surface with coarse, sub-squamose, transverse lines, of growth about six in two lines.

The whorls are often somewhat larger in proportion to the width than in the specimen above figured.

I have heretofore referred specimens belonging to this species to the *Euomphalus uniangulatus* (Hall), but the recent discovery of a number of good specimens leads me to regard it as a distinct, although a closely allied form. That species has the lower side deeply concave, forming a deep umbilicus like *Helicotoma planulata* (Salter); while in this, it is usually flat, and when concave, is only moderately so. The whorls in this species are also more compactly inrolled.

I have stated (*ante*, p. 236,) that the genus *Ophileta* was founded on species of *Maclurea*, with very slender whorls. The specimen above figured was discovered since that page was printed. It shows very clearly that the aperture has a sinus in the lower lip, and a notch in the upper, characters which are not at all exhibited by perfect specimens of *Maclurea Logani.* In *M. crenulata* (*ante*, p. 236,) there is a sort of spiral band, and, also, there are indications of a sinus in the lip on the flat side, but they are only incipiently developed. The two genera may be thus distinguished :—in *Maclurea*, the aperture is entire, and the whorls usually large ; but in *Ophileta*, it has a sinus below, and a notch above, while the whorls are usually slender.

All the species of *Pleurotomoria* and *Helicotoma*, of the Lower Silurian rocks of Canada, of which perfect specimens have been found, have this same form of aperture. And so have some of the *Euomphali* of the Devonian and Carboniferous rocks.

It would appear also that *Maclurea* is a dextral shell, and that the flat side is the umbilicus.

Locality and Formation.—This species occurs at Bedford, in Stanbridge, range 6, lot 20 ; in Farnham, range 5, lot 41 ; and at Cow Head, in Newfoundland, in Division P ; Quebec group.

Collectors.—T. C. Weston, J. Richardson.

HETEROPODA.

Bellerophon Palinurus. (N. sp.)

Fig. 302.

Fig. 302.—*Bellerophon Palinurus.* Side and front views. The specimen figured, being imperfect, does not show the form of the lip.

Description.—Sub-lenticular ; dorsum acutely carinated ; greatest width close to the umbilicus ; vertical diameter from one inch to one inch and a half. The outline on a side view is elongate ovate, the vertical diameter (from the upper side of the aperture through the umbilicus) being usually one-fourth greater than the horizontal diameter, and often more owing to a distortion to which the species seems to be subject. The greatest convexity is close to the umbilicus, whence the surface ascends, at first with a convex, and then with a concave slope to the dorsal edge. The latter is usually very acute, but in many specimens, it is minutely rounded but always with a concavity, of variable width, just within. The umbilicus is small, from one-sixth to one-fifth the horizontal diameter, rounded on the edge. The aperture is ovate, indented to the extent of one-third its height on the lower side by the penultimate whorl. Some fragmentary specimens shew that, in the perfect aperture, the lowest lip is much thickened next the umbilicus, and forms a thin layer, on the side of the whorl. The surface is usually obscurely striated, and sometimes irregularly undulated in the direction of the striæ; the latter radiate from the umbilicus to the dorsum in a gently sigmoid curve.

The width, or the diameter transversely through the umbilicus, varies from a little less than one-third to one-half the diameter.

This species is closely allied to *B. acutus*, (Sowerby,) but is in general not so much compressed.

Locality and Formation.—Stanbridge, range 6, lot 20; Quebec group.

Collectors.—J. Richardson, T. C. Weston.

CEPHALOPODA.

ORTHOCERAS ATTICUS. (N. sp.)

Description.—Shell short, rapidly tapering; section circular; septa from six to eight to the inch; siphuncle about one-seventh the whole diameter, half way between the centre and the margin, not much, if at all, inflated between the septa. Surface unknown.

The specimen is 4 inches in length; diameter at the larger extremity, 21 lines; and at the smaller, 7 lines. Diameter of the siphuncle about 2¼ lines, where the shell is 15 lines.

Locality and Formation.—Corey's farm, lot 7, range 8, Stanbridge, C, 1, section Geol. of Canada, p. 844; Quebec group.

Collectors.—Sir W. E. Logan, E. Billings.

ORTHOCERAS REPENS. (N. sp.)

Description.—Shell small, gradually tapering; section circular, or nearly so; siphuncle cylindrical, in contact with the shell; septa thin, strongly concave, numerous, about eighteen to the inch. Surface unknown. The shell appears to be obscurely annulated.

A specimen 5 inches in length has a diameter of 9 lines at the larger extremity, and 4 lines at the smaller. The siphuncle is 1¼ lines in diameter, and perfectly cylindrical, exhibiting no trace whatever of inflation between the septa.

Locality and Formation.—Phillipsburg, B 2, section Geol. of Can., p. 844; Quebec group.

Collector.—Sir W. E. Logan.

Orthoceras Catulus. (N. sp.)

Description.—Shell of medium size, slender, very gradually tapering, slightly curved, somewhat strongly annulated; section apparently circular; septa rather strongly concave, from 12 to 15 to the inch; siphuncle cylindrical, in contact with the shell, or nearly so. Surface unknown.

A specimen 7 inches in length is 10 lines in diameter at the larger extremity, and 4 lines at the smaller. The siphuncle at the mid-length is 2 lines in diameter, but appears to become smaller towards the apex. The annulations are about 3 lines distant from each other, but scarcely $\frac{3}{4}$ of a line in height; the intervening spaces broadly concave.

Closely allied to *O. repens*, but has more distant septa.

Locality and Formation.—Phillipsburg, B 2, section Geol. of Can., p. 844; Quebec group.

Collectors.—P. J. Farnsworth, E. Billings.

Orthoceras Perseus. (N. sp.)

Description.—Shell of the medium size, elongate, very gradually tapering; septa about nine to the inch; siphuncle small, cylindrical, in contact with the shell.

It is possible that the section of this species may be circular, but all the specimens, belonging to at least four or five individuals, are compressed laterally, giving an elliptical section, of which the diameters are in the proportion of about three to two. In all of them the siphuncle is situated, not on one of the broad sides, but on one of the narrow, rounded edges.

The species appears to have attained a length of about 18 inches, with a diameter of about $1\frac{1}{2}$ inches at the aperture. Diameter of the siphuncle from $1\frac{1}{2}$ to 3 lines.

Locality and Formation.—Phillipsburg, B 5, section Geol. of Can., p. 844; Quebec group.

Collectors.—Dr. P. J. Farnsworth, E. Billings.

ORTHOCERAS MISSISQUOI. (N. sp.)

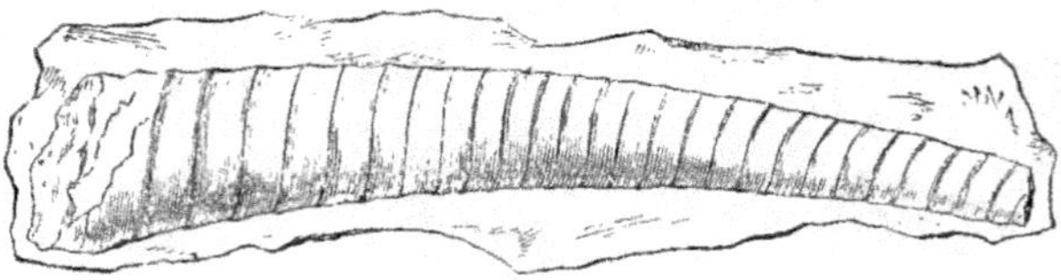

Fig. 303.

Fig. 303.—Siphuncle of *O. Missisquoi*, the most common form.

Description.—No specimens of this species with the septa preserved have been found, but the siphuncle, represented by the above figure, occurs in great numbers in one locality, in B 2, at Phillipsburg,. The most common form (of the siphuncle) is three or four inches in length, gently curved, tapering at the rate of about one line and one-third to the inch, and marked by from nine to twelve septal rings to the inch. As these rings are most distant from the apex on the concave side, it is evident that the position of the siphuncle, in the fossil, is near the shell on the dorsal side, or on the side of the concave curve.

Associated with this short curved form, there are numerous others, more elongated, somewhat straighter, and not quite so rapidly tapering. The septal rings are sometimes more rounded, or more like the annulations on such shells as *O. arenoliratum.* Similar differences are exhibited by the detached siphuncles of other species. I think all the specimens found at this locality belong to one species, variable to some extent in its length and rate of tapering. It probably is like a large gently curved *Cyrtoceras*, from six to ten inches in length, with the siphuncle on the inner instead of the outer curve, and with a diameter at the aperture of from one to three inches.

Locality and Formation.—Phillipsburg, B 2, section Geol. of Can., p. 844; Quebec group.

Collectors.—Dr. P. J. Farnsworth, and E. Billings.

ORTHOCERAS CATO. (N. sp.)

Description.—Shell of medium size, somewhat rapidly tapering; section apparently circular; septa nine to the inch; siphuncle very slender, cylindrical, in contact with the shell or nearly so; chamber of habitation deep; surface with rather strong thread-like engirdling striæ, about four in one line. The shell appears to be plain, but in one part there seems to be some indistinct annulations.

The specimen is 3¼ inches in length, somewhat flattened, evidently by pressure; diameter at larger extremity about 10 lines, and at the smaller about 5 lines; the rate of tapering being thus about 1⅔ lines to the inch; siphuncle ¾ of a line in diameter; depth of the chamber of habitation, so far as preserved, 2 inches.

Locality and Formation.—Phillipsburg, B 2, section Geol. of Can., p. 844; Quebec group.

Collector.—Dr. P. J. Farnsworth.

O. Cataline. (N. sp.)

Description.—Shell short, annulated, curved; chamber of habitation slightly narrowed towards the aperture, greatest diameter at the last chamber; section apparently somewhat ovate; septa from twelve to fourteen to the inch; siphuncle very slender, in contact with the shell on the side of the convex curve; annulations broadly rounded, slightly elevated, about two lines distant from each other; surface with fine thread-like engirdling striæ.

The length appears to be on an average from 4 to 6 inches; greatest diameter, at last septum, 9 lines; depth of chamber of habitation about 18 lines.

Resembles *O. Cato*, but is distinctly annulated, and has more numerous septa.

Locality and Formation.—Phillipsburg, B 2, section Geol. of Can., p. 844.

Collector.—E. Billings.

Orthoceras Sayi. (N. sp.)

Description.—Shell short, rapidly tapering; section elliptical, the diameters being in the proportions of nine to twelve; tapering at the rate of three lines to the inch in the lateral diameter, and about one and a half lines in the dorsal ventral; siphuncle cylindrical, in contact with the shell; septa twelve to the inch.

Surface with fine engirdling striæ. The specimen is a little curved towards the ventral side, in which respect only it differs from *O. servile*, which shows a tendency to curve in the opposite direction.

Length of the specimen 3¼ inches. In 2 inches of the length it tapers in the lateral diameter from 14 lines to 8 lines.

Locality and Formation.—Phillipsburg, B 2, section Geol. of Can., p. 844.

Collector.—Dr. P. J. Farnsworth.

Orthoceras Xerxes. (N. sp.)

Description.—Shell rather large, annulated, gradually tapering; section apparently circular; septa about six to the inch; siphuncle cylindrical about one-third the whole diameter of the shell, and either in contact with the shell or nearly so.

The specimen is distorted and, therefore, neither the section nor the rate of tapering (apparently between one and two lines to the inch) can be precisely ascertained. The annulations are broadly rounded, and the intervening spaces broadly concave. The surface of the shell, as well on the annulations as in the interspaces, is ornamented with sharp sub-imbricating engirdling striæ, about four in one line.

Length of the specimen 8 inches; diameter about 2 inches; diameter of the siphuncle 8 lines.

Locality and Formation.—Phillipsburg, B 5, section Geol. of Can., p. 844; Quebec group.

Collector.—Dr. P. J. Farnsworth.

Orthoceras Tityrus. (N. sp.) ?

Remarks.—In B 2 were found some fragments of a large *Orthoceras*, resembling *O. Xerxes* in every respect, except that the shell is not annulated. I propose the above name for it provisionally. It is closely allied to *O. velox* (*ante*, p. 173).

Cyrtoceras Aristides. (N. sp.)

Description.—Shell small, slightly curved, greatest diameter at the last septum, then slightly contracted towards the aperture, and tapering at the rate of about four lines to the inch towards the apex; septa thin closely crowded, from six to eight in two lines; surface and siphuncle unknown.

Length of a specimen which is entire but imbedded 21 lines; diameter at last septum 7 lines; depth of chamber of habitation 6 lines; diameter at the aperture a little less.

Locality and Formation.—Phillipsburg, B 2, section Geol. Can., p. 844. Quebec group.

Collector.—E. Billings.

CRUSTACEA.

Asaphus Pelops. (N. sp.)

a

b

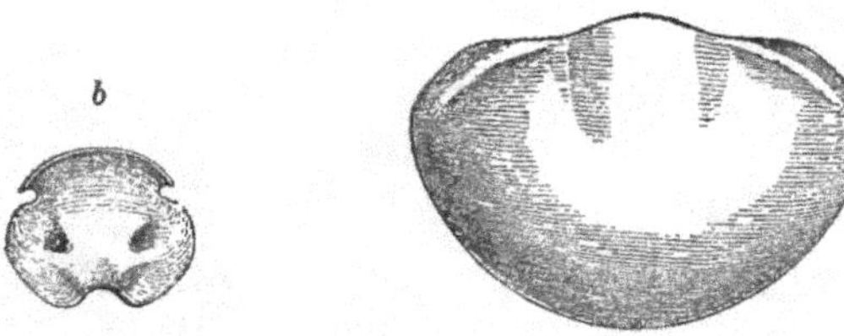

Fig. 304.

Fig. 305.

Fig. 304.—*Asaphus Pelops.* *a*, the pygidium ; *b*, the hypostoma.
305.—*A ? curiosa.* The pygidium. The specimen is somewhat distorted.

Description.—Pygidium rather strongly and uniformly convex, smooth, no marginal groove ; length two-thirds the width ; anterior angles obliquely truncated for about half the width of the side lobes ; an obscure pleural groove just behind the genal angle, and extending thence nearly to the dorsal furrow ; axis about one-third the whole width, scarcely elevated above the general surface ; dorsal furrows only distinguishable near the margin. The widest part of the pygidium is on a line drawn across it at about one-fifth the length from the middle of the front margin. The whole margin behind this line is uniformly curved, forming very nearly a regular semicircle. In some specimens the middle of the posterior margin shews a tendency to become more narrowly rounded or obscurely angular. The axis is in general, only distinguishable near the anterior edge. On the under side the fold of the crust, or doublure, is equal to full one-third the whole width of the pygidium. It has a small pit in it near the middle of the posterior margin.

The hypostoma is short, transversely ovate, its width about one-fifth greater than its length, the alar expansions at the anterior angles small and acute, the notch behind them also small and rounded ; the central portion in the anterior half is gently convex ; the two side lobes flat ; the notch in the posterior margin is shallow, rounded, its depth about one line where the whole length is six lines ; the muscular impressions are rather large, about one-third of the whole width distant from each other, and with their centres a little behind a line drawn across at the mid-length.

Fragments of the head shew that the posterior angles are rounded angular. The eyes are small, and situated a little behind the mid-length of the glabella.

This species resembles *A. platycephalus*, but the form of the hypostoma and the absence of a marginal groove on the pygidium appear sufficient to separate it therefrom.

Locality and Formation.—East side of the village of Bedford in the bed of Pike River, and upper end of the island of Orleans; Quebec group.

Collectors.—Sir W. E. Logan, E. Billings.

Asaphus? Curiosus. (N. sp.)

Fig. 305.

Description.—Pygidium sub-pentagonal, the anterior margin somewhat rounded, the anterior angles very largely truncated on a line subparallel with the longitudinal axis, a wide shallow concave groove all round; axis depressed convex in the anterior half, but becoming obsolete before reaching the marginal groove. Surface apparently smooth.

No perfect specimens of this peculiar fossil have been found, but from such fragments as have been collected it is clearly a new form. The shape of the pygidium, is what the same part of *A. platycephalus* would present, were its lateral angles cut away to the depth of about half the width of the side lobes. It has also somewhat the aspect of the tail of a *Bathyurellus*.

It is referred to *Asaphus* provisionally.

Locality and Formation.—Stanbridge, range 6, lot 20; Quebec group.

Collector.—T. C. Weston.

Bathyurellus expansus. (N. sp.)

a.

b.

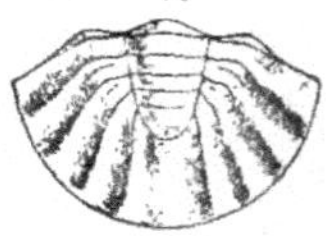

Fig. 306.

Fig. 306.—*Bathyurellus expansus.* *a*, the glabella, with part of the fixed cheeks; *b*, a pygidium, more convex and strongly ribbed than usual.

Description.—Head moderately convex, with a wide concave border. Glabella strongly convex, conical, sides in the posterior half, or two-thirds straight and parallel, in some specimens slightly concave just behind the eyes or between them, the anterior third converging to a narrow rounded point. The dorsal furrows extend all round, but they are not deeply impressed. Neck furrow all across. The fixed cheeks all round the glabella are gently convex, or, rather, the glabella seems to be a little sunk into them. In front of the glabella there is a convex slope ending abruptly at the inner edge of the concave border. The eyes are semi-circular, about one-third the length of the glabella; their anterior angles a little in advance of a line drawn across the glabella at the mid-length; their centres distant from the dorsal furrow about one-third the width of the glabella.

The pygidium is semicircular, its width a little less than twice its length and varying from moderately to depressed convex; anterior angles obliquely truncated for about half the width of the side lobes; sides and posterior margin uniformly curved into a nearly perfect semicircle. The axis is strongly convex, conical, slightly tapering backwards, a little more than half the whole length; apex obtusely rounded, somewhat abruptly terminated; four distinctly defined depressed convex rings (besides the half segment at the anterior margin, and a fifth terminal subtriangular segment at the apex, which occupies twice the space of one of the others). The proportional length of the axis varies a little, but in all the specimens it is distinctly segmented, and well defined at the apex. It also varies in width, being in some one-fourth, and in others one-third the greatest breadth of the whole pygidium. The lateral lobes have a small triangular space on each side, next the axis, which is flat or horizontal. It becomes gradually narrower backwards, and terminates in a point at the apex of the axis. Outside of this the whole of the pygidium is gently concave. There are four pairs of ribs in the side lobes. The first pair, in crossing the flat triangular space, are at right angles to the axis. They then turn backwards, forming an obtuse angle which varies from 120° to about 150°. The other ribs are more inclined backwards, and the last pair are nearly parallel with the axis. The first three pairs have an indistinct pleural groove extending outwards from the axis to the edge of the triangular flat space. The main grooves between the ribs are shallow and concave.

In several of the large specimens the side lobes are more nearly flat, and the ribs more obscure, than they are in the smaller ones.

The surface is not distinctly preserved in the specimens, but it is not tuberculated, apparently it is smooth. One of the specimens of a large pygidium exhibits some indications of concentric fissure-like striæ.

This species appears to have attained a length of 4 inches, but the majority of the specimens are fragments of individuals from 2 to 3 inches in length.

This species is closely allied to several of those described in the foregoing pages. The differences are as follows:

1. *B. marginatus.*—The head of this species, in the only specimen col-

lected, has the cheeks abruptly elevated from the bottom of the dorsal furrow at the side of the glabella to the eye. The pygidium has a very small axis, and the side lobes are nearly flat.

2. *B. nitidus.*—The glabella and eyes are surrounded by a semicircular groove, and the whole of the margin in front of the apex of the glabella is concave (*ante*, p. 265, fig. 249).

3. *B. formosus.*—Only one-third of the space in front of the glabella is concave; in this species the concave border is at least half the width of the same space.

4. *B. fraternus.*—The head is more convex, while the front part of the glabella is more depressed, being on a level with the general surface. The pygidium is, also, shorter, the axis wider and not elevated at the apex.

5. *B. validus.*—Head strongly convex; front of the glabella not elevated; the whole of the side lobes of the pygidium concave, and the axis not elevated at the apex.

Of all the above, *B. nitidus* and *B. marginatus* seem to be most closely allied to *B. expansus*. They form a remarkable group, and it may yet be found necessary to unite them all into one polymorphic species.

Locality and Formation.—Stanbridge, range 6, lot 20; Quebec group.

Collector.—T. C. Weston.

Other Species of Bathyurellus.

The following are named provisionally from specimens of the pygidium.

1. *Bathyurellus rarus.* The specimen is a flat and nearly perfectly semicircular pygidium, nine lines in length and seventeen in width. There are obscure indications of an axis extending one-third the length; it is scarcely elevated above the surface. There is a faint concave depression all round near the margin and the central one; half of the whole upper surface is slightly convex. Surface apparently smooth. It was collected in the upper part of limestone No. 2, at Point Levis, Quebec group, by T. C. Weston.

2. *Bathyurellus litoreus.*—Pygidium nearly semicircular, anterior angles obliquely truncated, sides and posterior margin rounded to the curve of a semicircle; axis not quite the whole length, from one-fourth to one-third the whole width, conical, the apex moderately well defined. There is an obscure groove close to the anterior margin on the axis and side lobes, but otherwise the whole surface is smooth. The side lobes are nearly flat, with a barely perceptible slope to the margin. Occurs with the former and also in band D, on the beach at Point Lévis.

Amphion Westoni. (N. sp.)

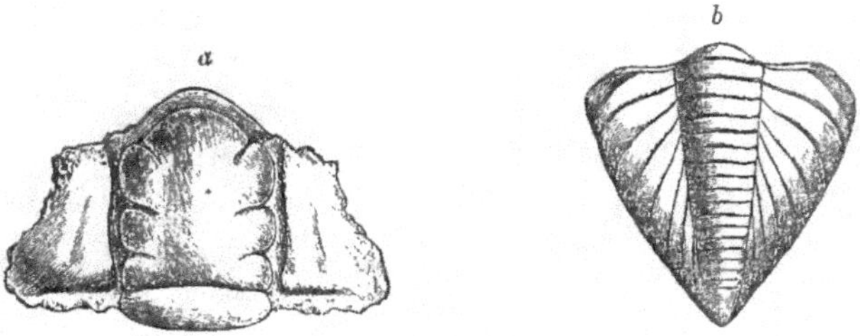

Fig. 307.

Fig. 307.—*Amphion Westoni.* *a*, the glabella with part of the cheeks (the specimen is a cast of the interior, and does not shew the eye); *b*, pygidium found associated with it.

Description.—Glabella oblong, pentagonal, depressed convex, most elevated along the middle; sides straight and usually parallel, sometimes slightly converging forwards; anterior margin of glabella rounded—angular in the middle, then straight or gently convex to the anterior corners which are rounded. Neck furrow extending all across. Three pairs of glabellar furrows; the second pair a little in advance of the mid-length; the first pair half way between the second and the neck furrow; the third pair running out just in advance of the anterior corners, sloping inwards at an angle of 45° to the longitudinal axis. The furrows all extend inwards about one-fourth the width of the glabella. In most of the specimens there is a small pit in the middle of the front margin. Sometimes the first pair of furrows curve backwards and partially isolate the posterior pair of glabellar lobes. The glabella is well separated from the cheeks by deep dorsal furrows. The position of the eye has not been distinctly made out, but it appears to be opposite the posterior glabellar furrow. Length of largest glabella collected 10 lines; width of the same 7 lines.

The pygidium above figured, although widely different from that of an ordinary *Amphion* in aspect, still exhibits, in its structure some affinity thereto. It is triangular, tapering uniformly backwards with gently convex sides to the apex which is pointed or very narrowly rounded. Axis cylindro-conical, about one-third the whole width, strongly elevated and sub-angular along the median line, becoming more depressed towards the apex where it is scarcely raised above the general surface; about eighteen rounded ribs, those towards the apex sometimes obscurely developed. In the side lobes there are about ten ribs. Of these, the last four or five are very imperfectly developed, and are nearly parallel with the axis. On a side view this pygidium is very strongly convex, the ribs being bent down so that only half their length is seen in a view of the upper side as represented in the above figure.

In general there are only five segments in the axis of the pygidium of an *Amphion*, but in *A. Julius* figured (*ante*, p. 290), there are ten, and in this species eighteen. It is possible that all behind the fifth may be regarded as equivalent of the long triangular terminal segment of such species as *A. Barrandei*, *A. Canadensis*, and others. The general form of this pygidium is also very like that of *Encrinurus*, a genus which is very closely allied to *Amphion*. Indeed, if the specimens had been found associated with the head of an *Encrinurus*, I would have had no hesitation in referring them to that genus; but there was not a vestige of anything that could be identified as belonging thereto collected. On the other hand the glabella and pygidium above figured were found in about equal numbers together, and in great abundance. Out of one small piece of rock scarcely a yard in length, there were taken twenty-seven specimens of the glabella, and twenty-four of the pygidium. In this mass of rock there was no other head to which the pygidium could be referred, nor any other pygidium to which the head could possibly have belonged. Notwithstanding, however, this remarkable association, it is with great doubt that I classify the specimens under one name, even provisionally. Should a separation be hereafter found necessary, I beg that the specific name may be retained for the head.

Dedicated to Mr. T. C. Weston.

Locality and Formation.—Stanbridge, range 6, lot 20; Quebec group.

Collectors.—J. Richardson; T. C. Weston.

Amphion convexus. (N. sp.)

Description.—Head strongly convex, apparently forming one-fourth of a sphere. Glabella convex, oblong, uniformly rounded in front; sides straight and parallel; dorsal furrows deep; neck furrow all across; three pairs of glabellar furrows; the second pair half-way between the neck furrow and the front margin, the first pair a little nearer the neck furrow than they are to the second pair; the third or anterior pair cutting the anterior margin half way between the middle and the sides, and extending obliquely inwards at an angle of about 45°. The furrows all extend inwards one-third the whole width. The eyes appear to be large. A line drawn across the glabella at the mid-length would pass through their posterior angles, and they seem to slope inwards from this point towards the middle of the third lobe of the glabella. The distance of the posterior angle of the eye from the dorsal furrow is equal to nearly half the width of the glabella. The cheeks are somewhat coarsely pitted.

Length of the head 3½ lines; width of the same 5 lines; width of the glabella, 2¼ lines.

The glabella of *A. Westoni* is nearly flat, and the eye situated not so far forward as it is in this species.

Locality and Formation.—Stanbridge, range 6, lot 20; Quebec group.

Collectors.—J. Richardson, T. C. Weston.

Cheirurus Glaucus. (N. sp.)

a b

Fig. 308.

Fig. 309.

Fig. 308.—*Cheirurus Glaucus.* *a*, side view of the glabella; *b*, upper side of the same with part of the cheeks. As this view is a vertical one, the spine seems to be further back than it is in *a*.

309.—*C. Satyrus.* Side view of the glabella, enlarged two diameters.

Description.—Head strongly convex with a small cylindrical spine just behind the centre of the upper surface of the glabella. Glabella obtusely conical; sides gently convex, a little converging forwards; front margin broadly rounded; neck furrow all across; three pairs of glabellar furrows; the first pair curving backwards and inwards, making the posterior lobes about one-third the length of the glabella from the neck furrow to the front margin, and one-third the width; the second pair at about the mid-length, and the third a little in advance of the second. These two pairs of furrows extend about half way up the sides, and have the convex curve forwards. On a side view, the outline is strongly arched upwards to the mid-length, just behind which rises the spine, from the base of which to the neck furrow there is a straight slope. The front of the glabella appears to be bordered by a very narrow rim. The surface of the glabella seems to be smooth.

This species is allied to *C. perforator*, (*ante*, p. 287,) but differs in having the spine not so far forwards. *C. Satyrus* has a much larger spine.

Locality and Formation.—Stanbridge, range 6, lot 20; Quebec group.

Collector.—T. C. Weston.

Cheirurus Satyrus. (N. sp.)

Fig. 309.

Description.—Glabella extremely convex, so much elevated as to become obliquely conical, gradually passing upwards into a stout spine, the base of which occupies the whole of the second one-fourth of the length from behind. On a vertical view the outline is oblong, the length two-sevenths greater than the width, the sides gently convex and sub-parallel, the anterior corners nearly right angles, the anterior margin moderately convex, and apparently with a very narrow rim. There are three pairs of glabellar furrows; the posterior pair leaving the dorsal furrows at rather more than one-third the whole length from the posterior margin, and sloping upwards and backwards until their inner extremities approach each other within one-third of the whole width; the other two pairs are situated in the anterior half, and are very short. The neck furrow extends all across, and the neck segment appears to have a small tubercle in the middle.

Length $2\frac{1}{4}$ lines; width $1\frac{3}{4}$ lines.

Locality and Formation.—Chazy limestone, Montreal.

Collector.—T. C. Weston.

Cheirurus Vulcanus (*ante*, p. 284).

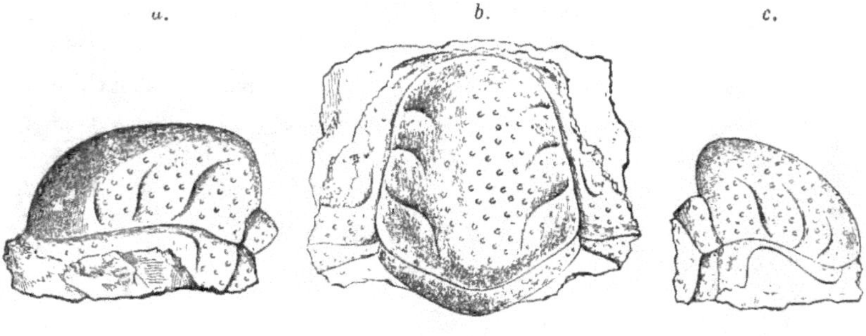

Fig. 310.

Fig. 310.—*Cheirurus Vulcanus.* *a*, side view of a large glabella; *b*, upper side of another somewhat larger: *c*, side view of a glabella in which the posterior part is extremely convex.

Remarks.—Since the description of this species (*ante*, p. 284,) was printed, a large number of specimens of the glabella have been collected at Stanbridge. The form varies greatly. In some the outline is uniformly arched from the front margin to the neck furrow; in others, the arch is depressed in the upper part, as in figure 310, *a*; while some (*c*) have the posterior part arising abruptly from the neck furrow, and so extremely convex as to exhibit a tendency to become prolonged into a spine. There is a regular gradation between these forms, and they seem, therefore, to be all of one species.

The specimens above figured were collected in Stanbridge, range 6, lot 20; Quebec group; by T. C. Weston.

CHEIRURUS PROLIFICUS (*ante*, p. 285).

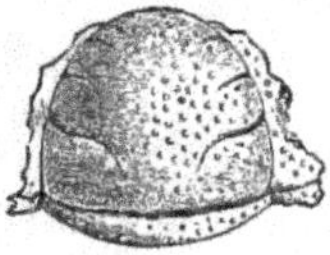

Fig. 311.

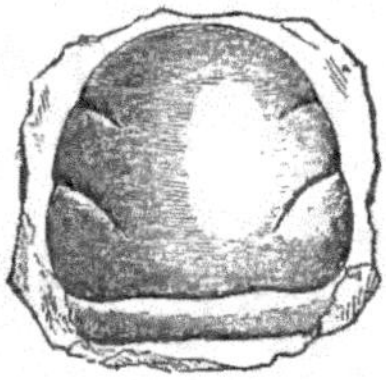

Fig. 312.

Fig. 311.—*Cheirurus prolificus*. Glabella from the Township of Stanbridge.
312.—A specimen from the Chazy limestone, Montreal.

Remarks.—This species occurs at Stanbridge along with *C. Vulcanus*. Fig. 312 is drawn from a gutta percha cast of the impression of the glabella of a *Cheirurus*, in a piece of Chazy limestone. It exhibits only two pairs of glabellar furrows, but it is evident that the whole of the glabella is not represented in the cast, and it is almost certain that there is a third pair. It is either *C. prolificus*, or a very closely allied species.

REMOPLEURIDES AFFINIS. (N. sp.)

Fig. 313.

Fig. 313.—*Remopleurides affinis*. Glabella enlarged two diameters.

Description.—Glabella rather strongly convex; width between the eyes a little less than the whole length; front abruptly elevated; width of the neck segment and also of the portion of the glabella in front of the eyes a little more than half the width between the eyes. The eyes are semi-annular, a little more than half the length of the glabella and neck segments; their posterior extremities touching the neck furrow, their anterior a little in advance of the mid-length; neck furrow all across. No glabellar furrows are visible.

Of this species four specimens were collected, all about 2½ lines in length each.

This species is most closely allied to *R. Canadensis* of the Chazy limestone (*ante*, p. 182), but is more convex, and shows no indications of glabellar furrows.

Locality and Formation.—Stanbridge, range 6, lot 20; Quebec group.

Collector.—T. C. Weston.

HARPES GRANTI. (N. sp.)

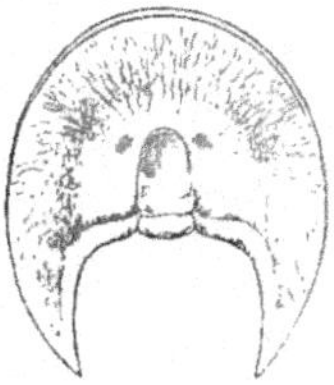

Fig. 314.

Fig. 314.—*Harpes Granti.* A perfect head, enlarged three diameters.

Description.—Head, including the border and spines, sub-elliptical; the front uniformly rounded; the sides also uniformly convex, but more broadly curved. Without the border, the head is very strongly convex, its width at the neck segment one-third greater than the length; front broadly rounded, sides nearly straight, slightly converging forwards. Glabella elongate conical, cylindrical, rounded in front, with two obscure glabellar pits at the sides; neck furrow all across. The eyes appear to be situated opposite the anterior extremity of the glabella, but their position is very obscurely indicated in the specimen. The border is gently concave, nearly flat, its greatest width in front of the glabella, where it is equal to one-third the whole length of the head from the neck segment to the front margin, a little narrower at the sides of the head, somewhat rapidly tapering from the line of the neck segment to the points of the spines. The length of the spines is four-sevenths of the length of the head from the neck segment to the front margin. The distance between the points of the spines is a little more than half the greatest width of the whole head, including the border. The neck segment, at the posterior margin forms an elevated plate which follows the inner edge of the spines to their points.

Surface of the glabella and elevated cheeks apparently smooth. The border is beautifully marked with radiating and irregularly branching striæ. This species differs from *H. Ottawaensis* (*ante*, p. 182), in having the glabella more elongate and parallel-sided and in having the border striated instead of punctured.

H. antiquatus of the Chazy limestone has the whole of the glabella punctate, and seems to have a narrower border.

Dedicated to Dr. J. A. GRANT, F.G.S., Ottawa.

Locality aud Formation.—Stanbridge, range 6, lot 20; Quebec group.

Collector.—T. C. Weston.

ILLÆNUS SIMULATOR. (N. sp.)

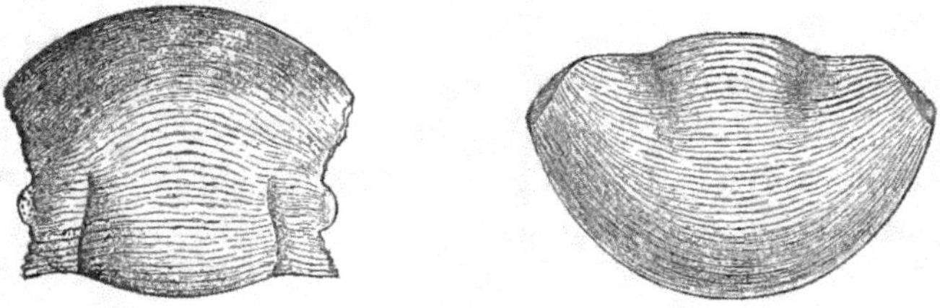

Fig. 315.

Fig. 315.—*Illænus simulator.* *a*, part of the head; *b*, the pygidium.

Description.—Head very convex, broadly rounded in front, usually uniformly arched from the posterior to the anterior margin; sometimes more abruptly bent downwards in the middle. The glabella is gently convex, its width equal to about half the length of the head measured on the curve. The dorsal furrows are strongly impressed, extending a little more than one-third the length of the head, and usually with a sigmoid curve. Eyes about one and a half lines in length; about their own length from the posterior margin, and a little more from the dorsal furrows.

Pygidium rather strongly convex, flatened in the axial region; anterior angles obliquely truncated, the line formed by the truncation forming an angle of about 45° with the longitudinal axis of the body. The length of the straight side on the angle is about half the width of the side lobe. The axis is gently convex and defined by the dorsal furrows for a little more than one-third the length of the whole pygidium. The sides and posterior margin are uniformly rounded. The length of the pygidium is about two-thirds of the greatest width.

The whole surface is covered with undulating fissure-like striæ, from three to five in one line.

This species is certainly most closely allied to *I. fraternus* (*ante*, p.

276), and has given me much perplexity on that account. The differences are that in this species the eye is proportionally nearer the glabella, and the glabella itself wider in proportion to the length of the head measured along the curve. Four specimens, A, B, C, D, gave the following measurements, in lines:

	A	B	C	D
Length of the head on the curve	24	18	18	18
Width of the glabella..	13	9	9½	9
Distance of the eye from the dorsal furrow	3½	2¾	2¾	?

From the above, it appears that the width of the glabella is about half the length of the head, and the distance of the eye from the dorsal furrow is a little less than one-third of the width of the glabella. In *I. fraternus* the eye is distant from the dorsal furrow at least one-half the width of the glabella, while the latter is less than half the length of the head. A specimen, of which the length of the head is 8 lines, has the glabella 3¾ lines in width. In this proportion an individual with the head 24 lines in length would have the glabella 8¼ lines in width, or nearly 4¾ narrower than the specimen of *I. simulator*, lettered A above.

A number of other specimens of the head of *I. fraternus* have similar proportions; none of them are more than 10 lines in length, and most of them have a small tubercle near the posterior margin on the glabella. *I. fraternus* appears thus to be a smaller species with a narrower axis, and the eye more distant.

I. Crassicauda has likewise a more slender axis, and the pygidium more broadly rounded.

I. Davisii (Salter) has the doublure on the under side of the pygidium less than one-third the length, while in this species it is more than half the length of the pygidium. The anterior angles are not so deeply truncated as they are in our species.

Locality and Formation.—Stanbridge, range 6, lot 20; Quebec group.

Collector.—T. C. Weston.

ILLÆNUS CONSIMILIS AND I. AMERICANUS.

In comparing these two species with each other, it was stated (*ante*, p. 278,) that the only differences were in the form of the middle lobe of the head, and in the surface markings. Having recently obtained a number of specimens of *I. Americanus*, and also some additional fragments of the head of *I. consimilis*, I am now enabled to shew that these are really quite distinct species.

Illænus Americanus (Billings).

Illænus Americanus (Billings). *Can. Nat. and Geo.*, vol. iv, p. 371, October, 1859.

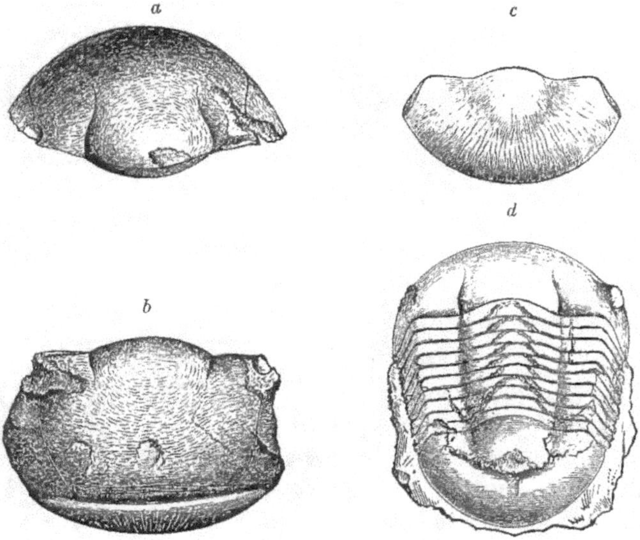

Fig. 316.

Fig. 316.—*Illænus Americanus.* *a*, upper side of the head of the original specimen; *b*, front view of the same; *c*, pygidium of the same; *d*, a specimen in the cabinet of Dr. J. A. Grant, of Ottawa.

Description.—Oblong, distinctly tri-lobed; length two or three inches; width from three-fifths to five-sixths the length.

Head large, strongly convex, its height usually a little greater than its length measured on a straight line, sometimes abruptly bent down at less than half the length from behind, often uniformly arched from the front to the posterior margin, equal to about one fourth of a sphere; length from front to posterior margin about two-thirds the width between the cheek angles in a straight line. The glabella is moderately convex; the dorsal furrows extend from one-fourth to a little more than one-third the whole length of the head, measured on the curve, and have an obscure sigmoid curve, at first outwards and then inwards, their anterior extremities usually turning a little outwards; they are distant from each other not quite one-half the whole width of the head. The eyes are of moderate size, about two lines in length, about half their length from the posterior margin, and half the width of the glabella from the dorsal furrows.

The cheek angles are rounded, and the posterior margin of the head makes with the lateral lower margin, as seen in a side view, usually a right angle, but in some specimens an obtuse angle of nearly 100°, owing to the variable extent to which the front part of the head is produced downwards. In some the portion of the posterior margin outside of the eye curves forwards, and brings the cheek angle to a position in front of the eye. In others, it is behind the eye. The space between the eye and the dorsal furrows is convex, and the eye itself seems to be rather strongly protuberant or sub-conical. The movable cheek is sub-triangular, its width at the posterior margin about one and a half the distance of the eye from the dorsal furrow, its length along the lower margin a little greater than its posterior width. The anterior margin of the whole head is uniformly rounded, with the exception of a slight concave curve just outside of the suture. In some specimens in which the front part of the head is most abruptly bent down the middle portion of the front margin is depressed convex or nearly straight.

Thorax with ten segments. Axis moderately convex, from a little more than one-third to nearly one-half the width of the whole animal, a little wider at the anterior than at the posterior segment; the sides sometimes straight, and sometimes slightly curved outwards. On each side of the axis there is a flat space between the side of the axis and the bend of the pleuræ. The width of this space is between one-third and one-half the width of the axis. The pleuræ are bent at the fulcra at an angle which varies in different individuals, from 25° to 45°, and at nearly one-half their length from the side of the axis.

Pygidium usually a little shorter than the thorax; varying from moderately to rather strongly convex; the posterior margin broadly and uniformly rounded; the anterior angles truncated nearly half the whole length of the pygidium; the straight sides formed by the truncation forming an angle of from 40° to 60° with the longitudinal axis of the body. The axis of the pygidium is well defined at the anterior margin by the dorsal furrows, which die out at about one-third or one-half the length, converging towards each other, and sometimes obscurely defining the apex.

The surface characters of this species are peculiar, although somewhat variable. The specimen on which the species was originally founded has the whole of the head and pygidium covered with short squamose fissure-like striæ; one edge of each fissure, being more elevated than the other, gives to the surface a wrinkled appearance. These striæ vary in length from half a line to two or three lines, and are from one-eighth to one-fourth of a line distant from each other. On the tail they seem to radiate irregularly from the axis as a centre. Near the front margin and parallel with it, are a number of straight continuous fissures. This latter character occurs in other species of this genus. In other specimens the striæ are more distinct and distant, but still are of the same character. In a specimen in Dr. Grant's cabinet, the middle portion of the front of the head is nearly smooth, and in addition to the striæ, is coarsely punctured. The following are the dimensions of the original specimen (A), and the one represented by fig. 316, *d*, (B), in lines.

	A. Lines.	B. Lines.
Length of the head in a straight line from the anterior to the posterior margin,........................	12	10
Following the curvature,...	16	14
Distance between the dorsal furrows,...............	7½	6¾
Width of head at the cheek angles, ...	18	15
Distance of the eye from the dorsal furrows,...... ...	4	3
Length of the eye,...............................	2	2
Distance of the eye from the posterior margin,.........	1	1
Length of thorax,................................	9	7½
Width of axis at first segment, ...	7½	6½
" " at last segment, ...	6	5
Bend of the fifth segment from side of axis, ...	2¾	2¾
Length of the pygidium in a straight line,............	7½	7½
Following the curve,.............................	9	9
Greatest width,..................................	14	12½

This species is allied to the *I. crassicauda* (Wahlenberg), but still is, I think, quite distinct. In the two specimens of the latter, figured by Dalman, the axis in one is 9 lines in length, and 5½ in width; in the others, it is 10 lines in length, and 7½ in width. In the specimen figured by Angelin, it is 10½ lines in length, and 7¼ in width. The axis appears thus to be proportionally longer and narrower than it is in *I. Americanus*. The pygidium is also larger in *I. crassicauda*, and the surface of the head marked by coarse undulating lines, not short wrinkle-shaped fissures.

From *I. consimilis* (*ante*, p. 277), this species differs in the form of the glabella, and in the surface characters, but more remarkably in the shape of the posterior angles of the head, as shown in the following figures:

Fig. 317.

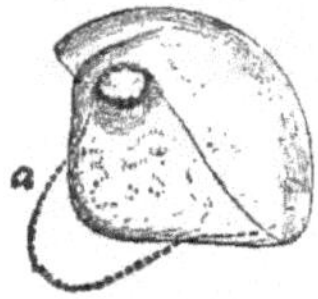

Fig. 318.

Fig. 317.—A detached cheek of *I. consimilis*.
" 318.—Side view of a head of *I. Americanus*. The dotted line, *a*, is an outline of the cheek of *I. consimilis*.

In *I. Americanus* the posterior margin of the cheek outside of the eye forms with the lateral margin, in some specimens, an angle of 90°, and in others from 90° to 100°. In *I. consimilis* the same two lines (without regarding in either case the rounded angle) are inclined towards each other at an angle of less than 50°; the posterior termination of the cheek being produced into an auriculate projection, altogether different from that of *I. Americanus.*

I. Americanus is a rare species, but I have examined three specimens with the head, thorax and pygidium in connection, two others with the head and thorax, and about thirty detached heads and portions of heads. The comparison of these shews very conclusively that it is quite distinct from *I. consimilis.*

Locality and Formation.—Most of the specimens are from Ottawa, but we have it also from L'Orignal and Lake Huron; Trenton limestone only.

Illænus incertus. (N. sp.)

Fig. 319.

Fig. 320.

Fig. 319.—*Illænus incertus.* *a*, upper side of a perfect head; *b*, side view of the same.
Fig. 320.—*I. consobrinus.* *a*, upper side of the head; *b*, side view of the same; *c*, side view of another specimen, with the posterior angles more produced.*

Description.—Closely allied to *I. consobrinus.* Head strongly convex, width twice the length, broadly rounded in front. Glabella wide, depressed convex, its width equal to one-half the whole length of the head following the curve; dorsal furrows straight and parallel. Eyes of moderate size, ovate, their length about one-third the width of the glabella, about their own length from the posterior margin, and the same distance from the dorsal furrow. The cheeks are subtriangular, narrowly rounded at the angle, the lower margin a little concave between the angle and the facial suture; the posterior margin outside of the eye, in length, equal to a little more than half the width of the glabella; the lower margin somewhat longer than the posterior.

The pygidium closely resembles that of *I. consimilis* (*ante*, p. 276),

* In the figures of this species (*ante*, p. 280), the facial suture is represented as curving outwards from the eye. On closely examining the specimens, I cannot make out the suture distinctly; the line (only seen on one side) appearing to be a fissure. The figures are therefore reproduced here with the line removed, to guard against error.

but is only one-fourth the size: its length is about half the greatest width, the anterior angles truncated, all the rest of the margin broadly and uniformly rounded; axis gently convex, extending half the length, narrowed to a point at the apex, where it is sometimes obscurely defined all round. Surface covered with coarse undulating striæ.

Length of a perfect head following the curve 8 lines; length from the posterior margin to a straight line erected vertically from the front margin 4½ lines; width in a straight line between the cheek angles 9 lines; width of the glabella 4 lines; length of the posterior margin of the cheek outside of the eye 3 lines.

Length of the largest pygidium seen 4 lines; width of the same 9 lines. A number of perfect heads and pygidia have been collected. The largest head is the one above figured; most of the specimens are one-third smaller.

On comparing a number of specimens of the head of both species, it is found that this one differs remarkably from *I. consobrinus* in the form of the glabella, the dorsal furrows being always straight, and either parallel or with their anterior extremities a little more distant than the posterior; whereas, on the other hand, in *I. consobrinus* they are never straight, but always curved inwards anteriorly. This character must give to perfect specimens a very different aspect, and will be found, most probably, correlated with other differences in other parts. The cheek angles are somewhat variable in both species, but they are always prolonged backwards in *I. consobrinus*, sometimes extremely so, as represented in the above Fig. 320, *c*. In *I. incertus* they are, as a general rule, only a little less than a right angle, while in some individuals they are rather more.

Locality and Formation.—Stanbridge, range 6, lot 20; Quebec group.

Collector.—T. C. Weston.

HARPIDES? DESERTUS. (N. sp.)

Fig. 321.

Fig. 321.—*Harpides? desertus.* An imperfect glabella.

Description.—Glabella conical, strongly convex; sides nearly straight or gently convex; front rounded and abruptly elevated. Neck furrow narrow, extending all across. Neck segment with a tubercle in the middle. The glabellar furrows are two deep elongate grooves extending from about the mid-length backwards and inwards nearly to the neck furrow; their posterior extremities separated by about one third the width of the glabella. There appears to be an exterior pair represented by a small pit on each side, but this remains still doubtful.

Length of the only specimen collected 5 lines; width at the neck furrows 3 lines. It is referred to *Harpides* provisionally.

Locality and Formation.—East side of the village of Bedford in the bed of Pike river; Quebec group.

Collector.—E. Billings.

DIKELOCEPHALUS? CORAX. (N. sp.)

Fig. 322.

Fig. 322.—*Dikelocephalus? corax.* *a*, the glabella; *b*, a pygidium found associated with *a*.

Description.—Glabella obtusely conical, depressed convex, well defined all round by a linear dorsal furrow, gently narrowed from the mid-length forwards; front obtusely rounded, the greatest width nearly equal to the length. Neck furrow extending all across, on each side of the middle with a slight curve backwards; the outer extremities curved forwards. There are three pairs of glabellar furrows, the last pair connected across by a straight line in the middle of the glabella; the other two pairs not so connected; all inclined forwards and outwards. In front of the glabella there appears to be a wide smooth border. On the neck segment there is a median tubercle.

The pygidium above figured was found in the same mass of limestone. It is not certain that it belongs to this species. It has a structure allied to that of the pygidium of an *Amphion*, and to some extent that of a *Bothynotus*.

Locality and Formation.—Point Lévis, in limestone No. 1; Quebec group.

Collector.—T. C. Weston.

Lichas Jukesii (*ante*, p. 282).

Fig. 323.

Fig. 323.—*Lichas Jukesii.* *a*, perfect head from Cow Head enlarged two diameters; *b*, portion of a head from Stanbridge enlarged two diameters.

Remarks.—A number of specimens of this species having been collected since the description on p. 282 was printed, it is found that the head varies in a remarkable manner. In some the glabella and side lobes, (between the glabella and the eyes) are divided by a transverse groove, as in fig. 323 *a*, above; in others the side lobes, only, are divided; and in some the groove is not visible at all as in fig. 269 (*ante*, p. 282). I cannot separate these different forms, as there is a perfect series from those with smooth lobes through others with the groove becoming deeper and deeper until the forms above figured with a deep furrow are reached.

In addition to the Cow Head locality, it is now found to occur abundantly in Stanbridge, range 6, lot 20, where it was discovered by T. C. Weston.

PROTOZOA.

Calathium ? pannosum. (N. sp.)

Fig. 324.

Description.—This specimen is a fragment of what appears to have been a wide cup-shaped individual. In fig. 324 *a*, is shown the inner concave surface of a portion of one side. The wall of the cup, so far as we can judge from the structure of this specimen, consists of an inner poriferous layer about three lines in thickness as shewn in the unshaded curved band in fig. *b*. Outside of this there are some appearances of a thick, rough spongy layer without regular rows of pores, but with an obscure lamellar concentric structure. On this point however there is much doubt, as the remains of the outer layer are imperfectly preserved. The inner surface seems to be smooth and compact. At what appears to be the bottom of the cup, there is a space where the pores have no definite arrangement, but from this space they proceed up the sides in regular slightly undulating rows. New rows are introduced at intervals according to the increasing expansion of the cup. Most of the pores have a thin, sharp, slightly elevated margin. The internal structure of the inner layer seems to be reticulated, all the pores communicating with each other by longitudinal and transverse canals of the same size as the external orifices of the pores.

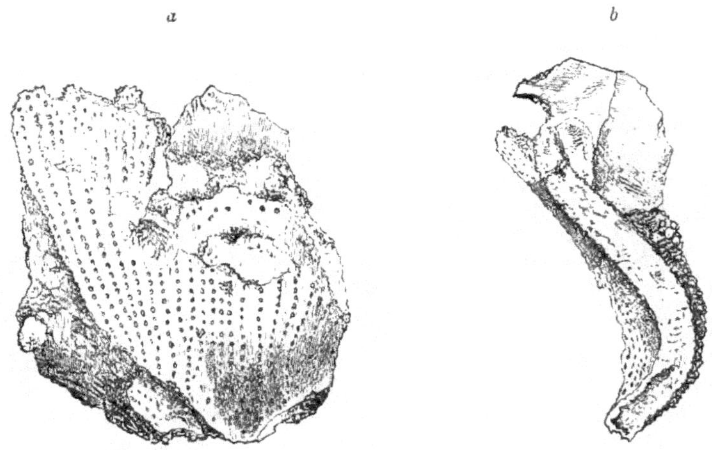

Fig. 324.

Fig. 324.—*Calathium? pannosum.* *a*, the internal surface; *b*, side view of the specimen showing the thickness of the inner poriferous layer.

From what remains of it, it is clear that the cup of this individual must have been at least 3 inches wide, and 1½ in depth. But as the edges are all broken, we cannot say how much larger it may have been when perfect. The rows of pores are on an average 1 line distant from each other, and there are about 6 pores in 3 lines of the length of each row.

The specimen is a silicified fragment, and was dissolved (by hydrochloric acid) out of one of the nodules of limestone, in which the species of Brachiopoda figured on pp. 73, 75, 79, 82, were found. That this species is generically allied to *Calathium* will appear by reference to the following, which will be described in this place for convenience of comparison.

Locality and Formation.—Point Lévis; in the upper part of limestone No. 2, Quebec group.

Collectors.—Sir W. Logan, J. Richardson.

Calathium Anstedi? (*ante*, p. 210.)

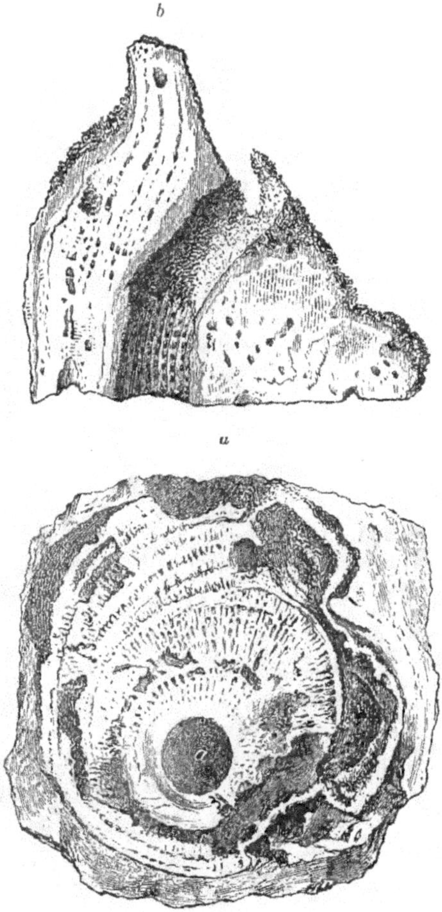

Fig. 325.

Fig. 325.—*Calathium Anstedi?* Transverse and longitudinal sections of the upper extremity of a specimen supposed to be of this species.

Remarks.—The specimen above figured, when collected, was imbedded in a piece of limestone, the transverse section, only, being visible. Of this, the above fig. 325, *a*, was first made, and then it was sawn in two longitudinally with a lapidary's wheel. The two halves were next treated with hydrochloric acid, and the cup was thus freed from the limestone with which it was filled. The section made by the saw passes lengthwise through the cup splitting it in two, one half of which is shown in fig. 325, *b*. It is evident that this specimen consists of only the upper extremity of the fossil, and that the upper right hand sloping side of *b*, above, represents one-half of the margin. From the form of this part it might be supposed, at first sight, that the fossil was obliquely terminated at the upper end, one side of the cup being lower than the other. But it will be observed that the narrow cylindrical cavity of the cup enters at a right angle to the general plane of this sloping side, and that, half-way down, it is curved so as to meet the lower straight side, also at a right angle. This proves that the fossil, when perfect, was considerably curved.

In the transverse section at *a*, is shown the diameter of the cup, five lines. Its centre is seven lines from the exterior on the lower side of the figure, which corresponds to the outer or convexly curved side of figure *b*. But it is eighteen lines from the exterior of the opposite side. Its position, thus, in this specimen, is very eccentric. In the specimen figured on p. 210, it is central. In the lower part of *b*, the structure of a portion of the inner wall of the cup is shown. It is perforated by small ovate or sub-quadrate pores, most probably the apertures of a system of radiating canals. These pores are arranged in straight longitudinal rows, and there are from three to four pores in the length of two lines in each row. There are four rows in the width of two lines. In the transverse section, *a*, the course of the canals radiating from the centre outwards is shown. The whole fossil appears to be composed of a number of concentric laminæ from one-fourth of a line to one line in thickness. Each of these is no doubt a repetition of the inner wall of the cup, and they are all perforated by the radiating canals. Between the concentric layers, another set of canals ascends from the base upwards, and it is probable that all communicate with each other, vertically, laterally, and in a radial direction. I cannot determine from these specimens whether or not this species had an external layer of a spongy texture, as seems to have been the case with *C. pannosum*.

Judging from the form of what remains of it, this specimen must have been 5 or 6 inches in length when perfect. It was found in division H, Pistolet Bay, Newfoundland, along with the specimen figured on p. 210.

I have referred it to *C. Anstedi* with doubt, because its structure seems to be somewhat different, being more compact towards the exterior. Should it turn out to be a distinct species, I propose to call it *Calathium crassum*.

8. *New Species of Fossils from the Calciferous Formation, with Remarks on some others previously described.*

INCERTÆ SEDES.

Genus RIBEIRIA. (Sharpe.)

RIBEIRIA. (Sharpe.) *Jour. Geo. Soc.*, vol. ix, p. 157, 1853.

Remarks.—Mr. Sharpe thus describes this remarkable genus. " Shell univalve, elongated, laterally compressed into the form of a Pholas or Lithodomus ; open at both ends and along the pedal margin, with a thick transverse internal plate near the anterior extremity, behind which is a very large corrugated boss for the attachment of a muscle.

" This curious shell appears related to the family of *Calyptrœidœ*, but it shows no trace of spiral growth ; as far as can be judged from the imperfect specimens seen, it is equilateral, and both the transverse internal plate, and the muscular attachment are placed along the middle of the back of the shell ; the external form may be described as a Calyptræa pressed together laterally till the sides nearly meet, leaving only a narrow opening for the foot of the animal." (Sharpe, loc. cit.)

One species, *R. pholadiformis* is described by Mr. Sharpe. It was found in the lower division of the Lower Silurian formation of the Serra de Mucela, and the Serra de Bussaco, in the neighborhood of Bussaco in Portugal.

J. W. Salter has, I think, referred this genus to the Crustacea, but I have not at present access to the publication containing his paper.

Our species agree, in all general characters with the description of Mr. Sharpe, except that the internal casts do not exhibit the impression of any large boss for the attachment of a muscle. This, however, may be due to differences in the growth of the shell of the individuals examined. It is not uncommon, in the Mollusca at all events, to find in the same species individuals with the muscular scars strongly developed, and others with it scarcely perceptible. In a fragment of a silicified specimen in our collection, the transverse plate is perfectly preserved. Just beneath the umbo, and in front of it, there is a small aperture, of a semicircular shape, which appears to be the entrance to a tubular passage running backwards over the transverse plate into the general cavity of the body. This is visible in so many specimens that I think it scarcely possible that it can be the result of the accidental destruction of the apex of the umbo or beak. My present impression is that it served the function of a byssal orifice, and that these species were anchored by a byssus passing through the beak.

Mr. Sharpe does not notice this character, although one of his figures shows a perfect exterior, and it may be that our species belong to a different genus. At present I shall place them in *Ribeiria* provisionally; and should a further examination show that a separation is necessary, I propose *Ribeirina* as a sub-generic name for their reception.

In England there appears to be one or two species of this genus in the lower part of the Llandeilo formation. (See Siluria, 3d. edition, pp. 50, 549.)

RIBEIRIA? CALCIFERA. (N. sp.)

a *b* *c*

Fig. 326. Fig. 327.

Fig. 326.—*Ribeiria? calcifera.* *a*, side view of a specimen with the shell preserved; *b*, anterior extremity showing the gape and the orifice beneath the beak; *c*, dorsal view.

" 327.—*R? longiuscula.* Side view.

Description.—Ovate, compressed, narrowed towards the posterior extremity, anterior broadly rounded; ventral margin more or less convex its whole length, sloping upwards nearly to the dorsal line from about the mid-length backwards; dorsum from the beaks to the upper posterior angle straight, usually a little concave in the posterior half. The beaks are not prominent, and their position varies from one-sixth to one-fifth the length from the anterior angle. The portion of the dorsum in front of the beaks is nearly straight, situated a little below the line of the portion behind, usually sloping slightly downwards from the orifice to the angle. The dorsum is entire, that is to say, it has no hinge, there being only one valve; it is very narrowly rounded or sub-carinated. The posterior extremity is abruptly truncated at an angle of about 100°, the straight margin formed by the truncation being in length about one-fourth or one-third the height of the shell from the ventral margin to the beaks. The gape of the shell extends all round both extremities and the ventral margin; and it is usually a little less than one line in width. Surface characters unknown, apparently smooth.

Most of the specimens collected are silicified, and some of them are empty. Several casts of the interior were procured. They show the oblique fissure beneath the beak occasioned by the transverse plate in a manner somewhat similar to that of casts of the interior of the genus *Cleidophorus* (Hall), but sloping backwards instead of forwards. There is a line also running round parallel with the ventral margin and near it, resembling the pallial line of the lamellibranchiate shells. The form is somewhat variable, the ventral margin not having always the same amount of convexity. Both sides of the shell are gently convex.

Length from 8 to 16 lines; width of the shell from the beaks to the ventral margin, about half the length.

Locality and Formation.—Counties of Leeds and Grenville; Calciferous formation.

Collector.—E. Billings.

RIBEIRIA ? LONGIUSCULA. (N. sp.)

Fig. 327.

Description.—The specimen on which this species is founded is oblong-ovate, the dorsal and ventral margin in the posterior two-thirds nearly parallel, the anterior extremity uniformly rounded, the posterior third apparently narrowed, as the ventral margin slopes upwards, as if to form a termination like that of *R. calcifera.* The dorsum is straight from the beaks backwards. The portion in front of the beaks nearly straight, lower than the portion behind. The orifice beneath the beaks is obscurely seen in the specimen. Both sides of the shell are gently convex, and from the beak there is a wide shallow concavity extending backwards and downwards to the ventral margin. The slope of the shell extends all round. The dorsum is entire and narrowly rounded, sub-carinated. Surface unknown.

The specimen when perfect was apparently about 16 lines in length and 7 in width.

I have some doubts whether this species is distinct from *R. calcifera*, as the two were found together in the same beds, but this one is extremely rare.

Locality and Formation.—Counties of Leeds and Grenville; Calciferous formation.

Collector.—E. Billings.

GASTEROPODA.

Pleurotomaria Canadensis. (N. sp.)

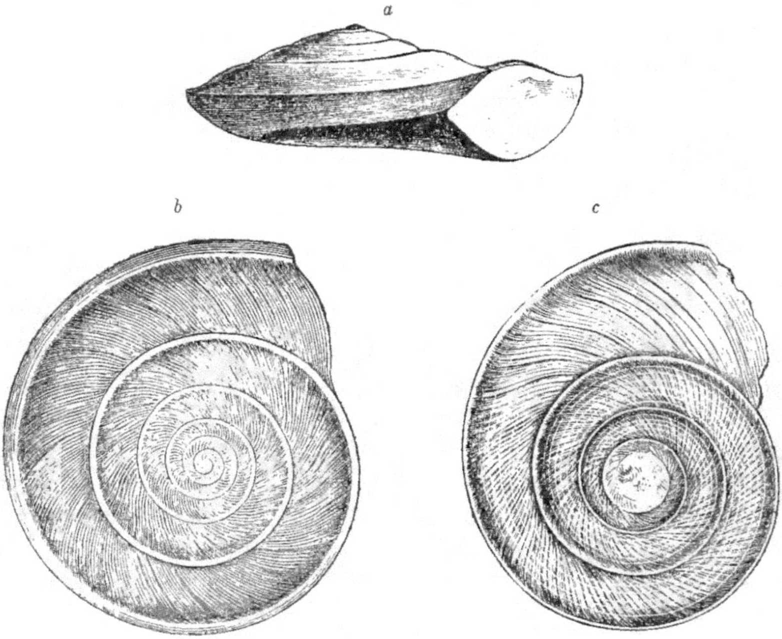

Fig. 328.

Fig. 328.—*Pleurotomaria Canadensis.* *a*, front view of a cast of the interior; *b*, spire of a specimen with the shell preserved with a wide smooth marginal band; *c*, a specimen with a sharp elevated margin, and with the surface reticulated by transverse and spiral lines.

Description.—Shell large, lenticular; spire varying from nearly flat to depressed conical; whorls about six, rather slender, a wide shallow concave band just within the margin, the inner two thirds gently convex; suture distinct. The margin in some specimens is acute and turned upwards; in others with a rounded band sometimes one line in width. Umbilicus wide, usually one-half or two-thirds the whole width, the margin sub-angular, and the slope of the whorls within flat or nearly so. The under side of the whorls have usually a slight concave band just beneath the margin; thence to the edge of the umbilicus uniformly convex, often strongly so. The aperture is transversely ovate or obscurely rhomboidal, the outer and inner angles acute, the contour corresponding to the form of the whorl.

Surface with fine sharp striæ of unequal size, the smaller four or five in one line, the larger twice the size of the smaller; usually with shallow undulations one or two lines wide conforming to the course of the striæ; all curving backwards to the margin, which they reach at an acute angle. In some the surface is reticulated with longitudinal spiral lines following the whorls to the apex. Diameter from 18 to 30 lines.

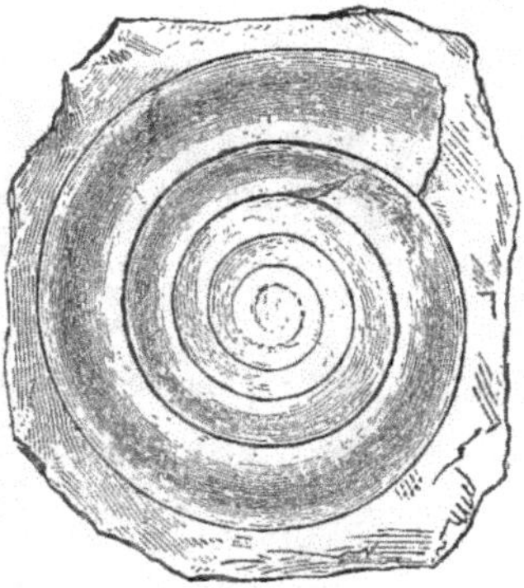

Fig. 329.

The whorls vary in their width greatly. Fig. 329 represents a cast of the spire of an individual with six whorls, and specimens have been collected which have them still more slender.

P. aperta (Salter) is the species most nearly allied to this, the transverse section of the whorls being precisely the same except that in the umbilicus they are not flat but rounded, and, besides, it is a smaller form and never has more than four whorls. The large specimen figured in the Geol. of Canada, p. 117, fig. 28, *d*, as a form of *P. Laurentina*, belongs to this species. The true *P. Laurentina* has the umbilicus scarcely one-fourth the whole width. (See also *ante*, p. 191, 229.)

Locality and Formation.—Counties of Leeds and Grenville, also Mingan Islands; Calciferous formation.

Pleurotomaria Arabella. (N. sp.)

Fig. 330.

Description.—Shell small, with four or five slender whorls; spire depressed convex, with the whorls turrreted above each other for about one-fourth their depth. On the upper side there is a deep narrow groove close to the margin following the whorls to the apex; all between the grooves and the suture rather strongly convex, the greatest elevation being at about one-third the width from the suture. The margin outside of the groove consists of an elevated rounded wire-like rim. The suture is deeply impressed all the way to the apex. Surface with moderately fine striæ curving backwards from the suture to the margin. Under side unknown, but evidently with a wide and deep umbilicus.

Fig. 330.

Fig. 331.

Fig. 330.—*Pleurotomaria Arabella.* View of the spire.
Fig. 331.—*Ophileta? disjuncta.* *a*, view of the spire; *b*, the lower side.

Belongs to the same group with *P. Canadensis*, but is a smaller species with more slender whorls, a narrower marginal band, and a deeper suture.

Locality and Formation.—Counties of Leeds and Grenville; Calciferous formation.

Collector.—E. Billings.

OPHILETA? DISJUNCTA. (N. sp.)

Fig. 331.

Description.—Shell about one inch across, consisting of two or three whorls which are usually a little separated from each other. Spire deeply concave with an acute, strongly elevated carina following the whorls to the apex, and situated about one-third the width from the outer margin. Within the carina there is at first a shallow concave band, and then a concave slope into the suture. Outside of the carina there is a similar but barely perceptible concavity, below which the periphery is uniformly convex. On the under side the whorls vary from uniformly convex to very depressed convex, and sometimes flat along the median line on approaching the aperture. The edge of the suture is usually at first rounded and then angular. Surface with rather strong sub-squamose striæ. The whorls are sometimes separated two lines from each other, but usually not so distant, and often almost in contact. The depth of the whorls is about equal to their width. It is difficult to say whether this species should be called an *Ophileta*, a *Helicotoma*, or an *Ecculiomphalus*. These genera seem all to run into each other.

Locality and Formation.—Counties of Leeds and Grenville; Calciferous formation.

Collector.—E. Billings.

MURCHISONIA ARTEMESIA. (N. sp.)

a

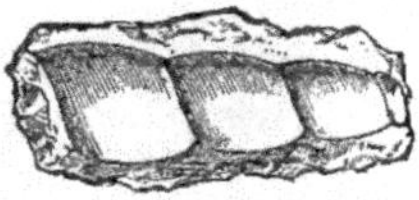

b

Fig. 332.

Fig. 332.—*Murchisonia Artemesia.* *a*, cast of the interior of a fragment of this species; *b*, a specimen partly restored.

Description.—Shell elongate, slender with from ten to twelve depressed convex whorls and a strong rounded spiral band. The whorls, in the cast are depressed ventricose, flattened in the middle and abruptly rounded into the deep suture. The casts of the exterior show a strong rounded band along the median line of the whorls: it is about one line wide on the large whorls. Surface with fine sharp striæ curving backwards to the band.

Length from $2\frac{1}{2}$ to 3 inches; apical angle about 15°.

Resembles *M. gracilis*, but is always more elongate and with flatter whorls, in which respects also it differs from *M. simulatrix* (*ante*, p. 231, fig. 218). *M. agilis* (*ante*, p. 235) has the suture not so oblique. *M. vesta* (*ante*, p. 32) is a shorter and more abruptly tapering form.

Locality and Formation.—Counties of Leeds and Grenville; Calciferous formation.

Collector.—E. Billings.

Murchisonia Ada. (N. sp.)

Fig. 333.

Fig. 333.—*Murchisonia Ada.* A gutta percha cast of the exterior.

Description.—Shell small slender with twelve or more whorls. Apical angle between 15° and 20°. The whorls are short, there being twelve in a length of nine lines of the apical portion. They are moderately and uniformly convex in the lower two-thirds of their width; in the upper third with a shallow concave band; close to the suture an obscure rounded carina which forms the sutural edge. Surface unknown; but on one of the whorls there appears to be a thread-like spiral carina about the middle of the most convex part.

Closely allied to *M. acrea* (*ante*, p. 231, fig. 216); but in that species the lower portion of the whorls is flat. *M. Anna* is a larger species, with a distinct band just below the middle, and not concave in the upper third.

Locality and Formation.—Counties of Leeds and Grenville; Calciferous formation.

Collector.—E. Billings.

Metoptoma simplex. (N. sp.)

Fig 334.

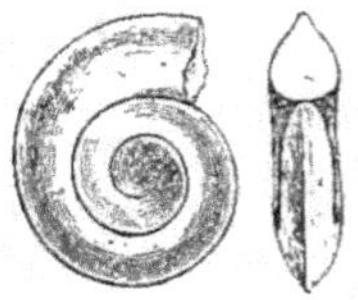

Fig 335.

Fig. 334.—*Metoptoma simplex.*

Fig. 335.—*Bellerophon macer.*

Description.—Shell small, varying from broad-oval to nearly circular; height, from one-half to five-sixths of the width; apex acute, incurved, the point is sometimes nearly over, but usually a little behind, the anterior margin. The most elevated part is just behind the extreme point of the apex, thence to the posterior margin the outline descends with a gently convex slope. The outline beneath the apex is, on a side view, distinctly concave. Length 4 to 7 lines; width a little less than the length.

Locality and Formation.—Near Mirrickville; Calciferous formation.

Collector.—E. Billings.

BELLEROPHON MACER. (N. sp.)

Fig. 335.

Description.—Shell lenticular, with three or four slender whorls ; dorsum acute ; greatest width close to the umbilicus ; vertical diameter from nine to twelve lines ; umbilicus large, exposing all the whorls, its width from one-third to one-half the whole diameter ; the whorls enveloping apparently to the depth of one-third. The edge of the umbilicus is narrowly rounded, and from it to the dorsum the side of the outer whorl has a convex slope becoming flat or even a little concave on approaching the periphery. The width or thickness of the disc is about one-fourth of the diameter or a little more. Surface unknown.

This species is smaller and more compressed than *B. Palinurus* (*ante*, p. 311,) and has a larger umbilicus, in which latter respect it differs, also, from *B. acutus* (Sowerby).

Locality and Formation.—Counties of Leeds and Grenville ; Calciferous formation.

Collector—E. Billings.

CEPHALOPODA.

ORTHOCERAS LAMARCKI (Billings.)

ORTHOCERAS LAMARCKI (Billings). *Can. Nat. and Geol.*, vol. iv, p. 362, October, 1850.

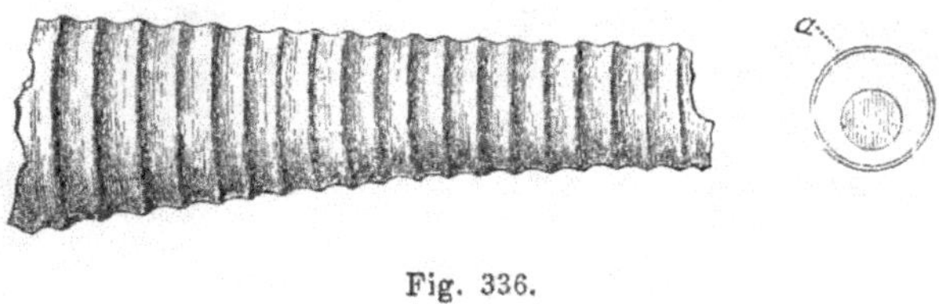

Fig. 336.

Fig. 336.—*Orthoceras Lamarcki.* Side view ; *a*, section shewing the large siphuncle.

Description.—Annulated, tapering at the rate of from one line to one and one-half lines to the inch ; section circular ; septa gently convex, eight in one inch where the diameter is eight lines, more numerous towards the apex ; siphuncle cylindrical, a little excentric, its diameter full one-third the diameter of the whole shell. The annulations are well defined rounded ridges, crossing the shell at right angles to the length, distant one line and a-half from each other in specimens from six to twelve lines in diameter. The spaces between the annulations are uniformly concave. All the specimens yet discovered are silicified, but with the surface characters of the shell not preserved. Several have been collected which are slightly curved.

The septa increase rapidly in number towards the smaller extremity of the shell, and it would appear also that, in some individuals, the distance between them varies in different parts. In one specimen, where the diameter is five lines, there are five septa in half an inch; but in the next half inch there are eight. The position of the siphuncle is also slightly variable.

There are several American orthoceratites which in fragments, not shewing the internal characters, could hardly be distinguished from this. *O. decrescens* of the Trenton tapers somewhat more rapidly, and has a small slightly moniliform siphuncle. *O. Priamus* (*ante* p. 253) has also a smaller siphuncle and tapers more rapidly.

Locality and Formation.—Mingan Islands, Township of Godmanchester, Counties of Leeds and Grenville, and Newfoundland. The specimens from the latter locality are doubtfully referred to this species (*ante*, p. 255). Calciferous formation.

Collectors.—Sir W. E. Logan, J. Richardson, E. Billings.

ORTHOCERAS FURTIVUM. (N. sp.)

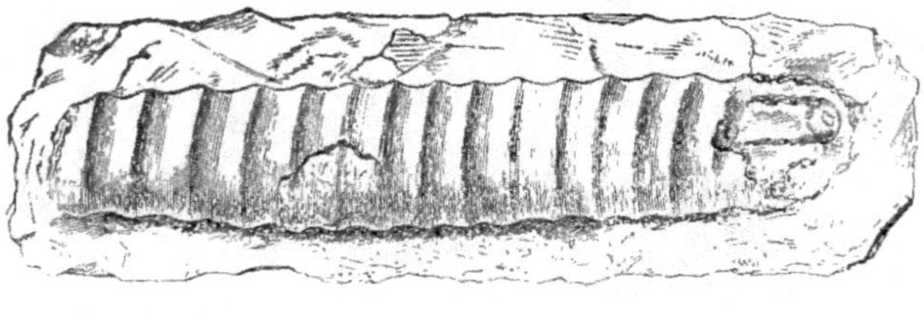

Fig. 337.

Fig. 337.—*Orthoceras furtivum.* *a*, the siphuncle.

Description.—Obliquely annulated, tapering at the rate of a little less than one line to the inch; section circular; siphuncle cylindrical, about one-third ? the whole diameter, in contact with the shell or nearly so. Septa and surface unknown.

The annulations are prominent, narrowly rounded, six or seven in the length of one inch, and slightly oblique; the intervening spaces uniformly concave. The siphuncle is obscurely seen in the specimen, but of its position, close to the shell, there is no doubt. Closely resembles *O. arcuoliratum* (Hall) of the Trenton, but that species has a small central siphuncle.

Locality and Formation.—From a rock-cutting in the Brockville and Ottawa Railway in the Township of Kitley; Calciferous formation.

Collector.—The specimen figured was procured from Mr. Francis Ballantyne, of the Township of Kitley.

Orthoceras indagator. (N. sp.)

Description.—This species is founded on some detached siphuncles retaining the marks of the septa, but no other parts. The best preserved specimen is three and a half inches in length, six lines in diameter at the smaller extremity, and about seven lines at the larger. Thirty-one septal rings. It appears to be flattened on one side as if by contact with the shell.

Another specimen, three inches in length, six lines in diameter at the larger, and four at the smaller, has twenty-seven septal rings.

This species resembles *O. Flavius* (*ante*, p. 255), but has the septa somewhat more distant. The spaces between the septa are also more concave, and, in one of the specimens, are transversely marked with several thread-like rough rings, which are not seen at all in the *O. Flavius*.

Locality and Formation.—Mingan Islands; Calciferous formation.

Collectors.—Sir W. E. Logan, J. Richardson.

Orthoceras edax. (N. sp.)

Description.—Siphuncle the same as that of *O. Missisquoi* (*ante*, p. 314), but with more distant septa. One specimen four inches in length tapers from nine lines to five lines, or at the rate of one line to the inch. Where the diameter is between six and seven lines there are four septal rings to the inch. They are most distant from the apex on the side of the concave curve, shewing that the position of the siphuncle is similar to that of *O. Missisquoi.* The curvature is very slight, the height of the arch formed by it being only two lines in a length of four inches.

It is barely possible that this may be a variety of the *O. Missisquoi*, but owing to the very great difference in the distance of the septal rings, I think it best to give it a separate name.

Locality and Formation.—Township of Oxford; Calciferous formation.

Collector.—E. Billings.

Orthoceras ordinatum. (N. sp.)

Description.—This species tapers about one line and a-half to the inch ; section apparently circular ; siphuncle cylindrical, about one line in diameter where the diameter of the shell is five lines, its centre distant one and a-nalf lines from the margin. There are twelve moderately concave septa to the inch. Surface apparently not annulated.

The specimens are very imperfect, but they show that this is an ordinary form, probably when full grown eight or ten inches in length. It is not quite certain whether the section is circular or ovate. At all events it must be very nearly circular.

Locality and Formation.—St. Ann's and Township of Oxford ; Calciferous formation.

Collector.—E. Billings.

Orthoceras veterator. (N. sp.)

Description.—A fragment of this species has a dorso-ventral diameter of nine lines, and a lateral diameter of eleven lines. Septa deeply concave, eight in three lines. Siphuncle cylindrical, three lines in thickness, in contact with the shell. Another specimen is eight lines in diameter ; siphuncle three lines ; septa nine in three lines.

This species has the septa much more concave than they are in the figure of *O. primigenium* given by Prof. Hall. Both of the specimens are distorted, and the section may be oval.

Locality and Formation.—Township of Oxford ; Calciferous formation.

Collector.—E. Billings.

Orthoceras glaucus. (N. sp.)

Description.—Small, slender, very gradually tapering ; section apparently circular. The siphuncle is cylindrical, three lines in diameter, and in contact with the shell. There are seventeen deeply concave septa to the inch in one specimen, and fifteen in another. The proportional diameter of the siphuncle to that of the shell cannot be made out with certainty, but it appears to be one-third of the whole section. The shell is not annulated.

This species has a larger siphuncle than has *O. deparcum.* It resembles *O. repens* (*ante*, p. 312), but has a larger siphuncle.

Locality and Formation.—Township of Oxford ; Calciferous formation.

Collector.—E. Billings.

Nautilus ferox. (N. sp.)

Description.—Shell large, apparently eight or nine inches across; whorls rapidly increasing, the third measuring nearly three inches in the dorso-ventral diameter. Section apparently nearly circular. The whorls are somewhat closely inrolled, the first three slightly indenting each other. In the second whorl there are six septa to the inch, and in the third whorl four to the inch, as seen on the median line of the side. The umbilicus is deep, exposing all the whorls to the apex. Siphuncle and surface unknown.

The specimen is a fragment consisting of a little more than three whorls, and as there are traces of the septa visible to the extremity or where the last whorl is broken off, it is evident that no part of the chamber of habitation is preserved. In the centre of the umbilicus there is a space eight lines in diameter, in which no indication of structure is seen, and is taken to be the size of the first whorl. The second whorl, commencing with a dorso-ventral diameter of five and a-half lines, enlarges to eleven lines in making one complete turn. The third whorl, commencing with a diameter of eleven lines, enlarges to thirty-three lines. Diameter of the whole specimen, consisting of about three and one-eighth whorls, six inches.

This appears to be quite distinct from all those described in the preceding pages. It approaches, in form, *N. tyrans* of the Chazy limestone, but is more compactly inrolled.

Locality and Formation.—Mingan Islands ; Calciferous formation.

Collector.—J. Richardson.

CRUSTACEA.

The following are all the species of Trilobites known in the Calciferous formation in Canada up to the present time :—

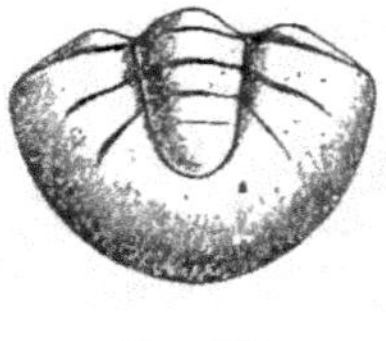

Fig. 338.

Fig. 339.

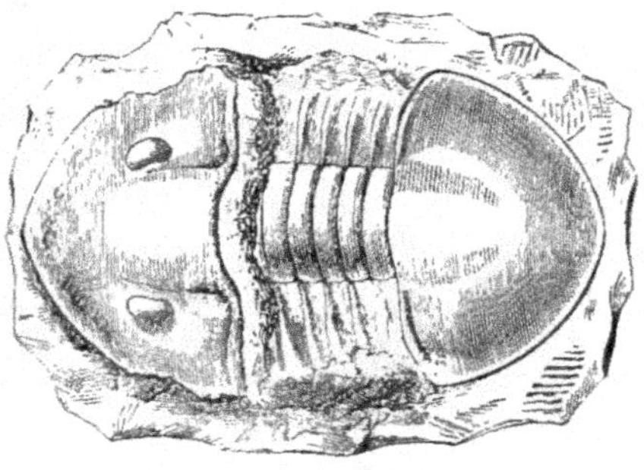

Fig. 340.

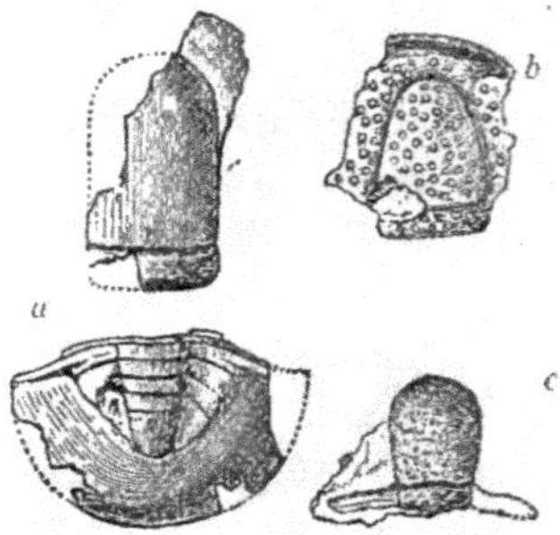

Fig. 341.

Fig. 338.—*Dolichometopus? rarus.*
339.—*Amphion Salteri?* enlarged two diameters.
340.—*Asaphus canalis?*
341.—*a*, *Bathyurus amplimarginatus*; *b*, *B. conicus*; *c*, *B. Cybele.*

Remarks.—The specimen of *A. canalis* above figured appears to me to be perfectly identical with those that occur in Newfoundland and the localities mentioned on p. 270. It was found in the Calciferous formation near Mirrickville by Mr. Francis Ballantyne, of the Township of Kitley.

The pygidium above referred to *Amphion Salteri*, cannot be distinguished specifically from the original specimen on which the species was founded. It was collected in the Calciferous formation in the Township of Oxford, by T. C. Weston. This species was first discovered by J. Richardson in the limestone of the Quebec group at Phillipsburgh.

Dolichometopus? rarus differs from *D. convexus* (*ante*, p. 269), in having the axis of the pygidium somewhat shorter, and having only two simple grooves in the side lobes. *D. gibberulus* (p. 269) has a shorter axis, which is smooth. These three species are certainly very closely allied to each other, and future discoveries may prove them to be identical. It occurs at Oxford with *A. Salteri.*

Bathyurus amplimarginatus (fig. 241, *a*) has been found only at the Mingan Islands in the Calciferous.

B. conicus (fig. 241, *b*) was originally discovered at St. Timothy, on the Beauharnois Canal, in the upper part of the Calciferous. It occurs also at Comstock's Landing, in the State of New York, in the same formation. A specimen, only distinguishable from this species by having the surface smooth instead of tuberculated, was collected in the Quebec group at Cow Head, Newfoundland, in Division P. In all these three localities it occurs associated with *Camerilla calcifera*, the most characteristic brachiopod of the Point Levis limestone.

B. Cybele occurs at the Mingan Islands, Beauharnois, and in the Counties of Leeds and Grenville. It has been found also at Orwell, in the State of Vermont, and at Comstock's Landing, in New York.

Bathyurus Minganensis.

Description.—Glabella rather strongly convex, sub-conical, sides in the posterior two-thirds of the length straight and nearly parallel, the anterior third converging so as to form a rather narrowly rounded apex. Neck segment large; neck furrow all across. Fixed cheeks moderately prominent. The eye appears to be semicircular; the posterior angle on a line crossing the glabella at almost the mid-length and three lines from the dorsal furrow. From the posterior angle the eye seems to curve forwards and inwards, so that its anterior angle is close to the side of the glabella. The pygidium, of which only a fragment has been collected, has at least four wide rings on the axis. It has also four, and perhaps more segments, in the side lobes. These segments, in the side lobes, are wide and flat, with an obscure groove along the middle. The margin of the pygidium is unknown.

Length of the glabella 9 lines; width at the mid-length 7 lines. The pygidium is apparently about 15 lines in length.

This species is founded on an imperfect glabella and part of a pygidium, of which however sufficient is preserved to show that it is distinct from any described form. It is most nearly related to *B. amplimarginatus*, but has the glabella broader and the ribs of the side lobes divided by a furrow along the middle.

Locality and Formation.—Mingan Islands; Calciferous formation.

Collector.—J. Richardson.

PROTOZOA.

Although the zoological rank of *Archeocyathus Calathium* and *Rhabdaria* is not positively established, I shall retain them among the Protozoa for the present, provisionally.

GENUS ARCHEOCYATHUS. (*Ante*, p. 3.)

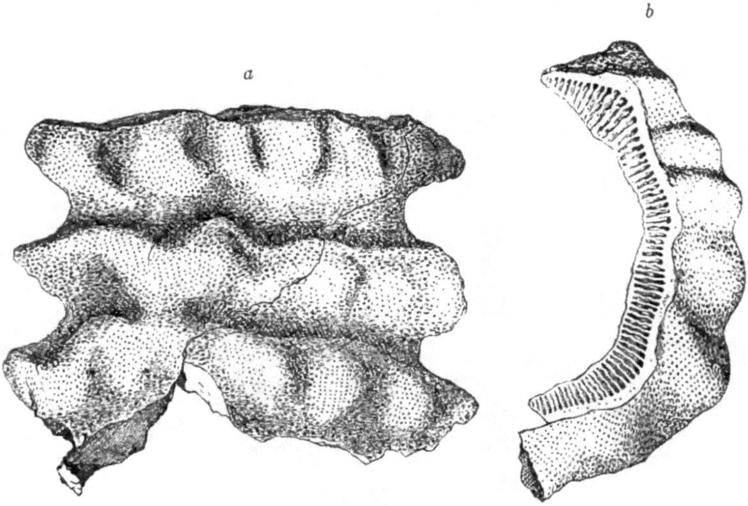

Fig. 342.

Fig. 342.—*Archeocyathus Minganensis*. *a*, fragment of the cylindrical portion of a silicified specimen of this species ; *b*, end view of the same specimen.

Remarks.—The following are some additional details of the structure of this remarkable genus. The general form, as exhibited by the three species at present known, is that of an elongated hollow cone, or, rather, a hollow cylinder, with one end narrowed to a point, the smaller extremity being closed and more or less curved ; the larger end open. They thus resemble certain large species of *Zaphrentis* or *Cyathophyllum*, and, in fact, from their form and septate structure were at first thought to be corals. Some of the individuals appear to have attained a length of two or three feet, with a diameter of three or four inches. All of the species are transversely and more or less deeply marked by irregular annulations. The structure consists of an inner, thin wall, or endotheca, lining the great central cavity,—an outer wall, or epitheca, forming the rough external surface and, between these, a system of radiating septa. The outer wall, in two of the species, *A. profundus* and *A. Minganensis*, is perforated with numerous small irregular apertures leading directly into the loculi or empty spaces between the septa. In the third species, *A. Atlanticus*, it (the outer wall) appears to have a compact smooth surface, with only a few perforations. The inner wall is very thin, with numerous pores leading from the loculi into the great central cavity. The septa consist of thin flat plates, arranged longtitudinally exactly as in the genus *Zaphrentis.* They extend from the outer to the inner wall, and are perforated with numerous small circular pores, so that the interseptal loculi all communicate with each other as well as with the central cavity and the exterior. The loculi are subdivided by very thin dissepiments resembling those of a *Cyathcphyllum*, but they are irregularly distributed, being in some parts entirely absent, and in other places so numerous that they completely fill the loculi with small cells constituting the "poriferous or cellular tissue" mentioned in the original description of the genus (*ante*, p. 3). The central cavity extends nearly the whole length, and constitutes a large proportion of the bulk of the fossil. Below it there is a portion of the smaller extremity or base, which is composed only of the outer wall, the septa and the dissepiments. The section across this part shows that the new septa, which are introduced from time to time, as the diameter increases, do not at first extend to the centre, and it would appear from this that they were developed on the inner surface of the outer wall, and gradually widened as in the genus *Zaphrentis.*

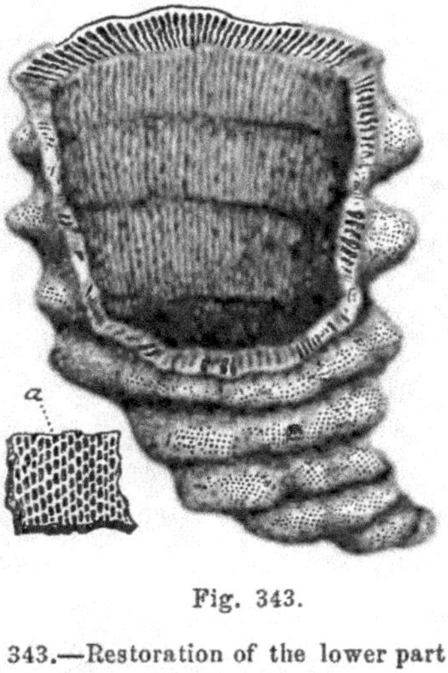

Fig. 343.

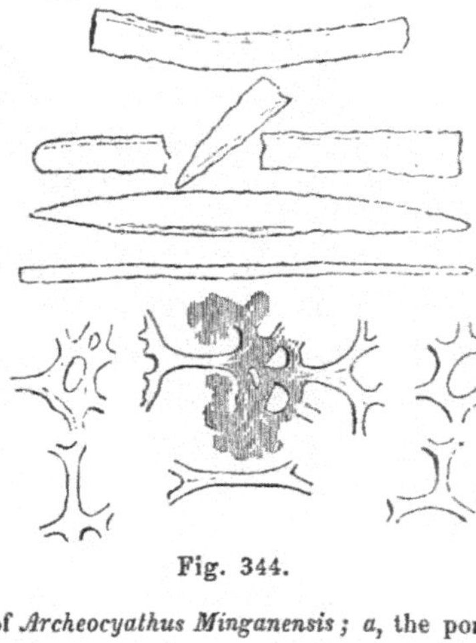

Fig. 344.

Fig. 343.—Restoration of the lower part of *Archeocyathus Minganensis*; *a*, the pores of the inner wall.

344.—Spicula found imbedded in the walls of the same species or associated in the same rock-specimens. Enlarged 50 diameters.

Close to the extreme point of the base the septa and dissepiments have an irregular arrangement, and the loculi sometimes here appear to be mere circular perforations.

The small branching spicula, above figured, are seen imbedded in and forming a part of the substance of the outer wall of *A. Minganensis*. The fusiform and cylindrical varieties are also seen, but rarely, either adhering to or partially imbedded in the same specimens. As they were obtained in thousands in the sediment left after dissolving pieces of the limestone holding fragments of this species, they were at first thought to belong to it. But I have recently, while treating other pieces of limestone from the same bed, also holding fragments of *A. Minganensis*, found that another large species, *Trichospongia sericea*, occurs in this rock, portions of which are crowded with, and seem to be almost altogether composed of, these spicula. It should therefore remain an open question whether or not these fusiform and cylindrical spicula actually form a part of the structure of *Archeocyathus*, or are those of *T. sericea*. There can scarcely be any doubt about the branched spicula, as they can be seen not only projecting from the surface of the silicified specimens, but also in the thin slices prepared for the microscope. No spicula have been detected in *A. profundus*. In *A. Atlanticus* there are several objects visible, in the only specimen of that species that has been collected, which resemble branched spicula. No silicified specimens of these two latter species have been procured, and I think it probable that if such could be examined spicula would be found in them.

As to the zoological rank of this genus there yet remains some doubt. The general structure is such that it may possibly be a sponge. The apertures in the external wall may be the homologues of the inhalent pores of the ordinary sponge, while those of the inner wall may represent the exhalent orifices. The great internal cavity, in that case, would have the same function as the large central cloaca of the fistulose genera of sponges. A radiated and more or less perfectly septate structure occurs in many undoubted sponges. In this genus, however, the substance of the septa is almost as compact as that of the true corals. The perforated character of the outer wall, and also of the septa, suggest a comparison with corals of the division *Zoantharia perforata*. The *Favosites* have also their walls perforated. Dr. J. W. Dawson, who has examined a number of the slices of *A. Atlanticus* and *A. profundus*, which have been prepared for the microscope, is of opinion that the structure of these two species is similar to that of the Foraminifera.* My own opinion is that all three species

* Can. Nat. and Geol. April, 1865.

belong to one generic group closely related to *Calathium*. This latter passes into *Eospongia*, which, in its turn, gradually merges into other genera that occur in more recent formations, such as *Rhysospongia*, *Scyphia*, *Siphonia*, and others. The resemblance between the whole structure and that of the palæzoic corals seems also to shew that in the Lower Silurian seas organic forms existed combining the characters of the Protozoa and the Cœlenterata.

Genus Trichospongia. (N. gen.)

Generic Characters.—This genus occurs in rudely hemispheric masses from one to five inches across. The skeleton appears to be minutely fibrous, and is full of elongate cylindrical or acerate spicula just visible to the naked eye. In silicified specimens that have been treated with acid there are seen numerous irregular branching canals from one to six lines in diameter.

Trichospongia sericea. (N. sp.)

Description.—The form appears to be rudely hemispherical, and from one to five inches in diameter. In one specimen an imperfect concentric structure is obscurely indicated. In a very small individual there is a deep concavity in one side, which may be the cup.

The specimens are very imperfect, consisting, in general, of portions which were sufficiently silicified to resist the acid, and very little can be determined with certainty as to the form. All the fragments that have been observed appear to belong to one species.

Locality and Formation.—Mingan Islands ; Calciferous formation.

Collectors.—Sir W. E. Logan and J. Richardson.

Genus Rhabdaria. (N. gen.)

Generic Characters.—This genus is proposed for the reception of certain small cylindrical bodies which were found in the residue left after dissolving pieces of the magnesian limestone from the Mingan Islands in acid. They are from one to four lines in diameter, with a rough surface, and have a small perforation along the centre. There are two species which I propose to name provisionally as follows :—

1. *Rhabdaria fragilis.*—Small cylindrical stems, with a rough exterior, and a central perforation or canal. At first these were thought to be silicified specimens of *Stenopora fibrosa*, but when others were procured shewing the central canal, it became evident that they could not be thus

referred. They have the form of crinoidal columns, but are not jointed. No structure can be made out in thin slices under the microscope.

2. *Rhabdaria furcata.*—A single specimen of this species only has been collected. The principal stem is three lines in thickness, and it sends off a number of branches at angles varying from 15° to 30°. The branches seem to be connected in one place by lateral processes as in *Syringopora.*

CALATHIUM? PARADOXICUM. (N. sp.)

a b

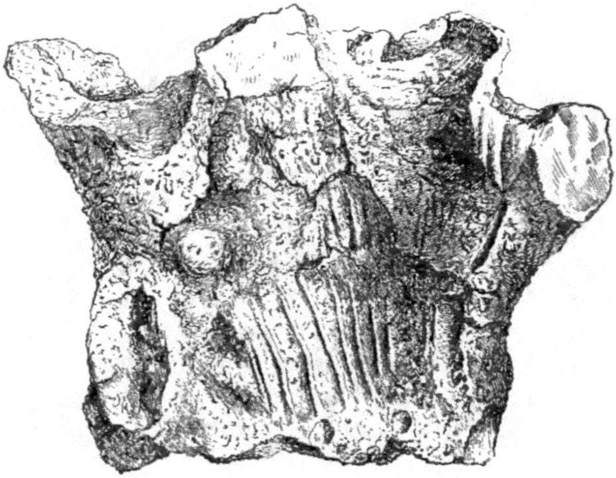

Fig. 345.

Fig. 345.—*Calathium? paradoxicum.* Side view of the upper extremity of a large specimen.

Description.—The specimen above figured is a fragment of the upper extremity of an individual which, when perfect, was probably six inches or more in length, and three inches across at the top. It is perfectly separated from the matrix, but split in two longitudinally, giving a vertical section on the side opposite that figured, but showing no structure except an obscure concentric lamellar arrangement near the outside. It is composed of compact chert or quartz. The lower half is cylindrical, slightly tapering. The upper half suddenly expands, and has two projecting lobes at *a* and *b*, each of which appears to be the base of a branch. On the surface of the lower half there are a number of somewhat prominent rounded longitudinal ridges.

Another specimen is four inches in length, and broken off at both extremities. Its diameter in the middle is about twenty lines, and at the upper extremity three inches. It appears to be lobed at the upper end as is the one above figured. The exterior to the depth of three lines has an obscurely concentric lamellar structure. The interior, as exhibited in the fracture of the large end, is a poriferous mass two inches across. The pores are rudely circular, from one-fourth of a line to one line in width, and about the same distances apart from each other. The fossil itself is composed of a whitish chert, and it is imbedded in dark-brown magnesian limestone. This dark-brown rock is injected into the pores, and defines them very distinctly. The external lamellar portion is perforated in a radial direction by small canals about half-a-line in diameter, as shown in one place; but in another place they seem to be much smaller. The central poriferous mass seems to be irregularly reticulated by the canals.

Judging from these two specimens this species appears to be a subturbinate form, which at the height of several inches produced several others by a budding process. It is referred to the genus *Calathium* provisionally.

Locality and Formation.—Mingan Islands; Calciferous formation.

Collectors.—Sir W. E. Logan, J. Richardson.

RECEPTACULITES CALCIFERUS. (N. sp.)

Fig. 346.

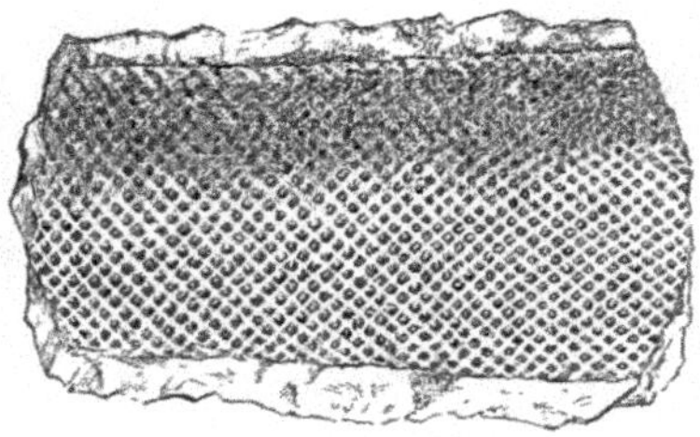

Fig. 347.

Fig. 346.—*Receptaculites calciferus.* A fragment of the inner surface of the ectorhin.
" 347.—*R. ? elegantulus.* A cast of the inside.

Description.—The specimen (fig. 346) is a fragment of the lower side, showing the inner surface of the ectorhin with the radial and cyclical stolons preserved. It resembles *R. occidentalis* (Salter), but differs in having the stolons of a somewhat greater length. This perhaps would not be sufficient to separate the species, but as the one is only known in the Calciferous, and the other in the Black River limestone, the whole of the Chazy intervening, it is most probable that they are distinct.

The squares formed by the stolons are on an average 1¼ lines on the side. The largest sized squares that can be made out in *R. occidentalis* are 1 line on an average, and in general they are somewhat less.

Locality and Formation.—Mingan Islands ; calciferous formation.

Collector.—J. Richardson.

Receptaculites ? elegantulus. (N. sp.)

Fig. 347.

Description.—This appears to be an elongate sub-cylindrical species, several inches in length, about one inch in diameter and probably tapering or more or less rounded at each end. The best specimen is a fragment of nearly half of the cylinder split in two longitudinally and empty. The drawing is made from a gutta-percha cast of the interior, and is too straight, the original being slightly undulated. The whole of the inner surface is covered with obscurely rhomboidal elevations arranged in oblique rows crossing each other at an angle of about 45°. These elevations leave corresponding rhomboidal pits in the gutta-percha cast represented above. There are on an average four or five pits in the length of two lines. The fossil is imbedded in a finely granular magnesian limestone, and, although the thickness of the wall can be very clearly made out, yet the tubes which ought to be apparent, if it be a true *Receptaculites*, are not visible. Supposing them to exist, they would be, in this species, very slender, and in this kind of rock all delicate structure is usually destroyed. The thickness of the wall is only two lines, and therefore, the tubes would be less than two lines ; while their diameter, if in proportion to other species, would be one-eighth of a line or thereabout.

It is referred to *Receptaculites* provisionally.

Locality and Formation.—Mingan Islands ; Calciferous formation.

Collector.—J. Richardson.

Genus Euchasma. (N. gen.)

Generic Characters.—The only species of this genus known to me is strongly convex triangular, inequilateral, equivalve, subcordiform. The posterior ? extremity is flat and gaping the whole length. The anterior ? extremity is rounded-angular, and seems to be gaping also ; but no specimens have been procured with this part perfect, and, therefore, this point remains doubtful. The hinge line is short, and seems to have an external ligament. When the flat side is ground down gradually, it is found that just below the umbones the shell of both valves has a large rounded protuberance on the inside. These leave an impression in the cast of the interior just behind the umbone.

E. Blumenbachia has been heretofore referred by me to the genus *Conocardium*, but that genus has not the two large posterior teeth ? possessed by this shell. It must be closely allied to *Eopteria* (*ante*, p. 221, 306, 307), but differs externally in having one extremity flat. This may not be sufficient to separate the genera, and should it hereafter turn out that the internal structure is the same in all the species, I beg that the *Euchasma* be retained for the group, and *Eopteria* withdrawn from science.

In the above description I have called the flat side the posterior with doubt, as the specimens are not sufficiently perfect to enable me to determine which is posterior or anterior.

I may explain here, also, that this genus would have been described on p. 220, only that I had then hopes of procuring better specimens, and thus delayed.

Fig. 348.

Fig. 348.—*Euchasma Blumenbachia*. *a*, side view of a small specimen ; *b*, the flat, posterior ? extremity, shewing the long narrow gape.

9. *New species of Fossils from the Quebec Group in the Northern part of Newfoundland, with a few from the Potsdam Group.*

(*Continued from p.* 300.)

GRAPTOLITIDÆ.

A number of species of graptolites were collected at Table Head, Bay St. Paul, Pistolet Bay, and Cow Head. Most of them are identical with those that occur at Point Lévis, but there are a few which may be new species. It would require a larger collection of more perfect specimens to decide.

Table Head.—Two species, in a bad state of preservation, were found at this locality in the black bituminous slates forming the upper part of Division N. One of them resembles *G. pristis*. The other, of which a single specimen only was collected, consists of twenty or thirty stipes radiating from a central point, but so imperfect and distorted that it cannot be determined whether it is a compound species or a number of individuals of one of the simple forms accidentally congregated together.

COW HEAD.—In the black slates of Division P, the following were collected, all of which occur at Point Lévis, and are described by Prof. Hall: *Phyllograptus typus*, *G. bryonoides*, *G. denticulatus*, *G. fruticosus*, *G. Headi*, *Callograptus elegans* and *Ptilograptus plumosus*.

BAY ST. PAUL.—From the black slates of this locality, belonging to Division *P.*, we have *G. bryonoides*, *G. denticulatus*, *G. fruticosus*, *Ptilograptus plumosus* and *C. elegans*.

PISTOLET BAY.—The graptolites collected here are very imperfectly preserved. The most common is a slender filiform species like *G. flaccidus*, but straighter; a species closely allied to, if not identical with *G. ciliatus* (Emmons) and a small *Phyllograptus* about three lines in length. The slates and black dolomite of this locality, in which these species occur, are undoubtedly of the same age as the black slates of the upper part of Division N at Table Head.

OTHER FOSSILS.

Murchisonia Anna, *Pleurotomaria Laurentiana*, and *P. calcifera* occur in Division *G*, at Port au Choix. At Cow Head in Division P, a trilobite was collected, only distinguishable from *Bathyurus conicus* by having the glabella smooth instead of tuberculated. *Asaphus Pelops* (*ante*, *p*. 317) also occurs at Cow Head. *Lingula acuminata* occurs in D, at Bay Ste. Barbe.

OBOLUS ? MURRAYI. (N. sp.)

Description.—The specimen is very nearly circular, broad ovate, width a little greater than the length, uniformly and moderately convex; the shell black and corneous and covered with fine concentric striæ. Length 7 lines; width about 8 lines.

Of this species only a single valve was found in a loose piece of grey argillaceous limestone by Mr. Murray at Maiden Arm, Hare Bay, on the east side of the northern point of Newfoundland. It belongs probably to the Quebec group.

Dedicated to ALEX. MURRAY, Esq., who discovered it.

BATHYURUS SOLITARIUS. (N. sp.)

Description.—Pygidium semicircular, length a little less than half the width, uniformly rounded behind, gently convex; the side lobes smooth with a flat border all round and a furrow close to the anterior margin; axis depressed convex, extending three-fourths the whole length, terminating at the edge of the marginal flat border, not elevated at the apex, distinctly defined at the sides by the dorsal furrows, about twelve narrow but well defined rings.

Length 5 lines; width 9 lines; width of marginal border 1 line; width of axis at the anterior margin 2½ lines.

This species is certainly closely allied to *B. Saffordi* (*ante, p.* 259), but differs from it in having the border wider and flat instead of convex, and in the axis having twelve instead of nine rings. These differences, although slight, give to the specimen an aspect distinct from that of any variety of *B. Saffordi.*

Locality and Formation.—Found loose at Hare Bay along with *O. Murrayi.*

Collector.—Alexander Murray, Esq.

BATHYURUS GREGARIUS. (N. sp.)

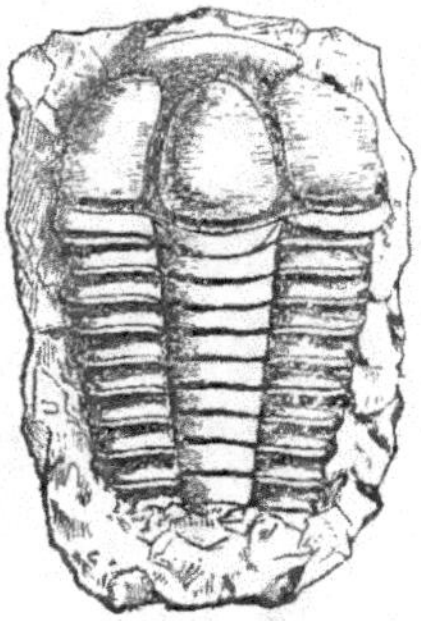

Fig. 349.

Fig. 349.—*Bathyurus gregarius.* Part of head and thorax, drawn from a cast in plaster.

Description.—Ovate, from one to two inches in length. Head semicircular, broadly rounded in front and with an elevated rounded margin. Glabella strongly convex; sides nearly straight, apex rounded, separated from the cheeks by deep dorsal furrows, a deep and wide groove in front of it; length including the neck segment full three-fourths the whole length of the head; neck segment rather large, rounded: neck furrow well defined all across. Cheeks strongly convex. The eye is situated on a line drawn across the head at one-third the length from the front margin, distant from the dorsal furrow rather more than one-half the width of the glabella. It appears to be a little more than one line in length where the length of the head is six lines. Thorax with at least nine segments, the precise number not known; axis narrow, less than one-third the whole width strongly convex sides straight, gradually tapering backwards; pleuræ with a very wide groove. Pygidium and moveable cheeks unknown.

The cheeks and glabella are very convex; the glabella separated from the cheeks by a deep groove; the margin in front of the glabella is elevated into a strong rounded cord-like rim between which and the apex of the glabella there is a wide and deep groove. These characters shew that it is closely allied to both *B. conicus* and *B. Cordai.* On comparison with these, it is seen that *B. conicus* differs in having the glabella more narrowed forwards and in the form of the space between the apex and marginal rim, that is to say, convex next to the glabella and concave close to the margin. *B. Cordai* has the glabella proportionally more elongated. The eye also in *B. gregarius* seems to be further forwards and more distant from the glabella than it is in the other two.

The surface characters cannot be made out from the casts.

Locality and Formation.—In the primordial slates holding *Paradoxides Bennetti* (Salter) at St. Mary's Bay in the south part of Newfoundland.

Collectors.—The specimens were procured by Mr. D. R. McKay of Montreal, who furnished me with a cast holding four individuals in a space of three inches square.

BATHYURUS PERPLEXUS. (N. sp.)

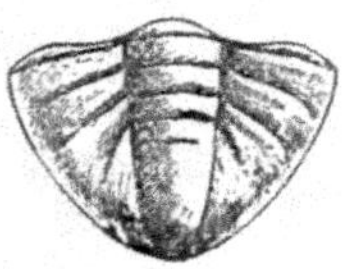

Fig. 350.—Pygidium of *B. perplexus.*

Description.—Pygidium semi-elliptical or sub-triangular, strongly convex; anterior margin gently convex, nearly straight; sides gently convex and converging to form a somewhat narrowly rounded apex; axis cylindro-conical, strongly convex, extending the whole length very nearly, rounded and rather abruptly elevated at the apex, with three distinct segments in the anterior half (besides the half-segment at the anterior margin), the posterior half apparently smooth. Side lobes with a narrow smooth border all round, and three depressed convex segments each, separated by narrow grooves. The anterior segment has a pleural groove close to the margin. These three pairs of segments occupy, with their inner extremities, the length of the anterior half of the axis being separated therefrom by the linear dorsal furrows. Behind the third pair there appears to be a fourth alongside of the posterior half of the axis, and consisting of two obscurely developed triangular or sub-ovate lobes. The specimen, however, is not well preserved in this part. Surface, apparently smooth.

Length of the only specimen collected 8 lines; width at the anterior margin 11 lines; width of the axis at the anterior margin 3 lines.

It is scarcely possible to separate this species from *B. extans* of the Black River limestone. The axis is more distinctly segmented, and this is the only difference exhibited by the specimen.

It may be that this is the pygidium of a species of *Olenellus* or *Dikelocephalus*, both of which genera are evidently allied to *Bathyurus*.

Locality and Formation.—B, east arm of Bonne Bay, Newfoundland; Potsdam group.

Collector.—J. Richardson.

Bathyurus vetulus. (N. sp.)

Description.—Pygidium semi-circular, obtusely rounded behind, length about half the width, rather strongly convex. Axis cylindrical, strongly convex, with three segments (besides the half segment), in the anterior two-thirds, the posterior third, smooth. Side lobes with three broad convex segments (besides the half-segment at the margin), a narrow smooth border all round. Surface apparently with fine tubercles.

This species differs from the last in its more obtuse form and more convex segments.

Length 6 lines; width at the anterior margin 12 lines.

Locality and Formation.—B, east arm of Bonne Bay, Newfoundland; Potsdam group.

Collector.—J. Richardson.

Besides the species of trilobites above noticed there are fragments of a number of other species probably all new.

In the Potsdam group, in B and C, *Olenellus Thompsoni* occurs in vast abundance, but no entire specimens were collected. In *C. Conocephalites Teucer*, and *C. Adamsii (ante* p. 11), were also found.

In the following catalogue, there are several species, such as,—*Scolithus linearis*, *Palæophycus incipiens*, and some others, which were collected on the north shore of the Straits of Belleisle; on the east side, and also in the southern part of Newfoundland, in rocks which have not yet been strictly identified with any of the divisions. Their position is, therefore, not indicated in the columns:—

CATALOGUE OF FOSSILS FROM THE POTSDAM AND QUEBEC GROUPS, NEWFOUNDLAND.

Page		A	B	C	D	E	F	G	H	I	K	L	M	N	O	P
	PLANTÆ.															
2	Scolithus linearis.															
2	Palæophycus incipiens.															
	PROTOZOA.															
5	Archeocyathus Atlanticus.															
4	" profundus.															
209	Calathium affine							*								
210	" Anstedi								*							
209	" formosum							*								
211	" Fittoni										*					
211	Trachyum cyathiforme							*								
212	" rugosum							*								
	GRAPTOLITIDÆ.															
362	Graptolithus bryonoides															*
"	" denticulatus															*
"	" fruticosus															*
"	" Headi															*
"	Phyllograptus typus															*
"	Ptilograptus plumosus															*
"	Callograptus elegans															*
	ZOOPHYTA.															
212	Stenopora fibrosa								*							*
212	Stromatopora compacta											*				
213	" rugosa							*								
	ASTERIADÆ.															
213	Stenaster Huxleyi									*						
	BRACHIOPODA.															
216	Acrotreta gemma															*
6	Obolus Labradoricus.															
362	" Murrayi.															
7	Obolella chromatica.															
8	" cingulata.															
214	Lingula Nympha													*		
215	" Iole															*
216	" Cyane															*
216	" Quebecensis															*
362	" acuminata				*											
217	Orthis delicatula												*			*
217	" Electra							*		*						

FOSSILS FROM NEWFOUNDLAND—*Continued.*

Page		A	B	C	D	E	F	G	H	I	K	L	M	N	O	P
	BRACHIOPODA—*Continued.*															
218	Orthis Hippolyta															*
218	Strophomena Aurora										*	*	*	*		*
219	" imbecilis															*
219	Leptæna decipiens															*
220	Camerella calcifera															*
220	" varians													*		*
305	" costata															*
219	" parva													*		
220	Rhynchonella Corinthia													*		*
	LAMELLIBRANCHIATA.															
220	Euchasma Blumenbachia							*	*							
221	Eopteria typica							*								
221	Ctenodonta Angela												*			
	GASTEROPODA.															
222	Holopea Ophelia											*				
223	Straparollina pelagica							*	*							
223	Subulites Daphne											*				
224	Pleurotomaria virgo								*	*	*	*				
224	" selecta								*	*	*	*				
225	" virguncula								*	*	*	*				
226	" sponsa													*		
226	" Etna							*	*							
227	" Hortensia								*							
227	" Harpya							*								
228	" Hyale						*									
228	" Normani							*								
229	" Numeria							*								
362	" Calcifera							*								
230	" Agarista								*							
230	" Calphurnia							*								
362	" Laurentina							*								
231	Murchisonia Catharina										*					
362	" Anna							*								
232	" Acrea							*								
232	" Adelina							*								
232	" simulatrix								*	*	*	*	*	*		
233	" Cicelia											*				
233	" sororcula								*	*	*	*	*			
234	" Augustina								*	*	*	*	*	*		
235	" agilis							*	*							
235	" placida							*								
236	Maclurea crenulata									*	*	*	*	*		

FOSSILS FROM NEWFOUNDLAND—*Continued.*

Page		A	B	C	D	E	F	G	H	I	K	L	M	N	O	P
	GASTEROPODA—*Continued.*															
237	Maclurea oceana						*	*	*							
238	" affinis						*									
239	" ponderosa															*
240	" acuminata										*	*	*	*		
241	" speciosa							*	*	*	*	*	*			
241	" transitionis										*	*				
242	" Emmonsi									*	*	*	*			
244	" Sylpha							*								
244	" Psyche							*								
245	" rotundata							*								
245	Ophilata Nerine						*									
310	" bella															*
247	Helicotoma Proserpina							*								
247	" Tritonia							*								
248	" Gorgonea								*							
249	" Eucharis											*	*			
249	Ecculiomphalus distans															*
250	" Atlanticus						*									
250	" superbus															*
2[illegible]1	Metoptoma instabilis											*				
	CEPHALOPODA.															
251	Orthoceras piscator									*	*	*	*	*		
252	" servile											*				
253	" explorator								*							
253	" Priamus											*	*			
254	" Allumettense												*	*		
254	" hæsitans									*			*			
255	" Lamarcki							*	*							
255	" Flavius									*						
256	Piloceras Canadense						*	*								
257	" Triton								*	*						
256	" Wortheni								*							
257	" gracile								*							
258	Nautilus insolens											*				
558	" desertus											*				
258	" calciferus						*	*								
259	" versutus								*							
259	Lituites Pluto											*				
	CRUSTACEA.															
262	Bathyurus breviceps													*		
261	" caudatus							*	*							

FOSSILS FROM NEWFOUNDLAND—*Continued.*

Page		A	B	C	D	E	F	G	H	I	K	L	M	N	O	P
	CRUSTACEA—*Continued.*															
362	Bathyurus conicus															*
259	" Cordai						*									*
260	" Nero						*	*	*					*		
16	" parvulus.															
364	" perplexus		*													
259	" saffordi															*
15	" senectus.															
261	" Timon							*	*							
365	" vetulus		*	*												
363	" gregarius.															
263	Bathyurellus abruptus						*	*	*							
264	" marginatus						*	*	*							
265	" nitidus															*
266	" formosus															*
267	" fraternus															*
268	" validus											*				
269	Dolichometopus convexus							*								
269	" gibberulus							*								
270	Asaphus canalis						*	*	*	*	*	*	*			
271	" Huttoni													*		
272	" Morrisii													*		*
272	" quadraticaudatus													*		*
317	" Pelops															*
273	Nileus macrops													*		
274	" scrutator													*		*
275	" affinis															*
276	Illænus fraternus											*		*		*
277	" consimilis											*	*	*		
278	" tumidifrons															*
279	" arcuatus															*
280	" consobrinus															*
281	Endymionia meeki													*		*
281	Holometopus Angelini													*		*
281	Harpides Atlanticus															*
282	" concentricus															*
282	Lichas Jukesii															*
283	Shumardia glacialis													*		*
284	Cheirurus Vulcanus															*
285	" Mercurius															*
285	" prolificus															*
286	" Polydorus													*		*
287	" perforator													*		
288	" Sol													*		*
288	Amphion Barrandei									*	*	*	*	*		*

FOSSILS FROM NEWFOUNDLAND—*Continued.*

Page		A	B	C	D	E	F	G	H	I	K	L	M	N	O	P
	CRUSTACEA—*Continued.*															
290	Amphion Julius															*
290	" insularis							*								
291	Triarthrus Fischeri													*		*
291	Telephus Americanus													*		*
292	Encrinurus mirus													*		*
293	Remopleurides Panderi													*		
294	" Schlothemi													*		*
295	Ampyx læviusculus													*		
295	" normalis													*		*
296	" Rutilius															*
297	" semicostatus													*		*
297	Agnostus galba												*	*		*
298	" Fabius													*		*
11	Olenellus Thompsoni		*	*												
11	" Vermontana		*	*												
12	Conocephalites Adamsii		*	*												
13	" Teucer		*	*												
11	" miser.															
	ENTOMOSTRACA.															
299	Leperditia turgida							*	*							
299	" concinnula											*	*			
300	" ventralis													*		
300	Beyrichia Atlantica											*				
	ANNELIDA.															
17	Salterella rugosa.															
18	" pulchella.															
18	" obtusa.															

Distribution of the Species.

The distribution of the species in the foregoing catalogue, may be discussed in the following order.

Potsdam Group.

In this group, consisting of Divisions A, B, and C, we have nineteen species, none of which are found in the Potsdam sandstone in Canada. But in that part of the group, which is usually known, in the State of Vermont, under the designations of the Red Sand Rock, and the Georgia slates, the following occur:—*Scolithus linearis*, *Palæophycus incipiens*, *Obolus Labradoricus*, *Obolella (Kutorgina) cingulata*, *Olenellus Thompsoni*, *O. Vermontana*, *Conocephalites Adamsi* and *C, Teucer*. As these are the most abundant species in the formation, both in Vermont and Newfoundland, there can be little doubt, but that the rocks in which they occur, in these two widely separated localities, are of the same age. None of these species have been found in the Potsdam sandstone of Wisconsin, and other parts of the Western States as described by Owen, Hall, Shumard, and Meek. We have, therefore, no palæontological evidence that the Potsdam of the West is precisely of the same age as that of Newfoundland and Vermont. The general affinities and aspect of the fossils and the physical relations of the rocks, however, prove that there can be no great difference. In the next overlying strata Division D, *Lingula acuminata* was found at Bay St. Barbes. I have compared the specimens from this locality with those that occur so abundantly in the upper part of the Potsdam, in the Township of Beverley in Canada West, and believe them to be perfectly identical.

Calciferous Formation.

The Calciferous formation is represented in Newfoundland, by all the Divisions from D to H inclusive. In this series of strata, there are sixty-three species, of which the following fourteen are found in Canada and New York; *Stenopora fibrosa*, *Stromatopora rugosa?*, *Lingula acuminata*, *Euchasma Blumenbachia*, *Pleurotomaria Calphurnia*, *P. calcifera*, *P. Laurentina*, *Murchisonia Anna*, *Ecculiomphalus Atlanticus*, *Orthoceras Lamarcki*, *Piloceras Canadensis*, *Bathyurus Cordai*, *Asaphus canalis*, and *Leperditia turgida*,—excepting *S. fibrosa* and *B. Cordai*, all of these occur in the true Calciferous in Canada. *B. Cordai* abounds in the same formation in New York. *S. rugosa* is doubtfully determined, and is probably distinct from the Black River species of that name. The beds in which *L. acuminata* occurs in Canada, are placed in the top of the Potsdam; but as *Pleurotmaria Canadensis*, and an orthoceratite, are associated with it, perhaps these particular strata should be more properly referred to the base of the Calciferous, and they would then correspond to Division D. Most of the species are found in Divisions G and H, the upper part of the formation in Newfoundland. Two of the species (*S. fibrosa* and *A. canalis*) range upwards into the Chazy, the former continuing to the Upper Silurian. The general aspect of the fauna is peculiarly that of the Calciferous, the most striking features being the great numbers of small *Maclurœ* and species of *Piloceras*, the latter a genus which seems to have culminated in this particular period.

Divisions I, K, L, M.

These four divisions consist of 235 feet of magnesian limestones at the base, above which we have 844 feet of light bluish grey limestones, making in all a thickness of 1084 feet. Only thirty-seven species of fossils have been collected in this series of beds; and of these, nine species are found in division H below, while ten of them pass upwards into Division N next above. Three of the species (*Stromatopora compacta*, *Orthoceras Allumettense* and *Asaphus canalis*) occur in Canada, the first two in the Chazy and Black River, and the last in the Calciferous and Chazy. The following are closely allied to Black River and Trenton species.

Ctenodonta Angela,	allied to,	*C. contracta*,	B. R.
Subulites Daphne,	" "	*S. parvulus*,	B. R.
Murchisonia simulatrix,	" "	*M. gracilis*,	B. R. & Tr.
" *Cicelia*,	" "	*M. perangulata*,	B. R.
" *sororcula*,	" "	" "	B. R.
" *Augustina*,	" "	*M. bellicincta*,	Tr.
Orthoceras hœsitans,	" "	*O. Bigsbyi*,	B. R.

The occurrence of great numbers of individuals of these species, in a silicified condition, and weathered out in bold relief, gives to the slabs of limestone an aspect so remarkably like that of the well-known specimens from Pauquette's Rapids, that at first sight one might be well led to say, this is surely the Black River limestone. But on careful comparison of perfect specimens, it is seen that notwithstanding the resemblance, none of the species are strictly identical. All present such differences that after a study of collections from both localities, they can be separated if mixed up together without their labels. Even *O. Allumettense*, which I have identified, differs by being much larger than any specimens that have been seen in the original localities.

If the succession were the same here as it is in Canada and New York, we ought to have the Chazy formation represented in these four Divisions.

But no one acquainted with the peculiar and strongly featured fauna of that formation could recognize it in this collection. Three of the species are, indeed, Chazy fossils, but then they are not characteristic forms. The typical and leading species which always go together in great numbers and in one compact army, as it were, in every exposure of the true Chazy, are totally absent.

The Lamellibranchiata, Gasteropoda and Cephalopoda of these beds have, so far as the genera *Ctenodonta*, *Subulites*, *Pleurotomaria*, and *Orthoceras* are concerned, an aspect very like that presented by the same genera in the Black River and Trenton formations. But species similar to most of those above compared have a great range, and are found in all the different groups of rocks up to the Devonian. Their occurrence here is not, in my opinion, sufficient to counterbalance the negative fact that (excepting those in question) not a vestige of any one of the species of the vast fauna of the Black River and Trenton has been detected. *Tetradium fibratum*, *Columnaria alveolata*, *Leptæna sericea*, *Strophomera alternata*, *Orthis testudinaria*, *Calymene Blumenbachi* and *Asaphus platycephalus* are sure to be found in every collection of any considerable extent from these two formations. If they occurred here as abundantly and persistently as they do in Canada and New York, it would be difficult to give any reason why these four Divisions should not be regarded as the equivalents of the Black River and Trenton. But not one fragment of anything which could by any possibility be referred to any one of these species can be seen in this collection. A piece of red limestone was found at Bay St. Paul which is full of *L. sericea*, but it was a loose and worn fragment, lithologically different from any of the strata in question. Judging from this specimen I should say that the Trenton may possibly occur somewhere near, but we cannot refer, on any palæontological ground, the series of strata constituting Divisions I, K, L, M, to that formation.

Divisions N, O, P.

The rocks of these divisions, in ascending order, consist of 277 feet of black, bituminous limestone, with some black shales, very fossiliferous; next 700 feet of sandstones, in which no fossils were collected or observed; and at the summit 700 feet of black shales, holding grey and white limestone conglomerates, abounding in fossils, although there are not a great many species. There appear to be, in this series of strata, two formations, distinguishable from each other, both by lithological and palæontological characters. The first includes the black, bituminous limestones and shales, forming the upper 277 feet at Table Head, and those of Pistolet Bay, and 4 miles N. E. from Portland Creek. The rocks at the latter locality appear to lie above the 700 feet of sandstone constituting Division O, and are, therefore, in the foregoing descriptions of species, referred to Division P. Taking these three localities to be on the same, or nearly the same, horizon, we have from them, in addition to a few not yet described, the following 48 species :—

Lingula Nympha
" Iole
" Cyane
Acrotreta gemma
Orthis delicatula
* Strophomena Aurora
" imbecilis
" decipiens (?)
Camerella parva
" varians *
Rhynchonella Corinthia
Pleurotomaria sponsa
* Murchisonia simulatrix
* " Augustina
* Maclurea crenulata
* " acuminata
Ecculiomphalus superbus
* Orthoceras piscator
* " Allumettense
* Bathyurus Nero
" breviceps
Asaphus Huttoni
" Morrisii
" quadraticaudatus
Nileus macrops
" scrutator
* Illænus fraternus
* " consimilis
Endymionia Meeki
Holometopus Angelini *
Harpides Atlanticus
" concentricus
Shumardia glacialis
Cheirurus Polydorus
" perforator
" Sol
* Amphion Barrandei *
Triarthrus Fischeri
Telephus Americanus
Encrinurus mirus
Remopleurides Panderi
" Schlotheimi
Ampyx læviusculus
" normalis
" Rutilius
" semicostatus
* Agnostus galba
" Fabius

In the above list those with an asterisk before them are found in some one or more of the Divisions below N ; those with an asterisk after them occur in the grey and white limestones of Division P, at Cow Head. *Camerella varians* is a Chazy species. *Orthoceras Allumettense* is both Chazy and Black River. *Holometopus Angelini*, *Endymionia Meeki*, and *Cheirurus Sol* occur in the Quebec group of Canada East. We find here, for the first time, among American trilobites the peculiar type of *Cheirurus*, with a spine upon the glabella—*C. perforator* (*ante*, p. 287). Another of the same structure, *C. glaucus*, was discovered in the Quebec group, in the township of Stanbridge ; and a third, *C. Satyrus*, in the Chazy, at Montreal, by T. C. Weston, last year, 1864 (*ante*, p. 323). This type has been known for several years among the Russian trilobites by *Sphærexochus cephaloceros* (Nieskowski) = *Zethus triplicatus* (Eichwald), which occurs in the Pleta limestone. The genus *Triarthrus* has not heretofore been found below the Trenton in America. *Remopleurides* occurs in the Chazy, and *Amphion* in both Chazy and Calciferous ; but neither of these genera have yet been reported as occurring above the Chazy in Canada or New York. The general aspect of the trilobitic fauna of this series of strata seems to me to be more like that of the Pleta limestone of Russia, and Angelin's two Swedish groups, B C and C, than it is to that of any of the American Lower Silurian formations heretofore illustrated.

The second formation, above mentioned, consists of the 700 feet of black shales with grey and white limestone conglomerates, at Cow Head. In no other part of Newfoundland do we meet with the remarkable fauna which characterizes the Lévis formation. It undoubtedly occurs here in full force. The following list contains the species collected at that locality, and also shows how many of them occur in Canada :

	C. H.	C. E.
Stenopora fibrosa (Chazy to Devonian)	*	
Graptolithus hryonoides	*	*
" denticulatus	*	*
" fruticosus	*	*
" Headi	*	*
Phyllograptus typus	*	*
Ptilograptus plumosus	*	*
Callograptus elegans	*	*
Orthis Hippolyte	*	*
* Camerella varians (Chazy)	*	
" calcifera, (Calciferous)	*	*
" costata	*	*
Lingula Quebecensis	*	*
Maclurea ponderosa	*	*
Ophileta bella	*	*
Ecculiomphalus distans	*	
Asaphus Pelops	*	*
Bathyurus Cordai (Calciferous)	*	*
" conicus (Calciferous)	*	
" Saffordi	*	*
Bathyurellus nitidus	*	
" formosus	*	*
" fraternus	*	
Nileus affinis	*	*
Illænus tumidifrons	*	
" arcuatus	*	
" consobrinus	*	
* Holometopus Angelini	*	*
Lichas Jukesii	*	*
Cheirurus Vulcanus	*	*
" Mercurius	*	*
" prolificus (Chazy)	*	*
* Amphion Barrandei	*	
" Julius	*	

In the above list those found at Cow Head are placed in the column C. H., and those which occur in Canada East (as well as Cow Head) C. E. The seven species of graptolites, with *Lingula Quebecensis*, occur only in the black slates ; all the others in the grey and white limestones. The three species with an asterisk before them are found in the next group of strata below. No one could compare the collections from Cow Head with those of Point Lévis and Phillipsburgh without some feeling of astonishment, that in localities nearly a thousand miles distant from each other, there should be such a perfect identity, not only in the fossils, but also in the character of the rock. The specimens, if mixed together, without their labels, could never be separated. Only a small collection was made at Cow Head ; and there can scarcely be a doubt that further examination will bring to light a greater number of species common to the two countries.

This fauna, although, upon the whole, specifically distinct from the one next below, consists of the same types of trilobites, with the exception of *Bathyurus Cordai* and *B. conicus*, which are Calciferous species, as is also the brachiopod *Camerella calcifera*. There are two species, *Amphion Sol* and *Endymionia Meeki*, which are found in Division N, in Newfoundland, and not at Cow Head ; but they occur in the limestones of Point Lévis, which are of the same age as those of Cow Head. There are thus five common species, instead of three, as would appear by the above list.

From Cow Head, Point Lévis, St. Antoine, Stanbridge, Bedford, and Phillipsburgh we have in all 219 described species. Of these, the fifty-one species of graptolites described by Prof. Hall, and also *Lingula Quebecensis*, *L. Irene*, *Obolella desiderata* and *Shumardia granulosa* have been found only in the slates and thin-bedded limestones interstratified in the slates. The other 162 species occur in the white and grey conglomerate limestones. That the slates and these peculiar limestones belong to the same group, is proved by their occurring together in widely separated localities ; although as yet we are unable to shew that any of the species are common to both. At Cow Head *G. Headi* was found in a loose piece of grey limestone ; but it is not quite certain that the specimen belongs to the conglomerates.

The evidence that the rocks at Cow Head in Newfoundland are of the same age as those of the Lévis formation in Canada East amounts to this—1, they are precisely the same in lithological characters, and—2, out of the 34 species collected at Cow Head 23 are perfectly identical with those collected at Point Lévis, Bedford, Phillipsburgh, and other typical localities of the formation. There is, however, in Newfoundland an important series of strata, consisting of all the Divisions from I to O inclusive, having a thickness of 2061 feet, lying below the Lévis formation and above the Calciferous, which has not been recognized in Canada. It thus appears that the Lévis formation not only lies above the Calciferous, but more than 2000 feet above it. Yet it holds a large number of trilobites of the Potsdam type, and several species, such as *Lingula Mantelli*, *Camerella calcifera*, *Bathyurus Cordai*, *B. conicus*, and *Asaphus canalis*, which certainly do occur in the Calciferous.

In the foregoing general catalogue (ante pp. 366–370) there are 62 species placed in Division P. But if we exclude from that Division all the species, except those collected at Cow Head, only those on the list on p. 375 properly belong to it. The others should be placed in Division N.

10. *Fossils from various Formations in the Silurian and Devonian Systems.*

PROTOZOA.

CALATHIUM CANADENSE.

Fig. 351.

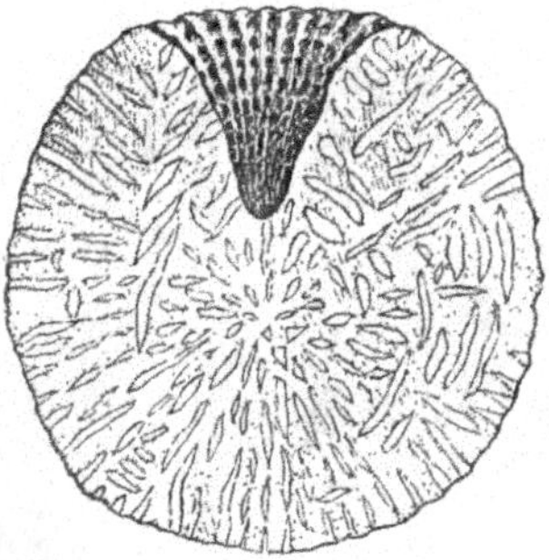

Fig. 352.

Fig. 351.—*Calathium Canadense.* A vertical section of a small specimen, showing the interior of the cup and the apertures of the radiating canals.
Fig. 352.—*Astylospongia præmorsa.* Vertical section of a specimen, copied from ROEMER.

Description.—Elongate, turbinate, expanding to the diameter of about one inch in a height of one and a half inches at the base, then becoming more nearly cylindrical. The cup is about one-third the whole diameter, and extends nearly to the base. The pores or canal-apertures are ovate, about eight in six lines of the length of each vertical row, and two in one line in the transverse rows.

The specimen above figured has the cup empty, but does not show the structure of the walls, even in a polished section. Another specimen, a fragment three inches in length, shows, in a longitudinal fracture, that the radiating canals curve downwards, in proceeding to the exterior.

This species probably attained a length of four or five inches, but only two fragments have been found. It differs from *C. Fittoni* (*ante*, p. 211) in having the pores, in general, one-fourth smaller, and from *C. Anstedi* (*ante*, pp. 210, 337) in having them larger.

The above figure, 352, is copied from Roemer, who gives it to illustrate the internal structure of *Astylospongia præmorsa*, a fossil sponge which occurs in the Lower Silurian rocks of northern Europe, and also, according to him, in rocks of the same age in Tennessee.* The structure of the inner wall of the cup is very much the same in both of the species above represented, but still I think they belong to different genera. In our species the walls are as completely reticulated to the depth of six lines, as in the inner surface of the cup itself. This is clearly shown by the fragment above mentioned. There is a great difference also in the general form of the two groups, the species of *Calathium* being elongate-turbinate like the corals *Zaphrentis* and *Cyathophyllum*, while those figured by Dr. Roemer are more nearly globular. The genus *Aulocopium*, also illustrated by Roemer, has some turbinated species, but the figures of the inside of the cup (of which several are given) do not show any perforations: their absence, however, in the figures may be owing to the imperfection of the specimens.

Locality and Formation.—Mingan Islands; Chazy limestone.

Collectors.—J. Richardson, Sir W. E. Logan.

Genus RECEPTACULITES, Defrance.

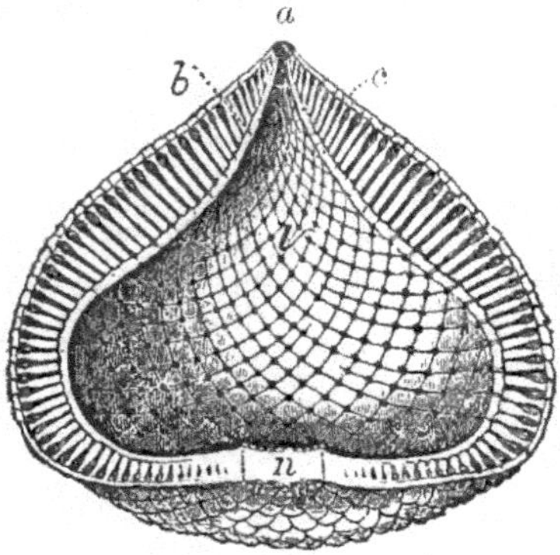

Fig. 353.

Fig. 353.—Diagram of the structure of *Receptaculites*, as it would be shown in a vertical section through a sub-conical species. *a*, the aperture in the summit; *b*, the endorhin or inner integument lining the central cavity; *c*, the ectorhin or external integument; *n*, the usual position of the nucleus; *v*, the great internal cavity. The unshaded bands running from the ectorhin to the endorhin represent the tubes.

* DR. FERDINAND ROEMER, *Die fossile Fauna der Silurischen Diluvial-Geschiebe von Sadewitz bei Oels, in Nieder-Schlesien*, p. 10, pl. II, fig. 6.

The structure and zoological position of *Receptaculites* have been more or less elaborately investigated by Goldfuss, Eichwald, Roemer, Salter, Hall, and other eminent observers, and yet, owing to the imperfection of the materials, a great deal remains to be done before the various questions involved in the relations of this curious genus can be regarded as positively settled. Since the publication of Salter's paper in the first Decade of our Geological Survey, numerous specimens of several distinct species have been collected in the Silurian rocks of Canada, and I am, by the study of these, now enabled to furnish a few additional details. The principal new points are, the perforated structure of the internal integument, the existence (in most, if not in all, of the species) of a great central cavity and an orifice in the upper side. The flat watch-shaped specimens which are usually figured as constituting the whole of the body, are probably only the basal portion of the body-wall of the discoid species.

The genus may be described as consisting of organisms, which, when full grown and perfect, are of a discoid, cylindrical, ovate, or globular shape, hollow within, and usually, if not always, with an aperture in the upper side. In or near the centre of the lower side there is generally to be seen a small rounded protuberance, indicating, most probably, the position of the primitive cell or nucleus from which the animal commenced its growth. In some species the lower side is more or less concave, and often the nucleus is not at all elevated above the surface adjacent thereto. Its place, however, in the absence of any other guide, may generally be found by observing the point towards which the spiral lines or rows of plates on the outer surface converge. The body-wall is of a somewhat complex structure. It consists of three parts,—an external and an internal integument, and, between these, the peculiar tubular or spicular skeleton presently to be described. The external integument may be called 'the ectorhin,' and the internal 'the endorhin.'

The ectorhin is usually composed of numerous small rhomboidal plates closely fitting together, and arranged in curved rows which radiate in all directions from the nucleus outwards to the peripheral margin of the base, and thence, ascending upwards, converge to the edge of the aperture in the upper side. Two or three of those rows of plates (the precise number is not yet determined) originate in the nucleus, and, as they diverge from each other, new rows are introduced between them. The rows diminish, in number, again on the upper side according as they converge towards the apex of the fossil. The plates at and immediately around the nucleus, and also towards the centre of the upper side, are somewhat smaller than they are at the widest part or middle region of the body. It seems probable that, in some of the species, this integument was of a flexible, coriaceous consistence. In others the plates were solid. In *R.*

occidentalis (Salter), when silicified specimens are treated with acid the plates are easily separable, and, therefore, although in close contact, they were not anchylosed together.

The endorhin is also composed of small rhomboidal plates arranged in curving rows; but it differs from the ectorbin in being perforated by numerous small circular orifices, one of which is situated at each point where the angles of four plates meet. From the centre of each of the plates of this integument there radiate four small canals, one proceeding straight to the middle of each of the sides of the plate, where it communicates with a similar canal in the adjoining plates. Each one of these plates is, therefore, connected by these canals with the four plates in contact with it. The canals are excavated in the substance of the plates, and communicate with the central canal of the transverse tubes. The canals are not always perfectly circular, but are often flattened or irregularly circular. The endorhin varies greatly in the extent to which it is developed. In some specimens the plates are well-defined and rhomboidal, with perfectly circular pores at the angles. In others the plates are not at all defined, the ectorhin being one continuous integument without sutures, but always with the full complement of pores. The latter in such specimens are not all circular, but are variously shaped orifices sometimes with rough edges. There are also specimens in which the endorhin consists of only a thin film, capping, as it were, the tubes and inclosing the canals, the pores being proportionally larger than they are in those with well-developed plates. The end of each tube, in these specimens, forms an irregular, rounded tubercle instead of a rhomboidal plate.

The tubular skeleton above alluded to consists of numerous small, straight, rarely curved, cylindrical tubes or hollow spicula, placed parallel to each other and at right angles to the planes of the body-wall of which they form the greater portion. They connect, and at the same time keep asunder, the ectorhin and the endorhin. One of these tubes springs from the centre of each plate of the ectorhin: it is, at its base, or next to the ectorhin, very slender, but enlarges so as to attain its full thickness at about one-fourth of its length, and then remains at the same diameter throughout until it reaches the endorhin, by a single plate of which its inner extremity is, as it were, capped. The outer extremity of each tube has four small slender stolons, one proceeding to each of the four angles of that particular plate of the ectorhin from the centre of which it (the tube) springs. It there seems to form a connection with the stolons of the three adjacent plates whose angles meet at that point. The stolons are so arranged that one of them always points inwards towards the nucleus, and another on the opposite side of the tube outwards or upwards.

It is proposed to call these the radial stolons; they form continuous lines radiating in all directions away from the nucleus. The other two stolons of each tube project at right angles to the direction of the radial stolons; they form circles round the nucleus, and may therefore be called the cyclical stolons. The connection of all these different parts may be better understood by studying the following figures.

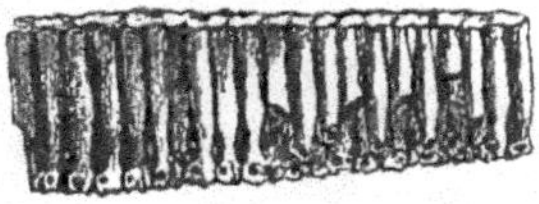

Fig. 354.

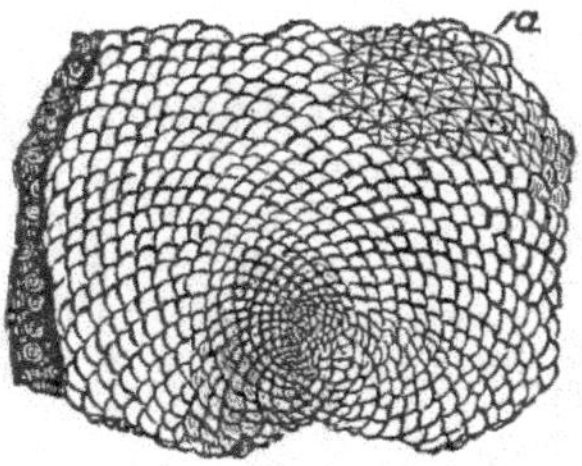

Fig. 355.

Fig. 356.

Fig. 354.—A small portion of *R. occidentalis* showing the tubes.

Fig. 355.—A part of the lower side of the same species showing the nucleus and ectorhin.

Fig. 356.—A fragment of the same, showing the endorhin, the pores at the angles of the plates, and the nucleus, which, on this side, is usually deeply concave.

At the lower side of fig. 354, is shown the ectorhin and the apertures in the hollow stolons, broken off in the specimen. The apertures are slightly enlarged in the figure. In fig. 355, the usual aspect of the central portion of the lower side of this species is given. It will be seen that the greater number of the plates are not truly rhomboidal, but approach the form of a spherical triangle with two of the sides concave. This form of the plates frequently occurs. The convex side of such plates is always outwards towards the periphery of the fossil, and the acute angle formed by the two concave sides always directed towards the nucleus. This shows that the consolidation of the plates commenced at the nucleus and gradually extended outwards. In many specimens the plates are all perfectly rhomboidal, and in such they may have solidified simultaneously all over the body. One corner of the specimen at *a* is represented as denuded of the ectorhin, showing the various markings beneath, which will be hereafter explained by other figures. By fig. 356 is represented the ordinary appearance of the endorhin of silicified specimens when cleared of the limestone matrix by treatment with acid. Although the pores have been seen in this species only, yet it seems quite probable that they occur in all others of the genus.

In the diagram fig. 357 the tubes are placed proportionately much farther apart than they are in any known species, in order to exhibit the structure with the greater clearness. The endorhin is drawn as if it were transparent to show the position of the tubes beneath it. The dotted lines give the outlines of the upper portions of the tubes, and also define the course of the endorhinal canals,—four radiating from the top of each tube. The endorhinal pores—one situated at each of the points where the angles of four plates meet—penetrate through the endorhin into the space between the tubes, and not into the tubes themselves, as might be supposed from a superficial examination. In the ectorhin the rough lines *k* represent the sutures between the plates; and it will be observed that they have the same direction as the endorhinal sutures in the upper part of the figure. The stolons have not the same direction as the endorhinal

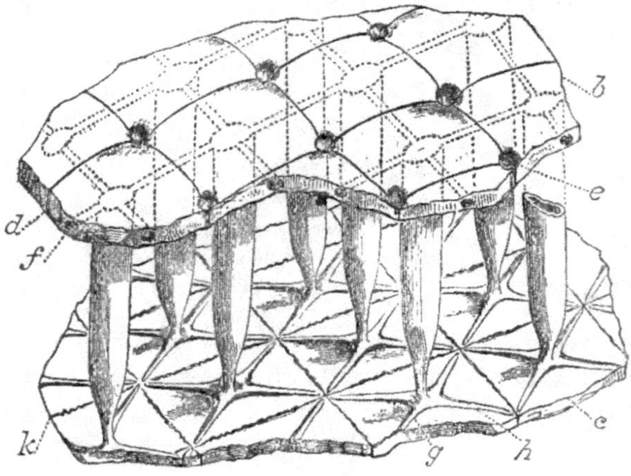

Fig. 357.

Fig. 357.—Diagram to explain the structure of the body-wall of *Receptaculites*; *b*, the endorhin; *c*, the ectorhin; *d*, suture between the plates of the endorhin; *e*, endorhinal pore; *f*, endorhinal canal; *g*, radial stolon; *h*, cyclical stolon; *k*, suture between the plates of the ectorhin.

canals, but are, as it were, turned one-eighth round, so that the two directions are inclined to each other at an angle of 45°. The stolons run along the inner surface of the ectorhin, but the endorhinal canals are excavated in the substance of the endorhin. The space between the tubes is almost always filled with the rock of the same kind as that in which the fossil is imbedded. In perfect specimens, the rock, while it was still in the condition of soft mud, must have found its way through the aperture in the upper side into the great central cavity, and thence through the endorhinal pores into the spaces between the tubes. In general the upper side or vault, as it may be called, over the central cavity is not preserved, and the specimens then consist of the whole or a portion of the base with the nucleus, as in fig. 355. These are also filled with matrix; the soft ooze having entered not only through the pores, but also through the broken margin. It is probable that the animal lived with its base partly buried, a portion of the vault with the aperture projecting above the surface of the mud. During the life the central cavity was perhaps kept free from sediment by currents of water which the animal had the power of exciting. But as soon as the currents ceased (with vitality), the mud would enter freely. The vault would also soon fall to pieces, and the fragments of all those individuals of which it (the vault) projected above the surface of the sediment would be soon scattered, while the partly buried base would be preserved.

The specimen represented by fig. 358 is a fragment of the ectorhin of *R. calciferus*, from the Calciferous formation, Mingan Islands. It shows only the inner surface on which the stolons are still preserved, but the tubes are worn nearly to their bases. It is rare to find specimens in that condition; and this one was not suspected to be a *Receptaculites* for several years after its discovery, until a large portion of the base of an individual of *R. occidentalis* was found, which, by having been slowly weathered down from the upper side, retains the tubes over an area of several square inches, while a considerable space around the nucleus is covered with the squares formed by the stolons, precisely as in this example. Fig. 359 is a cast of the inner surface of the ectorhin of *R. Oweni* (Hall), from the Lower Silurian rocks of Illinois. The integument itself is totally removed. The vertical lines are the impressions of the radial stolons, while the more irregular and slightly curved transverse lines are the imprints of the cyclical stolons. The dark points are the apertures of the cylindrical perforations in the rock once occupied by the tubes now entirely removed. On following any one of the lines, it will be seen that there is, between every two of the orifices, a point where two of the lines cross without an orifice at their intersection. Each one of these marks the point where the angles of four plates met. Four stolons also met at each of these points. This will be readily understood by comparing fig. 357. In specimens in this state of preservation we see no traces of the sutures between the plates, as the whole substance of the ectorhin—plates, sutures, and all—is destroyed.

Fig. 358.

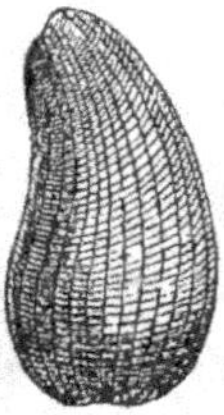

Fig. 360.

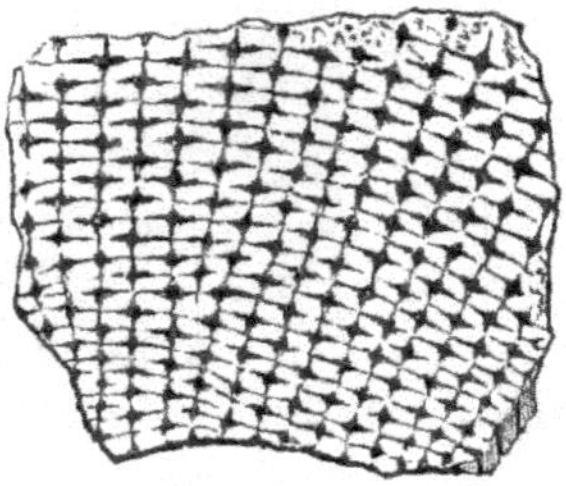

Fig. 359.

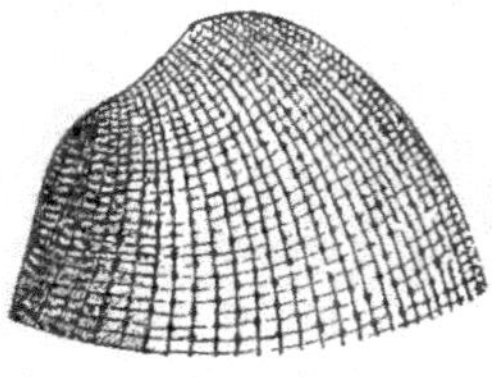

Fig. 361.

Fig. 358.—Fragment of *R. calciferus*, showing the inner surface of the ectorhin with the stolons remaining, but all other parts worn away.

Fig. 359.—A cast of *R. Oweni*, showing the impression of the inner surface of the ectorhin.

Fig. 360.—*Tetragonis Murchisonii* (Eichwald) reduced.

Fig. 361.—A portion of 360, natural size.

Fig. 360 is a reduced outline of *Tetragonis Murchisonii*, from Eichwald's 'Urwelt Russlands,' pl. iii. fig. 18. It does not show all the lines given in the original figure, as they could not well be represented on so small a scale. Fig. 361 is the upper part of the same figure, of the size of the original. The vertical lines are the impressions of the radial stolons, and the finer transverse lines the grooves of the cyclical stolons. By comparing fig. 359, it will be seen that the grooves in both figures have precisely the same arrangement; that is to say, the dark points, representing the openings of the cylindrical cavities, once occupied by the tubes, occur at each alternate crossing of the grooves. It would appear, therefore, that Eichwald's genus *Tetragonis* was founded on a species of *Receptaculites*, with the ectorhin removed. The genus *Ischadites* also exhibits very similar markings, as may be seen by comparing the figures of *I. Kœnigii* (Murch.), on pl. 12, 'Siluria,' and the following of *R. Canadensis*.

The specimen represented by fig. 362 has been figured by me in the Geology of Canada, p. 309, under the name of *Ischadites Canadensis*. It is the cast of the inner surface of the ectorhin, and differs remarkably from the similar specimen of *R. Oweni* (*ante*, fig. 359). It is deeply pitted all over with sub-quadrangular or rhomboidal depressions, the form of each cavity being such as would be made by the impression of a small four-sided pyramid. In the bottom of each is a small rounded orifice, from which radiate three grooves to three of the angles of the square.

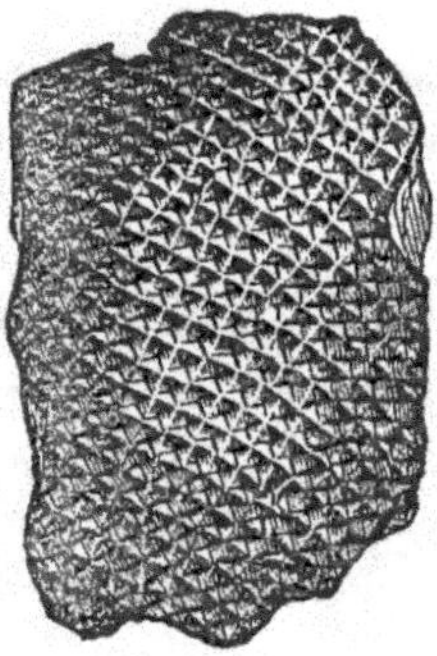

Fig. 362.

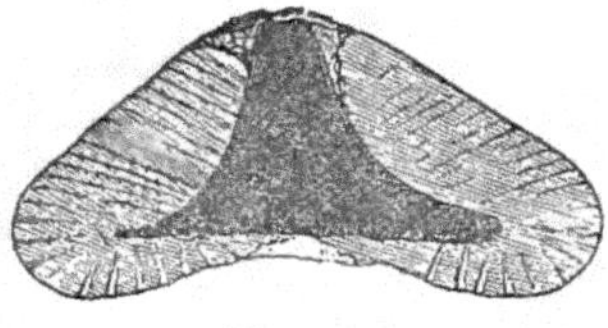

Fig. 363.

Fig. 364.

Fig. 362.—*R. Canadensis* (Billings), a cast of the inner surface of the ectorhin.

Fig. 363.—*R. Jonesi*, a polished section through a nearly perfect specimen, showing the central cavity and the aperture at the top.

Fig. 364.—*R. Iowensis* (Owen), a weathered section through a specimen, showing the aperture and the central cavity imperfectly.

These, I have not the least doubt, are the grooves of three of the stolons. The absence of the fourth stolon may be accounted for in this way. Among the detached silicified tubes of *R. occidentalis* which are found in the sediment left at the bottom of the vessel, after dissolving specimens of limestone holding these fossils in acid, numerous specimens have been collected with only three stolons in contact with the plate or at the end of the tube, but with the fourth a small distance from the end. It is evident that in casts of the inner surface of the ectorhin of specimens with all the tubes thus constructed, there would be only the three grooves of the terminal stolons visible on the surface, the fourth being buried beneath the surface. I have also ascertained that this fourth stolon is in *R. occidentalis*, one of the radials, and always when it can be seen *in situ*, the one pointing outwards away from the nucleus.

Fig. 363 is a vertical section of *R. Jonesi*, a small species which occurs in the upper part of the Lower Helderberg rocks of Gaspé. The shaded bell-shaped area is the central cavity. It is distinctly observed in several others of the same species. It will be seen that the body-wall in the vault above and on the sides of the cavity is thicker than it is in the base, but the tubes are much more slender. They here assume the form of the elongated connecting spicula of the true sponges. Fig. 364 is a similar section, through a specimen of *R. Iowensis* from the Trenton limestone at Ottawa. At *a*, the central cavity is distinctly shown, filled with the grey limestone matrix, which has also found its way between the tubes in the base of the fossil. The shaded portions *b b* are replaced by a reddish magnesian spar. The under side of the specimen is deeply concave, and the peripheral margin is so convex as to resemble a cylinder coiled into a ring. The aperture in one specimen of *R. Jonesi* is rounded, and resembles the umbilicus of an apple.

The figures given by different authors of foreign species show a considerable range of variation in the general form, and apparently also in the structure of the body-wall. The details given in this paper have been made out principally by the study of numerous specimens of *R. occidentalis*, which is undoubtedly congeneric with *R. Neptuni*, the typical form of the genus. In others, such as *Tetragonis sulcata* and *T. parvipora* (Eichwald), there appears to be a transition to species in which the ectorhin was a soft coriaceous integument, not distinctly plated, although connected with the interior by tubes or spicula. The genus *Tetragonis*, instead of becoming obsolete, might be retained for some of the species which have a structure different from that of *R. Neptuni.*

As to the zoological rank of *Receptaculites* there yet remains much diversity of opinion. At the present time the most ably supported view is that which places the genus in the Foraminifera near *Orbitolites*. Seen in this light, the diagram at the head of this paper would represent the soft and not the hard parts of the animal. If this be the true interpretation, then we must suppose that outside of the ectorhin there was a layer of shell, and another layer covering the endorhin, or lining the great central cavity. All the space between the tubes was also a compact mass of shelly substance similar to that of the Foraminifera. But not a vestige of any such shell has ever been discovered. The space between the tubes is invariably filled with the same kind of rock as that in which the specimens are imbedded, while all that is, in this paper, described as constituting the skeleton is in the same mineral condition as are the hard parts of the corals, crinoids and molluscs found buried in the same beds. In the ordinary limestone, whenever the solid portions of the other fossils are replaced either by calcareous spar or silica, or partly by one and partly by the other, the skeleton of *Receptaculites* is always found connverted into the same mineral substances. And again in the magnesian limestones, where the hard parts of fossils are, in general, totally removed, so that the cavities once occupied by them remain empty, we find *Receptaculites* in the same condition. We have not the tubes themselves, but only the cylindrical perforations in the rock which they at one time filled, while the existence of the stolons is only indicated by grooves such as those represented in figs. 359, 362. These facts seeem to prove clearly that the space between the tubes was not filled with shell substance, but either empty, or entirely, or partly full of soft matter, which was immediately dissipated after the death of the animal, and its place occupied by the soft mud in or on which the creature lived. Were it otherwise, we would now find the space in question a compact mass of calcareous spar or amorphous silex, while the tubes (or cells as they would be in that case) might be filled with limestone. In the magnesian specimens the ectorhin seldom, if ever, remains; and in species with flat plates the form (of the plates) can rarely be made out, the only markings on the surface being the grooves of the stolons. But where the plates were deeply concave the position of the sutures is indicated by more or less strongly elevated ridges enclosing rhomboidal depressed spaces with a tube cavity in the centre. Fig. 362 represents a fragment of *R. Canadensis* in that state of preservation. The rhomboids in this case are not the plates themselves, but only their impressions. In describing such specimens, the tubes are sometimes spoken of as having rhomboidal openings, but this is an error; the tubes when perfect, as can be proved by hundreds of specimens, are not open at all, but completely closed, at one end by the ectorhin and at the other by the endorhin. They all, however, communicate with each other through the stolons and endorhinal canals.

Were the tubes of *Receptaculites* to be closely crowded together so that their walls would everywhere be in contact, and no space between them, then the structure would be similar to that of *Orbitolites*, but with the system of connecting stolons arranged on a different plan. The genus would then also closely resemble *Dactylopora;* but I do not yet see that the evidence is sufficient to prove clearly that the tubes are strictly the homologues of the cells of any group of the Foraminifera. They appear to me to be more nearly related to the connecting spicula of the Spongidæ. Each tube with its cylindrical shaft, and plate at each extremity, resembles not remotely a birotulate spiculum. Or it might perhaps with more probability be described as consisting of two spicula united at their points. Thus the ectorhinal plate with the four stolons may be a peculiar form of the foliato-peltate spicula, of which many different kinds are figured by Bowerbank. The cylindrical shaft may be a spiculum approaching the acuate or acerate varieties with its point inserted into the nucleus of the foliato-peltate spiculum. Most sponge spicula are hollow; and we know how often it happens in the structure of the animal kingdom that organs may at one time subserve one function, and elsewhere a very different function. The cylindrical cavity, which in the spicula of the ordinary sponges seems to be functionless, may in *Receptaculites* be transformed into a canal for the transmission of fluids. But although the cavities of all the tubes in *Receptaculites* communicate with each other through the endorhinal canals, and perhaps through the stolons also, they may not constitute a canal-system. The so-called tubes are extremely slender, and may be solid in some species.

On comparison it will be found that the general form of *Receptaculites* and structure of its body-wall are almost precisely that of the seed-like body that plays so important a part in the development of *Spongilla.* This consists of a small ovate or spherical sac with an aperture on one side leading into the cavity within. The enclosing wall consists of a coriaceous membrane on the outside of which there are arranged, perpendicularly to the surface, numerous small birotulate spicula, exactly as the tubes of *Receptaculites* are arranged on the endorhin. The outer extremities of these spicula give off at right angles a number of small spines corresponding to the stolons above figured. These spines coalesce, and (if I understand the figures rightly) become connected together, so that they form by their union a plate similar to that of *Receptaculites*, only that it is hexagonal. The plates of all the spicula enlarge until all come into contact, and thus an outer tesselated integument corresponding to the ectorhin is formed. In this stage a section through the seed-like body shews an inner integument (or endorhin), and an outer plated integument (or ectorhin), the two being separated and at the same time connected by the pillar-like cylindrical shafts of the spicula representing the tubes of *Receptaculites.* The space between the tubes is, according to some authors, filled with a gelatinous silicious matter; but Bowerbank says he did not detect this substance in the specimens examined by him. This little sac or cell is a *Receptaculites* in miniature, and it is also one of the embryonic stages of a sponge. When we consider that the full grown and adult individuals of many of the long extinct tribes of animals never attained in their structure a more advanced organization than that exhibited by the embryos of orders living at the present day, it does not seem surprising that we should find in the palæozoic rocks a sponge which although often of large size, never became more highly developed, than is the recent genus *Spongilla*, when it has only advanced to the sac-like stage above described. It is not intended to assert here positively that *Receptaculites* is a sponge, or to determine the question of its zoological rank one way or the other, but only to direct attention to such peculiarities in its structure as appear to me worthy of being taken into account in the investigation.

RECEPTACULITES JONESI. (N. sp.)

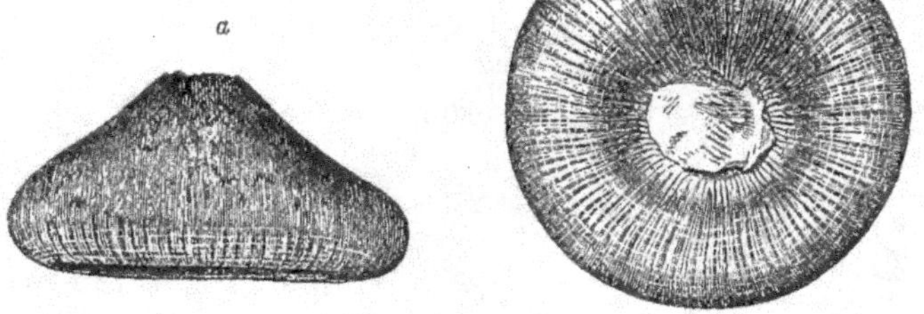

Fig. 365.

Fig. 365.—*Receptaculites Jonesi.* *a*, side view; *b*, view of the base. Owing to the peculiar condition of preservation, the grooves of the stolons are imperfectly seen in this specimen. They are well shown in the fragments of other individuals collected in the same bed with the one here figured.

Description.—The specimens of this species that have been as yet collected are small, turbinate, or depressed conical bodies, from one to two inches across, and from six lines to one inch in height. The broadest extremity, supposed to be the base, is usually circular, sometimes ovate, gently concave, and with an obtusely rounded margin all round, the thickness of which is from three to five lines. The smaller extremity, or the upper side, is a depressed cone, with an apical angle of 110° to 130°, with an irregularly rounded truncated apex. The grooves of the radial stolons, as shown in the cast of the interior of the ectorhin, radiate straight outwards to the margin, and run upwards over the rounded edge. There are here (on the peripheral edge) four or five grooves in a width of three lines. The grooves of the cyclical stolons are closer together, there being about nine in the width of three lines. From the margin to the apex both systems of grooves become more crowded together, and, at the apex, the ectorhin appears to have been of a somewhat pliable, coriaceous integument. At the apex there are indications, in all the specimens which have this part preserved, of a small irregularly rounded aperture, which is usually depressed, in form, somewhat like the umbilicus of an apple.

Several specimens have been collected which show the internal cavity. It varies slightly in form in different individuals, but is, in general, bell-shaped, as represented in fig. 363. (*ante*, p. 385.)

None of the specimens yet seen have the ectorhin preserved, and the form of the plates is not, therefore, yet known. Dedicated to (the eminent English naturalist) T. RUPERT JONES.

Locality and Formation.—Cape Gaspé, in the upper part of the Lower Helderberg group, in beds holding a mixture of Upper Silurian and Devonian fossils.

Collector.—Prof. R. Bell.

CLASS UNCERTAIN.

Genus PASCEOLUS, Billings.

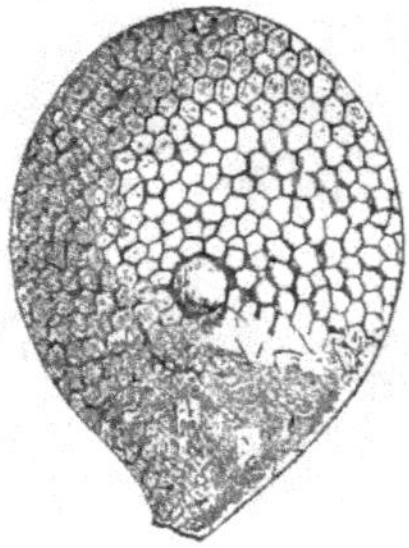

Fig. 366.

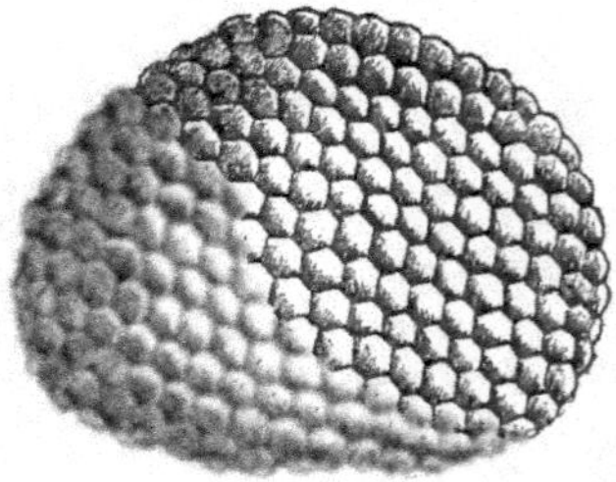

Fig. 367.

Fig. 366.—*P. Halli.* From the Middle Silurian, Anticosti.
Fig. 367.—*P. globosus,* Trenton limestone, Ottawa.

The fossils of this genus are of an ovate or globular form covered with an integument of small polygonal plates (?) and with one or more circular apertures. Two species are at present known to occur in the Silurian rocks of Canada, both of which are above figured.

P. Halli is of an ovate form, from one to two inches in length and about one-fourth less, in width. At one end there is a narrow prolongation which, most probably, constituted the pedicle by which the body was attached to the bottom. No trace of any other point of attachment can be seen; and it is almost certain, therefore, that this smaller extremity is the base. A little below the mid-height of the body there is a small circular elevation which appears to mark the place of an orifice; but as the integument is not preserved in this part, it cannot, at present, be positively determined whether there was an aperture here or not. All that can be said is that there appears to have been an orifice where this elevation occurs. The specimens collected are all casts of the interior, but of the one figured a portion of the integument remains attached to the matrix. It is about one-third of a line in thickness, of a translucent, horny color, the surface covered with minute corrugated wrinkles just visible to the naked eye. No sutures can be distinguished, and the form of the plates can only be made out as so many obscure convexities on the outside. But where the integument is removed the cast shows the place of the sutures most distinctly, and that the plates were deeply concave on the inside. The polygonal spaces, in the above figure, represent only the outlines of the casts of the inner surfaces of the plates, and, as those are deeply concave, of course the whole surface of the cast of the fossil is covered with small convex elevations. In some places these are so exceedingly convex that they present the appearance of a mass of small globular cells just so much pressed together as to produce the hexagonal outline along the boundary of contact. Many of these elevations have a small round knob in the centre with an obscure ridge radiating to the middle of each of the sides, where they meet similar ridges from the other convexities. These markings are very obscurely developed, and in some places cannot be seen at all.

P. globosus only differs from *P. Halli* in being larger and of a spherical shape. The specimens are sometimes three inches across, but the common size is about two inches. They are, usually, more or less compressed and distorted, in general of a hemispherical shape, the base flattened as if the body had been a soft globular sac of matter which had settled down by its own weight. They are, however, occasionally found of a nearly spherical form. On one side (the flattened side) of a specimen in the cabinet of Dr. J. A. Grant, of Ottawa, there is a small elevation which may have been the point of attachment. No orifices have yet been made out, but it must be observed that no specimen has been collected in which the whole of the surface can be examined. None that I have seen have a vestige of the integument remaining. The plates (or rather their impressions) are, in these specimens, for the greater part, strongly convex and precisely like those of *P. Halli*, only larger. In some they are partly concave and partly convex or flat. Individuals also occur which have them either convex, all flat, or all concave. Yet as these occur together in the same localities, I think them all one species. They have, as yet, been found only at the city of Ottawa in the Trenton limestone.

In one piece of shale scarcely a yard square, I collected about fifty individuals, but although they occur thus abundantly in certain spots, good specimens are exceedingly rare.

This genus was first described by me in the Report of the Geological Survey of Canada for 1857, p. 342, and placed among the fossils of uncertain class. The two species above figured are also there described. They have been on exhibition in the cases of our museum for the last ten years, and have been examined by a great many of the naturalists of all countries. But I do not think we yet know to what class they belong. *P. Halli* and *Ischadites Canadensis* are figured on p. 309 of the Geology of Canada, as members of the *Tunicata*. The latter, however, is a true *Receptaculites*. It is barely possible that the former may be a tunicate, but we have no positive evidence that it is.

Eichwald, in his Lethaea Rossica, has described and figured two species, *Cyclocrinus Spaskii* and *C. exilis*, which appear to me to be either congeneric with our two, or, at least, to belong to the same family. Both of Eichwald's species are small globular bodies covered with hexagonal or pentagonal plates. The plates of *C. Spaskii* have a tubercle in the centre and a number of obscure rounded ridges radiating to the sides. He says there is a small oral orifice on one side, and on the side opposite, a rudimentary pedicle. One of his figured specimens is covered with a tubular incrustation consisting of small cells which he considers to be a part of the integument itself. It may be, however, a coral. A fragment of one of the specimens of *P. Halli* from Anticosti is incrusted in precisely the same manner with what I take to be a species of *Stenopora*. Eichwald places his genus among the Cystidea; but the more general characters, such as a jointed crinoidal column, the arms or pinnulæ, and the peculiar orifices which characterise all true Cystideans, are not forthcoming. It is barely possible that his view may be the correct one.

The fossil called *Sphæronites tesselatus* (Phillips), from the English Devonian rocks has the surface covered with hexagonal plates, and resembles, in general aspect, a species of *Pasceolus*. Mr. Pengelly has figured a specimen in the Geologist, vol iv, which shows the interior, covered with a net-work of vertical and horizontal ribs, giving the appearance of the inner surface of the specimen of *Receptaculites calciferus* above noticed. He proposes a new generic name, *Sphærospongia*, for it. If the specimen figured by him be truly of the same species as that described by Phillips, it would seem that an internal structure like that of *Receptaculites* is not inconsistent with an integument of hexagonal instead of quadrilateral plates. I do not see, however, how the net-work figured by Mr. Pengelly can be made to fit hexagonal plates in the way that the squares formed by the stolons of *Receptaculites* are adjusted.

M. M. Edwards and Haime have referred Eichwald's genus *Cyclocrinus* to the *Zoantharia*. Whether they are right or not with regard to the Russian species, I can most confidently assert that *Pasceolus* is not a coral. It may be allied to *Receptaculites*, but its true zoological position is quite undecided at present.

ECHINODERMATA.

PETRASTER BELLULUS. (N. sp.)

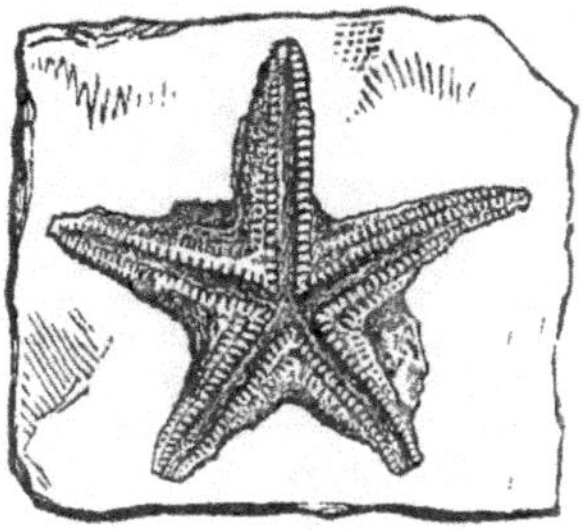

Fig. 368.

Fig. 368.—*Petraster bellulus.* Under side.

Description.—Deeply stellate, about eighteen lines across; disc five lines wide; width of rays, at the base, half the width of the disc, uniformly tapering to their extremities; ambulacral grooves, narrow and deep, with about thirty adambulacral plates on each side. These plates are strongly convex and nearly square. Outside of these there is a row of marginal plates, which appear to extend to the extremities of the rays, but on this point there is doubt, as the specimen is not perfect. There appear to be one or two small disc plates between the marginal and adambulacral plates just outside of the oral angles.

Locality and Formation.—Township of Grimsby; in the Niagara shale.

Collector.—Johnson Pettit, Esq., Grimsby, C. W.

CYCLOCYSTOIDES HURONENSIS. (N. sp.)

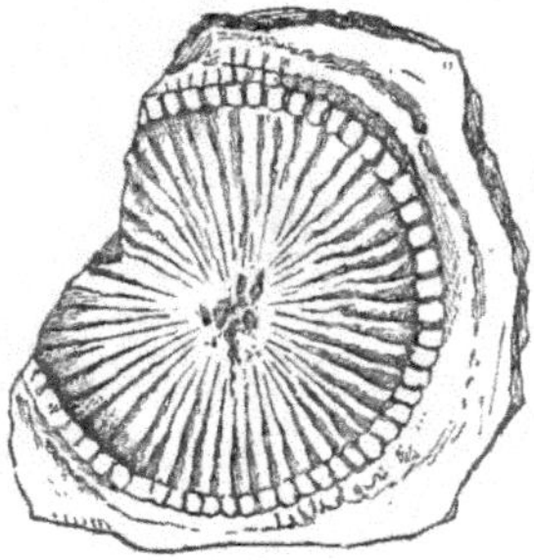

Fig. 369.

Fig. 369.—*Cyclocystoides Huronensis.*

Description.—The only specimen of this species that has been collected is sixteen lines across, and had, when perfect, about sixty marginal plates, of which forty-six are preserved.

It closely resembles both *G. Halli* and *G. Davisii*, but has a larger number of marginal plates, the former having thirty-six and the latter about fifty.

Locality and Formation.—Rabbit Island, Lake Huron; Hudson River group.

Collector.—Prof. R. Bell.

GASTEROPODA.

Chiton Canadensis.

Fig. 370.

Fig. 371.

Fig. 370.—*Chiton Canadensis.* *a*, view of the upper side of one of the terminal plates; *b*, side view of the same; *c*, underside.
Fig. 371.—*Metoptoma Montrealensis.*

Description.—The terminal plates of this species are, in form, like one-half of a hollow cone with an acute apex. The anterior margin (assuming this to be the posterior plate) is straight in one specimen and slightly undulated in another, and is so convex as to form an uniform arch equal, very nearly, to a semicircle. The anterior angles are narrowly rounded. The upper side in one specimen has an obscure lobe along the middle, and is covered with fine striæ parallel to the anterior margin. Just in front of the apex, on the under side, there is a thin plate, as shown in fig. *a*.

Locality and Formation.—Pauquette Rapids, on the River Ottawa; Black River limestone.

Collector.—E. Billings.

Metoptoma Montrealensis. (N. sp.)

Fig. 371.

Description.—Acutely conical; apex a little in advance of the centre; base obtusely elliptical, the antero-posterior diameter a little the longest. On a side view the outline is gently convex from the apex to the posterior, and concave to the anterior margin. Surface, when perfect with fine vertical striæ running from the apex to the margin, and with both fine engirdling striæ and obscure undulations of growth parallel to the base. In most of the specimens the fine striæ are not perceptible.

This species varies greatly in the elevation. In some the height is only about one-half the width of the base, while in others the height and width are equal, with every intermediate stage.

Locality and Formation.—Montreal; Chazy limestone.

Collector.—T. C. Weston.

11.—*Species from the Quebec Group, published in* 1860.

In order that descriptions of all the species of trilobites of the Lévis formation may appear in this volume, it is thought advisable to republish those described in the Canadian Naturalist and Geologist. This will be found to be convenient for those who may not have access to the volumes of that journal.

(*From the Canadian Naturalist and Geologist, vol. v, August* 1860.)

" On examining the specimens recently collected at this locality (Point Lévis), I find some evidence of several groups of species, each occurring in a rock somewhat different in appearance from that which contains the others. It does not seem improbable, judging from the fact that all the three varieties of limestone occur in close proximity to each other, that these species may yet be found more or less intermingled in the same beds, but for the present it is best to keep them separate. I shall designate the rocks simply as limestones Nos. 1, 2, 3, and 4."

The genera collected in each are as follows:

The species were collected by Sir W. E. Logan, the late John Head, Esq., Dr. T. S. Hunt, Prof. R. Bell, and J. Richardson. To save space I shall not repeat the locality and formation after each description.

Agnostus Americanus, (N. sp.)

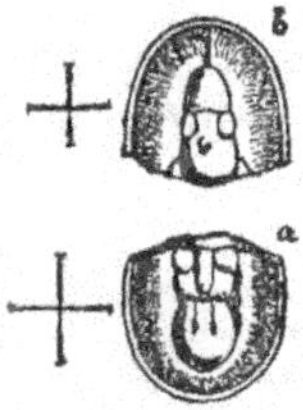

Fig. 372.

Fig. 373.

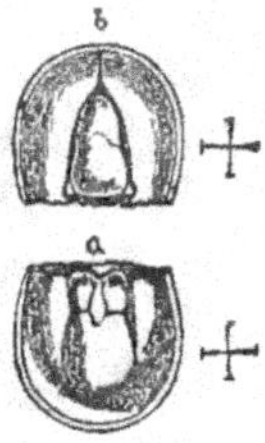

Fig. 374.

Fig. 372.—*Agnostus Americanus*; *a*, the tail; *b*, the head? Both a little magnified.
Fig. 373.—*Agnostus Orion*. Natural size.
Fig. 374.—*Agnostus Canadensis*; *a*, the tail; *b*, the head? Both magnified.

Note.—*All the figures in this article are of the natural size, unless otherwise specified.*

Description.—Head oblong semi-oval, rather strongly convex, most elevated at the posterior one-fourth of the length, thence descending with a depressed convex slope in all directions to the sides and front; margin with a very narrow projecting border. The glabella is elongate oval; width, one-third that of the whole head; length, rather more than two-thirds the length of the head. It has two transverse furrows which completely or partially divide it into three segments. The anterior furrow extends all across at one-third, or a little more, of the length from the front. The posterior furrow is interrupted in the middle and is only distinctly seen on each side, penetrating one-third the width, while its position is a little in advance of the posterior third of the length of the glabella. The space between the two inner extremities of the posterior furrows is occupied by a low conical tubercle, with the apex directed backwards. At each side of the glabella at the posterior extremity there is a small triangular lobe. The glabella is defined all round by a very narrow groove, just distinctly visible to the naked eye, and from the apex a similar groove runs straight to the middle of the front margin. The surface is ornamented by from fifteen to twenty irregular, slightly impressed, radiating rugose striæ.

In the pygidium the posterior segment of the median lobe is equal to the two anterior in size; and there are no triangular lobes at the anterior margin. The tubercle is well developed, and its backward sloping apex reaches nearly to the posterior furrow. It seems to divide the two anterior segments, so that each has a sub-quadrate lobe on each side. The surface is striated like the head. Two heads and one tail have been found.

Length of the tail three lines and one-fourth; of the largest head, three lines, and of the other, two lines and three-fourths. The width is about equal to, or a little less than the length.

The contour appears to be not a regular semi-oval; the sides and terminal margins being only gently convex, and the angles broadly rounded.

The structure of the tail is similar to that both of *A. tardus* (Barrande) and *A. glabratus* (Angelin); but in these species the median lobe of the head is smooth, and consists of one plate only, without furrows.

It may be that the tail above figured belongs to a different species, but even if that should be the case, it is specifically distinct from *A. tardus* and *A. glabratus*, for these are both smooth, while ours is striated like *A. exsculptus* (Angelin), and besides the proportions of the parts are sufficiently different to be of specific value, especially when the character of the surface is taken into account. *A. tardus* and *A. glabratus* both belong to the upper part of the Lower Silurian. *A. exsculptus* to Angelin's Region B, which is the upper division of the Primordial Zone in Sweden,

In Limestone, No. 1.

Agnostus Orion. (N. sp.)

Fig. 373.

Description.—Length and breadth about equal, sub-circular, convex, a very narrow margin all round, glabella not quite two thirds the whole length very convex, a transverse furrow at one third the length from the apex, a small triangular tubercle at each side next the posterior edge ; no tubercle visible on the top of the glabella. A fissure from the apex of the glabella to the anterior margin. Length two lines.

This species only differs from *A pisiformis* as figured by Salter in the 3rd Edition of Siluria by having the glabella proportionally shorter.

Limestone, No. 1. In No. 2 there are two specimens of an *Agnostus* which resemble this species, but more are required to decide whether they are identical or not.

Agnostus Canadensis. (N. sp.)

Fig. 374, *a. b.*

Description.—Head, obtusely oblong, semi-oval ; width, a little greater than the length ; a concave border nearly as wide as the glabella all round. Glabella in width, less than half the width of the head, and in length a little more than two-thirds the length of the head: a triangular tubercle on each side of the neck, and a transverse furrow a little in advance of the mid-length ; the tubercle is obscure, and appears to be indicated by the small indentation forward in the middle of the transverse furrow.

The specimen represented by Fig. 374 *a*, is provided with a tubercle, but I cannot see in which direction the apex is directed, and consequently am unable to say whether it is a head or a tail. It has the broad margin of Fig. 374 *b*, and I think therefore it belongs to the same species. The segment next the thoracic extremity is a little less than one-third the whole length, and about one-third the whole width. The posterior segment is large and convex, extending quite to the concave border, where it is full one-half wider than it is at the suture between it and the smaller segment. The tubercle is situated in the transverse suture, and makes a small indentation in the edge of the larger segment.

Length of the specimens, about two lines.

Limestone, No. 1.

Conocephalites Zenkeri. (N. sp.)

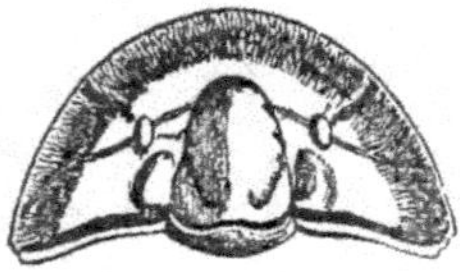

Fig. 375.

Fig. 375.—*Conocephalites Zenkeri.*

Description.—Length apparently about two inches. Head very convex nearly semi-circular, with a strongly elevated thin sharp margin all round the front and sides, and just within this a wide deep uniformly concave furrow, the width of which is equal to about one third the length of the glabella. The posterior margin is strengthened by the neck segment which extends the whole width of the head, and becomes much elevated on approaching the outer angles. Glabella conical, very convex, most elevated at about the mid-length, with a well defined neck furrow, the posterior lateral furrows directed obliquely forwards at an angle of 45° with the longitudinal axis of the body, their inner extremities separated from each other by full one third the width of the glabella; the posterior lobes sub-triangular, their anterior angles situated at nearly one third the length of the glabella forward excluding the neck furrow and segment; the middle lateral furrows represented by a small depression or indentation on each side situated on a line drawn across the head passing through posterior half of the eyes; in front of these a much smaller indentation on each side representing the anterior furrows. The eyes are small and conical, situated on a line crossing the glabella at one half the whole length of the head, their distance from the glabella equal to one-third the width of the neck segment; ocular ridge extending from the eye forward to a point situated a little in advance of the anterior lateral indentation or furrow of the glabella. From the eye a strong ridge runs outwards to the margin of the head in two of the specimens, but in another it is not seen. Between the eye and the posterior margin, and situated near the posterior lobe, on each side is a large sub-semicircular tubercle. This elevation is very slight in the small specimens. The surface of the glabella and cheeks adjacent thereto are apparently smooth, but the whole of the concave border around the head is ornamented with fine rugose striæ distinctly visible to the naked eye.

Length of head in largest specimen seen eight lines; length of glabella six lines; width of head fifteen lines; width of glabella four lines; distance between the eyes six lines.

Thorax and pygidium unknown. I have not ascertained whether the posterior angles of the head are rounded or produced into spines.

Limestone No. 1.

Genus DIKELOCEPHALUS. Owen.

In the species which I have referred to this genus, the general form and aspect of the glabella and pygidium and the course of the facial suture are the same as in *D. Minnesotensis* the type of the genus, specimens of which I have before me from the sandstone of the Western States. From numerous fragments of *D. Oweni* exhibiting the underside of the head, I have ascertained that the facial suture does not separate the cheeks from each other by cutting the fold of the margin. The head is therefore composed of three pieces only,—the glabella, hypostoma and united cheeks. This separates the genus from *Proetus*, some species of which, such as *P. striatus* (Barrande) have an expanded front margin and a spinose pygidium very like those of *D. magnificus*. The head of *Proetus* consists of five pieces. The hypostoma found associated with our specimens is much like that of *Proetus*, and it is also not unlike that of *Ogygia*. According to the figure givin in SILURIA, plate III, fig. 2, representing the sub-marginal fold of the cephalic shield, and the hypostoma attached thereto of *Ogygia Buchii*, the structure of the head of *Ogygia* must be the same as that of *Dikelocephalus*. The affinities of the two genera are still further indicated by the form of the glabella.

DIKELOCEPHALUS MAGNIFICUS.

Description.—Eight or nine inches in length. Head large with a short broad obtusely conical depressed convex glabella, in front of which there is a broad flat margin with from five to eight obscure radiating ridges. The neck furrow is represented by an obscure shallow groove which is visible in the middle two-thirds of the width, but dies out before reaching the sides of the glabella. In front of this there are from one to three shallow pits or faint depressions on each side of the median line representing the glabella furrows. A line drawn across the head at one-third the length from the posterior margin would pass through the centres of the eyes nearly. The eyes are annular about one-sixth the whole length of the head, situated their own length from the posterior margin and with their centres about the same distance from the side of the glabella. The facial suture runs from the inner anterior corner of the eye forwards and outwards at an angle of about 45° to the longitudinal axis of the body

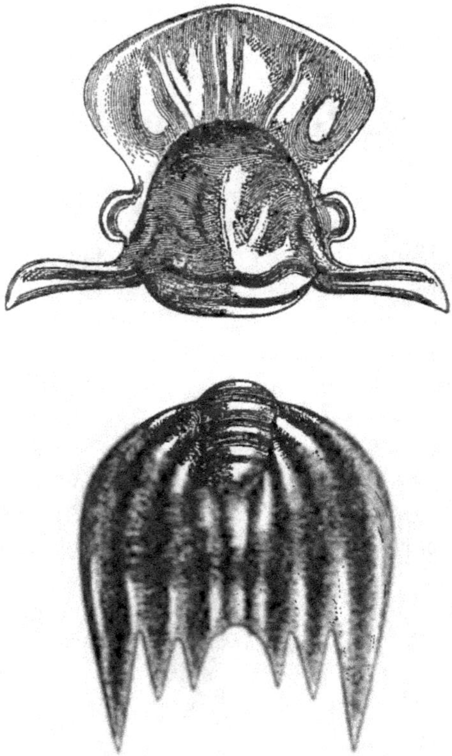

Fig. 376.

Fig. 376.—Glabella and pygidium of *D. magnificus*.

until it crosses a line drawn through the eye parallel with the axis of the body, and having gained a point situated outside of this line at a distance from it equal to the length of the eye or thereabout, it curves inward and reaches the front margin at a point somewhere near the line. It then appears to run round the margin. Behind the eye its course is, after a short inward and backward curve, directly outwards nearly parallel with the posterior furrow apparently one half the width of the cheek when it curves back, and cuts the posterior margin before reaching the angle. On each side of the glabella nearly opposite but a little behind the position of the eye there is an obscure rounded elongated prominence.

Judging from several detached cheeks the posterior part of the head must be very wide and the angles produced into moderately long triangular spines.

The pygidium is somewhat fan-shaped, the posterior margin terminating in six triangular points or spines, the outer ones of which are the longest and the inner ones diminishing in length so as to produce a semicircular emargination for the posterior outline. The greatest width of the pygidium is at about one-third its total length from the front measuring to the extremity of the longest spine. In front of a line drawn across at this place the contour is nearly semicircular, but behind the line the sides are straight or only gently convex, and somewhat parallel, slightly converging towards each other. The main body of the axis is about one-fourth the total length, convex conical and with four shallow concave transverse grooves; four ribs in each of the side lobes besides a rudimentary ridge along the middle being a continuation of the axis. The surface is marked by fine fissure-like undulating lines.

The pleuræ which seem to belong to this species are broad, flat, falcate, and with a moderately strong groove running obliquely nearly their whole length.

Judging from the form of the three pygidia figured by Angelin on Plate 41 of the Palæontologia Scandinavica, it appears probable that this species connects *Dikelocephalus* with *Centropleura*, a genus which occurs in the base of the Lower Silurian of Sweden, in Regio B and C of Angelin. It is perhaps an extreme form, but the course of the facial suture and characters of the glabella are the same as they are in *Dikelocephalus*. The pygidium differs from *D. Minnesotensis* in having fewer ribs and a greater number of spines, but this difference is not of itself, I think, of generic value.

Limestone No. 1.

DIKELOCEPHALUS PLANIFRONS. (N. sp.)

Fig. 377.

Description.—Head with a broad smooth margin in front, the width of which is about equal to the width of the glabella: the latter oblong conical,

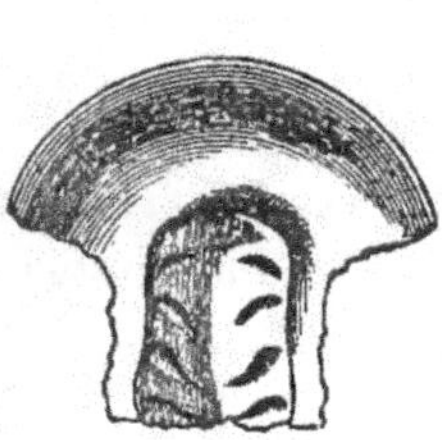

Fig. 377.

Fig. 378.

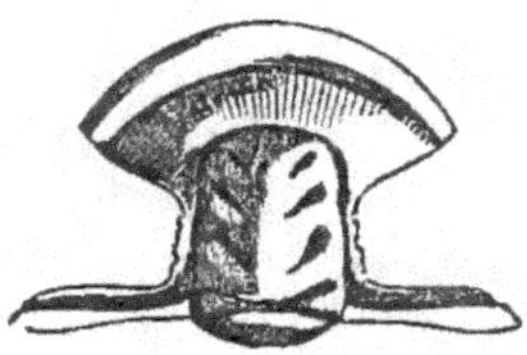

Fig. 379.

Fig. 377.—*D. planifrons.*
Fig. 378.—*D. Belli.*
Fig. 379.—*D. Oweni.*

rather flat, most elevated along the median line, broadly rounded in front, its sides nearly straight and sub-parallel, slightly converging from behind forwards. On each side of the median line there are three or four obscure depressions which represent the glabellar furrows. The length of the glabella appears to be about once and a half its width at the neck segment. Eyes, cheeks, thorax and pygidum unknown. Length of largest head seen, twelve lines; length of glabella, seven lines; width of glabella at base five lines, at front margin four lines and a half.

The head of this specis differs from *D. magnificus* in having a more elongated and depressed glabella with the wide border in front smooth instead of ornamented with radiating ridges.

Limestone, No. 1.

DIKELOCEPHALUS OWENI. (N. sp.)

Fig. 379.

Description.—Head with a broad punctured and striated margin in front of the glabella; the latter oblong conical depressed, most elevated along the median line, and with from two to four obscure depressions on each side, representing the glabellar furrows. The front of the glabella is broadly rounded, the sides straight or nearly so, sub-parallel or slightly converging from behind forwards; the posterior margin straight in the middle, turned forward at the sides. At the base of the glabella there is an obscure transverse furrow, and I am not sure whether this should be regarded as the posterior glabellar groove or the neck furrow. The front of the head is strengthened by a depressed convex rim just within which there is a curved row of punctures, four or five in one line. From these punctures fine somewhat flexuous striæ converge towards the front of the glabella. Eyes, cheeks, thorax and pygidium unknown.

Length of head of a specimen which appears to be of the average size ten lines; length of glabella, seven lines; width of glabella at neck segment five lines and a half, and at front margin four lines and a half; width of the marginal rim, one line and a half.

The depressions representing the glabellar furrows are sometimes obsolete, and sometimes only one or two are visible on each side.

One of the specimens has the anterior striated margin proportionally one fourth narrower than the above and only five punctures in the width of one line. The glabella is smooth and not narrowed in front. I do not at present think, however, that these differences are of specific importance.

In another specimen where the crust is preserved, the punctures are scarcely visible, but where it is removed they are distinct.

Dedicated to Dr. D. D. OWEN, whose extensive geological researches in the Western States have been of such great service to science.

Limestone, No. 1.

DIKELOCEPHALUS BELLI. (N. sp.)

Fig. 378.

Description.—Head semicircular, the width apparently twice the length or a little more. Front margin surrounded by a narrow convex rim, distant about its own width from the front of the glabella. The latter is obtusely oblong, conical, rather convex, well defined all round by the narrow groove of the dorsal furrows, the sides nearly parallel, straight or nearly so, the front rounded. The neck furrow extends entirely across, nearly straight in the middle third and directed obliquely forward at an angle of about 45° at the outer third on each side. In front of this, two oblique glabellar furrows on each side, their inner extremities separated by about one-third the width of the glabella, forming three lobes of nearly equal size. The eyes appear to be situated opposite the second pair of furrows from the front, and to be distant from the glabella about one third the width of the neck segment.

Length of head of medium size, six lines and a half; length of glabella five lines and a half; width of the same at base four lines; a little narrower towards the front; width of marginal rim half a line; width of space between the marginal rim and the front of the glabella, half a line. Surface smooth.

Cheeks, eyes, thorax and pygidium unknown. Dedicated to Mr. ROBERT BELL, the discoverer of the genus in the Canadian rocks.

Limestone, No. 1.

DIKELOCEPHALUS MEGALOPS. (N. sp.)

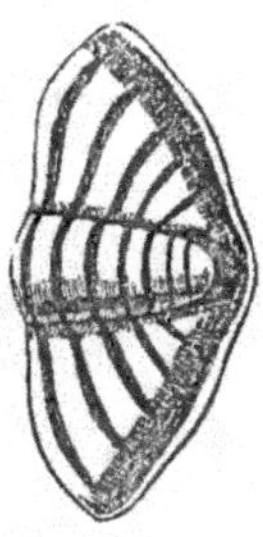

Fig. 382.

Fig. 380.

Fig. 381.

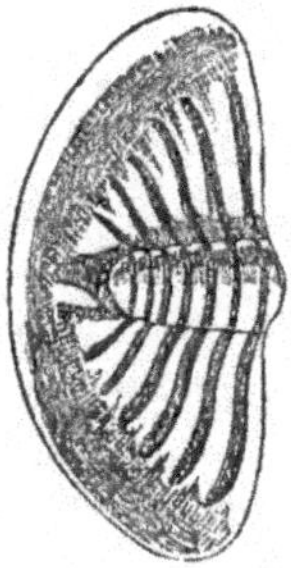

Fig. 383.

Fig. 380.—*D. megalops.*
Fig. 381.—*D. cristatus.*
Fig. 382, 383.—*Pygidia* common in Limestone No. 1.

Description.—Head apparently semicircular; anterior margin strengthened by a narrow convex rim a little more than its own width from the front of the glabella, just within which is a curved row of punctures with fine striæ as in *D. Oweni.* Glabella elongate conical, depressed convex, front rounded, sides nearly straight, slightly converging from behind forward Neck furrow straight in the middle, turned slightly forwards towards the ends. In front of this, two other short furrows on each side dividing the glabella into three lobes of which the anterior is the largest; the posterior furrows sometimes obscurely connected on the median line their outer extremities directed forwards at an angle of 45° with the longitudinal axis of the body; the anterior pair nearly at right angles, but sloping a little forwards, their inner extremities not connected. On the front lobe there appear to be indications of a third pair of furrows on one of the specimens. The eyes are semi-annular, nearly half the whole length of the head, their anterior corners a little in advance of the outer extremities of the anterior glabellar furrow; their centres distant from the sides of the glabella, one-third the width of the neck segment, their upper and lower angles, half that distance. Surface, except the striated front margin apparently smooth.

Cheeks, thorax and pygidium unknown.

Length of largest head seen five lines and a half; of glabella four lines and a half; width of glabella at neck segment three lines and a half nearly, and at front furrows three lines.

Limestone, No. 1.

DIKELOCEPHALUS CRISTATUS. (N. sp.)

Fig. 381.

Description.—Small, head apparently semi-circular; front margin with a strong rim abruptly elevated on its posterior edge and thence descending with a flat slope to the anterior edge, distant about its own width from the front of the glabella, with a row of punctures as in *D. Oweni.* Glabella oblong, front and sides somewhat straight, anterior angles rounded, neck segment and furrow well defined, no glabellar furrows. The glabella just in front of the neck furrow is abruptly elevated into a sharp rounded roof-shaped ridge from which it descends with a flat or gently concave slope to the front and lateral margins. Eyes very large, full one half the whole length of the head, their posterior angles close to the glabella at the neck furrow; thence they curve outwards so that their centres are distant from the sides of the glabella rather more than one third the width of the neck segment, thence more gradually curving inwards they reach the sides of the glabella (nearly) at a point a little in advance of its length.

Length of head in largest specimen seen four lines; of glabella about three lines; width of glabella at base two lines, a little narrower in front. Surface with the exception of the striated and punctured front, apparently smooth.

Limestone, No. 1.

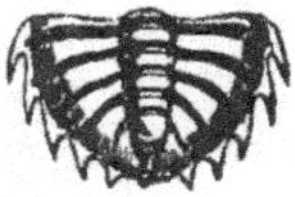

Fig. 384.

Fig. 384.—The pygidium represented by Fig. 384, appears to belong to a species of *Dikelocephalus*, but the small fragment of stone in which it occurs resembles Limestone No. 2, in which no recognisable fragments of that genus have been found.

Genera.—ARIONELLUS (Barrande) and MENOCEPHALUS (Owen).

These two genera seem to be closely related, and I shall therefore notice them collectively. In *Arionellus* the glabella is cylindrical or sub-conical with three or four lateral furrows. The facial suture proceeds from the eye forward with a slight inward inclination to the front margin which it cuts on a line drawn between the eye and the glabella parallel with the axis of the body. Behind the eye it cuts the posterior margin at a point situated on a line drawn between that organ and the outer angle of the head. In the thorax of *A. ceticephalus* there are from 7 to 16 segments according to the age of the individual. The pygidium is small.

The head (all that is known) of *Menocephalus* only differs from *Arionellus* in having the glabella exceedingly convex. Owen discovered the glabella and a portion of the cheek plate, but none of the other parts. He describes the former as being circular, highly arched, hemispherical and pustulated. Judging from this description and the figure given by the author, and also from the aspect of the associated fossils, it appears to me highly probable that the species which I have called *M. globosus* is not only congeneric with Owen's *M. Minnesotensis* but that it is closely allied thereto. *M. Sedgewicki* cannot be separated generically from *M. globosus*, and this latter leads us through *A. subclavatus* to *A. cylindricus*.

This latter appears to me to be an *Arionellus*. The specimens are too imperfect to enable me to prove whether or not our four species belong to two distinct genera or one only. I shall place the two most convex forms in *Menocephalus*, and the other two in *Arionellus*.

Arionellus cylindricus. (N. sp.)

Fig. 385.

a

Fig. 386.

Fig. 385.—*Arionellus cylindricus.*
Fig. 386.—*Arionellus subclavatus*; *a*, side view of the glabella.

Description.—Glabella sub-cylindrical slightly narrowed from behind forwards, the sides nearly straight and separated from the very prominent cheeks by a deep furrow; the front obtusely rounded or nearly straight. The neck furrow is deep and rounded and the neck segment well defined but apparently not very prominent. The posterior glabellar furrow is well defined all across, parallel with the neck furrow for half the width of the glabella and then directed obliquely forward on each side at an angle of 45°; it is about its own width distant from the neck furrow. The next furrows forward are situated a little in advance of the mid-length of the glabella; they are slighty oblique and their inner extremities are separated by about one-third the width of the glabella. In front of these are two other furrows on each side very inconspicuous and not always visible. The anterior margin of the head consists of a narrow elevated ridge separated from the front of the glabella by an angular groove of about its own width. From the summit of the terminal ridge the margin descends with an abrupt slope so that on a front view the head appears to be bounded by a flat nearly vertical band, the width of which is equal to rather more than one half the elevation of the glabella. The surface appears to be smooth or finely granular. Eyes, fixed cheeks, thorax and pygidium unknown. Length of longest head seen three and a half lines; width of glabella about two lines at neck segment and a little less at the anterior extremity. The form of the glabella of this species is almost exactly like that of *Dikelocephalus granulosus.* (Owen.) [See Geo. Rep. Wisconsin, Pl. I, Fig. 7.]

Limestone, No. 1, not common.

Arionellus subclavatus. (N. sp.)

Fig. 386,—*a*.

Description.—Glabella as long as the head, separated from the front margin by a narrow groove only, strongly convex and elevated in the anterior two-thirds, less convex, more depressed, and somewhat narrower in the posterior third; sides gently convex, nearly straight, sub-parallel, slightly more distant from each other towards the front than behind, front obtusely rounded. The neck segment and furrow are rounded and well defined all across; the posterior glabellar furrows are rather strong, directed forwards at an angle somewhat less than 45°, their inner extremities separated by one-third the width of the glabella, and distant from the neck furrow about the width of the neck segment. In front of these are two obscure, nearly vertical furrows on each side, at about equal distances from each other. The fixed cheeks are strongly elevated, and separated from the glabella by the deep, narrow dorsal furrows. The eyes are small, and situated on a line drawn across the head, passing about midway between the two posterior glabellar furrows. They are connected with the front lobes of the glabella, by slender ocular ridges, as in the genus *Conocephalites.* The distance of the eye from the glabella is a little more than half the width of the neck segment. The facial suture cuts the front margin, a little inside of a line drawn through the eye, parallel with the length of the body. Behind the eye it runs obliquely outward with a gentle curve, and cuts the posterior margin at a point between the line passing through the eye, and the posterior angles of the head. The surface in the large specimens is finely tubercular, but in the small ones apparently smooth. Length of largest head seen five lines and a half; the width of the glabella at one-third the length from the front, is about three-fourths of its own length, excluding the neck segment and furrow. Moveable cheeks, thorax and pygidium unknown.

Limestone, No. 1.

MENOCEPHALUS SEDGWICKI. (N. sp.)

Fig. 387.

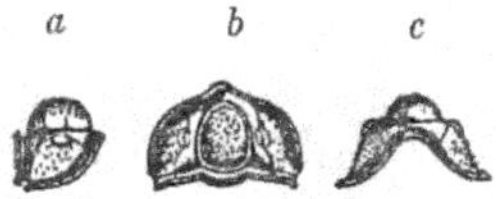

Fig. 388.

Fig. 387.—*Menocephalus Sedgwicki.*
388.—*M. globosus.* *a*, side view of the head; *b*, upper side; *c*, front view.

Description.—Glabella very convex, conical gradually tapering from the neck segment to the front, which is obtusely rounded. Neck segment and neck furrow well defined all across. Two glabellar furrows on each side, which divide the glabella into three pair of lobes, the anterior pairs a little the largest, the other two nearly equal to each other. The posterior furrows sometimes curve so far backwards as to isolate the lobes from the body of the glabella; their depth, however, is inconsiderable. The glabella is separated from the cheeks and front margin by the deep, narrow dorsal furrow which runs all round. The eyes are situated opposite the anterior glabellar furrows, and distant from the glabella about one-fourth the width of the neck segment. The front margin slopes from the front of the glabella downwards, and is then turned up to form a slightly elevated but well defined wire-like rim, which probably runs all round. Surface covered with small tubercles. Cheeks, thorax and pygidium unknown. Length of largest specimen collected, four lines; length of glabella, including neck segment, three lines; width of, at neck furrow, two lines.

In some specimens a third glabellar furrow is represented by an obscure indentation close to the front.

The facial suture is evidently the same as in *A. cylindricus* and *A. subclavatus*.

Limestone, No. 1.

Menocephalus globosus. (N. sp.)

Fig. 388—*a*, *b*, *c*.

Description.—Head globose, the posterior angles produced into small slender spines directed outwards, at an angle of about 45° with the axis of the body. Glabella exceedingly convex, almost hemispherical, its length slightly exceeding its width; either totally destitute of lateral furrows, or with two inconspicuous indentations on each side. Neck furrow and segment well defined; the margin of the head with a narrow, wire-like border all round, which turns up in front of the glabella, and forms an obtusely pointed rostrum; cheeks moderately tumid, but drooping on each side, so as to give a great depth to the outline of the head. Eyes about one-fifth the total length of the head, situated opposite the mid-length of the glabella, and about their own width from it. Facial suture as in *A. subclavatus.* Surface covered with small tubercles. Width of head in the specimen figured, five lines; length, three lines; length of glabella, two lines and one-fourth.

Associated with these are very numerous glabellæ of a larger size, in general four lines in length, which probably belong to this species.

Limestone, No. 1.

Genus Bathyurus. Billings.

This genus was described in the "Canadian Naturalist and Geologist," vol. iv, p. 364, in the article on the fossils of the Calciferous Sandrock. It differs from *Asaphus* by having nine segments in the thorax, the front of the hypostoma not forked, and the glabella well defined by the dorsal furrows. It somewhat resembles both *Megalaspis* and *Niobe* (Angelin), in the form of the glabella, but the hypostoma is precisely like that of *Ogygia*. I have some evidence to show that the head is composed of three pieces only, as in *Dikelocephalus*. The species heretofore described are, *B. amplimarginatus*, *B. conicus*, and *B. Cybele*, from the Calciferous Sandrock:—*B. Angelini*, Chazy; *B. extans*, (*Asaphus extans*, Hall,) as yet known only in the Black river limestone, and *B. spiniger*, (*Acidaspis spiniger*, Hall.) This latter species occurs both in the Black River and Trenton, in Canada.

The following species are referred to this genus provisionally. I am not at all satisfied that they belong to the genus, but I know of no other to which they bear so near a resemblance.

Bathyurus capax. (N. sp.)

Fig. 389.

Description.—Head convex, forming a depressed quarter of a sphere. Glabella oblong, separated from the flat, sloping rim of the front margin by a narrow angular groove; sides gently concave, nearly straight, with a short obscure outward curve opposite the eye, slightly converging towards each other from behind, forwards. The neck furrow is represented by an obscure transverse impression, which occupies the middle third of the width of the glabella, but does not reach all across. The anterior and

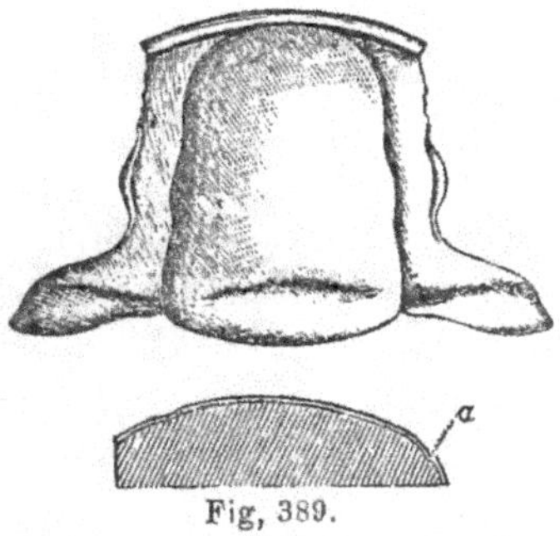

Fig, 389.

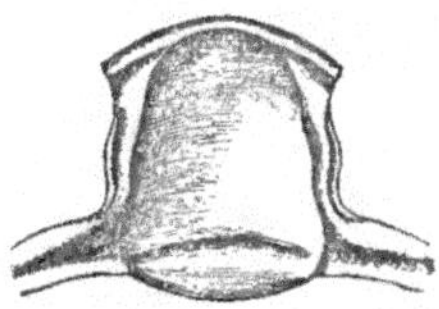

Fig. 390.

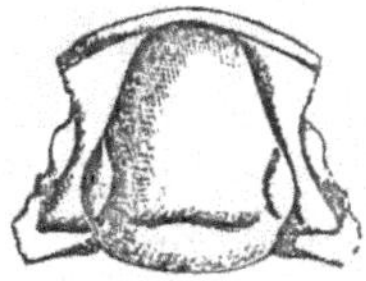

Fig. 391.

Fig. 389.—*Bathyurus capax.* The lower figure is a longitudinal section, showing the convexity of the glabella and the flat sloping rim of the front margin at *a*.

Fig. 390.—*Bathyurus dubius.*
Fig. 391.—*Bathyurus bituberculatus.*

posterior angles are rounded, and although distinctly defined all round, by the dorsal furrows, (which, however, are only slightly impressed,) the glabella in the anterior half is scarcely at all elevated above the general convexity of the head; it is moderately prominent behind. The eye is situated at mid-length of the head, semi-annular; its centre distant from the side of the glabella, two lines, when the length of the head is thirteen lines.

The anterior margin of the head to front of the glabella is strengthened by a flat rim, which slopes downwards and forwards at an angle of about 60°, with the horizontal plane of the body. This character is constant in head specimens of all sizes, from a length of six lines to thirteen. The width of this rim in the largest specimens, is one line and one-third. Cheeks, thorax and pygidium, unknown. Surface apparently smooth.

Length of large head, thirteen lines; width of glabella at base, nine lines, and at two lines from the front margin, eight lines.

Limestone, No. 1.

Bathyurus dubius. (N. sp.)

Fig. 390.

Description.—This species differs from *B. capax* in having the glabella more pointed and more narrowly rounded in front, and the marginal rim not flat but of a sub-cylindrical wire-like form.

Length of the head in largest specimens seen, nine lines; width of glabella at neck furrow, six lines and a half, and at two lines from front margin, five lines.

Limestone, No. 1.

Bathyurus bituberculatus. (N. sp.)

Fig. 391.

Description. Glabella the same as in *B. dubius*, but more pointed in front, and with an elongate-oval tubercule or lobe on each side of the posterior half. These tubercules are of an elongate oval form, pointed at both ends, bounded on the outside by the dorsal furrow which runs all round the glabella, and on the inside by a shallow, rather obscure groove, but which seems to separate them completely from the main body of the glabella. The lower pointed extremity of each terminates a little below the level of the neck furrow, and the upper, a little behind the mid-length of the head.

Length of the largest head seen, eight lines and a half; width of glabella just behind the neck furrow, six lines; length of each tubercule two lines and a half; width of same in the middle one line. Surface smooth.

Limestone, No. 1.

Bathyurus armatus. (N. sp.)

Fig. 392.

Description.—Head very convex, with a strong broad-based spine projecting backwards from the neck segment. The contour of the glabella is obscurely indicated by two faint grooves which appear to die out before reaching the front margin. It appears to be regularly conical, but scarcely at all elevated above the general convex surface of the head. Length of head in the specimen figured—excluding the marginal rim, which is unknown,—nine lines. Width of glabella at base, six lines ; at about the middle of the head, five lines ; the length of the spine is unknown. Surface smooth.

Limestone, No. 1.

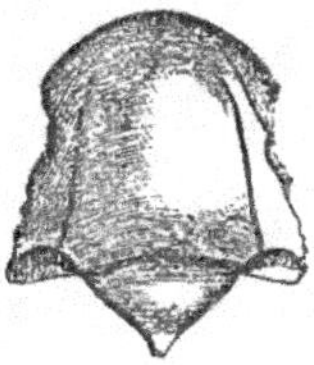

Fig. 392.

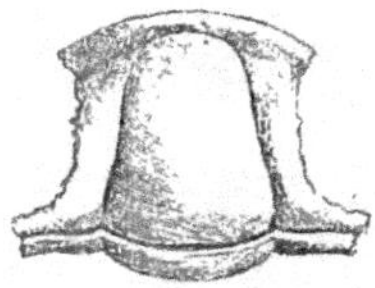

Fig. 393.

Fig. 394.

Fig. 395.

Fig. 396.

Fig. 392.—*Bathyurus armatus.*
Fig. 393.—*Bathyurus Saffordi.*
Fig. 394.—*Bathyurus oblongus.*
Fig. 395.—*Bathyurus Cordai.*
Fig. 396.—*Bathyurus quadratus.*

Bathyurus Saffordi. (N. sp.)

Fig. 393.

Description.—Glabella conical convex, much elevated above the general surface of the head, front angles rounded, sides somewhat straight in the anterior half, below which they curve a little outwards, and become parallel for a short distance next the posterior margin. The neck furrow in the cast of the interior is well defined all across, but when the crust is preserved it dies out on approaching the sides. The rim which forms the front margin has a flat slope inwards to the anterior edge of the glabella.

Length of the largest head seen, five lines and a half; width of glabella at neck segment, six lines, and at two lines from the front, three lines and a half. Surface smooth.

Dedicated to Professor J. M. Safford, State Geologist of Tennessee.

In Limestone, No. 2.

Bathyurus oblongus. (N. sp.)

Fig. 394.

Description.—The glabella of this species is oblong, convex with nearly parallel sides, well separated from the cheeks by the deep dorsal furrow, the front rounded, and the neck furrow rather deep all across. The eyes are small, situated a little behind the mid-length of the glabella, and distant from the dorsal groove a little less than one half the width of the neck segment. The marginal rim of the head is the same as in *B. Saffordi*. Surface smooth. Length of glabella four lines; width three lines.

Limestone, No. 2.

Bathyurus Cordai. (N. sp.)

Fig. 395.

Description.—Glabella conical, with a deep sulcus all round; in front an elevated rim apparently forming a rostrum similar to that of some species of *Calymene*; just within the rim a deep groove, between which and the furrow that surrounds the glabella, there is a rounded ridge. Neck furrow well defined all across. Eyes apparently about opposite the middle of the glabella. Surface smooth.

The glabella in some of the specimens is more narrowed towards the front than it is in the specimen figured.

Length of the largest head seen, seven lines; length of glabella, five lines; width just in front of neck furrow, three lines and two-thirds; at one line from the front, three lines.

Limestone, No 2.

Bathyurus quadratus. (N. sp.)

Fig. 396.

Description.—Glabella oblong, convex, only slightly rounded in front, well defined all round by the dorsal furrows, the sides straight and parallel, the eyes are small, and situated as in *B. oblongus*, an ocular ridge obscurely visible in one specimen. Neck furrow well defined all across.

Length of glabella four lines; width three lines and a half.

Limestone, No. 2.

CHEIRURUS APOLLO. (N. sp.)

Fig. 397.

Description.—Head convex, semicircular, width about twice the length or a little more. Glabella depressed, convex, somewhat circular or very broadly conical, the posterior margin convex, the sides and front rounded, the width at the posterior third equal to the length, the neck furrow in the cast defined all across three glabellar furrows directed obliquely forwards and outwards at an angle of about 30°, with the longtitudinal axis their inner extremities turned backwards, and distant from each other about one-fourth the whole width. The four side lobes of the glabella are sub-

Fig. 397.

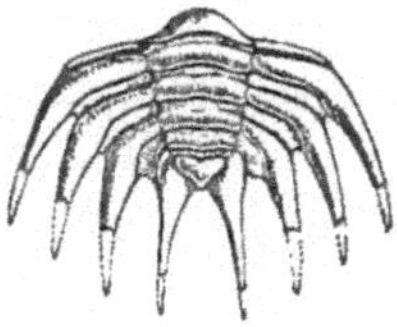

Fig. 398.

Fig. 399.

Fig. 397.—*Cheirurus Apollo.*
Fig. 398.—*Pygidium.* Limestone No. 2. This may be the tail of an *Amphion.**
Fig. 399.—*Cheirurus Eryx.*

equal, the posterior pair a little larger than the others. Eyes small, opposite the second lobe from behind, distant from it about the width of the lobe or a little less. Cheeks in the cast punctured. I have not ascertained whether or not the posterior angles terminate in spines. Length of head, five lines; length and width of glabella, a little less than five lines.

There are many European species of this type, and they range from the Landeilo Flags upwards to the Devonian.

Limestone, No. 2.

CHEIRURUS ERYX. (N. sp.)

Fig. 399.

Description.—Head semicircular, depressed convex, width twice the length or a little more, the posterior angles produced into short spines. Glabella elongate conical, moderately convex, rounded in front, sides

* This pygidium is figured in the Geology of Canada, p. 239, provisionally under the name of *Amphion Cayleyi.* It may, however, possibly belong to one of the species of *Cheirurus* above figured, perhaps to *C. Apollo.*

nearly straight or gently convex, neck furrow well defined all across, and continued on the cheeks to the outer angles of the head, four lobes on each side of which the anterior is largest, the posterior smallest, and the other two almost equal to each other, the furrows directed obliquely forwards at an angle of about 30°, to the longitudinal axis, their inner extremities distant from each other a little less than one-third the width of the glabella. Cheeks moderately convex, punctured. Eye opposite the second lobe from the front, and distant from thê glabella apparently about the width of the lobe.

Length of head nearly four lines; of glabella, about three lines and a half; width of glabella two lines and a half.

Limestone, No. 2.

Closely allied to a small species which occurs in the Chazy limestone at Caughnawaga. Another of the same size and type occurs at Phillipsburgh.

Asaphus Illaenoides. (N. sp.)

Description.—Head very convex, in shape like that of an *Illaenus*, equal to about one-fourth of a sphere, posterior angles rounded; width a little less than twice the length. Glabella obscurely defined, oblong, slightly narrowed just behind the eyes, thence a little widened both forwards and backwards. Eyes sub-globular, of a medium size, close to the glabella, the distance between their centres about equal to the length of the head. The facial suture runs from the inner anterior angle of the eye, with a scarcely perceptible curve outwards, directly forward to the front margin, being in this part almost parallel with the longitudinal axis of the body. From the inner posterior angle it runs outwards and backwards, and cuts the margin at a point in a line drawn parallel with the axis of the body, passing outside of the eye at a distance therefrom equal to one-half the width of that organ. The cheeks from the eye to the posterior angle of the head, descend with a flat slope of about 45° to the horizontal plane of the body. The surface appears to be smooth.

The pygidium is depressed, convex, semicircular, the posterior margin regularly rounded; the axis depressed, semi-cylindrical, sub-conical, sides a little concave, rather prominent, the extremity very obtusely round, the length varying from a little more than one-half to two-thirds the total length; its width a little less than that of the side lobes, five very obscure segments, of which the last two are sometimes blended into one. The anterior margins of the side lobes are almost at right angles to the axis for one-half or thereabouts of the width, then sloping backwards to the outer corners, which they reach at an angle of about 30° to the transverse diameter of the body.

Just behind the margin there is a single groove, obscure towards the axis but more distinct outwards. There are in some specimens, several faintly marked ribs, but in general the side lobes, with the exception of the anterior furrow, are smooth.

Length of head of a specimen of medium size, seven lines width, twelve lines ; distance between centre of eyes, seven lines.

Length of a pygidium of medium size, six lines ; width, twelve lines ; length of axis, four lines and a-half ; width of same at front margin, three lines and a half, and at half a line from the posterior extremity, three lines.

I have seen the underside of the head of this species and the sub-rostral fold is distinctly divided as in *A. platycephalus.* Had not this character been observed, I would have, without much hesitation, referred the head to the genus *Illœnus.*

In Limestone, No. 3.

ASAPHUS GONIURUS. (N. sp.)

The above name is proposed for a small triangular pygidium found in No. 3. It is evidently distinct from any described Silurian species of this country, but allied to one that occurs in the Chazy Limestone at Mingan. The form is triangular, the length three-fifths, or thereabouts, of the width, the axis scarcely at all elevated above the surface, and indistinctly divided into segments in the anterior half, but towards the extremity becoming strongly elevated, smooth and pointed. The largest specimen seen is about half an inch in length. It resembles the tail of a small *Homalonotus.*

Limestone, No. 3.

LIST

OF THE

ORGANIC REMAINS OF THE LEVIS FORMATION.

(Except where otherwise indicated, all the species of graptolites, in the following list, were described by Prof. J. Hall; all the others by E. Billings.)

PROTOZOA.

Calathium pannosum.
Eospongia ———— ———?

ZOOPHYTA.

Stenopora fibrosa, Goldfuss.

ECHINODERMATA.

Palæocystites tenuiradiatus? Hall.

GRAPTOLITIDÆ.

Graptolithus abnormis.
" alatus.
" arcuatus.
" bifidus.
" Bigsbyi.
" bryonoides.
" constrictus.
" crucifer.
" denticulatus.
" extensus.
" extenuatus.
" flexilis.
" fruticosus.
" Headi.
" indentus.
" Logani.
" Logani, var.
" nitidus.
" octobrachiatus.
" octonarius.
" patulus.
" pennatulus.
" quadribrachiatus.
" ramulus.
" Richardsoni.
" rigidus.
" similis.

Diplograptus inutilis.
" pristiniformis.
Climacograptus antennarius.
Phyllograptus angustifolius.
" Anna.
" ilicifolius.
" typus.
Reteolites ensiformis.
Reteograptus tentaculatus.
Dendrograptus diffusus.
" divergens.
" erectus.
" flexuosus.
" fruticosus.
" gracilis.
" striatus.
Callograptus elegans.
" Salteri.
Dictyonema irregularis.
" Murrayi.
" quadrangularis.
Ptilograptus Geinitzianus.
" plumosus.
Thamnograptus Anna.

BRACHIOPODA.

Lingula Mantelli.
" Irene.
" Iris.
" Quebecensis.
Obolella Ida.
" desiderata.
Leptæna decipiens.
" sordida.
Orthis gemmicula.
" Tritonia.
" Orthambonites, Pander.
" Euryone.

Orthis Electra.
" Hippolyte.
" Evadne.
" Mycale.
" Eudocia.
" Battis.
" apicalis.
" Corinna.
" Armanda.
" Minna.
Camerella varians.
" calcifera.
" breviplicata.
" costata.
" polita.
Stricklandinia Arachne.
" Arethusa.

LAMELLIBRANCHIATA.

Eopteria Richardsoni.
" ornata.

GASTEROPODA.

Ecculiomphalus intortus.
" Canadensis.
" spiralis.
" distans.
Pleurotomaria vagrans.
" Postumia.
" Quebecensis.
" rotundispira.
" Missisquoi.
Murchisonia Vesta.
" Hyale.
" Jessica.
" Cassandra.
" Sylvia.
" Missisquoi.
Helicotoma miser.
Ophileta bella.
" profunda.
" abdita.
" uniangulata, Hall.
Maclurea ponderosa.
" Atlantica?
" matutina? Hall.
" sordida?
Subulites Psyche.
Holopea dilucula?
" leiosoma.
" Proserpina.
Cyclonema Phædra.
Clisospira curiosa.
Bellerophon Palinurus.
Metoptoma Niobe.
" Eubule.
" Orithya.
" Melissa.
" Hyrie.
" Orphyne.
" Venilia.
" anomala.
" Augusta.
" superba.
" Quebecensis.

CEPHALOPODA.

Orthoceras Autolycus
" Atticus.
" repens.
" Catulus.
" Perseus.
" Missisquoi.
" Cato.
" Cataline.
" Sayi.
" Xerxes.
" Tityrus.
Cyrtoceras Aristides.
" Metellus.
" Dictys.
" Alethes.
" Syphax.
Cyrtocerina Mercurius.
Nautilus Pomponius.
Lituites Farnsworthi.
" imperator.

CRUSTACEA.

Agnostus Americanus.
" Orion.
" Canadensis.
Amphion Salteri.
" Cayleyi.
" Westoni.
" Julius.
" convexus.
Ampyx ——— ?
Arionellus cylindricus.
" subclavatus.
Asaphus illænoides.
" Pelops.
" goniurus.
" curiosa.
" canalis, Conrad.
Bathyurus conicus.

Bathyurus Cordai.
" capax.
" dubius.
" bituberculatus.
" armatus.
" Saffordi.
" oblongus.
" quadratus.
" strenuus.
" arcuatus.
" perspicator.
Bathyurellus nitidus.
" formosus.
" fraternus.
" expansus.
" rarus.
" litoreus.
Cheirurus Apollo.
" Eryx.
" Solitarius.
" Vulcanus.
" Mercurius.
" prolificus.
" glaucus.
" Sol.
Conocephalites Zenkeri.
Dikelocephalus magnificus.
" planifrons.
" Oweni.
Dikelocephalus Belli.
" megalops.
" cristatus.
" Devinei.
" Hisingeri.
" affinis.
" Sesostris.
" selectus.
" Missisquoi.
" pauper.
" Corax.
Endymionia Meeki.
Harpes Granti.
Harpides desertus.
Holometopus Angelini.
Illænus tumidifrons.
" arcuatus.
" consobrinus.
" simulator.
" incertus.
Lichas Jukesii.
Loganellus Logani.
Menocephalus globosus.
" Sedgwicki.
" Salteri.
Nileus affinis.
Remopleurides affinis.
Shumardia granulosa.

APPENDIX.

1. The first twenty-four pages, as noticed in the Preface, were reprinted in 1865, with the following alterations. On page 3 the parts in brackets in the reprint consist of new matter. On pages 4, 5, a new species (*Archeocyathus profundus*) is instituted for the specimens from Anse au Loup, originally referred to *A. Minganensis.* On page 8, *Kutorgina* is inserted in the name of *Obolella cingulata.* Page 11, *Olenellus* is adopted instead of *Paradoxides.* The notes on pages 10, 11, 12, of the original are withdrawn.

Pages 57 to 72 have been also reprinted, from 57 to 66 inclusive, and part of 67 being entirely new matter.

2. *Stricklandia.*—As this generic name is preoccupied, I have changed it to *Stricklandinia.* (See *Can. Geol., vol. viii,* p. 370.) The two species (*ante*, p. 85) must therefore be called *Stricklandinia Arachne* and *Stricklandinia Arethusa.* I have still some doubts as to the generic affinities of these fossils ; but so far as their internal structure can be made out, they appear to be more nearly related to this genus than to any other. They are also allied to *Camerella.*

3. *Fossils from the Black Hills.*—MEEK and HAYDEN have re-described the fossils from these localities (*ante*, p. 58) under the name of *Lingulepis pinniformis* (Owen), *Lingulepis prima* (Conrad), *Obolella nana, Theca gregarea, Agraulos Oweni,* and *Agraulos ?—?* (Palæontology of the Upper Missouri, by F. B. MEEK and F. V. HAYDEN ; published by the Smithsonian Institution, April, 1865.

4. *Fauna of the Levis Formation.*—The number of graptolites is put down at 53 species (*ante*, p. 62), but this includes *G. Milesi* and *G. secalinus*, which have not yet been found in rocks clearly identified with the Levis formation. The correct number (51 species) is given on p. 376, and also in the foregoing list, p. 417. There are also five species of *Asaphus* instead of four, as mentioned on pp. 62, 63—the total number of trilobites being 74, of which 73 are described. There are also 29 species of Brachiopoda. As to the total number of species of all orders, in this formation, I am satisfied that we are still far from the truth. Every new locality furnishes several new forms. I have stated (*ante*, pp. 62, 376) that there are 219 described species; but as several of these are doubtfully identified, it would be better to say that there are between 215 and 220.

CYRTOCERAS JUVENALIS. (*Ante*, p. 177.)

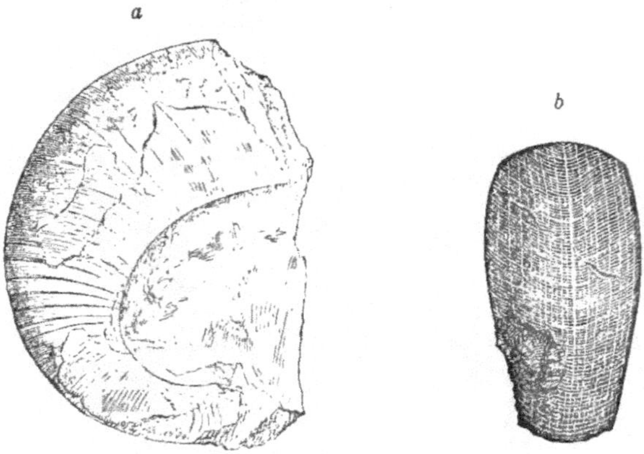

Fig. 400.

Fig. 400.—*Cyrtoceras Juvenalis.*—*a*, side view of a nearly perfect specimen; *b*, ventral view of the original, showing the surface characters.

Remarks.—Since the description of this species was printed, Mr. J. F. Whiteaves has discovered a nearly perfect individual, in the Trenton limestone near Montreal, which is figured above.

The specimen is $2\frac{1}{2}$ inches in length measured along the outside, and is curved to a radius of about 11 lines. It tapers, in the lateral diameter, from 8 lines to 3, and, in the dorso ventral, from 9 to 3 lines. Near the mid-length a number of the septa are well preserved,—6 in 4 lines measured on the side, and 7 in 6 lines on the median line of the ventral aspect. There appears to be a constriction near the aperture.

CLISOSPIRA CURIOSA. (*Ante*, p. 186.)

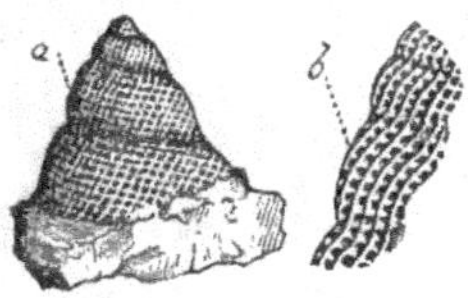

Fig. 401.

Fig. 401.—A portion of the spire of *C. curiosa*, which retains the shell and surface markings.

Remarks.—Among the specimens of this species lately collected by T. C. Weston is one which retains a part of the shell. The surface is beautifully reticulated by ascending and revolving lines as above represented.

INDEX.

Acrotreta gemma, 216.
Agnostus Americanus, 395.
" Canadensis, 397.
" Fabius, 298.
" Galba, 297.
" Orion, 397.
Amphion Barrandei, 288.
" Canadensis, 288.
" convexus, 322.
" Julius, 290.
" Insularis, 290.
" Salteri, 352.
" Westoni, 321.
Amplexus cingulatus, 106.
Ampyx Halli, 24.
" læviusculus, 295.
" normalis, 295.
" Rutilius, 296.
" semicostatus, 297.
Archeocyathus Atlanticus, 5.
" Minganensis, 354.
" profundus, 4.
Arionellus cylindricus, 406.
" subclavatus, 406.
Arthroclema pulchella, 54.
Asaphus canalis, 270, 352.
" curiosus, 318.
" goniurus, 415.
" Huttoni, 271.
" Illænoides, 414.
" Morrisii, 272.
" Pelops, 317.
" quadraticaudatus, 272.
Ascoceras Newberryi, 164.
Astylospongia parvula, 20.
Athyris Anticostiensis, 147.
" borealis, 147.
" Headi, 147.
" Julia, 146.
" Prinstana, 145.
" umbonata, 144.
Avicula Hermione, 40.
Bathyurus amplimarginatus, 352.
" arcuatus, 205.
" armatus, 411.
Bathyurus bituberculatus, 410.
" breviceps, 262.
" caudatus, 261.
" capax, 409.
" conicus, 352.
" Cordai, 259, 412.
" Cybele, 352.
" dubius, 410.
" gregarius, 363.
" Minganensis, 353.
" Nero, 260.
" oblongus, 412.
" parvulus, 16.
" perplexus, 364.
" perspicator, 205.
" quadratus, 412.
" Saffordi, 259, 411.
" senectus, 15.
" Smithii, 56.
" solitarius, 362.
" strenuus, 204.
" Timon, 261.
" vetulus, 360.
Bathyurellus abruptus, 263.
" expansus, 318.
" formosus, 266.
" fraternus, 267.
" litoreus, 320.
" marginatus, 264.
" nitidus, 265.
" rarus, 320.
" validus, 268.
Bellerophon Palinurus, 311.
" macer, 347.
Beyrichia Atlantica, 300.
Calathium affine, 209.
" Anstedi, 210, 337.
" Canadense, 377.
" Fittoni, 211.
" formosum, 209.
" pannosum, 335.
" Paradoxicum, 358.
Camerella antiquata, 10.
" breviplicata, 304.
" calcifera, 220.

Camerella costata, 305.
" Ops, 148.
" parva, 219.
" polita, 305.
" varians, 220.
Charionella Hyale, 166.
Chiton Canadensis, 394.
Cheirurus Apollo, 413.
" glaucus, 323.
" Eryx, 413.
" Mercurius, 285.
" perforator, 287.
" Polydorus, 286.
" Pompilius, 181.
" prolificus, 285, 325.
" Satyrus, 324.
" Sol, 288.
" solitarius, 206.
" Vulcanus, 284, 324.
Clisospira curiosa, 186, 420.
Conocardium immmaturum, 41.
Conocephalites Adamsii, 12.
" arenosus, 15.
" miser, 13.
" Teucer, 14.
" Vulcanus, 14.
" Zenkeri, 398.
Ctenodonta abrupta, 46.
" Angela, 221.
" Iphigenia, 152.
Cyclocystoides Huronensis, 393.
Cyclonema Hageri, 29.
" Montrealensis, 30.
" Phædra, 188.
Cyathophyllum Anticostiense, 109.
" Eriphele, 111.
" Euryone, 110.
" interruptum, 109.
" nymphale, 111.
" Pasithea, 112.
" Pennanti, 107.
" pelagicum, 108.
" Wahlenbergii, 108.
Cyrtia myrtea, 165.
Cyrtoceras Alethes, 193.
" Aristides, 316.
" Dictys, 192.
" Huronense, 176.
" Isodorus, 175.
" Juvenalis, 177, 420.
" Ligarius, 176.
" Lysander, 161.
Cyrtoceras Mercurus, 194.
" Metellus, 191.
" Orestes, 177.
" Orodes, 162.
" Postumius, 178.
" Syphax, 194.
Cyrtocerina Mercurius, 194.
" typica, 178.
Cyrtodonta Emma, 150.
" Harrietta, 149.
" Hindi, 151.
" Leucothea, 46.
" ponderosa, 150.
Cystiphyllum maritima, 112.
Discina Circe, 51.
" Pelopea, 52.
Dikelocephalus affinis, 197.
" Belli, 403.
" Corax, 334.
" cristatus, 404.
" Devinei, 195.
" Hisingeri, 196.
" Magnificus, 399.
" megalops, 403.
" Missisquoi, 199.
" Oweni, 402.
" pauper, 200.
" planifrons, 401.
" selectus, 199.
" Sesostris, 198.
Dolichometopus convexus, 269.
" gibberulus, 269.
" rarus, 352.
Ecculiomphalus Atlanticus, 250.
" distans, 249.
" superbus, 250.
Endymion Meeki, 94.
Endymionia Meeki, 281.
Encrinurus Mirus, 292.
Eopteria ornata, 307.
" Richardsoni, 306.
" typica, 221.
Eospongia Roemeri, 19.
" varians, 19.
Eunema cerithioides, 35.
" Erigone, 35.
Euchasmia Blumenbachium, 220.
" Blumenbachia, 361.
Harpes Dentoni, 183.
" Granti, 326.
" Ottawaensis, 182.
Harpides Atlanticus, 281.

Harpides desertus, 333.
" concentricus, 282.
Helicotoma Eucharis, 249.
" Gorgonea, 248.
" Miser, 309.
" Proserpina, 247.
" Tritonia, 247.
Holometopus Angelini, 95, 281.
Holopea Gracia, 159.
" Guelphensis, 159.
" Harmonia, 158.
" Lavinia, 28.
" leiosoma, 187.
" Nereis, 27.
" Ophelia, 222.
" Proserpina, 28.
" Pyrene, 27.
Illænus Americanus, 329.
" arcuatus, 279.
" consimilis, 277.
" consobrinus, 280.
" fraternus, 276, 331.
" incertus, 332.
" simulator, 327.
" tumidifrons, 278.
" Vindex, 179.
Ischadites Canadensis, 385.
Kutorgina cingulata, 8.
Leptæna decipiens, 74, 219.
" sordida, 73.
Leperdita concinnula, 299.
" turgida, 299.
" ventralis, 300.
Lichas Jukesii, 282, 335.
" Minganensis, 181.
Licrophycus Hiltonensis, 101.
" Hudsonicus, 101.
" minor, 100.
" Ottawaensis, 99.
Lingula Briseis, 48.
" Canadensis, 114.
" Cobourgensis, 50.
" Cyane, 216.
" Daphne, 50.
" Forbesi, 115.
" Irene, 71.
" Iris, 301.
" Iole, 215.
" Kingstonensis, 48.
" Nympha, 214.
" Perryi, 20.
" Philomela, 49.
Lingula Progne, 47.
" Quebecensis, 72, 216.
Lituites Apollo, 25.
" Farnsworthi, 21.
" imperator, 23.
" Palinurus, 25.
" Pluto, 259.
Loganellus Logani, 201.
Maclurea acuminata, 240.
" affinis, 238.
" crenulata, 236.
" Emmonsi, 242.
" Oceana, 237.
" ponderosa, 239.
" Psyche, 244.
" rotundata, 245.
" speciosa, 240.
" Sylpha, 244.
" transitionis, 241.
Menocephalus globosus, 408.
" Salteri, 203.
" Sedgwicki, 407.
Metoptoma Alceste, 153.
" anomala, 89.
" Augusta, 88.
" Canadensis, 394.
" Erato, 39.
" Estella, 153.
" Eubule, 38.
" Hyrie, 87.
" instabilis, 251.
" Melissa, 86.
" Montrealensis, 394.
" Niobe, 37.
" Nycteis, 38.
" Orithya, 38.
" Orphyne, 88.
" Quebecensis, 308.
" simplex, 346.
" superba, 172.
" Trentonensis, 40.
" Venilia, 88.
Modiolopsis Adrastia, 45.
" Gesneri, 43.
" Maia, 44.
" Meyeri, 42.
" Nais, 45.
Murchisonia Acrea, 232.
" Ada, 346.
" Adelina, 232.
" agilis, 235.
" Alexandra, 172.

Murchisonia Artimesia, 345.
" Augustina, 234.
" Cassandra, 189.
" Catharina, 231.
" Cicelia, 233.
" Estella, 157.
" Harmonia, 158.
" Hercyna, 158.
" Hermione, 33.
" Hyale, 33,
" Jessica, 189.
" Missisquoi, 307.
" Mylitta, 157.
" placida, 235.
" Procris, 34.
" simulatrix, 232.
" sororcula, 233.
" Sylvia, 190.
" Vesta, 32.
" Vitellia, 156,
" Xanthippe, 155.
Nautilus calciferus, 258.
" desertus, 258.
" ferox, 351.
" insolens, 258.
" Pomponius, 26.
" versutus, 259.
Nileus affinis, 275.
" macrops, 273.
" scrutator, 274.
Obolella chromatica, 7.
" cingulata, 8.
" desiderata, 69.
" Ida, 71.
" nana, 67.
" pretiosa, 68.
Obolus Galtensis, 168.
" Labradoricus 6.
" Murrayi, 362.
Ophileta abdita, 189.
" bella, 310.
" disjuncta, 344.
" Nerine, 245.
" profunda, 188.
" uniangulata, 246.
Olenellus Thompsoni, 11, 365.
" Vermontana, 11, 365.
Olenus Logani, 201.
Orthis apicalis, 301.
" Armanda, 303.
" Battis, 185.
" Corinna, 302.
Orthis delicatula, 217.
" Electra, 79, 217.
" Eudocia, 83.
" Euryone, 78.
" Evadne, 81.
" gemmicula, 75.
" Hippolyte, 81, 218.
" Iphigenia, 133.
" Laurentina, 138.
" Maria, 137.
" Merope, 139.
" Minna, 303.
" Mycale, 82.
" Orthambonites, 77.
" porcata, 135.
" retrorsa, 136.
" Tritonia, 76.
Orthisina festinata, 10.
Orthoceras Allumettense, 254.
" Atticus, 312.
" Autolycus, 91.
" Cataline, 315.
" Cato, 314.
" Catulus, 313.
" Darwini, 161.
" diffidens, 174.
" Drummondi, 173.
" edax, 344.
" explorator, 253.
" Flavius, 255.
" furtivum, 348.
" Glaucus, 350.
" hæsitans, 254.
" indagator, 349.
" Lamarcki, 255, 347.
" Lysander, 161.
" Menelaus, 26.
" Missisquoi, 314.
" ordinatum, 350.
" perparvum, 27.
" Perseus, 313.
" piscator, 251.
" Piso, 168,
" Priamus, 253.
" repens, 312.
" Sayi, 315.
" Selwini, 161.
" servile, 252.
" Tityrus, 316.
" velox, 173.
" veterator, 350.
" Xerxes, 316.

Palæophycus Beauharnoisensis, 98.
" Beverleyensis, 97.
" congregatus, 3.
" funiculus, 98.
" incipiens, 2.
" obscurus, 98.
Pasceolus globosus, 390.
" Halli, 390.
Petraia angulata, 103.
" aperta, 102.
" latuscula, 104.
" pygmea, 103.
Petraster bellulus, 393.
Phragmoceras Hector, 163.
Piloceras Canadense, 256.
" gracile, 257.
" Triton, 257.
" Wortheni, 256.
Pleurotomania Agarista, 230.
" Agave, 170.
" Amphitrite, 32.
" Arachne, 31.
" Arabella, 343.
" Calphurnia, 230.
" Canadensis, 342.
" Deiopeia, 155.
" Dryope, 170.
" Elora, 154.
" Etna, 226.
" Eugenia, 30.
" Galtensis, 154.
" Harpya, 227.
" Hortensia, 227.
" Hyale, 228.
" Laurentina, 343.
" Missisquoi, 191.
" Normani, 228.
" Numeria, 229.
" Postumia, 191.
" Quebecensis, 190.
" rotundispira, 191.
" selecta, 224.
" sponsa, 226.
" vagrans, 90.
" Valeria, 169.
" Viola, 169.
" Virgo, 224.
" virguncula, 225
" Vitruvia, 171.
Porambonites Ottawaensis, 140.
Ptychophyllum Canadense, 107.
Receptaculites Canadensis, 385.
Receptaculites calciferus, 359, 384
" elegantulus, 360.
" Iowensis, 385.
" Jonesi, 385, 389.
" Murchisonii, 384.
" Neptuni, 386.
" occidentalis, 381.
" Oweni, 384.
" parvipora, 386.
" sulcata, 386.
Remopleurides affinis, 325.
" Canadensis, 182.
" Panderi, 293.
" Schlotheimi, 294.
Rhabdaria fragilis, 357.
" furcata, 358.
Rhynchonella Anticostiensis, 142
" Corinthia, 220.
" fringilla, 141.
" glacialis, 143.
Ribeiria calcifera, 340.
" longiuscula, 341.
Rusophycus Grenvillensis, 101.
Salterella pulchella, 18.
" obtusa, 18.
" rugosa, 17.
Scolithus Canadensis, 96.
" linearis, 2.
Serpulites dissolutus, 56.
Shumardia glacialis, 283.
" granulosa, 92.
Sphærexochus parvus, 180.
Stenaster Huxleyi, 213.
Stenopora fibrosa, 212.
" Huronensis, 185.
Straparollus Daphne, 160.
" Hippolyta, 160.
Straparollina pelagica, 223.
Stricklandia Arachne, 85.
" *Arethusa*, 85.
Stricklandinia Arachne,
" Arethusa
Strophomena alternata, 117.
" antiquata, 129.
" Arethusa, 132.
" Aurora, 218.
" Ceres, 119.
" fluctuosa, 123.
" Hecuba, 126.
" imbecilis, 219.
" imbrex, 128.
" Julia, 127

Strophomena Leda, 120.
" nitens, 118.
" Philomela, 122.
" recta, 130.
" subtenta, 132.
" Thalia, 125.
Stromotopora compacta, 55, 212.
" rugosa, 213.
Strombodes gracilis, 113.
Subulites Daphne, 223.
" parvulus, 36.
Psyche, 188.
Telephus Americauus, 291.
Trachyium cyathiforme, 211.
" rugosum, 212.
Trematis Hurouensis, 53.
" Montrealensis, 52.
" Ottawaensis, 53.
Triarthrus Fiscberi, 291.
Trichospongia sericea, 257.
Trimerella grandis, 166.
" acuminata, 167.
Zaphrentis Canadensis, 105.

CPSIA information can be obtained
at www.ICGtesting.com
Printed in the USA
LVHW111955050422
715401LV00006B/218

9 783752 589269